DEATH ON THE WILD SIDE

By

Jack Corbett

Nirvana Printing Co.

Published by The Nirvana Publishing Co.

Copyright @ 1995 by Jack Corbett

2nd Edition
Published by Nirvana Publishing Co.
Printed by Createspace
January 2012

ISBN 978-0964714335

For information, address
P.O. Box 3181
Prescott, AZ 86302
United States

jack.corbett@gmail.com

http://www.alphapro.com

Frank Harring hates lawyers. He hates them so much that he dreams about planting as many as possible up to their necks in his fields--then decapitating them with his farm machinery. Frank Harring hates the institution of marriage. He tells his friend Stan: "Marriage is one hell of a shitty thing for the man. What I'm saying is that nothing could be more stupid than entering into a marriage contract, which is a contract enforceable by law, which will result in divorce 50 % of the time, and which will result in acute financial loss to the man. That is a really stupid thing for us to do. Since we are not stupid, the only reason we would do something that idiotic is that some very powerful forces are out there compelling us to do so."

Frank hatches his "great plan," which he claims will procure the greatest possible number of beautiful women at the lowest cost--"far cheaper than marriage," he promises Stan--and starts to implement his "great plan" in the St. Louis Metro-East area, home to at least twelve topless nightclubs, where anything goes. The "great plan" works--that is, until he becomes involved with Lori Mellon--one of the top strippers in the Metro-East. The "great plan" starts to unravel just as he predicted it would.

Like Frank Harring, this author believes that most lawyers are thieves and parasites sucking the life blood out of honest hard-working people. There is not enough legitimate business out there to support half of them. So they resort to stealing, using the legal system as a loaded gun pointed at our heads. Unlike Frank Harring, this author feels that women as well as men are preyed upon by these predators. Like vampires smelling blood, the lawyers home in on whomever has money--sparing no one regardless of gender.

When it comes to divorce, it is usually the man who has the money. Sometimes the woman has it. In either case the lawyers go after the money like blood hounds, greedily sucking up as much of it as they can. Marriage has outlived its usefulness--mainly because it supplies food for these parasites, who would otherwise starve.

And don't expect things to change for the better. The lawyers and judges all went to the same law schools. They all look out for each other. Thieves need to be punished and it doesn't matter if stealing is done by the law or outside the law. It will take a revolution in thinking and it will take action to get the job done. Frank Harring acts--and pays the price. Will you?

It doesn't matter if you are a man or a woman--if you question the rosy picture you are constantly getting of love and marriage--this book's for you. If you hate lawyers and judges, you should read *Death on the Wild Side*. You will feel better after reading it. And if you are interested in topless bars and strippers, *Death on the Wild Side* will take you into a new world, the world of the St. Louis Metro-East which this author has experienced in depth.

About the 2nd Edition of "Death on the Wild Side"

This book is based upon the author's life experiences until 1995 when the first edition was published. The people, places, and events in this book are all based on people, places, and events which the author had met, been or witnessed in his life experience and travels. None of the people in this book, however represents any specific person from the author's life. Rather, the people in this book represent much more. Each character in this work represents a combination of people and their problems, concerns and values--or lack thereof--that the author had witnessed, experienced, heard of and felt throughout his life. It is these representative characters and the events of their lives, as interpreted by the author, which the author uses as a vehicle through which to express his various philosophies of life.

All of the pictures in this second edition of "Death on the Wild Side" were taken after the year 2000, five years after the first edition's publication. The people in the pictures were not even contemplated by the author when he was writing "Death on the Wild Side."

By the year 2000 the author had already entered an entirely new realm of the adult entertainment industry. In this new arena he repeatedly encountered professionalism of the highest caliber at a level that is consistently underestimated by the misinformed. By then the author was sponsoring an exhibitor's booth at the Exotic Dancer Magazine's Expo in Reno and Las Vegas which featured a trade show exhibiting the entire spectrum of products and services available to the adult entertainment industry along with seminars geared for top club decision makers on how they could improve their clubs' bottom line while creating a better public image of strip clubs.

The author remembers hearing one of the speakers at one of his first conventions addressing more than fifty club owners at one of the seminars: "Today the United States is faced with a tremendous battle between the far right which wants to deprive Americans of their right to freedom of speech and expression and those who wish to preserve such freedoms. You gentlemen are on the front line of this battle which has been joined by all those who are trying to close your clubs down."

Exotic Dancer's annual conventions introduced the author to an exceptionally talented group of people who would introduce him to an incredibly rich and varied assortment of individuals representing many aspects of the world of adult entertainment. It was here that he met Anne Marie and Jim Hayek, the owners of the Pure Talent Agency, who would invite him to join their feature entertainers for four day long feature showcases across the entire United States in which he was given free hotel rooms in exchange for the pictures he took. He also met Sam Stimmel at one of the conventions, an Indiana club owner who would invite Jack and his friends to stay in his home while Jack did photo shoots in his club. It would be Sam who would introduce Jack to the owner of "Nudes-A-Poppin" which would later on provide so many opportunities for Jack's photography and magazine articles.

Jack would meet Vic Robinson at one of Exotic Dancer's expos who was the general manager of Club Maximus in Wichita Falls, Texas although technically he met Vic while he was waiting for his luggage to arrive at the Las Vegas airport before the convention was even underway. It was there at the baggage carousel that Vic hired Jack to be the Club Maximus photographer for the club's M.S. Texas pageant that was coming up the following fall. The author wound up being invited back to Texas to do more photo shoots for Club Maximus and its sister club in Abilene which was hosting its M.S. Texas West.

It was the day after Vic hired the author at the airport's luggage carousel that Big Daddy hired him to do photo shoots at a new club he was rebuilding in Dixon, Missouri. Jack had met Big Daddy when he was general manager for the Regina's franchise of clubs while shooting his first feature showcase for the Pure Talent Agency in Springfield, Missouri. The photo shoot led to a 2nd photo shoot, which led to bimonthly visits when he would stay as Big Daddy's house guest, which led to his becoming the official photographer and web site designer for S.P.E.W., an acronym that stands for Sexy Professional Exotic Wrestling.

He would meet Jeremy Mcteague, the editor of *Xtreme Magazine*, at one of Exotic Dancer 's expos and go on to writing over sixty magazine articles for *Xtreme* over the next several years including twenty gun articles in which he got to choose both the weapon and the model he wanted to write about provided she had the requisite good looks to satisfy the magazine's editor and owner.

Life simply doesn't get any better than this with so many incredible opportunities to work with such a huge variety of interesting, talented people. And ironically this side of the adult entertainment industry was one from which "Death on the Wild Side's main character, Frank Harring, would have been excluded from simply because he was looking for sex in the wrong places. The problem with Frank is, he misbehaves too much and he misbehaves far too often. In "Death on the Wild Side" he finds what he is looking for in some of the seediest parts of the adult entertainment world. But by the year 2000 the author found an entirely new spectrum of the adult entertainment industry which can be compared to a fraternity of kindred spirits who are for the most part fiercely individualistic, charismatic, hard working and talented people who are ahead of their time in a nation whose conservatism often seems to verge towards a neo Puritanism that is almost medieval in its outlook.

Dedication

To all those terrific people I have met in the adult entertainment industry who have given me the opportunity to develop my skills not only as a writer but as a photographer and in graphics arts design without which I would have been unable to produce both the front and rear cover of this book.

11

THE BARN

The place had once been a barn. That had been in the days when every farmer had eighty acres and some cattle and horses. Times had changed and so had the barn. A drive through hallway for trailer trucks now bisected the old structure. At ground level two wooden cribs holding grain now occupied both sides of the hallway. Upstairs were three holding bins which resembled little wooden rooms. In the old days a man had hung himself above one of them. But that was in the past and the old barn was now hardly recognizable. Eight large steel grain bins now surrounded the ancient structure. A one-hundred foot tower built to move corn towered over everything else.

"Now tell me, Candy, where you haven't looked."

"I've looked all over this farm except for those overhead bins." Candy pointed above her head at the heavy oak beams that supported the floor upstairs. "I hate it up there," Candy continued. "It's so dusty around those overheads and there's cobwebs all over. There's something about it that I just don't like--something spooky."

Frank had been around those overheads many times before. He and Stan had kept the place's dark secret from Candy. He pushed the thought from his mind hoping that it had not happened again. Then he took her by the arm and led her over to the narrow wooden ladder which had been bolted to the side of the hallway.

"Wait here," he told her. "I'm going up for a look."

Half way up he yelled down to her, "Turn on the lights," Candy. By the time he got to the top she had found the switch. A narrow opening in the floor allowed him to swivel his body away from the ladder and step onto the upstairs floor. Frank stood on the floor upstairs and looked around. The lighting was barely adequate but it was enough.

A rope was still tied to a wooden beam. Stan's body hung from the beam, its legs dangling into empty space over an empty bin. He still wore his cap, and his feet were almost level with the floor. *He couldn't have struggled*, thought Frank. *If he had dropped a few feet, perhaps only a couple, into the bin before the rope had tightened he would have died instantly from a broken neck. So he must have put the rope around his neck, stepped over the edge of the bin, and slowly strangled.* His hat was where he usually wore it, the bill centered and tilted slightly downward toward his forehead. Frank considered the raw courage and deliberation it took for Stan to hang himself this way, slowly strangling to death, knowing that he could save himself at any time simply by grabbing onto the rope and pulling himself up onto the floor.

It happened once before and in exactly the same way. Thirty years ago the farmer who had been living in Stan's house and who had been farming the same ground had hung himself from the same beam. It had been Stan's father who had found him and who cut him down. According to Stan's father the man had been wearing a similar cap and had stepped out into eternity without dislodging the cap

Frank went back down the ladder, took Candy by the arm, and walked her to the house. She asked immediately if he had found Stan and he shook his head trying his best to show no emotion. He took her inside and went into the kitchen with her.

"Make a pot of coffee," he ordered, "but first call Stan's mother and get her over here. While you are making the coffee, I'll call the sheriff."

Candy called Gloria and handed Frank the phone. Then she started the coffee. Gloria came in before the pot was ready. "Did you find him?" she asked.

"No," Frank replied. I'm going into the next room to call the sheriff while you ladies talk.

Frank went out of the room and into the living room. He sat on the couch and dialed the number to the county jail. A deputy answered the phone.

"Jim's not there. Is he?" Frank asked.

"No, he's home in bed," the deputy replied.

"This is Frank Harring. Stan Osterman has just hung himself. We are all at his house. Please wake Jim up and get him over here, and call the coroner and whoever else you have to call."

The voice on the other end sounded surprised. "Stan Osterman's hung himself? When?"

"Tonight. Please get over here fast. I have to get off the phone now and tell Stan's mother and girlfriend."

Frank hung up and went back into the kitchen. Candy poured three cups of coffee and looked him in the eye. "What's going on?" she asked.

"Sit down. Both of you. Candy, I'm sorry I've lied to you. I just didn't want to tell you over at those side cribs. Stan's hung himself."

"Hung himself? Is he----"

"Yes. He's dead. I'm very sorry. He's my best friend. The sheriff's on his way."

Three hours later, Frank went home. He went inside, flipped on a light switch, entered the kitchen, and sat down at the table. Putting his head in his hands, he reflected on the last year's events. *It was all me. I'm the reason he killed himself. And it was Carl.* Then he broke down. It had been a long time since he had cried, and he had never had this good a reason to--not in his whole life. Fifteen minutes later he regained control and went over to the refrigerator for a beer. Going back to the kitchen table Frank slumped back into his chair, took a long swallow of Budweiser, and thought about the last year. No, he reminded himself. It all started even before last year. Choking back his sobs, he went back to the beginning.

It all started at the Injection Pump.

THE INJECTION PUMP

It was 7:30 on a Friday evening and Frank had already downed four Michelobs. This was rare. First that he was drinking Michelob, and secondly that he was drinking anything at all that early. He and Jeff had started at 5:00 p.m. and would have had at least six each had they not broken for dinner. They had left Jeff's Chesterfield condo, eaten fast food, and were now parked in Frank's Pickup in a vacant East St. Louis lot facing the setting sun. A cooler of Busch lay on the pickup bed behind the cab. Frank reached for two cans through the sliding glass window above the seat. Both men were white; the neighborhood was black. There were other vacant lots scattered wherever they looked. All homes were derelict, in sad need of repair, junk lying in the tiny yards.

The sun was distant and glorious, in sharp contrast to the wasteland before it. Frank reflected on their situation. There they were in East St. Louis in a pickup, downing their fifth beer, two whites in a crime-ridden neighborhood, out of place, lots of money in their pockets. Surely they were out of their minds. He looked over at Jeff, the smaller of the two, no match for the trouble that could start easily at any time for them in this neighborhood. No sign of uneasiness there. Jeff was in his element. Relaxed, drinking a beer planning and plotting with his friend. Only 130 pounds and five foot eight, Jeff had total confidence in his ability to talk his way out of anything, anywhere, under any circumstance. Not only that--he could reduce practically anyone within arms length to laughter. One of America's greatest cultural disappointments was that Jeff Shannon had never been hired to appear on Saturday Night Live.

Obviously Jeff could just have easily been eating a salad in a West County restaurant. Jeff had balls of iron. The fact that a gang could appear at any moment and cause trouble was not even worth contemplating. They had one night together and each of them was planning to make the most of it. The next day Frank would have to go home to his wife 75 miles away while Jeff's wife would return from visiting her parents in Chicago. Trouble could come. Let it. They would have a good laugh with whomever would appear. They had beer to spare. He did not consider the situation to be potentially serious at all. The vacant lot was merely a convenient spot to drink beer and plan the evening. What was serious was what was not there--their problems at home.

"Frank, what do you want to do. I know several places. All

close. We can go to the one with the most girls first. It's a little classier than the others or we can go to this other one where the beer is cheaper and get warmed up."

That was typical of Jeff. He wanted to be well primed before getting into action. Frank didn't know if he was really all that cheap or if he just wanted to hit several places so that he could wow the most people with his wit. A smaller place would call greater attention to Jeff. The comedian would be unleashed.

"What's the first place like? Think we'd like it?"

"The first place doesn't have a cover. Dancers won't be as good there, but you never know."

"How many places are there?"

"I really don't know. There's Stormy's, the Injection Pump, PTs, East meets West, Ciceros and some others I don't know the name of."

Frank thought of the prospects before them. The setting sun was beautiful tonight. His wife, Karen, was a distant memory. He should never have gotten married. The evening ahead was going to be good. For the first time in years he felt free. And it was not just the evening ahead--it was as if this evening stretched into an eternity of evenings without end where Frank could go wherever he wanted--be with whomever he pleased, and dream of the possible and the impossible. But for now he ruled the night and there was no fear, of anything, anywhere.

"Okay Jeff, where to now? The sun just disappeared, and I want to check these places out."

"Just drive straight north for a few blocks."

Frank slipped the pickup into gear and drove out into the street. After five minutes behind the wheel Jeff asked him to stop. It was just a little roadhouse like you find in the country except this was not the country. This was East St. Louis and this whole evening was going to be different starting with this place whatever it might turn out to be. They walked into a place inhabited by women, most of them black.

A woman approached, swaying her hips, large breasts practically exposed.

"Hi. Can I get you anything? This lady's thirsty. Will you buy me a drink, honey?"

"Sure. Get us a couple of beers. Any kind of beer and get yourself whatever you want," answered Frank.

"Frank, you've got to remember one thing," whispered Jeff, "These girls are out after only one thing. Your money. Don't ever forget that."

"Don't worry about it. We've got one night. Just one night, and that's it. Let's take this one evening we've got and turn it first edgeways, then upside down. Let's give these women all the money they want, within reason. Let us be nice to them--nicer than they expect us to be. Then let's turn around and go to the next place."

They sat at a small table just off the center of the room. Within three minutes the woman was back. She sat down, close to Frank.

"Where are you boys from?"

"Jeff's from St. Charles and I'm from the country taking a vacation from my wife."

"Where's that?"

"Oh I live just eighty miles from here or so."

She slipped her hand onto Frank's upper thigh. Then she ran it up to his crotch and started to stroke him.

"Do you want to do a private?" she asked.

"What's a private? Seems like you've already got a hold of them."

"My name's Melissa. You give me twenty bucks. That's the important part. Then you follow me over there to that couch. I will take care of you over there."

"Melissa, my name is Frank. This is Jeff."

The girl grabbed Frank's elbow and started to pull him away from the table. Frank got up, uncertain as to what it was she was talking about, equally uncertain about whether he wanted to let go of twenty dollars just yet. There was nothing understated about this woman's appearance. She was well-formed, tall, and tight. Her breasts were ample and jutted out noticeably, tapering to wonderful erect points. She was sexual rather than sensual. Whitney Houston she was not. She was not pretty but curvaceous and utterly unforgettable. At the same time she was 100 percent vulgar, for they had not been in the place for more than five minutes and she was already feeling him up.

"I know you will like what I'm going to do to you."

"What are you going to do to me?"

"Just wait and see. Baby, you will like what you are about to get."

"Okay. Show me."

They walked across the room. She pushed him into a sitting position on the couch.

"Twenty dollars first."

"Okay. Here it is." He handed her two tens. She put the money in her G-string, bent way over placing both hands on his knees, and placed her mouth on his crotch. She started to rub her lips up and down his pants.

"Just a little hint of what I give my steady customers," she said.

Melissa got up on Frank's lap, her back facing him, then stood up momentarily as she tightened her buttocks. He took in her slimness. *God* he thought. *I forgot how they were. Their butts are so firm. The muscles have a certain elasticity to them such as white women rarely have.* She lowered herself onto his lap again, turned around looking at him, and grinned. Then she began to raise and lower herself on him, slowly at first, then picking up speed. She got off and repositioned herself, this time facing him, but still on his lap.

"No one's looking. You can suck on my tits. Make sure no one sees."

Melissa began to thrust back and forth. Frank bent forward and licked a nipple. It was dark red, almost purple and perhaps two inches long. She reached behind her backside and started to stroke him between his thighs.

Out of the corners of his eyes Frank could see at least fifteen people watching them. He didn't care. *Hell, he'd never see these people again. And this Melissa. She's straight from the Amazon-- a jungle cat, all sex, with no finesse.* Reminded him of a whore he'd had in Bangkok. That whore, who had been a Thai, who had theoretically been Chinese, was at least five foot eight, had big breasts, was darker skinned than most Thais, and was all animal. He had never forgotten her even though he'd been with her for three hours straight yet had never understood a word she had said. Most Chinese girls he had met were slender and short. Then there was this one. Her parents had probably had eight children or so, had little money, and had sold her into prostitution before she was twelve. In any event she was magnificent.

This Melissa was not the same. She spoke to him. There was the common denominator of speech. They could relate. Yet Melissa was from God knows where. She was from a different culture--she spoke differently, acted differently. She was uncouth, unlike many of the other black girls he had known. Melissa was without pretense. And she was thrusting her hips back and forth, her back arching. He smelled the smell of musk. Not faint, but very strong.

The whole thing lasted for one song on the jukebox. When it ended, Melissa climbed off of him, put her top back on, and hurried off. Frank turned to Jeff who was just getting off the floor.

"What do you think?"

"Let's go. I know another place."

The Injection Pump was a two-story building surrounded by an ample parking lot which was well lit and nearly full. The place was large enough to have housed a dance hall, promising enough bodies to immediately dispel any boredom or mental lapses. A tall staircase just inside the front door led upwards to a single room filled with people. Large, to Frank and Jeff, after the last place and after all the beer they had drunk, it seemed vast. At the top of the stairs sat a tall black man, perhaps as tall as six five although it was difficult to tell since he was ensconced comfortably in a chair taking everyone's money. Muscular, the man seemed more than capable of handling just about anything that could conceivably occur.

"How much to get in?" Frank asked.

"That'll be three dollars each."

The man took Frank's five and handed him two ones, not looking up from the roll of bills he was holding. Frank did not think the man was friendly or particularly interested in anything other than his job for the moment which was taking people's money. Frank sized him up as a man whose attitude was almost one of "Hey I won't hassle you, but whatever you do don't mess with me." The man might have been a boxer in his earlier years. Everything about him reflected a quiet confidence in his own strength and agility. He looked forty although he might have been as old as fifty. Certainly he had seen a great deal and he perhaps had fought a lot in his earlier years. But he didn't seem to be the type to be a troublemaker or to have ever been a troublemaker for that matter. Perhaps he never had been a boxer; perhaps he was an ex drill instructor for the marines--perhaps he had been a green beret. Or he might have been--Frank thought--just a simple war hero who had fought hard in Vietnam. Wherever he had been-- whatever fighting he had done-- had been officially sanctioned. He was not the bar room brawler type.

The man neither smiled nor scowled. He was relaxed. Totally comfortable with his surroundings, he was one to not get excited if a fight should break out. Frank believed he would just simply grab one of the offenders by the arm hard enough to get his attention and quietly talk him out of the place. The other troublemaker would probably look on immediately stopping whatever he had been doing. Then the man would remount the stairs and quietly ask him to leave. But it would probably never come to that. Anyone entering the place would know without being told that the large black man was in charge and that would be that. It was almost as if all the patrons regardless of age or circumstance were third graders and the man was the principal of the school. One didn't even think about crossing him.

Yet there was something else about the guy, a certain indescribable quality that made you like him, even though he made no particular effort toward amiability. Perhaps it was that so long as you didn't cross the line--for example you didn't insult the girls, throw glasses at the bar, or do something equally stupid--he would accept you as you were, as a man who was out for a good time and who should be allowed to do so, within reason. And it wouldn't really matter if you were getting a divorce or if you were an alcoholic; if you were addicted to drugs or if you had been under a psychiatrist's care. He understood.

Immediately ahead of them was a large bar which allowed seating on both sides of a walk through area where the bartender and waitresses hurried back and forth. The bartender, who was around twenty-three or so, was perhaps five foot four or five, weighed about 110. She was quick in her actions and very alert. She could pass for a college girl--had long brown hair, a firm derriere, and smallish breasts that would be firm to the touch except she wouldn't let just anyone touch them. The girl was busy mixing one drink after another or pouring draft beers for her customers. Every few minutes a phone that hung on the wall would ring and she would have to answer it telling the caller that this girl or that girl was here or not here tonight or giving directions to the place. She was going a million miles an hour Frank thought. Fifty feet behind him and to his left was a second bar tended by a pretty blonde.

As he and Jeff approached the main bar a waitress strode up to them, quickly fondled Frank's balls, welcomed them to The Injection Pump, and took their order. While waiting for their beers to arrive, Frank studied the place. There were four stages strategically placed throughout the room. At each stage girls were either dancing or sitting on the laps of the men seated in front of it. There were one or two girls at each stage except for stage number three which was occupied by three girls. Stage three was L

shaped. Seated in front and around this stage were five or six men.
The first three men had the three girls on their laps, each girl with
her back pressed against the chest of her partner. Loud music
blared as the girls slithered on the mens' laps. The three dancers
pumped back and forth, slowly rubbing the mens' groins with their
backsides to the beat of the music.

One girl got off her partner, took off her top, pushed his
chair a foot or so backwards, kneeled in front of him, and started
to rub her breasts against his groin. She was blonde, tall, with
large breasts, firm buttocks, and thin waisted. Five feet, eight 128
pounds, Frank guessed. She was laughing and talking to the guy.
The woman was gorgeous.

"Our kind of place," said Jeff. "Now we know why it is
called the Injection Pump."

"Was that my imagination?" continued Jeff. "Did I see that
waitress feeling you up?"

"No. It wasn't. She was feeling me up."

"How come you are getting all the early attention and not
me?"

"Because I think these girls know all about you Jeff. They
know you are cheap."

"Like I told you before, all these girls want is your money."

"That is basically all any girls anywhere want is a man's
money. It is just that girlfriends and wives utter meaningless
words like love, truth, and loyalty to camouflage their attempts to
get a man's money."

"Let's not get serious tonight, Frank. Let us move to the
finer things in life. For example, here is our beer."

The waitress had returned with two drafts. "I've never seen
you two here before. Is this your first time here?" asked the
waitress.

"My first time," replied Frank. "You mean you've never
seen Jeff here before? He tells me he's practically a regular?"

"No, I've never seen him around. Listen, I've gotta go. If
you need anything give me a holler."

"Okay Jeff, what's the deal here? What are all those girls
doing?"

"They are doing lap dances. Each one lasts for one song.
The men tip them a couple of bucks each time."

They walked around the room. At stage one two girls had
stripped a guy to his underwear pants, and had him lying on his
back in the middle of the stage while they were working him over.

One girl was kneeling next to his feet rubbing the upper muscles of his legs while the other girl straddled his face. She leaned forward and started to stroke his chest as she lowered her crotch into his face.

"Go on up there, Frank, Jeff urged. I dare you to get up on stage with them."

"Look who's talking. Have you done anything yet? We've been to two places already and all I've seen you do is walk around the inside of this place about twenty times."

"Frank, I hate to say it seeing that I'm here, but I'm looking for the perfect woman?"

"Yeah, and I'm looking for one that's totally imperfect. Full of character flaws, perverse, debaucherous, licentious, and absolutely demented. Think I can find someone here like that?" asked Frank.

"Considering that right about now there must be twenty girls or so working here, I'd say that you might even find one as depraved as you are? If you can't, I know another place called the Sports Bar that should do you. But that's for another night."

"Jeff, that should be my mission in life. To find a woman who is as hedonistic as I am."

"Ask and you will receive."

Every time three songs were played the girls were replaced by a new shift. Then the dancers who had been at the stage would go off to the dressing room or with their favorite customer of the moment. A short blonde with glasses knelt before one of the seated men at one of the stages. She unbuttoned the man's shirt and kissed him on the stomach. Then she moved up to his head, kissing him on his neck. She stroked his legs while she moved her lips back to his chest. There her lips lingered on his nipple. *She isn't as good looking as some of the girls but she is sure giving that guy his money's worth*, Frank thought. Frank sat at the stage sitting next in line. The guy gave her a dollar when the song ended. The girl sat on the man's lap ignoring Frank. The girl started to kiss the man's neck again; then got up off the floor from her kneeling position and straddled him. After five minutes, she left him and moved over to Frank.

"My name's Kathy. Sorry to keep you waiting."

"You are forgiven but only if you allow me to buy you a drink afterwards."

"You are on."

"Kathy, you gave quite a show."

"I try my best. That way a guy comes back to me the next night instead of to someone else."

Kathy climbed onto Frank's lap. She wasn't as short as he had thought. *About five four* he guessed. *One hundred and five pounds are so. Nice rear end. Beautiful breasts. Funny looking glasses though.* She kissed him on the lips first, then continued over to his ear and licked it. She reached into his shirt and stuck her hand down his pants caressing his groin. Frank reached out and felt her left nipple, then paused for a moment before bending his head to lick her nipple.

"Hey we've gotta watch it. We are on stage three. Not only do they have a camera on each stage but Bogart is over there watching us."

Frank looked to his right. The black man was looking over at him. Frank waved. The black man smiled.

"I guess you're right Kathy. We've got to watch it. I hate to get Bogart or whatever his name is pissed off. Is there some other stage where he can't watch us as well?"

"There's stage five. That's the best one. Or we can do a private."

"Well, he's still going to watch, isn't he?"

"Oh sure, he's still going to watch, but he tolerates a little more if the girl is doing a private."

"Why's that?" Frank asked.

"Bogart figures the girl is getting twenty dollars so she's not being taken advantage of as much as when's she's only getting a couple bucks for a lap dance. So as long as the girl seems okay, he lets her alone. Within reason of course."

"Kathy, the music just stopped. Let's get a table and order us a couple of beers."

She followed him to a table. Kathy motioned to a waitress and ordered two beers. *Now that's all right*, Frank thought--*she knows the waitresses by name, so she gets their attention a whole lot faster than I could.* Within five minutes the waitress was back.

"Didn't you two get one for me?" asked Jeff as he sat down across from them.

"Kathy, this is Jeff." Then Frank turned the waitress. "Get Jeff a beer."

"Do you want to do a private?" asked Kathy. "I give the best privates in the place."

"Lead on. I'll follow."

Kathy took him to a corner just to the left of the main bar.

Two small tables stood just a few feet from a couch. A customer sat at one of the tables talking to one of the dancers. Frank gave Kathy a twenty.

"Take off your shirt," she ordered.

Frank took off his shirt while Kathy took off her top. He stretched out on the couch. Without a word Kathy knelt in front of him, bent her head down, and kissed his groin. Parting her lips, she started to run them up and down the front of his pants. Glancing back at the bar, Kathy looked back and forth between Frank and the bartender. Seeing that the bartender was talking on the phone and looking away from their corner, Kathy turned back to Frank. "We've got to watch it. Ginny would fire me if she saw what we were doing."

"You mean the bartender?"

"Yes, that's Ginny."

The five minutes passed swiftly. The music stopped, signaling the end of the private. Kathy didn't make a move to climb off his lap.

"Kathy. You work here. You are doing your job which is to get us guys all turned on so we will come back. Can we get together outside of this place?"

"Frank, I would, but I'm really trying to work on my new marriage. I can't. At least, not now. But the next time you come here, I want you to look me up. I work Tuesday through Friday after 8:00 P.M."

"I'd better get back to Jeff. It's one o'clock and we should get going."

They found Jeff standing at the bar talking to Ginny who was still on the phone somehow handling two conversations at once.

"Frank, we've gotta go. Ginny asked me out, and I told her I couldn't go. Make me leave before she forces me into it."

"Kathy, looks like we're going." Lowering his voice Frank whispered, "Keep in mind that I'd like to go out with you if you change your mind."

"I will keep it in mind. Come see me now."

Frank and Jeff turned away and walked past the black man who nodded at them as they turned the stairs. The parking lot was fuller than it had been for the Injection Pump would be open until six.

And that was only Frank's first visit to the Injection Pump. It would not be his last.

KAREN

One and a half years passed since his visit to the Injection Pump. Then, one night, unable to sleep, Frank went downstairs to wait up for Nick who was an hour past his curfew. Nick had a date and had asked Frank if he could stay out till 1:30. Frank had considered letting Nick stay past his curfew deciding in the end that Nick would make a habit of asking for extensions to the 12:30 curfew that was already in place. Nick, Frank's stepson, was barely sixteen years old. *Twelve-thirty is already too late for a sixteen-year-old*, Frank reasoned. *Far better to snap this one in the bud*. Karen was gone when Nick asked Frank if he could stay out past curfew. Then Frank had left the house when Karen returned.

At 1:45 Frank heard a car drive up. Moments later Nick came in the front door. Seeing Frank sitting in the lazy boy, Nick walked past and went into the kitchen without saying a word. Frank heard the refrigerator door being opened as Nick helped himself to a snack.

"Nick, you are an hour and fifteen minutes past your curfew. Why are you late?" Frank asked.

Frank heard the kitchen cabinet door open as Nick reached in for a plate and a glass. *Funny*, thought Frank, *I can hear every move of Nick's yet he can't hear me when I ask him a direct question. The kid doesn't seem to realize that I bought the food he's eating, and that this house belongs to me. Here I am paying all of the bills while his mother takes college classes, drinks coffee with her friends, and watches television. I am the only person who works around here and Nick acts as if it's his mother who is clothing and feeding him.*

"Nick, come in here right now!" Frank ordered.

A minute later Nick walked into the family room, hands in his pockets, as he scowled at Frank. "What do you want?" Nick asked.

"I think you heard me the first time. Why are you late?"

"Mom came home when you were out. I asked her if I could stay out late and she said yes."

"Did you tell her that I had already told you no?" said Frank.

"I told her, but she went ahead and said I could stay out another hour."

"Why did you ask her when I already told you no?"

"You are not my dad, so I figured I could go ahead and ask

her."

"I notice that you brought your plate in. What are you eating?" Frank asked.

"A salami sandwich." Nick replied.

"And do you know who bought the salami, and the bread, and the plate?"

"You guys did."

"No Nick. Not us guys did. I did. Also, the house and the car you drove tonight. If you think about it, your mother doesn't work. Now don't you think that when your mother isn't home and you ask my permission to do something and I say no, that it means no."

"Like I said, you are not my father."

Frank felt her presence even before she entered the room-- felt her anger as she walked through the open door. Karen went over to Nick and stood next to the boy as she glared at Frank. *At least her height hasn't changed, thought Frank. Stand out in a crowd anywhere.* Still about six-one, Karen stood six foot three in her heels, making her even taller than Frank.

"Will you two stop arguing?" There was an undertone of menace in her voice that was directed at Frank. "Frank, will you let Nick get to bed?"

"He's past his curfew, Karen."

"No, he's not. I've decided to extend it to 1:30."

"Karen, he asked me first when you weren't at home."

"It was his first date with this girl. Nick told me that he didn't want to seem like a juvenile on his first date so I decided to let him stay out later."

"Karen, I was the person in charge since you weren't home when he asked. I resent his going behind my back after I told him no, and I resent the fact that you are siding with him, and I resent not having any authority in this house."

"You resent! You resent! Just who do you think you are Frank? You resent everything. You resent my kids, you resent me, you resent that you have to give up the family car to Nick. You have become a sour man, who can't stand the fact that people are having fun around you, who can't give in a little once in awhile. You want to control everyone around you like a dictator."

"Okay Karen, you've made your point. Now I'm going to make mine, and I don't care if Nick is here to listen to this. If I can't have some authority around here, and if I can't have a little say in a house I've bought, I'm going to make some changes around here, changes that I don't think either of you are going to like."

"Fine. Go ahead and threaten us," Karen said angrily. "Stew in your misery, Frank. Nick and I are going to bed."

Karen stormed out of the room as Nick went back into the kitchen. Frank was able to relax only after he heard the last footsteps disappear into the bedrooms. It had been a year since he had been at the Injection Pump. He had never gone back-- yet. Perhaps it was time for another visit, and for something more serious than lap dances. I no longer have a marriage, Frank concluded. He reflected on how one incident had followed another, each incident causing new damage to the marriage. At last Frank felt that he had no control over anything that went on in the house. More and more, he decided he was being treated like Karen's third child. Each time he and Karen argued over the children Frank hardly slept. Frank moved listlessly about the farm doing whatever had to be done. He was not alert, not energetic, and his performance suffered. Worse, at harvest time when he was constantly around potentially dangerous machinery, this lack of alertness made his work all that more perilous.

He considered his options. He could kick Karen out. If he did that, she might end up owning half of the farm if for some reason the prenuptial did not hold up. Frank reflected on the joys of marriage. *Marriage was a contract the man signed which automatically gave away half of what he owned. The fact that men had not risen en mass in arms against this institution was due to the simple reason that most men didn't own much to sign over in the first place. With a farmer it was different. Farming as an industry is extremely capital intensive. Producing a crop required a huge investment in machinery and land. In fact the investment required was so great that very few men could make it. Farmers were for the most part born into it. They got their start from their family. In time the young farmer ending up owning thousands of dollars of machinery and in many cases hundreds of thousands of dollars of land. If a farmer got married, he was signing far more than the average person over to his wife. With the divorce rate at more than 50% a farmer who got married was committing financial suicide.*

The lawyers, of course, would relish a divorce case involving Frank and Karen. Like weasels, they would lick their chops over the prospect of a hundred thousand dollar plus settlement. With land selling at $2000 per acre and with most farmers owning at least 160 acres, the stakes were high. By comparison the average factory worker or salesman or practically anyone else had relatively little to risk. It wouldn't be every day that the lawyers had such a plum to divy up, thought Frank. No, he would have kicked her out a long time ago. *No doubt*, he thought, *half the women in his township who were still married would be packing their bags by now. The problem was that the courts had interfered with the natural order of things. The man simply didn't have any clout anymore.* Frank decided that he'd like to be loyal to his mate, but this had become impossible. *Karen had run over him too many times and had gained too much weight. Slim and attractive before marrying him Karen had changed afterwards.*

Frank considered himself to be lucky. He and Karen had signed a premarital agreement which he hoped would keep her and the lawyers from stealing him blind once he decided to divorce her. Frank knew that other men were not so lucky. Once emasculated and stripped of his authority within the home the man didn't have many options left thanks to the judicial system which would come to the aid of the poor woman. *And what choice did the man have? He could live with it, he could kill his spouse, or he could divorce her while suffering financial ruin in the process. Some choice.*

THE THIEF

The Venture Discount Store was relatively quiet this Thursday at 2:00 p.m. Jeff Shannon had carefully chosen the day and the hour. Success could only be achieved if a minimum number of customers were in the store while he carried out his plan. On Thursdays he didn't have to teach until 4:00 in the afternoon. Jeff had been a drama teacher at Lindenwood College for ten years--had quit High School teaching soon after he had gotten his Masters. His wife, Susan, had just talked him into a two-week summer bicycling trip in Colorado. The trouble was, Jeff Shannon didn't have a bicycle.

He walked through the store, ambling along from department to department. He passed the magazine section, stopped, went back to it, and began thumbing through the latest "Consumer Reports." Jeff glanced at the bicycle section. *Yes it was still there.* He put down the magazine and walked over to the 15 speed mountain bike he had looked at just the last week. The bicycle section was close to the cash register. Just between the cash registers and the bicycle section was the fishing section. Rows of rods, some with reels attached, stood in racks on both sides of a walk-thru aisle. Boxes for lures and other fishing equipment together with the rods blocked the view between the cash registers and the bicycles. He had chosen this store carefully. The bicycle section was hidden from view not only from the cash registers but from the rest of the store as well.

Jeff Shannon chuckled to himself, "I am going to get a bicycle and it is not going to cost me anything." He considered the situation. *First, this store pays its employees next to nothing. That's the way it is in retail.* However, this particular store was on Lindbergh, a well-travelled street. The store did a lot of volume because of this location. Profits were bound to be high. Furthermore Jeff had a little problem with a North County Venture Store two years ago. He had bought a fan, and after six months it had stopped working. When he tried to return it, a sales clerk told him that the warranty had been good for only three months. *These bastards*, he thought--*they won't honor what they sell for six months. What a ripoff.* Well, he was tired of being ripped off. *The corporation is about to give me a well-deserved gift. After all, it is I who have helped educate their kids, and for very little money at that.*

Three mountain bikes, all identical, stood in a row. Jeff

looked around. Noting that no one was watching he began to take the tags off the bike. The last was the price tag which had showed $375. Then he wheeled the bike around into the main section of the store. The girls at the cash register were ringing up their customers--too busy to notice. He wheeled the bike up to one of the counters and waited his turn. The man ahead of him was dumping Styrofoam coolers, folding chairs, a Coleman lantern and other camping related items from his cart onto the counter. When he finished, Jeff smiled at the girl at the register.

"Excuse me miss. I'm not buying anything at the moment. I'm going to look around and come back. But would you do me a favor?"

"Sure, what can I do for you?" she replied.

"I bought this bike not too long ago and it was such a nice day that I rode it here. Could you have someone look after it while I look through the store?"

"I guess so. Why didn't you just leave it outside in front of the store?"

"I would have except I want to shop. You know how dishonest people are these days. That bike cost me practically $400 and I hate to have someone steal it when I'm not looking."

"Let me ring the manager and see what he can do for you."

She got on the phone and began to speak into it. Her voice was amplified onto loudspeakers throughout the store. "Mr. Scully" the voice called out, "You are needed at register four." Five minutes later a short stocky man in his early thirties appeared.

"Mr. Scully. This man here owns this bicycle and he's afraid it's going to get stolen. He wants to know if someone will watch it for him while he shops. I'm too busy at the register to be responsible for it."

Mr. Scully turned to Jeff. "How long do you think you will be shopping, Mr. -------?"

"I'm Mr. Harring. Dr. Frank Harring. I'll only be fifteen minutes at the most. I need some q tips and a few other things. I really have this feeling that bike is going to be stolen."

"Normally Dr. Harring, I'm too busy to do something like this but seeing that things are a little slow right now, I'll look after it myself."

"That's certainly nice of you Mr. Scully," replied Jeff. "I'd really hate to see either you or your store get blamed if something should happen to this bike."

"Don't you worry Dr. Harring. Nothing's going to happen to

this bike."

Jeff Shannon walked over to the pharmacy section and picked out a box of Q tips. Then he walked over to the prophylactic rack and selected a box of Trojans. The last item he chose was a small box of Preparation H suppositories. He went back to the counter. Mr. Scully was still there talking to the girl at the register while watching his bike.

"I don't know quite how to thank you Mr. Scully for dropping whatever you were doing so that this bike could stay in the right hands."

"Think nothing of it Dr._____."

"Harring. The name's Harring. Remember that," replied Jeff.

"Well, I've gotta go. Must count inventory."

Jeff turned to the checkout girl. "I've got only three things. Dirty ears, hemorrhoids, and a wandering penis."

"What did you say?" she asked.

"See the Preparation H, the rubbers, and the Q tips. I said I've got three things--dirty ears, hemorrhoids, and a wandering penis. The wandering penis is the important thing."

"That's what I though you said," she laughed.

"Well let's just forget the rest. I'm wondering if you can help me with the wandering penis?"

"Not a chance. Do you want these in a bag or around your neck?"

"In a bag. Oh by the way, thanks for helping with my bicycle."

"No problem. Have a good day." She put everything in the bag and handed it to Jeff with a pained smile. Jeff wheeled the bicycle outside to his parked van. He put the bag in the back with the bicycle which fit in easily. He drove away, a satisfied smile on his face.

THE WIFE

"Karen, do you have a minute?"

Frank was in the middle of paying bills in his farm office. He had just finished paying the chemical bills for his farm and had moved onto the household, medical, and other personal bills that related to the raising of a family. Like clockwork there were the expected medical bills--too many. Karen loved doctors--seeing them as often as possible and sending her kids even more often. If a dentist wanted one of the kids to come in every six months for a checkup, Karen would send the kid in every five months. This was easy for Karen to do since Frank was paying all of the medical expenses. The next bill was for his stepdaughter's acne medications. Heather's acne had never really been that bad. He had seen far worse having suffered from an acne condition himself thirty years ago. Both he and his sister had grown the amount of pimples that was normal in a 15-year-old, yet neither of them had run up the bills the way Heather and her mother had.

"Karen, I just got this bill for Heather's acne prescription. It's for one hundred-twenty dollars. Do you remember that book in our bookshelf called The New Handbook for Prescription Drugs?"

"Oh that book. I told you, Frank, that it didn't apply to Heather. Heather's skin is very sensitive, and besides--the generic drugs in that book aren't always the same as the real thing."

"They are the same thing and you can cut some bills by half, some as much as by two thirds if---------"

Karen interrupted. "Frank, you are always thinking about money instead of me and the children. You are such a hard hearted man. We are dealing with human beings here who have feelings. Why if Heather thought that you were risking her face for a few dollars. I should tell her just what kind of man you are."

"Well you don't have to. She's in the other room listening," Frank replied. "I know it doesn't mean much to you, but we could have saved fifty or sixty dollars on that prescription."

"You are such a goddamn know it all. I suppose you think you know more than Dr. Finch. Well he prescribed that drug for Heather. He knows what he's doing. That's the trouble with you. You are such a self centered, selfish man--always putting human feelings last. Heather is only fifteen. She could be disfigured for life."

"That is highly unlikely. There are other prescriptions,

Karen, and besides, Dr. Finch drives a Porsche."

"What's that supposed to mean?" she hissed.

"It means that Dr. Finch is out of touch with the common man--that he is out to show the world that he has arrived--that he can drive a Porsche which costs $60000--that he doesn't care if you and I have to spend $50 for a prescription, $100, or $500."

"I have never heard anything so asinine in my life. And as for Dr. Finch driving a Porsche. Well he deserves it. He went to medical school. He works long hours. Maybe you should work harder yourself, Frank. Maybe you should get a Porsche. Maybe that will make you happy so you will get off of my back and Heather's. The trouble with you is that you are going through a mid life crisis." Karen was shrieking at him now. "You have finally come to realize that after all these years you haven't gotten as far in life as you had planned and now you are really pissed. So you begrudge honest hardworking men like Dr. Finch what they have worked hard to get."

"Karen, this Dr. Finch---"

"Don't interrupt me, Frank. You've brought this up. It is you who have ruined my day. Do you realize what you have done--are doing to our marriage?"

Blood started to course through his body swelling the veins in his neck. He wanted to hit Karen in the face. His arms started to rise of their own accord off his desk. *I can just read the papers now*, he thought. *Abusive man beats up his wife. Karen Harring admitted to St. Luke's Hospital with severe bruises, concussion.* He counted to ten . . . to twenty. He made an effort at controlling his breathing. *I've got to get out of this marriage*, he thought. *I don't know how or when, but I've got to get out.*

"Karen. I've got just one thing to say-------."

"Oh just one. I thought that by now you'd have at least ten. What do you have on your list now? Your hate list for me and my kids."

"I want you to get a job. End of subject."

"Oh you want me to get a job," she replied sarcastically. "What else do you want?"

"That will do it for now."

"Oh that will do it for now," she harped.

"Excuse me Karen. I really have to work. Sorry we argued."

"Well it's about time you apologized for something." She slammed the door shut. Frank looked out the window. He thought about Kathy and wondered if she was still at the Injection Pump.

UP TO NO GOOD

Jeff Shannon had been home only a few minutes when the phone rang. It was Frank Harring. They had not seen each other for months. In fact Jeff had not even talked to Frank on the telephone for at least two months. It had seemed to Jeff that every time they got together something happened. That something usually was good and memorable, and sometimes it was a kind of tour de force level of adventure that they both remembered for years afterwards. What would it be this time?

"Jeff is that you?"

Frank seemed excited. That spelled trouble. 'Yessiree, life was starting to look better', Jeff said to himself.

"You've got me. Hey Frank, I just want to warn you about something."

"What's that?"

"I just stole a bicycle from Venture. You should see it. A fifteen speed mountain bike. Just took off the tags when no one was looking, brought it to the checkout counter, and asked the manager to watch my bike for me. You should have seen the little dipshit watching that bike."

Frank pictured the whole scenario in his mind complete to the little manager watching the bike while sucking his thumb. "Hey, you've got to watch yourself, Jeff. Someday you are going to get caught and then it's goodbye Lindenwood College. Hello to your new career washing dishes. But don't worry---I'll still be your friend. I'll bring you brownies in prison."

"You make it sound so tragic, Frank. By the way, there's one little thing about it."

"What's that?"

"When I had the manager watch the bike, he wanted to know my name. So I told him I was Doctor Frank Harring."

"Great, Jeff. That's just great. You are a true friend."

"Well anyway, I doubt if anyone will call you or anything, but just in case they do, just tell them that you don't know anything about it. So what's up?"

"Jeff, I've got a great idea. Let's go to East St. Louis again. If I recall, you never had to teach on Tuesdays. Is that still the deal?"

"Yes, but I've got my preparations to do, and I've gotta do some research in the library."

"Oh piss on all that. We are talking about women. Beautiful, succulent women all decked out to make our lives better."

"I don't know Frank. It sounds good but if my wife ever caught me at one of those places."

"Yeah, I know. It would be the best thing that ever happened to you. Jeff, you need a breather. I know just the girl for you," Frank lied. "She likes the cerebral type or at least that's what she told me. Exact words honest to God. I told her I knew this college professor and she begged me to bring you by. Now what do you say? Is this an offer you can't refuse or is this an offer you can't refuse?"

"You talked me into it. When and where do we meet?"

"How about twelve noon at the Injection Pump parking lot on Tuesday. We can eat there. It's on the house." Frank threw that in knowing that Jeff couldn't pass up a free meal. "After we eat, we can get free passes to go to this other place." Frank promised a free meal knowing that there would be no way Jeff could stay away now.   "See you there, Frank. You can count on it."

"I know. See you there. Noon. Bye."

NIPPLES

The van was already there when Frank drove into the Injection Pump parking lot. Frank was surprised to spot Jeff in the van. If he had arrived first, he would have waited over a beer or even a coffee inside. After all, he had only four hours or so before he would have to go home. *Time, more than money, was therefore the essence, and why not,* he asked himself, *spend it with the girls upstairs? Surely that was far better than idling around in a parking lot watching the second hand of his watch.* Then he saw that Jeff was not alone. A man several inches taller than Jeff was sitting next to him on the front seat. The man was in his late thirties. Bedroom eyed with wavy hair, his stomach betraying a slight paunch, he appeared to Frank to be an ex High School jock, perhaps years ago a football player.

"Frank, good to see you. Do you want a beer?" Jeff and his friend were drinking beer from cans. A large cooler lay on the seat between them.

"Have you two eaten?" Frank asked. "They've got food upstairs. It's free."

"I don't know about you two, but are you sure you want to go up there? There's another place down the street that doesn't have a cover," Jeff's friend replied.

"I'm Frank Harring," said Frank. Frank sized the stranger up as a know it all.

"Tom McGinnis. I'm a friend of Jeff's. We live next door to each other."

"Tom, you can tell us about that other place later. I'm hungry. The cover's only three bucks, and I've just gotta eat," said Frank. "Let's go upstairs."

Without looking back at the other two, Frank went up the stairs, paid his way into the Injection Pump, and took a seat at the bar. He ordered three beers and waited for Jeff and Tom to walk in five minutes later. Frank spied a pretty blonde coming out of the restroom. The girl's hair hung long around her face, blonde to a light brown in color, not quite straight with just a little curl to it. She wore a white dress, just a little on the short side to accentuate her legs, but not short enough to show off her thighs. The girl seemed out of place in a topless bar. Perhaps it was her hair or perhaps it was the dress that did it, but the girl appeared too innocent, too much like the girl you were taking to the Prom. She walked demurely over to the far side of the bar and sat alone.

Frank went over to the bar and sat next to the blonde. She looked up at him and smiled as the bartender came over. "I'm getting a Bud Lite. Can I get you anything?" he asked the girl.

"I'll have a Coke. I really don't drink."

"Then you want a Bud Lite and a Coke?" the bartender asked Frank.

"Please."

The bartender came back with the drinks which Frank promptly paid for. He turned again to the girl. "My name is Frank."

"Hi. I'm Chanel," the girl replied shyly.

"Chanel, you seem different from the other girls. I haven't been here a lot--only once and that was almost two years ago. The girls were more aggressive if I remember, but then I was pretty loaded."

"You really don't think I'm aggressive?" Chanel laughed. "Perhaps it's because I'm only nineteen or maybe it's because I don't drink."

Frank looked across the room and saw that Jeff and Tom were already seated at a table. Two girls had joined them, one of them sitting next to Jeff, the other on Tom's lap.

"Chanel, see my two friends over there at that table with the two girls. Care to join them."

"Sure."

Frank brought Chanel over to the table. Soon after everyone had introduced themselves, a waitress came over. The girl on Tom's lap asked, "Will someone buy me a drink?" The girl looked at Tom.

"Sure. Waitress. You there. Bring this woman a drink. He's buying." Tom pointed at Jeff.

What do you mean? Jeff asked.

"Your turn."

"But I brought the cooler, Tom."

"Look, Jeff, I didn't bring a lot of money. I'll get the next round."

Once, Chanel had to leave to dance at her stage. Frank went over to a small buffet table where he helped himself to a plate of spaghetti and a bowl of peach cobbler. By the time he returned to the table with his plate of food, Tom was kissing the girl on his lap on the neck. Jeff was still sitting next to the other girl smoking a cheap cigar--the kind that sells for ninety-eight cents a pack. A few minutes after Chanel had rejoined them from her stage, Tom looked up at all of them while checking his watch.

"I'm sorry to break up a good thing, but we've gotta go meet some friends down the street."

"I forgot all about that," Jeff replied. "Don't worry girls. We will be back." Jeff and Tom got up from the table and started to walk down the stairs. Frank still sat at the table.

Frank turned to Chanel. "I really don't know this Tom at all, and I don't know what he's got on his mind. How long are you going to be here?"

"I started at noon, and I'm done at 8:00."

"Can't promise, but I'll try to get over here before I go home."

"If you don't, I'm usually here during the day on Tuesdays through Saturday. If I'm not here, I might be down the street at Ciceros. When they don't have enough girls there, they call down here since the same guy owns both places."

Frank left and joined his friends outside who were already waiting for him in the parking lot. Jeff was reaching into his van for another can of beer.

"Want a beer Frank? You Tom?"

"Always. You don't even have to ask," replied Tom. "Hey did you see what I was doing to the girl I was with. I got to feel her tits. You should have seen it. I was rubbing her nipples and I was feeling her ass under the table. And I didn't have to do a lap dance or even buy her a drink. This is great. Just stick with Tom and you guys will be all right."

Frank turned to Tom. "Okay, so what does a guy tell his wives after he's been here all day. I've gotta get home by six."

"I don't believe you guys. You two are a couple of pussies. I just tell my wife I ran into a couple of friends, went out and had a few beers, and I just got home late, that's all. It's all part of training the little woman."

"So you just pass yourself off as a guy who goes out and has a bunch of beers with some guys and your wife buys into that?" asked Frank.

"You better believe it. It's no fucking big deal. Why? Does your wife have a problem with that? Hey you two, I told those broads upstairs that I had to go. This place is too damn expensive. There's this place down the street called the Sports Bar. The girls aren't as nice looking, but there's no cover. Plus they've got this limo. You pay a hundred dollars for the limo for one hour. I rode in it once. Made friends with the driver who had seen me in the bar a lot. He told me things were slow, and then he asked me if I'd like to take a ride in the limo? I rode around and you should see that limo. They've got everything you need in there. Rubbers, champagne, beer, cigars. Everything."

Jeff handed Tom a beer. "Let's see if I've got this right. We just go in there, meet a girl, and more or less ask her to fuck, and she says 'Sure. The limos on you. The fuck's on me.'"

"Well not quite like that. You meet these broads see. You play up to one like I did back at the Injection Pump with that broad. Get on her good side, and if she begins to like you, you can bang her in the limo. I got all these girls eating out of my hand, but I just couldn't see paying a hundred bucks plus the tip to the girl."

"So you gotta pay the girl too. I thought she'd like you so well Tom that she'd do it for free. What does that cost?" asked Frank.

"Oh anywhere from fifty to a hundred and fifty."

"Sounds like a deal I can't pass up. Good thing you got me out of the Injection Pump. Too expensive for my blood." Frank headed for the pickup. " I'll follow you two to this sports complex bar."

The bar was down the street less than two miles away. Frank pulled into the parking lot next to the van. Before the other two could get out of Jeff's van, Frank was already walking into the Sports Bar. Just inside the door was a long bar. Several men lounged around it on both sides. The bar was in the form of an elongated U so that customers could sit all around it. A middle-aged woman with a bored expression stood behind the bar. Seven or eight women either sat at the bar or walked around the room. Frank walked around to the other side of the bar where he spied a blonde sitting there next to another woman. She looked more than thirty. She hardly noticed Frank as he approached her. He didn't have a lot of time and decided that she was probably the best looker in the place.

"Can I buy you a beer?" Frank looked directly at the thin woman in front of him purposely avoiding the woman sitting on the woman's right.

"Sure. Go ahead. Hey Nadine. Get me a Budweiser and get him whatever he wants." She nodded toward Frank.

Frank paid for the beer just as Tom and Jeff walked in. Jeff stood just inside the door studying the situation. Tom eyed Frank and immediately came over.

"Hey buddy, can you buy me a beer?"

"Sure. You get the next one. Just have Nadine bring you whatever you want. Tell her I'm paying. This time."

Tom ordered a Miller Lite and turned to the girl.

"Hi Nipples."

"Hello. I haven't seen you in here in awhile." She looked up at Tom. She did not smile.

Frank looked at her with new interest. "Did he just call you Nipples?"

"Yes, that's my stage name. Everybody calls me that."

"Why do they call you Nipples?"

The girl stood up and looked directly at Frank her eyes meeting his. She took off her top. Her breasts were small, though firm and compact. In the middle of each was a large nipple two or three times larger than average. Frank could see that she was around five foot five--and around one hundred-ten pounds. She had a thin waist and no stomach, was slender in the hips, yet there was just enough flair in them to keep her from appearing masculine.

Tom advanced on the girl, beer in hand. "Let me feel them, Nipples. I want to see if you've changed." Tom grabbed the girl's breasts roughly, one in each hand. "No doubt about it--you're the same Nipples."

"Tom, I think Jeff wants to talk with you. He's over there." Frank motioned to Jeff who was still at the other side of the bar. He turned to the girl.

"Let's grab a table."

"Fine. How about that one over there?" Nipples motioned across the room where ten tables with chairs surrounded a single stage. Frank noticed for the first time a girl walking off the stage toward him. She walked by the other men seated between Frank and the stage.

"Hey, you're new here. Do you want to tip me for my dance?"

The girl looked vaguely Oriental. Frank sized her up as neither Japanese nor Chinese. Obviously she was of mixed blood and probably born in the U.S. He noted that she was short and good-looking which brought the number of good-looking girls in the place up to two.

"What do you mean, do I want to tip you? I'm sure that your dance was very good, but you haven't been on my lap. I just got here." Frank remembered the table or lap dances he had with the girls at the Injection Pump. He considered this form of request for payment strange. "Look, you're really good looking, but I promised . . . what's her name" . . . he gestured toward Nipples, who had already seated herself at a table . . . "wealth, my body, and beer."

"Oh that's all right. Have a good time." She sidled past Frank toward Tom who was just behind him. Frank joined Nipples at the table. He noticed that she was wearing an incredibly narrow bikini top with a bottom half that was just as skimpy. Close to the stage now, the neon lights had come into play. *Neon green. That's the color she's wearing. Such audacity. First, she takes off her top and lets Tom feel her up. But the color of her outfit. A real attention getter,* thought Frank.

Jeff came over and sat next to Nipples. Frank slipped into a chair across from her.

"Hi, I'm Jeff. Somebody told me that you have great breasts. I've got a great penis. Don't worry, I'm not bragging--it's just that that's what all the girls tell me."

For the first time the girl laughed. She turned to Jeff.

"Show us then. I just showed my tits over there. Put up or shut up."

"I would but my mother made me promise that I wouldn't let anyone else touch it--today I mean. However, tomorrow you can meet me at Best Western."

Frank leaned across the table and grabbed the girl gently by the arm. She turned toward him.

"What should we call you? Somehow I don't want to call you Nipples."

"You can call me Lori. But I don't care. You can call me Nipples."

Frank studied the girl. One moment she would be sitting erect, attentive to everything that was said around her. She was like a sponge taking in everything, missing nothing. She seemed an innocent, quiet and receptive to what was going on around her. Unwilling or unable to make waves, she would let the men do most of the talking. No longer did she seem the sallow, unsmiling girl whom he had first met at the bar. Her face reflected a peacefulness and contentment which seemed out of place in a strip bar. Yet underneath it all he knew--had in fact seen when she had taken off her top just minutes before--another side. That other side was that of an imp, of a woman who made her own rules, who played jokes, and who really didn't particularly care what anyone thought of her. She was a Dr. Jekyll and Mr. Hyde, so quickly had she changed from being uninhibited to becoming Miss attentive. He had misjudged her. She was not more than thirty after all, but in her early twenties. And the boredom that had been written all over her when she was seated at the bar was no longer there.

"Lori, I like that much better than Nipples," said Frank. "Don't get me wrong, you've got great nipples, but I think there's much more to you than just great nipples. Your nickname is too one dimensional. I have a feeling that you are a very interesting woman."

"Thanks Frank. You know, I really don't know you, but you are different from most of the guys who come in here."

"You are right on that. Take Jeff over there. He's one of my best friends yet he and I are totally different." Jeff was leaning back in his chair, talking to a woman sitting at the table behind theirs. The woman was wearing a Cowboy hat.

"Can I borrow that hat? Jeff asked the woman. I'll give it back."

"Sure, go ahead and take it, but buy me a drink first."

Jeff stood up and took the hat off the woman's head. Putting it on, he went to the bar and ordered two beers. Tom came over and asked Jeff for a beer.

"Get your own beer. What do you think I am? Made out of money. Tom, I don't think you've bought a beer yet."

"The hell I haven't. I've bought several."

"All right then. But you've got the next round. Okay? Get him a beer." He handed the bartender a ten. When she brought him his change, Jeff went back to the table.

"Hey Nipples. What do you think of this hat on me? Makes me look like a good guy doesn't it?"

"No. I'd say it makes you look perverted."

"You are right. I am perverted. Give this woman $1000 for answering the question." He was showing off for the woman at the next table. Jeff leaned over and kissed Nipples. "And you my dear--here's a beer." He turned around to face the other woman who was still sitting at the next table.

"Thanks for the beer. Do you mind if I join you and your friends?" The woman pulled up a chair and sat next to Jeff.

"No, I don't mind at all, but first you have to answer a question."

"What's that?"

"Do you believe in sex on the first date?"

"Well . . . that all depends."

Jeff pointed at Frank. "With him I mean. Would you have sex with him if he asked you out?"

"Well, I don't know."

"How about an easier question? Do you think she'd have sex with him--Jeff pointed at Lori and Frank-- if they didn't have a date?"

"Sure she would." The woman caught Lori's eye. "You don't care if I answer that for you, do you, Nipples?"

"Yes I do," Lori replied. Lori looked at Jeff mischievously. "I tell you what. Jeff, why don't you have sex with that girl up on the stage?" Lori waved at the dancer on the stage who waved back at her. The dancer was a little on the heavy side, blonde, and totally nude. She was gripping a pole in the middle of the stage which rose from the platform into the ceiling.

"In my underwear," said Jeff. "I'll only do it with her in my underwear. For you, Nipples, I'll let you take my underwear off, but that's for you only."

"I'm sorry to be rude, but I'm Kim." The other woman addressed the group. "I'm up next. Be back in a few minutes."

Kim got up and went over to the jukebox which stood behind the bar. She made three selections for her music. The girl who had been on the stage put her top and G-string back on and came over to the table. Standing just inches from Frank, she pulled her G-string away from her body. Her vagina gaped at Frank. Frank reached into his pocket for a dollar bill and stuck it between her stretched G-string and pubic hair. The woman bent over and kissed him.

"Thanks hon. I'll be back."

She went over to Jeff. Lori touched Frank's hand and giggled.

"Don't say a word. I know exactly what you're thinking."

"Good. I'll save it till later," said Frank.

The dancer was still standing in front of Jeff. She had already pulled her G-string aside. Jeff fumbled in his pockets.

"I thought I'd brought my wallet. Just can't find it."

"That's all right. You can get me next time."

"I can't wait," said Jeff.

The woman went to two men who sat at a nearby table. Each gave her a dollar. She kissed each man, then moved to the next man who sat alone at the bar.

Kim climbed onto the stage and grabbed the pole. The

jukebox came alive with her first selection. Kim leaned away from the pole which transferred her weight from her feet to her right arm which held onto the pole. Tentatively she began to move around the pole. She performed one 360 after another, her feet never completely leaving the floor, her body twisting away from the pole. The jukebox started to play the next selection. She stopped and looked over the audience taking in three newcomers who had just come in the bar. Then she took off her top and G-string and started on the pole again.

Frank noticed her body for the first time. Kim was a large woman, but not fat. *She'd go around five eight, one-hundred and forty pounds*, he thought *A little too heavy for doing gymnastics off the pole and she knows it.* He preferred women who were thin but not so thin as to be on the frail side. But all in all he found her attractive.

"Do you have a dollar for the jukebox?"

Frank hadn't noticed the woman who had walked up to him carrying a bowl. He slipped a dollar into the bowl which was already filled with dollar bills. He turned to Lori after the woman left.

"How do some of these girls make a living?"

Lori's eyes lit up. "See I told you. I knew what you were thinking. You don't like fat women and you were wondering how we can all make a living here."

"You read me right. I just don't see how everyone can make a living here especially girls who are overweight. The place is small and there just aren't that many guys here. But there are a lot of dancers."

"It's a rough go."

"And you, do you make a lot of money?"

"Sure. I do all right. I have my regulars who come in pretty often. You wouldn't believe what some of them pay me just for my company."

"I won't ask. Want another beer?"

"Sure. And how about a shot to go with it?"

"What kind of shot?" Frank asked.

"I'll handle it." Lori spied the waitress, several tables away. "Hey Pat," she yelled out, "bring me a shot and two beers?" She looked at Frank. "She knows what I want."

"Want to tip me for my dance?"

It was Kim. Frank had not noticed that her set had ended and that another girl had already taken her place on the stage. Kim stood before him, bare breasts practically in his face. They were what one would define as ample. Her skin was a light brown. Her nipples were darker brown in color and about one third the size of Lori's. They were a little more elongated than usual though pyramidal in shape. Looking at them he could scarcely taste the mouthful of beer he had just swallowed. He could anticipate what one of those nipples would taste like. *Not imagine, but anticipate*, he thought. This close to them, it was almost like having one in his mouth already. He could feel the nipple just below his tongue jump in his mouth of its own accord so that it was above the tongue. He could feel the warmth of her breast as it swelled against his face and the nipple itself became larger in his mouth. Frank reflected on the true meaning of the word titillate. Synonyms flashed through his mind like excite--arouse--stimulate--kindle.

And speaking of stimulating--Kim had pulled her G-string away from her body displaying her vagina. Her pubic hair was short and few in number. Frank pulled out a dollar bill and gently tucked it in front of her G-string.

"Can I call you Nancy?" Frank asked.

"No. My name's Kim."

"I know. But you really remind me of this Nancy I know. I'm really complementing both of you. It's like I've known you for a long time, and here I've just met you."

"Sorry, but you've got to call me Kim."

She moved over to Jeff and pulled her G-string out.

"What a nice bush!" Jeff exclaimed.

"Jeff, do you want to tip me for my dance?"

"I'll make you a deal. When you come back, I'll buy you a drink instead."

"Sure. When I come back."

She moved to the next table. Jeff looked over at Frank and Lori, shrugged, then got up and followed Kim. Coming up behind her, he put his arm lightly around Kim's shoulders and addressed the two men sitting there.

"Give her two dollars for her dance. Hell of a dance, wouldn't you say. Just think. If she does what she just did for two dollars, what will she do for ten?" Jeff asked the two men.

The two men each gave Kim two dollars. She went to the next man who was standing at the bar. Then she went to another table. Jeff followed her until she had received an extra dollar from six men asking each man to tip her an extra dollar. Then he went back to Frank and Lori. Jeff sat next to Lori leering at her from beneath the cowboy hat.

"I know you want me baby. You just can't fight it." Before Lori had time to react, Jeff bent over and started to kiss her.

"You are really rude," she started to say.

Before Lori could finish, Frank grabbed the brim of the cowboy hat that had been squeezed down tightly over Jeff's head. It was almost as if the hat were permanently attached to Jeff's head. With one quick flick of the wrist Frank flung Jeff back into his chair. Jeff stood up

"I'm going to go check on Tom."

"You won't have to Jeff. He'll be out of beer soon. Look at him. He's at the bar talking to two women. Are they buying him drinks? After all, we haven't seen him for at least twenty minutes. Oh by the way, Lori is my woman. At least she is while I'm here. No hard feelings."

"Don't worry about it. I just thought she was in love with me. See you lovebirds later."

Frank turned to Lori. "I'm sorry not to have stopped him earlier. I didn't think you cared. In fact, I thought you liked him. He's terribly funny you know."

"He's funny all right, but he's also very rude. Here, I'm sitting with you. You are buying me drinks. I'm obviously with you, and here he's supposedly your friend and he's trying to kiss me every chance he can get."

"There won't be a next time," said Frank.

"I've gotta go. It's my turn to dance." Lori got up and went over to the jukebox to punch in her selections. Kim came over and sat next to Frank.

"Frank, do you want to do a private?"

"Kim, I'd love to do a private with you, but I don't think I can right now." Frank couldn't believe that Kim would come over and sit next to him right after Lori had to go up on stage. He was incredulous that she would ask him for a private when he hadn't even done one with Lori.

"Why not?"

"It's not fair to Lori. That's why."

"Lori would do the same to me."

"What do you mean?"

"She'd horn in on a guy I was with."

"Kim, doing a private with you sounds intriguing. What could I expect?"

"You'd love it. Let's just say you'd be well satisfied. I always make sure of it."

" You are very tempting, Kim, but it'll have to wait for some other time. As long as I'm with Lori, I'm with Lori. It's just that simple."

"You don't know what you're missing. Frank, I've just gotta do a private with someone. I've hardly made any money today."

"Why don't you do a private with Jeff?"

"I would, but I don't think he likes me."

"Oh he likes you all right. He's just clowning around. That's all. Tell you what--I'll convince him to do a private with you."

"You think you can?"

"All I've got to do is remind him he's got a penis, that's all."

Frank had all but forgotten about Lori. The first song had just ended. She was taking off her G-string and top. The next selection from the juke box came on. The singer was Garth Brooks. Lori grabbed the pole with one hand and began to circle it. At first her feet stayed on the platform. In seconds she picked up speed. Her feet rose off the platform climbing higher and higher into the air. Lori's weight, all 110 pounds of it, was evenly distributed between both arms now, as her legs circled the pole three feet above the stage. Her body pirouetted around the pole as centrifugal force held her slender form nearly parallel to the stage. Frank excused himself and pulled up a chair in front of the stage. He rested his feet up on the edge of the stage, his legs slightly apart. Lori saw him and came off the pole. She stood over him, looked down into his eyes, and smiled. Then cupping one breast in both hands, she started to play with her nipple. Then she did the same with the other breast flicking her nipple with her fingertips. Lori stepped forward a little bit so that she was almost on top of Frank and offered him her breast. He leaned forward and reached out. Lori smiled once again at him, then shook her head. Taking a quick step backwards she turned around so that her back faced him. She placed her hands on her buttocks and squeezed them together. Frank could see the muscles contract. Then she spread her legs from a standing position and pulled her buttocks apart. The muscles that had been jutting out tightly against her skin relaxed. Grabbing both of her buttocks firmly with both hands Lori spread them so that her vagina peered out at him. She took a little step backwards so that her vagina was inches away from Frank's face and bent over at the waist almost touching the floor with her head. The motion spread her buttocks even farther apart at the same time bringing her vagina even closer to his face. Like a breath of warm humid air, he could feel the heat from her body pouring over his face. Lori twisted her neck as she raised her head so that she was facing backwards from between her legs. Smiling at Frank from this position she took her right hand off her backside and started to stroke her vagina with quick little flickering movements. With an outward twist of the wrist Lori gestured to the audience in general and to Frank in particular as if she were throwing a gift toward them.

Frank understood this gesture to mean *I'm offering myself to you to do whatever you want.* And he wanted her. The neon light had distorted Lori's face making her look haggard and old. Deep shadows had appeared under her eyes. The Garth Brook's selections did not help. Frank's overall impression was one of sadness, of a woman whose life was almost tragic. But Lori's body--that was an entirely different matter. She was so light on her feet and so quick in her movements. Yet she had been very strong and well coordinated on the pole. She could have been a star athlete--perhaps a figure skater, ballet dancer, or even a cliff diver. Her legs were obviously strong, yet not heavily muscled like a runner's. Her entire form flowed together as if she was of one piece. She was put together--beautifully. Frank thought. And here she was--performing for twelve men or so, around a pole at three o'clock on a Tuesday afternoon. Naked, she stood before him, her light brown pubic hair on public display.

Her replacement mounted the stage as soon as she climbed down. Lori ignored Frank and went from table to table, from man to man, collecting her tips. Frank went back to their table.

"Hey buddy, can you get me a beer?" Tom called out loudly.

Frank ignored him, walking over to the bar where he ordered two beers, one for himself, and one for Lori. By the time he got back to the table, she was standing before him, G-strings pulled out. Tom, Jeff, Kim and a brunette were already sitting at a table.

"Would you tip me for my dance?"

"Now that was a dance that's worth tipping for," he replied. He slipped a dollar into her G-string, fighting off the urge to let his fingers linger there.

"Hey, where's my beer?" It was Tom.

"Same place as your money," replied Frank.

"What do you mean?"

"I mean it's nonexistent."

"Hey look, I've been buying you beers all afternoon," said Tom.

"You haven't bought anyone a beer that I know of," said Frank.

"Oh bullshit," grumbled Tom.

Frank stared at Tom stonily. "Look, collect from my insurance agent." Then he turned to Lori. "Let's sit down and drink this beer. I despise people who don't pay their share," he said out loud.

"Do you have a dollar for the jukebox?" It was one of the overweight women who worked for the Sports Bar. Still looking at Lori, he put a dollar into the jar she carried. The woman went over to Jeff who declined.

"Lori, this thing with the jukebox and all the dancers wanting their tips is getting very annoying. You're with me and I could care less about anyone else, so I wish they'd just leave me alone."

"Frank, you really don't have to pay. Just say no."

"Really hate to do that. I suppose I shouldn't even be here if I'm not willing to play the game. I want to play the game so I fully expect to pay even though I know it's all a hustle. You almost feel sorry for all these fat women. I don't want to just shut them down entirely. But these interruptions are making it damn hard to carry on a conversation."

"Do what you've got to do."

"Hey, do you girls want to have a party sometime with us. That is, if we can get away from our wives?" Jeff looked over at Lori, then at Kim sitting next to him.

"Sure," said Lori, "What do you have in mind?"

"Well, I'm really not sure. Any ideas, Frank?"

"I've got one. There's this drive inn movie theater near me. It's fifteen miles from where I live, seventy from here. We could all go there except there might be people who would know me, who would tell my wife. However, that's the exciting part. Playing with fire. I could get burned."

"Well, we could just all camp out at my house some weekend," said Lori.

"Aren't you married?" asked Frank.

"No. I've got a boyfriend. And a brother. They both live with me in my house."

"I can just see it now," said Frank, "We can invite our wives. You invite your boyfriend and brother and we all get together in some kind of pile." He turned to Lori. "Any kids?"

"I've got five kids, but I can get a babysitter. My boyfriends in jail right now and I can just send my brother away for the weekend."

"Why did your boyfriend go to jail?" asked Tom.

"He got into a fight in a bar. He broke the other guy's jaw after the man stabbed him in the thigh. He's in for thirty days."

Frank whispered in Lori's ear. "How about lunch sometime. Or how about going out at night, just you and I? Perhaps an outdoor theater. Ever been to the Muny Opera?"

"I've never been there, but I've heard about it. Sure, I'll go with you."

"I want to ask you one thing," said Frank.

"What's that?"

"Are you a dependable person?"

"Sure. I've missed work only once and I've been here eight months. Ask any of these girls."

"What I mean is, can I depend upon you? There's two kinds of people in this world. Those you can count on and those you can't. I don't have anything to do with anyone I can't trust, male or female."

"You can count on me," said Lori.

"You want to do a private?" Frank asked Lori. "I can't stay here much longer."

"I'd love to. Now?"

"Definitely."

Lori got up from the table and went into the next room. The room was open to the bar. The kitchen and a restroom were down a hallway close by. The room didn't offer much privacy but it was better than the main room. Lori led Frank to a chair in the back corner. He handed her a twenty and took off his shirt as Lori took off her top.

"Sit back in the chair," she ordered.

He slumped into the chair as she climbed onto his lap with her back facing away from him. She started to thrust back and forth as she rubbed her backside along his groin. Then suddenly, not happy with their position, she got up and turned around. She climbed onto his lap this time facing him. He started to kiss one of her nipples. Then his mouth wandered up to find her lips. They kissed until the song was over. Then she got up.

"I'd stay longer, but they're watching me. We've gotta get back to the table," said Lori.

They went back to the table where Kim was trying to talk Jeff into doing a private.

"Hey, all I've got left is two bucks. Honest. Isn't that right Tom?"

"Yeah. We are both just about broke."

Frank interrupted. "Kim, can't you talk Jeff here into five minutes of perfect bliss and contentment?"

"No. He says he's broke."

"Jeff, I'll tell you what. I'll lend you eighteen dollars so you can get a private. Remember though, it's a loan. Not a gift."

"Well, okay then."

Jeff took the money from Frank and went to the adjoining room with Kim. Five minutes later they returned. He was smiling.

"Hey you guys. We've gotta go. Jeff, don't you have a class or a game to referee or something?" Tom's voice was urgent.

"No, No, No. You guys don't have to go," said Frank.

"Sorry Frank, but Tom's right. We've gotta go," said Jeff. The decision had been made. The two were leaving.

"Well Frank, this has been great. Let's do it again next week," said Jeff.

"Girls, are you working next Tuesday?" asked Frank.

"We'll be here," Lori replied.

"How about 1:00 next Tuesday then?" Frank's eyes were fixed on Lori.

"I'll be here."

"Then let's all be here at 1:00," suggested Jeff.

Tom was walking out the door into the parking lot. Jeff turned to follow him when Frank grabbed his arm.

"Look, I'll meet you here on Tuesday, but don't bring Tom. The man doesn't pay his fair share plus he's a total know it all. I know he's your friend and I respect that. Just don't bring him around me."

"I understand Frank. See you on Tuesday." Jeff hurried outside to rejoin his friend. Five minutes later Frank was in his pickup headed for route 64. Except that he was not going to go home yet. There was the little matter of Chanel. After all, he had told her he would try to get back to her.

SHANNON BLOWS IT

"Tom, I don't know about you, but I could really use another beer for the ride home. I'm pulling off the main drag to let that cop get ahead of us."

"What cop? I don't see one."

"He's behind us, I think. In any case, I'm taking this side street. When I pull over, grab us two beers," Jeff ordered.

Jeff turned right and drove nearly a block when he pulled over. Tom reached into the cooler and grabbed two cans of beer. He opened one and handed it to Jeff. Then he opened the other. After several minutes had passed, Jeff went around the block, turned right, and got back onto the road they had just left. They drank their beers in silence as they headed toward the interstate. They scarcely noticed the two cars that had been parked along the side of the road pulling in front of them. The van was traveling much faster than the car that had just pulled in front of it. Jeff noticed that its driver had turned on his right turn signal. The car started to turn right, slowly at first, then accelerated into a side street. The car that it had been following had its brake lights on. Jeff's van was traveling thirty miles an hour. The first car loomed in front of them going two miles an hour. Jeff slammed on the brakes. It was too late. The van responded, losing speed rapidly, but the car was too close. The van hit the rear end of the car. There was a dull thud, and Jeff and Tom were thrown forward.

"Are you all right, Tom?"

"Yeah, I'm okay. I almost poured beer all over myself. What happened?"

"Goddamn niggers pulled in front of me, that's what happened. I didn't see that this car had stopped in the middle of the fucking road."

"The cops are going to get here. You're going to get a ticket. Holy shit, we've got beer in this van! We've gotta do something!" Tom exclaimed.

"Listen up. I'm getting out to talk to the driver of that car. I want you to throw everything out of the van. The beer, any cans, the cooler, everything."

Jeff got out and walked up to the car he had just rear-ended. Tom started to rummage around for any empty cans which remained in the van, putting them in the cooler. Then Tom got out of the passenger side of the van with the cooler, and noticed that someone had put a fence around his yard. He threw the cooler with everything in it over the fence and returned to the van. By this time Jeff was already talking with the driver of the car.

"Look, we're sorry that this happened. It's our fault."

"You better believe it's your fault. I'm gonna sue your ass," the driver of the car threatened.

"Don't worry. We've got insurance. What do you think-- should I make a call to the police so they can make a report?"

"No they'll be here in a minute anyway. They're policing us niggers all the time. I'm still gonna sue your ass."

"I'm going back to my van. I've got a friend with me."

Jeff returned to the van as a squad car approached. He started to survey the damage that had been done to his vehicle and noticed that his friend sat inside looking morose. Then Tom lowered the window.

"I hope we can get this over with. My wife's going to kill me," Tom complained.

"Your wife! What about my wife? This is our van, not yours. Hey, I thought you had this thing with your wife all figured out. Don't you remember telling Frank that you'd just tell her you met some guys, had a few beers, and everything's just fine? Don't you remember mentioning something about training the little woman?"

"Yeah, but that was before the accident. This is different."

"Then how do you explain this Tom? Why is it that you were having to leave the Sports Bar so soon? Could it be that your wife keeps strict tabs on you, and you had to be home?"

"My wife doesn't keep strict tabs on me. I've got her under my thumb unlike you," Tom said belligerently.

"Don't bullshit me. I'm your neighbor. I know what goes on in your house. Same thing that goes on in my house, Frank's house, most guys' houses. The woman has got to have a rein on the man. Except that you won't admit it."

"May I see your licence and registration?"

The cop was standing at the driver's side of the van. Jeff took out his wallet and handed his licence to the cop. He opened the glove compartment where the registration was kept, found it was there, and showed it to the officer.

"Have you two been drinking?" the cop asked.

"No sir," said Tom.

"Look here, I'm talking to the driver," the cop snapped.

"Officer, there was another car that had been driving ahead of me. Suddenly he turned right and there was this guy out parked in the middle of the street. The guy was hardly moving at all. I couldn't see him on account of the first car until it was too late. I think we were set up," Jeff explained.

"So, where's the other driver?" asked the cop.

"I don't know. Probably home by now."

"Well then, that's too bad. There's no witnesses that will verify your story. Looks like you fell asleep. Looks like you simply ran that car down," said the cop.

SHANNON EXPLAINS

Jeff drove into his driveway at 5:30 noticing that his wife had still not returned home. He fixed a pizza for the kids and made a sandwich for himself. He grabbed the Post Dispatch, sat in his lazy-boy, and started to look through it while he waited for Susan to return home from work. At seven Jeff heard her car pull into the garage. Since Susan had started her latest job, it had become Jeff's responsibility to feed the boys who were always hungry well before she got home. Somehow, somewhere, Jeff had gotten the distinct impression that Susan thought it was beneath her dignity to fix meals at night now that she was working again. He would even go so far as to admit that she had probably searched for a job that would keep her away from her maternal duties. It didn't matter that the two boys were hers from a previous marriage. 'After all, as she so often pointed out, 'You have said your vows and have taken me for better or worse.' Jeff wondered *when the better would arrive* when Susan walked into the room. She was a tall woman with red hair. She was also forty pounds overweight.

"Well, did you get the kids fed?"

"As always," Jeff replied.

"I'm tired, and I haven't had a thing to eat. Do you want to go out and get something?" she asked.

"No. I've had a sandwich. Susan, there's something I should tell you."

"What's that? Tell me later."

"I wrecked the van."

She looked at him, eyes fit to kill, her face livid. "You what? You stupid idiot. Let me get this straight. You wrecked the van. Our van!"

"That's right. I ran into this guy. He pulled in front of me. Actually the guy who was following him, who was in front of me, pulled over suddenly. At the same time he put on his brakes so that I would rear-end him. His car was a ... "

"You rear-ended a car," she interrupted. "Were you on drugs or what?"

"As I was saying, Susan, it was a setup deal. His car was a junker. He's trying to get some money out of the insurance company. Can't work for a living so he has to rip off the system."

"Oh, how utterly disgusting. And what happened to you?

Didn't you see this happening? Were you drunk? Where did this happen anyway?"

"No. I wasn't drunk. The whole thing was unavoidable."

"If you-rear ended the guy, you must have a ticket. Let me see it. Where'd you say this happened?" she asked.

Jeff reached into his back pocket and pulled out the ticket. He handed it to her. "Somewhere in Washington Park Illinois."

Susan was already reading the ticket. "Goddamn it Jeff! Isn't that over by East St. Louis? What were you doing in East St. Louis anyway?"

"I was in a strip bar. What do you think I was doing in East St. Louis?" he asked angrily. Jeff had decided that he had enough of her bullying.

"You were what? Say that again Jeff. I was in a strip bar."

"You asked for it. You've got it. I-w-a-s i-n a s-t-r-i-p b-a-r."

Jeff spoke each word with exaggerated deliberation.

"And just what were you doing there?"

"I was watching these women dance. What do you think you do in a strip bar?"

"Why? Why'd you do it? Don't you have enough to do around the house? Don't the kids and your work give you enough to do? Why would you go and watch those awful women?"

"Because I like to watch a bunch of naked women. What did you think?"

They argued until three in the morning. As always, she won. He had classes to teach the next day, and he needed to be sharp. She got him to promise to never again go to a strip bar. It was a promise he had no intention of keeping.

THE MEANING OF MARRIAGE

It was a hot summer day in August, and Frank was in the last place he wanted to be. He and Stan were standing ankle deep in a pile of corn shoveling it toward a hole that was a few inches wide. The overhead bin needed to be cleaned out since they were loading semi trailer trucks the next day with beans. The overhead bin was fifteen feet above a driveway which went through the storage area where he and Stan kept their grain. A number of large grain bins surrounded this storage area which had once been a barn. A grain leg towered over the whole complex rising over one-hundred feet off the ground. At harvest which occurred in the Fall, grain would be dumped into a pit which would transfer the grain all way to the top of the leg. A valve one-hundred feet up in the air could be set at ground level which would channel grain to whatever bin they selected. These bins were thirty-six feet in diameter and more than thirty feet high. Eight bins surrounding the leg held the year's harvested grain. When they sold the grain, they would auger the grain out of the bottom of the bin into the pit. The grain would be brought up from the pit into a second leg or tower from which it was dropped through a long tube into the overhead bin in which they were standing. This overhead was one of several, all of which were made out of wood. Each was like a little room although each one held enough grain to fill a semi. Semis would pull up underneath the overhead bin. Frank or Stan would then open the door in the floor of the overhead, and the grain would flow out into the semi truck below.

Periodically these overheads needed to be cleaned out. For one thing, not all the grain flowed out of them without a little additional help. The floors sloped toward the center so that gravity caused most of the grain to flow into the open doors in the center of these floors. Usually there still remained close to two-hundred bushes in the bottom of the bins. Stan and Frank were contending with those last two-hundred bushels in overhead number one. Each man held a large aluminum shovel which had been specially designed for scooping up grain. Each of these shovels had a head on it which was almost 2 feet wide.

It was almost totally dark in the bin. The door in the center of the floor was a frame of white being practically the only source of light. Underneath the door in the center of the drive-thru was a harvest wagon. Frank thrust his shovel into the pile of corn, lifted it full of grain, and dumped it into the open door. He drove the shovel head into the pile again and scooped another shovel full into the door. The grain fell into the wagon bed. Each time he scooped, Frank moved a half bushel of grain from the overhead to the wagon. He shoveled with short strokes of his arms moving quickly without rest. Stan stood on the other side of the door, legs slightly spread. Stan picked up the pace, scooping faster. Dust from the ground up kernels of corn filled the inside of the overhead. Neither man wore a mask which would have filtered this dust away from his lungs. Frank started to shovel faster to match Stan's pace.

"Stan, are you ever going to start wearing a mask?"

"I doubt it. I hate masks. I can scarcely breathe with one on. Then I can't work as hard or as fast."

"Well, after I get out of this grain dust, I can scarcely breathe for a week."

"Yeah, I'm the same way. It's a good thing we don't do this every day. We'd get the white lung for sure," said Stan.

"I wonder if there is such a thing as white lung. This dust can't be good for a man. All the truck drivers I know who get around this grain dust use masks. Bean dust, though, that's the worse. It coats my throat and gets into my system so that I'm not quite the same for a while."

"You want to have coffee at my house or yours afterwards?"

"Mine. No one's home. We can talk without being overheard," said Frank.

The two men picked up the pace again, shovels flying. Frank wanted to rest. His arms ached. He knew that Stan probably felt the same way but wouldn't admit it. Neither man wanted to show any sign of weakness to the other, both of them working nonstop. Finally, the pile began to dwindle. At last only a couple of inches of corn remained on the floor of the bin. Frank started to use his shovel as a large scraper pushing or pulling the corn across the floor into the door. Scraping noises filled the bin as the edge of Frank's shovel head scooted across the floor. Several minutes later all of the corn had been moved from the overhead bin to the wagon below. They would deal with the wagon later. It was coffee time.

Frank fixed a pot of coffee as Stan sat at the kitchen table. When enough coffee had been brewed to fill two cups, Frank quickly removed the glass container that had come with the coffee maker. Before any coffee could get away, he put a cup underneath the appliance to catch the coffee that was dripping out. Filling the two cups, he replaced the glass pitcher so that the rest of the coffee could drip into it as it was brewed. Then he sat across from Stan after handing him a cup.

"You and I both work hard for our money," Frank began.

"I don't know if we always do, but we just did--that's for sure," said Stan.

"Do you think it's worth it--working as hard as we do?"

"Have you got a better plan in mind?"

"As far as how hard we've gotta work, no. However, when it comes to how we spend the money or how we live our lives I have some new ideas," said Frank.

"You're always coming up with new ideas, Frank."

"You and I are in similar situations. We both farm, we are both married, and we both have lost control over our lives when it comes to our marriages. Am I right?"

"What do you mean?"

"What I mean is that our wives run us. But most men around here are in the same predicament."

"You are right on that score, Frank."

"Have you heard about Sally Seiffert and what she did with her Dad's credit cards?"

"Not really. What happened?"

"She's up at college you know. Well, Alan gave her a Visa card to be used for emergencies. This last semester when he got the bill, it turned out that Sally had charged it to the limit. Alan got so mad that he found her purse and cut her credit cards to pieces with a scissors. Then he did the same with all her other credit cards. When his wife Brenda came home, little Sally complained about what her daddy had done. From what Alan told me, they argued about it all night. Sally, of course, was there most of the time listening in."

"That sounds like a typical husband wife fallout for around here," Stan replied.

"So here's the picture. Little Miss Spoiled Rotten runs up her Dad's credit card to over a thousand dollars, and Big Mama comes to Little Miss Spoiled Rotten's aid when Big Mean Old Papa Bear gets upset. The lesson to be learned is that Little Miss Spoiled Rotten should do it again."

"That sort of thing happens to me all the time. Happens to you too, I've noticed." Stan sipped his coffee plunged in thought.

"Do you remember last winter when our daughter, Heather, was on the girl's basketball team, and the coach lined up a bunch of games with St. Louis teams. Those games were more than eighty miles from here. I brought the matter in front of the school board. Told those idiots that they should be more concerned with academics, and that it was ridiculous to schedule a slug of games that far away."

"Girls' basketball is ridiculous anyway," replied Stan.

"In any case, Karen found out about my talking to the school board. She argued with me all night about it just like Brenda did with Alan."

"No wonder the whole United States has such a shitty school system," said Stan. "The whole school system rotates around sports. The be all and end all."

"Well, I've decided that I'm going to get a divorce. For two weeks I've thought about it. I've been taking this crap for far too long. This thing with girls' basketball was the last straw. It used to be that a man had some clout, but those days are over. I cannot continue to have Karen run over me. This whole thing is undignified. Bunch of bullshit to have the wife whip her husband around."

"Excellent decision Frank. So when are you going to do it?"

"Next summer. I've got a year. Then her kids will be in college and it won't disrupt their lives too much."

"It's going to be a tough go, knowing what you're going to do and still living with Karen for a year."

"I've got some ideas I'd like to share with you. Let's start with Tee Pee etiquette."

"What in the hell are you talking about Frank?"

"I was reading a book about the American Plains Indian. Most of the tribes had a set of rules of Tee Pee etiquette that they enforced. Things like, the man entered the Tee Pee first and the squaw deferentially followed the man, and the children while in the Tee Pee, at least, kept their mouths shut until they were spoken to. Also, that all the men in the village were like uncles to the Indian boys, and that they were to be obeyed at all times."

"Sounds like the way things used to be around here fifty or sixty years ago," said Stan.

Frank went on. "Take the cave men for example. Their job was to go out and hunt. To put food on the table. The woman's job was to make clothes, take care of the children, prepare the food, etc. The man always had the last word just like the American Indian. Take most of your primitive cultures, and you will find that the man had the last word. "

"More than that," added Stan, "women had it pretty rough. They got all the crappy jobs. The men--when they got done with what they had to do--got to bullshit with the other men in a special tee pee, drink beer, smoke Peyote or eat it or whatever you do with Peyote."

"Exactly. And then those Virginia Slims commercials had to come out and ruin it all."

"I can picture those commercials perfectly. The new modern woman giving herself cancer while dressed stylishly as her family goes to hell in a hand basket," Stan replied.

"Well, we both know that those cutsie pie commercials depict the downfall of the United States. Those commercials are telling women to be liberated--to be their own person--to not take crap off of anybody. Am I right or am I missing something?"

"No, Frank. You are absolutely correct."

"Yet God, if there is a God, designed men and women to be entirely different. The first thing a woman wants to do is to have children. That is, most women. Watch little kids when they get around babies. The little girl, when she sees a baby, she wants to look at it, hold it, care for it. The little boy, when he sees a baby, he ignores it. He goes back to his toy gun or whatever else he was playing with. Take a man and a woman now when they are grown up. They are sitting in a restaurant and another couple comes by with a baby. The man either sits there bored or he talks to the other guy if he knows him. The woman makes over the baby as if she was seeing the Great Wall of China for the first time. She holds the baby, she plays with the baby, she comments on how cute the baby is."

"And after the man and the woman get in the car, she continues to talk about how cute the baby was," added Stan.

"You've got it. Most of them are designed that way by their maker. It's as if these women were wind up toys. After they are wound up or created by God, they have only one direction to run. The spring is wound tight and the toy slowly winds down with the wind up key turning in only one direction. That's how they are with babies. Now, once the woman has kids, she's like a female lioness with those kids. Everything revolves around the kids. She will do anything for them--even kill for them. One of them turns into a murderer, it doesn't matter, she will protect the murderer till hell freezes over. And what happens to the man--her husband?"

"She forgets about him. He becomes superfluous," said Stan. "Going along with what you're saying, Butch Drover once told me that he used to watch birds for hours on end. Once the eggs hatched, the female bird starts bringing worms to her little ones. Then she has the male bird bringing worms to the nest. But she'd chase him away from the nest as soon as he delivered the worms. All he'd do for hours on end was to bring worms to the nest yet she wouldn't want him near her or the nest. Well you know Butch. He's cynical as hell. He went on to say that women look upon men as their worm getters. That is all that they amount to. Their chief function becomes making money for the kids. Aside from that the women don't care if the man is happy, if he's well fed, if he has a say in the house, if he is satisfied sexually. Now I don't know if I agree with Butch, but that's what he thinks."

"Butch is a little extreme. Many would consider him to be almost demented, but the truth of the matter is, he's usually not too far off the mark." Frank got up and poured himself another cup of coffee. "Did you really want to get married, Stan?"

"Not really. I was going out with my wife just soaking up life and enjoying myself. I had my friends and things to do. I had a woman who kept me sexually satisfied. Then she more or less told me that I had better start getting serious or start looking for someone else."

"Same thing happened to me," added Frank. "I had everything going my way when I first met Karen. I had lots of money. I traveled a lot. I had several girlfriends. When we first started going out, she did everything for me. She was Miss Perfect. She brought meals out to my tractor when I was out in the field. Wherever I wanted to go was fine with her. Karen wanted to screw all the time. Then she told me she was losing her heart to me. She said she didn't want to get hurt. She said I'd have to make a decision--to either make a greater commitment or lose her. Hell of a sales job."

"Frank, I'd say that happens to just about all the guys. The girls pressure them into marrying them."

"Now here's the fundamental difference between women and men. The women have this terrific biological urge to have children. The men--they're ambivalent. They want to be free. They want to be with their friends, pick up women, drink beer, go waterskiing, and do a little screwing. But kids and marriage-- That's the last thing on their minds. Women on the other hand are programmed to have children. They are like wound up robots-- Gotta find a man, any man. Gotta make babies. Must perpetuate the human race with my offspring. So the woman goes out to find some guy who's just going through life doing his own thing and she begins to work on him. She does this incredible sales job to make him think she's better than sliced bread. She convinces him that he can't do without her and that he's going to lose her if he doesn't marry her. So what does he do?" Frank left the question hanging there.

"He marries her and then the fangs come out."

"Exactly, Stan. The fangs come out. All the meals brought out to the tractor while the man is putting in his sixteen hour days putting in a crop--she stops bringing them out. Now it is she who decides what they will do and when. What she used to do while she was selling marriage to the guy, she stops doing."

"So, it's a broken contract. All the things she has promised during the courtship period are forgotten. Is that what you mean?" asked Stan.

"You bet. But all's fair in love and war, right?"

"That's utter bullshit," said Stan. There was venom in his voice.

"Look at it this way. It's a contract all right. A verbal contract. But marriage--that's a written contract. And as you probably know, Stan, a written contract overrules a verbal one. Any lawyer will tell you that. So what we have are all the things a woman promises a man which induces him to marry her, she reneges on. He has of course married her on the strength of her promises, and if he breaks the written contract by divorcing her, he loses the farm."

"Frank, you have a most painful way of cutting to the heart of the matter."

"I learned at the feet of the master. Butch Drover."

"Our resident local guru," added Stan.

"We need someone to set us on the right path. I believe the women all read this little red book, like Mao Tse Tung had for all of his Communist followers. This little red book, which is kept secret from all men, is entitled *How to rope in your man and then pluck him*."

"You didn't say fuck him, did you?" asked Stan.

"No, I said pluck him, as in pluck all his feathers off. But it's not just the sales pitch that gets the men into this state of marital bliss--excuse me, Stan--I really meant marital blasphemy. It's God."

"Come again."

"God. You see someway, somehow, we men have been

designed to almost always gravitate to one woman. Let us suppose, Stan, that you are single and that you are going out with several girls."

"Okay, that sounds good. I'm going out with several girls."

"And," Frank continued, "invariably you end up preferring one to the others--often for purely physical reasons."

"Sure--one is better looking than the others," said Stan.

"One might think so. But the one that you would choose, assuming they are all pretty good looking in the first place, is she the one I would choose?"

"Not necessarily," countered Stan. "It becomes a matter of personal preference."

"So it would appear. But there's something just a little different about the one you choose. Something about her hair, the way it envelopes your face as you are kissing her. Perhaps it is her voice that gets to you or the way she walks. Now the fact that you prefer her because of these kinds of things really isn't a question of looks is it?"

"No, but those kinds of considerations are related to looks," said Stan.

"True, but they are not the same thing. Let us take it a step further. So what happens is, you prefer that one girl and you end up spending more and more time with her. Eventually you end up dropping the other girls. You keep spending more and more time with her. You begin to think that no one else is like her. Physically I mean. No one else can fuck you the way she can. No one else feels quite like her. No one else smells quite like her. You develop a bond with her that's magnetic. By magnetic I mean that the two of you continue to gravitate toward each other, and that other women fail to break that bond."

"I can see your point," added Stan. The bond that develops sucks the two in. And the attraction becomes more and more intense until the man and the woman decide they can't do without each other."

"That's right. And our creator designed us to be that way. However, read the Bible and you get entirely different ideas--like God wanted Adam to have a companion, and men and women should be helpmates, that sort of thing. He didn't intend that at all. As proof of this, I think that you and I both entirely agree that most men's wives make terrible companions. No, it's a sexual thing. One body calling out to another. Drawing it in. Sucking it in. It's about one girl's vagina feeling better around one's penis than another's. It's about come and 69ing and fucking. The whole biblical idea of love and marriage is rubbish. God's concern is really to perpetuate the human species, and He doesn't really give a shit about how He's going to do it."

"Frank, I hope you never get on a pulpit."

"I don't intend to. But let me go on. So the guy who is so physically attracted to this woman, what does he do? He gets married because of her high pressure salesmanship and promises that she will break in the future. Then the years go by, and guess what happens? The man becomes less and less physically attracted to her. Even if she takes care of herself, the prospect of screwing another woman becomes more appealing to him. It's like an old farmer friend of ours said once, 'If you could have steak every day, you'd eventually get tired of it and want to try something else.'"

"So who's that?" Stan interrupted.

"Your Dad."

"You've gotta be shitting me."

"I'm not. But in any case, for one reason or another, most of the time the magnetic and irresistible attraction that once existed begins to wear off until it is gone."

"It's gone because the guy would like to try something new. Am I correct?" asked Stan.

"Either that or the woman has gotten fat and ugly or she has turned into such a bitch that he doesn't want her anymore. My main point is that the bond is broken."

"But there's children in the marriage by that time," added Stan.

"My whole point. Mission is completed. God's intentions, and I might add-- the woman's, have been fulfilled. Or perhaps I don't want to say the woman's intentions. Remember that she has been wound up. She can go only one way. She doesn't really have free will in the matter. But God's will has been done. And it is not according to the Bible. The woman is a terrible companion. Furthermore the marriage was based on a bunch of broken promises on her part and upon a sexual attraction which is both impersonal and magnetic. Almost a demonic force. And lastly, happiness does not result from this marriage, only children."

"So, you don't think much of God?"

"I didn't quite say that," Frank replied. "What I am saying is that His intentions are to perpetuate the human species and that these intentions are as honorable as perpetuating a race of crickets.

I am saying that what He is doing creates unhappiness instead of happiness. Actually I admire Him. He's a great strategist."

"I am beginning to see your point. It is a good thing that I'm not going to Church."

"Speaking of which--ever notice how people get married in churches. Not to mention how these churches keep promoting marriage. Now go into a church. Any one of them. Do you see more men or women?"

"There's a lot more women. But then women outlive men so there's bound to be a lot more older women than older men," added Stan.

"Take a closer look. There's more younger women than younger men too. It's because the church is telling women what they want to hear. Now look at the judicial system. Most of the guys around here, if they got divorced, they'd lose 50% of what they've got. Since most of us are farmers and we own land, most of us could stand to lose well over a hundred thousand dollars right off the bat. What would happen if a woman would end up with nothing if she got divorced?"

"She probably wouldn't ever get divorced because she'd lose too much," Stan replied.

"And don't you think she'd be very careful to make sure she wouldn't be thrown out? If her husband told her to jump, she'd jump. But with the court system the way it is today, she's protected. She can be the biggest bitch in the world, and if her husband doesn't like it, she can run off with his money. And the legal system and the church will condone what she is doing."

"So what we are saying," added Stan, "is that the leading institutions are holding men in bondage."

"You bet your ass, that's what I'm saying. Not only that but take a guy who's single. What do the girls who have already got husbands or boyfriends want to do? They want to set the poor guy up with their friends, who they can't wait to marry off to the guy. Not only that, but I'm convinced that most of the married guys secretly want the guy to get married too just as much as the women."

"You've lost me there," said Stan.

"It's simple. First, they want the other guy to share his pain--to find out what it's really about. Second, human nature is they don't want the other guy to be better off than they are. The single guy is free whereas they aren't so they want to bring him down to their level."

"So what you're saying is that it's a plot against the single man's remaining single."

"What I'm saying," Frank replied, "is that you and I both have rotten marriages like most guys we know. What I'm saying is that marriage is one hell of a shitty thing for the man. What I'm saying is that nothing could be more stupid than entering a marriage contract, which is a contract enforceable by law, which will result in divorce 50% of the time, and which will result in acute financial loss to the man. That is a really stupid thing for us to do. Since we are not stupid, the only reason we would do something that idiotic is that some very powerful forces are out there compelling us to do so."

"So what can we do about it?" asked Stan.

"What we should do is to kick all the women out of their jobs, usurp control over the money supply for ourselves, live in dormitories, have the women live in dormitories, and raise the children the way we think they should be raised instead of how they think the kids should be raised. We should disbar any lawyer who thinks a woman is entitled to anything out of a divorce. Child Support yes--any form of alimony, no. If this sounds familiar, it's because that's the way it used to be, except for the dormitories although some cultures had them in one form or the other. I mentioned the idea of dormitories as a kind of metaphor. The men would be able to do things together any time they wanted, and the women being in dormitories represents the fact that they would have limits placed on their influence. But there's one thing I'd do before even that."

"What's that?"

"I'd do away with the Virginia Slims commercials."

"Well, it's unlikely that we are going to shuttle the women into dormitories not to mention the men," said Stan.

"Collectively, it is unlikely that we are going to accomplish anything. Individually we can do something, however."

"Such as."

"I am reminded," continued Frank, "of a black guy who was a good friend of mine. I will always refer to him as Saint Perrier. Actually his name was Bob Perrier, but I call him a saint because his ideas promise redemption for the man who follows them. Anyway, this Bob Perrier, or Saint Perrier had an agenda which he called his Three Point Plan."

"Mind if I get myself a fresh cup of coffee," asked Stan. "You don't have to get up." Stan went over to the coffee pot and poured himself a fresh cup. "That's what I like about you, Frank, you've always got some new all comprehensive plan."

"That's because I am of Germanic extraction. We Germans like to pigeon hole everything, categorize things, summarize. We like theories and models. It's because we cannot stand disorder. Anyway, Saint Perrier was probably the only black German in the world because he certainly liked to put everything into nice little theories. Saint Perrier suggested that men tend to get stuck on one woman and that is what ruins them. He informed me that he used to have at least three girlfriends which he categorized as plans. He had a Front Program, a Homestead Program, and a sneak Program. The Front Program was the girl you took out. She was the girl you'd introduce to your mom and dad and to your friends. She was the one you'd take to the Junior Prom in High School. The Homestead Program was a girl who was above all things your friend. Maybe you screwed her, maybe you didn't. That was immaterial. If you needed a button to be sewed on your shirt, she'd do it for you. If you wanted to go to a movie on the spur of the moment, she'd go with you. She'd drink beer with you. Above all, she was your confidant."

"So what's the Sneak Program?" Stan asked.

"I knew you'd be interested in that. That stood for a girl whom you'd have sex with. Not that you didn't necessarily have sex with the others, but this girl you didn't parade in front of your friends. She would be there for sex and that would be it. She didn't have to be especially good looking. She didn't have to be smart. And she didn't have to have good manners or a good personality. One more thing."

"What's that?"

"You don't have to be limited to just one. You could have as many sneaks as you wanted. In any case Saint Perrier contended that a man could be 'together' only if he successfully maintained a three-point plan. There's one more thing."

"What?"

"At the time I was Single, and Saint Perrier was married. I asked him about married guys and the Three Point Plan. He laughed and said, 'It didn't matter. All guys should have a three-point Plan.' I used to think that was horrible since I believed that a man should be faithful to his wife. Now after having been married after all these years, and after having been abused the way I've been abused, I know he was right."

"Why's that?" asked Stan. "How can you justify a man

cheating on his wife now, but you couldn't then?"

"Because then I believed that people were honest. I used to believe in the principle of give and take. I used to believe that men and women could jointly make decisions together and that neither should run over the other. Now I've come to realize that the woman promises to observe this principle until after she's gotten married. Then she starts to run the man. Then she literally runs over him. What she has done is that she has broken the verbal contract she made with the man which convinced him that marriage was an okay deal after all. This then gives him the moral right to commit adultery. Furthermore, if we go a little further with this line of reasoning by contending that there was an implied contract between God and man, we find out that God broke his end of the bargain by promising companionship. As a result man can go ahead and commit adultery."

"So, if this three point plan's so good, why don't more men practice it?"

"Because it's practically impossible to maintain," Frank replied. "For one thing there's that trap that the man gets hopelessly pulled one woman over the others. And he can be pulled by one of his sneaks just as easily as by his front. The other thing is that a three-point plan is so terribly time consuming. It takes a lot out of a man to keep three or more women occupied. He'd just about have to quit his job and be born rich to accomplish this. Nevertheless, the three point plan is an ideal like the Holy Grail that men should aspire to. They should attempt to follow it whenever and for as long as possible."

"Did you say that you had some ideas? I take it you have a better idea?" Stan asked.

"I'm not sure if it's better or not, but I've got an idea. Actually, it's a takeoff of the tree point plan. Let me ask you a question? Or let me ask you two questions? Both are personal. How many times do you get laid per week is the first. The second is how much more does it take you to maintain your wife and your children over what it would cost you to live by yourself?"

"I'd say I get laid once a week on the average, and it costs around $28000 more per year to be married and to have children than what it cost me by myself. Believe it or not I've often thought about the second question because I've often thought about the question of divorce and what I could save out of pocket."

"Now, Stan, listen carefully. Let's break that $28,000 down. Let's say that you want to continue having sex once a week except that you take two weeks off on account of illness or any other reason. Dividing $28000 by 50 gives you $560 a week. That means that you can pay someone for sex any amount up to $560 and be better off than you are now. And don't come back and give me the standard retort that money can't buy love and all that crap because let's face the fact that our wives do not treat us with love. They might say they love us, but that's just words. Empty, meaningless words. The day we got married, we started paying dearly for sex. And out of all the options, marriage was the most expensive option for getting steady sex."

"Hey, I won't argue that one bit." Stan spoke eagerly. Stan was fully attentive now, knowing that something would come out of this conversation after all.

"Now what do you think it would cost you to get a decent looking prostitute to spend the night with you?"

"I haven't checked lately. In fact, I haven't checked at all. But I'd say $200 for the night, $100 for a fuck, maybe less," Stan guessed.

"I would venture to say that in today's sorry economy that you'd probably get a decent prostitute to spend the night with you for $150 once she got to know you and if she liked you. Stan, you could have two different prostitutes each week for $300 which is $260 less than you are presently spending on your wife and kids. Consider the benefits. Variety in your women. Greatly reduced cost. More time to do what you want with your friends or otherwise. And best of all you are a master of your fate. That is you no longer have to kowtow to a bossy, castrating, bitch."

"Yeah, I'll be master of my fate all right," Stan replied. "I'll get aids."

"I don't have that figured out yet. I'm working on a cure," laughed Frank. "In any case we'll just have to worry about that later."

"In spite of the aids you're about to convince me I could get, this sounds interesting."

"You remember Jeff Shannon, don't you?"

"How can I ever forget him?"

"Jeff once warned me that if I ever got divorced the first thing I'd do was to go out and look for another woman. He told me he'd do the same thing, and that either one of us might do even worse."

"That's probably true. They say that divorced men often go on the rebound, and that many of them get married within a year of their divorce. So, Frank, what are our options?"

THE GREAT PLAN

"What are our options? The obvious option is that we can get divorced and hang around singles bars waiting for Miss Right to allow us to get her phone number," Frank said with sarcasm. "That's what would be expected of us, and that's what most guys do after they get divorced."

"Sounds humiliating, "Stan retorted.

"Definitely unappealing. The prize isn't worth pursuing anyway because the whole thing leads to unsuccessful marriage number two. All right, consider this one. How about the Personals? You know. Advertise your credentials in a newspaper. I can see it now. Personal for Stan Osterman, *Lonely outdoorsy type wants company of attractive single woman 25-40 who enjoys tennis, drinking, the opera, and the good life. Women with kids need not apply. Please send photo and bust size.*"

"I can't see many applying who don't have kids, "Stan replied.

"Or maybe the answer is to go on a Cruise and just hope that the right girl just happens to meet you."

"Or how about the wrong girl or just any girl?" said Stan.

"Now you're onto something. But why the indirect approach. Why not go with a more direct method of procuring a girl? After all, you just said that you'd go for any girl, assuming I take it that she's pretty attractive?"

"You've definitely lost me."

"Have you ever been to East St. Louis or that area? Places like the Injection Pump, Ciceros, and others?" Frank asked.

"A few times. But surely you don't think that those places can offer anything, do you?"

"Depends on what you want. Seems like you just told me you wanted female companionship. I believe we agreed that Singles Bars were a bunch of crap, and that a serious relationship leads to the pitfalls of the marriage trap."

"Well those places are only clip joints. They just take your money. You leave and all of a sudden, you realize your pocket just had a hole in it," said Stan.

"So, what's marriage, Stan? Keep in mind and don't ever take your mind off one little number."

"What's that?"

"$28000 per year. I didn't think I'd mention it again, but since we're talking about holes in one's pocket."

"I agree with you, Frank. Marriage is very expensive, and going to places like the Injection Pump doesn't begin to compare when you look at it that way."

"I've thought about this a long time, and I've been to the Injection Pump and several places like it recently. I think we can have a pretty good time with the girls working out of those places if we just analyze it from the right perspective. Now what do you think these girls hate the most about their customers?"

"Not paying enough," Stan replied after a moments deliberation.

"That would be one thing. Another, and I'm only saying this because I've been there recently, is they probably despise guys who come in, sit with them, and immediately start putting their hands all over them. On the other hand, if a guy comes in fairly often, and provided he tips them enough, I would think the girls would each try to outdo one another trying to get his business."

"Especially," added Stan, "if the guy seemed to have several girls whom he was spending time with."

"Shades of the three point plan. Can't ever let one of them think she's got you. If we start doing this thing, we've gotta make sure we don't get stuck with one girl. Gotta make them compete. Make them think they must do something special for us for them to be competitive."

"How far do you think they'll go?" asked Stan.

"I think it pretty much depends upon the girl. Some will do anything for a buck. Some will probably not do much at all. And don't forget about Aids. I believe you mentioned that earlier," Frank warned.

"That would seem to put a fly in the ointment."

"So, one doesn't want the easy ones, but just wants to set up something with the ones he likes for later--after the big Divorce."

"He's still got the problem with aids."

"By that time, perhaps he knows the girls better. Gets a feel for which ones have been around more than the others. Hell, I don't know. We'll just have to cross that bridge when we come to it."

"Then what's the whole point?" asked Stan.

"To have fun. Worry about the future later. Oh, and there's something else that's very important."

"What's that?"

"The girls should have fun too. Our rule is that each girl that we have anything to do with should be better off after we met her than before. That means that we don't take advantage of them. Pay them enough that we're worthwhile to spend time with. Treat them with enough respect that they don't look upon our money as a kind of blood money."

"Jesus," explained Stan, "you're going to codify the whole thing."

"You're damn right. Remember my Germanic heritage. Yours too. We'll call it the Code of the West."

"That's a funny name, Frank. Are you sure you're not carrying this just a little too far?"

"Not really. Let's say you promised me that you'd be somewhere or that you'd do something for me. You'd honor it right?"

"Sure, but so would you."

"And so would most of the people we know," added Frank. "But we live in a rural setting. Here a man's word is his bond. Let's say you called an implement dealer on the phone and you agreed with the salesman or owner to buy a John Deere tractor for $65,000. Two weeks later John Deere starts a rebate program which would reduce your cost by $10000 to $55,000. You could deny buying the tractor over the phone for $65000. You could go to a competing John Deere Dealer and buy the same tractor for $55000 thus saving yourself $10,000. But you wouldn't do it, would you?"

"No, because the word would get out into the community that I could not be trusted." Neither man spoke for a moment, then Stan continued. "But that's pretty small potatoes. If I sold 50,000 bushels of my corn crop over the phone, and the buyer was slow in sending out a written contract, and the price went up 50 cents a bushel, I could maintain that I never spoke to the buyer over the phone, and never made the sale. Then I could turn around and sell the 50,000 bushels to someone else at 50 cents a bushel more profit. That's $25,000 extra for me. But my word would be no good."

"That's my whole point. Most of us out here on the farm would rather be men of principle than rich. But the rest of the world doesn't think that way. In St. Louis, Chicago, L.A. or any other large metropolitan area people seem to think that they should screw the other guy before they get screwed themselves."

"So what does this have to do with the Code of the West?" asked Stan.

"Everything. Rural communities such as this one are relics.

The old West had a set of frontier values similar to what we practice every day. We take these values for granted, thinking the rest of the world plays by the same rules. And our value system is clearly superior. Back in the old West if a man did not hold to his word, he was considered a lowlife scumbag--an earthworm. I consider all men who fall short of their word lowlife insects, who deserve no consideration at all."

"Have we gotten off of the subject or have we gotten off the subject?" Stan was shaking his head. "You've lost me. What does this have to do with those titty joints?"

"What I'm saying is that we should be men of our word in those places. That we should treat the women with respect. And that we should bring our own values with us when we visit those places and not accept those values other people play by."

"Such as what values?"

"Most people would say that a man is hard up to go to such places to begin with," said Frank. "Most people believe that a man can't get sex somewhere else and that's why he goes to such places. We must on the other hand firmly believe that it is our choice to go to those places and that choice is better than the other options. We must be totally convinced in our own minds that this is an intelligent use of one's time. We should not care what others think, and believe that we are being far more rational than those who would condemn us."

"Why do you think people would condemn us? That is, if we start going to those places often?" asked Stan.

"Women hate prostitution. The reason they hate it is that it introduces an element of competition. A Woman who is married to a guy or who is the guy's girlfriend can no longer use sex as a bargaining chip. That is something that can be held back or given to the man so long as he does what she wants. Then there's the old adage, *why buy the cow if you can buy the milk free*. Prostitution is not free, but it's one hell of a lot cheaper than marriage. Women know in their hard little hearts that many men would never get married if they could buy sex from whomever whenever they wanted. These places we have in mind are not whorehouses, but who can tell what all this might lead to."

"If I had my way, to prostitution," Stan interjected.

"Did you know, Stan, that men would condemn us for going to these places just as fast as the women will?"

"Why's that?"

"Ego. Most guys don't want other guys to think that they'd

buy sex. Why? Because they need to feel superior to other men.
No matter how common the man. No matter how ugly his wife or
girlfriend, that man will condemn the man who sleeps with a
beautiful prostitute. It's really simple. That man doesn't feel good
about too many things in life. Now he can feel superior. So he
will often say things such as 'Me? I never have to buy sex."'

"That's funny Frank. I used to think that way myself."

"But you wouldn't if you lived out in one of those counties
in Nevada that legalizes prostitution. And I can tell you that where
it is legal, it's great. You walk into this house which is usually
called a ranch. You are typically greeted by the Madame who
asks if she can bring you a drink. Then she asks if you want to go
to the bar or if you'd like to meet the girls right away. If you say
you'd like to meet the girls, she will usher before you as many as
fifteen women whom you choose from. Now, you've got to
understand that the woman you choose knows there's a lot of other
girls she's competing against whom you might choose over her the
next time. So when she's with you, she's only too anxious to
please. And because the whole prostitution game out there is so
competitive, she is typically a good conversationalist who acts
truly interested in you and your problems."

"So when can we go, Frank?"

"Because prostitution is legal and there's no cops to pay off
or risk of going to jail for the women, sex is relatively cheap. I've
seen the District Attorney of Carson City, Nevada and an eighteen
year old boy in a ranch at the same time. What I'm saying is that
out there prostitution is highly regarded by the men. I think they
believe they're entitled to it simply because they are men.
Unfortunately, here in the Midwest prostitution is illegal so we
have to do the next best thing."

"Which is the Injection Pump, Ciceros, and the like."

"Right. And we shouldn't bat an eye about going just as the
D.A. of Carson City, Nevada didn't care whether an eighteen-year-
old kid saw him or not in a whorehouse. Stan, it is really the way
to go. That is if we do it right."

"What do you mean, do it right?"

"As I've already mentioned--we pay the girls enough to
make it worth their while and we treat them with respect. Next,
we go in a position of strength rather than from a posture of
weakness."

"What position of strength?" asked Stan.

"Although one prefers a certain girl to others, he must not act as if he's infatuated with her. In the final analysis he must make clear that he can easily make do with one of her competitors who is only too glad to steal her best customers."

"Are you saying then that we should follow the ideas of the three point plan when we're in those places?" asked Stan.

"Basically yes." Frank replied. "Keeps them guessing. Besides women value most what they can't have, so if you play the game cool and not commit to being a girl's only customer, the girls will like you better."

"I don't know if I agree with you."

"Stan, you can do what you want, but I'm going to get to know a few of the girls. Hopefully they'll like me or at least like my money, which is apparently about all my wife is interested in. Then I'll just sit back and watch what the girls will do to compete for my business. I might get laid. I might not. But I guarantee that I will have lots of fun."

"What if a girl has a boyfriend or husband and you're trying to set something up with her on the side. For example, a hotel room?"

"First of all," Frank answered, "whoever the boyfriend or husband is, he's beneath my consideration. Any man who lets his wife or girlfriend work in such a place has no pride. If he has no pride, he would not be a man of his word. That man, if we can call him a man, is either using his woman to get money from her, or at bare minimum allowing her to be abused. Remember, not all the guys that go to these places are as considerate of the girls as we're going to be. The girls have to let all kinds of men feel them up. The girls squirm all over the guy's laps until they come in their pants. Now, would you let your wife do that?"

"I'd divorce her in a minute, but I'd never let her work in a place where she would be manhandled by all her customers. And, if I needed the money that she could make in that kind of bar, I'd eat dog food instead. Or I'd shoot myself."

"That's what I mean by Code of the West. You have got principles that are so much a part of you that you'd kill yourself rather than violate them. Do you know that at the end of World War II," Frank continued, "the Russian soldiers gang raped thousands of German women right in front of their husbands, and that many of those husbands would run forward to stop their women from being raped?"

"What happened?"

"The Russians hated the Germans so much for what they

did to their people that they became like animals when they got the upper hand. So, as they raped the German women, their friends would circle around with submachine guns to shoot down any German men who might protest. Many German men couldn't endure the shame of watching their women get raped choosing death instead."

"So what you're saying," said Stan, "is that you absolutely detest any man who could put up with having his woman more or less molested in a strip bar."

"Right."

"What about the women?"

"Well, that's different. Suppose you are good looking, but you can only make five dollars an hour at some low end job. I would really be pissed at a system that would only give me five bucks an hour when living costs are as high as they are today. If I could work in a strip bar and make say thirty dollars an hour, I would be making intelligent use of my assets. Now if it were me, I'd discipline myself to save enough money to buy my own business. Then I'd quit working in the strip bar. Or I'd work there long enough to meet some nice guy who I could settle down with. Someone like me." Frank laughed.

"So, you think the girls are all right who work there, but the men who let their women work in those plays are total bums?"

"That's right. A real man doesn't want to share his woman with anyone. He wants to put her on a pedestal. He might want to tell her what to do, but the one thing he won't put up with is someone else messing with her. Now the woman who works at a strip joint might have a couple of kids, and she might have real financial problems which she decides to work through on her own. The job, disagreeable as it might be, nevertheless gives her the means of paying back her debts instead of sticking someone else with the tab." Frank got up to get another cup of coffee.

"Well I think that a lot of those girls are real sleezeballs just like their boyfriends," said Stan.

"I don't know. Let's find out. What are you doing Tuesday?" asked Frank.

"I can go. I'll just tell my wife I'm going to a farm sale."

"Then let's do it."

TEAM EFFORT

Stan's pickup truck was a dark green Ford F=150 four wheel drive. Now only minutes away from the Injection Pump, Stan accelerated to sixty-five as Frank eyed the speedometer.

"Don't get overeager, Stan. You don't want to invite a ticket."

"I suppose that's one of the provisos of our Code of the West?"

"Has nothing to do with it, but it's a good idea anyway. Just remember this. You are a far better man than the guys these girls are with. Just remember those Germans rushing into Russian submachine gun fire to save their women. Also that you are going to be nice to the girls keeping in mind of course that they're lucky to be with you in the first place. Remember that if one of the girl's treats you for any reason in a way that you don't think you should be treated, that it's her loss, not yours. There's plenty of others in the wings. Then there's that little adage: 'Money talks; bullshit walks.'"

"So you think that if I set up a date with a girl and she fails to show up, it is her loss and not mine?" laughed Stan.

"Absolutely. One--Her boyfriend or husband is not anymore of a man than your wife's pet parakeet. Two--The minute she doesn't show, you're coming right back here for her replacement. Three. You're going to have a good time regardless. Four. Her replacement will get the money she would have made. Five. She won't get a second chance with you but her replacement will make any future money she would have made. Six. She might have had a chance at a deeper involvement but she's blown it, and Seven. You will have just gotten the opportunity to better yourself by spending your time with a better woman than her. Need I go on?"

"No, that should do it."

"Look Stan. This economy is very tough. You and I have talked about it many times, and we have both agreed it's getting tougher all the time. You and I farm. We do all right, and we will probably continue to do all right. Most guys--their job situations are either nonexistent or as unstable as hell. We are very lucky. It's not that we're better than a lot of other guys. But we do have more to work with and that's the bottom line. What we are about to do is to use one of our number one assets--money--to bypass the whole dating game-- marriage trap that holds so many guys in bondage. Hey, we are almost there."

Frank paid Bogart the cover for both of them. A tall blonde waitress took their drink order at the door. They walked past one of the nightclub's two pool tables to the buffet and helped themselves to a plate of roast beef, mashed potatoes, green beans and a bowl of pudding. Then they sat down at the main bar.

"That'll be four dollars." The waitress handed Frank two Bud Lights.

"Thanks. You've got a lot of girls here today. Not too many customers," said Frank.

"You two have got it made. Not much competition. For a while. Of course, the place will get more crowded. Then at eight the night shift comes in and by then the guys are coming out of the wood work."

"What do you think of our waitress?" asked Frank.

"She'll do."

"Do for what?"

"I think she'd be good as a dancer. I like the way she's put together. She's nice too," commented Stan.

"I'd like to spend time with her if she were a dancer. I'll bet you she remains a waitress though. She seems just a little too prim and proper to get into all the lap dances."

"So that's what all these girls are doing. To me it looks like they're all dry fucking the guys. Lap dances. Great name," said Stan.

"They don't do them at the Sports Bar."

"Sports Bar? Where's that?"

"That's where we are going next."

"Frank, we don't have much time then. I'm going to run off and find someone."

Stan disappeared into the far end of the room. Once again Frank noted how the place was so large that two men could come in together and not see each other again for an hour or two. He went up to the bar, noticing that several girls sat alone, obviously available. The place wasn't busy. Yet. One of the girls, a slender girl with short reddish brown hair, sat by herself on her bar stool, quietly nursing a drink. Frank went up to her and sat down on the stool next to her.

"Hi. I'm Frank. You look like you could use another drink."

"Could I? I'll have a Jack and Coke. I'm Susan."

He stayed with her for the next hour, buying her one drink after the other. He never joined her on stage yet she always came back to him. Jeff had called his house several days before and left a message that he could not meet with Frank. He would have brought Stan with him anyway and the two of them would have met Jeff at the Injection Pump. As it was, he still had promised Lori that he would meet her at the Sports Bar around 1:30. He would have liked to stay with Susan a little longer, but a promise was a promise and that was all there was to it.

"Susan, we've gotta get going. I've brought a friend with me and he promised to meet someone at this other place."

"What other place?"

"The Sports Bar."

"Uhhhh. You guys are going there. I heard that's a biker bar."

"Well I don't know about that."

"And the women. I've heard they are pretty big."

"Not all of them Susan."

"I think you agreed to meet someone there. Not your friend. But that's okay."

"I will try to get back here, but I won't promise."

"You know where to find me."

Frank found Stan at a table just off the main bar. A woman of around thirty-five drank next to him. She smiled at him when Frank approached their table.

"Hi, I'm Nirvana. Stan and I have just been talking about his farm."

"I'm Frank. I'm Stan's neighbor." Frank turned to Stan. "We have to go, Stan. We promised the other guys we'd meet them at The Sports Bar," Frank lied.

"The Sports Bar!" Nirvana exclaimed. "Uhhhh, do you guys have to go there?"

"Oh Nirvana, it's not all that bad. I actually went there once and lived. Besides, Stan here will take care of me," said Frank.

"Nirvana, it looks like we've gotta go. Are you going to be here next week?" asked Stan.

"On Mondays, Tuesdays, Wednesdays, Thursdays, and Saturdays. I've always got the day shift."

"I'll be back."

KIM

At the Sports Bar one of the local heavies was doing the elephant walk up on the stage. Frank saw Lori sitting at the bar with a customer. Frank went over and stood next to her and ordered three beers from the bar. After the bartender returned with the beer, he turned to Lori.

"Hi Lori. I bought you a Budweiser. That's what you drink, isn't it?"

"For now. Hey, I thought you were coming in around three or so."

"No. We all agreed on 1:00. Actually I'm late. One of those tables in front of the stage all right?" Frank pointed toward the front of the stage, ignoring the man who sat next to Lori.

"Let's go," she replied.

Lori and Frank left the bar and sat down as Stan meandered around the room, joining them a few minutes later. Frank handed Stan a beer and gulped hungrily from his own.

"God, this tastes good today. Either I'm thirsty or this is an uncommonly good batch."

"I think you just want to get drunk," said Lori.

"By the way, Lori, this is Stan. He's my bodyguard. Are there any women around here you think he'd like?"

Stan made a show of looking around at the other girls. Then he laughed.

"Got any good looking friends around, Lori?"

"Oh, there might be one or two. You can't have me though. I'm Frank's."

"Yeah, I own her," Frank warned. "You can take my advice or leave it Stan, but I'd recommend Kim." He looked at Lori. "Can you bring her over?"

"Sure. Be right back."

Lori returned a minute later with Kim who looked as if she'd just gotten out of bed, She looked puffy eyed and more than a little run down. "Hi guys. Boy did I get fucked up last night. Too many tequilas. I really shouldn't be here."

"Her boyfriend gave her a hard time," said Lori.

"Speaking of boyfriends"--Frank turned to Lori--"Who's that guy you were sitting with at the bar?"

"Oh him. He always comes in here. Doesn't spend a lot of money. Just comes in to talk about his problems."

"I can see where he might have a few," Frank replied.

"You want to tip me for my dance?" The heavy set woman who had been dancing had thumped off the stage and found their table. She had dark red hair and freckles on her body. Frank produced a single one dollar bill and stuck it in her G-string. He tried to appear totally absorbed in Lori, hoping she would get the hint and move on. The woman bent over and kissed him.

The woman went over to Stan--then getting a tip from him disappeared somewhere near the bar. No one watched her go. Frank noted that Lori's back and neck were ramrod straight yet she seemed perfectly at ease. Her face was contemplative as if she were down at the beach quietly watching a bunch of seagulls. It was almost impossible to believe that Lori was a stripper. She seemed too serious, too thoughtful, and too beautiful. *She could have any man she wanted*, thought Frank. *So what in the world was she doing here?*

"Excuse me, I'll be back in a minute. A guy just came in–someone I haven't seen for a while." Lori walked over to the door. Two men had just walked in. She started talking with the older man, who was wearing a cap that at first glance appeared to be a Greek fisherman's cap, but wasn't as rich looking. Frank thought that goofy looking cap summarized the man who was around fifty-five to sixty. He had a pronounced beer gut. Lori pulled her top off for the two men who studied her breasts. The older man took a step forward and started to feel her nipples. After a moment or two, for by this time he must have studied their unique formation to his satisfaction, he stopped fingering Lori's nipples. The three talked for a minute or two. Then the men loitered to the bar and Lori came prancing back--a different Lori.

"God, I can't believe I'm doing this shit. I've got an MBA and here I am working at a strip bar!"

"What? You've got an MBA," said Frank. "Where from?"

"From Slue," Lori replied.

"From where?" Frank tried to make Slue register with the colleges and universities he knew by name. *Slue, Slue, sounds like sewage or something made out of sewage. Then it dawned on him. St. Louis University.* The term was slang for St. Louis University. Frank had gotten his MBA there, but he had never heard anyone actually call St. Louis University Slue.

"Lori, that's one hell of a coincidence. I got my MBA from St. Louis University except we never called it Slue. When did you graduate?"

"Two years ago."

"Did you ever have a professor named Corker? The man was an Israeli. He was very young when I had him. Used to wear suede jackets."

"There's two of them now," she replied.

"Two of what?"

"Two Corkers. I think it's a father and son. One's older than the other."

"How old's the older one, would you say?"

Frank's voice betrayed keen interest. He had been impressed by Dr. Corker when he had studied for his MBA. That had been almost twenty years ago.

"I'd say he's maybe fifty-five. "

"The Corker I knew," Frank continued, was blonde and very good looking. Didn't seem Jewish or Semitic at all. Looked very Teutonic."

"He's still a very attractive man. In fact he even comes in here every so often. He comes in and buys all the girls drinks. The first time he came in, he was sure surprised to see me."

"You mean his prize student?"

"Hey, do you want to do a private?" Kim asked. Up to now Stan and Kim had been pretty quiet. Stan had not been very eager to talk, and Kim was very hung over. It was obvious they were not hitting it off.

"What's that cost?" asked Stan.

"Twenty dollars. I'll give you a good one."

"Then let's go."

Stan and Kim disappeared. Lori leaned forward smiling.

"Will you get me a beer and a shot?"

"You want them both? What kind of shot?" Frank asked.

"Nadine will know."

"Sure. Why not."

"Hey Nadine. Get us a couple of Budweisers, and bring me a shot, will you. Hey, when's my set?" yelled Lori.

"You're up next," Nadine replied.

Several minutes later, Nadine came back with the drinks. She looked at Frank with disapproval. He considered tipping her $5.00. *The woman obviously needs an attitude change,* thought Frank. He reached into his pocket and found five dollars.

"To my favorite bartender." Frank looked at Nadine and gave her the best smile he could muster. "This is for leaving us alone and having everyone else leave us alone during our private."

"Sorry, can't do that. House rules. Keep it clean," she

warned.

"Hey Nadine, you ever catch anyone screwing back there during a private?" Frank asked.

"One month ago. I had to kick the customer out and we had to fire the girl," she replied.

"Yeah, it was during the night shift," said Lori. "You should have been there that night, Frank. We got really drunk."

Nadine left them for her castle which was the bar. *It was,* Frank decided, *her private bailiwick. She didn't make the rules, but she'd enforce them according to her interpretation.* He promised himself that he would try to stay on her good side.

"Frank, I'll be right back. I have to go pick my music."

Lori looked small standing by the juke box punching in her selections. One of the resident heavies stood next to her talking about the men in the place. By contrast, Lori seemed to have no stomach and no ass whereas the other girl had both in abundance. Lori's movements were quick. Even standing still, her whole being radiated uncommon vitality. Frank pondered how any other woman could make a living in this place. Lori came back to the table, quaffing her beer down as she walked. The shot glass stood empty on the table. He hadn't noticed her chugging it before going to the juke box.

"Do you want to come up while I do my set?"

"Why not. Do you like having me in front of the stage? Most of the guys don't do it?"

"It doesn't bother me a bit. You can do whatever you want, but it's kind of nice having you up there."

Frank followed Lori to the stage, sitting in a chair which had been placed next to it. Lori set her beer bottle directly in front of him. Frank considered it a little odd for a woman to be drinking directly from the bottle, but Lori was acting more and more cut off from the mainstream every minute he was around her.

"Aren't you afraid you're going to kick it off the platform? You've got that bottle right in front of us," Frank suggested.

"No. Never kicked a good beer over yet. The stuff's too good to waste."

The voice of Garth Brooks filled the room. Lori took one last swallow from the bottle. A waitress came up and took Frank's order for two more beers. Lori began circling the pole holding onto it with her right hand as her feet left the stage. Her form glided effortlessly in the air as Frank watched. Later, finished on the pole, Lori turned her attention to Frank. She eyed the crowd--

then looked down on him and smiled. In one fluid motion she took her G-string off and threw it aside. Then she popped off her bikini top. She came over to him standing just six inches in front of him. Lori lifted her right leg and set it gently across Frank's shoulder. He stared into her light brown pubic hair close to his face. Setting her leg back down she brought her left leg up against his neck as she inched closer to him. Close--so close that her public hair almost grazed his lips.

Lori took her leg off Frank's shoulder and jumped back shaking her finger at him as if to say 'Naughty boy, I know what you're thinking.' She looked up at her audience and smiled. Then turning around, thrust her rear end into his face. Lori leaned forward bending down at the waist, grasping her ankles with her hands so that her head almost touched the floor. Her buttocks tightened from her stretching. It was the rear entry position--Lori offering herself to him just inches away as she spread herself open to him. Except that they were both in public and she was also showing herself to everyone else in the room. Lori took her right hand off her ankle, reached up between her legs, and briefly fondled herself. Then she made a throwing motion with her fingertips toward Frank as she stuck her head between her legs out at him and smiled.

He wanted her. The question was, did she want him? No-- of course not. Frank didn't dwell on the possibility. Other guys might be lulled into believing that for some inexplicable reason she or someone like her might be attracted to them, but he wasn't like other guys. This was her way of making money. Lori would have developed a talent for making each of her customers feel that he had a very real chance of fucking her. The customer would think that it would only be a matter of time and for the right moment. Frank knew this was the lure that brought the fish to the bait. For Frank, there were dozens of women like Lori who were all playing the same game. Today, it was Lori. Tomorrow or next week or in one hour, Frank could play with someone else. He was secure in the knowledge that he enjoyed the game whichever turn it might take and that he could afford it. It would only be a matter of time and Lori and several other girls as well would wake up to the fact that Frank would go on tipping only so many of them. They would learn that he was a prize customer, and that it was in their best interests to offer him more than they offered their other customers--a whole lot more.

Lori came off the stage and began her rounds, collecting a

dollar off each man in the bar. She rejoined Frank at the table and stood in front of him pulling her G-string out as she smiled at him.

"Do you want to tip me for my dance?"

"You bet I do. That was worth more than all the other dances together."

The waitress brought over the beer he had ordered from the stage. Lori sat down next to him, leaned over, and kissed him. She slid her tongue into his mouth, her tongue flickering rapidly back and forth in his mouth. Her tongue was thin and firm, not flaccid and broad like many others he had in his mouth over his many dating years before Karen. He lifted her onto his lap, still kissing her, not stopping until she got off and sat back in her chair.

"Frank, we've gotta stop that. Nadine will get pissed. She doesn't like for a girl to get too friendly with a customer. What time do you have to leave?"

Frank looked at his watch. It was later than he expected. "We have to leave right after you and I do our private."

Just then, Stan and Kim came out of the corner and returned to the table. Kim was smiling. Stan's face betrayed no emotion whatever.

"Frank, we have to go soon. We are a couple of married men."

"You might be," said Frank, "but right now I don't feel married at all. In fact, we are headed to our private little couch back there."

Frank and Lori left Kim and Stan with one of the dancers who had come over with the jukebox bowl. Stan was fumbling in his pocket for a dollar as they rounded the partition that obscured the chair from the rest of the bar. Lori put her hands on Frank's shoulders and started to kiss him. Then she took his shirt off, pulling it over his head and tossing it on a nearby table. She pushed him into the chair and sat on his lap facing him. He reached down to feel her nipples, rolling them between his fingertips as she french-kissed him. Frank reached underneath her, placing the fingertips of both hands gently on both sides of her G-string as he gently massaged her pubic hair with his fingers. Lori pressed her breasts against his chest and wiggled around on his lap with a sideways motion of her hips.

In a few minutes, the private was over. Nadine came around the partition to check up on them. She glanced at Lori who nodded over to her.

"We've gotta go back to the table. Nadine's being like an

old mother hen."

"Well, we can't get you fired now can we?" said Frank.

They went back to the table. Stan drank what was left from his beer glass and got up. Kim looked around the room, her eyes going from one man to the other, sizing up where her next customer would come from. Frank turned to Lori.

"See you in about a week."

"We'll be here."

"See you guys. Don't forget us now." Kim's voice was low and husky.

Frank drove onto route 64, careful to obey all traffic signals. He could not afford to take a chance of getting a ticket. He pulled out a pack of Anthony and Cleopatra cigars and offered one to Stan.

"Okay, I'll have one. You know, Frank, that I don't smoke, but we'd better have a cigar or two to get rid of any possible smell of perfume."

"What do you think, Stan?"

"I liked the Injection Pump. That girl I was with there. Nirvana was her name. What did you think of her?"

"Not bad. Seems real friendly. A little older than the rest, but not bad. I liked her," Frank replied. "Didn't you like Kim?"

"Oh, we didn't really hit it off. Her eyes were real puffy. She didn't look too good. Maybe on another day she'd be better if her eyes weren't puffy. And that place! We're going to call it the money trap. God, the way the girls want to be tipped for their dances all the time. And the jukebox. They're always bugging you about a buck here and a buck there."

"That's a real pain in the ass," Frank added. "So, you liked the Injection Pump?"

"It's heaven on earth. I can't believe what goes on there. And everybody's so friendly. Why, if I lived near there, I'd be there every day."

"Hate to break it to you Stan, but soon we are going to be back with our wives for every day."

"Who needs them."

One hour later, they pulled in front of an old red barn. The barn along with several other buildings stood on one of Frank's farms 2 miles from his house. Both men got out of the pickup and changed into their older jeans. Stan hung his trousers and dress shirt on a nail just inside the barn while Frank threw his good jeans and sport shirt behind the seat.

CHANEL

Frank and Lori were just finishing their fourth beer together. A tall blonde swung listlessly around the pole, her feet planted firmly on the stage as if they had been set in concrete. She finished and headed Frank's way.

"Why do they always come to me first?" Frank asked.

"Because they think you're a nice guy," Lori replied. "And you are. You tip them. You talk to them. You let them kiss you."

"I still don't know what so many girls are doing here. There just aren't enough guys around."

"Most of the girls just like hanging around. And sometimes they have their moments. Especially as the afternoons wind into the evenings. Guys get drunker and more careless with their money then."

"Here she comes. Where can I hide?"

"Hello Frank, you wish to tip me for my dance?"

He tipped the woman as she kissed him. Frank turned to Lori, turning his back on the woman.

"What would you think of having lunch with me next week? Something a little different. Perhaps Japanese. We could drink saki together, get drunk, eat sushi, and get to know each other better?"

"Sounds good to me. Just name the day."

"How about Monday? Can you get the whole afternoon off?"

"Sure, as long as I give a day's notice. But if it doesn't work out for you, call me at least by the day before so I can tell Nadine."

"Let us meet at the Tachibani Restaurant off of Olive Street Road in Creve Coeur. Do you know where that is?"

"I know the area pretty well. I used to clean houses around there."

"Then do you know where Fee Fee Road is about 2 miles west of 270."

"Sure I know where it is."

"Good. Here, let me draw you a map." Frank pulled a pen from his pocket. Lori went up to the bar and returned with a piece of paper. She tore a corner off and wrote the Sports Bar's telephone number on it. She handed it to Frank who started to write on the paper.

"That's the number here. Just in case things don't work out," said Lori.

"Will do. Now this is how you get to the Tachibani." He continued to draw a map explaining carefully how to get to the restaurant. Lori got up and sat next to him. She listened attentively. Then she carefully folded the map and put it in her purse.

"I have to go home now," said Frank, "I'll meet you there at 12:00 on Monday."

"You've better be there, Frank. That's clear around St. Louis for me, and I'm taking off of work!" Lori called out to him as he walked out the door.

Frank drove slowly, being careful to obey all stop signs to the letter. Highway 64 was nine or ten blocks from the Sports Bar. The Injection Pump was on the way. Although it was getting late, Frank could not pass it up. If it wasn't for Lori, there would be no way he would pick the Sports Bar over the Injection Pump. Stan had joked that the Sports Bar should be called the Money Pit since girls were always pressuring men to donate to the jukebox or for tips. Although a man would occasionally be asked to donate to the jukebox at the Injection Pump, it wouldn't be that often. As far as tips, the only way a man was expected to tip a girl was if he had a private or a lap dance with her. It was entirely up to him if he wanted to do either. He could sit at the bar or at a table and quietly drink by himself or with a friend. Frank could play pool if he preferred. He could watch the dancers from afar. If he wanted to have a girl squirm all over his lap, he only had to walk up to a stage and sit in front of it. He could do what he wanted when he wanted. There were many girls to choose from, and very few of them were fat. The waitresses were all exceptionally friendly, and Ginny, the bartender, was very attractive.

He paid his way in and walked up to the bar. Ginny came up to him smiling.

"You're in here a little late. Don't you usually come in here right after lunch?"

"I've been at the Sports Bar drinking with a friend."

"Ugh. You've been there. How can you stand it? I understand the women are all fat. And don't a lot of derelicts hang out there?"

"You're right Ginny. a lot of unsavory types go there. Doctors and lawyers. Then, there's me, for instance."

"Oh, you're all right. You should spend most of your time here. You'd be much better off. Anyway, what can I get you?

"Coffee. I need something for the long ride home."

Ginny brought him his coffee in a glass. He looked around, but he didn't see anyone he knew. He looked at his watch. The absolute most he could get away with was twenty minutes. Too late to get to know one of the girls--even on the most superficial level. He looked toward the rear of the room. A small blonde sat on a man's lap. It was Chanel. He went to the back stage and sat down on the man's right. The tune ended, and Chanel stood up studying her prospects. The man she had been entertaining remained in his seat hoping she would come back to him. She looked over at Frank and smiled, then climbed onto Frank's lap laughing.

"I remember you. You came in here with your friends a few weeks ago."

"You have a good memory."

"Well, I'm glad you found me back here. Things are getting pretty boring."

She drew herself up tight against his chest and put her arms around his neck. Then she started to rock back and forth. Leaning back, she started to roll her hips in rhythmic circles. The tune soon ended.

"My set's over. That's too bad."

"How about us doing a private?" asked Frank.

"Okay. Let's do one then."

Frank followed Chanel to the small couch off behind the main bar. He gave her a twenty and sat down as she reached over and pulled off his shirt. Kneeling in front of him she parted his knees with her hands, pulled off her top and leaned down so that her bare breasts pressed hard against his groin. She rubbed them back and forth against his crotch. After the first ended, she switched positions and climbed onto his lap. Chanel leaned backwards, resting her head against the wall behind them and started to move her pelvis back and forth across his lap. She parted her lips slightly and started to shake her head slowly from left to right.

Chanel's eyes drifted away from Frank, her concentration focused somewhere else. She started to play with her G-string as she moved her buttocks across his lap. The twisting of her head, the leaning back of her body, the unfocused aspect of her eyes, and her fondling of her G-string--all combined to produce in Frank the impression of total abandonment--of utter lasciviousness.

Still leaning against the wall Chanel willed her body to relax. As she rocked back and forth across Frank's lap she thought of far away places and far away things. Her eyes became slits. Through them the room became a blur; the man she was sitting on became an amorphous shape like all the rest that had come before him or that would come after. It was as if she were a patient waking up in recovery after an operation. Everything and everybody around her were both there and not there in surrealistic fantasy. Chanel thought of Colorado. She had been there only once as a child. She thought of herself childlike, the mountains all around her, the fresh clear water of a mountain stream just at her feet. Slowly, almost daintily she walked out into the water, the water cold around her feet. Waves of riveting coldness coursed upwards from the stream through her feet and into her body. Then the coldness stopped and flowed backwards, downwards through her body, back into her feet where it remained. Chanel breathed the fresh thin Colorado air and let it fill her lungs. She was alone in a world of pristine beauty where everything was perfect, where things were as they should be. There under that deep blue Colorado sky, people didn't hurt one another and they didn't let you down. They didn't because they weren't there. Chanel was there alone, a part of her surroundings, fused in perfect harmony. She felt the coolness of the stream on her feet, the warmth of the sun on her back, the fresh air in her lungs. She wanted to stay there for hours waiting for a deer or a squirrel to appear. The music of the Injection Pump had been there all the time. As Chanel's consciousness drifted away from her surroundings, the music playing on the jukebox seemed to get softer and softer until it was hardly there at all. Yet it had never gone away entirely, remaining as a low hum in her head. This is the way it always was when she did a private. The hum stopped. That meant that the tune had ended and the private was over. Chanel got up and started to dress as Frank put his shirt back on.

"Chanel, I'm glad we could get together for a private. I've got to get going. Sorry I can't stay longer, buy you a drink, and get better acquainted."

"That's all right. We'll get together some other time," she replied.

Frank left the Injection Pump, walking quickly, pausing only for the flight of stairs leading to the exit door. The air was warm outside and the sun was shining. His mind was clear and sharp, his body quick and powerful. Everything was perfect. Frank climbed into his pickup, lowered the power windows, and drove away as he lit an Anthony and Cleopatra. He thought of three women: His wife, Lori, and Chanel. He quickly dismissed his wife for he knew the thought of her would ruin his day. Chanel had been wonderful. There had been a certain wantonness about her that none of the others had. She was also very pretty.

Then there was Lori. Slender and quick in her movements she had a mind that was as agile as her body. She could read a man like a book. Always alert, she listened to everything he said, yet her eyes would occasionally move about the room like a ferret's to make sure that one of her other customers didn't walk in and leave without her saying hello or goodbye. She'd smoked cigars with him and drunk a lot of booze with him. She had been serious and she had been impish. He pushed a cassette into the tape player. It was Tom Petty. *Very appropriate,* thought Frank. Lori was a master of her craft. She could make all her customers feel important at all times, and she was always the perfect companion.

Tom Petty's voice filled the interior of the pickup. He was singing *A Face in the Crowd.* It was Frank's favorite selection on the tape. Definitely not a ballad, it had nevertheless always made him think of the Old West, and for some reason, that he couldn't quite put his finger on, about Billy the Kid. He had first heard that tape while visiting a friend in Oregon. The two of them had listened to that tape while driving to Mount Hood with their skis in ski racks on top of a Mazda. The friend was a very good friend--a fearless skier, who had left a secure job in the Midwest, in order to live how he wanted to live in the West. This friend was the only person in the world Frank wrote to, the written word being the form of communication chosen by both men to bridge the 2000 miles separating them. The man had never had a secure job since moving to Oregon, but he had nevertheless carved out a life of his own choosing on his own terms. Larry had been born one hundred-fifty years too late. For that matter so had Frank. The souls of both men were alike in that they did not belong in a century of civilized constraints.

They had driven to the Oregon coast where they had stayed for several days along the ocean, picking their way around the boulders littering the beach and hiking through Oregon's rain forests. Larry and Frank had drunk lots of beer together in Oregon's brew pubs where homemade ales were served. They had skied Mount Hood together to see who was the fastest that year. The two men had ridden chair lifts while getting soaked as wet heavy snow fell on them from the skies. And through it all they discussed anything and everything: their marriages, their careers, politics, farming, history, life, death.

Frank couldn't make out most of the lyrics in *A Face in the Crowd.* What was important was the impression he got out of the music. It was tied to the West--the Old West--even though no one but Frank would get the connection. And it was tied to Lori. The crowd was all those people out there going about their daily business, scurrying about between job and grocery store and all those mundane things and places that most people preoccupy themselves with. An individual becomes lost in the crowd--crying out for someone like him--but the crowd is too busy frantically trodding the treadmills of life to notice or to care. The soul sees a river of faceless people flowing around him and drifts away in lonely isolation. Then out of the crowd appears a light--a face. It takes shape and touches the soul. Perhaps for a fleeting moment, an instant of time only, the isolation is penetrated as one soul touches another. The two recognize one another, and both know that they are not alone.

And so it was with Lori. The woman had five kids. She had a young and violent boyfriend who was going nowhere fast. Once Lori left work her life had to be one of despair and hopelessness, of little children tugging at her from the time she got home till the time she went to bed. And Frank's life, not nearly as bad by contrast, was saddened by the constant realization that he would soon divorce the woman he had once loved. He and Lori had met in a strip bar in the midst of the crowd where the strippers sought to rip off their male customers while the customers tried to use the bodies of the dancers. Whether it was by merely watching the naked women or by doing privates with the girls and in many instances getting off, these male customers were using money as a way of getting something they wanted without showing any interest in the girls as human beings. The girls in turn saw the men as a meal ticket--easy marks--to be exploited for money. The girls were not really interested in their customers. After all, what kind of a man would allow himself to be fleeced so easily? The promise of a little sex for so much cash. These guys had to be hard up.

Frank thought the whole thing had to be a kind of love--hate relationship. The girls and their customers were so nice and polite to each other while they were getting physically intimate with one another. Yet most of the men probably despised the woman for working in a strip bar while the dancers in turn despised the men for going there in the first place. The women, in constant competition with one another to get and to keep the best paying customers would treat the men like kings, each woman telling her customers what they wanted to hear, and holding their hands as if in love. Lori was a master at this. She pretended that Frank was the most important person in the world. Lori had told him once that he had a wonderful body, asking him what he did to keep in such good shape. She made out with him openly and she remembered every little detail he had ever told her about his life.

In spite of her need to play an act in order to keep him as a customer, Frank knew that she liked him. He didn't stiff her, but he didn't pay her exorbitantly either. He was used to giving her just $1.00 for her stage dances and $20 for a private and all the drinks she could drink. Certainly there were other men who paid her a lot more for her company. Yet she would drink beer after beer with him for hours at a time. No, she genuinely enjoyed his company. He enjoyed her company as well. Her company was something to savor through the hard days of farming and the trying times with Karen. He knew that she looked forward to his visits as well. How much, he didn't know. Perhaps he was her face in the crowd. But then again, that was all part of the game. The dancer's job was to make the man feel special. The fact that Lori made him feel totally special meant perhaps that she was just that much better at the game than all the other girls.

CHOPSTICKS

Frank had been sitting at the sushi bar in the Tachibani restaurant since 11:55. It was now 12:15. Lori was either very late or she had stood him up. He figured she had stood him up and ordered a beer and an order of Suchi Yaki. The waitress brought the beer at 12:20. She put the Suchi Yaki in front of him at 12:25. *That's too bad*, he thought, *I was really planning to have some sushi. It's no fun eating sushi alone. Now why did Lori stand me up? If she likes me, it doesn't make sense. Now, let's say she doesn't particularly care for me. Suppose it's all an act. It is still in her best interests to keep me as a customer. Lori should have made up an excuse as to why she couldn't come here in the first place such as 'I can't leave my kids'. Since she agreed to meet me here, she should have at least left a message at the restaurant that an emergency had occurred and that this was the best she could do considering that she didn't have my home number. Lori should never have stood me up--not just because it isn't a nice thing to do, but because she would risk losing me as a customer. This woman's got to have a short circuit in the brain.*

The Suchi Yaki's not bad. Frank ate the meat and vegetables with chop sticks, then looked around to see if anyone was looking. Picking the bowl up with both hands he brought it to his lips and drank the broth. *What the hell,* he thought, *that's the way the Japanese do it.* He moved onto the subject of Lori. *It's just past 12:30 and I've got three hours of time invested in getting to and from St. Louis. I'm not going to let her get me mad. When I was eighteen I'd be pretty upset. I'm going to have one hell of a time today, and I'm just going to act as if it didn't even happen. However, there will be no ski trip for Lori. So what are my options? Going to a bookstore? No. Too tame. Not worth the one and a half hour drive here and the one and a half hour drive back. The Injection Pump? Sure, why not? Find someone new.*

Frank cleaned off the little wooden chopsticks and carefully put them back into the little wrapper they came in. The name of the Tachibani Restaurant had been stamped on the wrapper. He put the wrapper in his shirt pocket, finished his beer, left a dollar tip, paid for his meal, and walked out to his pickup. He slid behind the wheel, started the engine, and pulled out of the parking lot onto Olive Street Road. Two miles later he was on 270. Soon he was on Highway 40 traveling East. His thoughts returned to Lori. *She's got five kids. Probably is so strung out at home that she hates even being there. Whole life probably revolves around the Sports Bar and what goes on in there. Gets drunk in there and has one hell of a time with the customers and the girls she works with. Laughs a lot, plays practical jokes on the other girls, and perhaps even on some of the customers. Gets oblivious to the dark circumstances of her real life. So, she's got this thing set up with me, but after I leave, she decides to fuck with me--to make light of the whole situation. What the hell, I'll just go over there and observe how the other girls treat me. That way I'll know. Then, no matter what happens, I'll go to the Injection Pump.*

In thirty minutes he was pulling into the parking lot of the Sports Bar. Frank observed that just a few cars were there. He walked into the bar and spied Dotie at the other end. Frank caught Nadine's eye who came over to him.

"What can I get you, Frank?"

"How about a Budweiser? And while you're at it, why don't you send a beer down to Dotie."

While Nadine was getting the beer, Frank strode over to Dotie. She looked up at him and smiled. Lori had once told him that Dotie was her best friend in the place.

"Dotie, Nadine's bringing you a beer. Since Lori's not here, I thought I'd drink one with you. Speaking of Lori, do you know where she is?"

"She's not here yet. This isn't like her. She's hardly ever late."

"Don't tell the whole place, but she was supposed to meet me for lunch at 12:00. She didn't show."

"That's not like Lori. If she said she'd be there, she'd be there. Do you suppose she got lost?"

"I doubt it. She said she knew the neighborhood and I gave her a good map."

"Well, she probably doesn't know the neighborhood. She's probably just out there driving around trying to find it."

"Is there a phone around here?"

"There's a pay phone outside. Nadine probably doesn't want you using the bar's phone."

"Phone book?"

"Over there."

Frank went over to where Dotie was pointing. A St. Louis phone book lay on a small shelf. He picked it up and walked outside. There was a phone booth in the south parking lot. Since he had always parked on the north side of the bar, he had never noticed it. Frank thumbed through the white pages and found the Tachibani's number and dialed it, being careful to use the 314 area code. An operator answered and instructed him to deposit $1.25. He fumbled in his pocket for a bunch of quarters, found them, and placed five in the coin slot. A woman's voice answered on the third ring.

"Tachibani Restaurant."

"I was eating Suchi Yaki in your restaurant just forty-five minutes ago. Did a woman come in looking for someone?"

"What did she look like?"

"Blonde, twenty-six years old, five foot five or so."

"No. No one like that came in here."

"Did anyone call for me?"

"No, no one called."

"Thanks."

Frank hung up and walked back into the bar. Dotie was still sitting where he had left her drinking the beer he had gotten her. A customer was sitting next to her.

"She's here. She just walked in. She's in the dressing room."

"Who?"

"Why Lori, of course," replied Dotie.

Frank sat next to Dotie, on her left, and started to drink the beer that had been placed before him. It was good and cold. He gulped it down and ordered two more.

"A Bud for me, and one for Lori when she comes over here," he ordered.

"You mean Nipples?" answered Nadine.

"Yeah. Nipples."

Just then Lori came out of the dressing room looking haggard. Looking at Nadine, she came over to him. She had not bothered putting any makeup on.

"They took my car. I couldn't come. My brother and my boyfriend. They just took my car and it was gone. I'm so fucking pissed off. I oughta kick both of their asses out."

"You mean not only your boyfriend, but your brother lives with you as well?" asked Frank.

"Both of them. And my five kids. I'm sorry I couldn't make it, but I just couldn't get there."

"Did you ever think of calling the restaurant? Hell, I would have called a cab for you."

"I don't have a phone right now. I'm in the process of

moving to a new place and I had it disconnected. I'm moving this week."

"Couldn't you go over and use one of your neighbors' phones?"

"What, with five kids hanging on me?"

"Sure. After all, I only drove eighty miles to get there. Lori, if I drove eighty miles to get there and my pickup broke down just ten miles from the restaurant, I'd pay for a cab just to be able to keep my appointment with you, but then that's just the kind of guy I am. Maybe you hang out with a different crowd than I do, but people can count on me."

"Look, Frank, I don't blame you for walking right out of here right now. I've probably really blown it with you."

"Drink your beer Lori. I'll have one with you. Maybe two. Then I'm going to the Injection Pump."

Frank reached into his shirt pocket and pulled out the wrapper with the chopsticks in it. He pulled out the chopsticks and handed them to Lori. Part of him wanted to stay and drink with Lori. He couldn't forgive her for standing him up, but maybe she had panicked. The other part of him was saying: *Leave her for dead; go on to the next girl.* Nadine had just placed two beers in front of them. He gave Nadine a five.

"Do you know how to use those?" Frank asked.

"No," Lori answered.

"Well, since we don't have any Japanese food here that popcorn in the bowl in front of you will have to do. Here, hand those chopsticks to me. And the bowl."

Lori put the bowl in front of Frank and gave him the chopsticks. He handed her the wrapper. Frank placed the chopsticks between his fingers and picked a kernel of popcorn out of the bowl. Then he put the kernel back in the bowl and picked up another with his chopsticks raising it to his mouth as if he were going to eat it.

"See how easy it is. Like so. By the way, these came in that wrapper I just handed you. Notice that it says Tachibani on it. Now you know I was there. You missed a good meal. Here, you try it."

He handed her the chopsticks. Lori picked them up and reached in the bowl for a kernel. She got it between the two sticks, picked it up, and then dropped it just as she started to bring it to her mouth. She reached in for another. This time she brought it to her mouth. She tried for still another, dropping it just as it reached her mouth.

"Will you tip me for my dance?"

The voice had a husky quality to it. It was Kim, standing before him bare breasted. Frank slipped a dollar into her G-string.

"Look Kim--We are eating popcorn with chopsticks. Watch."

Lori reached into the bowl and brought out a kernel which she brought up to her mouth. Eating it, she took out another kernel. It was coming easily to her now. The coordination she had shown on the stage was apparent in her ability to learn how to use chopsticks. Frank thought it was too bad that he wouldn't be taking her skiing. She would have been good at it, and she would have loved it.

"Can I try?" asked Kim.

"Sure," Frank replied. He turned to Lori. "Hand them to me. I'll demonstrate first."

Lori handed Frank the chopsticks. He inserted them between his fingers, looked at Kim, and grinned.

"I just put a dollar into your G-string, right?"

"Right."

"Laid it right in your pubic hairs and it didn't bother you, right?"

"Oh, Frank, nothing you could do would ever bother me," replied Kim.

"Good, because Lori here is getting just too good with those sticks. I need a bigger challenge than popcorn."

Frank eyed Kim's chest and reached out toward her breast with the chopsticks. He placed the two sticks around one of Kim's nipples and gradually started to apply pressure. He pulled her nipple back, stretching and elongating the nipple with the sticks. Frank leaned forward so that his mouth was only inches from her nipple and pulled the nipple into his mouth.

"Just getting hungry," said Frank. "Now you know why Orientals use chopsticks. Imagine doing this with a fork. Here, you try it Kim."

Kim took the chopsticks from Frank, placed them between her fingers, and reached into the popcorn bowl. She grabbed onto a kernel with the stick ends, but was unable to get the kernel out of the bowl. She handed the sticks back to Frank.

"I'll be back to try it some more. I'm going to get some more tips."

Kim went on to the next customer. Frank placed the

chopsticks back between his fingers and reached into the popcorn bowl. In rapid succession he grabbed several kernels one by one, eating each kernel after bringing it to his mouth. He looked over at Lori.

"Now I'm ready for you. Would you please take off your top and give me a bite out of one of your breasts?"

Lori took her top off showing off her large prominent nipples. Frank leaned over her and grabbed her right nipple between the chopsticks. Squeezing them together he was able to put enough pressure on her nipple so that he could drag it to his mouth. Elongating the nipple until it was over an inch long with the chopsticks, Frank swallowed the nipple.

"The Saki Yaki was good but this is better."

"Okay, Frank. So you're good. Let's see what I can do. Take your shirt off."

"What! In here? We're sitting at the bar. Nadine will get upset with me exposing my chest at the bar."

"Hey, Nadine, you don't mind if I take Frank's shirt off here at the bar do you?" shouted Lori.

"No honey, but I draw the line at his pants. Keep them on if you don't mind."

Lori started to unbutton Frank's shirt. He pulled it off the rest of the way and placed it over the back of his bar stool. Lori grabbed the chopsticks and put them between her fingers. She placed them around Frank's nipple and started to apply pressure. Then she pulled his nipple back into her mouth as she hovered over him. Lori swirled her tongue around his nipple for a few seconds--then pulled away. Setting the chopsticks down on the bar she raised her mouth to his lips and started to kiss him. She french-kissed him for twenty seconds, stopping only when she noticed the look Nadine was giving her.

"Nadine, can you get us two more beers?" This time it was Lori who ordered. Then she turned to Frank. "I'm going to put my makeup on. Then I have to play my music. Are you staying?"

"For awhile. I'm still going to the Injection Pump."

"Then come up to the stage. Okay."

"Sure."

Lori disappeared into the dressing room. As if on que, Kim appeared.

"God, am I horny."

"You what?"

"I'm really horny. It's raining outside. Every time it rains I want to make love. Do you ever get that way, Frank?"

"I'm always ready, but I don't know that the rain has anything to do with it. I suppose you want to make love with me?"

"If I wasn't working here right now, I sure would be thinking about it."

"Do you know that Lori stood me up today?"

"She what? Come again? She never tells me anything."

"She was supposed to meet me at the Tachibani Restaurant at noon and she never showed. She told me that her boyfriend and brother took off with her car."

"Did she call to tell you that she couldn't make it?"

"No."

"That's pretty stupid. If you had offered me lunch, I would have been there."

"I'll keep that in mind. Maybe I'm with the wrong girl. But I'm going to give her the benefit of the doubt. Perhaps she really got screwed up."

"She probably did," said Kim. "That's not like Lori at all."

Lori came out of the dressing room and went over to the jukebox where she made her Garth Brooks selections. Then she went on stage to dance. She looked over at Frank and Kim. Frank decided against sitting in front of the stage. *What the hell*, he thought, *even if she lost her head, she still stood me up. This seat is already warm and Kim is in a talkative mood.*

"Kim, do you want a beer?" he asked.

"Are you buying?"

"Sure. Why not?"

"Get me a Busch."

"Nadine, get Kim a Busch and bring me another Bud." Frank had already caught Nadine's eye, and she was already approaching their end of the bar.

"Do you want another one for Nipples?" she asked.

"Definitely."

Nadine returned with three beers. Frank took the Bud and brought the bottle to his lips, not bothering with the glass. He continued to chug it, not lowering the bottle until it was all gone. Kim sat and watched wide eyed.

"I can't do that."

"I haven't done it for years. Just felt like it."

"I suppose you and Nipples are going to do a private."

"We just might. What are your privates like?"

"They're great. You'd never forget one."

"Not now. In spite of Lori and I not having lunch together, I'm not doing a private with anyone else, but sometime you and I will have to do one."

"Well, I don't want to get between you and Nipples. She'd probably feel pretty bad if you and I just went off and did one with her here."

"There might be another time."

Lori came off the stage. The jukebox had played all three selections and Frank had scarcely noticed. She came over to Frank and Kim.

"Do you want to tip me for my dance?"

"Sure, here's a dollar." Frank put it in her G-string. She moved onto the next customer. Two minutes later she was back, her G-string full of dollar bills.

"One of my customers just came in. Hate to leave you, but he'll get mad if I don't go over to him," said Kim.

Lori sat next to Frank. She saw the full bottle in front of her and poured it into her glass. She swallowed one third of it.

"I feel like a shot. Want one?"

"No. Go ahead."

Lori called out to Nadine who returned with a shot of Tequila. She quaffed it down; then turned to her beer.

"You'd better watch it. You're going to get me drunk, Frank."

"I doubt it. I'll bet you could drink me under the table several times over."

"Probably not. You do just fine. But I can drink a lot. I'll say that much."

"Look, Lori, I must go pretty soon. Normally we'd do a private, but to tell you the truth I'm not really in the mood. I'm going to give you a twenty and take off."

"No, you've gotta do a private with me. I'm not taking your twenty."

"Look Lori, your job is to do privates for money. Now, I've spent a lot of time with you and your time is money. And let's face it, it isn't that you girls exactly get off when you do a private even if some of the guys do. I'm just not into it today."

"What do you mean, we girls don't get off during a private. I got off when we did a private."

"Right. You just got off just like that. Who do you think you're kidding?"

"No. Honest. It was that first time you and I met. You had

your two friends in here. It was the only time I've ever come while I was working here."

"Okay, I won't dispute you. You came when I wasn't looking. Look I'm wearing khaki pants. Suppose I came in my pants while you and I were doing a private. I probably wouldn't, but let's just suppose I did. Jesus, I'd have one hell of a stain to show off to everybody and it would stand out big as life on khaki."

"Then you should do what a lot of the other guys do."

"What's that?"

"Wear some protection."

"A rubber?"

"Sure. A rubber."

"Where would I find one?"

"In the men's room."

"There aren't any rubbers in the men's room."

"You've been going to the wrong men's room. Try the one to the left of the bar. You've been going to the one around the right side of the bar."

"Okay. You've sold me. But on one condition."

"What's that?"

"That you put it on me."

"You're on."

Frank got up and walked to the men's room. To the left of the bar was a hallway. Twenty feet down the hallway he found a bathroom that was not labeled for men or women. He entered and saw that Lori had been right. There were three prophylactic machines on the wall. One machine had a picture of a bare-breasted blonde woman. Her mouth was slightly parted and her eyes were half closed. She was stroking her large breasts, the expression on her face one of total ecstasy. The caption underneath the picture read "Arouse her to her fullest. Special tip ensures maximum stimulation." Another machine, this one having no picture, had a caption reading "Contents are to be used for protection against disease only." The third machine read *Special sex stimulant. The woman in your life will love it.* Frank chose the third machine and deposited two quarters. A small packet dropped down into the special tray underneath the machine. Frank picked up the packet and studied it, for he had not used a rubber in years. Didn't have to. This packet was small. Wondering if the rubber inside would fit him, he carefully split the packet open. A red viscous substance began to ooze out of it. He put it in his pocket and went back to the chair where they had always done their privates. Lori was waiting for him, her top already off. Frank took his shirt off and sat on the chair.

"Let's take a look at it," said Lori.

Frank reached into his pocket and showed it to Lori. She looked at it, studied it, turned it over, then turned it over once more. It was Frank who broke the silence.

"This thing is awfully small. And you've really got to watch it. I've seen lubricated rubbers before but this thing is really messy. I think they've got a quality control problem."

"Frank, this isn't a rubber. This is just a sexual jell of some sort. Rubbers don't come in packages that small."

"Well, I didn't think it would fit me. I thought it might fit certain friends of mine. Jeff Shannon for instance. But not me. Did you just say that this is not a rubber?"

"That's what I said."

"Well I thought they didn't make them like they used to. Jesus, and they don't even use much packaging."

"Frank, you're going to have to get another one."

"No Lori, you're going to get another one. There were three machines in there. With my luck I'll probably buy some special French tickler that you wear on your tongue or a pair of rubber gloves that gynecologists wear. Just what does one do with that red gel anyway? Spread it between a woman's legs to take the smell away."

"I don't know either, but you've probably got the right idea. Got two quarters?"

"I'm out. Can you give me a loan? I'm good for it."

"Sure."

Lori got up and walked briskly back to the restroom. Thirty seconds later she was back. She pulled up a chair which had been next to a nearby table.

"Here, sit here. Face the wall with your back toward the bar. If anyone comes around, they won't see what I'm doing to you."

The partition that shielded the couch from the bar and the main room was perhaps five feet high and ten feet long. No one sitting at the bar or in the next room could see the couch or anyone on it. However, someone could easily walk around the partition to check up on those doing a private. Frank sat on the chair as Lori kneeled in front of him. She loosened his belt, pulled down his zipper, and pulled his fly open. She reached inside and grabbed his penis, pulling it out. With quick short strokes of her hand she got him to a full erection and placed the rubber on the tip of his penis. Lori started to roll the rubber onto Frank's shaft, starting with the top then continuing with the bottom. In seconds she had deftly rolled seven inches of latex all the way down to his balls. Then she climbed onto his lap, facing him.

"This time I'm going to make you come for sure," she promised.

DEBBIE

One week later Frank went back to the Sports Bar. Dotie saw him as he came in. She hurried over to him just as he was ordering his beer.

"Guess what happened to Nipples? It happened yesterday. Her brother shot himself, and she was here working and someone came to get her. It's awful. Just as she was starting to get her shit together. She just moved into her new house. She's been putting some money away. He must have done it when the kids were home. That's terrible--those young kids having to see all that blood and everything. Probably brains all over the place. Poor Nipples. It's going to take awhile for her to get over this."

"That's terrible Dotie. She'll probably not be back here again for a couple of weeks at least. She might never come back."

"Oh, she'll be back all right. I don't know when, but she'll be back."

"Is Kim here?" asked Frank.

"Yes. She's in the dressing room."

"Dotie, I'll buy you a beer if you will do me a favor."

"Nadine, get me a beer?" Dotie demanded. She turned to Frank. "Okay, what's the favor?"

"I want you to get me a piece of paper and a pen. I'm writing Lori a note. Can you get it to her?"

"Sure. I'll put it in her locker for her." Dotie went over to the other end of the bar and took a small piece of paper and a ballpoint from her purse. She returned and handed them to Frank. He started to write on the paper. When he finished, he handed it to Dotie. It read:

Dear Lori
Sorry to hear about your brother. I was hoping that the move into your new house would go smoothly instead of ending with tragedy.

Will look forward to seeing you when you return to work.

Frank

Just then Kim came out of the dressing room. She saw Frank and Dotie and grinned.

"Hey Frank, do you want to help celebrate my birthday. I'm going to really party this Friday night. How about stopping by?"

"Kim, I'd love to. But I'm married, and my wife just won't let me out of the house on weekends unless I'm with her."

"Why are all the nice guys married? Just my luck."

"Kim, I'm not really that nice a guy. And remember, I'm not happily married."

"That's what most married men say. They come out with their sob stories, find a woman who listens to them, and screws her as long as she lets him. She falls for him, and then when the chips are down, he refuses to leave his wife. I'll bet you're just like all the rest."

"I know I can't convince you otherwise so I won't even try. For the record, and Kim, I want you to remember today and what I said, I will either be divorced or separated by July of next year."

"What's so special about July? That's a long way off."

"I know. I wonder if I can last that long."

"What do you mean?"

"My wife, Karen, has two kids. One's still in High School. He will graduate next June. He feels he has a home on the farm. Did I tell you I was a farmer? Well, anyway, if he goes in the military, gets a job, or goes to college, or whatever, he will more or less be on his own next year. Now it would disrupt his life too much if I kicked Karen and him out of the house."

"How do you and Karen get along?"

"We don't. I'll tell you Kim, it's pure hell living with someone you once loved knowing that after so many months you're just going to tell her to get out of your life as if she never existed. And she's really not a bad person. You'd like her. It's just that she's not good for me. Bossy as hell. Wants to run everything. If I was pissing in the toilet and my urine were spraying the bowl low and to the right, she'd come in and tell me I should direct my stream more the center. Some guys can put up with that. I can't and I won't, but speaking of toilets, I've gotta go. Be right back. Get us a couple of beers. I'll pay when I come out."

Frank went to the men's room on the right side of the bar. He locked the door behind him since it was small and anyone opening the door while he was inside would showcase his bathroom etiquette for the whole north end of the bar. Frank did not believe in showing strangers that he sprayed urinals low and to the right. He stood before the urinal and started to urinate. Just then there was a loud pounding on the door. The pounding stopped. Then it started again. Frank finished and started to wash his hands.

"Hey, what's the matter? Are you afraid? This is a strip bar, not the opera." The voice outside was loud and demanding. Frank went out. A large man stood just outside the door, obviously drunk.

Frank looked the man directly in the eye and said softly, "I'm not afraid of anything. I just like my privacy. Do you mind?"

The man looked at him stupidly. "No. Not at all. Just need to go." Then he walked in. Frank rejoined Kim at the bar and sat down.

"So Kim, are you married?"

"Was. I've got a boyfriend. I don't know how long I'll have him, but I've got a boyfriend. My ex-husband--he's got my kid. He's taken off and I can't find him. He just kidnaped my kid. I've got the police out looking for them."

"So how long has your ex-husband and your boy been gone?"

"Over six months. That fucker! He should leave my kid alone!"

Nadine came over with two beers, hand stretched out for payment. Frank gave her a ten.

"Keep the change Nadine. I don't always tip you when I'm here. In fact I hardly ever do. Take it for the good service you've always given me."

Frank turned back to Kim. "Look, right after this beer I have to take off. For one thing, I don't want Lori to come back here in a week or two to find out that I've been messing around with one of the other girls. With her brother getting shot, that's all she needs. And you've got your other customers. There's money to be made, and it's not right that it be made off of me."

"Oh what the hell Frank. Nipples won't know. Let's you and me do a private."

"Can't do it."

"Why not?"

"Sometime I'll explain." He drank the rest of his beer. "I have to go. Sorry I can't come to your birthday party."

Frank left Kim before she could answer hurrying out the door to his pickup. He was disappointed that Lori wasn't there. He was saddened that there was a very good possibility that he might never see her before he started harvest. And harvest, he knew from past experience, might very well keep him out of life's mainstream for weeks. He would be working eighteen hour days, seven days a week. He could not afford to go out and party. It was not only the time involved, it was also his need to keep focused on the job at hand. Since thousands of dollars were at stake, he knew that he had to concentrate on farming 100% of the time. He remembered the bitter lesson he had learned when he had first started farming. He had cultivated the weeds out of his beans the first time. Later, when the soybean plants had reached a foot and a half in height, a secondary infestation of weeds had started between the rows. He knew that he should cultivate a second time, but there had been a party in St. Louis. Frank had gone to the party expecting to cultivate the next day. However, the next day it rained. The next week it rained. And the week after. The field had gotten muddy and it had stayed muddy, and both the beans and the weeds had gown larger. After three weeks, the soybeans were more than three feet tall and the weeds were out of control.

Frank also felt sad for Lori. He remembered how she had told him that she should kick her brother and her boyfriend out after they had run off with her car. Perhaps her words now haunted her. And her brother had probably been her chief babysitter. *What would she do now?* thought Frank. Nevertheless, it was a beautiful day. The sun was out and it wasn't too hot. Soon he'd be in the Injection Pump, and who knows what would happen there.

He got in his pickup and drove slowly out of the parking lot. He was in a poor black neighborhood. Two black youths watched his pickup pull out into the street. Frank wondered what they thought of him--a white man coming out of the Sports Bar. They no doubt envied him for having the money to throw around. For a second or two he felt guilt. Then he thought of other things such as who would be in the Injection Pump. *Now that*, thought Frank, *was an example of progressive thinking.* Within minutes he had reached the Injection Pump.

The place was crowded. As he paid Bogart, he saw Stan Osterman sitting at the bar. Nirvana sat next to him, one arm around Stan's shoulder. Frank hurried over to them.

"Lori's brother shot himself and she's not at the Sports Bar. There's no telling when she'll return."

"What happened?" asked Stan.

"She had just moved to her new house with her five kids, boyfriend, and brother. They all live together. She was at work when someone came in and told her that her brother had shot himself. She hasn't been back since."

"That's unreal," said Stan. "Hey, I know that Lori stood you up and I know that you aren't planning to do anything with her anymore, but I think you ought to give her a second chance."

"Why's that?"

"Because she's something else. I mean, she drinks like a fish, tells jokes, smokes cigars. I don't know any woman who smokes cigars. She's one of a kind. You could really have fun with her. The two of you are made for each other."

"I might never see her again. If she doesn't go back to work, I don't have her home phone number. I doubt if Kim would get me in touch with her. She wants me for a customer or a boyfriend. I don't know which. Nadine doesn't give a shit, and Dotie's always too drunk to remember her phone number anyway. But maybe, I'll ask her to lunch again if she comes back."

"Where's this?" asked Nirvana.

"The Sports Bar," replied Stan. "Franks got this woman he's interested in over at the Sports Bar."

Frank noticed a woman over on stage three. She was sitting on a man's lap swaying back and forth in a languid manner across his groin. Her long light brown hair was held in place by a band which she wore around her forehead. Her skin was light olive colored. She was long legged and gorgeous.

"Hey Stan. See the girl over on stage three. Watch her. Is she into that lap dance or not?"

"She's interested in getting the guys money. Look at all the bills she's got in her G-string. She sure is good looking though. Why don't you give her a try?"

"I might. I just might. Nirvana, who is that girl?"

"That's Debbie. She's all right, but you've got to watch her. She likes money."

"Don't you all?"

"Sure we do, but Debbie likes expensive places and nice things. She's always going off to Cancun or San Diego or the Bahamas. The guys pay for it."

"Your kind of woman," laughed Stan. "She sure looks classy though. I'll give her that."

The tune ended. Debbie got off the man's lap. She walked off the stage over to the pool table as the man followed her. Frank walked up to the bar and watched Debbie and her customer play pool. One of the dancers came over and sat next to him drinking with him until she had to go up on stage.

He saw that Debbie was sitting at the bar alone. She could

have been a pretty girl in a West County Pub--a woman from Ladue or Frontenac out for a cocktail or coffee. You did not approach someone like that unless you already knew her. Nothing about this woman suggested that she was a stripper.

"Can I get you a drink?"

He could have said something inane like "Can I get you a drink. You must be tired after that game of pool." Or he could have asked her "Mind if I sit with you?" *Well that was what he would be expected to do in a singles bar. What a bunch of crap,* thought Frank. *Sure she wanted him to sit with her. And yes, she wanted him to buy her a drink. It was better than her buying herself a drink with her own money. He chose instead the direct approach. He'd buy her a drink. They'd have one together. She was after his money so she was hardly in a position to refuse. And he was perfectly willing to give her some of his money, just so long as it was in perfectly controlled dosages.*

"I'll have a root beer schnapps." Debbie looked up at him measuring him. Her voice was noncommittal.

" I'm Frank . . . You're Debbie, right?"

Ginny came over to take their drink order. It was obvious to Frank that Debbie was no beer drinker. Frank sized her up as someone who was trying to stay sober, for if she had been like many of the other strippers she would have ordered something stronger. Perhaps she was watching her weight. Drinking in the line of work was a sure fire way of getting old in a hurry. Many of the girls drank with their customers, matching them beer for beer, drink for drink. The difference was that the customers didn't do it every day or at least they didn't drink every day at the Injection Pump. The girls who treated the drinking as part of the job became bloated in a hurry. Root beer schnapps was a way of drinking with the customers while keeping the calories down.

"How did you know my name was Debbie?"

"Nirvana told me. I figured I'd get half the introduction done early so I could get to more important questions."

"What other questions?" Debbie shrugged with disinterest.

"Oh, the usual, such as are you married? How long have you worked here? Why did you become a stripper? I'm not boring you, am I?"

"No, not at all. Answer to the first question is I am not married, but I do have a boyfriend. He's Swedish. He wants me to move over there."

"Will you?" Frank asked.

"I really don't know. Maybe I will and maybe I won't. It all depends."

"Depends on what?"

"How I feel the next time he asks," Debbie replied flippantly.

"Must be a hell of a deal commuting back and forth to Sweden."

"Oh, he doesn't. He just visits me from California. That is when I'm not visiting him over there. We get together every two or three weeks. Keeps the fire burning."

"So you really like your boyfriend?"

"I'm nuts about him."

Frank didn't think it was very smart for Debbie to be telling her customers how much she adored her boyfriend. It kept them from harassing her, but at the same time it told them that they had no chance of ever getting anywhere with her. Perhaps he was wrong, but Frank considered it to be important for a dancer to lead a man on. If she could keep him convinced that sometime when everything was just right he could get her to bed, she could keep sucking money out of him. Many of the men, perhaps most of them, liked to believe they were special. A smart stripper would do everything possible to make a man feel that he alone held the keys to her heart. Debbie either was not smart or didn't care.

"Debbie, have you ever done any skiing?"

"Water skiing? I've tried it, but I don't like it."

"Why not?"

"I'm not really good at it, that's why."

"How about snow skiing? That's what I do. Now that is something worth doing."

"Never tried it."

"What do you think of it? Think you'd like to try it?"

"I don't know."

"Why don't you?" Frank asked.

"Because I've never tried it."

"Suppose your boyfriend took you. You like him. Now let's say that he wanted you to like skiing, and here you are, a dancer, with a far better than average body and probably of good athletic ability--would you go to please him?"

"I don't try to please anyone. No, I probably would stay in the lodge. It's too cold out there."

"You mean you would just let life pass you by while you sat around the lodge?"

"No, life would probably be flowing around me as I was sitting in the lodge."

Frank had to hand it to her. She was right. Girls like her were so good looking that all they had to do was sit there and wait for men to come knocking. For this kind of girl, men were adventure enough. How different he was from her. Even if plenty of girls were always available--and there never seemed to be enough--he would always be out risking his neck doing some dangerous thing or another. Frank had jumped off cliffs with his skis on. Even sky dived. He had raced motorcycles. He compared Debbie to Lori. Frank suspected Lori to be capable of anything for a laugh or for fun. Not only would she jump off a cliff--hopefully with skis on--but she would probably be the first one to the edge.

"I'm up next. Want to follow me over?" Debbie asked.

"Go ahead. I'll be over in a minute or two."

Five minutes later Frank found Debbie over on stage five sitting on a customer's lap. After rocking back and forth on his lap for a short time she partially opened her G-string and lewdly looked down her crotch before raising her eyes into her customer's with a little half smile. The customer stuck a five in her G-string as Debbie smirked. Frank interpreted this to mean *I know you want this so bad that you can taste it. Look at yourself drooling as I pull my G-string down just the littlest bit. Now I've got your five and now I'm leaving you, you old fool.* Debbie pulled the bill out of her G-string and with a quick flick of the wrist tossed it behind her onto the center of the stage. She quickly got up and came over to Frank.

Debbie crawled up onto Frank's lap and looked into his eyes. She arched her eyebrows as the little half smile returned to her face. She pulled herself into his chest. Her smell was sweet and distant, of far away places and scents. The feel of her was substantial, her body long and lean, her breasts in their prime thrust against his chest.

Debbie leaned back and took off her top showing off firm breasts that were crowned with tight light brown nipples. She rested her back against the edge of the platform and pulled her g-string down almost exposing herself, but not quite. He could almost feel her in his hand, his fingers running up her leg between her thighs searching and stroking to get inside her. Yet his hands were a foot away. He raised his arm and rested it against her leg. His hand moved down to her G-string. She laughed, pulling her

G-string up to cover herself and shook her head form side to side.

"Oh no you don't," she teased.

Frank pulled his hand away. Debbie stood up, her feet resting on the stage. She pulled her G-string out and beckoned. Frank fumbled in his pocket, found a five, and put it in her G-string while she smiled down on him.

"Are you staying?" she asked.

"No, I'm going back to the bar for one last drink. Then I'm going home."

"Enjoy your drink then."

Debbie tossed his five onto the center of the stage. A man sat across the platform. Debbie strutted over to him and hollered, "Arriva." That was for Frank. She had just collected a five from her previous customer and she had just gotten five from him. If she got yet another five from the new guy, that would make $15.00 for fifteen minutes work. With two tunes left--they always played four in a row--there would still be the chance that someone else would appear which could mean still another five. Then again, any one of the guys might stiff her--giving up only a one. Nevertheless, Debbie had the opportunity to make twenty bucks every time she got up on the stage.

"Arriva." *Now what in the hell did that mean?* Frank asked himself. It was as if Debbie had announced--'One down and one more to go' or 'Hey you other girls out there, I just nailed me another sucker.' The flippant way she tossed her money out onto the stage displayed an indifferent attitude toward her customers who had probably worked hard for that money. Tossing money around like that was like an Indian taking a scalp--shouting "EEEEEEEEAH," as he lifted it off his victim's head before thrusting it into the air for his companions to see. Debbie's "Arriva" completed the image. Frank wondered if Debbie was announcing to the other girls 'Look, see my trophies. Look at all the money I'm making. Another one bites the dust.'

Frank found Stan and Nirvana sitting together at a table. He ordered a beer from a waitress.

"Nirvana, this Debbie--is she Jewish?"

"What do you mean? Are you asking me if she likes money?"

"No, I mean, is she of Jewish blood as in is she Semitic?"

"I don't think so," Nirvana replied. "I think she's part Indian though."

"Just how much money does a girl like Debbie make?"

"Debbie. Debbie makes a lot of money. I'll bet--oh let's see--well this is just a guess--perhaps, hmmmmmm--maybe $200 per day."

"Now, does she have to split any of that with the bar?"

"Not really. We all pay $18.00 a day to the Injection Pump just to work there. What we make after that is all ours."

"So that's how the Injection Pump makes money," added Frank. "I knew it couldn't make it on $2.00 beer. Each girl contributes $18.00. There's perhaps ten girls on the day shift and ten on the night shift. That's twenty total. Times $18.00--that makes $360 a day plus what the place makes on the alcohol."

"And that's not all," continued Nirvana. "There's also the fines."

"The what?" Stan's face lit up with interest. "Fines. Are we talking gold dust here?"

"Might as well be," replied Nirvana. "Gold for the owners of the Injection Pump if a girl fails to show up for any reason. If she's scheduled to work, even if she calls the day before to explain that she can't make it, and she doesn't show up, she gets fined $135.00."

"Well, I can see their point. Management has to be able to count on these girls. If one of them doesn't show up it's bad for business," Frank explained. "A $135 find helps insure reliability in these girls."

"Yeah, but, the girls are fined even if they have valid excuses for not being able to work, and even if they call a day or two ahead of time."

"How does management collect from the girls then?" asked Stan.

"The girls are expected to pay $35 a day unless they owe more than $1000. Then they have to pay management back $50 a day until their debt is paid back. That's in addition to the $18 they have to pay in the first place. Many of the girls have kids. The kids get sick. Have to go to the doctor. The girl has to miss work because of a family emergency. Cars won't start. Whatever. There are three girls I know of who owe more than $2000."

"Well, that's business," Frank commented. The waitress returned with his beer. Frank paid her and drank from the glass. "I imagine that in a business such as this, you've got to keep a close handle on the girls. They probably are drunk, hung over, on drugs, got a new boyfriend they're lying down with-- whatever. As a group they are probably not very reliable. Cruel as it might seem, management has to keep control over them."

Nirvana's eyes shifted to the staircase. A man was paying his cover to Bogart. "Sorry, but one of my customers just came in. I've got to go over to him for a while. How long are you two staying?"

"Not long," Frank replied. "I don't know about Stan, but I'm going right after this beer."

"I probably won't stay very long either," answered Stan.

Nirvana got up to greet her old customer. Frank looked over at Stan and grinned. "I figure I've got maybe twenty minutes, and then I'm headed home. Time for one more lap dance." He left the table and walked over to stage two. Just then the music stopped. It was the fourth song. The two girls who had been at stage two walked off the stage. A pretty blonde walked up to Frank, large breasts bulging out of a skimpy bikini top. Across the top of both breasts were tattoos, each of them large enough to sprawl across the whole top of her breast. Frank stood in front of her path and smiled.

"Do you mind if I look at your tattoos?"

"That's what they are there for, she replied good-naturedly."

"Those are really different."

"So am I. I am the best."

"Meaning what?" Frank asked.

"Come up on the stage sometime and see for yourself," she replied.

"Mind if I ask you a question?"

"Go ahead." Her voice was bubbly and friendly.

"Those two tattoos. You have a similar one on each breast. Can you make them meet?"

Her smile brightened. "I sure can. Watch this." She removed her top exposing two breasts that had obviously been implanted with silicon. *A breast man's delight*, thought Frank. She took a breast in each hand and pushed them together so that they touched. The two tattoos now joined to form one image. It was of a butterfly, its wings spread in flight. Each breast had one wing on it and half of a butterfly body. Together they formed one butterfly, the breasts being a mirror image of each other.

"Now that's really something," said Frank. "Do me a favor. Come meet my friend and show that to him."

"Be glad to. Where is he?"

"Follow me." Frank led her to Stan who was still sitting at the table nursing a cup of coffee. Frank turned aside and nudged the blonde gently. She stepped in front of him.

"Stan. This--excuse me--I didn't get your name."

"Passion. My friends call me Passion."

"So what does your boyfriend call you?" asked Frank.

"As I have said. Everybody calls me Passion."

"Unforgettable as are your breasts."

"It helps in this business to be unforgettable. I am. You'll find that out. These are just tips of the icebergs." She looked down at her breasts and winked. "No, they're not icebergs. They're much too hot for icebergs. That was just a figure of speech."

Frank looked at her in disbelief. "Miss Passionate--do I have this right? Would you please show Stan what you just showed me."

Passion broke into laughter. "Just call me Passion. Passionate is more appropriate for my customers." Once again she took off her top. Passion thrust her breasts in front of Stan, giving him a good look, and then squeezed them together. Stan smiled and looked at the tattooed breasts, his eyes lit up with good humor.

"Now I thought I've seen everything. Passion, sit down with me. I'm going to buy you a drink. Anything you want."

"And I'm going. Whatever else happens next in this place has got to be boring," said Frank. "Nice meeting you, Passion. See you later Stan."

His pickup truck started as always. Frank reflected on the day's events as he drove home. Only at the Injection Pump could a man see the mating of two breasted tattoos. Actually it could probably have occurred at any one of a number of places similar to the Injection Pump. The point is it had happened at the Injection Pump along with everything else that had happened to him. Or almost everything for he had momentarily forgotten about the Sports Bar. Frank considered for a moment that he could have gone to a Singles Bar. There he could have observed the mating of a Brooks Brothers suit, double breasted at that, as he watched any one of a number of well-dressed men try their best moves on whatever available women they could find. Not to mention that he could participate in such mating rituals, trying his best lines on the women present.

His thoughts returned to his wife, Karen. She was better looking than most of the women he could hope to encounter in a singles bar. Yet he was terribly unhappy with his life with her. So, did he hope to do better at a Singles Bar in terms of personality or some other attribute he might find in another woman? *Probably not.* So what did he hope to achieve there? That was a tough one. He answered himself with a single word. *NOTHING.* After all, he had already determined that marriage was nothing but an empty hope. Practically every marriage he could think of was unhappy. Then, how about sex? Well, what about it? With his luck he'd get aids. His days of indiscriminate sex were over. The equation had changed as if a heavy weighted steel door had closed over him forever. Then, there was companionship--perhaps he could find that. No--absolutely not--that led to marriage.

Then what about other avenues where he could meet women? Frank rejected them out of hand. *They all lead to the same thing. Companionship--then to marriage. How God had erred.* He had created what Frank termed the "Horror of the Inhuman Condition" Allegorically the story was best expressed in Genesis by the fable of Adam and Eve. Man and woman were living in harmony until they had tasted of the apple. The apple represented sex. Once they had eaten the apple things were never the same again. The harmony that had existed between the man and the woman was destroyed once and for all. *Forget about all that crap about Heaven and Hell, Death, and Life after Death. Concentrate Frank on one thing and one thing only--that one thing that consumes you. The relationship between the man and the woman was never the same again once the apple had been tasted. And let no one misunderstand for a moment what was being explained here, for the serpent represents nothing other than the man's penis--that throbbing erect thing that relentlessly seeks release.* Frank laughed to himself, *let the Bible thumpers ponder that--that sex is represented by the apple and the temptation of the serpent is nothing other than a blood swollen penis looking for a place to erupt--leading to a future that held no answers.*

The Injection Pump beat the living hell out of any Singles Bar. It was worth the price of admission if one could afford it. It was great entertainment, and if one were there often enough he would find that it offered all the elements of great theater: comedy, excitement, and ultimately, if one was perceptive enough to look for it, tragedy.

Frank's thoughts turned toward Passion. She had an eager smile. She was super friendly and had a great personality. So, why had he been so willing to turn her over to Stan? *Was it because he might still be interested in Lori? Perhaps. No, probably not, for Lori had let him down. Then how about Debbie? No, and for two reasons: One--She had made it very clear that she was totally in love with her boyfriend, and two--He didn't think she was his type no matter how good looking she might be.* He couldn't put his finger on it. Maybe it was the tattoos. Or perhaps it was because he was looking for something else and he just hadn't found it yet. The question was, would he recognize it when he found it?

Before he knew it, he was pulling into his driveway. He had become so absorbed in thought that he had not even bothered turning on his radio.

CANDY

"It looks like we're going to have to miss the Injection Pump tonight," said Stan.

"Your idea of using the Cervantes Center Farm Show as an excuse was a good one," said Frank. "This way we don't have to get home before six, but Karen and Louise are going to wonder if we come home at midnight--especially since you are not known as a drinker."

"What's the name of this place again?"

"Houlihans. I think there's one at Union Station, but this is the first one in the St. Louis area. Just remember that we're right off hi way 270 and Manchester Road--just in case you ever decide to come here by yourself."

They had come in early--around five o'clock--had finished their dinner in what Frank had called the Jungle room--and were on their last beer after having settled with the waitress. Houlihans had several main sections in addition to a number of private booths set up as little alcoves where a man could be alone with his date. Frank called the room where they had eaten their dinner the Jungle room because of the large number of indoor plants hanging from the ceiling and walls.

"I saw a bar around the corner when we came in," said Stan.

"Should be very busy right about now. Six o'clock is happy hour time and it's Friday night. Let's check it out."

"Don't worry, I've got the tip," Stan told his friend as he followed Frank to the next room. The bar, just to the left of the entrance, was packed. Stan noticed that the bar itself didn't have seating room for two, and that the booths up against the wall were occupied as well. That left the tables in the center of the room, but these were taken also. A dozen or more people, all men and women from twenty-five to forty, milled around the room, either alone or talking in small groups.

"Looks like standing room only," said Frank. "Wait here while I get us a couple of beers."

"Are you going up to the bar?" a woman's voice asked from behind him.

Frank turned around to answer and saw three women sitting at a small table directly behind him, only three feet away. One of them, a woman in her late thirties, several inches taller than her two friends, was looking right at him.

"I'm getting us some beer," replied Frank.

126

"I heard you saying there was standing room only," said the woman. "You can sit with us if you want but you must buy us all a drink. That is, if you girls don't mind." The woman glanced at the woman on her left, then the blonde on her right, searching for eye contact, looking for approval that it was all right to invite Frank and Stan to their table.

"It's my birthday. The service is slow, and I'm out to get drunk," replied the blonde. "As far as I'm concerned, the more the merrier."

"I'm Candy," said the tall woman. "This is Tina." Candy nodded toward the blonde. "And that's Judy to my left."

"I'm Frank and this is my neighbor Stan," said Frank. "Now what can I get you girls?"

"Judy's drinking Vodka Gimlets and Tina's getting bombed on Black Russians. I'm having a Bloody Bull, which is kind of a house specialty," Candy replied.

"Got it," said Frank as he started for the bar.

Five minutes later he returned with the three mixed drinks thinking *this wouldn't happen in Springfield, Illinois. The women up there are too uptight--too stuck in a conservative rut to invite us over. Now I know why I like St. Louis.* Then he went back to the bar for the two beers he had gotten for Stan and himself, returning to the table which was now surrounded by five chairs. Somehow Stan had managed to find two extra chairs in the crowded room.

Sitting next to Judy, Frank was just in time to catch Candy asking "So you live close to Springfield, Illinois?"

"We both live thirty miles south of there," Stan replied.

"So why aren't you up there? Isn't this a long way from home?" Candy asked.

"There's a farm show downtown," said Frank. "We're both married, and it's really tough for us to get out on a Friday night. Stan's wife will hardly ever let him get out of the house, and the farm show is a perfect excuse."

"We're all married too," said Candy. "Judy's birthday is our excuse."

They left at ten o'clock, four hours and eight beers later. In the pickup, on the way home, Frank asked: "What is your wife going to say when she sees that you've been drinking? After all, she doesn't think you drink."

"Right now, I really don't much care, Frank. What did you think of Judy?"

"A little too plump for me, and she's too short. Besides, she's married."

"I don't think Candy's happily married," said Stan.

"Why's that?"

"She's told me so."

"You really get down to the nitty gritty; I'll say that for you."

"I got Candy's phone number. We're going to go out."

THE AFFAIR

"So, how's it going between you and Lori?" Frank.

"Nowhere. We just sit in the bar and drink for hours. I've tried to get her to meet me in a restaurant, but she never shows. I can't understand it. She'll stay with me in the bar. I don't tip her and she ignores her other customers. I'll do a private with her later on--for twenty bucks. That's it. She'd make a lot more money if I wasn't there."

"She likes you," said Stan. "She likes you so much that she forgets about making money."

Stan had slipped away from his farm preferring to drink coffee at Frank's instead of in his kitchen, his wife lurking close by. Frank's stepchildren were in school while Karen was off in Springfield looking for a job. Frank's kitchen table had become the favorite meeting place for the two men--a quiet spot with a coffee pot within arms' reach, where they could discuss their adventures in the Metro East.

"How about you Stan? I know you're going down there a lot. We both are."

"You remember Candy, don't you?"

"Sure. I remember Candy."

"I met her for lunch at a place you told me about. We hit it off just like the first time we met, and we ended up going to a motel. She said afterwards that she had a great time and she meant it. For the last two weeks we've been going to a motel. Then--and this I can't really believe." Stan paused, lost in thought.

"She's told me that she loves me." Stan continued.

"Doesn't she have a husband?"

"Sure she does but he's totally worthless."

"Does he work?"

"Not really. He does odd jobs when he feels like it. Candy supports him."

"Does he know about you and Candy?"

"He knows all right, but I don't think he really cares."

"How often do you two get together?

"Three times a week. Maybe more. I wonder if my wife suspects anything."

RECKLESS

Stan's wife suspected that Stan was doing something that he shouldn't be doing. Almost as tall as Frank at five ten or so and weighing less than one-hundred and forty, Louise came over to Frank's when Frank was in the machine shed changing the oil on his tractor. He had just finished putting in the new filter and was putting fresh oil in the crankcase when she walked into the shed.

"Frank, I've gotta talk to you."

"What's on your mind, Louise?"

"It's Stan. I think he's having an affair."

Frank laughed. "Stan? Having an affair? He's always in his machine shed working on something. Probably having an affair with that International tractor he just bought."

"I'm serious, Frank. He's seeing a woman. I just know it."

"What makes you think so?"

"He's staying out all the time. Two weeks ago he didn't come home for dinner. He didn't call or anything. And you know how Stan is. He's a homebody. Last night, he didn't come home until after two in the morning. I asked him where he had been. You know what he told me?"

"What?"

"That it was none of my business."

"He said that!" *So Stan's gone off the deep end. Has to because he's not even bothering covering his tracks*, thought Frank.

"Then I asked him what was wrong, and he called me a bitch. Then he accused me of all kinds of horrible things, and then he said that he was going to do whatever he wanted to do from now on. There's something wrong with him, Frank. I think he's doing a lot of drinking, and Stan never drank before. I think he's gone crazy. He needs a psychiatrist. Do you know anything, Frank? I still think he's got a girlfriend."

"Can't help you there Louise."

"But you're his best friend. He'd tell you. I want to know."

"I don't know anything Louise."

MAMA, PROTECTOR AGAINST EVIL STEPFATHERS

Frank sat in his office totally absorbed with the accounting figures on the computer screen. He had an appointment with his CPA for the next day. He was doing his final revisions to the balance sheet and income statement for his farm corporation, and he had to get done for his taxes. Frank had always prided himself that his CPA had to do very little work on his return since all the groundwork had been thoroughly done by himself beforehand. The door to his office was suddenly opened. It was Karen.

"What is this about your asking Nick to get off the phone," she demanded.

"I needed to call the implement dealer for some parts. Harvest is less than a week away, and I needed to get some new bearings for the transport auger."

"So why did you have to wait till four o'clock in the afternoon to call your dealer?" she asked.

"Why shouldn't I call at four? What's the significance of four o'clock?"

"The significance is that both kids are home around then. The kids need to use the phone a lot then."

"So?"

"Well don't you have any feelings for them and their needs. Do you always have to weigh things in dollars and cents. You're not that terribly busy yet. Your call could have waited till the next day. Either that or you could have called earlier."

"It takes several days to get the parts. If I don't have that transport auger fixed in a week, I'm not going to be able to put any corn in any of my bins."

"Our bins," she corrected him. "Those storage bins are our bins just like that corn is our corn. And didn't you say that harvest isn't starting for a week? If it takes three days to get the parts, then you had time to spare. Right?"

"No Karen. That's not right. I want to line that auger out now-- not next week. Next week there's other things I need to do."

"But you have a week. Right? So you don't really have to have the bearings right now. Am I correct?"

"Karen, I've told you before, and I'm going to tell you once again--I don't need you to tell me how to run my business. So what's your problem?"

"My problem is that I don't like the way you told Nick to get off the phone."

"At a quarter to four Nick was on the phone with his girlfriend. Fifteen minutes later he was still on the phone. I said 'Nick, I have a very important phone call to make. I need the phone for the next ten minutes.' Nick got off the phone. There was no problem."

"Well there was a problem. Nick gets embarrassed in front of his girlfriend when you ask him to get off the phone."

"Then, why doesn't he come to me about it?"

"Because he's afraid to."

"Let's see if I've got this straight then," said Frank. "Nick is afraid to ask me to hold off on my phone call because he's on an important phone call to his girlfriend. Well, he should be afraid of putting his call to his girlfriend ahead of my business calls. He knew that my phone call was more important than his. Nick also knew that I'm paying the phone bill--not him and not you. He also knew that I was pretty nice to him about it. Now Karen, I've been trying to tell you that my business calls are very important. If I can't handle the farm business, I'm not going to be able to make enough money. If I can't make enough money, then I'm not going to be able to pay the phone bill. If I can't pay the phone bill, then no one's going to have a phone to use."

"You and your high and mighty business calls. Just who in the hell do you think you are around here anyway? The king? Oh yes, King Frank--that's what you want to be, and all of the rest of us are your subjects!" Karen genuflected at the waist as she spat out the words.

"So, what you are telling me is that I should hold off on my calls until the kids are off the phone whatever time that should be, or at least that's what I am reading between the lines." Frank spoke deliberately, white anger evident in his tone.

"No. What I am telling you, is there is a better way to ask them to get off the phone. You should have said 'Nick, I know that you are on an important phone call right now. Can I ask you to please complete your conversation sometime during the next five minutes? Then, when I get done with my call, I'll tell you so that you can continue with any unfinished business with your friend."

"In other words, you want me to kiss his ass!" Frank bellowed.

"No, all I'm asking is that you show just a little human decency toward the others who have to share this house with you if that's possible."

"Karen, you are making it damn difficult for me to carry on my business. I've been more than nice to your kids, both of them. You don't appreciate that. I think it's high time that you and your kids get your own phone. I'll have one installed as soon as possible. But you are paying for it."

"Poor Frank. Poor, poor Frank. You've got it so rough. Everyone's picking on you." Karen's voice ripped with sarcasm as she pantomimed the playing of a violin, one hand holding it while the other pulled the bow back and forth across its strings.

"You are making me very angry. Now get the hell out of my office. NOW! Get the fuck out of here right now before I really get mad!" Frank came out of his chair and towered over Karen. Setting both hands on her shoulders, he pushed her firmly out of his office.

PRIVATE WITH KIM

Harvest and the post harvest fieldwork had taken over six weeks to complete. It had taken nine grain bins to hold all of the grain he had raised, and Frank had still run out of space. The rest he had to take to town. This year's harvest had been exceptional, the best Frank and his friends had ever seen. With the help of good weather, America's farmers had outdone themselves.

Frank was proud of his operation, having an excellent line of farm machinery, most of it John Deere. Through the years he had proved to be a capable manager, and as a result there was very little debt on his farm. His bookkeeping system was all on a computer which kept track of every dollar that was taken in or spent and where it came from or went. The prices of grain and other commodities reached him by satellite where they were fed onto a computer screen. Prices out of the Chicago Board of Trade were received on this monitor only ten minutes after they changed in Chicago. Not only that, but this same monitor displayed weather maps that changed every hour, and agricultural news. Frank received USA Today at five each morning on this screen before his urban counterparts received their newspapers.

Once again Frank had been successful. True, he had displayed a lot of skill, but he also had been very lucky. His thoughts turned to the Injection Pump, and to the Sports Bar. It had been six weeks since he had stepped feet in either place except for once just one weeks before on a day it had rained him out of the field. He had gone into the Sports Bar for only a half hour where he had a beer with Lori. Against his better judgement he had set a lunch date with her. Stan had talked him into giving it another shot. Once again she had not shown up at a restaurant. This time he thought something had happened to her. After all, her brother had either shot himself or been murdered in her house. When he drank that last beer with Lori one weeks ago, she had told him that the police now believed that her brother had been murdered.

But she had stood him up a second time. Frank entered the Sports Bar having waited in the restaurant for only fifteen minutes before leaving. The restaurant he had chosen this time was close to the Sports Bar. He had deliberately chosen one close by so that he would waste little time in the event of a no show. Lori was not in the Sports Bar. Kim was sitting on the other end of the bar. She motioned him over.

"Will you buy me a beer, Frank?" she asked.

"Sure. Ask Nadine to bring us both one. Let's sit over at that table over there." He pointed to a table that was out of the way, next to a wall. Frank followed Kim to the table where they sat next to each other.

"So how are you doing Frank?"

"I"m fine. Do you know where Nipples is?"

"No. She's supposed to be here though."

"She's supposed to be in a restaurant right about now with me sitting across from her."

"Oh no. You didn't."

"I did. I pulled a really dumb shit move by giving her a second chance."

"I don't know why she did that. That's not very smart."

"Tell me about it."

"Frank, there's something I have to tell you about Nipples. I don't mean to cut her down or anything, but she's a liar."

"I know."

"But you don't know how bad a liar she is."

Just then a tall blonde walked by. Kim grabbed her by the arm to stop her. The woman looked down at her and smiled.

"Christie, sit down with us for a second." The woman pulled up a chair. Her eyes sparkled with good humor.

"What's up Kim?"

"Christie, tell Frank about Nipples."

"You mean about?"

"Yes, tell him about her brother."

"Well, Nipples told everyone--all her customers and all of the girls who work here that her brother shot himself. Well, he didn't. Someone she knew shot himself or at least that's what she's telling everyone now."

"How did you girls find this out?" asked Frank, surprised.

"Dotie went over to Fastasy's house one day. She's about Nipples's only friend here," Christie continued. "Nipples's brother walked in the room. He didn't even have a hole in his head or anything." Christie broke out laughing.

"So anyway," said Kim, "All of us hate her guts now. After we thought her brother had been shot, we all gave her a party. Got Nipples really drunk. She didn't buy one drink." Kim paused for a moment; then continued. "She lied to us all. She always lies."

"So, I picked the wrong girl, didn't I?"

"You sure did. You invite me to a restaurant--baby I'll be

there."

"Maybe we should sometime."

"Tell me when."

Kim's hand moved under the table onto Frank's lap. She undid his zipper sliding her hand into his fly as she worked her fingers under his shaft and around his balls. Christie peered over the table at him.

"I'm new here," said Christie. "I used to work at the Injection Pump."

Frank choked back the urge to laugh. He was having his balls massaged right in front of Christie, who didn't suspect anything was going on. Christie continued her story.

"I really didn't like working at the Injection Pump. Here, you don't have to put up with someone unless you want to. I guess in a way you do, but at least you make twenty bucks for a private. What I like about this place is there's no lap dances whereas at the Injection Pump you are expected to do lap dances. And sometimes a guy only gives you a dollar after you've been all over his lap for a song or two and after he's been slobbering all over you."

"So, how long did you work at the Injection Pump?" Frank asked .

"One day. I didn't know quite what to do. I was up on the stage with this other girl. I was just more or less dancing around the stage. The girl knew I was scared, so she told me that I could just keep dancing and that she'd take care of all the men. All day long all I did was dance while she went into overtime bouncing from one man's lap to another."

" So, who made all the money?"

"She did by rights. After all, she took care of all the men while I did zip. But you know what? She gave me a lot of her money. I don't know if it was half or not, but I sure didn't deserve it."

"I hate to interrupt, but do you want to do a private?" asked Kim.

"Sure, it's about time that I find out what one of your privates is like," replied Frank.

"Then lead on. I'm right behind you. You know where it is, don't you?"

Frank was already out of his seat heading for the chair in the back. Frank sprawled into the chair taking off his shirt as Kim took off her top. He watched in amazement as she took off her G-string, then turned around to face him. She undid his belt and in one quick motion pulled both his pants and his jockey shorts down to his ankles. Turning around so that her back faced him, Kim started to squat on his lap. It all happened so fast that Frank was caught totally by surprise. Kim hovered one inch over his lap, her vagina already wet as his penis started to swell. In seconds he would be inside of her.

This was unplanned and unwanted. Nevertheless, it was going to happen. Kim started to reach behind her buttocks, stretched out fingers groping for his shaft. Suddenly she jumped off of him yelling "It's Pat. Holy shit, it's Pat over here to check up on us." It was true, for a slender brunette in her early thirties had walked around the partition. Kim frantically started to put on her G-string as Pat walked by purposely acting as if she didn't notice anything out of the ordinary. Frank pulled up his jockey shorts. She got back on his lap.

"Oh Jesus Christ!" she exclaimed. "Oh Jesus Christ! Pat almost caught us. Pat would have had my ass."

"Oh, she probably wouldn't have done anything now, would she?" asked Frank.

"I don't know, and I really don't want to find out," said Kim. Then she started to kiss him probing his mouth with her tongue. Frank was glad it had not happened. He did not like to do things that he had not planned, especially something that could lead to aids. He was surprised that she had set him up for this, but then Kim had always wanted to get him away from Lori.

The private was over. Frank and Kim went to the bar. Christie was seated with two men at one of the tables. Nadine came to take their order. Frank waved her off.

"Nadine, thanks, but I've gotta get going." He turned to Kim. "That was a great private Kim. You are full of surprises. See you later."

A minute later he was in his pickup on the way to the Injection Pump.

Frank saw Debbie sitting by herself at the bar. A waitress asked for his drink order as he was paying Bogart his cover at the door. "Just get me a beer. And get Debbie a root beer schnapps. I'll be over there."

Frank saw Chanel walking toward him. Chanel walked quickly looking puzzled. Not recognizing him, she was about to walk past him when he stepped in front of her.

"Chanel, now where are you hurrying off to?"

"Oh hi. I'm looking for this guy who's supposed to be here. He's supposed to be around here someplace." Chanel appeared as if she had left her shoe someplace and had not remembered where it was.

"Chanel, you and I have to get together again sometime," said Frank.

"Well you see, right now I have to find this guy. He called to tell me he would be here. He usually spends an hour or two with me. Maybe when he leaves."

"Sure, I'll tell you what Chanel. After he leaves just come over. I might be with Debbie."

"If you're with Debbie, I'm not going to separate you. Maybe some other time."

"Fine with me. See you later Chanel."

Frank went over to Debbie and took a seat on the bar stool next to her. The waitress came over with their drinks.

"Is this for me?" Debbie asked.

"It's not for me. I'm drinking the beer."

"You remembered what I drink. I'm surprised."

"How's your boyfriend?"

"Great."

"Get married yet."

"No and I'm not going to."

"Why not?"

"I don't feel like it."

"You felt like it the last time. Last time I talked with you--the only time I talked with you--you were telling me how he was from Sweden and how much you were in love with him."

"That was before. Now I feel different about it."

"And you're going to feel different again the next time I'm here, and I'm not going to let you answer that one."

"Good, because it's time for me to get on stage. Come and join me," said Debbie.

Frank followed her over to stage one and sat at one of the chairs in front of the platform. Debbie stood in front of him leering down on him. Then, laughing, she climbed onto his lap. Out of the corner of his eye, Frank saw Chanel scurrying back to the bar. A short fat man around fifty who had just paid his cover stood next to Bogart. *So that was Chanel's customer*, thought Frank. Frank found himself craning his neck looking 180 degrees behind him. Cool fingers closed over his eyes.

"You seem distracted," Debbie said calmly; then laughed. "I'll just cover your eyes so you won't look at the competition."

"Debbie, I'm not looking at anyone. I just heard some commotion back there and looked to see what was going on," Frank

138

lied.

"I'm sorry, but I forgot your name. Tell me again?" asked Debbie.

"Frank."

"I won't forget again. Sorry about that."

Debbie clasped her hands behind his head and leaned away from him with her back pressed up against the edge of the stage. She arched her pelvis upward and started to move it up and down suggestively, using the muscles of her stomach and groin. She looked into his eyes; then rolled hers at him. Then laughing, she started to toss her head from side to side.

She's mocking me, thought Frank. She's mocking the whole situation. Well two can play this game. He grabbed her shoulders gently but firmly so that she couldn't move. Debbie looked at him quizzically. For the first time since coming to the stage she became serious.

"What's going on?" she asked.

"I'm taking my shirt off."

"Suit yourself."

Frank pulled off the short sleeved sport shirt he was wearing. The weeks of farming, with all the long hours, the skipped meals, had taken their toll. He had lost ten pounds and all traces of a gut. His muscles rippled. For weeks now, he had worked hard physically, shoving and pushing large heavy objects that refused to be moved, shoveling corn in his bins, and climbing forty foot ladders to get to the top of the bins. He had been up and down those ladders so many times that he would have lost count long ago. Farming had made his muscles hard as steel. Debbie winked approvingly.

"So Debbie, what do you think of being single?"

"Single life sucks."

"You're sure spelling out your opinion. I think it's great. Of course, I'm married."

"Most of the guys who come here are. I noticed your ring."

"I might not be wearing it for that much longer," he warned. "You'd better look out Debbie."

"Is she still screwing you?"

"Sure, but we really don't get along. We haven't for years, and it's getting worse."

"But she's still sleeping with you right? I'd stay with it if I were you Frank. With aids and all the weirdos out there, I'd put up with a lot of crap."

"Well I have been, and I'm not going to much longer."

Debbie pulled out her G-string. Frank slipped a five behind the elastic. Looking him directly in the eye she held his gaze and said: "There's another guy who just sat next to you. I can stay with you if you want or I can go over to him?"

"Stay with me. You're talking sense. I don't agree with you, but at least you are putting a different light on single life. Do you think I'm one of those weirdos out there Debbie?"

"Sure. You come here don't you? Everybody who comes here is weird."

"What about the girls who work here then?" Frank countered.

"We're getting paid."

"But look what you have to do for it. Is it worth it? Take a look at some of the guys you have to put up with. Some are old farts. Some have two heads, some have hare lips, some are green, and some are orange. I mean we're talking about the losers of the earth."

"Beats pumping gas."

"What?"

"I'm saying I used to pump gas for a living before I started to work here. One of my girlfriends got me drunk and dragged me in here. I thought *No way can I do those lap dances*, but look at me now."

"The moneys really good then?"

Debbie pulled out her G-string and beckoned toward her vagina. Frank gingerly slipped in another five. "See what I mean. We haven't been here more than six or seven minutes and you've already given me ten dollars."

"You are utterly shameless. And you are heartless as well. Taking my money like that."

"My boyfriend doesn't think I'm heartless."

"Neither does my wife. She still thinks I'm a nice guy, but I'm not what she thinks I am."

"And what's that?"

"Heartless."

He ended up tipping her another five after the last song ended. They went back to the bar, ordered another round of drinks, and continued the conversation. Soon it was time for Debbie to go back on stage. He followed her over to stage three. She did one lap dance with him, promised to come back to him, and climbed on top of the man who was sitting on Frank's left waiting his turn. Frank got up and wandered over to the bar.

He sat next to a dancer he had never seen before who was eating her lunch. The girl had long curly black hair, was thin waist ed, and had large breasts. Every now and then, between mouthfuls, she would look up at him slyly.

"Is the food any good?" he asked. "I've heard it isn't."

"It's not bad," she replied. "Roast beef and potatoes today. When they have chicken, I eat at McDonalds."

"I don't believe we've met. I'm Frank."

"I know you. I'm Susan. You come here a lot."

"You're not Susan. Susan has short reddish brown hair. So who are you?"

"I'm Susan. I'm wearing a wig. Today I'm a brunette. Tomorrow," she laughed, "Who knows."

"I'm taking your advice. Be right back." Frank went over to the buffet table. There were only several items on it: mashed potatoes, roast beef, green beans, and cherry cobbler. Still, it was a good deal. He had paid only three dollars to get in. Beers were $2.00, and the coffee was free. He helped himself to some roast beef, skipped the potatoes and beans, and scooped onto his plate a large portion of cherry cobbler. Then he returned to his bar stool. Susan was just finishing her lunch when the set ended.

"Sorry we can't talk longer, but I've gotta go onstage. Come on over."

"I will some other time. I've gotta leave before long."

Moments after Susan left Debbie returned from the stage. She took a seat by herself at the opposite end of the bar. For a minute or two she ignored Frank, then she turned around to face him and stuck her tongue out at him. He got up to join her.

"What's this with the tongue business?"

"Always gotta run off and talk with the other girls. You really can't stay with one person for more than ten minutes at a time, can you?"

"Debbie, I would have stayed, but you just couldn't be loyal to me. Had to do a lap dance with someone else," Frank kidded.

"You know that's the way it is. I'm here to make money and all these guys are paying. I would have come over to you."

"I get bored real fast waiting around. Besides, I've got itchy feet. By the way, I have to go home."

"I'll see you the next time you're here," she said gently. Debbie got up and walked across the room. In less than ten seconds she was already talking to another guy, then sitting at the man's table. Frank left the Injection Pump walking briskly down the stairs to the parking lot. The parking attendant, a short chubby black man, sat on the hood of someone's car. He nodded at Frank.

"Beautiful day isn't it?" said Frank.

"Not bad. A little warm out though."

"I have to go home. If my wife calls tell her she can catch me here next week."

The attendant broke out laughing. Frank gave him a knowing smile, then started to laugh as he walked over to his pickup.

JUST SHOOTING A LITTLE POOL

Frank went to Ciceros alone, but he only had one beer there before deciding to go to the Injection Pump. He drove out of the lot in his pickup not in any particular hurry to see anyone in particular, but anxious to get to the Injection Pump. Soon he was there. He mounted the stairs, paid Bogart, and went to the bar for a beer. He bought himself a glass of Budweiser and brought back a large mug of Lite for Bogart. Large meant 48 oz of beer, in a mug almost the size of a pitcher.

He sat with Bogart with his back facing the bar so that he could see the other customers come in. Frank felt totally relaxed, wanting for once to stay away from the girls--at least for a little while.

"Is this for me, Frank?" asked Bogart, surprised that someone had bought him a beer.

"Gotta be for you Bogart. I'm not going to try to handle that. Not with the long drive I have ahead of me."

"Where do you live then?"

"Middle of nowhere better than an hour from here on a farm."

"You don't look like a farmer to me," said Bogart.

"That's what they all say."

Small cool hands were suddenly placed over Frank's eyes. They were a girl's hands--the question was which one's. Whoever had sneaked up behind him apparently expected him to guess whose hands they were. He didn't know where to start.

"Must be Chanel," he guessed.

"No." The voice was mature yet melodic.

"Susan?"

"Not even close."

"How about Debbie?"

The girl took her hands away. He turned around to find that it was Debbie after all. This was a surprise because he had not seen nearly as much of Debbie as he had of some of the other girls. He had also assessed her as cool, almost aloof--definitely not the kind of girl who would seek him out this far away from the bar. Then he remembered the old saying *Money talks and bullshit walks.* He had been more than generous with his money and with more than one girl at that. Here he had just bought Bogart what amounted to a pitcher of beer and Bogart wasn't even one of the girls. He had recognized Debbie as having a keen nose for money. This was after all a competitive business, and he was probably viewed as one of the better paying customers around. That obviously explained it.

"It's about time you got around to my name," Debbie replied good-naturedly. "You've just been with too many girls. Come join me at the bar and buy me a drink." Frank followed Debbie to the bar. They sat on stools next to each other. Ginny came right over to take their order, the bartender's face somehow reminding Frank of a pixie's.

"Well, what are you two going to have?"

"Ginny, bring me a beer. Get Debbie a...whatever she's having." For a moment Frank thought he remembered what Debbie drank. Whatever it was, it eluded him. Perhaps it was that he had been around too many of the girls. He told himself that he just wasn't as attentive as he should be.

"Just bring me a root beer schnapps," said Debbie.

"You always get the root beer schnapps," replied Frank, "and I keep on forgetting."

Debbie laughed. "Like I just said, you've just been around too many girls. Now where have you been? I haven't seen you for a while."

"I've been here. Several times. Must have been on your days off. Then I've been over at the Sports Bar. Ciceros."

"Why don't you just spend more time here? You'd be better off."

"To tell you the truth, I like it better here, but I always run into a girl or two at one of the other places who I have to check up on once in awhile."

"You just haven't been with the right girls here."

"Debbie, what's the night shift like here? I was here once at night a long time ago."

"You don't need the night shift. It really gets hectic. Just come on over here during the day."

"You think I'll be taken care of by the day shift?"

"Sure. As long as you come see me."

"Think I can handle that?"

"Sure. Why not? Hey, you want to shoot some pool?"

"Let's go." Frank climbed off of the bar stool and went over to one of the two pool tables. Close by, on the wall was a rack containing five or six pool queues. He picked several of them out examining each one in turn. All with the exception of one were either too light or not straight enough.

"Give me some quarters. I'll rack the balls," Debbie volunteered.

Frank reached into his pocket and found four quarters which he gave to Debbie. She stooped over the head of the table and inserted three quarters into the slot. The balls rumbled around inside the guts of the table and started to roll into the receiving bin just underneath the coin slots. Debbie scooped up the balls and put them on the table. Frank found the ball rack and handled it to her. She racked the balls tightly together being careful to put the eight ball in the center.

"Your break," said Debbie.

"Here goes then." Frank placed the queue ball on the table and drove it into the stacked balls. It hit just to the left of the lead ball just as he intended. The momentum was there, but nothing went in. Debbie took the stick from him and surveyed the table. The one was lined up with the left corner pocket. Debbie lined up for the shot and put it in. The seven now lay close to the queue ball. It was an easy shot and she made it. The three was the only open shot and five feet of green stretched between the white ball and the far corner pocket. Debbie lined up and missed.

Frank took the stick from her and looked over the possibilities that now lay before him. Although nothing had gone in, his break had been a good one. Several open shots presented themselves. A stripe was lined up with the right corner pocket. It was a long shot, but if he could make it he would be lined up with the fourteen and the right side pocket. He shot carefully with a soft touch. The slate bed was true. Even though the queue ball traveled slowly it went straight. The ball went in and he was lined up for the side shot. This time Frank hit the queue ball low and hard giving it a backwards spin. The shot was good and the queue ball spun backwards so that it rolled next to another stripe which was close to the left side pocket. Frank put it in easily. That left another long shot. Frank took it and made it.

He was on a roll. Four shots without a miss. He had always considered himself to be a better than average pool player, but he had never thought himself to be a good one. He looked over the bar. Chanel sat there sipping a glass of orange juice. He had seen her alone several times before although usually she had a guy with her. Rarely had he seen her with the other girls. She sat on a bar stool only fifteen feet from the pool table, a puzzled look on her face, as she watched the game. Or was she watching him?

Frank took the next shot. It was not a particularly difficult one yet he missed. He thrust the butt end of the stick downwards against his foot in disappointment. It was not a particularly obvious gesture.

Debbie hardly noticed but Chanel, still over at the bar, broke into laughter. Frank went over to her.

"You shouldn't laugh. Debbie's probably the resident pool shark. Root for the underdog--me."

"Debbie's good. This'll be interesting." Chanel replied.

Debbie took her shot and made it. Once again, she lined up quickly for the next shot which she missed. Frank watched her and then turned to Chanel once more. "I keep seeing you with a guy. Now you are alone, and I'm with Debbie. I'd like for us to get together sometime."

"Our timing never seems to work out. I'd like for us to get better acquainted also."

"Chanel, I hate to leave you, but it looks like it's my time to shoot."

Frank returned to the table and dropped the next two balls. This put him ahead by three balls. Debbie sank the next two, one of them a long shot. On her next shot she missed, which enabled Frank to sink his remaining balls. He then took the eight ball calling his shot as he made it.

"You got real lucky," said Debbie.

"What do you mean? I'd say that was skill."

"You did well, but it's my turn to get up on stage. If you hadn't won as soon as you did, we'd have to leave the table anyway, and it would be a tied game."

"No, it wouldn't have been," replied Frank, "I was way ahead."

"Doesn't matter," Debbie teased, "it could be anyone's game, and my getting up on the stage would have tied the game."

"In cases like that the person who's ahead wins," said Frank.

"Oh no. It's dealer's choice."

"What's that supposed to mean?" asked Frank.

"It was my idea to play--therefore I was the dealer. So I get to make up the rules as we go."

"You're heartless."

"Let me show you how heartless I am. Follow me up on stage so I can take your money."

Frank sat in front of stage II. Debbie stood in front of him as two other customers took seats close by. For a moment, Frank thought Debbie was going to go over to them first, but she eased onto his lap and threw her arms around his neck.

"Tell you what. I'll do two songs with you. Then I've got to go over to those two guys. Then, if you want to go back to the bar, go ahead. I'll join you afterwards." The time passed swiftly. Frank sensed that Debbie had changed. She seemed relaxed. As before, she teased him. She pulled her G-string aside allowing him a quick glimpse. She played with her breasts, daring him to touch them, then when he reached out for them, pulling back away from him at the last moment. This time, however, she didn't mock him as she had before, as he had seen her mock the others. The change was subtle. It was as if she felt comfortable being with him. It was as simple as that. Or was it the other way around?

She moved onto the next guy as Frank returned to the bar. Ten minutes later she was sitting next to him ordering another root beer schnapps.

"What's that other place you go to?" Debbie asked.

"Sometimes Ciceros. Usually the Sports Bar."

"You really shouldn't go there. You're likely to get into trouble."

"Debbie, trouble can be fun. Besides, I really don't see much wrong with the place. A guy has to have several places to go. That way if things are slow at one place or if his favorite girls are not there, he can go to one of the others."

"I'm here Mondays, Wednesday, Saturdays, and Sundays. Come then and things will never be slow."

"You probably won't be here all the time when you are scheduled."

"Most of the time I'll be. Two weeks from today I'm going to California. I'll be there for ten days. Then I'll be back. Must be with my honey. Then it's back to the grindstone."

"One last beer, Debbie, and then I'm going home."

"And a root beer schnapps?"

"And a root beer schnapps," said Frank.

"Ginny, get us another beer and root beer schnapps," Debbie ordered.

Ginny brought the drinks right over. By now it was obvious to Frank that Debbie had some clout with the other girls. He had often found Ginny to be a little slow to get a girl a drink. Sometimes he had even seen her refuse to bring a girl a drink. Ginny, as bartender, had the right to refuse to give a dancer alcohol if she felt the girl had too much. Ginny did not hesitate to exercise her right of refusal. Although she was cute, young, and almost dainty, Ginny knew when to draw the line and often did so. With Debbie, Frank sensed that Ginny was anxious to please. For this reason, Debbie never waited more than several minutes before Ginny returned with her drink.

Frank lifted his glass of beer and clinked it against Debbie's glass which remained on the bar. "Toast Debbie. Let us drink to the next time we drink together, to good times, and to your having a good trip to California."

"I'll go for that. To good times, California, and the next time we drink together." Debbie reached out for her glass and raised it to her lips. "And here's to even better times."

"Debbie, you really are a tease. So here's to you." Frank drank greedily from his glass.

"I'm not such a tease. It's just that---I can't help it. Oh well, that's me, I guess."

He finished with the beer just as she finished her schnapps. "I've gotta go. See you next time, Debbie."

"I'll be here. Be careful."

Frank walked the stairs. He looked over his shoulder just as he started down them. Debbie had already found someone else. Frank shrugged. *Just part of the game. It's a business after all and the girls gotta eat.* Soon, he was in his pickup idling out of the parking lot. On the way home he thought about his friend, Stan, who had called to tell him that he was planning to divorce Louise.

THE WHITE WOLF

The white wolf stood just on the other side of the wire on her hind paws. Her body was stretched to the limit, her head reaching 5 1/2 feet above the ground. Fully one hundred-twenty-five pounds, Circle was easily capable of crushing a man's arm or leg in her massive jaws. The wolf's fore paws rested against the wire of the pen. Frank Harring studied the wolf while he stroked her head through the wire.

The pen had been built with concrete footings 3 feet deep so that the wolves could not dig underneath the wire. Heavy wire ten feet high formed the walls of the pen. A gray wolf skulked twenty feet behind Circle. This was Cosmos, a male timber wolf, fifteen pounds heavier than his mate. Or at least the owner of the two animals had believed they would be mates when he had bought them as pups three years ago. What he had not counted on was the immutable social order of the wolf hierarchy. As a rule each wolf pack had two Alpha animals which were the leaders of the pack. The others were Beta wolves. Only the two Alpha animals would bear young--the rest would spend their lives helping to support the Alphas. Since only the Alpha animals bore pups, all wolves would cooperate in bringing down large game as well as bringing food to the pups. Baby-sitting chores would be assumed by other members of the pack.

Circle was proud, fearless, and beautiful. Her white coat shimmered in the sun. Her posture was erect and alert. Even now she muzzled through the gaps of the wire, licking Frank's hands. When Frank moved around the pen, she would follow. Her eyes followed every movement hoping he had a treat hidden in his coat or behind his back. When he stopped walking around the cage, she would get up on her haunches hoping he would rub her ears. Cosmos lurked in the background apprehensively watching Frank. When Frank called out his name, he skittered away. When Frank stood in front of the pen and Circle rose on her hind paws, Cosmos would nervously inch forward. Cosmos and Circle would never mate for Circle was an Alpha whereas Cosmos was the archetype of the Beta animal. Frank sat on the ground in front of Circle. The female wolf followed his movement and got down on all fours. She reached through the wire with a paw. Frank stroked it.

This was one magnificent animal, he thought. He wouldn't give two cents for the male, but he would give thousands for the female. She was strong enough to destroy any dog or man foolish enough to challenge her. Her owner, a distant neighbor of Frank's, had once told him that a wolf only respected humans who were fearless in its presence. The owner had told him that he would let no one in the cage with the two animals. He had explained that the wolves tended to view humans as members of a wolf pack and would treat them accordingly. In the wild a wolf would stay clear of humans, but in a pen it would be a different matter. The man who would enter the pen would be entering the wolf's inner territory, and would be considered a member of the pack. The animal would size the man up as being inferior, equal, or superior, for the wolf's sense of social order was so acute that the trespasser must be given his proper hierarchical position. Show the smallest trace of fear, and the human who entered the pen would be gambling with his life. The animals might disdainfully ignore him. Then again, they might turn on him.

Frank had never been in the cage. The owner didn't know him that well, and in todays lawsuit happy world, letting a man into a wolf pen with two healthy wolves was stupid. However, if he should venture into the pen, Frank was sure the male wolf would retreat into the farthest corner. Circle would probably run up to him and encircle his neck with her paws. After all, Frank was an Alpha animal and she knew it.

Frank was a farmer. He lived seventy miles from St. Louis on the Illinois side of the river. Having spent years outside and having spent most of his working hours alone, he had many quiet moments to study his environment, the animals around him, and mankind in general. The wolves intrigued him because they reminded him of people.

He had long ago concluded that Nature allowed only the fittest animals to survive. Coyotes ate only those pheasants which were too old, too slow, or too dumb to get out of their way. Coyotes which were not resourceful and quick starved. With wolves only the Alphas mated. Lesser animals were doomed to extinction. Frank wondered if the same was not true for humans. It seemed to Frank that there were two types of people--leaders and followers. The leaders, it seemed, were born to lead, while the followers were destined to do whatever the Alphas wanted. Down deep the Alphas didn't care what others thought while the followers meekly observed what was going on around them; then followed the examples set before them. Like pack animals the followers didn't really choose for themselves. Others dictated their music preferences as well as how they dressed, acted, and thought. Frank believed that only the Alphas mattered. The follower would go on to breed, unlike the Beta wolf, but his life would be irrelevant.

Frank called out to Cosmos. The animal retreated, head lowered, his tail between his legs. Then he turned toward Circle. She looked like a Siberian husky except that she was twice the size of one. *What would it be like having her at his farm?* The owner had told him that if such an animal were confined to a house, it would chew all the furniture to pieces. Frank looked over at the doghouse which the owner had built for the wolves in the center of the pen. Many of the shingles had been ripped off its roof. Very little paint remained on the wooden sides which had been clawed, scratched, and bitten. Frank decided that keeping her in his house was out of the question.

He would have to build her a pen. He looked at Circle. No, he thought, she is too fine an animal to have in a pen, this one included. Frank took in her eyes, and noticed that they had a strange look to them. In a way they were like the eyes of a dog, but they were more alert, more intelligent. It was almost as if the animal were saying, "I exist in the present and I hold in me the past, a past that goes way back, but I have no knowledge of a future." Was the animal silently saying that there was no future for something so wild and so magnificent?

The white man had killed off most of the wolves. Only a few hundred remained in Minnesota, a few thousand in Alaska. In an age without telephones, automobiles, and vcrs; in an age before the wolf had become practically extinct, the wolf and man lived close together. The Indian was able to study the wolf at close hand and had come to admire it The American Indian recognized early on that this wonderful creature truly embodied the best characteristics man could have. The wolf was strong, courageous, faithful to its spouse, family oriented, disciplined, intelligent, and immensely capable.

And humans? No wonder the divorce rate was 50%, thought Frank. *They were too quick to sleep with each other, then get sidetracked with the wrong sexual partner, finally ending up with that person because of convenience or because the man and woman had gotten used to each other.* Frank had noticed long ago that most marriages, even those that lasted, were mediocre affairs at best. He had also learned from history that there were also those love affairs, so intense and permanent, that the lovers would sacrifice anything to be with each other.

Take Mark Anthony, for example. Frank recalled from his Shakespeare how at the very pinnacle of success and with the keys

151

to Rome in his grasp he fell in love with Cleopatra. Frank remembered how this strong, disciplined, capable Roman general suddenly turned into a love sick puppy, aimlessly pursuing love while weaker men defeated his army. Then, beaten and cornered, both of them committing suicide. He recollected how King Edward VIII gave up the thrown of England so that he could marry Mrs. Wallis Simpson, a commoner from the US? *There had to be a difference,* thought Frank, *between the ordinary love affair and the extraordinary one--the latter so intense that a king would give up a crown for love or a Mark Anthony giving up his life.*

The bond between lovers has to be altogether different, thought Frank. He knew that for most people, that bond was sexual. Easily started and just as easy to end, the intensity of the bond would start to fade in a year or two. *The other type of bond, so magnetic and riveting that the two lovers would give up anything to stay together, has to go beyond sex,* thought Frank. *The chemistry has to be just right so that the two lovers feel every fiber of their bodies crying out for each other. It happens when their minds focus on each other completely--consciously and subconsciously. And it happens suddenly and unexpectedly, perhaps once in a lifetime and perhaps not at all when each lover finds the one he is destined to be with.*

And that's the way it is with wolves, thought Frank. *Somehow the Alpha animals find each other and stay with each other until the end. Sometimes it is the same way with humans, but only sometimes, and only then does the word love have any meaning.*

Frank heard the phone ring in the house. The owner went inside to answer it. *Now's my chance,* thought Frank. *It's only a question of balls.* In the wild the wolves would leave him alone. In the pen, alone with the two animals, who could tell? He had to know. Would the wolves accept him or would they panic, turn on him, and rip him to pieces? It was the ultimate gamble--to jump in with the two animals and take his chances, the prize being the certainty from within that he was unafraid. Of anything.

Frank walked to the other side of the cage. Within seconds he had jumped up, grabbed the top of the fence, pulled himself up, and dropped onto the ground on the other side. Landing on his feet, Frank started to approach the two wolves. Cosmos lowered his head, cowering next to Circle before retreating to the far end of the pen. Frank stood erect, standing still for a moment, his blue eyes boring into the eyes of the female wolf. Then he started to advance toward her, his movements slow and deliberate. For a moment Circle watched Frank; then she trotted up to him. Frank felt the adrenaline flow, not from fear, but from his mastery over it.

That was it. Suddenly everything became crystal clear to him. It would come with a burst of adrenaline if it would come at all except it wouldn't be adrenaline but a much longer lasting high. The moment would seem to be fleeting at first--when he knew for sure-- and then it would become forever.

Frank studied Circle. She watched him. Looking into the eyes of the wolf, Frank knew that she understood. And somehow he understood that she knew that he knew.

THE DREAM

Frank walked along the stream into a small grove of spruce trees skirting the high mountain. The pack had gotten heavy and he needed a drink. Soon he would be climbing above tree line, with the world below him as the mountain air became colder with altitude. Up there he could not build a fire for there were no trees or wood. He found a small clearing in the grove, saw a large boulder next to a tree, and sat down. Leaning backwards against the boulder Frank rested the pack against it taking its weight off his shoulders. With sixty pounds off his back he was able to slip his arms out of the straps. Frank stood up, his shoulders aching from where the pack had been and walked over to the stream. Lying down on his stomach next to the water, he started to drink the cold water. After he had enough, he went back to the boulder and sat up against it.

From where he sat he could peer out into the distance looking away from the mountain on his left toward a range of high peaks forty or fifty miles away. Between where he sat and the far away mountains a flat valley stretched for miles. Two specks appeared on the horizon and started to move toward him. As he watched, the specks grew larger moving rapidly in his direction. *Must be some kind of deer*, thought Frank, as he observed the two specks approach. Now only half a mile away, he saw that they were coyotes. *I am far away from civilization, and there can't be any dogs out here*, he thought. *Can't be wolves either which are extinct in this part of the country.* Except that they were wolves. Still coming toward him, he saw that the two animals were much too large to be coyotes. Both were white, the color of the arctic wolf. Not seeing him or ignoring his presence, the wolves approached to within fifty yards. One of the animals was larger than the other, *obviously the male*, thought Frank. This animal continued to ignore him as the female turned her head in his direction. It was Circle.

What is she doing way out here? thought Frank. He had left her in a cage back in Illinois. *And the male--it is not Cosmos.* Larger and heavier than the gray wolf he had seen in the cage, this male was white, like Circle. Unlike Cosmos, this male was confident, holding his head high, his gait arrogant as it approached him. Then both wolves stopped as both animals became aware of his presence. Still, the male continued to ignore him, as if it were disdainful of this trespasser in his territory. Circle, who had been looking in his direction, now looked directly at him.

The eyes of the female wolf met his. There was that eerie

sparkly quality about them that all wolves' eyes had. As Frank returned her gaze the eyes gradually lost that sparkly quality as her eyes focused into his thoughts.

She's trying to tell me something, thought Frank. Taking her eyes off his for a moment, Circle looked over at her mate. *That's it, she's no longer with Cosmos. She never belonged to him in the first place, and out here she found the wolf she belonged to--the one she had been destined to be with, and the one she would die with.*

The eyes once again looked into Frank's as Circle walked toward him. She stopped twenty feet away from him her gaze still focused on him. Circle didn't need to talk--her look, her willingness to approach this close to him, her looking over at her mate, her being out here in the first place said it all. She had been with the wrong male wolf. Somehow she found the right one out here--against all probability, somehow escaping from her cage and ending up out here in Wyoming. And she had found Frank to tell him something. Still she looked into his eyes as words formed in his mind as if they were coming from her and intruding into his thoughts. *Soon Frank, you will find the one who was meant for you. Only you must look; then hold onto her when you find her. You will know.*

Except it was all a dream. Frank woke up in the middle of the night, thinking about wolves, and about a woman. It wasn't Karen.

Tiger Kiara

Kiara came down from Iowa with her husband to Jack's apartment for a photo shoot. Tiger Wayne who Jack had met at Big Daddy's Cabaret provided the white tiger club, Smokey. Kiara and her husband would later go with Jack and Tiger Wayne to Club 64 in East St. Louis where the owners allowed the tiger the run of the club. The rifle in the picture is a Mauser 98 German WWII battle rifle which the author wrote about for *Xtreme Magazine* featuring Kiara and Smokey as his models.

156

Kiara with Smokey at Club 64. Most club owners would probably not have allowed the tiger in their places due to concerns about liability. Frank and Sherry Marcella, the owners of club who had been friends of the author for years thankfully decided in favor of the Tiger.

Arianna a del. Jack would meet Arianna at a Pure Talent Showcase at Big Al's in Peoria He had just bought a new 2002 Mazda Miata special edition sports car and had not yet had a woman with him in the car. Arianna would be the first.

Arianna a del at the Candy Store in Mobile, Alabama

Selena

On your knees

http://www.bigdaddyscabaret.com

Jack Corbett

Promo for Selena who would model with the Springfield 03 for Jack and *Xtreme Magazine* with Harley, both of them working for Big Daddy's Cabaret in Dixon, Missouri. Jack hit it off famously with Big Daddy the club owner and drive his sports car down to Big Daddy's often after initially getting hired as a photographer. That led to S.P.E.W. with the help of the Lumberyard's Big Mike. Big Daddy, the author, and Hawkeye, a 10 year friend of Big Daddy's who was Djing for B.D. then got their PADI scuba diving certification together in Missouri . A few months after they became certified divers, the threesome went on their first trip to Thailand together to sample the warm waters of the Gulf of Thailand.

Darien Ross poses with Vic Meyers M-15 full auto rifle for Jack's Xtreme Magazine gun article at Vic's Missouri home. Later she'd pose for more M-14-M-15 shots in Texas, this time with Jack's own M-14 he bought several months after the shoot at Vic Meyer's house. Vic would partner with Jack and Xtreme Magazine to produce the Xtreme Weapons calendar and while working with Jack and his models for many of Jack's over 20 Xtreme Weapons and Babes articles for the magazine. Darien Ross also appears in the author's gun article on the 1861 Springfield Civil War rifle.

Arianna a Del at the hotel in Mobile, Alabama during the Pure Talent Feature Showcase at the Candy Store. When the author was shooting feature showcases he would often share a room with one of the features as there were only a limited number of rooms the clubs hosting the feature showcases were contractually bound to pay for.

Marketing seminar held by the Exotic Dancer Exotic Gentlemen's Expo at Caesar's Palace Las Vegas. When the author first met Jim and Anne Marie Hyatt, Jim was the M.C. for the seminars. Later Jim would quit Exotic Dancer to join his wife to run the agency. Exotic Dancer's seminars are geared for the club owner who wants to improve on such aspects of club management as marketing, how to improve his club's image in the community, how to retain good employees, insider theft prevention, etc.

Anne Marie and Jim Hayek, the owners of the Pure Talent Agency at one of their feature showcase. Anne Marie and Jim put Pure Talent on top as one of the premier talent agencies representing features entertainers. Pure Talent became renowned for its feature showcases which it scheduled across the country in which it worked closely with clubs that sponsored the events. Although other agencies would oftentimes schedule feature showcases, Pure Talent put a particularly strong emphasis on them which was made possible by the tireless efforts of not just one individual but two extremely talented people who were equally devoted to the success of the agency.

Carrie Bare, Michael Dunn, a fellow professional
photographer who often showed up at the same adult
events as Jack, and Jim Hayek. At this point the
author had written close to 20 gun articles for "Xtreme
Magazine" and the Xtreme Weapons calendar is
already underway. Vic Meyer a gun owner friend of
Jack's, Xtreme Magazine and the author had entered
into a three way partnership to produce the calendar.
Pure Talent was hosting another of its Feature
Showcases at Big Al's in Peoria, Illinois. The photo
shoot was held on a farm owned by Tommy Gun a few
miles outside the club. Vic had come all the way from
Missouri with an AR-15, a Russian Dragonov sniper's
rifle, and an FAL while the author supplied his
Springfield M1-A, M-1 Garand, and Ruger .454
Casul. Pure Talent even supplied Gary, a makeup
artist-hair designer to be at the photo shoot. The three
feature entertainers, Carre Bare, Serenna Star and
Kelly Taylor would become three of the twelve
models for the 2004 Xtreme Weapons calendar.

Serenna Star on the left, Carrie Bare in the middle, and Kelly Taylor on the far right, three Pure Talent Feature entertainer about to pose for the Xtreme Weapons calendar. The three women had to wake up early after performing their shows at the Pure Talent Feature Showcase at Big Al's in Peoria, Illinois.

Jim Hayek firing the author's Ruger .454 Casull. Jim had told the author months before the Feature Showcase that he was looking forward to shooting a few weapons. The author had written his first gun article for "Xtreme" about the .454 Casul, a handgun that has as much power as a .45-70 buffalo rifle. The author decided to play a little joke on Jim by buying the most powerful shells he could find. After firing five of the six rounds in the cylinder, Jim handed the gun back to the author, while telling him, "I've had enough." Jack then nonchalantly fired the last round without paying attention to where he had placed his thumb. The recoil caused the cylinder latch to cut deeply into Jack's thumb resulting in a spurt of blood.

Promo the author was working on for Club Maximus's 2003 M.S
Texas Pageant in Wichita Falls, Texas. Montana Steele had won
the 2002 pageant after staying up nearly all night before the last
night of the pageant which was a three day affair. Each contestant
was judged for each night with the title going to the entertainer who
had the best three night average. Exhausted, Montana would still
manage to do a photo shoot with the author for his coming "Xtreme
Magazine" article "America's Gun, the lever action Winchester". It
is women like Montana who represent the true professionals of the
adult entertainment industry, as they are hard working women
dedicated to their craft, who don't know the meaning of quitting.
During the entire competition, it didn't matter how tired or busy she
was, Montana conducted herself in a manner worthy of a president's
first lady, putting on a bright face for the judges, while chatting
amiably with the club's customers between her shows.

167

SOUTH AMERICA

They were already on their second pot of coffee only this time it was Stan who kept on going back to refresh his cup. Frank had never seen his friend so animated. Usually it was Frank who kept refilling his cup asking Stan each time, "Do you want more coffee?" Stan would allow his cup to be refilled several times, then said firmly "hold" on the fourth cup.

"South America, Frank--that's where the money is going to be made. Both Argentina and Brazil are raising more soybeans every year, and all that extra production is driving the price of soybeans down on the world market. The future is there, and I'm going to cash in on it."

"If we're not going to make any money here by raising soybeans, just how are you going to do it over there?" Frank asked.

"The price of our land is getting too high," said Stan. "With soybean prices going as low as they have been during the last few years, a farmer has to get bigger and bigger just to survive. And hell, you and I both know that we can't afford to buy more land with the price of land being as high as it is. In Brazil the land is dirt cheap. All a man's got to do is burn off or bulldoze away the rain forests and put the ground down there in soybeans. And down there a man can buy a lot of small cheap tractors to farm the ground. That's better than buying the expensive stuff up here. Labor in Brazil is so cheap that the landowner can hire a lot of tractor jockeys to run his machinery and maintain it as well. A guy can't miss."

"So what's this about your setting up a corporation?" Frank asked.

"I got a lawyer named Carl Chicanery to set the whole thing up for me," Stan replied. "I'm President and he's Vice President. He's borrowing four hundred-fifty thousand dollars against the acres I already own, and he's putting in fifty thousand of his own money. That makes a half million dollars to start the operation. Of course, I'm getting the lion's share of the profits, but then again, that's as it should be seeing that I'm supplying most of the money."

"So, who's the corporate treasurer, Stan?"

"That will be Carl."

"I don't know if I would do that Stan. Making Carl

Treasurer gives him too much control over the finances. He's going to write the checks, and he'll have the power to borrow money for the corporation."

"Oh, he's okay, Frank. The man's been a lawyer practically all his life. So far his reputation's been pretty good around here."

"So far," Frank replied skeptically. "The guys a lawyer. Most lawyers are snakes in the grass."

"He'll be all right," Stan replied. "What are you going to do--sit around here in the US watching your income shrivel up with each new year?"

"That's what I'm going to do if it ever comes to that, and I'm not going to have a scheming lawyer take control of my business."

"Nothing ventured, nothing gained."

"So when are you going to put in your first crop?" Frank asked.

"Six months from now. I'm going to go to Brazil next month and get started hiring people and buying machinery."

"How much do you think the machinery will cost?"

"Two hundred thousand to get started."

"Then you'll be in for $650000."

"The rest we're going to borrow short term for seed and fertilizer," said Stan.

"It goes without saying, Stan, that if this doesn't work out for you, you will be finished," Frank replied ominously.

"I have to do something, Frank. When I divorce Louise, the courts are going to ask me to support her for the rest of her life. Louise will never have to go out and work. Of course, they're going to practically ruin me in the process. If this thing works out, I'll be able to start over again and I'll be able to provide a nice home for Candy and me. "

"Isn't there another way out?" Frank asked.

"I have two choices. One--to live the rest of my life unhappily with Louise. Being browbeaten, humiliated, and bossed around. Two--to divorce her and suffer financial ruin for taking control of my life. And three--to take this gamble. And I don't even know if Candy will have me in the first place."

LOAN SHARK

Frank came into the Injection Pump alone on a Sunday night. He was on his way to meet Jeff Shannon, had some extra time, and expected to find the bar to be closed. He hadn't brought much money since he didn't expect to find the place to be open. But it was, and both Nirvana and Debbie were there.

He found Nirvana sitting by herself at the bar. Frank ordered two beers from the bartender, reached in his pocket for his money, and found that he barely had enough for the two beers.

"What are you doing here Nirvana? I didn't know you worked on Sundays."

"We're open on Sundays even though it's a little slow. I don't always make the money I usually do, but sometimes it's kind of nice to just kick back and have a few."

"Do you like working here, Nirvana?"

"I'm getting kind of tired of it."

Suddenly he felt cool hands being placed around his eyes as he sat on his bar stool.

"Gotta be Debbie."

He turned around and saw her smiling at him.

"Debbie, this is great finding you and Nirvana here. I was just passing through on my way to see Jeff Shannon, and I thought this place would be closed."

"We're always open on Sundays, and I'm usually here," Debbie replied.

"I've got bad news," said Frank. " I only brought five dollars and I've just spent it on two beers. It's for a good cause though." He nodded toward Nirvana and smiled. "I've got my checkbook but a lot of good that's going to do me here."

"I'll cash a check for you," said Debbie.

"You will?"

"Sure. I trust you."

"Wait here for me then. I'm going to my car to get it."

Frank left the two girls sitting together at the bar and went outside to get his checkbook. When he returned, they were still there.

"How's forty dollars sound, Debbie?"

"You can write one for a hundred if you want. The only condition is that you've got to spend it all on me," Debbie replied.

"Can't do that. I can't even stay long, Debbie, but I'll tell you what. I'll buy you drinks for as long as I'm here. Same goes for Nirvana."

"Okay, you're on."

He wrote the check for forty as Debbie gave him the cash from her purse. He spent the next hour talking to both girls. Frank found Nirvana, as always, to be very comfortable to be around. Surprisingly he enjoyed being around Debbie as well. Frank had found her to be very attractive, but then he found many of the girls to be that. This time he began to feel that perhaps he had misjudged her. She didn't seem to be as money hungry as he had first thought her to be. Tonight, more than ever before, she seemed to be relaxed to be around him. More willing to talk than on previous meetings, she was more sincere and more serious than she had been in times past.

When he left to meet Jeff Shannon, for the first time he seriously contemplated asking Debbie out.

DEBBIE AGREES TO LUNCH

"Then let's get together outside of this place, Debbie. How about us meeting for lunch?"

"I'll meet you, Frank, but only on one condition."

"What's that?"

"I'm not going to one of these Pakistani, Mexican, or Thai restaurants you keep bringing up. How about Italian?"

"Fine with me. Anyplace that you recommend since I'm not all that familiar with the Italian restaurants near you?"

"There's a place called Caledonia's next to Northwest Plaza. It's close to where I live. Do you know the area?"

"If it's close to Northwest Plaza, I'll find it," said Frank. "When do you want to go?"

"I'm off next Monday. Why don't we meet at 12:30?"

"I'll be there," said Frank.

When he left the Injection Pump that afternoon, somehow he knew that she would be there.

THE LUNCH DATE THAT DIDN'T HAPPEN

Someone died. The father of a friend of his had a heart attack on a golf course. By the time the man's friends reached him, he was already dead. The funeral was scheduled for Monday at 1:30 in the afternoon. When Frank found this out, he felt sick. The friend was a close friend, so it was one of those funerals he couldn't miss, and his date with Debbie was scheduled for 12:30. This would normally not have been a problem, but this time it was since he didn't have Debbie's phone number. He had tried calling information--after all--he had her real name in his check registry, but information didn't have it either. He called the Injection Pump on Saturday and Sunday, but she wasn't there on either day. Ginny was tending bar on Sunday so he had asked her for help. She didn't have Debbie's phone number either.

Frank had never stood a girl up before, but this time there were no answers. He talked to Stan about it.

"I'm going to be with Candy in St. Louis on Monday. Tell you what. Candy and I will go into the restaurant and tell her what happened," Stan told him.

The funeral was far away from the clubs and just as far from home. On his way home Frank stopped at the Injection Pump at 3:30 for a beer or two. He found Chanel saying goodbye to one of her customers and went up to her when the man left.

"Are you alone?" he asked her.

"I am. Can you believe it?"

"Well, so am I. This must be the first time in a long time that neither one of us is with someone. I think we need to get better acquainted."

"I've been wanting to but it seems like things never worked out."

They sat at a table where he ordered her a Coke and a beer for himself. Then he told her about Debbie and the funeral. "That's terrible luck," she said. "What are you going to do?"

"Nothing I can do. I'll just stay here with you today," said Frank. "Worry about tomorrow when tomorrow comes."

He sat with her in front of the stage several times that day. She was content to sit on his lap with her arms around his neck, the two of them entwined in each other's arms as they talked. Before he left her, they agreed that he would see her the following Thursday.

"Please call me at twelve so that I'll be sure that you're coming," said Chanel. "Then if anyone else calls or if any of my other customers come in, I can put them off."

"Sounds like a date to me."

"It is except that it will be here."

THEY HAVE FEELINGS TOO

He found Chanel walking around the room looking for someone, *probably me,* thought Frank, and took her to a table. He had called earlier to remind her that he was coming, and she had been at the Injection Pump as she had promised.

"Any of your other customers coming in?" Frank asked her.

"One of them called, so I told him that I was busy because of a previous commitment."

"You're pretty businesslike."

"Don't you think I should be? If I wasn't, I'd have a lot of customers mad at me, and then they'd go on to someone else."

"How old are you Chanel?"

"Nineteen."

Well, you never can tell, thought Frank. *She's only nineteen so she's probably the youngest girl here yet she has all her customers call in to see if she's available. Sets up appointments with them just like she's done with me, not for dates outside the club, but for her time inside the club. Smart woman. The other girls could learn from her.*

"What made you come into the Injection Pump and apply for a job here in the first place?" Frank asked.

"I saw an ad in the paper. You might think that I'm weird but I've always been interested in kinky stuff. I read a lot of exotic romance novels, and I've always been a little curious. And I like sex."

"With?" Frank left the question hanging there.

"Guys and girls. I like them both. Right now I'm living with a guy, but I don't think it's going to last much longer. In the meantime I'm with him."

"Did you know anyone who was a dancer before you applied here for a job?"

"No. I just saw the ad and I just dropped in. Most girls who work here have a friend who convinces them to come in to work. I guess I'm just a little different from the other girls."

Two hours later he saw Debbie up on stage two and decided that he had better go over to her. Excusing himself from Chanel, who had to dance across the room at stage five and promising that he would return to her as soon as she got off stage, Frank went over to Debbie's stage. After all, he and Chanel had already been up to the stages several times already, and Chanel had mentioned that she didn't want Debbie to get mad at her, so they both agreed that Frank's seeing Debbie for a little while was a good idea.

Someone was already sitting in front of the stage. Frank sat next to the man. Debbie came over, not to Frank, but to the other customer. She usually came over to Frank first, but this time she kept him waiting until the last song of the set. Debbie did not smile when she sat on his lap. Her movements were mechanical and listless. By the time the song ended, she had still not said a word to him. He studied her trying to read her thoughts and found her lifeless as if her spirit had been squeezed out of her.

"Sorry I couldn't make it to lunch on Monday. I had Stan explain everything to you."

"That's okay. Things happen."

"I had no way to get hold of you."

"I should have given you my phone number."

"I'll have to get it from you later," he replied.

"I see you and Chanel are hitting it off."

"On my way back home from the funeral I stopped off here. When I walked in today, I spotted her right off, but I didn't see you."

"I've been here the whole time. You just weren't looking."

For the first time since he had started to come to the clubs, he realized that he had to choose. He had started seeing Lori over at the Sports Bar, coming to the Injection Pump afterwards to see other girls. Since Lori had stood him up the last time, he hadn't been back at the Sports Bar for months. This time it was different since Chanel and Debbie worked at the same club. That afternoon he chose Chanel, spending the rest of the afternoon with her although he still managed to get Debbie to give him her phone number before he left.

He had gotten to like Debbie although he had found her to be flippant and insincere at first. Each time he was with her after the first time she had let her guard down a little more becoming more serious, more genuine. Chanel, perhaps ten years younger than Debbie, had been straightforward with him from the start. Perhaps the prettiest girl in the Injection Pump, Chanel wore the kind of dresses that were out of place in a topless bar. To the casual observer she looked innocent yet she had just told him that she had started dancing out of exotic curiosity. The other girls seemed to avoid her yet she was one of the most popular girls with the customers. And he couldn't shake the image of Debbie sitting in a ski lodge while everyone else was out skiing. In the end, he decided that Debbie was the kind of woman who didn't want to get her hands dirty, who didn't want to do wild and crazy things, and who was just a little too concerned over what others thought of her.

Frank ended up making a date with Chanel for lunch at a Chinese restaurant, a place where Debbie would never meet him where they served food that was too ethnic and too different for her tastes. He went home thinking, *These girls are supposed to be professional. They are not supposed to show their feelings on their sleeves. They have feelings and they can be hurt, and I can't take advantage of them or use them.* And although he didn't want to, he would end up using them in the end.

TAMARA

Frank paid his cover into the Injection Pump as a waitress came up to take his drink order. Nirvana was sitting by herself across the bar. She waved as Frank ordered a Bud Lite from the waitress. A few moments later the waitress returned with a glass of beer which Frank paid for leaving the waitress a dollar tip. Frank saw Chanel leaving Stage Five and went over to her.

"Let's grab a table Chanel. I have to get home early so I can only stay for two or three hours."

"That will work out fine. One of my customers is supposed to be here in two hours," Chanel replied.

Frank pulled a chair up for Chanel at one of the tables close to the bar. A waitress saw them sitting down and came over to ask them what they needed. Barely into his beer, Frank ordered a coke for Chanel and looked over at the board behind the bar to see what girls were working today. His eyes stopped at the name Tamara.

"Chanel, I couldn't help but notice that they've got a new girl working today called Tamara. I always check the board just to see who's here. I remember that name from somewhere, but I can't remember where."

"She just started working here two weeks ago. She's really nice or at least she's nice to me."

Frank noticed a tall woman in her late thirties or early forties approach them on her way to the bar. Long legged, the woman walked confidently past them. Frank noticed that she was right at six feet which made her the tallest dancer he had seen in any of the clubs.

The woman went up to the bar and ordered herself a drink. Several minutes after the bartender had brought her a drink the woman turned in their direction.

"I know her Chanel. That's gotta be Tamara. I met her years ago in a topless bar only ten miles from my farm. We used to talk a lot then. Never did any lap dances with her, but she sure can talk. I remember having several interesting conversations with her. I can't remember what they were about now but I remember her as extremely bright and as having worked all over the United States as a dancer."

"Why don't you ask her to sit with us," Chanel suggested.

The woman started to walk toward them again. When she drew even with their table, he reached out and grabbed her gently by the arm. "You must be Tamara," said Frank.

"How'd you know that?" asked the woman.

"Does the name Carol Lewis ring a bell with you?"

For a moment Tamara looked puzzled--then she recognized him, surprise registering in her face. "Hold that thought. I'm sitting down with you two. You don't mind, do you Chanel?"

"Please sit down Tamara. Obviously you and Frank are old friends. This is going to be interesting."

"Carol Lewis is my Mother-in-law. She ran the bar where I used to work. You used to come in and talk with me. Sorry, but I've forgotten your name."

"I'm Frank Harring."

"Do you still live on a farm south of Springfield?"

"I'm still there."

"Jesus, Frank. We're practically neighbors. I only live eighteen miles from you. Of course I have to drive almost sixty miles to work each day. What brings you way out here?"

"So my wife will never find out. Seventy miles is a pretty good distance. I can come here and have a good time and chances are she will never find out."

"Makes sense."

Frank noticed that Nirvana was sitting at a table across the room. Tamara sat with Frank and Chanel until it was her turn to dance; then she left them, promising to return later. Chanel had to dance at the same time as Tamara and left for her stage which left Frank alone at the table. Nirvana had just gone over to the bar with another girl. Frank decided to go over to them knowing that it would be worth the price of a drink to avoid the boredom of sitting alone.

Nirvana saw Frank walking to the bar, jumped off her stool, and intercepted him.

"I was about to break down and buy myself a drink. You'll buy me one, won't you?"

"I'll be glad to buy you a drink, but only if you keep me out of the clutches of these other women. I'm waiting for Chanel and Tamara to come off the stage. You can drink with us if you want."

"I might just do that," said Nirvana. "In the meantime, it's just you and I."

Frank went home early, but not until after had arranged to meet Chanel for lunch the following Saturday and after he had spent nearly a hundred dollars for drinks in an hour and a half. He had met Chanel at a Chinese restaurant the week before. This time he decided to take her to Houlihans.

CANDY'S HUSBAND

They drove to Houlihans in Stan's pickup. It was Frank's idea that they go to St. Louis together since Karen was planning to be home the whole day. Nevertheless, he had called Chanel to confirm their lunch date. He couldn't stay out late--not with Karen keeping an eye on him--so he had told his wife that Stan and he were spending Saturday afternoon looking at used farm machinery. Stan had then invited Candy for lunch, telling her that he had to cut it short because of Frank.

Both girls were late. A waitress led them to a booth close to the bar where they ordered coffee. "Two women are going to meet us here," Frank said to the waitress. "They are not coming in together since they don't know each other. One is short, blonde, and very young. The other is tall, brunette, and in her late thirties. If you see them, send them over to us."

"I'll keep an eye out for them," said the waitress. "I'll bring your coffee right over."

As soon as the waitress left, Stan looked across the booth at Frank, winked, and asked mischievously: "Do you think Chanel will show?"

"These dancers are not very dependable, but Chanel's different," said Frank. "She's only nineteen, but she's got a mind like a steel trap. I think she knows that if she doesn't show, she's going to lose me as a customer."

"I don't know about Candy," said Stan. "Perhaps she'll be the one who won't show."

"Come off of it, Stan. You've got to admit that Candy's been reliable. She's not a dancer for one thing."

"It's over. Candy told me on the phone that she decided to stay with her husband, and that she thought it best that we stop seeing each other. I just want to say goodbye to her, that's all."

"Stan, her husband doesn't care about her. He proved that when he didn't try to stop you from going out with her in the first place. Now, he's just worried that she will leave him for you. That's serious now because without her he loses his major source of income. You told me yourself that he's lazy and that he doesn't hold down a regular job."

"I know. I know. I just can't convince her of that."

Chanel, ten minutes late, found them at the booth, and slid

in next to Frank. Five minutes later, Candy walked in, no makeup on, looking flustered. "Sorry I'm late. Ralph and I had an argument. I almost didn't get away, and there's a chance he followed me here."

"How's that?" Stan asked.

"One of his friends was visiting him. I was halfway up the street on my way here when I saw his friend's car backing out of our driveway."

"That's just great," Stan replied. "But what the hell. We're all here together and that's what counts."

"Here comes our waitress," said Frank. "Anyone care for something to drink?"

"I'll just have a coke," said Chanel.

"Candy and I are having beer, aren't we Candy?" Stan turned to Candy and grinned.

"I need a beer. Maybe several," Candy replied. "I'm pretty nervous."

They had almost finished their dinner when two men walked in, seated themselves at the bar, and ordered beer from the bartender. Frank knew they had ordered beer--they all knew they had ordered beer--because one of the men, the shorter of the two, the one with the protruding pot belly--spoke loudly in a belligerent tone. Frank knew that it was Ralph when the man swivelled his stool around and started staring at them.

"Just ignore them," said Frank. "Don't even give them the satisfaction that we've noticed them."

"That's hard to do," said Candy whose eyes had been nervously glancing back and forth from her friends to the bar.

They all saw Ralph jump off his bar stool and motion angrily toward the booth, holding his hand out them as he wiggled his finger at them. There was no mistaking the gesture--it was meant for Candy--telling her, "you've better get over here."

"I've better go up there," said Candy. Then turning to Stan. "Look out for me, Stan. I'm coming right back, and I mean right back."

Candy went up to the angry, stubby man, who was her husband, and came back moments later. "Ralph wants you to go up there and talk to him, Stan."

"I have nothing to say to the man," Candy continued.

"I'll go up there with you, Stan," said Frank.

"You don't have to. You're better off staying here with the

girls."

"There's two of them, Stan. Better that there are two of us."

"If you insist."

Ralph looked at the two men standing in front of him, one well more than six feet and weighing well over two hundred pounds--the other right at six feet but much thinner at one-sixty or so, the smaller of the two poised yet like a coiled spring--ready for a fight.

"I'd like to talk with Stan alone," said Ralph. "Stay clear. Will you?"

"There's two of you so there's going to be two of us," Frank replied. "But I'll tell you what. I'll just sit a few seats down the bar from you so you can have a little privacy."

Frank sat several stools down from Ralph and Stan, motioned the bartender over, and said: "Here's three dollars. I want a bottle of Bud. Keep the change." At first facing the bartender, Frank continued to look straight ahead, even after his beer arrived, pretending not to pay attention to the conversation close by. He had chosen wisely, for Ralph, obviously angry at Candy and Stan, was speaking much louder than normal. Suddenly, there were a few moments of silence. *Ralph must have lowered his voice*, thought Frank. Then he heard Stan say: "No, I'm not staying away from your wife, and I really don't care what you think." "Don't say I didn't warn you," he heard Ralph reply. Stan was easy to hear now, obviously angered by the threat, he continued: "I don't think you've been very good to Candy. I know I am so it looks like we are both going to have to take our chances, doesn't it Ralph?"

Frank turned to face the two men and saw Ralph look over at Candy, glaring at her. Once again, Ralph gestured at her. Candy excused herself from Chanel and went up to the bar. This time, Frank didn't have any problems hearing Ralph, who was raising his voice, obviously angry over Stan's latest remark.

"Now I want you both to hear this," said Ralph. "I'm not leaving Candy and she's not leaving me, but if she does, I'm going to make sure that Stan's wife hears all about it. I know where you live Stan. I know that you live in a small community, and I know what that's like because I'm from a small community myself. If you don't stop messing with Candy, I'm going to make sure that everyone there knows about what you've been doing."

"Candy," Ralph was speaking to her directly now. "Who do

you love now? Him or me?"

Candy looked at her husband, then looked over at Stan. "I don't love you any more Ralph. You know that. I love him, and I'm going to continue seeing him."

Stan stared at Ralph icily. "You can do what you want, Ralph. Go ahead and tell everyone what we are doing. But after you do, don't let me catch you around St. Louis and don't come anywhere near to where I live because I'll kill you with my bare hands."

Frank watched Ralph turn red in the face and saw him stomp out of the bar, followed closely by his friend. Then he went up to Stan and Candy. "I'll say one thing, and that is--you both have guts. I'm buying you both a drink."

"We both need one," said Stan. "Thanks for coming over Frank."

"That's what friends are for. You'd do the same for me, Stan."

Then Frank turned to Candy. "How about a shot of Tequila?"

"Right now, that sounds good," she replied. "Hey Stan, wanta do a shot with me? Frank's buying."

"About time he buys something for me." Stan winked at Frank, then broke out laughing.

"Bartender, bring my two friends two shots of Cuervo. And give them some salt and limes, please. I'm leaving a twenty on the bar. Give Stan the change after taking out a dollar for your tip."

Turning once more to Stan and Candy, he excused himself saying: "I'd better sit with Chanel. She probably feels left out."

"She's lucky," said Candy.

Frank slid into the booth next to Chanel who looked up at him quizzically. "Sorry, you had to miss it all, Chanel. I guess you didn't expect all of this when you decided to go to lunch with me."

"I caught some of it, but not enough to really know what's going on," she replied.

"It's all really simple. Ralph warned Stan to stay away from his wife. Stan told Ralph that he wasn't any good. Ralph got mad at Stan and threatened to tell everybody where Stan lives about Stan's affair with Candy. Stan threatened Ralph that he would kill him if he did that."

"The repercussions of all this," Frank continued, "is that

Ralph might very well tell Stan's neighbors and friends about Stan's affair with Candy. Then, Stan will have a very nasty divorce, and it's going to cost him practically everything he's worked for."

"So, that's all going to happen?" Chanel asked.

"I really think the die is cast," said Frank.

Frank saw Chanel to her car soon afterwards, going back in to have several more drinks with Candy and Stan. Agreeing that it was best that Candy not go home to Ralph that night the three of them went to a motel close to where Stan and Frank lived. They left her in a room after Stan promised that he'd check up on her the next morning.

On the ride to Frank's house from the motel, Stan told Frank: "I really don't care what happens at home. The only thing I care about is her."

BLACKMAIL

Frank had the mower out by the windbreak behind the house, this time enjoying the job as it took his mind off his worries. Mowing next to the Colorado blue spruces he reached the corner where they turned at a right angle to the South and brought the mower around to keep even with the trees. Suddenly he saw someone standing there just a few yards away. For a moment Frank shuddered, surprised that someone had been there watching him; then he saw that it was Stan. Frank shut the mower down, got off the seat, and walked over to Stan.

"How's it going Stan?"

"He's doing it, Frank, just like he said he would."

"You don't mean."

"Yes. Ralph is spilling his guts. My wife knows. He called her up and told her all about Candy and me. The kids know too."

"So what did Louise say to you about it?"

"About what you'd expect. She yelled and screamed. Called me all kinds of things. Blamed you for everything."

"Me?"

"Damn right she did. She told me I didn't have the guts to have an affair. Said that you had to lead me into trouble, and that it would not have happened except for you. She even said that she hoped you'd rot in hell."

"What did you say to her?"

"I told her I didn't love her anymore. I told her that I loved Candy, and that I wanted a divorce."

"It sounds like that's what you're going to get."

"That's right. Ralph has told Louise that I was sleeping with his wife. Well, I really don't care anymore, but now Louise has got it in her head that you are going out with me, and that we are picking up women together. He's also told her that your women are young girls. Sooner or later Louise is going to tell your wife, Frank. She's already told my parents. She called them up to tell them that you've been providing me with women, and that now I've fallen in love with Candy."

"The truth is that Candy is one fine woman. You know how she is Frank. She is comfortable to be around, understanding, supportive, and she cares more about me than anyone in the world. She's everything Louise isn't. And Candy listens to what I have to say."

"I don't care what anybody thinks," Stan continued. "I think I've done a good job raising my children. At least I've done the best job I could, and I've tried hard. I am an outstanding farmer and I've always paid my debts on time. I don't break promises. In spite of all this, Louise has always griped over what the neighbors have that we didn't have. She's embarrassed me in public. She's made a habit of interrupting me in front of company. Louise has pushed me to the edge, Frank. Now, for the first time in twenty-five years I feel alive. I have a woman who makes me feel good-- who makes life seem worth living. They can all talk all they want because I know who I am, and I know Candy is not what they are going to say she is."

"So what are you going to do, Stan?"

"I'm going to end up divorced. My kids won't think much of me, which is really a shame, and I'm going to get Candy away from her husband. Then I'm going to go on loving her."

"For how long, Stan?"

"Until she stops loving me."

OUT IN THE OPEN

Frank sat alone in his office with his paperwork reconciling his corporate checking account with the bank's. *Hell of a thing to be doing at eight o'clock at night*, he thought. Then the phone rang.

"Frank, let me talk to Karen."

It was Stan's wife on the other end. Always bitchy and demanding, this time there was no doubt what she had on her mind. Her marriage on the rocks, Frank had heard from the grapevine that she had blamed him for Stan's affair with Candy. After all, Stan had always stayed at home unless he had something to do on the farm, and now he was staying out into the wee hours of the morning. Then Candy's husband had told Louise that Stan was seeing his wife. The voice on the phone, a voice he had gotten to know well throughout the years, told him that she was going to spill her guts to Karen. Now that Louise had succeeded in ruining her own marriage, she was going to lay the blame on someone else. On Candy and on Frank--never mind that she had been impossible to live with. She didn't see it that way, thought Frank. Outside forces of evil had entered her marriage--outside seductive forces of corruption and sin--which had torn her husband away from her. And those forces centered around him, Stan's pied piper to the bars. Now she was going to tell Karen what an evil man Frank was--without considering what it would do to Karen and Frank's marriage--without thinking at all.

He couldn't stop her. He could say that Karen wasn't home--could even refuse to let her talk to Karen, but she'd call again, and again until she finally got hold of Karen. *What the hell! My marriage is in ruins anyway--in ruins before I started going to those bars. Let it happen because it's going to happen anyway.*

"She's home. I'm putting her on." Frank told her.

Going back to his paperwork, Frank didn't see Karen again until she came bursting into the house an hour later, her face a white sheet of anger. *She left the house and all this time I thought she was on the phone,* Frank said to himself. Karen strode up to him, with clenched fists, as he stood inside the family room.

"I've been next door. Louise told me all about what you and Stan have been up to."

"And."

"Are you proud of yourself, Frank? Ruining their marriage

by providing women for Stan. Taking him to all those pickup places. You know how he was. He wouldn't dream of doing anything like that. Then you had to take him down to see all those women--some of them young girls. Look what you have done. You've destroyed a family, and you've known his kids all their lives."

"And you've destroyed our marriage," Karen added. "You're just like your dad. How many girls have you gone to bed with Frank? Five? Ten?"

"I've been keeping score, Karen. According to the latest revised Frank Harring scorecard, the number is zero. But you won't believe that so why don't you pretend that you didn't even hear it. As for Stan, he's old enough to know what he wants. And he doesn't want Louise, and who can blame him."

"You are a selfish bastard, Frank. You're not sorry about what you've done at all, are you?"

"No. I'm not. Why should I be? As for our marriage, I'm going to see an attorney this Monday. I'm divorcing you, Karen."

"You don't have the guts, Frank."

"Try me. Monday, and that's a promise. I'd do it today, but it's Saturday and no one's open. The fact that I've been going to bars proves that I'm very unhappy in this marriage. You have taken away all of my authority in this home. You and your children have been running the whole show around here long enough. You forgot that I have a life. Now I'm taking it back. Oh, and one more thing, Karen. Next time you're out shopping for a man, look for a mouse."

LEGAL ACTION

"I wish more people would do what you've done, Frank," said Randy Green. "A Prenuptial would solve a lot of the problems we are having in the divorce courts. There might be a problem or two with yours, but I think we can manage all that. It should hold up."

Frank had called for an appointment first thing Monday morning. Saturday evening he had started sleeping on the couch wanting to make a clean break with Karen. The law firm Randy Green worked for had been handling some of Frank's corporate work. Another lawyer had been handling all of that while Randy Green handled much of the firm's divorce work.

"What problems do you see with the Prenuptial?" asked Frank.

"For one thing, there's this clause on the fourth page about giving Karen $7000 less any money you paid during the marriage to support her two children. Some of the Illinois courts have taken the view that an obligation to pay one party cannot be limited by one's payments to a third party. In this case her children are the third party."

"It's one and the same," said Frank. "Those are her children. She'd support them before she'd support herself. I paid for those kids. Since I paid over $50000 for their support Karen has been able to go out and get a college degree while she could stay home and study. With the degree she can be in the job market and make more money than she ever could hope for before."

"I agree with you, Frank. I think the judge will also agree with you, but I can't promise that. The judge might decide to invalidate the paragraph in the Prenuptial dealing with the $7000 because of the phrase about your support for Karen's kids. He might decide to rule against the whole agreement because of that phrase. The court system has taken the position that a Prenuptial has to provide something meaningful to the woman. If the judge rules that your Prenuptial gives her nothing, he might declare the whole thing void and against public policy."

"You were smart," Randy continued, "by having her get her own attorney to advise her on what she was signing. It's going to be hard for her to prove that she was forced into signing it. The judge might also decide that if her attorney thought the Prenuptial was giving her nothing because of the statement on the financial support to her kids, he should have said something about it. Therefore it can be said that both Karen and her attorney felt that you were giving her something of value by supporting her children."

"Like shaking dice, isn't it, Randy? The judge can decide whatever he wants to decide."

"Unfortunately that's true."

"And if the Prenuptial doesn't hold, what then?" asked Frank.

"We can appeal the decision to a higher court. In the meantime the judge will award her one half of your marital assets which are those assets which you and Karen picked up during your marriage."

"Any other problems Randy?"

"You attached a balance sheet to your Prenuptial Agreement Frank. Her attorney is going to contend that your balance sheet either does not adequately reveal your financial situation at the time of your marriage or that it is not accurate. We are going to have to prove that it is accurate. The assumption here is that a woman signing a Prenuptial Agreement is agreeing to give up her financial rights that arose out of the marriage agreeing instead to take what the Prenuptial offers her. There is an obligation for the husband to spell out exactly what rights she is giving up by providing an accurate financial picture of what he has. Your balance sheet was not made up by a professional accountant. You did it. Therefore there is the assumption that you falsified it. The presumption is that it is fraudulent and it is up to us to prove otherwise. This means that you are going to have to have someone do a lot of work on your behalf. I will have to do some of it. Your CPA or Accountant will have to do a lot of it, not to mention that the other side is going to try to drive you crazy in having you come up with all sorts of financial data."

"Such as."

"Financial reports going back through your eight years of marriage, income tax returns, bank account statements and all your checks, and a whole lot more. One helluva lot more."

"Best that a man never gets married in the first place," said Frank.

"My sentiments exactly."

"Any other problems, Randy?"

"They are going to argue that $7000 is a paltry amount

considering your income and net worth Frank. We are going to have to prove that it isn't. We are going to have to establish that her college degree is worth a lot and that it is part of the settlement. I can also argue that your net worth or income isn't all that great to begin with."

"A man supports a woman's kids for her for which he receives no thanks. The kids run over him and act like he's not even there. The man deprives himself of all the vacations he used to take when he was single and of all the other nice things he used to do for himself just so that the woman can spend all of his hard earned money on her kids. He sends her to college at his expense so that she can get a better job later. Then she sues him for the family farm, which is his whole means of support. And the court system goes along with it."

"Hopefully not," Randy replied.

"Thank God she's out of my life."

"Not yet she isn't," Randy replied.

CRAZY MAN

Frank went directly from Randy Green's office to the Injection Pump hoping that Chanel would be there. No longer was he hoping for divorce. He wasn't planning it either. He had come out of the closet and had acted, initiating legal proceedings just like he had promised Karen he would. Frank had hoped to wait it out until the summer, but Stan's wife, Louise, had spilled her guts to Karen telling her everything she knew about Frank's excursions to the topless bars in the Metro East. After Karen confronted him with this, Frank decided in an instant that he wouldn't put up with her any longer. She had harped at him constantly about what a tightwad he was. She had fought him tooth and nail about the kids, always getting her way in the end. She had nagged him to no end about other matters, great and small. Now for the first time he knew she had legitimate reason to be upset. *Sure she should be upset, but she'll never realize that I had already decided it was over and that I just had to get away and do something that would take the pain away*, Frank said to himself.

He found Chanel sitting at the bar with a skinny little guy in his forties Frank had often seen in the nightclub. Frank had never seen the man spend much money there, and the girls had pegged him as cheap. Frank went right up to them, glad to see both of them, ready to buy both of them a drink.

"I'm in a good mood today, a great mood," said Frank. "I'll buy you both a drink."

"I don't drink," the man replied, "but thanks anyway."

"I'll have a coke," said Chanel.

After Frank paid for her coke and a Bud Lite for himself, he lifted his bottle to both of them. "To divorce and freedom." He chugged half of his glass as he smiled at them.

"You didn't," said Chanel.

"Oh, but I did. I had an appointment with my lawyer this morning. I have now officially started divorce proceedings against my wife."

"You've done it. You've finally done it." Chanel was smiling now.

The man left them, excusing himself with "I'm going to leave you two lovebirds alone. Have fun now."

Two hours later, Frank had Chanel on his lap over on stage three. A man in his late twenties came over and sat in the chair next to them. Frank saw the man pick something he had laid next to him off the floor and watched the man start to play with it. It was a little doll.

"Oh, oh," Chanel whispered. "I know him. He keeps following me around. He's weird."

"When does he follow you around?" Frank asked.

"He was in here last week. I could hardly get rid of him. I'm afraid to be rude to him because then he gets really upset and starts to cause trouble. I think the best policy is to lead him on a little, and then to excuse myself later. Usually I say I have a customer in here who expects me to get back to him. The last time he even got mad at me for saying that."

"If I were you, I'd stay clear of him," Frank suggested. "Don't give him an inch. Ignore him. If you don't, the man will keep coming back, and he'll think you are giving him the go ahead."

"That'll really make him mad."

"So what! You don't owe him anything."

"I've met people like him before. They belong in an institution. I'm afraid of what he'll do."

"I'm telling you," Frank warned, "Ignore him and you'll have a whole lot less trouble in the long run."

But he didn't convince her. Chanel went over to the man and sat on his lap next. Frank took her back to the bar when her set was over. Perched up on her stool, Chanel caught the bartender's eye. The girl came over.

"Ginny, I don't know what to do about that strange guy with the dolls. Any ideas?"

"If you ask me, he's trouble. I'd stay away from him."

"I'm thinking maybe I should spend a few minutes with him. If I don't he just might fly off. There's no telling what he'll do."

"I don't know Chanel. You might try it, but I have my doubts," Ginny replied.

"Frank, you don't mind if I sit with the guy for a while. I'll come back to you."

"I can't stay that much longer, Chanel. I don't think you should, but that's your decision."

Chanel excused herself and went over to the man. A few minutes turned into half an hour. Frank decided to leave when he saw them sitting at a table together across the room. Frank walked up to the table, looking at Chanel but ignoring the man.

"I've really got to leave Chanel. I'll see you the next time."

"You've got to leave?" Chanel asked, surprised that Frank was actually leaving.

"Yes. I have a lot of things to catch up on."

Frank went over to the staircase that led to the parking lot below and turned around to wave at Chanel. Just as he started to wave, he heard the man yell out. "Bye you old goat." Chanel sat there next to the man, smiling, only this time her smile wasn't innocent. If Frank read her right she was thinking *I've helped stir this up. Let's see what happens when these two guys fight over me.*

By the time the insult registered Frank had already taken a step down the stairs. Implacable rage took over his body. He wanted to turn right around, go up to the man, and knock him out of his chair. *It would be so easy.* Frank felt the rush of blood surge into his arms, felt the adrenalin go to his head, felt the power that was in him. Suddenly he would become a whirling unstoppable force bent on destroying or even killing the man. It would be over in three seconds with the man helpless on the floor. But Frank knew he would be kicked out of the bar. And there was a very good chance that Karen already had someone watching him. Someone in the Injection Pump. Right now. So he continued to walk down the stairs, hating himself for it.

CHANEL QUITS

He had been trying to get hold of Chanel for over a week, and in that week she had not been back to the Injection Pump once. However, he did have a phone number, not hers, but a phone number where he could leave a message.

She called him back the day after he called the number, collect as he had instructed so that she wouldn't have to pay for the call.

"Frank. It's Chanel."

"I've called down to the Injection Pump several times. They told me you haven't been there in a week."

"Didn't they tell you that I've quit?"

"No, why did you quit?"

"Because I don't belong there. You don't either, Frank."

"What do you mean you don't belong there?"

"Because I'm not like the other girls. I detest doing all the lap dances, and I can't stand doing what we all have to do just to collect tips from them."

"So what are you going to do?"

"I don't know. But I'm not going to work in any of those clubs."

"Call me in about a week. Let me know how you are doing."

"Okay. Just one thing Frank and remember it. Stay away from those clubs."

BACK TO LORI

Frank sat alone at the bar in the Injection Pump. Already he was on his third beer and he had not been there an hour. Although several girls had approached him as he sat there, he had acted disinterested in them. He weighed his options. He could look for someone new. That would entail a number of visits to the Injection Pump and a lot of money on tips. He could sit there and get drunk, perhaps for the last time there. That seemed the best approach. Or, he could go back to the Sports Bar and get drunk there. Perhaps Lori would still be working there. It had been months since he had seen her. If not, certainly Kim or one of the other girls he knew would be there. That was it. He had suddenly gotten bored with the Injection Pump. Perhaps he had been there too often--which would have been okay if Chanel had been there-- but since she wasn't, and since none of the other girls he had favored were working there that day--he felt the sudden urge to leave.

Nadine recognized him as soon as he walked into the Sports Bar. "Do you want a Budweiser?" she asked.

"Yes. Thanks Nadine."

"If you're looking for Nipples, she's right around the bar next to the jukebox."

"Get her whatever she's drinking."

He found her across the bar standing behind one of the room's support pillars. She was talking to a customer, her back facing Frank, as he strode up. Without giving the man a glance, Frank placed his hands around Lori's waist. She turned to face him. Her face brightened.

"What are you doing here?" she asked.

"I came here to see you," he replied.

"Let's sit over there, close to the stage." Lori led him to a table.

She sat close to him, her slenderness making her appear vulnerable and as desirable as always. She was wearing her green top and bottoms. It had been so long ago that he had drunk with her that he had forgotten how comfortable she was to be with.

A waitress brought their beers to them. A new girl, dark headed and alert, she appeared to be part Hispanic. Frank paid her five dollars, four for the beer and one dollar for her tip.

"Hi, I'm Cindy."

"I'm Frank. I'm an old friend of Nipple's."

"You're not that old, Frank, "Lori replied.

"If you need anything, let me know." Cindy didn't linger, returning to the bar. Frank sized her up as a girl who was always efficient at work and who didn't indulge in idle chatter. He turned back to Lori.

"Lori, I'm getting divorced. I've already filed. Stan is getting divorced also. A lot has happened since you and I last talked."

"You're actually doing it, Frank. You are really divorcing Karen?" Lori asked surprised.

"You sound glad. Didn't you think I'd do it? I'm no bullshitter."

"I've kicked Travis out. We're splitting up."

"That's great. Looks like things are working out for both of us."

Kim came out of the dressing room. When she saw Frank, she grinned and walked over to their table. Frank noticed that she had gained weight since he had last seen her. Her waist was broader and her legs had gotten heavier since he had last seen her-- a sure sign of too much drinking.   "Hey Frank. What is that stuff you gave Nipples that makes people piss blue?"

"It's called methyl blue. It's a blue powder."

"Can you do me a favor? Can you get me some? I want to give some to my boyfriend."

"I'll try to bring you a little the next time I'm here," Frank replied.

Frank had not noticed the tall woman who had been sitting over at the end of the bar when he had come in. She had been sitting with a customer and had not noticed him either. It was her turn to dance and she now came up to their table.

"Hi stranger. I didn't notice you when you came in," said Tamara. "I've really been drinking a lot of shots. That's one of my good customers over there, and he's been getting me loaded. She pointed at a man in his early sixties quietly nursing his drink at the bar. "Well I've gotta dance. Talk to you later."

"When did Tamara start working here?" Frank asked Lori.

"Right after she quit the Injection Pump. Around three weeks ago."

"This place is getting better all the time."

"You like Tamara?"

"Sure, we've been friends for years. Probably six years now. She used to work at a topless place only twelve miles from where I live. I used to go there and sit with her just talking."

"Frank, will you buy me a shot?"

"Let's both have one."

Frank caught Cindy's eye. She came right over, took their order, and returned moments later with two shots of Cuervo. Then she left.

"To us being friends." Lori looked at Frank seriously. "You must chug it now." She gulped hers down in one swallow. Frank started to chug his, taking half of it down with one gulp, leaving the rest in the glass.

"To our friendship," he replied. "The tequila is too good to chug all the way down. I'm savoring the rest."

"You just can't admit that you're a wuss," said Lori.

The hours flew. They drank. They talked. Suddenly it was eight o'clock, and she had to leave. They said goodbye and she was gone. Then he realized as he sat there on his last beer that he felt terribly alone.

THE BIG TRACTOR

In some ways it was like piloting an airplane alone on a dark night. The sky was jet black and the stars were pinpricks of light scattered all over. One could see forever except it was so dark that you could only see lights in the distance--of farmhouses, of tractors working late, and the steady stream of cars on the interstate two miles away. The big tractor moved relentlessly forward at a steady five miles an hour, its own lights revealing an endless sea of corn stalks. Like a pilot on a solo, Frank sat alone at the controls looking out over the long green hood of a John Deere 50 series machine at the corn stalks he was chisel plowing. Small round gauges told him his oil pressure, fuel situation, tractor operating temperature, rpms, and speed. The investigator two monitoring system would alert him to any possible malfunctions and their cause. The tractor reached the end of the field and Frank downshifted into eighth gear, reduced his throttle, and began his turn. He would cut another eleven-foot swathe through the corn stalks cutting them up and throwing dirt all over them. Each time he would go a half mile he would have to turn the John Deere around and cut another eleven-foot swathe. Frank marveled at the smoothness of the fifteen speed power shift transmission and at how he could shift up or down two or three shifts at once without clutching. He had never tried it but the John Deere rep had told him that he could shift from forward to reverse without stopping and without clutching. You couldn't even do that in a Mercedes.

His lower back hurt from shoveling corn at midnight the night before. He had been putting corn in the bin from his harvest wagons and the spreader had quit at the top of the bin. The corn had piled in the center of the bin and the dryer fan would not push the warm air through the mound of corn as fast as it would through the corn along the sides of the bin. He had worked for an hour shoveling from the center pile to the sides until the bin was level enough.

Now his back ached, but not as badly as it did when he got up in the morning. Frank reached back to adjust the lumber support. The seat now hit him just right in his lower back. He reached down for the hydraulic seat control lever and pushed it up raising the seat another inch. Frank reached in his pocket for a cigar and pushed in the lighter. He was alone. The tractor stereo was playing something from Led Zeppelin leaving the tractor sounds muffled and far away. Led Zeppelin was the only thing he heard except for his thoughts.

Another tune came on from Led Zeppelin. It was one of those nights where the disc jockey would tell the history of several rock groups and play 12 songs from each group. Tonight all the groups were from the 60's. Frank marveled at how the tractor isolated its operator from the environment. Outside it was cold. In the cab he was still wearing his running shorts, for he had taken a twenty-five minute break from chisel plowing to run his four miles. The cab temperature was just right. Fifty feet ahead of the tractor was a possum. Frank noted that it was nocturnal and ugly.

He had shot possums before, dozens of them, and each time he asked himself why. They were easy to hit. Half of the time they played dead before he could get the first shot off. Frank had given up on shooting deer, rabbits, and practically everything else. But possums were always in season. They were that ugly. Groundhogs and ground squirrels had fallen before his guns in large numbers, but they were different. Groundhogs ate his beans, in large thirty foot circles. Ground squirrels, which resembled chipmunks, ate his corn just as the tender little shoots were breaking the ground. He hated the ground squirrels the most because they destroyed the first two rows of corn along the edges of his fields wherever they had a drainage ditch for a border.

Because of his desire to shoot on sight any ground squirrels within range, Frank always carried a pistol. The one resting on the little shelf in front of him was his favorite and the one he took on his tractor more than any other. It was a 45 automatic, but it was not ordinary. It was a chopped 45 Colt, the handle having been cut down to hold six round clips instead of the standard seven, and the five-inch barrel having been reduced to three and a half inches. He had a special dark grey finish applied which made the gun impervious to moisture. Orange fixed sights had long ago replaced the original and he had the gunsmith place them so that the gun would shoot slightly high at 25 yards. The three 1/2 inch barrel was a custom barrel so that the pistol would shoot tighter groups than one ordinarily would expect from it. The last feature of the gun was a lighter trigger than stock so that it was now utterly smooth throughout its pull.

It would have been a simple matter to get out of the tractor cab, run up to the possum, and shoot it as it scurried about. He didn't bother. As the heavy tractor moved through the field, Frank switched to a tape. The Led Zeppelin session had gone off the air. The tape selection was Rachmaninoff's Concerto in C Minor. Sound filled the cab--music that described a whole landscape, the Russian steppe, in all its vastness. Frank had read that Rachmaninoff had tried to depict a whole countryside with its people, its history, and its tragedy with this one concerto.

Russian history was full of tragedy on a grand scale. Twenty-six million Russians would die in World War II after Rachmaninoff wrote his concerto. Russian literature was rich and deep. For Frank there was nothing like Dostoevsky and Tolstoy, not to mention Gogol, Lermontov, and Pushkin. He remembered reading "Crime and Punishment" in college in which Dostoevsky's main character, Raskolnikov, considers whether he can commit the perfect murder and not only not get caught, but have his soul remain unscathed by the experience. He reflected on *"The Brothers Karamazov"* in which Dostoevsky ponders the question "Is there a God?*" It was too bad that Americans didn't study Russian literature. Their loss*, thought Frank.

The Concerto was as big as Russian literature and Russian wars. The Concerto reverberated with music so incredibly sad, so utterly descriptive of forlorn landscapes and of tremendous loneliness. And it described this half deserted land, of endless fields, large sky, and of man's isolation. Frank had already been working eighteen hours. No one had checked up on him. No one had seemed to care. He pondered the question of death. If he died tomorrow, he would soon be forgotten. Fifty years would pass, and it would be as if he had never lived. His farm would still be farmed, and in much the same way as he had farmed it. His home would be a gutted unpainted shell along the road, and passers by would wonder what kind of man had once lived there. He looked out the window of the tractor cab. The Illinois prairie, like the Russian steppe, was an unforgiving land that always reminded one of the stark reality of man's existence--one which offered no life after death. The Prairie just outside his cab was just a forbidding land that swallowed each life up in its own relentless timelessness.

His tractor lights lit up an object standing alone in the field to his right. As the tractor got closer, Frank saw that it was a coyote. The coyote watched the tractor as it approached. Seconds later the tractor passed it. Frank guided the tractor to the end of the field and turned around. Minutes later he had returned to where he had seen the coyote. It was still there, closer than before. Frank had never seen a coyote that large before. The night did strange things. It made foxes appear as large as average sized dogs. He got to the other end of the field, reduced the throttle, and applied his left brake. That brought the tractor around sharply to the left turning it in a tight 360. *Thank God that tractors used brakes, and two of them at that, for turning,* thought Frank. The use of brakes on a tractor allowed a heavy machine to literally turn on a dime. The chisel plow followed the tractor's path. Frank gave the wheel a tug to the left straightening out his course. Soon he was up to the coyote again, closer than before.

The coyote was a curious animal, watching the tractor move back and forth from one end of the field to the other. Each tractor pass in the field brought the John Deere twelve feet closer to the animal. Frank observed that at least something was interested in what he was doing. There was something a little different about this coyote, however. Frank couldn't quite put his finger on it. The tractor lights made things look a little different at night, but it was more than that. Then he saw that the coyote was white and that it was larger than a coyote should have been. Many passes later the tractor came within forty feet of the animal which stood alone watching, its yellow eyes illuminated by the tractor's lights. As the tractor drew abreast, those yellow eyes met Frank's. The coyote raised its tail as if to say goodbye and started to lope across the field. Its fluid motion was as graceful as any deer's, its pace unhurried. Thirty seconds later it was out of sight.

Had it been what he thought it was? Frank knew that was impossible. There were only a few hundred timber wolves in the lower forty-eight states, all of them in Minnesota. According to *Britannica* a coyote only got to thirty pounds or so although he had seen them reach fifty. This animal, whatever it was, went one hundred-twenty-five to one fifty. Could it have been the magnifying effect of the night and the lights which transformed an ordinary coyote into a white wolf? No, it had been too large, appearing out of the night as twice the size of a wolf. It had been white and he had never seen or heard of a white coyote whereas white wolves were fairly common. So where had it come from, and why was it watching Frank?

Sound continued to fill the cab. The concerto, so full of sadness, of love, of heroism of the past and of the future was from another world. Was the wolf also?

THE SPORTS CAR

Frank bought the MGB in perfect condition except for one major defect--the engine hardly ran, but that didn't matter since Frank had no intentions of owning an MGB. He had driven one while in college--extensively since it belonged to a good friend who had liked to drink a lot and who wisely had gotten into the habit of letting Frank do the driving while he did most of the drinking. Frank had loved the car--liked the way it looked, the way it handled, the feel of the open air when the top was down. The car had two major problems, which Frank soon became aware of, but which his friend, the car's owner, had to deal with. First, it had an unreliable engine. Second, the electrical system, even more than the engine, was an on again off again affair. Twenty years later Frank bought his first MG having it towed to Dave McGuire's home, not bothering to have it delivered to his place. The car had always been garaged and rarely driven by its previous owner. The body had no rust, was in mint condition in every respect, and was painted British racing green--according to Frank the only color for an MG

Dave McGuire heard the tow truck enter his driveway and came out to greet Frank. Dave had worked on Frank's tractors throughout the years. Frank had soon learned that Dave could do anything with machinery and it didn't matter what the job was. Of a wiry build, Dave was quick and sure with his hands while his mind could absorb the intricacies of how machinery fit together and worked. Once Frank had brought a Mini 14 rifle over to Dave's house. One week later Dave had transformed the gun into a fully automatic rifle complete with a selector switch so that the weapon could be fired semi-auto as well as fully automatic. Dave was not a gunsmith, and had never worked on a gun before yet he had been intrigued by the project. The whole thing was illegal yet both Dave and Frank had gotten off on the idea of converting a perfectly good rifle into a fully automatic assault weapon. This new project of Frank's was far more challenging, time consuming, and expensive, but Dave had been looking forward to it.

"So. You finally got the car. Can't even drive it, can you Frank? When do you want it back?"

" I suppose next week." Dave approached the little car, studying it as the tow truck operator lowered the front of the sports car.

"How about two months? I know that's pushing you, but I know you like challenges. Don't worry about an engine. One will be delivered to you within two days. Also a transmission. I want to get rid of as many British parts as possible. The Brits were always great on design but hopeless when it came to execution. I also brought you some catalogs which should give you something to go on for parts."

"What did you get for an engine?" asked Dave.

"The engine's a V-6 from a Mazda MX3. Around 130 horsepower which already trounces the little 94 horsepower engine the MGB came with. But I've already had it bored out for a little more displacement and horsepower. It's a very small V-6. You should have no trouble getting it under the hood. I want the car to be well balanced like the original. I suppose we could try a V-8 but that would make the car too heavy and we would end up with an unbalanced car. I want this machine to be very responsive, and I want it to out handle anything on the road. This includes Porsches, Vettes, what have you. You have a supercharger coming to you also. This should with the larger engine give it all the power it will need."

"You're spending a lot of money Frank. Why didn't you just go out and buy a Vette or a Nissan 300 Z? Something like that."

"I want to be different, Dave. I want this to be my car. I want it to reflect my individuality, and I want it to look like something much slower than what it really is. This car will be a wolf in sheep's clothing."

"What else do you want done to it, Frank?"

"A new electrical system. This one I'm leaving entirely up to you. It has to be stone reliable. Use all Japanese stuff."

"How about instruments?" asked Dave.

"New speedometer. I want it to show more than 120 mph. When you're done, the car will top that by a longshot. New tachometer. And a boost gauge to go with the supercharger."

"But that's not all," Frank added. "I want a new suspension. The MGB handled well in its day, but it won't handle with what's out there now. Get larger wheels and tires. Stiffer springs and make sure that you get them short enough to lower the car by about an inch. Put on the best shock absorbers made. And Dave, even when you get all that done, the car still won't handle quite right, so I'm going to let you decide where you're going from there. This will be your greatest challenge--how to make an MGB out handle anything that's out there."

"This is really going to cost you Frank. Sure you want to do all this?" Dave asked.

"It's either the car this way or an airplane. I don't want an airplane so we'd better just get this car right," said Frank.

"Then you've better go home and let me get started Frank. I'm going to need every minute of the next two months."

"Give it your best shot, Dave. I'm counting on you."

Frank drove his four wheel drive home, thinking about the car that would finally emerge from Dave's resourceful mind. Dave was not just a skilled mechanic. He was a prodigy--the kind that emerges only so often, one out of ten thousand. He and Dave had done a lot of drinking together throughout the years. Frank knew that Dave understood intuitively just what Frank wanted since Dave understood the way Frank thought. Frank went home confident that the sports car would not only be the best of its kind, but the only one of its kind.

SOMEONE NEW

Frank walked into the Sports Bar with the methyl blue that he had packed for Kim. Frank had put it in a small vial which he had enclosed in a plastic baggy for additional protection. The bag was in his front pocket. He had learned from bitter experience that just one grain of the stuff could raise havoc, and he had blue stains on a favorite pair of shorts to prove it. Lori was sitting at the bar. Standing close by was Tamara. A man sat at the bar next to her. Frank sat next to Lori and ordered two Bud Lites from Nadine.

"Lori, is Kim here? I brought her some methyl blue."

"She's here, Frank."

"What did you get her?" asked Tamara.

"It's methyl blue. It's a very potent blue dye they use in hospitals. Well actually I don't know and I don't care what they use it for. All I know is what I use it for. Put just a little of it in someone's drink, and it makes the person piss blue. For about a day and a half. And Tamara, it's not just a light blue, but a deep rich blue color the color of the sani-flush you put in your toilet bowl. It really gets the person's attention in a hurry. The person often thinks he has a disease."

"I want some. Got enough to give me a little?" asked Tamara.

"Oh, I think I can spare a little."

"Let's all grab a table," suggested Lori.

Tamara followed Frank and Lori to a small table close to the stage. "I can stay just a bit. Then I've got to get back to my customer," said Tamara. Tamara walked halfway back to the bar, pointed at Frank and Lori's table--then the bar to show her customer that she was coming right back. The man at the bar nodded.

"Lori, I have just one vial of methyl blue," said Frank. "You are much more coordinated than I am. Why don't you find another bottle or something and go to the bathroom and measure out some for Tamara." Frank handed the vial to Lori. Lori eyed it suspiciously and headed for the lady's room as Kim came over.

"Hey Frank, will you buy me a drink? I'm really pissed. This customer came in and we did a private. He asked me for a blow job when we were in the corner. Now he won't keep his hands off me."

"Kim, you are going to have to buy your own drink.

Harring's rules. I only pay for the girl I'm with, and that is Nipples. However, I have great news. Today, I am Dr. Harring and Dr. Harring is here to rescue you. Nipples is in the ladies room measuring out the methyl blue you asked for. Now. Here's what you do. Take a small bit of the blue powder, just about enough to fill a contact capsule, and slip it into your customer's beer when he's not looking. Then keep the beer flowing. Buy him a drink if you have to just to keep him in a drinking mood. Sooner or later he'll have to piss. It takes about an hour to take effect. If we're lucky, we'll all have a laugh."

Lori stormed back to the table, a fiery ball of energy, fists clenched, her eyes searching for Frank's. "That is a bunch of shit you've got there, Frank. Look at me? I've got this blue dye all over my leg, and I can't get it off. And you should see the bathroom floor. Just a little of it fell on the floor. There's a little water on the floor, and now I've got a hell of a mess." Lori looked over at Kim, who sat there grinning like an idiot. "Here's your shit, Kim." She handed Kim the vial. "I hope to hell you make good use of it because it sure has caused me a lot of trouble." Lori sat on Frank's lap and raised her leg to show him blue streaks above her knee.

"There, look what you've done to me, Frank. I'll be back. I've got more work to do thanks to you." Lori hopped off his lap and left.

"See you later, Frank. I've got a customer to take care of. Thanks lover." Kim walked over to her customer giggling. Kim and the customer sat at the bar together and ordered a drink.

Frank looked across the table at Tamara who raised her eyebrows and laughed. "Looks like it's you and me, Frank. Sorry to cause you all this trouble. Maybe I should never have asked for the stuff. Nipples is having a hell of a time."

Frank looked at Tamara and laughed. "Nipples needs something like this to happen. She thrives on it."

Ten minutes passed before Lori returned. She sat next to Frank and ordered a Jack and Coke from a waitress while he ordered a beer. "Do I still have any of that stuff on me?" she asked him raising her leg once more.

"I don't see any," he replied.

"Nipples, raise your arms. Let me look," said Tamara. Lori raised her arms rotating them as she studied her elbows. "Yep, you've got some on your arms," said Tamara. "It's not that bad though. You can get it off the next time you go to the ladies room."

"Now this is some evil shit. It goes from the bottle to my leg, then to my arm and gets all over the floor at the same time. And you two oughta see the bathroom sink. It's still tinted blue even though I used Comet."

An hour later a large man ran out of the men's room his face red as a beet, the veins of his neck protruding from the blood pumping rapidly from his heart. He plumped himself down at the bar. Kim was on the stage, dancing. The man glared at Nadine.

"Where's that bitch?"

"Don't call one of my girls a bitch," said Nadine.

"All right then. Where's the fucking cunt?" The man spat the words out, his face still livid.

"She's still on the stage dancing. Now mister, if you've got a problem with her, you must go through me first. And I want you to watch your mouth."

"I oughta go up there and rip her heart out."

"Okay. What did she do?"

"She must have put some shit in my drink. I'm pissing blue and the tip of my penis is burning."

"Okay. I don't know anything about it. I'm getting you a beer on the house. I'll talk to her about it."

Twenty feet from the bar Frank and Lori were sitting alone, drinking and laughing. Tamara had left them earlier to entertain a customer. Frank raised his beer can and tapped Lori's glass. "And this, Lori, is to methyl blue. Great shit that it is."

"This is great. This guy is an animal. Listen to him. Ever hear anyone that mad about a drink before. I mean, Frank, it's just one little drink." Lori started to chug the Jack and Coke and broke out laughing-- then choked as the liquid entered her throat. "This is just too much," she sputtered.

"Frank. I don't want you ever to bring any of that shit in here again. And keep it away from my girls. I don't need to have any more of it going to my customers." Nadine had walked up to them unnoticed. She stood next to them seething, hands on her hips.

"All come on Nadine. Look at the situation from the bright side. That stuff gives color to this place," said Frank.

"Frank, I don't need any shit from you. And you Nipples. You've made a mess of the Ladies room. I don't want to ever catch any of that stuff on you. Do you hear me?"

"Yes Nadine. But how do I get this stuff off me in the first place?" Lori raised her arm to show Nadine a blue streak that remained on her arm. Nadine stalked off huffily.

Lori looked up at Frank, laughing. "I'm saved by the bell. It's time for me to dance. Nadine won't be back bothering us anymore, especially if you come up to the stage with me. By the time I'm done, she'll have calmed down."

Lori went over to the jukebox to punch in her selections. A blonde, thirty-five to forty was on the stage. The woman was well built, tall and slender, though not as slender as Lori. Lori turned from the jukebox to face Frank. "That's Janey over there on the stage. She's having a bad day. Let's go over there and aggravate her," said Lori as she led Frank to the stage.

"Hey Janey, how's it going? We've come over to aggravate you."

"I'm having a hard time, baby. I'm not making any money."

"Here, let me lend Frank to you. Frank, get up on stage with Janey," Lori ordered.

What's she up to now, thought Frank. *Just what twisted perverted scheme is she concocting now.* He got up on the stage. "Now what?" he asked her.

"All right now. Lie down on your back," Lori instructed. Frank lay down on his back. Lori kneeled next to his head and grabbed him by both arms placing his hands under his head. "Now just relax Frank. You're going to love this." Lori now turned to Janey. "I want you to straddle his face. Then I want you to pick this dollar off him." Lori pulled a dollar from a stack of bills that she had brought over and placed it on Frank's face so that it rested lengthwise across his nose and forehead. "Now pick it off of him," she ordered. Janey lowered her body across Frank's face. It took only a second. The only thing he felt was the dollar being lifted gently away. There was no discernable contact between Janey and him, she was that good.

Lori pulled another dollar from her G-string and placed it across Frank's face. Again Janey stooped over him. This time he felt only the gentle almost imperceptible breeze of the dollar displacing the air above his nose as it was lifted away. Lori pulled out another dollar, then another, and each time Janey lifted it away. Once or twice the dollar fell back on his face as she tried to lift it away. Repositioning the dollar on his mouth the moment it fell Lori watched Janey pick seven dollars off Frank's lips. "Okay, that's enough. I'm going broke," Lori said.

Frank got up from the stage dumbfounded over how she was willing to spend her own hard earned money to help another dancer who was having an unprofitable day. Then he led her back to the table.

Several drinks later, he watched Lori go to the ladies room. She came out staring straight ahead, a wound up spring of hostility, tense and angry. This time she did not sit next to Frank, sitting across the table from him instead. She attacked the Jack and Coke he had gotten her, practically inhaling it.

"What's wrong?" he asked.

"It's that Janey. I went to the john and she wouldn't even speak to me. And I just spent seven dollars of my own money on her. I don't understand it. These girls are so mean to me. And I'm so nice to them. All I want is to get along."

"Lori. I want you to get one thing straight. You are by far the best looking girl in this place. It doesn't hurt that you've got a great personality too. So you get the most customers. This place is dog eat dog with all the girls competing for customers. They are all jealous of you. It's that simple. Then you go up on stage with Janey and me. She's having a bad day which means that she's hardly making any money. You're with me and making money off of me or at least that's what she thinks. You give her seven dollars as if to say--*Hey I'm doing great while you're doing hardly anything so I'll tell you what--I'll throw you some crumbs. Here's seven dollars. I'll let you pick it up off his face.*"

"I never thought of it that way before," said Lori.

"That's just the way it is. Same way with me. Back home, I do better than most of the other guys. Down deep many of them would secretly like to see me fail simply because I make more money than they do. They will smile to my face, but the resentment--it's still there."

"Sometimes I just want to quit. I come way out here. Work my butt off for me and my kids. I might be a stripper, and I might take off my clothes and worse, but one thing I'm not. I'm not on welfare. Nobody takes care of me and my kids but me. I can't help it if I'm the best dancer here, and I can't help it if I'm better looking than the other girls . . . " Lori was in tears. "Why do they hate me so much? I just don't understand it."

"Come on Lori. Snap out of it. I'm the real reason you're so blue." Frank touched Lori on her arm and eyeballed the streak the methyl blue had left there.

"Don't mock me Frank. I'm serious." Lori sniffled a few times. Then, reflecting on the methyl blue incident, burst out laughing.

Three men walked in the door wearing identical windbreakers. Although they were the far side of thirty Frank thought they brought back memories of all the frat guys he had known in college. *Identical jackets. Jesus--what next. Rigid conformists.* Lori got up to greet them.

"Be right back, Frank. I know these guys."

She stood twenty feet away from him chatting with the three men. Five minutes passed. One of the men leaned down to examine one of her nipples. Another reached over and touched her breasts.

Lori cried out, "No. No. Stop it," but the man kept feeling her. Frank felt lightheaded. He had quite a few beers. His initial impression was that the three men were friends of hers. Now he wasn't quite sure. In any case she had been away too long. His time was valuable and these three fraternity look-a-likes were stealing his time. And she was crying out for them to stop. He had to accept this at face value now didn't he?

"All right--that's enough. Leave her alone. She's sitting with me, and when she's sitting with me, I take care of her." Frank threatened. He steeled himself for a fight. *Let them come,* he told himself. *Fraternity type yoyos are sissies and I'm no sissy. I'll knock the first two down,* he promised himself. *By that time the whole thing will be broken up anyway.*

At first Lori seemed shocked. Reacting quickly, she placed her little body between the three men and Frank. Frank watched her tugging at the arms of one of the men and heard her say, "This guy is a friend of mine. He's very protective of me. Don't fight him. He's okay."

One of the men came over to Frank's table holding his hand out in friendship. "We're not trying to cause any trouble. Nipples tells us that you are very protective of her and that's okay by us."

"Sorry to have threatened you guys. I did not understand the situation. I thought you guys were giving her a hard time," said Frank.

"No hard feelings then," the man said.

"None whatever," Frank replied.

The man went back to his friends. Lori returned and sat down close to Frank. "I can't believe what you just did and that someone would fight just over little old me. Especially three guys at once."

"I'd fight ten guys if I thought you were getting hurt," said Frank.

Frank looked at his watch. It was close to eight and she would leave him. *God, the time passes swiftly when I'm around her*, he thought.

At eight o'clock, Lori looked at her watch and excused herself. "Gotta go get dressed," she said. "I'll be back." She went into the dressing room. Five minutes went by. Ten. She never came back. He felt cheated. Abused. He had been willing to fight for her--three guys at that--and she couldn't even come back to say goodbye.

The night shift came on. He had never seen any of these girls before. They came in--had been coming in since 7:30--one by one, rarely in pairs. Sometimes a boyfriend or husband took them to work. More often they drove themselves. First stop was the dressing room. There you could see one or two of them applying makeup or lipstick just inside the door which was wide open. Most of the girls were heavy set just like the day shift. Several were well endowed yet still a little too heavy for Frank's tastes. Five pounds overweight was for him five pounds overweight. That translated out to five pounds of fat which repelled him.

He remained at the bar drinking alone. *Can I outlast the night shift?* He had drunk with Lori all afternoon. *Six more hours of drinking will qualify me as a contestant for the Derelict Hall of Fame. Can I make it home--seventy miles of driving--without getting a DUI and without wrecking my car? That will be a challenge. Therefore, it is worth doing.* One girl in particular intrigued him. She was around five foot seven. Thin and small breasted, she had a tight rear end clad in equally tight cutoffs. She wore ankle high leather boots. Whenever she needed money, she would kneel down, partially undo the bootlaces on her right boot, and pull a wad of bills out that she had wedged between her sock and ankle. Frank caught her eye and motioned her over. Smiling over at him, she joined him at the bar.

"Hi, my name's Lena. Would you like to buy me a drink?"

"Sure. What are you having? I'm Frank Harring."

"I'll have a rum and coke."

Two minutes after the bartender returned with their drinks, Lena popped the question that Frank was waiting for. "Do you want to do a private?" she asked.

"You're pretty quick. Aren't you Lena?"

"About asking you for a private? Why not? A person doesn't have a lot of time and time is money. Am I right?"

"Yes. If that's the way you see it. Sure. I'll do a private. Twenty bucks, correct?"

"Wrong. The day shift gets twenty bucks. The night shift gets thirty. Reason is we have to give Ten bucks to our boss."

"Okay then. I'll expect a little more regardless. All right by you?"

"You always get more when you choose me. You're about to find that out."

Back in the corner, Lena wasn't shy doing her private. She fondled him, not once or twice, but constantly. Frank sized Lena up as a free spirit. This time he popped the big question.

"What would you charge me to fuck me here in the corner if we do another private?"

"To fuck me in this corner. Let's see. We could get caught. Someone could come in on us any time. That would cost me my job. How about sixty dollars?"

"Lena . . . Lena, I'm not asking what you would charge to screw some other guy here in this corner. I'm asking what it would be to fuck me. I'm not just some other guy. How's forty sound to you?"

"Okay then, but we'd better not get caught."

"Let's have a couple more drinks first," Frank suggested.

They went back to the bar. As they drank, Lena started to rub the inside of Frank's thighs. An hour went by. The bartender asked if they wanted another drink. Frank ordered another beer and a rum and coke for Lena. Then he realized that he only had a hundred-dollar bill on him.

"I hate to break this hundred."

"Here. Let me do that for you." Lena bent over, loosened her bootlaces and pulled the wad of money out of her boot tops. She gave him four twenties and two tens. He gave the bartender the ten and awaited his change. Then he gave Lena two twenties.

"Let's do it, Lena. I'm ready."

They returned to the corner as soon as his change arrived.

Frank sat in the chair and pulled his shorts, then his jockey shorts, down to his knees. She undid the belt on her cutoffs and slipped them off. Then she mounted him. He was ready, but he was very drunk.

Lena kissed him on the mouth. Then she drew back momentarily. "You are inside of me. How does it feel?"

"It feels great," he lied. He wasn't all that sure whether he was in or out. They were both in a contorted position. And he had drunk a lot of beer. *Perhaps yes, perhaps no. Whether we're doing it or not, this sure beats staying at home in front of the television.* The selection playing on the juke box ended and he saw someone come in around the partition. It was the owner. They ignored him, hoping the owner would not notice their state of undress, both of them pulling their shorts back on.

Frank went to the bar. The owner followed them in motioning for Lena to come back and talk with him. *Probably did catch us after all*, thought Frank. *She'll get fired while I'll just get warned . . .* Lena and the owner disappeared. The place closed soon after and he never saw her again that night.

AFTERNOON PLANS IN THE COUNTRY

The following Thursday found Frank back in the Sports Bar looking for her. Nadine had a can of Budweiser for him before he even asked. *One thing about the old girl--she sure as hell gives me great service,* Frank thought. "Nipples is in the dressing room, Frank. She'll be out in a minute. That'll be two dollars for the beer."

"You might as well get Nipples a Bud Lite as well. Here's five dollars with one for you, Nadine."

"Thanks honey."

Lori came right over from the dressing room. "I missed you Frank."

"I did too."

"We have a lot of fun every time you're in here, don't we?"

"Definitely."

"Let's grab a table." They sat far to the right of the stage.

"Lori, I want to take you to my farm. We can spend a couple of days there. I'll help pay the babysitter. You've got to understand that this farm is an extension of myself. It is me. I want you to see it--no one else."

"Frank, I'd go out with you in a heartbeat. You're what I want, but what I never had. Now I've screwed up my life. I've got five mistakes--my five children. But I love them all and I'd never give them up. If we do go out, I want to take it slow. I'm really scared of getting involved with you. I don't want to get hurt and I don't ever want to hurt you."

"What about this Saturday? Can you come down with me Saturday night? After work. I hear what you're saying about getting too involved too fast. I won't pressure you to sleep with me, but I want you to visit me in my element. See what I've done and how I live. That would be different from this artificial environment we keep meeting in--getting drunk together, and having fun."

"Okay. Why don't you meet me here in the afternoon. I'll quit early and leave with you."

"Count on me. I'll be here in the middle of the afternoon. I'll even mow the yard for you."

"What should I wear?"

"Bring some shorts. Jeans. Things like that. We'll go out to a nice restaurant Saturday night. Or if you prefer, we can put some steaks on the grill."

"Actually, I'd prefer the steaks on the grill. I can always go to restaurants."

They continued to plan the weekend. This time Frank left early. He had to get back to his farm and smoked a cigar on the way home. The hour drive passed quickly.

THE BLACK CAT

Saturday morning came. Frank woke up early enjoying the thought of having Lori at his farm. At the same time he had the gnawing feeling that she was going to fail him once again. He went out into his machine shed to work on a tractor. He heard loud meowing inside the building. *It's 45 automatic time again*, he told himself. Frank walked to his pickup thinking *I hate shooting cats, but I don't like them eating the wildlife around my place.* Frank pulled down the padded armrest which nestled in the seat. He pulled the chopped 45 automatic out of its hiding place and stalked back to the machine shed. *I know it's against the law to keep guns hidden in my truck*, he mused, *but then what respect do I hold for the law anyway. Men used to carry guns on horseback as they went around their chores. This pickup is the same as my horse, and I, a farmer, am the modern day counterpart of the cowboy of the Old West.* Frank reflected on his habit of drinking beer in his pickup which was also against the law. He could justify the 45 as a tool that was essential for disposing of cats and other varmints on his farm--but what about the beer? *Simple*, he told himself, *I drink it while driving because it feels good--end of subject.*

He entered the machine shed and pulled back the slide of the 45. Frank walked through the building but did not see the animal. *Now where is that damn cat? No sign of it anywhere.* He did his best imitation of a cat letting out a meow and heard a meow coming from the Northeast corner of the building. Frank meowed again, and once again the cat answered him. And then he saw it come out from underneath his planter. The cat walked briskly toward him. Frank leveled the 45 and pushed the safety off with his thumb. If he shot now, the bullet would go right through the cat and through the aluminum siding of the building. He would wait till it got less than ten feet away. He would shoot it then. The bullet would angle downwards and bury itself in the dirt floor of the building. The cat was now in his sights--then Frank noticed that it was not a cat but a half-grown kitten. Jet black with green eyes, the kitten was now running--running too fast for a humane shot. Now it was too close. Suddenly the kitten jumped into his lap.

No, he couldn't do it. Any animal that had the foresight and the good taste to jump into his lap was far too bright to put away just like that. Frank took the little animal into his house. Looking in a closet he found a small can of cat food that his wife had forgotten to take with her when she moved out with her two children and the family's pet cat. He fed the kitten. *Now what am I going to do with it? Keep it for a pet?* It was a beautiful animal. He'd have to wait and see. If he didn't want to keep it, he could always give it away. For now, he had his date with Lori, and it was time to clean up and drive to the Sports Bar.

The hour long drive to the Sports Bar seemed to take longer than usual. Frank walked in, took the room in with a glance, and didn't see her. Cindy came up to take his order.

"Nipples quit. What can I get you babe?"

"What did you say, Cindy? Did you say she quit? When?" Frank asked in disbelief, his voice crestfallen.

"Yesterday. She stormed out of here. She's quit before. A couple of times. But she always came back. This time I don't think she's ever coming back."

"Why's that? And I need something strong. Straight vodka. Just a little lemon."

"Because this time she made a complete ass of herself. She called all of us girls a bunch of holes right before she stormed out of here." The voice came from behind him. He turned around. It was Tamara.

"Why in the world did she say that?" he asked.

"I'm not sure what exactly happened, but a couple of the girls said she was doing a private with a guy. He must have gotten real handsy with her. Nipples screamed at him. No one came to tell the guy to watch his manners. Later she said that he practically raped her in the corner. Then she got mad and said that management did not back her up--that it backed up the customer instead. She was very drunk. Last couple of days she was crying a lot and drinking heavier than usual. So Nipples told all of us that we were a bunch of sluts or holes. And then she was gone."

"Tamara, what do you think she was crying about?" Frank asked.

"I'm not sure. Something about Travis no doubt. Who knows?"

Cindy, efficient as always, brought the vodka straight over. Frank chugged it down.

"Now I'll pay for this and one just like it. Also bring Tamara whatever she wants."

"I'd like a Bud light," said Tamara.

"Sit with me for a few minutes Tamara. Then I'm leaving."

"You don't seem to be in a good mood, Frank. Guess you really like Nipples?"

"Good observation Tamara. I was going to meet her here. Then she was going to come home with me for the weekend at my farm. I'm pissed."

"So was she."

They had another drink together. Then they had another. First he was with Tamara. Then one of Tamara's steady customers came in and he was with Kim. He was still drinking when eight o'clock arrived and the night shift took over. That's when Lena came in.

"Hi Frank. Remember me?"

"Sure, the little girl in the corner. We had a great private together."

"Yes, we had a great private. And we're going to have another great private. You been here long?"

"For hours."

"Thought so. You seem a little drunk."

"Lena. Right now I feel a little low. Glad you're here."

"Then let's do a limo."

"A limo! I've never done one of those before. How does it work? The other girls have told me about it, but I want to get it straight from you."

"You get a good half hour with me in the limo. You pay one-hundred-seventy bucks total. A hundred goes to me. Seventy goes to the bar. You and I are alone in the back seat. We can do whatever we want."

"We can do exactly what we want?" By this time Frank was slurring his words.

"You've got it. Exactly what we want. And it's going to be good. Real good."

"Just so that we've got this down right. At least as good as the corner, right?"

"Much much better than the corner," Lena replied.

"Then let's do it. Let's make it happen. Now!"

"Do you have cash or do you want to put it on your Visa?"

"Visa."

"Mary, get out the Visa forms," Lena told the bartender. "We are doing a limo." Frank looked up and noticed that Mary had replaced Nadine as the bartender. She asked Frank for his card and brought him a form to sign. He saw that it was made out for one hundred-seventy dollars, signed the form and waited for Mary to hand him his copy and five twenties.

"Now, you give me the hundred," said Lena. "The limo is already here. It waits outside on weekends. So anytime you're ready, I'm ready."

Frank gave Lena the hundred. "Let's go then."

The limo was outside waiting. It wasn't a stretch limo but it had a large back seat area. The driver held the door open for Frank and Lena. The driver closed the rear door behind them, walked up to the front of the car, and sat behind the wheel where he lit a cigarette. The back seat area was a separate compartment with a glass partition separating the driver from his passengers.

"I thought the glass would be blacked out, but I can see the driver lighting his cigarette. Does this mean he gets to watch? Not that I care. I just want to know."

"It's a one way glass," Lena replied. "We can see him, but he can't see us. The parking lot is lit up so we can see him here. "However, when we get onto the highway, it won't be as bright outside so we will hardly see him at all."

The driver eased the vehicle out of the parking lot. Frank took his clothes off and smiled to himself that he had done it before they had left the parking lot. Twenty seconds later, Lena sat next to him naked. He leaned over and kissed her as she started to rub him between his legs. Then, satisfied with what she had done, she pulled out a condom and expertly pulled it out of its wrapper.

"Don't move, I promise this won't hurt a bit." And she put it on him.

Fifteen minutes later he was still inside her. He was surprised that he had not felt pressured for time. They had each brought a beer from the bar and there was still time to drink and talk. It was Lena who broke the silence.

"That was good, Frank. We were good together. I think this worked out pretty well. We got a chance to know each other. Next time we can spend a little more time and get to know each other even better."

"Next time Lena, I'd like to take you home with me. That way we can do it several times instead of just once."

"I think--maybe we should do one more limo. Then the

time after, you can take me home with you."

By the time they had finished their drinks the limo was pulling into the parking lot. They entered the building together and sat next to each other at the bar. Lena sat close to him and started to rub his crotch. They drank for the next hour or two until the place closed. The next day he would not remember exactly what they did or what they talked about except that she sat very close to him and that she couldn't keep her hands off him.

Then he headed home. When he walked into his house, the black kitten ran right up to him. *That's strange*, he thought. *She should be shy, acting a little lost. But she's treating me like we've known each other for a long time. Most cats are not like that-- especially with a new home and a new owner.* It was the same way with Lori. They had taken to each other from the beginning as if they had always known each other forever. He had no way of getting hold of her--no phone, no address, no last name. Nothing. Somehow, Frank reasoned, *her quitting seems tied to me. Funny too, how the little black kitten, develops an instant bond to me, and shows up at the same time she disappears.*

FRANK FINDS HIS NIPPLES

He thought about forgetting her, but every time he looked at the black kitten he remembered. She was trouble--always had been. She was also very special. He had taken the cat in when he had originally intended to shoot it. She had turned out to be the most affectionate cat he had ever been around. Perhaps, just perhaps, as unlikely as it might seem, there was something around the corner with this girl. He decided to find her.

Frank went back to the Sports Bar on the following Tuesday. His friend, Tamara, was there sitting with a customer as usual. He went to their table without even bothering to get a beer.

"Hi Tamara. I don't want to interrupt you and your friend, but I've decided to find Nipples come hell or high water. Got any ideas?"

"Her best friends are Dotie and Goldie. One of them should be able to tell you. Are you planning to go over to her house?"

"Damn right I am. I'm not going to mess around. I'm finding her and that's that."

"Just like that. I'm sure Travis will love this," Tamara replied.

"Screw Travis. The fucker's a pimp living off her the way he does. Understand, I'm not calling her a whore or anything. It's just that I know he does not work and that he lives off her earnings. And the girls tell me he beats her up."

"Goldie's right over there. Go ask her."

Frank strode up to Goldie. "Goldie, I'm thirsty for a Bud light. Can you get me one? You look like you can use a drink yourself. I'll buy you one if . . . "

"Sure Frank. If. Now what must I do for my drink?"

"First, you must drink it with me. I know you're a waitress and that you're busy, but there's not that many people here yet so I think you'll manage. Second, I'm going to ask you to do me a favor. I have a proposition for you."

"Are you going to proposition me? And all this time I thought you were a nice guy."

"Goldie, just get us our drinks, okay?"

Goldie returned with his beer and her drink, which turned out to be a Jack and Coke and a shot of Cuervo. *Must hang around Nipples a lot*, thought Frank--*drinks the same drinks*. She charged him twelve dollars.

"Okay Frank, what's the favor you're going to ask me?"

"I want to find Nipples and I want to find her right away. If you can get me to her house today, I'll give you twenty bucks."

"That's pretty generous Frank. I've got a great idea. My boyfriend, Jim, is coming in here in a few minutes. Have you met Jim?"

"No, I haven't."

"I think you will like him. Anyway, I think he can find her house. You two can drive over there together."

"That's super. Great idea, Goldie. By the way, do you trust Nipples?"

"I love Nipples. Do I trust her? No."

"You mean she tells you as many stories as she tells me?"

"Probably more. I'm around her more."

"How much of what she says do you believe?"

"Maybe five percent. No. Probably not that much."

Thirty minutes later, Jim came in. He was around five nine--one-hundred and fifty pounds or so. He wore his dark hair in a ponytail. Goldie went up to him and kissed him on the lips. Then she motioned for Frank to come over.

"Hi, you must be Jim. I'm Frank Harring."

"Glad to meet you, Frank. I understand you want to find Nipples. I can find her. Let's have a beer together. Then we'll go see her. At least I can show you where she lives."

They drank together talking about Nipples. When they finished, they walked out to Frank's truck. "I hope you don't mind my driving. This whole thing is to my benefit. Besides, if I drive, I can more easily find my way a second time," said Frank.

When they got to route 64, Frank pulled out a pack of Anthony and Cleopatras and offered a cigar to Jim.

"Thanks." Jim took the pack and took out a cigar. He pulled out his lighter, lit the cigar, then lit Frank's. They smoked in silence for five minutes. It was Jim who broke the silence.

"So, you must like this Nipples a lot to go through this trouble."

"Yes. Unfortunately I do. Jim, what do you know about this Travis that she's living with?"

"He's younger than her. He's very much in love with her. At least that is my impression. He picks her up at work. She keeps him waiting on her a lot. And I don't think he really knows what she does. I think he's pretty naive."

"Just what are you saying Jim?"

"Well, you know--these dancers have the opportunity to do a lot of shit. Sometimes they do bachelors' parties, and who knows what goes on there. Then there's the limo. Anything goes in there. And Nipples does a lot of limos. Now I don't know what she does on those limos. That's none of my business, but I'm sure Travis would kick her ass if he knew she was even doing them."

They crossed the Mississippi River to the Missouri side. Jim guided him to route 55 South which they took to Arsenal Street. They went a few blocks, making a few turns along the way.

"Now turn right," Jim instructed, "This is her street. Look for a pale yellow Grand Prix. If we see it we're in luck because it means for sure that she's home." They drove two blocks. "I believe we are in luck. There's the car. Park right behind it."

Frank parked behind the Grand Prix. He turned to Jim and asked, "Shall we go up together? I want to meet Travis. Lori makes him out to be a real tough guy."

"Who? Travis? Shit. He's probably hiding inside. I'll bet it will be Nipples who comes to the door."

"Let's do it Jim. Let's go see how Lori lives."

The house was a typical South St. Louis home, all brick with no yard. They knocked on the door and waited a few moments. Then Lori appeared. She was wearing jeans and no makeup. She looked thinner than usual. One would never have guessed that this rather ordinary looking woman was a top stripper.

"Hi Jim. What's up?" She ignored Frank showing no sign of recognition. Lori did not smile.

"Is Travis home?" asked Jim.

"Yeah, he's back there somewhere."

A little girl around three years old appeared in the doorway followed by a boy who was around six. *Looks like she has kids all right*, thought Frank. *At least two.*

"Lori, this is my idea to come here. Jim's just showing me the way."

"Shhhh. The kids might hear you," Lori whispered. "I'll walk you to the truck."

Jim led the way followed by Lori. No one could have guessed that she knew Frank. When they got to Frank's pickup she whispered to him, "I'm working at the Pink Giraffe now. I have to be there at eight o'clock tonight." Then she walked back to her house.

On the way back to the Sports Bar, Frank pondered his situation. Eight o'clock was a long way off. Yet he had intended to find her. Now that he had, what was he going to do about it? He decided to have a few more beers at the Sports Bar, then look for the Pink Giraffe.

"What have you decided?" asked Jim.

"I'm going to the Pink Giraffe."

"Makes sense."

When they went back into the Sports Bar, Tamara greeted them, smiling. "You two probably need a stiff drink after that. Did you find her, Frank? Did you meet Travis?"

"Didn't meet Travis," Frank replied, "but we found Lori. She's working at the Pink Giraffe tonight at eight."

"You mean that's where she says she's working. I'll bet she won't even be there."

"Why's that?" asked Frank.

"Because they do a lot of lesbian shows there. Knowing Nipples, she won't put up with that. And they require it in there. At least that's what other girls tell me. So, my guess is that Nipples isn't even working there."

"I'm gonna give it a shot anyway."

The next three hours passed quickly. The beer went down easily. Frank got directions to the Pink Giraffe and was starting out the door to his truck when he saw Lena walking toward him.

"Where do you think you're going?" she asked.

"Home," he lied.

"Not until you buy me a drink."

"All right. One drink. Then I have to go."

They sat at the bar and ordered two Budweisers. Lena put her hand on his crotch and started to fondle him. "You know what we ought to do?" she asked.

"What?"

"I think we need to do another limo," said Lena.

"Lena, that would be a great idea, but not for tonight."

"Why's that?"

"Because tomorrow I have to meet with my lawyer about my coming divorce. I need to be sharp. So I've got to go home."

"I think you need to do a limo with me. We'll really get it

on. Then you'll feel so relaxed tonight that you'll sleep like a baby. You'll wake up refreshed and ready for your appointment."

"It won't work Lena. I've gotta go. Besides, we've already done one limo. It's one hundred and seventy bucks for the limo. The bar gets seventy and you only get a hundred, and I'm out one hundred and seventy. It would seem to me that there's a better way. Look, here's my business card. It's got my home number on it. Call me and we'll get together at my place."

"Frank, I know it's one hundred and seventy bucks, but my rent is due. I'm trying to get into this new place. I can't do it unless I have enough money. This will help me out."

"Lena, I've given you two reasons why I can't do it tonight. Now you've seen me heading out the door. I was going home."

"Oh come on Frank. Let's do a limo. It'll help me out. You'd like to help me out. Wouldn't you?"

"Sure I would, but I've already told you the score. Now you've got my number. Please call me. Call me collect."

"I'm not calling you. You don't give a shit about me. So I'm not calling you."

"Look, I'm going. See you later."

Frank got up and walked out. Frank drove away in his pickup, anxious to get away from Lena and close to Lori. He did not like being hustled. He did not care for a girl who had no respect for his hard earned money. And he didn't like her sniveling. It was time for the Pink Giraffe.

THE PINK GIRAFFE

The Pink Giraffe was one of several nightclubs off of route three near the stockyards. They were in a cluster close together. There was a sign outside of one place advertising that the place offered a customer time in a hot tub. Frank assumed that a man could pay so much by the hour to sit around in a hot tub with a female companion. This did not interest him. One thing, it seemed low rent to him. The other was that he was focused on one goal--Lori--and if she wasn't going to work at the Pink Giraffe tonight, he was going to leave--in a hurry. Several miles away from the Pink Giraffe the smell of the stockyards reached his nostrils. He had a premonition that in some way Lori had lowered herself when she left the Sports Bar for the Pink Giraffe. The thought saddened him.

There was a little street which separated the Pink Giraffe from the nightclub next to it. He had heard of the other place before but he had never heard of the Pink Giraffe until today. The Pink Giraffe had its own parking lot which was watched over by an attendant. Frank found a parking spot and pulled in. He walked into the nightclub reaching for his wallet knowing there would be a cover charge. A doorman greeted him in an alcove just inside the door from which a person was unable to see the main room.

"That'll be five dollars," said the man.

Frank paid the doorman and entered the main room. An attractive brunette intercepted him, barring his way to the bar. She stood close to him and smiled. "I'll bet you're new to the Pink Giraffe."

"This is my first time," Frank replied.

"Stand still. I have to frisk you." The woman placed her hands underneath Frank's arms and ran them along his sides. She ran her hands down him quickly until she got to his groin. She rested her hands there momentarily before continuing. She felt his thighs next. "Okay, you can go in," she said.

The woman had fondled him next to the jukebox just inside the entrance. To the left was the bar, which was shaped like a square so that customers could all sit around it while facing the bartender who stood inside of it. Throughout the room small tables were placed around the bar. The bar was in the center of the room, the tables just outside the center. Farther from the center were three stages where the girls danced. Unlike the other places he had been to, the Pink Giraffe had a second level. A staircase went up to it. Just off the top of the staircase was a small platform. The disk jockey, a large bald black man, perched there surrounded by sound equipment. The upper level was a large circular loft, its floor perhaps ten feet wide. A heavy wooden railing four feet high circled this floor. It existed to keep people from falling to the main floor below. The center of this upper level was kept open so that anyone who sat or stood on the upper level could look out and down into the main room to watch the dancers perform at their stages. Small tables large enough for two or three people were placed around this upper floor. Each table was accompanied by two chairs. Every so often a single chair was placed against the wall on this upper floor. Private dances were usually done at these chairs. A large globe light hung above the exact center of the room just over the bar.

Frank walked around the room searching for Lori. He remarked to himself that he was early and resigned himself to a seat at the bar. He ordered a bottle of Budweiser from the bartender and considered his situation.

Perhaps Lori worked here. Perhaps she didn't. Now that he was here, he was going to have a good time. He could see that most of the girls who worked here were attractive. He'd have the best time with Lori, but he was certain that he could find a suitable substitute if she failed to show. For him anything was possible. His wife, Karen, had moved out after all. Frank could call any telephone number he wanted with impunity with no regard for how and when the charges would show up on his bill. He could stay out as late as he wanted. He didn't even have a male friend with him who would hold him back. No one to restrict him on account of having to go home early. The best part of the whole situation was his mental attitude. Other than showing common courtesy to whomever he should meet Frank felt no compulsion whatever on pleasing anyone. Nor did he feel the need for picking someone up or for impressing anyone. For the first time in his life he felt totally free to act as he pleased and to chart his own course with no regard for what others should think.

He thought about how men went through life constantly compromising. They wore suits to impress their boss or to win over a client. They took people to dinner they didn't like just to get ahead and drove mini vans to house their families. They insisted on air bags in order to protect their loved ones. They kissed everybody's asses to keep ahead. It was all done in order to continue their precious petty little lifestyles--which Frank referred to as Middle Class Mediocrity. Here he sat in his shorts and T-shirt wearing a pair of moccasins feeling above it all and not wanting any part of it.

A pretty woman stood next to him and ordered a drink from the bartender. He knew that it was no accident that she was standing next to him. She was there to get his attention. Once she got it, it was going to cost him. He'd have to buy her expensive drinks, and it might be expected that he do lap dances with her. As long as he had the money and was willing to spend it, so what, he reasoned.

And then he saw her. She was standing on the stairway almost at the top talking to the D.J. *It was going to be more than a good night. It was going to be a great night.* He never saw her look over at him. At first he thought that she had not seen him. Then she came over to him. *She must have eyes in the back of her head*, he thought.

"Hi Frank. Been here long."

"Just got here."

"I feel like just sitting down with you and talking, but I'm up next. Want to come see me dance?"

"What do you think?"

Frank followed her to one of the stages sitting in front of it as Lori mounted the platform and went over to the pole. Lori began to pirouette around the pole, slowly rotating her body around its axis as she took in the crowd. Suddenly, she stopped and started climbing, hand over hand, as she pulled her legs after her until she reached the top, twelve feet in the air. Then she climbed back down, halfway to the platform, turning her body upside down so that her head almost touched the floor. Hanging like a bat with the insides of her feet firmly grasping the pole, Lori started to talk to him, but Frank couldn't hear a word above the jukebox.

She dismounted from the pole and took off her dancing clothes, standing there completely nude as the second song ended. Frank was shocked to see that Lori had shaved her vagina. "I don't want to dance," she told him as she sat in front of him hanging her feet over the platform.

"I can't come down onto your lap," said Lori. "We can't do

lap dances here so why don't you just lean forward."

He pulled his chair closer to the edge of the platform. Lori sat close to him and wrapped her legs around Frank's neck. He tucked his face tightly between her legs and pressed his lips into her. Suddenly she jerked back.

"I can't do that when I'm undressed. I almost forgot. Hope no one saw that."

"I did, and it was very nice."

"So, why did you quit the Sports Bar?" he asked.

"I had a guy almost rape me during a private. The trouble is a lot of the girls are really putting out in the corner. Some of them are giving blow jobs. So this guy thinks he can get by with that kind of shit with me. Wrong! But he kept at it and no one came to help me. I had been having a rough week anyway so I called all the girls a bunch of holes and left. I doubt if they want me back there now, but I don't care."

Frank didn't ask why she never called him. She was unreliable and that was all there was to it. Whatever excuse she could give would be inadequate at best. *How can you not find a phone over a three-day period?* he asked himself. At worse she would come up with a bullshit story that would absolutely stultify the imagination and he didn't want to put up with that. *Far better to let it go for now. Just lean back and enjoy her.* He did, and as before, time passed as if on wings. At two o'clock he asked her if she wanted to do a private.

They went upstairs. He gave her a twenty and she took him to one of the tables. He sat at one of the chairs and took off his shirt. She took off her top leaving her bottoms off. Lori reached down and grabbed one of Frank's nipples which she put into her mouth. When it was good and wet she took her mouth away and bit down on his other nipple at the same time rubbing it between her finger tips. After both nipples became hard, she reached into his shorts and fondled him beneath his jockey shorts. He slid his fingers underneath her bottoms and started to stroke where her pubic hair should have been. She started to get wet which made him get even harder. Then she started to kiss him her tongue probing his mouth as he bit down on her lips. They continued feeling each other heedless of who might see what they were doing. Several songs were played. What should have ended with the end of the selection continued far longer than the time allowed. Finally she got up, startled.

"I lost track of the time. I'm having too good a time, that's why. We have to go downstairs.

"And I've gotta go home," he added.

"Why?"

"Because I've got a big day ahead of me, that's why. I have to meet with my divorce attorney. It's important."

They came down the stairs together and went to the door holding hands. Frank walked out to his truck and slid behind the wheel. One mile down the road he thought about going back. He had passed up the chance to do another limo with a girl who had been a good time before--a $170 chance--for a private. Yet it had been one helluva private. Sex with Lori would be more than good. He had never been that sure of it before. He needed her now--he wanted her--more than he had wanted anyone in years. He'd go back and claim her--he didn't care where or how. It could be in a closet, a stall in the men's room, or in the corner. He'd do it in front of one thousand people--right before his own father's eyes. But he kept going. Five miles up the road he decided once and for all to go home.

PINK T-SHIRT AND GARTERS

Three days later he came back to the Pink Giraffe. She found him at the bar. He ordered two Bud Lites while she sat on his lap. A girl with long brown hair walked up to them. He remembered her from the Sports Bar where she had used the stage name, Brittany. Frank and Stan had come in together, and Lori had introduced Brittany as her little sister. The girl had gotten a lot of very expensive drinks off Stan, then turned around and had him pay for her dinner. Stan had never let Frank forget the incident, reminding him each time that Lori was capable of pulling some nasty practical jokes on either one of them. Frank had gone to Lori's defense, but Stan had cut him off with the remark "If she didn't know us very well it would have been one thing, but Lori has been around us enough times that she should never have pulled off the 'fake sister' story."

"I give up, which one of you do I call Brittany?" Frank asked.

"Do you know each other?" asked Lori.

"Your little sister from the Sports Bar, remember?"

"I almost forgot. Her real name is Rozanne."

"Hi Rozanne. I still think I should call you Brittany or perhaps I'll just call you Little Sis."

"Oh, now I remember you. You're the one who came in that time and brought your friend."

Rozanne stayed until she was called up to the stage. Clearly she looked up to Lori, big sister or not. After she left, Lori ran up the stairs and talked to the D.J. for a minute. She returned carrying a pink T-shirt which she showed to Frank. "Do you want to buy this T-shirt from me? I get a commission off it. It's only ten dollars, and it can be a souvenir that you can remember me by."

"Sure, I'll buy it from you." Frank studied the T-shirt. On it was written *The Pink Giraffe--World Class Men's Club.* He pulled a ten from his pocket and gave it to Lori.

"Frank, I've got an idea. Do you want to do a hot tub with me?"

"What do you mean, do a hot tub with you?"

"Haven't you seen the hot tub? Maybe you haven't. It's not big and they keep it covered. It's over there." Lori pointed toward one of the stages. Just below it was a rectangular object which protruded a few inches off the floor. The object was approximately eight feet long and five feet wide. The fact that it appeared to have a brown Naugahyde covering and the floor was tile proved that it was portable and could be easily removed. Now that he looked at it closely, Frank determined it to be a hot tub cover, the hot tub itself being recessed into the tiled floor. Although the brown cover contrasted with the tiled floor, it still camouflaged the hot tub so that it was not obvious to the casual observer.

"Okay, I see it. Is the hot tub better than a private?"

"I think so. It will cost you $50. $30 to me and $20 to the club. We will just have to try it and see what you think."

"Let's do it then."

"We'll wait for an hour or so. But I must put in for it now. I'll see you back here in a few minutes after I talk to the D.J. about it." Lori stood up and headed upstairs. Frank went to the bar to order another beer. He spied Rozanne dancing on stage.

"Bartender. I'll have another Budweiser. And get me whatever Rozanne is having please."

"Rozanne's drinking Bloody Mary's. That'll be $6.50." Frank pulled some bills from his pocket and counted out $7.00 while the bartender made the Bloody Mary. The bartender then opened a bottle of Budweiser and put the drinks in front of Frank.

Frank went over to Rozanne's stage with the drinks. Only one customer sat at the stage. The man started to get up, reached into his pocket, and put several dollars in Rozanne's G-string. Then he left. Frank sat down in the man's chair handing the Bloody Mary to Rozanne who accepted it greedily.

"Hi little sister. How are things going?"

"I'm not making any money. Just not having a good day. How about you?"

"Lori and I are doing a hot tub. Are these rumors I keep hearing about splendor in the suds true?"

"I don't know. I haven't worked here long and I haven't talked to anyone about doing a hot tub."

"Lori's talking to the D.J. about it now. We'll let you know how it is later."

"I'd like to do a hot tub. Will you do one with me when you get done with Lori?"

"Can't. Like to, but Lori probably won't like it. I wouldn't."

"Then why don't you take me with you. We can all do one."

"Rozanne, why don't you find a guy and do the hot tub with

him. I'm sure you won't have any trouble finding someone."

"But I don't know any of the guys well enough. Besides, I want to do one with you and Lori."

"All right. If you really want to do one with us, we'll take you along," said Frank.

"Let me know when? I'll be there."

"We'll come get you." Frank looked over at his table. Lori was back looking bored. "Catch you later, Rozanne. I've gotta rescue Lori." Frank returned to the table.

"Got everything squared away?"

"It will be a little while yet. I need fifty dollars."

"Rozanne's coming with us. She said she's never done one before and that she wants to do one with us."

"That little shit. She's just after the twenty-five dollars that's all." Lori spat the words out. "As if she can't get her own customers. Why does she have to horn in on mine?"

"What do you mean by twenty-five dollars?" asked Frank.

"I mean it's now going to cost you seventy-five dollars instead of Fifty. She gets twenty-five, I get twenty-five and the club gets twenty-five."

"So you make less."

"Exactly. And you pay more. And it won't be as much fun for us. We won't be able to move around as much," said Lori.

An hour later, the hot tub was ready. Frank had paid Lori seventy-five dollars and she had just paid the D.J. She returned from upstairs carrying a towel and men's swimming trunks.

"Here, take these and go get dressed," she ordered.

A few minutes later Frank returned from the men's room dressed in the swim trunks. They fit perfectly. Bare chested and bare legged, he stood in sharp contrast to the fully clothed men around him. "Let's go Lori. I'm ready."

"Order us some drinks first. I'll get Rozanne."

Frank found a waitress, gave her twelve dollars, and ordered a round of drinks. "You can bring them to the hot tub. I'm going for a swim."

"You've got to wait for the girls," the waitress warned.

"All right, look for me at pool side."

Frank kneeled on the bare tile next to the hot tub. Moments later both girls came over to him. Lori pushed a button that was recessed into the tile. The water started to churn as Frank slipped into the tub. The girls followed him into the water, Lori easing behind him hardly causing a ripple. Rozanne, twenty pounds heavier than Lori, splashed hot water on his face as she tumbled into the tub. Rozanne crawled onto Frank's lap as Lori wrapped her legs around his back. Lori reached around his chest and grabbed one of his nipples in each hand. Squeezing tightly with her hands she thrust her pelvis against his rear. His nipples hardened instantly. Then she got up, chasing Rozanne off his lap. Rozanne got out of the tub and reentered it so that she was now behind him as Lori repositioned herself so that she now faced him. Thrusting her nipples against his chest she started to kiss him on the mouth--then, lowering her head, bit into one of his nipples until it started to hurt.

Rozanne sat behind him halfheartedly kissing the back of his neck. Fifteen minutes later the last song ended, signaling the end of the hot tub session. Frank went to the men's room to get dressed. When he came out, he noticed that Lori was already up on stage, several men already sitting in front of her. Two or three others stood watching close by. Frank ordered a Jack and Coke from the bar and brought it over, placing it on the stage in front of her. She smiled at him as she took off her garter--then tossed it to Frank while the men cheered.

Lori rejoined him at the table when her set was over. "Well?"

"Well what?"

"How'd you like the hot tub?"

"Oh, I think it has possibilities."

"Yeah, if Rozanne wasn't there."

"You didn't care for her horning in, did you?"

"Like I said, we could do a lot more without her."

"She sure didn't do much for me, "Frank complained--"Just sat behind me clinging onto me like a log."

"Rozanne's lazy."

"And not nearly as good looking as you."

"No. Probably not. Let's leave her behind the next time, okay?"

"You're on. Just the two of us."

The next two hours passed quickly. Frank left two hours before closing. He drove home wondering what would happen the next time he came to the Pink Giraffe.

THE HOT TUB

This time he didn't come alone. He brought Jerry, a good friend, who farmed near him. He had called Jerry and had asked him to go out for supper. Like most married men, Jerry was not getting along well with his wife.

Frank picked Jerry up in his sports car, the top down. "Don't ask me where we are going. You'll see when we get there," he told his friend. "Just trust me." One hour later, they arrived at the Sports Bar. Frank had a quick bite--the special was only $3.50 and was always a good deal. They had only a beer or two with a couple of the girls Frank knew; then they left. Then they went to Ciceros which was practically next door. They sat at the bar while several girls vied for their attention, but Frank had decided long before where the money in his pocket was going. This time it was Jerry's turn to eat. The buffet, which was on the house, had offered tacos and all the good things that go with them. Jerry, a big man at six three and over two hundred pounds was unable to control himself, going back to the buffet several times. On the way to route 64 they stopped off at the Injection Pump where they played pool and drank beer.

They entered the last place, the Pink Giraffe. She sat at the bar, alone. Paying the $5.00 cover, Frank hurried over to her while Jerry still fumbled with his change. Without so much as giving his friend a second thought he sat next to her and took her by her hand. Lori looked up at him seeing him for the first time. Her face that had seemed almost forlorn took on the trace of a smile.

"Lori, you look like you need a drink."

"Just get me a bud light, Frank."

"You seem sad."

"I'm just a little bored. That's all. I'm glad you came."

"My friend's coming over. I want to introduce you to him. He's one of my best friends."

Jerry walked over, a big grin on his face. Lori stood up.

"Let's get a table--back there where we usually sit," suggested Lori as if she were playing the hostess.

"Lori, this is Jerry. Jerry's kind of like a bodyguard to me. Keeps me out of trouble. Kept me out of several fights."

"Glad to meet you, Jerry. I've seen Frank almost get into several fights." Lori's mood had brightened considerably. It always did when Frank was around as if a mysterious form of alchemy had been at work. "Then I had to get him out of them too."

"Let's sit over here," suggested Frank. He pointed to a table close to the back wall. A waitress came over to take their order.

"A Bud Lite for Lori. Two Busches for us," said Frank.

"I don't believe it. I'm up already," said Lori. "Bad timing."

"You don't mind if Jerry and I just sit back and talk while you dance?" asked Frank. "I'll bring your beer to your stage."

"Not if you join me during the next set." Lori hurried off to her stage. Several minutes later the waitress returned with their beer.

"Looks like you and Lori know each other pretty well," said Jerry.

"It's been almost a year now. Be right back, Jerry. Gotta take her beer over to her."

Frank paid the waitress leaving her a two-dollar tip. Then he went over to Lori's stage where he found her on a man's lap. Hardly looking at the man Frank set Lori's beer on the stage in front of her.

Now looking at the man for the first time, Frank winked at him. "Excuse me. I hate to interrupt what's going on. I've gotta keep Brittany in beer just so that she can keep putting up with all this kind of shit. No offense. I mean, you look all right to me, but Jesus, you wouldn't believe some of the guys who come in here."

The man looked up with a bewildered look on his face. "What do you mean by that?" he asked. But it was already too late. Frank had been too quick for him. By the time the man had fully taken in what had happened, Frank was already half way back to the table.

The man then turned to Lori. "Who in the hell was that?"

"Just some guy I know. Don't mind him. He's just joking."

Fifteen minutes later, Lori came back to the table. For a moment she stood there, her legs spread slightly with her hands on her hips. She tried to look stern, but a telltale hint of a smile crossed her lips.

"I oughta kill your ass, fucking with my customers like that," she warned.

"I was just joking. Sit down Lori. Let's kiss and makeup."

Lori snuggled into Frank's lap and put both arms around his neck. She started to smile, at first a lovable innocent smile. But it was all an illusion--the smile quickly changed to the perverted Lori grin that Frank had seen so many times before. She started to kiss him on his lips, then moved down to his neck. At first she was tender, her lips gently grazing his neck. Then she started to suck, hard. He started to laugh.

"You're giving me a hicky. That's the kind of stuff people do in High School."

She didn't reply, continuing to suck on Frank's neck. Then she started to suck hard, angrily. It started to hurt. *How could a woman that small suck so goddamn hard*, he started to ask himself? Then she bit him. Suddenly she let go releasing his neck from her mouth.

Lori started to laugh. "That's what you get for being here with me."

"Well as long as you're going to give me a hickey, you might as well make sure you do it right. I've seen goldfish suck harder than you can, Lori."

"How true. You know, your neck is really muscular. That makes it hard to really make sure."

Lori bent over his neck once more and clamped down with her mouth on the same spot. She started to suck his neck, very hard this time. He could feel the bruise forming--feel it rising on his neck from the pain. Once again she released him from the vice like grip of her mouth. Then carefully and almost tenderly she backed her head away and studied what she had done as she ran her fingers gently across his neck. Satisfied with what she had done, she twisted his head around to expose the opposite side of his neck. This time there was no buildup to what was coming. She came on like a leech violently biting down on his neck almost drawing blood. She started to suck him with a force that was unbelievable. A few moments later she eased her mouth off his neck to inspect the damage.

"You've got a real shiner on the right side of your neck, but I can't seem to do much good on the left. Seems like you have even more muscle there," said Lori.

"Excuse me. I don't mean to interrupt or anything, but I've gotta piss!" exclaimed Jerry. "Put everything on hold. I don't want to miss out on anything. By the way, where's the John?"

"Straight behind you and way over to the left," said Frank.

Then, watching Jerry walking toward the restroom, Frank turned to Lori. "Do you think he's having fun?"

"My honest opinion? No."

"Then maybe we should get a girl over here for him," suggested Frank.

"Show time is coming right up. Someone will get him then. Just watch."

"I don't know if he's in the mood. You know, Jerry's awfully quiet tonight. You don't know him, but he's got a very outgoing personality. There's this Confederate general during the Civil War back in the 1860's. Name of Jeb Stuart. He was in charge of all of Robert E. Lee's cavalry. A real swashbuckler. Wore a slouch hat with a feather in it. Total showoff but a damn good general. Rode his cavalry around the whole Union Army just to show that it could be done and missed the next battle because of it. Jerry looks exactly like him and sometimes acts like him too. I gave Jerry a picture of Jeb and even Jerry agreed that the two of them looked like twin brothers. You've heard of Jeb Stuart of course?" Frank asked.

"Sure. The Confederate general. A real derelict," Lori lied.

That was choice. Real choice. Not one person out of a hundred would know who Jeb Stuart was. Frank almost choked on his thoughts. *But Lori will never admit she doesn't know something. Not that she's a braggart. It's just that she never wants to admit to any shortcomings to her knowledge.*

"I'm really feeling badly about Jerry. I should never bring anyone in when I come in to see you. You and I always get into our own little world and--we totally forget about time," said Frank.

"So. Do you want to do a hot tub?" suggested Lori.

"Why not. Put in for it right now."

"I'm really upset with Rozanne. Last week she cut herself in for the hot tub. It ended up costing you $75 instead of $50. And we didn't have as much fun as we could have. We could have moved around a lot better without her."

"Did you have to split your money evenly with Rozanne?"

"That's right, Frank."

"Okay, this time it's just you and me Lori. You and I have never made love before. Think we can in the hot tub?"

"I don't know but we can sure as hell try," said Lori.

"There's only a hundred people in this place. Does that bother you?"

"Not in the slightest."

"Just what in the world are you two planning now?" It was

Jerry returning from the men's room.

"Frank and I are going to go off and have fun together in the hot tub," Lori teased.

Just then the P.A. system came on. The disk jockey's voice boomed. "It's Show time, gentlemen. All dancers over on stage two."   "See you two later. I'm telling the disk jockey to have someone get the hot tub ready. Wanta back out, Frank?"

"Not in this world I don't."

"Then get your money ready. Remember, they collect in advance," said Lori as she left them.

A dozen girls collected over on stage two forming a single line. The jukebox started and the girls started to dance in unison, but only for a few seconds. The girls walked or jumped off the stage and dispersed throughout the room. The hustle was on. Each girl would single out a man. If the man was sitting down-- either at a table or at the bar, the girl would sit on his lap and start to squirm around. If he was standing, she would sidle up to him, thrust her rear into his groin and start rubbing against him rapidly. Each girl would do this for thirty seconds, perhaps as long as a minute, and then move onto the next customer, but not until she had collected her dollar tip. Show time lasted long enough for each girl to hit on three to five customers.

A tall buxomly brunette came over to Frank.

"Go over to him. I have to go to the men's room," Frank told her abruptly as he pointed at Jerry. The girl went over to Jerry and Frank headed the men's room. Frank almost made it. He had been quick but not quick enough. A slender brunette whom he'd seen in the club several times before intercepted him. She grabbed him by both shoulders. Then she turned around and placed her rear deep into Frank's groin.

"Funny, how as many times as we've seen each other here, we should finally really hookup like this," said Frank.

"That's because you are always with Brittany. You should really give some of the rest of us a chance," the girl replied.

"Brittany and I are close. We go way back," said Frank.

It didn't last long. He gave her a dollar, then escaped into the men's room, taking his beer with him. He really did have to go. Luckily no one was over at the stool although both urinals were occupied. After he had finished, Frank called out to one of the other men.

"Hey, are you having a good time?"

"Great, but I just had to go. I'm going back in there."

"And I'm staying in here. One of the dancers is my girlfriend. She gets insanely jealous if one of the other girls starts to get intimate with me," Frank lied. *Actually she doesn't give a shit*, he told himself. *I'm just a cheap ass mother fucker.*

"You mean you've got a girlfriend who works here?" the man asked visibly impressed.

"Yeah, I do. She's my girlfriend as long as I'm in here," Frank laughed. "And she claims me as long as I have money."

"Oh, I see what you mean," the man answered. "See you later buddy."

"Is it safe out there yet?" Frank called out.

"I'm not sure," the man replied as he walked out.

Frank returned to the table where he found Jerry sitting with the brunette who had first come over. A blonde came over, climbed onto Frank's lap, and started to jam her butt into his privates.

"Is this better than what the last girl did to you?" Lori asked.

"Definitely. I've been hiding in the john, but one of the girls waylaid me before I got there."

"I'm up." The brunette looked at Jerry. "Why don't you come with me over to my stage?" Then she got up, grabbed Jerry by the hand, and led him away from the table.

"Got fifty bucks?" asked Lori.

Frank reached into his pocket, found a wad of bills, and handed it to her. Lori started to sort through it, separated out two twenties and a ten, and handed the rest back to him.

"You're getting awfully sloppy with your money," said Lori. "I'm going to pay the D.J., then I'm going to get you some swimming trunks, and a towel. Be right back."

Ten minutes later she was back with the towel and the trunks. She handed him the trunks and pointed toward the men's room. "Go on in and change and bring back a rubber."

He took the trunks from her and headed the men's room. Once inside, he looked around. *Funny, I'm sure I saw one in here before.* Frank started to stalk around the room. There were no machines inside. He wanted to cry, no, better yet, he wanted to kill someone. *No fucking rubber machines*, Frank muttered to himself. *Every goddamn strip joint I've ever been in has at least one rubber machine. Even my favorite restaurant back home has a prophylactic machine. What kind of place is this--a church--a congregating spot for the great moral majority.* He had been so confident when he left home that he had seen a rubber machine here that he had never thought twice about it. Frank eyeballed the wall and took two swings at it--a left jab followed by a right. The wall was solid. If it hadn't been, Frank would have put two holes in it. Both of his hands started to throb. *Fuck it*, he said to himself, *now I couldn't put a rubber on if I wanted to. Probably broke my goddamn hands.*

"Jesus Fucking Christ!" he exclaimed aloud.

"You call." He had not noticed the middle-aged man standing at the urinal taking a leak.

Frank started to change into the swimming trunks. "Yeah, you're damn right I called."

"So, what's the matter?"

"Nothing. Nothing at all. Just that I almost got into a fight out there with a guy and now I'm back in here letting off steam."

By this time Frank had gotten his shorts off and had started to pull on the swim trunks.

"How come you're putting on swim trunks?" the man asked.

"Because I'm about to do a hot tub with one of the girls."

"No kidding. They do that here?" There was surprise in the man's voice. "Well she'll sure like you."

"Why's that?"

"Because you've got a really good build. Just what do you do to stay in such good shape?"

"Well I didn't think I really looked all that good, and if I do look all that great, a lot of good that's going to do me right now. I run a lot--maybe twenty-five miles a week or so. And I do a little boxing."

"I wish I could force myself to do all of that," the man replied.

"Nothing to it," said Frank. "Well, thanks for the compliment. I have to go."

He followed the man out the door and found Lori waiting for him at the table.

"There is no prophylactic machine in the place!" Frank said angrily. "Just last week I was sure I saw one in here."

"Frank, you've gotta be kidding me!" "Tell me you're kidding me."

"I'm not. Any suggestions?"

Lori looked puzzled for a moment. Then her face brightened. "We could try doing it without a rubber."

"Now you have got to be the one who's kidding," said Frank.

"No, I'm not. Now let's think about this for a minute."

"Sure, let's think about it. There's this thing out there called aids. It has many ways of killing you. The fastest has to be making my dick shrivel up and then rotting off or making you burn up inside from your vagina to your brain."

"That's if one of us has aids."

"Okay, I'll admit to screwing my wife for seven 1/2 years and not screwing anyone else. Then there's that girl who works the night shift at the Sports Bar. The one I told you about. I used a rubber and I can guarantee that it didn't break or slip off. What about you?"

"You're not going to believe this, but I've only screwed three guys in my life. A guy in High School, my husband--the one I'm still married to, and my boyfriend Travis. That's it. No one else would believe this. The girls all think I do tricks."

"You can get pregnant in that hot tub."

"No, I can't. I can't have kids anymore."

Frank didn't know whether to believe her or not. The idea that she only had been with three guys was absurd. *Or was it? Could he trust her?* After all, she had probably only lied to him 90% of the time before. Not to mention all the times she had stood him up. Yet there was something very serious about her this time. Okay, so how did she know he didn't have aids? She was going to trust him, and she knew he could kill her. If he had been having unprotected sex with other women, and if it had been he who was lying, he could be the one giving her aids instead of vice versa. So, how did he feel about her? Close, very close. And how did he think she felt about him? She liked him--one hell of a lot. All logic told him she had been toying with him in the past, but down in his guts he felt that she had very strong feelings for him. He just knew it.

And then look at how hard he had tried just to get her to go to lunch with him. He had known her for a year, and he felt that she liked him for a year, and still for some unfathomable reason she had always failed to show. Now, he could be in the hot tub with her--in her, making love to her, in front of one-hundred people. Everyone would suspect, but he knew from having been there before that no one could see under the boiling surface of the water. They could be 99% sure but they could never be absolutely certain. It was worth doing. It was derelict. And she was worth getting. Suddenly he didn't care any more about the dangers--of getting caught--of getting aids--of getting arrested--of embarrassment.

"Let's do it, Lori. Let's goddamn do it. Give the bastards a real show. Let them cream in their pants. Above all, let's make love, because we want to make love to each other, and we don't give a shit about anybody else or anything."

"Are you two going or not going?" It was Jerry returning to the table with the brunette.

"Damn right we are going and right now. See you later, Jerry." Frank got up and started for the hot tub with Lori right behind him. The D.J. saw them approach the tub. The D.J.'s voice over the P.A. announced:

"Ladies and Gentlemen. We have a special act for you right now. We have the lovely Brittany approaching the hot tub with her friend. Now normally we have girls together in the hot tub, but this evening we have made special arrangements to have a guy and a girl. Some ring side seats have been sold in advance. Feel free to watch."

"Did he announce anything about us earlier that I missed?" Frank asked.

"I believe he did, but I missed it too," Lori replied.

Already men started to gather in the seats around the hot tub. Within two minutes perhaps fifteen men were seated within six feet of the water's edge. *This is unbelievable*, thought Frank. *Unfucking real that people would be so hard up and brazen as to come right up to the hot tub to watch two people perform a sex act. Now this place is really something, isn't it? Well, I'm going to just have to stick it in their ears.* Frank and Lori walked up to the sunken hot tub. Lori found the button close to the water and punched it. The water started to boil and churn.

"Do you need a drink first?" she asked him.

"Hell no. I just need you." And he got in leaning back against the back side of the tub. Lori entered the water snuggling up against him with her back against his chest. With one fluid motion Frank pulled his trunks off under the water allowing them to slide all the way to his ankles. For one second the trunks gathered about his ankles, as the air pockets in his trunks forced both his ankles and the trunks to rise to the surface of the water. How many people saw it, Frank didn't care. But Lori, still sharp, caught it, and she did care.

"What are you trying to do, Frank, get me fired and you thrown in jail? Put those trunks back on!"

Frank hastily reached down for the trunks and pulled them up. Lori climbed onto his lap and pulled his shorts to the side so that he came out of his shorts. It was not the same as having them off but it was the next best thing. Frank knew from the onset that they would have no lubrication. Past experience had taught him that swimming pools and hot tubs did not promote good sex. The fleeting thought that Lori might have aids struck him again--but only for an instant. He remembered something he had read once, probably in Time Magazine--*Would you risk your life to make love to this person you didn't really know that much about?* Or was it, *would you give your life to make love to this person?* He considered Lori and answered the question with a *"*Hell yes I would! In a minute!*"*

"Come on--You've got to help," Lori urged.

He had just answered the question of life and death versus making love with Lori without a rubber with a yes. *Was it because she was pretty and he was more lustful than average? Was it because he had been trying to get her alone for almost a year-- without success--and he was now so frustrated that he was going to go for it with no count of the cost? Or was it because he had known her for nearly a year and he liked her that much?* Perhaps he'd never know the answer.

Whatever it was--it worked. He wanted Lori so badly and that was what counted. Seconds later he was inside her. Everyone watched while they made love. Frank smiled to himself. *Don't they realize that I've hardly noticed them? I'm making love to her and this place is presenting itself to us as a convenient bedroom.* He gloated over his sense of superiority over them. *They are thinking they are really seeing something whereas I've dared to do what they would never do themselves. And I'm reducing them to total insignificance by ignoring their very presence.* And then the true significance of what they were doing hit him. He and Lori were the Alpha animals in the wolf pack. Those close to the hot tub were the Beta wolves who were not allowed to mate. *We are mating right in front of the pack while these lesser animals slink in the background seeking a cheap vicarious thrill in being allowed to watch.*

Never better than this he told himself. Suddenly reality forced itself on the Alpha complex. He popped out.

"Face me!" he ordered. "Be quick." Quick as a cat, Lori spun around on his lap. Seconds later he was inside her again. They started to kiss. She went from his lips to his neck, her tongue first probing his mouth then licking him all over--his chin, his neck, getting him wet and hot all over. And then the music stopped. Frank slipped his head under the water. Someone came over. Frank never saw the man as the intruder asked a question that he never heard since his ears were under the water.

Lori jerked his head upwards so that his ears came out of the water. "Do you want to go another song?" she asked. "It's another fifty bucks."

"Fuck yes." Frank judged this to be the appropriate answer considering the situation. "Start the music again!" Frank ordered. The man went away. A dreamy look appeared on Lori's face.

They were making love--after nearly a year of not even coming close. He had to make it complete. If for some reason he didn't, he felt that it would be as if they had never started. He had only five more minutes. Never had he been in this situation before. He had a time limit. A hundred people were their audience, and he had to make it happen. The hundred people didn't matter--not a bit.

And he made it happen. It was the first time and he decided it would not-- could not be the last time. Suddenly she relaxed. Her back straightened, Her form went limp. She smiled, a little smile like that of an angel.

And everybody watched. Too soon they had to get out of the hot tub. He went to the men's room to change. When he came back to the table she was there waiting for him as a waitress came to take their order. It was the new girl--the best looking of the waitresses.

"That was great. You two were absolutely fantastic. I couldn't help watching the whole thing. What can I get you?"

"Two shots of Cuervo," said Lori. The waitress hurried off.

"When do you want to come to my farm?" Asked Frank. "Now that I know you want to come."

"Tomorrow night. Come see me tomorrow night. Travis is leaving for two days. I'll leave with you and spend the night."

"I'll be here tomorrow night then, but I'll be late. I want you to know, Lori, that farm is an extension of myself. I have not invited any women there since my wife left. You are very special, and that's why I want you to be there."

The evening ended too quickly. Jerry and Frank said goodbye to the girls and went out into the night, which had been perfect. They climbed into the sports car. Frank started the engine and eased the little machine out of the parking lot.

"Frank, I'm not going to ask you what you two did in the hot tub, but there for a while her head sure was bobbing up and down."

"It sure did, didn't it Jerry."

BETRAYAL

Two hours of sleep had not been enough. He woke at seven wondering where he was. The tequila--not to mention the beers and vodka had done the job. Of course--he was home. He knew that. Trouble was, it took thirty seconds to realize it. An awful taste hit him even before he got out of bed. When it dawned on him, who he was; where he was--it struck him that alcoholics got this way. *How well would he function today?* Probably the same way alcoholics functioned on the day after. He deduced that he was Frank Harring about the same time that he realized he had a full schedule. Trouble was he couldn't think of anything he had to do. He went downstairs looking for a bathroom. That taste just had to go. Some mouthwash, a toothbrush, and a lot of toothpaste--that's what he needed. The coffee would wait. He shuffled into one of the two bathrooms and found the toothpaste and a half-worn out brush. *Oh well, at least it was red.* He started to brush only to get a bristle stuck between his teeth.

Suddenly Frank realized that he was supposed to meet Lori tonight. He was going to bring her home to show her his place. Since she quit at four, they'd be starting the evening together in daylight--sometime around five, if he was lucky. They'd stay awake the next day together eating breakfast, drinking, making love, riding motorcycles, perhaps swimming. Except that it would not happen. She had let him down 100% of the time in the past. *Was there any reason to believe that would change? What would happen this time? Would she even be there?* Or would he get there only to have her come up to him to say, "Travis isn't leaving after all. Can we make it some other time?" Or perhaps somewhere around two or three she'd get a phone call or at least claim she got a phone call. "Oh, Frank," she'd say, "One of the kids got sick." So it wouldn't really make much difference how he felt. Whether he was in good form, felt good, or whether he felt like ground up road kill. It wasn't going to happen and that was all there was to it.

Frank went into the kitchen and started to make some coffee. Slowly he started to recover some degree of functionality. Since there was no question that she wasn't going to come tonight, he'd try to set her up for another night. Frank would look for some ski pictures--his best ones. He'd show them to her and tell her to keep them for a week or two. He'd ask her to take them out and look at them from time to time, and then to ask herself whether she wanted to go or not. He decided to dump it in her lap. If she wanted to go for an incredible week, she would have to call him. It would be her move. Lori would have to connect with him outside of the nightclub. She was the one who had to make it happen because she had always been responsible for making it not happen. Those pictures, he reminded himself to select with the utmost care those he'd give her, would be a tangible reminder to her of something she had never had. They'd be something she could pull out over the next few days to look at, and hopefully to dream about.

She had to know that he'd treat her like a lady. Always. He was confident of convincing her he could take her where she had never been, to a world of fast downhill skiing followed by fine dinners, good drinking, great entertainment, romantic evenings. She could forget who she was, what she did, her kids, and everything else that was weighing her down. *And who knows-- maybe that would be just a start,* Frank said to himself. Perhaps it would be the first of many vacations together. After all, he was not tied down, and he wasn't ever planning to be. But she had to want it--she had to reach out for it. She had to say to herself, "I know I'm stuck with five kids and this mess I've created for myself, but I'm a good person. I'm good looking and I'm fun to be with. I'm going to just take off. Get a sitter. Learn to ski. Fall on my face and have a great time."

The day went quickly. He cultivated in the sun, taking off the tractor's protective canopy. He stripped to his jockey shorts and took off his T-shirt so that he could get the most from the sun. When he finished the field, he switched to another tractor, the one with the Woods mower on it. Frank crawled in the cab, pushed the PTO lever up which started the mower blades, and guided the John Deere forward. Frank turned the stereo up, switched the air conditioner on, and lit the first of several cigars. He mowed some set aside ground. Then he started on his field lanes, mowing into the dark.

Lori would probably get to work around 9:30. He had told her he'd be there, but that he might be late. Frank reminded himself that she worked till four in the morning. *No hurry then.* He went in the house and changed to his running shorts and a pair of New Balances. Then he went out to run.

He struggled until he started to run South when he caught a moderate headwind. The full moon made it possible to see. His lungs took in the fresh air, and he started to feel whole again. The headwind caused him to slow down, but it cooled him off at the same time. The four miles passed swiftly. Twenty-five minutes later he was in the shower. In five minutes he had finished. He put on a pair of khaki shorts, a dark green knit shirt, and a pair of boat shoes and headed for his truck.

It took him one hour to reach the Pink Giraffe. It was now 12:30. He had felt tired soon after pulling out of his driveway which was unusual after a run. Usually he felt revitalized after a run but this time he felt let down. Frank didn't feel good about starting an evening this late, but he felt even worse when he contemplated staying up all night. But as soon as he got within a few miles of the nightclub, he started to feel better. He always had a good time in those places. If he didn't know any of the girls or particularly care for any of them, he could always have a few beers. That seemed to put things in the proper perspective. After a few, the girls always got better and he almost always got friendlier.

He paid the five-dollar cover and was about to walk in when the doorman smiled at him.

"Hey, you know what you should do?" the doorman asked genially

"What should I do?" Frank answered.

"You ought to get a VIP membership. It costs 50 bucks but you get in free all year long. Even when there's special entertainment and the cover goes to ten dollars, you still get in free. Not only that, but you can get your guests in free, and you can bring as many people as you want. As much as you come here, you really ought to consider it."

"I will. Sounds decent."

Frank walked in and was immediately stopped by a pretty brunette who started to frisk him. She gave him a quick go over. *Must recognize me from before,* Frank thought to himself. *Probably figures I'm heading right over to Lori and she won't have a chance to latch onto me. Smart woman.*

He walked toward the bar and was immediately met by Lori. She ran up to him.

"I thought you weren't coming!"

"No, I told you I'd be here, but that I would probably be late. You're still planning on coming with me tonight aren't you?"

"Yes, but I can't leave till seven."

"Why's that?"

"Because that's the time Travis is leaving."

"Can you keep me awake?"

"You're damn right I can."

"How about a drink?"

"I'll have a Bud Light. Where do you want to sit?"

"The bar for now."

There were two empty stools on the back side of the bar. Frank sat at one. Lori stood next to him very close. There was nothing contrived or fake about it. She didn't snuggle up next to him to make tips. She wanted to be close at his side because she liked him. *But*, he reasoned, *that was her job--to make all of her customers think they were special.*

"I've missed you." Her eyes met his as she said the words.

"I've only been gone for one day. You've forgotten last night already?"

"I'll never forget last night. It's just that Frank, you are my best friend in the world, and I've missed my best friend."

"Now you are really good, Lori. I've told you before, at least I think I've told you before that I like associating with those who are the best in their field. You are the best at what you do, and I like that. You're good looking--you are a great dancer--and you have the ability to make your customers feel that you really care for them. What the hell Lori--you know that I know the way this game is played. Trouble is, you have me almost believing you."

"Believe it Frank. You are my best friend in the world. The girls I worked with--they always get mad at me because they think I'm always taking their best customers away from them. I never took anybody's customer away. I can't help it if the guys like me better because I'm skinnier than they are or because I'm more fun than they are. The guys come over to me. You know yourself that I don't go over to them. Why are they so mean to me? I never did anything to hurt any of them."

"You just said it. They're jealous. So they're going to tear you down. And they do. But some of them really like you."

"I don't think so. No one over there's done anything for me-- none of the other girls anyway. But you, you like me because I am me. I always said you'd find me no matter where I was. You know who I am, how I feel. I've told you things, Frank, that I've told no one before. I love you Frank. You are kind. You are smart and brave. You're fun. And you've got a great body."

"I've got a great body?" There was mild surprise in his voice. Frank knew he had a thin, strong body. Especially for someone in his forties. He was not aware that a young girl who stripped for a living, especially a girl as pretty as Lori, would consider it to be all that outstanding.

"Yes Frank. You've got a great body. It's a hard body. Like mine."

"So what does this have to do with friendship?"

"Not much I suppose. It's just that . . . I trust you. You'd never hurt me. I hope I never hurt you."

"Like I've said, Lori, you are good, real good. You are utterly believable."

"I am because I'm telling you the truth. I could make a lot more money than spending time with you. Don't take me wrong. I want to spend the time with you. When you're here, I forget about the money. We always have a great time, have a lot of laughs, get drunk, and the time passes so quickly. Don't I always come over to you, no matter who I am with? And don't I always stay with you? Think about it, Frank."

"You're right. But I'm still not convinced."

"We'll continue this conversation later. Right now they're calling me up on stage. Come with me."

Lori slid her hands under his arms and lifted upwards. Frank hopped off the stool. She took him by his hand and walked quickly to her stage holding his hand in the air higher than normal. The gesture was meant to show the whole place that she was proud to be with him. "I'm playing some new music. It's for you. I think you'll like it." The jukebox came alive. Lori kicked off her shoes and started to dance around the pole. Then she began to climb it, a blonde monkey, her heels pressed together around the pole while she used her arms to pull herself up. She went fifteen feet up in the air so that she was almost level with the upper floor. Lori hung there above the stage for a few seconds smiling down on Frank, a little puppy looking for approval. Then she started down. He handed Lori her glass of beer. She stood in front of him drinking it down, eyes darting around the room taking in the crowd. Lori would miss nothing. It would be next to impossible for one of her customers to come in unobserved. Then she swiftly stepped backwards and stood on her hands. Gently lowering herself so that she now stood on her head Lori pulled her legs over her head so that they rested on the edge of the stage just inches away from Frank. Doubled over before him she offered herself to him, her legs practically straddling his face.

He fought back the urge to do something to her that would get them both kicked out of the place. He looked for her pretty face and found it somewhere beneath her contorted body. Her eyes were slits while her forehead seemed to contract with the effort of balancing herself. Her hair seemed blonder, her face smoother, younger. She was a different Lori, practically unrecognizable. He spoke to the pretty face that was upside down against the stage.

"I feel a little foolish up here," said Frank. "I want you, but I can't make myself do anything about it. These guys all look so ridiculous up here on stage with their tongues hanging out bending all over the dancers in order to suck their breasts or worse."

"You just feel uneasy because we're friends. You didn't feel that way with me when I was over at the Sports Bar."

"Yeah, and you weren't doing what you do here over at the Sports Bar either."

"What's different about my act?"

"You are much cruder now. You show it all and stick it in the guys' faces. They probably expect that of you here though."

"Didn't I do those things at the Sports Bar too?"

"You did, but it's not the same. Here you really flaunt your pussy. There you just showed it. There's a difference."

Lori pulled her legs back over her head whipping her body backwards so that she now sat in front of him on the edge of the stage. She took his beer glass from him and started to drink from it.

"I like it when you watch me dance. I really like showing off to you."

"I think you just plain like showing off."

"Can you believe that two years ago when I first started dancing I was real quiet?"

"I believe it."

They talked for several more minutes. Frank sat at the edge of the stage in shorts, his bare knees resting against it. Lori kneeled in front of him her face almost touching his.

"Gotta dance Frank. We've been talking long enough. Here's a dollar to tip me. Put it in my shoe and be obvious about it." She pulled a dollar from her G-string, folding it before she handed it to him. He put it on the stage. A minute later he unfolded it and stuffed it into her shoe. Lori smiled down on him.

"Thank-you for tipping me for my dance."

It was the last selection from the jukebox. She took her G-string off allowing it to slip around her ankles. With one fluid motion she kicked it off. She stood close to him her lower body almost touching his face. He leaned forward to kiss her, then thinking better of it, backed off slightly.

"I want you but I can't do what I want to do here. This bothers me. I can get in the hot tub and make love to you in front of the whole room, but I just can't cut it on the stage."

"We know each other too well. Is it that much different from what we used to do at the Sports Bar?" she asked.

"We didn't do that much at the Sports Bar. Besides, I've changed since then. I just can't get into this stuff anymore. I'm not here for the lap dances, or the privates. I'm here because of you."

"Hey I've got a great idea. There's this new girl. This is her first night. She's up next. Do you mind if we go over to her stage after I'm through?"

"I'll do it. What are you up to Lori? Another of your derelict games?"

"You'll like it. I guarantee it."

The song ended. Lori gathered her clothes and led him over to one of the other stages. A brunette, perhaps twenty-one, five foot seven, one hundred-twenty or so stood there.

"Frank, this is Laura. Laura, this is Frank. You can dance for him. Just don't let me bother you even though I'm watching. Do whatever you want to do to him."

Frank sat in front of the stage as Lori sat in the chair to his right. Lori motioned for Laura to come over to Frank. Laura came over to Frank so that she kneeled close to him her naked breasts almost touching his face. That was it. She did not thrust them into his face, and he didn't try to kiss them.

"Come on Laura. You've got to put them right in his face. All the customers like that. Let him kiss on them. Just don't let him suck on them too hard." The voice was Lori's. *Just what was she up to now?* thought Frank. *Was she really trying to get the girl off to a good start by teaching her or was she trying to stir something up? With Lori it was difficult to tell.* Laura leaned into Frank so that her left breast gently grazed his mouth. He took it into his mouth softly and held her nipple between his teeth as he licked it with his tongue.

"Time out. You two don't have to do that forever," warned Lori. "He's my boyfriend."

"I didn't know you cared, Lori," said Frank.

"Okay. Okay. Laura--sit on the edge of the stage so that you are facing Frank." Laura sat on the edge of the stage allowing her legs to dangle over the edge and touch the floor.

"No, you can't have your legs over the edge touching the floor. You have to be on the stage--all of you. And he can't get up on the stage," said Lori.

Laura brought her legs up in front of her.

"Now just relax. You look like you're about to go into labor. Now spread your legs and wrap them around his neck. Then take the weight off your ass and onto your arms." Laura followed Lori's instructions, wrapping her legs around Frank's neck, but her butt remained firmly planted on the stage.

"Lift your ass off the stage. Levitate your body by raising yourself with your arms." Lori almost shouted the instructions. This time Laura raised herself horizontally with her arms lifting her backside off the stage.

"Okay Laura, you've got the idea. Now go do that to those other guys." Lori pointed at three men who sat at the other end of the stage. Then Lori opened her purse and handed Frank a five. Laura got up and started to walk away.

"Hey Laura. Come back here." This time Lori was shouting. "You forgot the most important thing. Your tip." Laura walked back to Frank, pulling her G-string away from her stomach, depositing the five as he did so. She then went over to the three men at the end of the stage. By the time her music ended she had only gotten to the second man staying with him for several minutes only. At the end of the song Laura picked herself up off the stage and walked away.

"Laura, come over here," Lori shouted. Lori and Frank remained seated in order to observe Laura with the men at the end of the bar. Laura came up to Lori and Frank.

"How much money did you collect?"

"Three. Why?"

"Didn't you collect from both those guys?"

"No, but I was only with the second man for a few minutes."

"But you did dance for him right?"

"Sure, but."

"Then you stay with him until he tips you. You danced for him. He owes you a tip. It's that simple."

"Brittany---to the door--Brittany--to the door." It was the PA system.

"Frank, they're having me cover the door. Frisking time.

Come with me, please."

He followed her to the door. A waitress came over to take their drink order.

"I'll have a Budweiser. Lori, are you still drinking Jack and Coke?"

"Sure."

Frank looked at the waitress. She was in her thirties--close to forty. Pleasant looking--a little overweight.

"I'm Frank. Lori and I are buddies. We've known each other for a year."

"I'll say you two are buddies. I watched you two in the hot tub last night. Both of you put on quite a show. By the way, my name's Jean."

"I'll never forget that name, Jean. I like it."

Jean went away to get their drinks as two black men walked in. Lori intercepted them.

"Sorry but I've got to frisk you. We do it to everyone." She ran her hands up and down the first man's body leaving his crotch to the last. Then she frisked the second man. After they walked out of earshot, she returned to Frank.

"If there's one thing I hate is niggers. I don't know why, but I just don't like them."

"Well I think they're all right. At least most of them," said Frank.

Lori started for the stage. Four men were already sitting there. Frank knew that she would slight them to spend more time with him. She wasn't so foolish as to ignore them, but she would be obvious about whom she preferred.

"Lori, why don't I stay out of it this time. I'll talk to the waitresses or whoever will care to listen to me. Meet me back at the bar, okay?"

"Sure."

Frank went to the back of the bar and ordered a Budweiser from the bartender. By the time he had paid for his beer and received the correct change, Lori was well into her act. She straddled a man's face as the man tried to lick her between her legs. She pulled back and shook her finger at him. Lori turned around and crouched on all fours with her rear in the man's face. He started to grab her by her buttocks at the same time shoving his face between her legs. She pulled forward so that he had to let go. One of the other men pointed at Lori. Another man laughed. It was obvious that all four were friends. Lori got up and walked up to the next man kneeling before him. He put his finger in her navel and started to make circular motions with his hand. The other men looked on laughing among themselves.

For these men Lori was a piece of meat, thought Frank. *She's here to be fondled.* He saw insensitive eyes bulging with lust. *They could not know--would never know how she had just tipped the new girl, Laura, with her own money. They'd never find out that she loved her five children. And they would never guess that she'd fight for what she believed in or stand in between two men in order to protect one of her favorite customers. They would never see her smile her tender Lori smile, and they could never conceive that this woman cried--a lot.*

But she was here, and she was allowing this to happen. This was her choice. The question for Frank was, *why? Was it possible that she really enjoyed doing this? Or was she only doing it to maximize her income--using what she considered her best asset-- doing the dancing bit better than anyone else--taking it to the limit- -all the time knowing that she was being cruelly exploited just so that she could raise a family?*

He was going to show her the pictures as soon as they sat down again. If she was coming home with him, he wouldn't have to show her the pictures yet. She had almost convinced him that she was going to follow through this time, but he knew better. He kept on thinking about the Statistics class he had once taken. In class he had learned that if one flipped a coin 15 times in a row and the coin turned up heads each time, one could figure that the coin had a probability of coming up heads something like 99.99 % on the 16th toss. Since the normal coin would show heads 50% of the time if one tossed it often enough, one could determine that there was something wrong with this particular coin. Lori had never followed through on meeting him on the outside, not even for lunch. Frank decided that there was absolutely no way she was coming home with him tonight. Even now, he figured she had no intentions of doing so, and that the reason why she failed to keep her other promises was the same reason why she would fail him this time as well. The only thing that surprised him is that she had not yet told him that she couldn't come.

Someone came up behind him. He felt a woman's arms being placed around his waist. Then for a second he felt her hands fondle him.

"I hope that you know me."

"I know you quite well. Better than you think." It was Lori. "Didn't you notice me coming off the stage? You must really be out of it."

"Not really," said Frank, "Just plunged deep in thought. It's noisy in here. Do you think we can go upstairs?"

"I'll ask the D.J. See what he says."

She led him upstairs holding his hand. The D.J. looked up at them as they came up.

"We're not doing a private. We just came up to talk. It's really noisy. You don't mind, do you?" Lori asked.

"As long as you stay close to here, it's all right by me. Management doesn't want you doing anything on your own so just stay within my sight."

"Come on Frank. Let's go over there. We can sit over the hot tub. Two girls are going to do a show in a little while."

They sat at a small table upstairs. Their view of the hot tub was excellent since the balcony was only a foot away from their chairs. Frank pulled the envelope of pictures out of his back pocket and handed it to Lori.

"These are pictures of my favorite ski resort, Sun Valley. I'm showing them to you because I would like to take you there this winter. The only thing is that I'm afraid you wouldn't show up just like you haven't shown up for anything else. So I'm giving you the hard sell in the hope that you will show me that I can count on you. I want you to look at these pictures carefully. Drink them in. Imagine the big mountain, skiing down it, dry snowflakes coming off your ski tips gently bouncing off your face. Imagine a town of only three thousand people having sixty excellent restaurants with you having your choice of any one of them. Beautiful scenery, superlative entertainment."

"This is the Sun Valley that I know. It's got one great big mountain. Baldy. More mountain than most people can handle. The place has better food than most people can appreciate. You, Lori, have excellent athletic ability. You'd pick up skiing faster than practically anyone I know."

"I'd probably fall all the way down the mountain and end up in a wheelchair. Frank, how do you expect me to learn how to ski?"

"Simple. I'll put you in ski school. Sun Valley's got an excellent ski school. They'd put you on the little mountain, Dollar.

They'd coddle you. I'm willing to bet that within three days you'll be ready for the big mountain, Baldy."

"Suppose I'm not ready in three days?"

"Doesn't matter. We'll have a great time together in the mornings and especially at night. But I've seen you dance, and I've seen you with chopsticks. I've never seen anyone master chopsticks so fast. Lori, I kid you not, you have uncommon athletic ability. But you've got to really want it. You've got to want to go there. I want to take you because I want to take someone I can have a great time with. And you need to go. You deserve to go. Get a babysitter. Tell Travis you have an Aunt Martha who's off dying in Philadelphia or somewhere. Tell him you need a week to bury her. Explain to him that the power went out, all the local men are fighting in a war somewhere, and that you have to dig every shovelful of dirt yourself and that it will take you a week. Tell him something. Anything. What the hell! You've paid your dues. You've paid more than your dues."

"I can just see me on skis. I'll probably get a ski pole up someone's butt."

"Probably, but look at the fun you'd have doing it."

Lori pulled out the first picture. Frank had taken it from the second story of the Sun Valley Inn. In the foreground was the hot tub just outside the Inn. The pool was circular, perhaps fifty feet in diameter. Spruce trees surrounded it on three sides. The Sun Valley Inn itself furnished the fourth boundary. The film showed steam rising off the water's surface. A fence just inside the evergreens surrounded the pool. Looming in the background and dominating its surroundings was Baldy , steep white ribbons going down it in all directions, these ribbons being the ski runs themselves. One quarter mile away from the Sun Valley Inn and directly in line with Baldy was a large building that appeared to be made of logs.

"That's Baldy," said Frank. "The coach of the American women's ski team that won all Olympic Gold metals a few years back is the owner of a French restaurant, named Michelle's. He considers it the best ski mountain in the world and moved from France to Sun Valley to ski it. I agree with him except I don't like the food in his restaurant."

"Why's that?" Lori asked.

"His steaks taste as if they are flavored with Vitalis. Thank god for Kristin Cooper and Debbie Armstrong that he's a better coach than a chef. That large building in the background framing the mountain is the Sun Valley Lodge. It was built in 1936 to accommodate the rich. Looks like it's made of huge logs, but it's actually built of concrete so that the whole building could be made fireproof. You can't tell it though until you get several feet away and thump the concrete with your fist. Take a look at the next picture."

"What's that?"

"That's a hot tub. I actually stayed in Ketchum, the town Ernest Hemingway built his house in. Ketchum is a real town nowadays filled with restaurants, bars, and shops. It is less than 1 mile from Sun Valley. Sun Valley is a large development of Condos, shops, a golf course, restaurants, nightclubs, and the Sun Valley resort itself. It is owned by the Sun Valley Corporation. The Sun Valley Road which goes from Ketchum to Sun Valley is lined with a low fence which has strings of Christmas tree lights down its entire length. The hot tub in the picture as you can see is bathed in red light. It is outdoors yet protected by a roof. I stayed in a Condo only sixty feet from it. Was in it a lot after skiing and met a few of the locals there. Hey, I stayed at Horizons Four for the whole month of January two years in a row. I know the Sun Valley area like the palm of my hand. I can tell you this--I wouldn't have spent four months of my life there if I didn't find it clearly superior to all other ski resorts."

"Why do you want to take me there?"

"Because you deserve it. You think you can't go. You think because you have five kids and a boyfriend that you are never going to get away. Believe it will happen and it will happen. Believe me, Lori, I make things happen. I want to take someone I can truly have a great time with. We'd have a great time. You know that and I know it. Except."

"Except what?"

"You've got to stop standing me up. You've got to start showing me that I can count on you. I don't know why you do it, but the way things look, I could never buy you an airline ticket. You'd never make the plane. But you deserve to go, and no one else can take you where I'd be taking you, the way I'd be taking you."

"Look, I'm coming home with you tonight."

"Sure you are," Frank said doubtfully.

"Oh, one of the managers wants to talk to me. Be right

back."

Lori was gone a minute. She came back cursing under her breath, brusquely pulled her cigarettes off the table, and stood there looking at him still muttering under her breath.

"What's the matter?" he asked.

"I've got to get up on stage again. This time with a couple of girls. A Lesbian act."

"Sounds exciting. Something for the jaded. None of those types in here are there?"

"Oh, there's a few. Come on." She led him to the center of the stage and pulled a chair out for him. There up on stage close to the pole two girls joined her. Lori put her arms around the pole, her hands close together, as they tied her wrists together. Then they started to work on her from opposite sides. One, a tall thin blonde in her thirties stood in front of her while the other, a brunette, perhaps ten pounds overweight stood behind her as she kissed her neck. The brunette's lips brushed the back of Lori's neck, then started working down her back. At the same time the blonde began kissing Lori's nipples, alternating from one to the other. Then she tilted her head upwards and kissed Lori on the lips turning her mouth slightly.

So, the whole performance is simulated, thought Frank. The blonde was almost kissing Lori's lips except that her head was turned away ever so slightly. There could be no doubt that her lips were touching Lori's. However, the illusion that the two girls were frenching was believable at a distance. For Frank sitting in the center of the stage only five feet away from the three girls, the illusion didn't quite come off. Just then the brunette started to kneel between Lori's legs and began to lift her face upwards. The brunette's tongue flickered out and up into Lori's opening. Or did it? Even from where he was sitting it was difficult to tell.

Suddenly more men came over. Several took seats at the stage. Others stood close by watching intently. Lori looked over at them and smiled. The men gathered closer now in order to observe every detail of the act. Frank poured what was left of his beer into his glass and started to play with the bottle. He started reading the Anheuser Busch label. Then he began to tear off the label. A minute or two later he was finished.

Five minutes passed. Then the brunette came over to Frank while the blonde started to untie Lori. She sat on the stage with her legs up in the air around Frank's neck. He bent his head so that he could kiss her between her legs, but only for a moment.

Big fucking deal, thought Frank. *I can't believe that these guys like a lesbian show when for me the only meaningful or interesting thing about sex is what happens to me and the person I'm with. Do these guys actually get turned on by watching two girls fondle and kiss a third? Especially when management requires that the three girls carry out the act. How much difference is there between what I've just seen and what I've observed twelve year old girls doing in Thailand? How could men ever think of exploiting twelve and fifteen-year old girls? And how or why would they even dream of exploiting twenty-five year old women? After all, just ten years ago, Lori was fifteen, young and vibrant and full of dreams.* It surprised Frank that she could still be vivacious and full of life at all. And now perhaps as many as fifteen men had gathered around the three girls almost panting over what they had just seen.

These guys deserve to be taken. They deserve to be pickpocketed as they watch. So what was he, Frank, doing in the center of this whole thing? It was Lori. She had led him to where he was now sitting, lovingly by his hand. Perhaps it was easier for her having him there. If so, then was he glad to be there? The beers had taken their toll. Was he happy to be there after all? Did he want to be on the earth at all--in a world such as this one?

After the act was over, the other two girls drifted around the room collecting tips. Lori remained in the center of the stage, smiling, as men came up to tip her. After the last man had come up, Lori jumped off the stage, and approached several others who had watched but who had not yet tipped her. *Could it be that she was in her element?* Her smile, her alert posture, her whole bearing suggested the born entertainer. Frank could almost hear her saying, "Could you tip me for my act? Did you like it? Perhaps I'll do it again for you if you come see me."

After she had collected her last tip, she came back to him.

"I need a drink. Do you mind buying me a shot? Let's do a body shot."

Frank motioned for the waitress. A short thin brunette came over.

"We're going to do a body shot. We need two shots of Cuervo, some limes, and some salt. We'll be right over there." Lori pointed to a table a short distance from the bar. Frank led Lori to the table.

"What's this on your lip, Frank? Looks like some kind of burn." She touched his lip lightly.

"I was riding my dirt bike while looking at my crops. Riding it slowly the whole time smoking a cigar. A hot ember blew back into my lip and burnt the living hell out of it."

Lori bent her head toward him and started kissing him, her tongue probing the inside of his mouth. He liked the way she kissed him. Her mouth was small, her lips firm. Even her tongue, now darting quickly inside his mouth, seemed narrow and compact.

Then the waitress arrived with the Cuervo. No matter. Time for the body shot. Frank paid for the liquor--eleven dollars--while Lori got the salt ready. As soon as the waitress left, Lori unbuttoned Frank's shirt and started to suck on his nipple. When it was completely soaked in her saliva and hard, she rubbed salt all over it, after which she continued to suck it, rolling the nipple back and forth with her tongue until she had licked all the salt away. Then she picked up the first shot glass and chugged its contents. Lori finished with the lime taking it between her teeth then passing it deep into her mouth. She grabbed Frank and started to kiss him. Moving the piece of lime toward the front of her mouth Lori passed it outwards into his mouth. Frank sucked the lime backwards and then moved it toward her mouth with his tongue. Lori sucked it back into her mouth and then into his. After he had returned it to her once more, she swallowed the lime. Frank started to lick her breast. When it was wet enough she applied salt which he licked off. Lori took the shot glass, put it up to his throat, and started to pour. It came down his throat so fast that he almost choked, but he got it all down. He then took out the slice of lime and put it in his mouth. He started to kiss her again, passing the lime from his mouth into hers.

"Let's do a private. I've got an idea," Lori suggested.

"You're on, but I think we are in trouble if you have an idea."

"Let's go."

He followed her upstairs. "Let's go over there." Lori pointed to the upstairs stage which had a couch on it. Next to the couch was a pole. "Let me have your belt!" she demanded. Without another word she reached down and undid his belt buckle. Then she pulled it through the loops in his shorts. Lori now looped it tightly around his wrists and tied the other end to the pole while she forced him down into the couch.

"You are now mine." Lori dropped to her knees, parted his

legs slightly with her hands and began to run her mouth up and down his groin. Suddenly she reached under the leg of his shorts and started to stroke him. Lori started to turn her head toward the open leg of his shorts. Then she jerked upwards.

"Damn, it's Odin, the manager. Every time I come up here he's around checking up on me." She was right. A man appeared across the railing on the other side of the balcony. He came their way, walked silently past them, and disappeared down the stairs. Lori breathed a sigh of relief, and then turned to Frank.

"You're not getting away from me. Not now or ever."

"I'll bet I could get away."

"Frank, I don't think you can. Oh you might get this belt loose if you tried hard enough but you can't get away from me now. Up till now you've been the hunter. You're asked me out to lunch. You're tried to get me to your place. You've tried everything. Now the tables are reversed. Consider yourself the hunted. And I've got you all tied up."

They understood each other. He understood her now and she knew it. This was scary. He had never had that kind of bond with a woman before. Now she more than any other had a kind of power over him. What was even scarier is that he knew he wielded the same power over her.

"I am going home with you tonight, Frank. Can you believe how good it's going to be?"

"It would be good, but I won't believe it till I see it."

"I'm leaving my car in a safe place. First you are going to take me home. Then you are going to wait for me just off of Highway 55 at the Arsenal exit. There's a shell station there with a large parking lot. I'm leaving my car there all night. I'll be there as soon as Travis leaves."

The private would have been over. One song--twenty bucks--that's how it went. Several selections were played--perhaps four, five, or six. Suddenly Lori got off the couch. She took his belt off the pole and slipped it off his left arm leaving it still looped around his right.

"I think I'm up. Come on." She led him downstairs. Suddenly her face brightened into a smile. She took the belt off his arm and put it around his neck before he realized it. Lori darted in front of him and started to pull him toward the stage.

"You are my sex slave. Follow me."

Then, just as quickly as she had tethered him with his belt,

Frank bent down and scooped her off her feet lifting upwards. Lori was light as a feather. He spun her in the air in a tight circle, then carried her thirty feet to the nearest bar stool, placing her firmly upon it.

"I am not your sex slave. Don't ever forget that I am the one who's in control here."

She started to laugh, mocking him. Then she started to kiss him, her lips fluttering across his while her tongue darted back and forth inside his mouth as quickly as a snake's. Suddenly she stopped and led him to her stage. There they talked. Once or twice she asked him for a dollar tip telling him to be obvious about it so that the other employees would know that she was doing her job. A man came over to the stage and sat to their left. Lori went over to him and sat on the man's lap. The man looked forty, was short and stocky, and ugly. *Or did he just look mean?* Frank left the stage and went over to the back of the bar where he ordered a beer.

Not long after, Lori left her stage, taking her customer with her. They went upstairs. *Jesus*, thought Frank, *the guys these girls have to put up with. That man is definitely whipped with ugly stick. Besides that I don't think he's got a good bone in his body. Must get this woman out of this place. At least for tonight. Except, something's going to go wrong. Either that or she's got something up her sleeve.*

Ten minutes later Lori came downstairs. This time they sat at the bar. Suddenly the D.J. announced that the place was closing. All of the customers must leave and the girls had to go to the dressing room. Within thirty seconds every dancer had disappeared including Lori. Several of the male employees walked through the room.

"Everybody out. Come on. We're closing. You have got to leave now."

There was nothing subtle about the evacuation procedure. No last call. No chance to linger over the last half glass of beer. Frank went outside and got in his sports car to wait for Lori. Five minutes passed. Ten. Fifteen. At last she walked out the door with Rozanne. Frank then noticed the small pickup sitting next to his sports car its engine idling. It was the ugly man he didn't like. Like Frank he had waited fifteen minutes. *For which girl? Or was he simply some kind of pervert waiting for the girls to leave?* Lori started to walk by his sports car staring stonily ahead as if Frank wasn't even there. *What in the hell is going on?* Frank reached for the pack of cigars on his dash and pulled one out.

"Hey pretty woman, want a cigar?" he called out.

Lori came over and took the cigar. "It's Travis," she whispered. "I've gotta go."

"Where are you meeting me?" asked Frank.

"Over at the gas station I was telling you about. Wait there for me." Then she walked away to a car where the other girl already waited. Half a minute later the car left. At the same time the small pickup next to Frank left the parking lot only a hundred yards behind the girls.

Frank left to look for the Shell station. He already felt like a fool. Somehow he knew he had been had. But he had promised to be there and he always fulfilled his promises. *So who was the ugly man in the little pickup? Was Lori meeting him somewhere? Had he offered her a lot of money to screw her? Surely he's not Travis. Travis is young whereas this guy's around forty. And even Lori would not have a boyfriend this ugly or mean looking.* Then again, Frank was pretty drunk. Perhaps he had vastly overestimated the man's age.

Fifteen minutes later, Frank found the Shell station. He went inside to buy a coke, bought a paper, and went back to his pickup to read. The next hour passed slowly. Very slowly. She never came.

PLAYPEN

The next week, he came back. Frank walked into the Pink Giraffe not as a love sick puppy, hat in hand, hoping to do another hot tub with Lori, but as a man who was totally confident in himself and who believed he could do whatever he wanted and get away with it. Lori had left him in his convertible just last week feeling like a total idiot. She had stood him up once more. This time he wasn't even going to attempt to get her to go out with him. This time he was going to get a date with the waitress.

It was going to be the tall cute waitress who had watched them do their hot tub thing--the new girl. He had set her up perfectly. Last week she had come over to his table while Lori was in the dressing room. He and Jerry had ordered a round of drinks and he had asked her with feigned innocence "what really goes on in the hot tub." He remembered how she had laughed and said, "the sky is the limit." Frank had replied, "I was just asking because Lori and I are going to go in." And this was after Lori and he had already agreed to make love in the hot tub. Later, when she complimented him on his fine performance, she had whispered to him: "Now I guess you have found out about what goes on in the hot tub."

The girl had brought up the hot tub incident to him for a reason. It was no accident that her eyes had lit up as she talked about it. The girl had wished she had been in the hot tub with Frank instead of Lori. Then she went out of her way to communicate this to him. It was not just the words that conveyed this to him. It was the way she said it--the sensual lilt to her voice, her smile, and the way she had positioned her body close to his.

All he had to do was to show up and suggest their doing something together. Frank considered the various alternatives he could offer her such as "How about you and I doing a hot tub together" or "Come on home with me tonight" or "How about you and I taking a quick drive together in my little green sports car when you get off?" As a waitress she probably could not do the hot tub with him, but she would probably come back with something like "God, I wish I could." Then he'd reply "Well since we can't, let's just go out and make love together--not next week or tomorrow but tonight. It doesn't matter where for it can be in the parking lot for all I care just so long as we do it now." If she got in the car with him, he would pull off somewhere, pull a blanket from his trunk, and take her to the softest spot he could find on the ground.

He could get away with it with her because she had already admitted to him that she got off on the bizarre and the spontaneous--such as his hot tub performance. Totally absorbed with his thoughts about the pretty waitress, Frank strode to the rear of the bar. Hopefully Lori wouldn't see him right away. He sat back in the shadows and quietly ordered a beer from the bartender. He looked around the room for the waitress. One good thing about sitting at the back of the bar was that he could observe most of the room without being easily noticed himself.

The waitress was not in sight. *Had she quit? Was this her night off? It really didn't matter. All that counted was that Lady Luck was not riding with him tonight.* It looked like he'd have to go with option number 2--Miss Undependable. He'd come back for the waitress some other time. Frank slunk deeply into his bar stool, trying to make himself as inconspicuous as possible. It would be interesting to see how long it would take for Lori to realize that he was there. He looked over toward the lady's dressing room. Two women came out. One, a pretty blonde came right over to him.

"Mind if I sit with you?" she asked.

"Have a seat. I don't mind at all, but you are going to be disappointed."

"Why's that?"

"Because I'm waiting for Brittany. However, I'll buy you a beer while we wait for her. What kind do you want?"

"Will you buy me a shot instead?"

Frank turned to the bartender. "Bartender, will you get her a shot of whatever she wants."

"I'll have a shot of root beer schnapps." The girl looked over at the bartender who quickly returned with her drink. Frank paid the man who promptly returned with his change.

"Do you want me to go get her?" the girl asked.

"No. Let's just see how long it takes her to find me."

"Does she know you very well?"

Frank laughed. "We sat in the hot tub together last week."

"Now I remember you." The girl studied him closely. Then she got up and positioned her bar stool closer to his.

"So how many guys do the hot tub?" he asked.

"Not many," she replied as she seated herself. "Usually it's the girls. They've not really pushed the hot tub here except for the lesbian shows. Most guys don't even realize it's available to them."

Just then Lori came out of the dressing room and walked right up to them. Frank didn't even see her look over at them. *It was*, he reasoned, *almost as if she has a nose for Harring.* He laughed to himself over his private little joke. Certainly she would have appreciated it. *Time for the blonde to go. Too bad. She was good looking. a lot of them are, he mused, but there will always be another so long as I have the money to play.*

"Hi Lori. If you get someone's attention, I'll buy you a beer." Lori grabbed the barstool that was on his left and positioned it close to his. She sat down and leaned over him. The message was not lost on the blonde who immediately stood up and headed for the dressing room.

"I'm up next, so I had better get over to the dressing room. Thanks for the beer."

"I don't like her," said Lori.

"Because she was sitting with me probably."

"No. I just don't like her. She's always cutting down the other girls. She gets mad when they get more tips than her."

"She's good looking enough to do all right," said Frank.

"Oh sometimes she does okay, but I think some of her customers get onto her and move onto other girls."

"Okay, Lori, what happened last week? What do you think about the fact that I sat for over an hour in a gas station parking lot looking like a complete dork? Funny thought, isn't it?"

"That was Travis in the car when Rozanne and I went out. He found out about us in the hot tub. You see Frank, Rozanne got very jealous of you and me in the hot tub. She cut herself in with us the first time because she is so money hungry. Then she figured that she could get in with us the second time except I wouldn't let her. She told me that I had no right to keep you all to myself. Then I told her that you and I had been friends for years. So when she got in the car with Travis last week, she told him that she thought we had been fucking in the hot tub. When I got in the car, I could tell that he was really mad. Then when we got home he beat the shit out of me. Instead of meeting you I had to go to the hospital to get these." Lori bent her head down to show Frank the stitches.

Frank carefully put his fingers into her hair and probed tenderly. There was a raised area along her scalp over an inch long. It was too dark to see the stitches but the swollen area was very noticeable. He considered the question of her getting beat up for supposedly fucking him in the hot tub. *Maybe, maybe not.*

Probably another one of her stories, but the important thing is that she's here and so am I and we are going to have some fun. He caught the eye of the bartender and ordered two beers.

The beer arrived. Lori grabbed hers and drank from the bottle, greedily. "I feel like getting a little drunk. Can I get a shot to go with this?"

"Bartender, can you get Lori a shot of whatever she wants," said Frank.

"Make that a shot of Cuervo," said Lori. "And bring me two limes."

When her drink arrived, Lori drank it down at once as she picked up one of the limes. Putting it in her mouth, she motioned to Frank. Lori then grabbed his head with both hands and pulled him toward her. She started to kiss him. She thrust the lime into his mouth with her tongue. After he passed it back to her, Lori retained it at first, then ever so slowly worked it back to his mouth. Frank swallowed the lime, then suddenly started blowing into her mouth. He exhaled without inhaling, eventually running out of air. Not to be outdone, Lori started blowing into his mouth. It was a question of who could hold one's breath the longest. Frank's lungs started to hurt. When he felt he couldn't hold on any longer, Lori pulled away so that she could breathe again.

"I hope you two are having fun. Anything I can get you?" It was Jean.

"No, Jean, not at the moment," said Frank.

"Come on over to the jukebox with me. I'm going to be up soon. You can help me pick out my music," Lori urged. She took him by the hand and led him to the jukebox. "Anything on there you want me to play?" She asked.

Frank pored over the listings on the jukebox. *Somehow, it wouldn't make any difference what she played*, he thought. *What was it about her that caused him to lose track of things*? He didn't care what was playing. He didn't care what he was drinking. Time eluded him, flying by unnoticed until suddenly they both woke up to the fact that hours had passed. He had been right that first time he had thought of her when he played *Face in the Crowd* on his truck stereo. There was something that pulled them together-- impossible to explain to others--and that he didn't quite understand. It would have been easy to call it infatuation. That would have been a one way emotional overflow in one of them, and not necessarily the other. If he were the one who was infatuated, then how could one explain that she had just traipsed through the room with him hand in hand to pick out her music selections? Not to mention the fact that whenever he was there, she had practically forgotten all of the other men in the place. Not to mention that she was giving up income potential to be with him when he was there. She had told him and other girls had told him as well that a good-looking stripper who knew her business could easily pull down $300 on a decent night. *What did she make when she was around him? Perhaps $100-$150, and much of that from her lap dances and privates with other men?*

Other girls did not wander around the room hand in hand with their customers. He never saw any of the other girls bring their customers over to the jukebox to help pick out their selections. He had been stood up, time and time again. It would bother him when he woke up the next morning, but at this moment of time, he had forced that unpleasant reality into the back of his mind. In the long run, he reasoned he would be dead. In a few short years he would be old and feeble. Lori had five children, so there was no way that they could make a future together. It was the here and now that counted as if both he and Lori were perched on the knife's edge of the present, both of them acutely aware of the sheer drop off on either side of them that represented both the past and the future. Yet that knife's edge of time, so precarious, so thinly devoid of substance, meant everything to them.

Frank thought about the message from Tom Petty's *Face in the Crowd*. For him at least, that face was one out of many-- perhaps out of millions--one face that showed itself--possibly for only a few seconds-- to the other as a bright light different from all the rest. There was the meeting of the eyes, the flash of recognition from one to the other that there was a soul out there like one's own, then the parting which ended with the incredible sadness that they would never meet again. A vision in his mind appeared of a traveler of life on a train, which had just stopped for a few moments to pick up and drop off passengers. The other appeared suddenly outside the train, on the railing. The passenger and the one who had just gotten off saw each other--there was the flash of understanding--and then the train closed its doors--and began to creak forward. Seconds later, the vision--gone.

Five minutes later Frank was sitting on the edge of a stage feeling like a total fool yet enjoying it because Lori was with him. It didn't matter what they did together--they had fun. If he had been sitting at someone else's stage he would have stayed only for a moment, gotten up, gone to the bar, and ordered the stiffest drink he could imagine. Lori approached the pole and grabbed it in her right hand. Then she started to walk around the pole all 108 pounds of her being slowly transferred from the floor to the pole as she picked up momentum. Soon her feet left the floor as her body spun around the pole. Centrifugal force brought her legs almost to a horizontal position parallel to the floor. Lori shifted her hand position ever so slightly and started to slow down. A few seconds later her feet once again touched the floor. Then she started to dance. Her face took in the crowd. She smiled, arched her eyes the way a little girl does after having pulled off a prank, and looked down at Frank. She pointed at him. Then she started to talk to him, except that he couldn't hear her. *What's she doing?* he asked himself. *Trying to discuss the conditions of the dance floor? Describing one of the other men in the bar? Or telling me she wants to make love to me? Who knows?* As she danced, Frank noticed a curious phenomenon that he had noticed before. Her face became radiant as her shoulders started to swell. *Was it his imagination or did she start to grow before his very eyes?* She became taller as her chest became broader, and her back became wider. Perhaps the act of dancing had started to make her high, to cause the adrenaline to flow. Or was she now expanding her chest by breathing deeply as she took in more oxygen. Illusion or reality, Lori was obviously getting into her dancing, and for one reason or another, because of it, becoming a different Lori. She was--beautiful--perfect in form--tall and strong--a blonde sex goddess.

Lori started to climb the pole like a boy climbing a rope. Soon she was fifteen feet up and as high as she could go. She looked down, not at the crowd, but at him. She smiled as she gazed into his eyes. Then she came down, and started to stand on her head. Upside down she looked out at Frank through slitted eyes and started to jabber away. *She might as well be speaking in tongue*, he thought, *the place is too damn loud*. Lori then began to lower her legs behind her head as she started to arch her back. She soon had her legs and back bent way over her head behind her with her legs touching the floor.

Finally tired of her acrobatics, Lori came over to Frank and sat down on the platform with her legs hanging over the edge of the stage. They talked and talked until finally she looked up at the floor manager who sat near the bar shaking his head. Lori slipped onto

Frank's lap.

"Looks like I'd better do a lap dance. There for a while I forgot where I was."

She put her arms around Frank's neck and started to rock back and forth on his lap. Without warning she got up and remounted him, this time with her back facing him. She reached back with her hand and started to play with him.

"Just a hint of what is to come," she teased.

"What's that, Lori?"

"The hot tub. I'm going to have a ball. Two of them. Your balls," she laughed.

"Then put in for it right away. You know how they are around here about being slow."

After the set ended Lori stood up on the stage and started to gather her things while he waited. Lori put on her top, walked off the stage, and took him by the hand. "Let's go over there and sit at that table." This time she pointed at a table in front of the bar. After they had seated themselves, Jean, their waitress, came up to take their order.

"Now what can I get you two lovebirds?" She asked.

Lori looked at Frank and grabbed him by both hands, her eyes studying his. Then she arched her eyebrows and smiled.

"Jean, I think Frank wants to do a body shot with me. He's going to need one because we're going to do the hot tub together. Bring us two shots of Cuervo, some limes, lots of salt. Bring me also a Jack and Coke and get him a Budweiser."

After Jean hurried off, Lori turned to Frank to say "I'm leaving you for a minute to tell the D.J." Then she rushed off leaving him alone at the table. Frank reached into his pocket and found that he only had thirty bucks left. *No matter*, he told himself, *there's more in the car*. He went out to the car where he opened the little center glove box with his key. There, inside the little compartment that rested behind the gear shift lever between the seats he found a hundred dollar bill and several twenties. He took out one of the twenties and the hundred and went back into the Pink Giraffe. He found Lori upstairs talking to the D.J. Frank handed the man the hundred.

"Come on back into the manager's office with me for a second. We'll get some change, towels, and swimming trunks," the D.J. told them. Then he got out of his seat and walked over to a little room a short distance away. This was the first time that Frank had seen the D.J. when he was not sitting down. The man was totally bald--probably had his head shaven-- but Frank had already noticed that before. What surprised Frank was the man's size. A good six feet four or so, the D.J. probably tipped the scales at 240 or better. *Probably doubled as a bouncer.*

A short chubby man in his early thirties was waiting for them in the office. *So this was the club manager*, thought Frank. *Has to be because he sure as hell isn't the bouncer. Definitely doesn't tend bar, and he doesn't work the door either.* In fact, Frank had never seen the man before.

Lori went over to the manager and started to discuss something with him. The manager handed her a pair of swim trunks and a towel. The D.J. strode out of the office after giving the manager the hundred. Lori returned to Frank grabbing him by the hand. Her face broke into a grin. "Guess what. I didn't know this before, but we can stay in the hot tub as long as we want just so long as no one else wants to use it."

"Come on," she urged. "We've got a body shot down below. Jean's down there waiting."

They returned to the table. The drinks were all there--the two shot glasses, the Jack and Coke, his beer, and the salt and limes. *Good job Jean*, Frank said to himself almost aloud.

"Come on--let's do it!" Lori exclaimed. "What are we waiting for?"

This time she unbuttoned his shirt all the way, slipping it part way off his shoulders. "Sorry, but the place won't let us take it off," Lori complained. "I want to show you off." Lori got down on her knees and started to lick his nipple. Then she went over to the other one, licking and sucking it also. "Let's do a double." She laughed. After thoroughly wetting both nipples and a good part of his chest with her saliva, Lori started to apply the salt which stuck to him. Bending over him once more she resumed her sucking, first biting down hard on his nipple, then taking it firmly into her mouth. At first she pulled her head back and forth while clenching his nipple in her teeth. Elongating his nipple, then contracting it just as quickly Lori started to go faster and faster until it started to hurt. Then she turned to the other nipple until she had sucked and bitten all the salt off it as well.

"Oh, oh," some salt just fell down here." She started to lick his chest exploring it from the top to the bottom with her tongue. Then she got to his belly and began to lick his navel."

"Did you know I was in the Naval Academy?" she asked. "Learned a lot there too."

"When you said that, you just caused me to lose my erection," said Frank. He tried his best to act disgusted.

"My turn." Lori reached behind her back and loosened her top which she now slid over her head. Frank eyed a large nipple and started to lick it with the tip of his tongue, then engulfed the nipple in his mouth. He played with the nipple, swirling it back and forth with his tongue until it got hard. Taking it from his mouth, he now licked her breast wetting it down with his saliva. He turned to the other nipple and dragged it into his mouth. When both nipples and breasts were thoroughly soaked with saliva, he started to apply the salt. Then he reached for the shot glass and started to drink the Cuervo.

"Here, let me help." Lori took the shot glass from his hands and began to pour the whole shot of Tequila into his mouth. She snickered while she poured. "Come on now, be a good boy and drink it all down." When she had finished pouring it down Frank's throat, she once more kneeled on the floor and pulled his knees slightly apart. Bending over his lap, Lori started to rub her breasts against his groin.

"Brittany to the door." The P.A. system blared.

"Oh shit!" Lori exclaimed. "I've gotta go frisk people. Will you come with me?"

"Be right behind you."

"Then let's do the hot tub. Get in it early."

Lori got up and sauntered over to the door leaving her drink on the table. Frank followed close behind. For the moment no customers were coming in. She went to the cigarette machine and bought a pack of Marlborough Lights. Next to the machine was a chair. Frank climbed up on the chair and perched on its back, his sandaled feet resting on the seat. Two men came, paid the cover, and were about to walk past when Lori stopped them. She frisked the first, then the second. Frank was surprised that she didn't fondle them. Usually the girls did this in order to entice the customers to their stage.

While Lori was busy frisking them, Frank evaluated his own appearance. He was wearing a light blue pair of shorts with a navy-colored belt which perfectly matched a short sleeved sport shirt of identical color. He had chosen the colors carefully. Dark blue or navy would pick up the blue in his eyes. It would also serve to show his tan off to advantage. Since he weighed only 165 pounds, the shorts would show off his long and well-muscled legs as well as to accentuate his narrow waist. Long ago he had decided that the other guys could wear long pants and white shirts or whatever. He had worked long hours on the farm and had become quite brown in the process. Frank had run many miles which had kept him trim. Most people were not disciplined enough to run the miles he ran and their bodies showed it. *Let them hide their bodies*, he reasoned. He also decided that there was no more appropriate place than a strip joint to show off his.

But there was a little more to it than that. Since he had started the divorce, he had felt free for the first time in his life. He had thrown off the smothering influence of Karen and her two children. Since he had done that, he had a lot more spending power and a lot more time to do what he wanted. He felt freer than he had ever felt as a single man prior to his marriage. The reason, he believed, was that he had always been looking for someone with whom he could develop a close relationship. Now with seven and some half years of marriage behind him he clearly understood the error of his ways. Close relationships led to marriage which was the worst institution that had ever been inflicted upon men. Therefore, close relationships were a thing to be avoided at all costs. He could now--and should-- refrain from looking for the "right woman." This left him free to pursue all the wrong women-- a goal which ensured that more women would be available to him than ever before. The sandals, the shorts, and even the little sports car were symbolic of his new outlook on life--that life was short, that there were no answers, and that he had no one to answer to. He was going to dress the way he liked--because he could. He would drive whatever he wanted to drive because it felt good. Let others drive their idiotic looking vans so they could have more room for their families or because mini vans were now the "in thing." He had his truck and he had his sports car, and if the sports car wouldn't hold enough, he'd just take less baggage along the way.

Lori came over to him and snuggled up next to him. Now if he had her doing this back at home, other women would say: "she's way too young for him, or look at the way she dresses showing off her legs and ass the way she does." He imagined himself replying: "Oh, but she feels so good in my arms" or "She dresses the way she does because she has the legs and an ass to show off, unlike the rest of you."

"Come on, we're done here. Let's go back to our table," Lori suggested.

Someone was sitting at their table. Lori had left her Long Island Tea at the table practically untouched. A tall man sat in Lori's seat. She reached over him and grabbed her drink. The man glared at her.

"Stay the fuck away from my drink," he warned angrily.

"Your drink. That's my drink. He bought it for me." Lori pointed at Frank.

"Give it back to me," the man growled.

"Leave her alone," said Frank. "She's with me and you are at our table."

"Shut up. I'm talking to her. Not you."

"Up yours!" Frank replied.

The man got out of his chair glaring at Frank. Frank couldn't believe how big he was. At least six foot five, the man had to weigh 240 or more. Why did he, Frank, have to get into it with a man who was undoubtably the largest man in the bar? If he wasn't the biggest, then by now he was certainly the maddest. They would have already started swinging at each other, but the man had been sitting on the opposite side of the table from where Lori and Frank were standing. The man started to come around the table so that he could get at Frank. Frank asked himself whether he should hit the man in the head or whether he should punch him in the guts. He tucked his right hand low alongside his waist and mentally started to measure the distance from his hand to the man's head. Because of the man's height he would be hard to reach. Frank considered jabbing him with a hard left to the face; then hitting him as hard as he could with the right hand which he prayed would be the finishing blow. It had to be because by that time Frank would be under 240 pounds of fury. Just as the man cleared the table, Lori jumped between them.

"Get out of my way bitch!" the man roared.

Jesus, thought Frank, *now this is one hell of a bitch. She might be a lot of things. She's undependable and she makes up a lot of stories which are total bullshit but she's one glorious woman. A hell of a woman. She's going to get clobbered by this guy. I'm going in. I'm going to get my ass kicked, but I'm going to get first blood and that guy's going to get hurt.*

"Out of the way, Lori!" Frank ordered. "Let me at him."

Just then the D.J. got among all of them. Then the bartender came up and grabbed the bully around the shoulders. *Two big black men*, thought Frank. *Thank God for big black men*. He loved them both. Within two seconds all hell would have broken loose. Lori would have been decked, and he and the bully would have been at each other. He wondered if he could have knocked the man down with the first several punches. It would have been a bad scene and he might have been kicked out of the place along with the bully. That would have meant the end to hot tubs for him--at least at the Pink Giraffe. *But then he would have gone through fire for Lori.*

"Come on, Frank. Follow me," Lori urged. "Let's go over there."

She led him across the room to an area they had never sat at before. She pulled a chair out for him. "Here, sit down. And calm down. I'm finding Jean to buy us a couple of beers. My treat." Lori started off when Jean appeared obviously looking for them.

"I'm sorry that happened," said Jean. "We don't normally have that kind of trouble here, and I shouldn't have let him take your table. He comes in here every now and then and usually he's all right. Never causes trouble. I don't know what got into him tonight. Must be real drunk. What can I get you two? The bartender told me to bring you whatever you want on the House."

"Oh just get us a couple of beers," said Lorry. "That is unless Frank wants something different."

"No. Two beers will be fine," replied Frank.

Jean rushed off as Lori sat next to him. "That sure was close. That guy was big, Frank, and mean. I wonder what got into him. And the son of a bitch took our drink."

Frank looked into Lori's eyes and studied her. This was the second time that she had stood between him and a fight. He recollected the last time he had seen Chanel. He remembered that day he had left her with that nut case, the imbecile with the dolls, sitting at a table at the Injection Pump. Frank had felt so vulnerable then, and had truly believed that Karen had him under observation. At the time, he believed that Karen had hired a private detective who had followed him to the Injection Pump. He had never forgotten how the nutcase had called out to him, "You old goat" as he walked down the stairs. He remembered how badly he wanted to remount the stairs to tear the nutcase in half-- how he would have done so in a minute except for his paranoia about being watched. And Chanel had just sat there, a little smile on her face, drinking it all in. And so it was with most women, thought Frank. They would deny it, but secretly they probably felt a little glow of self-satisfaction about having helped cause the fight. Then they would cry afterwards and talk about how horrible it all had been. In the final analysis, however, there could be no denying the little warm glow of self-satisfaction no matter how fleeting it might have been. Either that or they would just sit back and watch it all happen--totally ignorant that they had somehow helped cause it, perhaps not directly at fault, but nevertheless implicated in some way or another. Perhaps the woman would cause one man to get jealous. Of course later she would deny her role in this.

And so it was here but with one big difference. Lori had stood between the big man and himself with total disregard for her own safety. She was behind him--all the way. That was something he could never accuse Karen of--standing behind him. Lori was with him, heart and soul.

"Here's my theory," answered Frank. "For some reason the guy's got the hots for you. He watches you. He watches us together. The guy knows he can't have you, but he sees us having a good time--a great time. He figures I can have you whereas he can't. Then, to make matters worse, he's probably seen me around my car or he's seen it in the lot, and the way I'm dressed or act, that it's mine. That really pisses him off because not only do I have THE GIRL but I have THE CAR."

"How are you two doing?" It was Jean returning with their beers.

"We're ready for the hot tub," Frank replied. "That's one hell of a lot better than a fight and getting kicked out. Do you know, Jean, how long Lori and I have known each other?"

"No idea, Frank."

"About a year now. I keep looking her up because she's a great drinking companion. The best."

"Jean, this is my buddy. Frank and I are buddies'." Lori threw her arms around Frank's neck to emphasize her point.

"You two enjoy the hot tub together, okay," said Jean, her voice almost motherly.

Frank gave her a two-dollar tip, then turned to Lori. "What are we waiting for? Let's go for it."

"You've got to change first Frank," said Lori as she pointed to the dressing room.

"Why bother? I don't care who sees me."

"Change Frank," Lori laughed. "I really believe you would go up to the hot tub nude in front of all these people."

"I would," said Frank as he got up to go to the dressing room.

"One more thing Frank."

"What's that?"

"Your trunks." She handed them to him and smiled, a sweet Madonna smile, that only she out of all the girls he had met, could deliver.

In the dressing room Frank changed quickly. Others shared the men's room with him, but this time he didn't bother bantering with them. Coming out of the men's room, Frank noticed that Lori was talking to the doorman. Carrying his clothes and towel he strode over to them, bare chested in his trunks. Lori took his hand and led him over to the hot tub. Frank slid into the water while she turned on the agitator. Then she slipped into the water and crawled onto his lap, facing him.

"Remember, we can stay here as long as we want just so long as no one else wants it. There are no lesbian shows scheduled so we might have awhile," said Lori. She put her arms around his neck and started to kiss him, reached into his trunks, and fondled him.

"Lori, I don't want you to get big-headed about this or anything, but guess what?"

"What?"

"You've almost got me by the balls."

"Oh really Frank. I thought I already had you by the balls, but don't you worry. I've got plans for you. Plans you don't know anything about."

"Should I ask you what they are?"

"No. I'd rather you didn't. Not now anyway."

"Let's go for a double header. Straddle me."

Lori flipped over so that her back faced him. For some reason it was easier to get inside her when they were in that position--at least in the hot tub. He slid in easily. She twisted her head sideways so that she could kiss him. He took her mouth in his. She put her tongue in his mouth and started to explore it, not ferociously as she usually did, but slowly as if she had all the time in the world. He loved the way she kissed. Her mouth was small, her tongue firm and active. Although she smoked, there was not a single trace of smoker's breath from her mouth.

"I love your body, Frank. God, do I love your body. It is a

hard body, like mine."

Like hers. Frank thought about her body. That was it. A hard body. Her breasts were small, but her nipples were large. She had not a trace of a stomach. Her waist was slender while her hips were narrow yet feminine. Lori was fully five foot six yet her body dimensions were those of a woman of around 5 foot two or three. She was so quick though and so strong that one could not really consider her to be skinny.

Other women might have large breasts and pronounced curves. *So much window dressing,* thought Frank. *It would all turn to fat. Even now it would slow them up if they had to do something meaningful like climbing the Grand Canyon.* Lori had told him once her little secret why she never picked up weight. He knew she would never get fat. *Good God, she had already had five kids, and she still had the body of a teenager.*

He loved her body too. *Wouldn't trade it for any other. Of course he wouldn't tell her that. She was probably big headed enough already. Think about it Frank, just think about it a second-this woman was never going to be fat. She'll always be able to keep up with you and she'll never turn you off because of extra pounds. And that, dear old Frank, is your number one turnoff. Think again Frank about all those women out there. Most of them can be divided into two categories--those who are fat and those who are going to get fat.*

Whatever her body had going for it, he was plugged into it. Here he was making love to her while she was kissing him, and he was able at the same time to analyze her physical attributes. At least he was thinking of her. That was far better than screwing someone while thinking about one's work or screwing someone else.

"Hey, wake up. I'm not boring you, am I?" Lori laughed. "Okay. That does it. I'm shifting positions. I'm going to make sure that you never forget me." She turned over so that she faced him. Then she clasped his lips in hers, kissing him wildly with her tongue. Suddenly she stopped kissing him, pulled her face away from his a bit, and studied him, looking into his eyes.

Once again she started to kiss him. Then she stopped abruptly and lowered her head so that her mouth could take in one of his nipples. Once she had swallowed it in her mouth, she bit down on it, hard. At the same time she raised herself off him once more.

Even in the hot tub, it was getting to be a little much. He wanted her. Frank took her around her chest with his arms and pulled her body into his. He returned her kiss, his tongue darting back and forth. He started to bite her lip. Frank bit her lip harder, and harder almost drawing blood.

When it was over Frank lay still in the water making no attempt to hide the smile on his face. Lori saw it and smirked. Frank saw her mouth narrow and the dimples form on her cheeks and knew he was in trouble. She leaned over to kiss him once more, then before her lips touched his, she grabbed his head and pulled it under the water.

"There, wipe that shit-eating grin off your face. That's not polite, "she laughed.

"What do you want me to do after coming in you? Be like this?" Frank screwed up his face and opened his mouth in his interpretation of a half-witted pervert.

"No, no--you did a much better pervert imitation up on the stage," she teased.

"Here's what the pervert looks like." Lori sucked in her cheeks while doing something with her eyes that made them bulge. They both broke out laughing.

"Don't worry about your stage dance Brittany. I've got you covered."

One of the other girls had come over. "Do you want one of the waitresses to come over?" the girl asked.

"If you don't mind, just have Jean bring us a couple beers." Lori turned to Frank. "That means we can stay here longer. I don't mind. Do you?"

"I'm loving it. Do you give blow jobs under the water?"

"Watch."

Lori put her head under the surface and started to brush her lips up and down his penis. Suddenly she jerked her head out of the water gasping for air. Then she broke out laughing. "I couldn't suck it. I would've drowned."

"That's the first time I've been blown under the water. And I've thought I've seen it all."

"Uhuh--no Frank--you have not seen it all."

"Is that a promise you are making of showing me new and interesting things?

"You might call it that. I'll show you when we go out."

"When we go out. Now that's a laugh. Lori, why have you

always stood me up?"

"I always wanted to go out with you. I've always loved you. Thing is, I wanted to be sure."

So she risked losing me for good by standing me up. I never allowed a girl to get away with that before, thought Frank. *She has to be lying. I could have stopped coming to see her, and the whole thing would have ended just like that.*

"Did you know, Lori, that love is a four-letter word? Like fuck, and shit, and damn, and piss. Things like that. Doesn't mean a damn thing. I mean no offense-- I am complimented that you are telling me that you love me, but I just don't believe you."

"Correction. I love you Frank. And you should believe me because I am telling you."

"Okay then, I'm glad you love me."

"Are you ready, Frank?"

"Yes I'm ready for a beer. Where's Jean? She should be here by now."

"I want you to face me. I want you to kiss me. I like the way you kiss, Lori."

She shifted positions so that she sat in his lap while facing him. She started to kiss him. Without warning Lori pulled away and screwed up her face in her pervert imitation. She narrowed her eyes and stuck out her tongue.

"Now just what is it that you like about the way I kiss?" she asked, becoming serious again.

"I like your mouth."

"What about my mouth?"

"It's small, so when you're kissing me there's no room for you to bullshit me."

"I don't bullshit you, Frank."

"You do Lori."

"Tell me what I've lied to you about?"

"I don't even want to start so I won't."

"You two seem to be enjoying yourselves. I brought you two Bud Lights. Hope that's okay. You can pay me later if you want." Jean raised her eyebrows ironically when she said 'enjoying' and gave them a knowing smile.

"The money's in his pants pocket over there." Lori pointed toward Frank's shorts which were lying ten feet away on the tiled floor. "Bring them to me Jean. Would you?"

"The water's great Jean. Why don't you jump in with us?"

asked Frank.

"I would in a minute but I don't think Brittany would appreciate it."

"You're right, Jean. If you or anyone else comes near Frank, I'm going to kick the shit out of them." Lori laughed good-naturedly.

"You're getting pretty possessive about someone you've never gone out with. Someone you've always stood up," said Frank.

"That was before. Now it's different. Please don't remind me again of all that."

Jean brought Frank's shorts over to Lori who reached into his front pocket. Luckily there were a lot of one's. Lori gave Jean seven dollars. After Jean left, she turned to Frank. "I gave her a one dollar tip. Hope you don't mind?"

"I don't. How about a toast? Come up with something good, Lori."

Lori grabbed her beer and twined her arm around his after handing him his bottle. "To a new beginning." She drank from her bottle watching him as he chugged his down. Then she started to splash him getting water all over his face.

"You little imp" Frank grabbed Lori's head and dunked her. She came up sputtering. For a second he relaxed, concerned that she had taken in too much water. Without warning Lori took her beer and poured it over the top of his head.

"I love you. I don't know why. I just don't know why, but I just do," she exclaimed as she started to splash him.

"I want you again, right now. Listen to me Lori. Stop splashing me and kiss me softly. I want to feel you, think about you, and you only. I want to breathe you in--drink you in--to be overwhelmed by your presence." He grabbed both her shoulders and squeezed them in his strong hands to emphasis what he had just said.

Lori began to kiss him allowing her lips to flutter slowly across his mouth. Then her lips stopped flowing across his. It all happened so swiftly. One minute she was splashing him, getting water into his nose--the next they were joined together--two lovers out of touch with everyone but themselves. Later-- an hour-- two hours later a voice intruded into their private world.

"Brittany. I hate to interrupt you two. You look like you're having so much fun, but it's your turn to go up on stage again." Jean had come up suddenly.

"Thanks Jean. We'll be right out," said Lori.

Lori turned her head to face Frank. "When you get dressed, come see me on stage."

Frank climbed out of the hot tub, grabbed his clothing and towel lying close by, and dried himself off. Then he strode to the men's room. Once inside he pulled his trunks off and put on his shorts and short sleeved shirt, and thought: *Outside the door Lori would be waiting for him on stage, other men no doubt gathered around her. By this time she would be almost oblivious to them going through the motions as an entertainer, thinking only of him.* Frank walked out of the men's room surveying the main room as he entered it trying to catch sight of her before she saw him. He spied her on the stage that was behind and to the left of the bar. He noticed that she was already smiling in his direction. Frank went over and took a seat next to a man who anxiously awaited a lap dance. Lori climbed onto the man's lap and gave him the officially mandated three minutes before going to Frank. The man left.

"Good. He's gone. Bastard only gave me a buck too."

"Calm down Lori. You didn't exactly set his world on fire either," said Frank.

"Guess what Frank? You're taking me home."

"I'm taking you home. How do you figure?"

"I don't have a ride with anyone else. We're going to be done right after this set. Don't wait outside the way you did last time. Just tell the bouncers and the manager that you are my ride and that you are waiting inside for me."

"You're on. I'll wait for you."

The last selection of the set was soon over and the place almost instantly evaporated. The dancers were immediately hustled into the lady's dressing room. The bartender, the manager, and the bouncer hurried around the room saying "Everybody out. The place is closed. You've got to leave. Now." Just minutes before, the place had been a going concern, filled with dancers, waitresses, and male customers, all drinking until four in the morning. Suddenly nearly everyone was gone. The bouncer looked over at Frank, saw with surprise that he was still there, and asked loudly, "Hey you, you've got to leave."

"I'm Brittany's ride home," said Frank.

The bouncer turned to the manager. "Did you hear that? He says he's taking Brittany home."

The manager looked at Frank surprised. "Weren't you in the

hot tub with her?"

"Sure, but I'm taking her home. We're good friends."

The manager exclaimed to the bouncer, "You heard that! He's taking her home! If she leaves with him, she's fired! As of right now, she's fired." Then he looked over at Frank. "You're going to have to go outside. You can't stay here."

Frank went outside and started his sports car. Then he got behind the wheel and parked the little convertible near the night club's front door so that Lori could easily see it. He lit an Anthony and Cleopatra and climbed out of the car. Two men came over. They were very ordinary looking being neither well dressed nor disheveled. They were not big men nor were they particularly small.

"Hey buddy, that sure looked fun what you were doing in the hot tub." The man smiled at Frank.

"And what do you think I was doing in the hot tub?" asked Frank.

"Oh you know it looked to my brother and me that you were doing it. Now tell us you weren't," the man laughed.

"It just looked that way, but it wasn't," replied Frank. "Besides, the girl and I have been good friends for a year."

"Man, how long did you two stay in there? Two hours?" This time it was the other brother who spoke.

"I don't know," answered Frank. "Think it was that long?"

"Had to be," said the second brother. "Man you must be loaded with money."

"Not really," Frank replied, "Just paid the standard amount. The girl and I like each other. That makes a difference."

"I still say you must have paid her a lot." The second brother who was blonde seemed to be the younger of the two. He was definitely the more talkative.

Frank took a step backwards not noticing the side mirror of the pickup truck behind him. His shoulder bumped the mirror, not hard, but hard enough to knock it off onto the ground. The blonde brother noticed what Frank had done immediately and rushed forward to retrieve the mirror.

"You knocked my mirror off of my truck." The man looked the mirror over carefully. "It's fucked up. My mirror is fucked up. Al did you see what he just did to my mirror?"

"Yeah. I see what he did. Well get his name and address. That's my advice."

"Yeah, and I'm calling the cops. Here, I'll get his name and address. You go call the cops."

Just what I need, thought Frank. *I finally get Lori to go with me in my car and these idiots come up with a mirror that falls off their pickup. They must have fastened it on with scotch tape. Well I can't let them spoil it. I'll have to buy my way out of this one. Last thing I need is to be tied up with a bunch of cops for the next forty-five minutes.*

Frank addressed the younger brother. "Look. I'll pay for the damage. No need to get the cops here. How much do you think it's worth?"

"Oh, I don't know. Probably fifty bucks. Yeah, I'd say it costs fifty bucks."

Frank saw Lori walking dejectedly out of the Pink Giraffe, her face a mask of anger. "Guess what Frank? Those fuckers fired me. They just fired me for going home with you."

"Come here Lori. We've got another problem. I just knocked this guys mirror off his pickup and he's asking fifty bucks or he's calling the cops."

Lori hurried over. "Frank, that mirror's not worth fifty bucks. Let him call the cops."

"Lori, we need to get somewhere where we can relax. You just got fired. That's the main thing. I just looked in my wallet, and I don't have fifty bucks. Give me fifty bucks. You know I'm good for it even if he doesn't." Frank pointed at the younger brother.

Lori glared at the younger brother. "We're giving you $35.00. That's more than that damn mirror of yours is worth."

"It's fifty bucks or I'm calling the cops. Look at what he did to my mirror. It's fucked. Look at it. My mirror is fucked."

Frank went over to the older brother. "Tell him we're giving him fifty bucks even though it's not worth it. Lori just lost her job and that's our problem now. This mirror is secondary. And one more thing."

"What's that?" asked the older brother.

"Tell him to stop sniveling before I flatten him." Frank now looked at Lori. "Lori, give this kid fifty bucks," he ordered firmly. "And don't argue. You and I are settling this later."

Lori pulled a fifty out of her purse and handed it to the younger brother without argument. Then she turned to Frank. "Now let's get the fuck out of here before I get more pissed than I already am."

Frank opened the door of the car for her. Lori got in and stared straight ahead at the windshield. Frank got in the driver's side and eased the little car out of the parking lot.

"Come on Lori. Snap out of it. We're in this together. We'll figure your job situation out over a cup of coffee or beer. Don't worry about the fifty. You know I'll pay you back."

"Those guys. Those little pricks. They think that because you have a nice car that you are rich and that they can take advantage of you. They probably had this all planned to set you up," she said angrily.

A few minutes later, Frank had the little car out on the expressway. The night breeze was cool with morning coming on. For one year he had tried to get this girl to go out with him. He had made love to her three times in the hot tub and now she was alone with him, in his car. And she was angry. Too angry to enjoy the drive. He wanted to take her in his arms and tell her that everything was all right--that she was with him--and as long as she was with him everything would be all right. If he had to fight the two brothers in the parking lot, he was sure she would have helped him just as she had been willing to throw her little body between the big man and his in the Pink Giraffe. He'd fight ten men for her. She was that special to him.

"I've seen this sort of thing happen before. They really took advantage of you Frank. Now I've lost my job and I've lost my fifty bucks."

"You might have lost your job for now, but you haven't lost fifty bucks. I'm paying you back. Real soon."

"Take me home, Frank. Just take me home."

She gave him directions. He crossed over to the Missouri side. They were soon in South St. Louis.

"See that used car parking lot over there. I live just a few doors from there. Let me out there."

Frank let Lori out. He watched her walk dejectedly to an apartment's outside door and waited for her to go in. Then he drove off, carefully noting where she had gone in and the street address. It was 5:30 in the morning and he had better than an hour's drive ahead of him. He had a wonderful time in the hot tub. And yet the whole thing had gone sour on him after all. Worse, he knew it had gone sour for her as well.

ABANDONMENT OF THE GREAT PLAN

A week passed. Frank called the Pink Giraffe. The voice on the other end said, "Brittany, I don't know what happened but they suspended her for three weeks." This brought him back to the Sports Bar. He walked in, a gyroscope for a mind, bent on tracking her down. Cindy greeted him at the bar.

"Hi Frank. What can I get you?"

"How about Nipples?"

"It's here, all around you, Frank. Women, half naked-- women to drink with--and play with. Welcome to Fantasy Land. All yours until you run out of money. " Cindy laughed. "I can't help it Frank, but I just couldn't resist. No, I haven't seen her."

"Hey Frank. One of her old customers just came in. He told me she's at the Pink Giraffe." It was Goldie.

"Goldie, are you sure he said that she was working at the Pink Giraffe?" Frank asked.

"Honest Frank, he left here just a few minutes ago. He told me he bought her several drinks today. What are you drinking?"

"Girls, I might see you later, but I'm off to the Pink Giraffe. I have a weakness for Nipples." Within seconds Frank was out the door and already turning the key in the sports car's ignition. Fifteen minutes later he was pulling into the Pink Giraffe's parking lot. Charles, the doorman, greeted him.

"Charles, is Brittany here today?"

"She's inside. Are you sure you want her?" A puzzled expression came over the doorman's face.

"You bet I do. Five dollars, right?" Frank handed Charles a five and went in. He took in the room at a glance but didn't see her. *Probably in the dressing room*, he thought. He sat at the far side of the bar and ordered a beer.

"Need some company. My name's Lisa." A tall brunette sat on the bar stool next to him. "Buy me a drink?" she asked.

"I'll buy you a drink if you'll bring Brittany over here."

"I can probably do that. I'll have a whiskey sour."

"Bartender, bring a whiskey sour over with my beer, will you?" Frank didn't have to raise his voice. The place was pretty quiet. Only four or five girls were working and there were only six or seven customers. It was early in the afternoon and the bartender was close at hand. Frank payed for the drinks and turned to Lisa.

"So you know Brittany?"

"Known her for years. She's a good friend. I'll go get her." Lisa disappeared. *That was odd*, Frank thought. He had never met anyone before who had known Lori for years. Too much turnover in the clubs. And Lori had only been at the Pink Giraffe for a month or so.

A few minutes later Lisa reappeared with a blonde. The blonde was around five foot six, one-hundred and ten pounds. Perfectly proportioned, she could have passed for Lori's sister except she was not Lori.

"Lisa, I don't know him." I thought you said he was a customer of mine. "I'm sorry. My name's Brittany. Now where do you know me from?" The girl smiled aT Frank.

"I've never seen you before. My name's Frank. I know a girl who worked here under the name Brittany very well. Her real name's Lori. I thought you were her. Someone told me at another bar that she was working here today."

"There was another Brittany. People are always getting us confused. She worked nights and I work days and nights. Only she's suspended."

"I know. And I think I'm the reason she's suspended."

"Why's that?" asked Lisa.

"I took her home one night when she was warned not to go out with one of the customers."

"They have a rule that the dancers cannot leave with their customers. The reason is that the club can get busted for prostitution." Brittany paused for a moment, then continued. "The Brittany you know got in a fight with one of the other girls. The cops came. One of them cracked her over the head with his nightstick when she attacked him. That's why she got suspended."

"I've gotta find her. We used to do hot tubs together and we had some great times. Hell, I've known her for a year now. Used to drink more beer with her than any other human being on the planet--during the last year I mean."

"How about doing a hot tub with us?" Lisa suggested.

"I'm sure you girls would be fun, and you're both very pretty. It wouldn't be the same. This Brittany and I are close. I mean real close and the hot tubs were special."

"Hey Lisa--I've got a customer over there waiting on me. I'd better get back to him." Brittany looked back at Frank. "Nice meeting you, Frank. If you're ever in here again, look me up. I'd like to help you forget this other Brittany."

"It would be interesting to have you try, Brittany. If you see me in here again, give it a shot. I'll have another drink with Lisa if she's ready."

"I'm up on stage now. You can bring me a drink and join me up there."

"I'll bring you a drink, but I don't think I'll join you up there. I'm in the mood to talk. I'm sad about what happened to Lori and I'm disappointed not to find her here."

"You're forgiven. I have to get up on stage or they're going to suspend me too."

Brittany joined her customer. Moments later Frank found himself at the bar, alone, ordering another beer and a whiskey sour. He took the whiskey sour over to Lisa's stage. A man sat alone at the stage. She was already on his lap when Frank set the whiskey sour next to her. Lisa smiled and nodded at him. He went back to the bar, this time taking a seat at the front where he could watch her dance. Two songs later, the man tipped Lisa, got up, and went to the back of the bar where Frank had been sitting earlier leaving Lisa on the stage alone. Frank hated to leave her there. He was tempted to do a lap dance and almost went over. Instead, he sat sipping his beer alone, rooted to his bar stool unable to think or do anything except think about Lori.

The woman on stage was around five foot eight and probably in her late twenties. She was thin in the waist and long legged. *Very attractive*, he thought, *but totally forgettable. Thanks to you Lori*, he whispered into his beer. The girl was now pirouetting around the pole. Five minutes later Lisa took a seat on the bar stool next to him. *Probably has one to two children*, thought Frank. *Most women do. In a bind financially. Is doing this between jobs. How many times will I have to visit her before she'll come home with him? She will come home with me. That is almost a certainty. The only question that needs to be asked is how long will it take.*

"I'm in the middle of a divorce," said Frank. "How about you? Are you single or divorced?"

"Divorced. You have any kids, Frank?"

"No. The two kids are in college and they are my stepchildren."

"I've got two. That's why I'm here. I want to give them the best."

Aha--the Butch Drover Worm Theory in action. This girl could be in an office somewhere working as a legal secretary or whatever. Definitely has the personality and probably has the brains. She's lost her husband for whatever reason and now all she can think of is to gather as many worms as possible. So now she's doing this to maximize her worm production. Now, if I only play my cards right, I can be going out with her soon, and not too long after that she'll be looking at me as the chief worm gatherer.

"How long have you worked as a dancer?" asked Frank.

"Seven or eight months now. I'm looking for some other line of work. The only thing is nothing much out there pays. That's what I'm doing this for. A girl can make good money at it if she works the guys right and works hard at it."

Frank sipped on his beer and studied the woman who sat next to him. *Nice looking woman. A good conversationalist.* If he handled things right he could work her into his great plan that he and Stan had engineered a year before. He could end up giving her so much a month or per week and she'd end up having enough worms for her children. Frank didn't doubt that she'd come across for him. He could use her for sex whenever he wanted or someone else for that matter. Perhaps he should do just that. *Push Lori out of his mind. Give up on her. Take this girl out and one or two others like her. This woman is probably a pretty nice person,* he thought. *So, can I work her into the plan? Do I want to?*

The image of Lori lying in the hot tub with her splashing water on him beckoned at him. Lori, crying out, "I love you, Frank. I don't know why but I just do." *Reckless, irresponsible Lori. Full of fun. Full of life.* He could chase her down. Find her. Such a hopeless, irresponsible, romance--one without direction or an end. The fly in the ointment of his plan. The death of the three point plan. Stupid, stupid, conclusion that he was making. No, he couldn't walk all over this woman who sat next to him nor anyone like her. The plan--that beautiful plan he and Stan had concocted-- so logical, so full of substance, so eminently workable--sucked. *Fuck it. Fuck the plan.* He was going to go out and find Lori and nothing was going to stop him.

"Lisa, look, I'm sorry. I've gotta go and I've gotta go now. I'll catch you some other time." Stan rose from his stool, his beer unfinished.

"You love her, don't you?"

"I do. I don't know why. I just do."

And he left.

Pure Talent feature entertainers being briefed on what to expect at the feature showcase in the dressing room at the Candy Store in Mobile, Alabama. To the left is the club's owner. Anne Marie who created the Pure Talent Agency on Darrel's left.. In his outings with Pure Talent the author had access to the hosting clubs' dressing rooms .

Pure Talent Agency Features at a feature showcase

Pure Talent Feature Entertainers

"Friends, Romans, Countrymen, lend me your ears" Jack
Corbett with Darien Ross at Caesar's Palace at Exotic Dancer
Magazine's Expo 2004

Jack and Leah Layne with Darien Ross as the
photographer

When it was turn for her to put on her show, all the other feature
entertainers would drop whatever they were doing to watch.
Aspen did everything in a big way and even had her own Aspen
Reign tour bus.

Jack with Pleasure and Paine at the Exotic Dancer Expo at
Caesar's Palace

Lolly Tops met the author while competing for M.S
Texas at Maximus. Later after the author was no longer
writing for "Xtreme" she invited him to come up to a
new club in Iowa hoping they could get the club
advertised in one of the two small Midwestern adult
magazines the author was writing for. Lolly Tops got
Jack a room next to the one she was staying at with her
boyfriend. Then she made a lunch appointment with the
club's general manager for the author and her to discuss
advertising. The general manager was sold. The trouble
was neither magazine was interested and both
disappeared soon afterwards. The author never found a
Midwest Magazine even close to Xtreme's caliber. The
author feels that feature entertainers represent an
exceptionally intelligent and motivated group of
women who are well in front of the average in most
respects.

Aspen Reign and Jeremy McTeague, Jack's editor at "Xtreme Magazine". The author met Jeremy at the 2002 Exotic Dancer Expo at Caesar's Palace who was writing a "Horror Scope" (not a misspelling) and "Adventures of the Backdoor Man" short story series for Xtreme along with performing his duties as editor. Jack brought his satiric Dick Fitswell, the man searching for the Perfect Fit" short stores over to Xtreme to go along with Jeremy's off the wall horror scopes. Later, Jack would do feature entertainer interviews, club owner profiles, cover key adult industry events such as the Exotic Dancer Expos and Nudes-A-Poppin and his guns and babes articles for Xtreme. The problem was Xtreme being an East Coast adult magazine that is funded entirely by its advertisers ultimately was not a good fit for Jack and vice versa. The author living in the Midwest had great contacts in the Midwest who were club owners and general managers. The problem was that club owners spending say a thousand dollars a month in advertising on the East Coast would not welcome Xtreme's covering Midwest clubs who were not advertising in the magazine. And of course, a Big Daddy, Big Mike or Big Al wouldn't benefit from advertising their clubs in New York or Massachusetts. Ultimately Jeremy would head the Xtreme Magazine Pennsylvania–New Jersey franchise and find himself having less and less time for his writing due to his demanding workload.

Darien Ross and Carrie Bare at the Pure Talent booth at an "Exotic Dancer Magazine" Expo. Nearly everyone attending the convention stays at the same hotel–casino, eg. Mandalay Bay, Caesar's Palace, etc. The trade show is held in a large convention hall. Pure Talent and other talent agencies typically have booths that are attended by the feature entertainers they represent. Visiting club owners stop by the booths to discuss potential future bookings.with heads of the agencies such as Anne Marie and Jim Hayek The booths also provide individual entertainers excellent opportunities to network with club owners, top managers, photographers, writers etc to hopefully advance their careers.

Carrie Bare showing her moves at a Pure Talent Feature Showcase. Jack would write two articles on Carrie for *Xtreme Magazine*

This is not what it looks like. The guy..well, that's Kenny, one of Big Daddy's DJ's. The woman is Pleasure at a S.P.E.W. wresting event at Big Daddy's Club

Hawkeye, Big Daddy's other D.J., at Angkor Wat, Cambodia. Jack, Big Daddy and Hawkeye got their PADI scuba certification together in Missouri, then they traveled to Thailand together three times. In the classroom, Hawkeye was the star straight A student getting perfect scores in his PADI exams while finishing the tests long before everyone else. Short of a Masters in Anthropology by just the final dissertation upon arriving at Angkor Wat, Hawkeye said, "This is what I really came to Thailand and Cambodia for."

Heather would be one of Jack's first models for the Xtreme Weapon's articles he wrote for *Xtreme Magazine* first as "Dirty Heather" with the Colt Python .357 magnum revolver, and here with the 30 caliber Browning M-19 machine gun. Heather, who's from Iowa, and Killer Kloey from Big Daddy's Cabaret in Missouri would be the first entertainers to get S.P.E.W. rolling. The match pitted Iowa's champion against Missouri's best.

Lauren Kaine is the robot on the left. Feature entertainers such as Lauren have thousands of dollars invested in their props and outfits they wear while doing their shows. An example would be K.C. Cannons who had several thousand invested in a single robot prop she often used in her feature acts.

The robot reveals herself

Posing for an Xtreme gun article in Wichita Falls, Texas, Pleasure and Pain billed themselves as a Mother-daughter stripper duo. After initially meeting the author at Nudes-A-Poppin, Pleasure and Pain would travel from Columbus, Ohio all the way to Dixon, Missouri and Des Moines, Iowa for S.P.E.W. Wrestling pageants. When the author suggested that they compete in Club Maximus's M.S. Texas pageant they came all the way over to Texas. In this picture they are at Vic Robinson's house for the weapons photo shoots after performing in the club's competitions. The author feels the general public does not realize how hard feature entertainers work to get discovered or how much they will spend traveling hoping they will become the next big name star.

There has never been anything quite like S.P.E.W. Men and women alike would fill up the clubs to enjoy the spectacle provided by Big Daddy and Big Mike and their teams of ten strippers. The events were well planned and rehearsed the morning before the matches. There would be grudge matches between sisters who weren't really sisters over one sister stealing the other's boyfriend. Contrived riots would break out into the ring requiring club security guards to be called in. There was talk even of a little blood letting when one of the entertainers would suddenly start bleeding from the forehead. There is of course no proof that Big Daddy or Big Mike might have done it, Big Daddy had once been a professional wrestler who had appeared several times on television so her certainly knew all the tricks the real pros used to excite the crowd.

Showing off their promo before the wrestling matches begin, the girls of S.P.E.W. Pleasure and Pain to the far left, the mother daughter duo, wearing hats. Second from Pleasure's left is Killer Kloey, Big Daddy's champion.

The wrestlers make their grand entrance.

Big Daddy, the father of S.P.E.W. with his co-partner Big Mike on the far right, Ron Jeremy porn star and Nudes-A-Poppin master of ceremonies in the middle. Ron Jeremy had earned a bachelor's degree in education, then a Masters Degree in Special Education before becoming a school teacher. After that he tried his hand at acting, but after being unable to support himself as a Broadway actor, Ron turned to adult movies which he was so successful at that he's been rated in the Guinness Book of World Records as having been in more adult movies than any other actor with 2000 films to his credit. Ron is an incredible M.C. When there are two or three M.C's and the others falter, time and time again, Ron has picked up the slack and come through. The author has never seen him demean or diminish his co-M.C.'s or members of his audiences in any way.

What the general public does not realize is how gifted so many members of the Adult industry are. Big Daddy is an incredible D.J., for example, but after mistakenly believing he had throat cancer, he turned to club management as a means to support himself. Marilyn Chambers who is the first woman to put adult movies on the map when she starred in "Behind the Green Door" which was produced by the Mitchell Brothers Night Club in San Francisco, was an actress with an incredible on screen persona who could really act but once she did her first adult movie any potential future as a Hollywood star was compromised. The author feels that many, perhaps even a majority of feature entertainers are extremely intelligent and competent women who at heart wish to be Hollywood actresses but who intuitively know there is small chance of their realizing their dreams.

LITTLE GIRL

The next day he drove to St. Louis, taking 55 past the Arsenal exit. He tried to remember what he had done when he had taken Lori home the last time he had seen her at the Pink Giraffe. This time his memory did not fail him. He was now on the South side looking for the apartment she had entered. He was surprised that he was on the right street. He found the used car lot which he remembered had been close to the apartment. There, close by, in the building next to the lot were two doorways. One of them led to Lori. He drove the little sports car past and parked on the street a block away. He strode up to the second doorway and knocked.

A girl, dressed in jeans, fourteen or fifteen years old, answered the door. She stood in the doorway waiting for Frank to speak.

"Hi. I'm Frank. I'm a good friend of Lori's. Is she here or does she live in the apartment next door?"

"Oh, you're a friend of hers. You've got the right place. I'm Becky. I'm Travis's sister. We're all living here temporarily until we can get our feet back on the ground again. Lori's asleep right now. Can you come back later?"

"Becky, I have something important to tell her. Can you wake her up? I know she'll want to talk to me."

"Sure. Come on in."

Frank followed Becky into the apartment. There were two main rooms. The second was not a second room but a separate section of the first with a wall stretching halfway across so that the two sections were partially partitioned off from one another. A television set, a single chair, an old couch and several mattresses lying on the floor were the only furniture in the first section. Five small children, the oldest around eight, sat, stood, or were running around in the apartment. A young man just under six feet tall, who had been watching T.V., silently stared at Frank. Frank walked by him following Becky into the second room without giving the man a second glance. A large bed lay just on the other side of the partition. Lori was lying stiffly on her back asleep. Becky went over and shook her. Lori opened her eyes and saw Frank, jumped out of bed and put on a bathrobe. "What are you doing here?" she asked. She did not smile.

"Looking for you. Next time call. It's a lot easier.

"What time is it?."

"It's noon. Why?"

"Travis. The fuckers going to be here any minute. You've got to leave."

"First, you've got to talk to me today. Promise me that!"

"Okay. Where can I find you?"

"Ill be at the Sports Bar. Where you used to work. You know the phone number. You know how to find it. I'll wait for there for you."

"Okay, okay. You've got to leave. Travis will be here any minute."

Lori walked him to the door. Frank walked out onto the sidewalk and headed for his car. Just then he heard a car drive up, heard it park next to the apartment, heard doors clam, and then, loud voices. He kept walking without turning around, got into the little car, and drove out into the street.

He drove out to I-55, taking it to route 64. A few miles later he got off on the road that would take him past the Injection Pump and onto the Sports Bar. Frank stopped at the top of the exit ramp.

"Hey Frank. Wait up. Look behind you."

The sports car's top was down. He looked behind him and saw a man and a woman on a Harley gesturing at him. At first Frank didn't recognize the two riders underneath their helmets. *Amazing how the little green sports car made it so easy to recognize me*, thought Frank. He waved as the motorcycle pulled up to him.

"It's us. Jim and Goldie," said Jim.

I don't know what you two are up to but I'm going to the Sports Bar for a beer, said Frank. "I'll buy you both a beer if you join me."

"You're on," said Jim. "Meet you there."

"Hey, did you hear that I quit waitressing there? They gave me a bunch of shit so I just took a vacation," said Goldie.

"I didn't hear about that. Tell me about it when we get there."

Frank was already sitting at the bar when they got there. Jim took a seat on the bar stool next to him as Goldie talked to the bartender. Nadine came over with a bottle of Budweiser in her hand.

"Nadine, what would I ever do without you. I can't even sit down before you have my favorite beer out for me. I'm getting Him and Goldie some beer unless Goldie wants something different. Jim, now, I know wants a beer."

"I'll have the same as Frank. Goldie wants a Jack and Coke."
"Goldie. You drink the same drink as Lori," said Frank.

"I know. And God knows how many we've had together."

"I just look her up."

"How's she doing?" asked Goldie.

"I don't know. She looked asleep to me. I woke her up."

"What'd you do–go over to her house?" asked Jim.

"Not a house at all. Hardly an apartment even. She might come here. She said she'd come here, but you know how she is."

"Yeah, there's no telling anything with Nipples. I don't even think she knows," said Jim, a touch of sarcasm in his voice.

"Now Goldie, you've worked with Lori. And she thinks the world of you. How much do you believe o what she tells you?"

"Not much."

"How much? Five percent?" asked Frank.

"If that much."

Just then the door opened and Lori walked in. She walked up to Frank, still looking tired, no makeup on at all.

"Well, I'm here. I look like hell, but I've made it."

"That sure was fast, said Frank. "I didn't think you were coming."

"Well, I did." Lori turned to Goldie, put her arms around the ex waitress's neck, and hugged her. "I'm so glad you're here, Goldie. I've missed you so much. Frank, I've gotta talk to Bill. Maybe I can talk him into hiring me back."

"He's right over there." Frank pointed to the back room. Lori released Goldie and went over to Bill. Five minutes later she was in the dressing room putting on her makeup and T-bar. Jim winked at Frank.

"Bill must have hired her back. Leave it to Lori to sweet talk Bill."

"Is he a soft touch?" asked Frank.

"Oh, he can be," said Goldie. "But not always. Usually though."

A few minutes later, Lori emerged from the dressing room. Makeup on and clad in her skimpy outfit, she was a new woman. She came up to Frank and snuggled next to him. He couldn't put his finger on it but it felt so right having her close to him. She felt so small and fragile in his arms yet he knew how strong and vital she could be.

"Got my drink?" she asked.

"Jack and Coke. Right?" He handed the glass to Lori.

"You know what I feel like doing today?" Frank asked.

"What?"

"I feel like breaking down and getting us a limo. What do you think?"

"I think it's a great idea. You're sure now, aren't you?"

"Never been surer. I'll do it anywhere, anytime with you."

"Nadine. We're doing a limo. Come and get Frank's money," Lori called out in a loud voice.

"Lori, aren't you a little loud. I mean, I really don't care, but You're telling everyone here that we're about to do a limo."

"I don't care either because I'm proud to do a limo with you. Why keep it a secret? We didn't keep the hot tub secret. We were there for everyone to see."

"Now it's going to take a few minutes for it to get here. We might as well have another drink while we are waiting for it," suggested Lori.

"Nadine. Get us another Jack and Coke and another Budweiser."

Frank paid for the drinks. Before Nadine returned with his change Lori's eyes brightened as she called out:

"Nadine, we're both going to do a body shot. Bring us some limes, salt, and two shots of Cuervo."

"We're not going to do one of those here sitting at the bar now are we?" Frank asked Lori.

"Sure, why not."

Frank thought about how doing body shots with Lori had become a tradition. Twenty minutes later, the driver came up to the bar.

Frank thought about how doing body shots with Lori had become a tradition. Twenty minutes later, the driver came up to the bar.

"Are you ready?" the driver asked.

"We're ready," Lori replied.

The driver led them to the back room and out into the parking lot. He opened the back door of the limo for Lori who stepped in as Frank followed. The driver wished them a good time and closed the door after them. Frank took his clothes off as Lori watched.

"Well you're not wasting any time, are you?"

"Why should I?"

"I was just asking. We haven't left the lot yet. What do

you think Frank? Do you think thirty seconds have elapsed?"

"More like twenty. If you don't count my socks, it took fifteen seconds for me to get my clothes off."

He watched her take off her T-bar. Then, both of them laughed, as they realized they were both naked and that the limo had still not left the parking lot. Lori lay against the far side of the seat and spread her legs slightly, leaning back, willing to accept whatever would happen.

"Are you nervous?" Frank asked.

"A little. No, a lot. We've never done it before in daylight."

"We've never done it outside of the hot tub."

Frank lay on top of her and started to kiss her between her legs. For the first time it dawned on him what she really was. She was a little girl with a shaved pussy waiting for him to plunge inside of her. No longer was she the strutting stripper whom every man in the place wanted. She was no longer the wonderful dancer whose body followed her will in perfect harmony. She was a tender woman, almost childlike, apprehensive of what would follow.

He took her with her legs up in the air, plunging inside of her. *Not good enough*, Frank said to himself as he grabbed her from behind, twisted his body around so that he was sitting on the limo's rear seat, and pulled her on top of him. Lori now straddled him, facing him as he started to kiss her. Now she was where he wanted her to be--at his level, face to face--an equal. No longer was she beneath him, legs spread out underneath his body, her face hidden under his arms. Pressing their bodies tightly together, they kissed each other, oblivious to their surroundings--forgetting that they were in a limo and that there was a driver with them. When it was over, he realized that he had never considered the use of a rubber.

The limo entered the Sports Bar's parking lot. Frank lifted Lori's head tenderly in his hands and kissed her once more on her lips. "When we go back in, let's go in hand in hand as if we've had a ball."

"I have had a ball. Two of them in fact," she teased.

They got out of the limo. Frank thanked the driver and tipped him a twenty. They walked back into the bar both of them smiling and holding hands and sat down ordering two more drinks from Nadine. Dotie came over to them grinning.

"Well how was it Nipples?"

"It was great, Dotie. A real good time. You shouldn't do so many limos. You'd appreciate them more."

Dotie sidled up to Frank and started to play with the buttons on his shirt. "Nipples, Frank sure has a great tan doesn't he? I'll bet he's got a great body."

"Frank, unbutton your shirt and show Dotie how brown your chest is. You don't mind, do you?"

"No, if you girls insist, I don't mind at all." Frank unbuttoned his shirt as Dotie slipped her hand inside, feeling his chest.

"He's pretty muscular. More than I originally thought. How big is he, Nipples?"

"Big enough." Lori laughed.

"Look Dotie, if you're that curious, why don't you check it out for yourself."

Lori shuddered, almost turning away. For a moment she looked sick. She had worked with Dotie for over a year and knew what she was capable of doing. Frank did not know what he was getting into in his effort to appear nonchalant. Within seconds, Dotie had bent over Frank. Without a word she unzipped his pants, parted his jockey shorts, and pulled out his penis. She stooped a little lower and started to suck on it-- but only for a few seconds. Then she put it back into his shorts and zipped his pants back up.

"Didn't think I'd do it, did you?"

"No, I really didn't," said Frank. "Amazing. Simply amazing."

He looked over at Lori and saw her stiffen, then felt her elbow jabbing him in the guts. "Let's get a table," she hissed. "Just you and I."

She led him to the far corner of the room, close to the stage, yet far away from the bar. "I want to get as far away from that bitch as possible. How could you let her do that to you?" Lori held his eyes in hers, demanding an answer.

"Simple. I didn't know she would actually go down on me."

"You should know better. You know what Dotie is capable of."

"Not really, but apparently you do."

"You damn right I do. Jesus, Frank, how can you be so fucking nonchalant about it?"

"Oh, don't take it so hard Lori. She's just having a little fun is all."

"Yeah. Fun with my boyfriend's penis. God, you act like it's a lolly pop or something. Well, it's not."

"Okay, if it bothers you all that much I'll try to refrain from doing that again."

"Frank, do me a favor?"

"What?"

"Don't ever do that sort of thing again. With other girls maybe, but never do it with me around, and one more thing."

"What's that?"

"Don't ever fuck any of these girls."

"C'mon. Give me a break. You're the one with the boyfriend. Remember. Travis. I believe that's his name. Do I have the right now to say, Lori, I don't want you fucking Travis any more?"

"Well, it's not the same."

"Yes it is."

"Okay then. Use a rubber then. And I want to know who you are doing it with."

"I'll do that much. Do you want a written report or will an oral one do?"

"Just let me know, that's all."

Frank went home that evening knowing that she cared. She had gotten jealous. She had showed the bar that she considered him her private property, not to be shared with anyone. He knew that he was not anyone's private property, but now he knew for the first time that he had influence over

Lori. Perhaps she loved him the way she said she did in the hot tub.

GONE AGAIN

Bitter disappointment struck him as soon as he entered the Sports Bar several days later. Lori was not there. Frank got that sinking feeling that something had happened to Lori and that she was not going to be back. Tamara sat by herself at the other end of the bar. She motioned him over.

"Will you buy me a drink?"

"Why not."

Nadine took their order. She came back with a Jack and Coke and a Budweiser. Tamara sipped from her glass, then looked up at Frank. "Nipples quit again," she said. " She got really drunk the other day. Then she threw a fit. Called us a bunch of holes. Even called me a hole. Then she stomped out of here. My guess is that Bill will not hire her back."

"So she really got pissed."

"No one knows where she is."

"So what else is new?"

"She does this to people you know. She gets a guy interested in her, then when he gets to know her, after he gets onto her games, she dumps him. Disappears. She knows you're onto her head games. She knows that you don't believe her bullshit anymore, so what she has to do is find someone else. Someone new. My guess is you won't hear from her again. Either that or she'll resurface somewhere in a few months after which she'll try to get money out of you in one of the clubs."

"Unless she leaves the state, she won't disappear from me. We'll find each other."

"I hope so, but don't count on it," Tamara replied skeptically.

Several drinks later, he went home. Was it his imagination that the Sports Bar was more dimly lit than usual? Had it stopped being fun without her being there? He could not let himself get this way. *Frank, old boy, grab hold of yourself, you must rely only on yourself--for your internal sense of well-being and for good times. There will always be another girl close-by. Enjoy her, whomever she might be.* He reminded himself that this should be his modus of operandi. But he was leaving and he was leaving early, and that said it all.

INJECTION PLUS

Two days later, he found her--on his answering machine. That voice, with just a trace of a Southern accent told him that she was working at the Injection Pump. Two hours later the phone rang. It was Lori.

"Frank, did you get my message?"

"That you're at the Injection Pump?"

"Yes. I'm working there now. Will you come see me?"

"Now?"

"I've gotta talk to you."

"Why?"

"I just want to see you, that's why. Can you come over? Right away?"

"Okay. Give me an hour and a half."

He drove eighty miles an hour all the way. Leaving his car in the lot, he walked up the stairs into the Injection Pump. He saw her clear down at the other end of the bar., practically out of sight, other dancers and their customers in the way. Yet Lori had seen him first, for she was already smiling and looking over at him. *Unbelieveable,* thought Frank. *The girl has eyes in the back of her head.* He told himself that he could never sneak in on her unobserved.

He paid the three-dollar cover and went over to her. She beamed at him. "I'm over here because of you."

"Because of me?" Frank asked.

"Yes. You always wanted me over here. You told me this was your favorite place and that you would like for me to work here. So here I am. And all because of you. Are you happy?"

"I heard you stomped out of the Sports Bar pissed as hell."

"Sure did. This guy and I were doing a private. He practically raped me back there. I asked him--what makes you think you can do this? He said that the other girls all do it. Then it started to get physical. I kept telling him no. I got louder and louder. No one came to help me. Then I talked to Bill. He told me that I had no reason to get upset and that I shouldn't have gotten his customer angry. Then I told him that all the other girls were giving blow jobs in the corner and that the guys thought they could do whatever they wanted with me. Frank, I got so mad. I called the other girls a bunch of holes and walked out of there."

"So the customer is always right. Let me get you a drink. Jack and Coke, right?"

"You've got it. And you are having a Budweiser or a Bud Lite. Third choice would be a Vodka straight up. See, I know you, Frank. I know you well."

Mary was bartending today. She was a tall girl around one-hundred and thirty. The way most guys like them. But not Frank. He liked them thin, a little on the narrow hipped side, with small breasts. Like Lori. Mary brought their drinks and set them down on the bar as Frank tipped her a dollar. Frank quaffed his beer down, noticing that Lori was almost chugging hers.

Out of beer, Frank looked across the bar at Mary who was on the phone. Five minutes passed. Frank tried to get the bartender's attention. He tapped his beer glass lightly against the bar, trying to get eye contact. Then, exasperated, pulled a five from his pocket and held it in front of his face hoping she'd notice. Mary turned away looking at her feet as she smiled into the phone.

"Why that bitch. She thinks she owns this place just because she's fucking the boss," Lori whispered. "And just when we're thirsty."

"When aren't you thirsty, Lori?" Frank teased.

"Shut up Frank. Shut the fuck up. We've gotta have a drink." Then raising her voice she shouted, "Mary, we're thirsty. Will you get off the phone?" Only then did Mary get off the phone and come over to them.

"All right, Britanny, what do you want?"

"We both want shots. We're going to get drunk. Mary, do you know my friend Frank?"

"Sure. He's here all the time."

"I know." Lori gave Frank a dirty look. "He was always here instead of being where he's supposed to have been. Seeing me."

"You are a jealous wench," said Frank.

Five minutes later the drinks arrived. Lori drank hers in one gulp, then took Frank's glass and lifted it above his face placing the rim on his mouth. He parted his lips knowing too well that if he hesitated one second she would spill it all over him. Lori tilted the glass nearly 90 degrees so that the Tequila emptied into his throat all at once. He started to choke, then regained control--barely. One second later the liquor was on its way to his stomach.

"I'm coming down tomorrow," said Lori.

"Where?"

"With you, to your farm. I'm going to spend the whole day with you. I'm telling Travis that I'm working tomorrow. I don't work

Thursdays but he won't know the difference."

"I'll believe it when I see it."

"This time I promise. Hey, I have to go dance. C'mon, I want to get you up on the stage."

"You need another girl for that," said Frank. "Go find one."

"Why don't you pick one out?"

"I'll go ask Denise. She'll go for it. She's from Texas."

Frank found Denise close to the bar. She was a tall woman, close to 5' 9" in her early thirties. She had short dark brown hair which accentuated her lankiness. Frank had bought her several drinks in the past on several occasions.

"Denise, Britanny's up. She wants me to go up on stage with her. Want to join us?"

"Sure. This'll be fun." Denise snatched up her drink and followed Frank to stage number two. Lori was already there standing on the platform grinning. Frank mounted the steps and walked over to her. Lori started to undo his belt, her hands moving deftly. Denise came up behind him and began to pull off his shorts while Lori unbuttoned his shirt. Then Frank finished taking it off. Seconds later he stood bare chested and bare legged, clad only in his jockey shorts.

"Now get down on the floor," ordered Lori.

Frank lay down on the stage. Its cool surface chilled his bare back. Then Lori lay down on top of him. She had taken her top off while he was positioning himself on the stage. She started to slide her body up and down his, rubbing her bare breasts down his chest and into his groin. Then, wetting her palms and fingertips in her own saliva, she took his nipples in both hands and started to rub them with small circular motions.

"Denise, sit on his face. And don't let him come up for air," yelled Lori.

Denise straddled him, placing her legs on both sides of his head. Then she lowered herself so that her g-string was only an inch above his mouth. Frank stuck out his tongue and started to probe for her opening. Lori inched backwards so that her mouth was on his groin. Then she seized his erect penis in her teeth through his shorts. Suddenly she released him and went down on him once more this time taking a shallower bite so that her teeth gripped only his underwear. Jerking her head upwards she tore a hole in his shorts. Lori lowered her face so that she could place her mouth around the hole. Then she inserted her tongue and started to lick him. Without warning she jerked her head upwards and started to laugh.

"Not big enough. Have to try again."

Lori went down on him again. She bit into his jockey shorts and came up spitting cotton. This time the hole was bigger. She pressed her mouth into the opening and started to probe with her tongue as Frank arched his tongue against Denise's g-string and moved it aside. Suddenly Denise got up.

"C'mon Brittany. Move aside. We're trading places."

Denise inched upwards, straddling his groin as Lori stood up and picked Frank's belt off the floor. Hiding his belt behind her, she sat on his chest. Suddenly she whipped the belt out and started to loop it around his wrist. Frank saw it coming--saw the belt before she could fasten it around him. His arm shot out--displaying his boxer's instinct. His fingers grasped the belt as his arm muscles contracted. Not expecting such quickness Lori relaxed her grip. Frank tore the belt away from her before she knew what had happened and threw it across the stage.

"I know that you'd like to tie me up sometime, but I'm not letting you do it here," said Frank.

Lori knelt down across Frank's face. She lowered herself across his mouth. With one hand she moved her g-string aside as he probed with his tongue. Denise hovered above his groin and started to lick his shorts. Minutes later Frank was thinking only of Lori. *I have to get her to my place tonight,* he thought.

"Our turn. Our turn." The voices belonged to the next two dancers who had just arrived to relieve Lori and Denise. The set over, Frank tipped Lori and Denise each a ten.

"Let's go get another shot, Frank," said Lori obviously anxious to get away from Denise.

Lori and Frank grabbed a table close to the bar. Mary brought them two shots of Cuervo. Once again, Lori took hers in one gulp. She expected him to do the same. He did.

"I've got an idea," suggested Frank. "Why don't we go to my farm tonight?"

"What about tomorrow?" asked Lori.

"You can still come tomorrow if you want. But I would like for you to come tonight."

"I don't know what I'm going to do about Travis. He's picking me up here at eight." Suddenly Lori's face brightened. "I've got it. I'll tell him I'm working a double shift. Then we can stay out till four a.m."

"Sounds good to me."

Eight o'clock came. Lori disappeared into the dressing room and came out ten minutes later with her duffel bag. She sat next to Frank, reached down the front of her shorts, and pulled out a wad of bills, which she placed on the table.

"Here help me count this. This is the money I've made."

Frank sorted the bills into tens, twenties, and fives placing them into three piles. He counted one hundred and sixty-five dollars. Then he stacked them into one pile and handed them back to Lori.

"Wait here for me. And get us a beer. I've gotta go give my money to Travis. By the way, you're going to have to give me some money tonight so that he'll think I actually worked."

"Sounds like Travis is your pimp."

"He's something. Whatever. Here watch my shit and make sure no one takes it." Then she darted across the room leaving the duffel bag at Frank's feet. A few minutes later she came back smiling. Frank had used the time to get two glasses of beer from the bartender. Lori sat next to him and started on her beer.

"He believed me. We'll just finish our beers which will give him time to get out of here. Then we can go."

They left at 8:30. He took her to his little sports car and opened the car door for her. She gave him a puzzled look which told him that she was not used to having men open doors for her.

"You don't have to do that," said Lori.

"Look. Let's get one thing straight. When you're with me, you're a lady. My lady. Now don't argue," Frank replied.

He started the engine and backed out of the parking lot. They were soon on highway 55 heading North. He reached under the seat for the white chauffer's hat which he had put there earlier. Putting it on his head he turned to Lori and grinned. "What do you think? Little car with no top on and then this hat. A little much, right?"

"No, it looks good on you."

"But, it'll look even better on you." He took the cap off and put it on Lori's head. He dropped the car into 4th and punched the accelerator just as Lori started to stand in her seat. The car's sudden acceleration made her fall backwards almost causing the hat to fall off. Frank brought the car up to 100 mph. The supercharger's response was instantaneous, unlike a turbocharger's which would have experienced a slight delay before kicking in, a phenomenon known as turbo lag. The engine began to whine as the supercharger kicked in. Frank looked over at Lori who was watching the scenery rush by. Observing that she was doing something with her hair, he asked himself, *What is she doing?* Even at a hundred miles per hour, he could see that Lori was braiding her hair into the hat's adjusting band.

"Lori, what are you doing with your hair?"

"I'm fixing it so that it won't blow off my head. This little tightening band isn't enough to keep it on if I get in the wind. If I tie my hair around the band, I won't lose the hat."

Lori continued to play with her hair. Finally, satisfied with her work, she stood up in her seat, hat firmly in place. By this time Frank had the little car down to eighty. Lori stood on the seat enjoying the night air--her face radiant--showing not a trace of fear that she might fall out.

They stopped at a tavern along the way. The place was not far from his farm. His cousin, Dick, sat at the bar talking to Tony Barnes, who farmed one of the farms in his area. Dick was thirty-five while Tony was in his early sixties. Frank was amazed that Lori remained quiet and attentive to the conversation around her. Finally, she excused herself to go to the ladies room.

"Hey Frank, said Tony, that girl is something else. But I don't think you're wired right for her." Tony laughed as he talked. Frank did not consider the comment to be an insult at all--that was just Tony, that's all. *But what did he mean by being wired for a particular girl?*

"Dick, what does Tony mean by wired? I never heard that one before."

"Neither did I," laughed Dick. "I think I know what he means, but I'm not sure."

"What does he mean?" asked Frank.

"Probably that she's too young for you."

"What did you mean Tony?" Frank looked right at Tony who sat there laughing in his beer.

"Nothing Frank. Just that you and Lori are wired differently, that's all. And it's not just age."

"Then what is it?"

"You'll just have to find that out," said Tony.

They left after Lori came out of the ladies room. Frank's farm was close by. A motion detector turned an outside light on when the car pulled into the driveway. The house was nestled inside a windbreak of Colorado Blue Spruce trees which shielded the house from the wind on all four sides. He had planted them--all 150 of them 15 years before. They were just now starting to get some height, being a slow growing tree to start with. Not only had they begun to protect the house from the wind--they also kept anyone outside the trees from seeing his house from any direction--thus lending an air of mystery to the farmstead as well as to its owner. A modern machine shed 100 feet long lay just outside the windbreak. In it were several tractors, a planter, and other machinery and tools. Frank had placed it outside the windbreak by design. He was a farmer, and painfully aware of the stresses that farming puts on a man--the twenty-four hour days, the ravages of the weather, the wild fluctuations of the grain markets, the dangerous machinery he had to work around--had deliberately tried to keep business and pleasure separate. When he was in his house and for that matter in his yard, he wouldn't see the machine shed which served as a reminder of the kind of work he had to do. And when he was in the machine shed he couldn't see his house, which would remind him of the soft life waiting for him inside.

An old barn lay inside the windbreak. Frank was very proud of this old barn and had renovated it. Inside he had built a recreation room. He had a bar put in which he had obtained from a local tavern just before it closed. In the middle of the floor he had placed a pool table. Then Frank had put in two oak tables with chairs. The room was rustic in appearance for the walls and ceiling were of the 1880's when the barn had been built. Heavy wooden beams in the ceiling supported the hayloft above it. Frank had built this rec. room in the barn as a place where he and his friends could get together and not disturb Karen and the kids. It was also a place he could escape to.

The house was new, having replaced the old house that had been there since Civil War times. It was not large, having only five rooms downstairs: a large family room, a kitchen, a utility room, one bedroom, and a bathroom. The upstairs was a loft. Two small bedrooms and another bathroom were up there. Frank had designed the house, like the yard, to be more at home in Colorado than in Illinois. He had patterned it off several of the larger condos he had stayed in on his many ski vacations. One example was the oak shake shingle roof. The loft was another example. Then there was that sunken portion of the floor in the family room with its focal point being the large fireplace. This sunken area was twelve feet square. Where the sunken portion rose to meet the upper level, Frank had placed cushions for people to sit. All of this replaced the need for a couch and chairs. Heavy oak beams stretched across this room from wall to wall. Frank was using one of the upstairs bedrooms for his office. The other he was using for a weight room. Frank showed Lori the whole place. He showed her the machine shed. Had her sit in one of his tractors. Then he walked her around his yard. The house was last. Frank took her into every room. He showed her his photo albums. She showed genuine interest in whatever he showed her, listening attentively to what he had to say. She was like a sponge--remembering everything while missing nothing.

The bedroom was the last thing he showed her. After they made love, Frank hoped that she'd come back again and again. And then they had to leave. Suddenly it was 2:45 a.m. It would take him one hour to get her back. The Injection Pump closed at 4:00 a.m. If Travis got there early and saw them come in at 3:45 when Lori was supposed to be in there working, she'd be in trouble. He thought of all this. Lori had however even forgotten what time it was.

He brought her back to the Injection Pump's parking lot at 3:45. They went upstairs and had a beer together. 4:00 rolled by. 4:15. They did not want to leave each other--could not leave each other, not until the last moment. They were the last to leave and Travis was outside waiting, waiting for sixty dollars, which Lori would give him after telling him she had a slow night.

ON THE FARM TOGETHER

The next day Frank was having his first beer at the Injection Pump bar at noon. Lori arrived fifteen minutes later. *Now this is a landmark event*, thought Frank, *for it's the first time except for work that Lori ever showed up somewhere she had promised to be.* He bought her a beer. An hour and a half later they were at his farm.

"Before we do anything else, I want to take you on a bike ride," said Frank.

"Do I need a helmet?" asked Lori.

"Not where we're going."

Frank went out to the barn and pulled his dirt bike out. It was a 500 c.c. Honda XL. The bike had one cylinder and plenty of horsepower. *Just the thing to scare the shit out of Lori*, thought Frank. He straddled the seat and started the bike with the kick starter.

"Lori, hop on before it dies," he urged. "It's cold blooded and takes a while to get warmed up."

She hopped on the seat behind him and put her arms around his waist. Frank piloted the machine down his driveway and into the field behind his farmstead. He took off easy in 1st gear knowing that if he did a wheelie things could get nasty in a hurry in the soft dirt. Frank accelerated quickly through 2nd and 3rd gear down the dirt field lane that wound between the neighbors field and his. Then he turned off into his field. He hit sixty before his nerve left him. It was one thing to do sixty or even a hundred on the street, but it was another thing to go sixty in a bean field on a dirt bike. The front tire started to wobble on him as it wandered into one cultivated ridge after another. Frank slowed and turned toward a drainage ditch.

Without proper drainage his farm would be a swamp. In fact it had been a swamp one-hundred years or so before. Back before the turn of the century, farmers had drained this swampland with field tile and drainage ditches. Field tiles back then were made of concrete or clay. Long ditches three to four feet deep and a foot or so across were dug by hand across farmers' fields. Field tiles, whether of concrete or clay, were hollow cylinders a foot or two in length. These were placed end to end in the ditches to form a long hollow tube under the ground which would serve as a conduit for water. Such ditches were typically a quarter mile long. Every hundred feet or so a new ditch would be dug and field tiles placed in its bottom. At the end of the field there was usually a drainage ditch some of which were ten or twelve feet deep. The underground field tiles ran into these ditches emptying tons of water into them. Frank headed his bike into one of these ditches.

The bank was almost straight up and down. He aimed his front tire straight into the ditch at a ninety-degree angle. He could feel Lori's fingers tighten around his waist. The bike plunged down the bank. Not able to turn sharply enough Frank rode up the opposite bank part way before he could get the bike around to drive down the length of the ditch. Riding down the bottom of the twelve-foot ditch Frank managed to do twenty-five miles an hour--or that was what his fear threshold would allow him to do. After one-half mile the ditch made a ninety degree bend to the left. He could turn left and continue riding in the bottom of the ditch. Instead he went straight on slowing to fifteen miles per hour. Frank hit the bank dead on. The bike's momentum took them over the top and out of the ditch.

Frank drove out onto the county road.

"So you're going to do something sensible for a change," said Lori.

"Not if I can help it," replied Frank.

He took her a mile down the road to one of his farms. It was there that Frank stored most of his corn. He kept it in 36 foot diameter circular steel bins which were twenty to thirty feet tall. Each bin had its own perforated steel floor which was 18 inches or more above ground level. Large electrical fans blew hot or cold air into this air space and into the perforations of the floor. This air then blew upwards through the corn which filled the bin. In this manner Frank was able to dry his corn down so that it would not spoil.

A tall steel tower, known on the farm as a grain leg, carried the corn one-hundred feet into the air. The corn then plummeted down steel tubes into the grain bins below. Frank parked the bike next to this tower which was only several feet across. A ladder ran up its side one-hundred feet to a steel platform at the top.

"I'll bet you can't make it up that ladder to the Frank Harring observation center that we are now looking at up there." Frank pointed at the platform. "Follow me, Lori."

Frank walked over to the ladder and started to climb it. He didn't go up there that often. It was a good workout being a hand over hand foot over foot affair. He looked behind him. Lori was right there. She hadn't even stopped to consider what she was doing or how she was going to do it. Frank knew that only one out of ten women would even attempt to go up that leg and that out of that 10% most girls would lag badly behind the guy. Frank climbed rapidly hoping to test Lori. He didn't look down until he had reached the platform. Only then did he look down. She was still right behind him. *Amazing*, he thought. *She's one of a kind. Fearless, strong, and very agile. Anyone who prefers a woman with a big ass and large breasts, just let him try her up here and see how she does.*

He pulled himself up onto the platform. Thirty seconds later Lori stood beside him. Up there they could see for fifteen miles or more. Frank put his arm around Lori.

"You're some woman to be able to scamper right after me like that."

"Frank, was there a reason for bringing me up here?"

"Sure. Two reasons. One. To enjoy the view. Two. To see if you would do it."

"You knew I would. You knew that all the time."

"True, but I had to see you do it."

Back on the ground a few minutes later, Frank had a brainstorm. Lori didn't even whimper when she was on the bike. Never said a word afterwards. She had just climbed the grain leg and had made it seem as easy as climbing out of bed.

"Let's go mow some grass," suggested Frank.

"You've got to be kidding."

"No, I'm not. I planned to do it a week ago. If we don't do it today, I'll hate myself."

"Whatever."

He took her to another one of his farms, this one being 7 miles away from his house. He had a 4450 John Deere tractor there. A seven-foot Woods mower was attached to the three point hitch on the back of the tractor. Frank climbed up into the cab. She followed sitting close in the seat next to him. He shut the door, turned the key which started the tractor, and turned on the stereo. His hand found a little knob above his head and turned it to the right.

"See, even has air conditioning," said Frank.

"I thought when you said mowing you were thinking of a little lawnmower," said Lori.

"Nothing's little on this farm, Lori."

Frank drove the tractor to a ditch which bordered one of his cornfields. Driving down the roadside just to the left and parallel to the ditch, Frank guided the tractor closer and closer to the ditch. Cutting the tractor's front tires at a slight angle Frank managed to slip the right front tire into the ditch. Soon he had the right rear tire in the ditch. He turned the steering wheel to the right and brought the right front tire up on the ditch bank. This brought the tractor's right rear tire up on the bank as well leaving the tractor's left tires, both front and rear, riding in the ditch. The tractor now rested at a precarious angle with its right side high up in the air on the ditch bank while its left side was down in the ditch. Frank turned behind him so that he could see out the back window of the cab. Using the hydraulic three point control lever Frank was able to lower the Woods mower deck so that it was only a few inches off the ditch bank. Then Frank pushed in the PTO lever. This engaged the PTO shaft that ran from the tractor's transmission out the back of the tractor. This shaft then engaged a shaft on the mower which turned the mower's blades.

He guided the tractor forward, the mower cutting down the grass and weeds on the ditch bank as it went along. The ditch gradually became deeper and deeper. In order to cut the whole ditch bank, Frank had to take the tractor higher and higher up the bank. This caused the precarious angle the tractor was leaning to become steeper still. Frank dropped the tractor down another gear. It was now crawling along at only one mph. Frank took it further up the bank until he could feel the weight shift. The cab made the tractor top heavy. The angle was now so severe that Frank could sense that the tractor was about to go over. One false move and she'd go. Another foot or two or a turn of the steering wheel in the wrong direction, not to mention the movements of Frank and Lori in the cab, would turn the tractor over.

He turned to look at Lori. She could feel it too. Frank saw it in her face. Lori felt the tractor's weight start to shift, and knew that the heavy machine was about to turn over, not on the right side but on the left side--her side of the tractor. For the first time he saw fear in her eyes.

He held her eyes and asked softly, "Do you trust me?" And then he guided the tractor off the embankment. They could feel the weight of the tractor shift. Seconds later they were out of trouble.

"Do you want to drive, Lori?"

"Yes, but not in this ditch."

Frank drove the tractor out onto the road. Lori got up into his lap and took the wheel. He showed her how the controls worked. Five minutes later she was guiding the tractor down the road at twenty miles per hour.

He had her drive the tractor back to the farmstead. After they got out, Lori gazed out into Frank's field. The corn was seven feet tall, still green for harvest was a month and a half away.

"Can you get me an ear of corn?" asked Lori. "I want an ear from your farm as a souvenir."

"The corn is premature. The ears are just starting to form so there's no corn on the cob. We'll have to come back later," Frank replied. "Lori, I'll tell you what. It won't be the same, but I'll pull some shelled corn out of the bin."

A grain bin stood a hundred feet from where they were standing. Frank ran over to it and scampered up the ladder which was bolted to its side. Reaching the top of the ladder he unlatched the small door on the lower part of the bin's roof. Then he entered the bin and walked down another ladder inside the bin. Grabbing a handful of loose corn which the combine had taken off the cob, Frank retraced his steps, climbing up and down both ladders with one hand. Running up to Lori, he handed her the corn. For a second or two she studied the corn--and then threw it at him. Corn ran down Frank's shirt. Grinning wildly Lori started to run away, but she wasn't fast enough. Frank caught up with her easily and scooped her off her feet. She put her arms around his neck and started to kiss him. He carried her back to his pickup, kissing her all the way.

BOGART LAYS DOWN THE LAW

The following Tuesday he found her at the bar. It seemed to Frank that business had been slacking off at the Injection Pump. *Was it the economy or was it because new topless bars were sprouting up in the area?* He bought Lori a Jack and Coke, the drink of choice of more than one dancer. They went to the stage together where she sat on his lap. They talked until her set was over when they went back to the bar for another round of drinks. Time flew. And then Bogart came over.

"Brittany, you're up on stage. Don't let me remind you again."

"Jesus Frank, I lost track of the time. Don't do this to me."

He followed her over to stage two. He set her glass down on the stage and started to drink from his glass. Suddenly Lori looked down on him and started to laugh.

"Okay. What's so funny?" asked Frank.

"Nothing. I just got an idea. Come on up here. You're getting up on stage with me."

"Don't we need another girl?"

"There's no law against just the two of us being up here," said Lori.

"I've been here a lot and I've never seen one girl get a customer up on stage before," replied Frank. "There's always two girls."

"We're just going to have to start something new," said Lori.

Frank walked up the stairs onto the stage. Lori came up to him and threw her arms around his neck. He kissed her.

"Off with your clothes Frank. I really want to fuck your brains out. Can't do it here so we'll just have to have a little fun."

Frank pulled off his shirt while she helped him pull off his shorts. He lay on the floor on his back. He had worn the same jockey shorts he had worn in there the week before. The holes that Lori had torn in them were still there. She lay down on top of him and started to kiss his nipples. Then she got up and lay down on him once more so that her head was even with his groin. She thrust her pelvis into his face and started to lick his jockey shorts. Moving across his shorts with her tongue she found one of the holes--and inserted her tongue. Frank slid his tongue next to her G-string and moved it aside. His tongue found her opening. Then he forgot where he was.

"Just what in the fuck are you two doing?' bellowed Bogart.

"I want you both off the stage now. Brittany, you know better than to do that."

Frank jumped up, found his shorts, and put them on. Snapping up his shirt, he leaped off the stage. Lori stayed on stage as he put his shirt on. Frank looked at Bogart sheepishly. "Bogart, we didn't mean to cause you any trouble. We won't do that again."

"You're goddamn right, you're not going to do that again. I've got a job to do, and you two are going to get my ass in trouble. Now I want you both to behave." Bogart stalked off to his table where he could watch the door.

Lori looked across at Frank. "We'll just have to go somewhere afterwards, that's all."

"I'll take you home with me. But first I'm going to take you to one of the neighborhood taverns. They have a pool table there. You can't beat me on my turf," said Frank.

"I'll bet I can," replied Lori. "We can play some pool here and get warmed up."

Several drinks and several pool games later, Frank looked at his watch. "It's eight o'clock. Who's your ride?"

"You."

"No. I mean who's supposed to pick you up?"

"Travis."

"Do you think he's out there yet?"

"Order us both a beer. I'll go get dressed, then check it out."

Lori went into the dressing room. Frank finished half his beer before she came out. Lori sat down at the table and stared at her glass intently. Without a word she picked it up and chugged its contents. Then she turned to Frank. "See you in a few minutes. Stay right here." Then she was gone. Frank looked under the table. Her bag was there. *She'll be back*, he said to himself.

Five minutes later he saw her come in. Smiling broadly she quickly crossed the room over to his table. "I gave him the money I made. Then I told him I was working a second shift, just like before. Order us another beer."

They left at 8:30. He took her to a little town five miles the other side of his farm and they headed to one of the town's two taverns.

"Where are we anyway?" asked Lori.

"Anyplace U.S.A. Just one of many little towns around here. They're all practically alike so it just doesn't matter where we are," replied Frank.

The tavern was on the town's main street. Lori followed him in. There was only one long narrow room. At the far end was a pool table. Five or six men sat at the bar stooped over their beers while several overweight women sat around the bar. Everyone looked up from their drinks studying the pretty newcomer.

"Everyone's looking at me," whispered Lori.

"They always do that when anyone new walks in here. Don't let it get to you. That's just the way it is in these country towns. And every town's the same. They're going to size you up and they're not going to be very shy about it. Two years into my marriage they were still staring at Karen every time we walked into one of these places."

A large blonde headed man saw Frank come in, grinned, and jumped off his barstool. The man had worked for Frank in the past-- had driven all of his tractors. He had been a good worker, but because of his habitual frequenting of taverns, had never been able to hold down a steady job. This was his place, his home away from home. Like a piece of furniture, he was a part of this particular bar's scenery. The man came up to Frank and put his arms around him.

"Hey Frank, I see you've got a new woman. Man, I haven't seen you in a long time. Where have you been?"

"Haven't been home much, Tommy. Haven't been here either," Frank replied. Frank turned to Lori. "Lori, this is Tommy. He used to help me farm."

"Glad to meet you, Tommy. Frank says he's going to beat me in pool. What do you think?"

"Ah, you can take him. He's not much good as a pool player. Can I buy you two a drink? What are you having?"

"Two Bud Lights," Lori replied. "Come on and watch me beat Frank."

"You two go ahead and play. I'll have the bartender bring you your beer."

Frank went over to the pool table, put three quarters in, and waited for the balls to rattle down into the waiting slot. Then he racked them up. Lori went over to the queue stick stand.

"These aren't heavy enough. I need a heavy stick."

"Just pick the best one," replied Frank.

This night Lori and Frank were an even match. Halfway through the first game Frank lined up with the eleven. The queue ball was at the far end of the table from the eleven back in the corner. It was a long shot. To make matters worse the eleven was not lined up with the corner pocket. To make it Frank would have to cut the eleven on its far left side.

"Don't shoot the eleven," warned Lori. "You can't make it. Take the combination shot. Hit the seven over here just left of center." Lori stepped over to the right side of the table and pointed at the seven. "It will hit the nine right here and bring it back to the right rear pocket."

Frank ignored her, took his shot, and missed.

"See. I told you not to take that shot. You never listen to me Frank," Lori said angrily.

"Christ Lori, it's just a game. Don't take it so seriously."

"To you it's just a game. You could be a decent player if you'd just listen for once."

"Maybe I really don't care to be a good pool player. I just want to have a good time, that's all."

Half an hour later they were already on their third beer. Lori came up to Frank, took his pool stick away from him, set it against the wall, and pressed herself up against him. She threw her arms around his neck and started to kiss him. He opened his mouth and stuck his tongue in hers. Lori sucked his tongue back into her mouth. He tried to pull it out but couldn't as Lori continued to suck his tongue. Finally, she released him. Then she started to lick his mouth working upwards to his moustache and finally to his nose. She inserted her tongue into his nostril. Then she pulled away.

"Come on," said Frank. "Let's get out of here. I want to take you home with me."

"Let's go then."

He took her to his house, went into the kitchen, and made her a Jack and Coke. She came up to him and started to take off his shirt. Moments later they were both naked on the floor. Suddenly she jumped up.

"Turn over Frank."

She got down on him again. Then she did something to him that he never forgot. Did something he'd never tell anyone about and that she'd remind him about over and over again for months afterwards.

At two-thirty Frank started to feel the full effect of the beer. He had to go to the bathroom. Lori went into the bathroom upstairs. He went into the other bathroom on the other side of the house, opened his fly, pulled out his penis, and aimed into the bowl. Just when he was about to let go, Frank had that feeling that he was not alone. He looked up and saw her standing in the doorway, watching him. Then she came in.

"Now just what are you doing, Lori?"

"Watching you."

"Why?"

"Because I love you, that's why."

"Well I get nervous when people watch."

"Just ignore me then."

When he had finished, they went back into the family room. She put her arms around Frank's neck and pulled herself tightly against him. "I wish I could stay here all night," said Lori. "What time is it anyway?"

"Time to get back."

It took them an hour to get back to the Injection Pump's parking lot. It was a quarter to four, fifteen minutes before closing time. They both knew that if Travis had already arrived there would be no way for her to sneak back in. Lori doubled her body down into her seat so that it would appear that Frank was in the car alone.

"Do you see my car in the lot?" asked Lori.

Frank looked for the old Grand Prix. He couldn't be sure--a lot of cars looked like hers--but he didn't think it was in the lot. "It's not there," said Frank. " We're lucky. We've been cutting it too close. We should start getting back by 3:30 at the latest," he warned.

Lori sat up in her seat, visibly relieved. "Then let's go grab a beer. We both need one."

Halfway through their first beer Lori looked up at Frank. "I hate this. I want to be with you more, but it looks like I'll have to be content with fucking you only once a week. Wednesdays are my day off, and I've got Travis convinced that I'm working Wednesdays."

"Tomorrow is Wednesday. Want to meet me here tomorrow at noon," asked Frank.

"Sure."

"We can have a standing arrangement to meet here at noon on Wednesdays and just take off," said Frank.

Once again it was impossible for them to leave each other. At a quarter after four the bouncer made the decision for them, chasing them out. She walked down the steps. Frank knew it was stupid, but he followed her closely. Travis was outside in the car waiting and watching.

WHAT ARE BEST FRIENDS FOR?

Frank waited half an hour for Lori to show. She never came. *Was she up to her old tricks?* he asked himself. He drank his beer when suddenly an idea hit him and smiled inwardly. *Okay Little Miss Unreliable, there's no excuse for not showing or at least for not calling. Let's see how you like my latest little plan.*

He went to the Sports Bar. Tamara was there. Then he spied Dottie sitting alone at the bar. He waved at Tamara and went over to Dottie.

"Dottie, let's grab a table. I'll buy you all the drinks you can drink." Frank had never sat alone with Dottie before.

"Go grab one. I'll be right behind you." Then Dottie looked over at the bartender. "Cindy, get me a whiskey sour and get Frank a beer."

Frank picked out a table and they sat down. Dottie leaned forward, placed her elbows on the table, and looked directly at Frank. "Have you seen Nipples lately?"

"She just stood me up."

"I thought you two were going out. She likes you a lot you know. Why'd she do that?"

"I don't know. We went out last night. I took her to my farm again. She was supposed to meet me at the Injection Pump at noon today but she never came."

"Sometimes I just don't understand her. Lori likes you though. That's for sure."

"Yeah. She sure has a funny way of showing it, doesn't she? Hey Dottie, how would you like to help me pimp Nipples?"

"How?"

"What do you think of my buying you out of this bar? We can go somewhere--get drunk--get a hotel room. Whatever. The other girls will tell her and you and I can have a damn good time."

Dottie started to grin, then broke out laughing. Frank knew he could rely on three fundamental truths that would work in his favor. *One. Dottie like most of the girls in these places would be money hungry. Two. Dottie was well known for becoming intimate with many men. And Three. Like many women everywhere, Dottie would not only take advantage of an opportunity to move into another woman's territory but would revel in doing so.*

"You two are good friends," said Frank.

"She's my best friend," said Dottie.

"She deserves to get pimped. Right?"

"It sounds like fun to me."

Cindy brought over their drinks. Dottie sipped from her whiskey sour. Frank pointed at her glass and raised his beer bottle. "Here's to you and me having a great time then."

Dottie chugged her drink. "I'm ready for another." Then she glanced at Tamara. Frank followed Dottie's eyes and decided to bring Tamara in as well.

"Come on over here, Tamara. I'm buying you a drink."

Tamara walked over and sat next to Frank. "What's up?" she asked.

"Nipples just stood me up today."

"She hasn't changed, has she?"

"I thought she had, but it doesn't look that way, does it?"

"She'll never change. Not until she grows up."

"Dottie and I are hatching a little plot. What do you think of my paying a hundred bucks and buying Dottie out of this bar? We go drinking somewhere and then go to a motel room."

Tamara doubled over with laughter. "Tremendous. That's tremendous. Nipples needs to learn her lesson. But I've got even a better idea. Why don't you and Dottie do a limo? Nipples knows what Dottie does on limos. No offence Dottie, but Nipples has been on a limo with you and one of the customers before. We all know about it."

Dottie started to giggle. "What do you say, Frank? Me and you on a limo."

"I think it's a great idea. Then let's do it."

"I've gotta go pee. Make sure I get another drink, okay."

"Go ahead. Tamara and I will sit here and talk."

Dottie got up and headed for the restroom. Tamara pulled her chair up closer to Frank's. She pulled a tiny packet from her pocket and handed it to Frank.

"Here's a rubber, Frank. You be sure you use it. Promise me. Dottie does a lot of limos. She fucks everybody. You be careful now. Promise me."

"I'll put it on twice," replied Frank.

Tamara looked up, saw Cindy close by, and waved her over. "Cindy we all need a drink. A shot of Cuervo for me, whiskey sour for Dottie, and a bud for Frank. Frank's doing a limo with Dottie. Nipples stood him up today."

Frank handed Cindy a twenty. Cindy took it, looked away,

and went to get their drinks. It was obvious that she liked Lori and didn't want to see her get hurt. Several minutes later she returned with the drinks and gave Frank his change.

"Now you be careful, Frank," said Cindy.

"Yes mother," Frank replied.

After Cindy left, Frank turned to Tamara and asked very seriously, "How will Lori take this when she finds out?"

"She'll probably not have anything more to do with you. Lori doesn't like to share and she knows Dotie will fuck anybody and that she does drugs. She probably won't fuck you with somebody else's dick if you ask me."

"Excuse me, Tamara, but they've got the paperwork waiting at the bar. I've better take care of it now so that Dotie and I are here when the limo arrives."

Frank went up to the bar and gave Cindy his Visa. She charged $170 on his card and had him sign the form. Then she gave him $100 in cash keeping back $70 for the owner. Standard procedure was for the girl to make $100 whereas the bar always got $70 out of which it paid the driver $20. Sometimes the girl charged more than $100. There were also incidents where the girl charged less if she was hard up for cash and her customer was not hard up for sex.

When Frank got back to the table, Dotie was already there waiting. The driver walked up to them from the rear entrance of the club.

"Hi, my name's Jack. The limo's ready."

Frank knew that the Sports Bar had two different procedures for the limo. At night the limo was always there in the parking lot. During the daytime the driver was on call--more often than not--at home. The day shift girls who worked from noon to 8:00 p.m. did not do a lot of limos. Since there wasn't much demand for limos during the daytime both the limo and the driver were kept off the premises. The night shift was a different matter. The girls were usually less laid back and more pushy. Management encouraged them to do limos and the girls responded. The limo was kept outside, always ready for the next joyride.

Jack led the way through the rear entrance. He opened the rear door of the large car for Dotie, who crawled in giggling. Frank followed, bringing beer with him. Jack closed the door behind them, got in the driver's seat, and started the engine. He waited until he drove into the street before he pulled the privacy screen across the rear window which separated the driver from his passengers.

Frank looked over at Dotie, grinned, and started to take his clothes off. Thirty seconds later they were both naked.

"Dotie, does that privacy screen really work? I can see the driver through the window. I've heard he can't see us though."

"Don't let it worry you, Frank. Believe me, he can't see us at all."

"Well, I want to find out for sure. Watch this." Frank sat up in his seat and leaned into the window sticking his tongue out at the driver. Then he turned back to Dotie.

"He didn't acknowledge me. I'm trying again."

This time Frank brought his whole body to the window. He could see Jack watching the road ahead, both hands on the steering wheel occasionally glancing through his rearview mirror. Frank pressed his penis up against the window and started to stroke it. Just then Jack looked through the rearview mirror but only for a split second after which he continued to watch the road.

"You're right. He can't see us," said Frank.

Dotie was laughing so hard that she spilled part of her drink. Frank watched her double up as she choked on the rest of it. "If he could see me, he'd be laughing just like you are, Dotie. Instead he's so serious; he's so conscientious about his driving, you'd think he was a prison guard at Alcatraz."

Dotie edged up to him so that she could kiss him on his lips. Her tongue started at his mouth and quickly moved down his chest and into his groin. A few moments later she saw that he was aroused. Breaking away she stopped, and pulled a small packet from her purse. Pulling the rubber from the protective foil, she slipped it onto him. Once again she took him into her mouth. Dotie sensed the right moment had arrived and pulled away. Lying on her back against the seat she pointed between her legs.

"Come on Frank. Let's do it. Come on in."

He climbed on top of her. She put her legs around his waist as he entered her. Only then did he get a good look at her. He liked her as a person and didn't consider her a slut regardless of what others told him. She had always been cheerful around him even when he refused to tip her or buy her a drink. Dotie always told him what she thought. She always acknowledged him and always made him feel important. Dotie was pretty but she was overweight. As he entered her Frank noticed the rolls of fat around her stomach. His body did not betray him or then again perhaps it did. Instantly it became a

338

traffic signal for his thoughts. He was not turned on. Frank didn't really want her. He was doing this as a joke, as a way of getting back at Lori. His hard-on died--immediately. He didn't know if he had gotten inside of her or not because he got soft at the critical moment.

Frank couldn't tell her. "Sorry but you're too fat. I can't keep it up for you. You're not Lori." He liked Dotie too much. He continued to rub up against her as if nothing had happened. Maybe, just maybe, he could fake an orgasm. Probably not, but it would be worth it if he could get away with it. He pretended to get excited. Then he pulled away.

"Here, let me pull that thing off your dick," offered Dottier.

"No. Have a cigarette. Relax. I'll do it," Frank replied, thinking *God, I don't want her to see how little it is and that I haven't left anything on it or on the rubber*. And he pulled it off himself, hiding it from her, as he grabbed Kleenex from the limo's dispenser and stuffed the rubber into it. Then he threw the rubber into the limo's trash can.

They had started early and they had ended early. With fifteen minutes to kill Dotie and Frank were both grateful for the drinks they had brought along. They finished them just as the limo pulled up at the Sports Bar. They went inside after Frank tipped the driver. He bought her a drink; then she excused herself to go to the bathroom. Two people came up to Frank whom he had known a long time.

"Frank, why you old whore. Goddamn you are a whore you know."

It was Kathy, a woman who lived thirty miles from him who had gone drinking with him and with her girlfriend several times before. She had come in with Patrick, a man who now drove a truck for Anheuser Busch, who at one time had earned a well-deserved reputation as a bar room brawler.

"Hi, Kathy. I see you and Patrick are still together. Looks like you've settled him down a bit." Frank looked at Patrick. "You are a little quiet, Patrick. You always let her do all the talking?"

"Only when I want to let her," replied Patrick.

"You old whore Frank. I heard you just took Dotie on a limo. Did you get a good fuck?" asked Kathy.

"We're just friends enjoying the sights of the greater East Side," replied Frank.

Dotie never came back. Later Frank heard she did three more limos after him. But that was later on another day, and it didn't really matter after all. So he went home and thought about the things that did matter.

MR. HEDONISTIC

The card shop specialized in the kind of cards you didn't send to Mother. There were racks upon racks filled with cards of well-built men with huge penises, naked three hundred pound women, women giving head, etc. Frank poured through hundreds of cards looking for the right one. At last he found it. On its front it read MAN OR WOMAN. Inside was a picture of a naked man standing ten feet off the ground in the fork of a tree staring at the ground, his muscles tense, ready to leap. Underneath the picture the card read I'M FUCKING THE FIRST PERSON WHO COMES BY.

Several days had passed since Lori had stood him up. He walked into the Injection Pump with a package that he had carefully gift-wrapped. She was waiting for him at the bar.

"Hi Lori. How are things going?" Frank asked.

"Better now that you're here. Who's that for?"

"It's for you. Who do you think?"

"For me? A gift? I suppose you wrapped it yourself."

"Just for you and I did wrap it myself. Open it."

Lori started to unwrap her present. Meanwhile several other girls came over, curious over what he had gotten her. She tore off the wrapping paper and opened the box that Frank had purchased from Hallmark. In the box was a single ear of corn and the card that Frank had bought for her. She read the card and laughed. Then she showed it to the other girls.

"I'm taking it into the dressing room so I can put it in my bag," said Lori. Then she left for the dressing room still smiling. One of the other girls came up to Frank.

"I think that's awful what you did to Lori," said the girl.

"Why?" replied Frank.

"Giving her an ear of corn. And that card was really disgusting," said the girl.

"It's an inside joke between Lori and me. You noticed that she wasn't crying."

"Still, I think it's a rotten thing to do," said the girl. Then she left.

Lori came out of the dressing room smiling. She came up to Frank who was by this time sitting at the bar. "Will you buy me a drink?" she asked.

"Sure. What would you like?"

"I'll start with a Bud Lite."

He ordered two beers from the bartender, then turned to Lori. "When you stood me up last week, I decided not to get angry. That was hard to do because I thought we had stopped all of that. I really believed that your unreliable days were over. I had driven seventy miles to pick you up, one hundred and forty miles both ways. You didn't even call."

"I was sick."

"Lori, there's only Three hundred million phones in the United States. Do you mean to tell me that you couldn't find one of them?"

"Frank, you know that I don't have a phone. And I was too sick to go to one of the neighbors. Besides, I don't know the people around me."

"Okay, I'm not going to get mad. Life is too short for that. I just want you to understand how disappointed I was in you not showing. So I ended up going into the Sports Bar where I found your old friend Dotie. We ended up doing a limo together."

"I know. I heard all about it. So you decided to get even with me."

"That's not getting even. I was having a good time, and she was willing."

"So you fucked my best friend."

"More or less."

"Drink up Frank," Lori ordered. "We are getting drunk."

Two beers later she was up on stage with Frank. Lori waved a waitress over. "Get us two shots of Cuervo and keep them coming."

After the waitress left to get their drinks Frank pulled Lori off the stage onto his lap. "What do you want Lori? What do you really want?"

"You." She said it in a little girl's voice. "That's all I want, is you."

The hours flew by. Soon it was eight o'clock. Travis would be outside waiting.

"I have another bar to take you to. It's close to where I live. Think we can sneak another one by Travis?"

"We sure as hell can try," replied Lori. "I'll go outside and see if he's there."

Lori picked up her money which she had set on the table earlier and ran down the stairs. Five minutes later he saw her walking toward him, a cigarette hanging out of her mouth. It struck Frank that she sometimes walked like a man, quickly and confidently. The cigarette which she kept in her mouth as she walked completed the image.

"Okay, it's all set. He went for it. He thinks I'm working a double shift again. Let's have one more beer."

Twenty minutes later they were in his sports car heading north. When they reached I-55 she leaned toward him and started to kiss him. When it became clear to him that he was almost running into things he asked her to stop. Lori reached down, undid his belt buckle, and unzipped his shorts. Frank pulled them down over his ankles after which she pulled his jockey shorts down. Then she went down on him. He had the top down. Since the car was about the lowest vehicle on the road there was no doubt in Frank's mind that they were keeping the truckers well entertained.

Frank put his shorts back on only when they reached a little town seven miles from his farm. He took her to a tavern on the main street. They walked in, hand in hand, and took a seat at the bar as everybody watched them.

"I need a drink," said Lori.

"And I need something to eat," Frank replied. "Are you hungry?"

"I'll have a little something."

"I think they only have pizzas. I'll order one."

The bartender, a pretty woman wearing glasses, came up to wait on them. "What will you have, Frank?"

"We'll have two bottles of Bud Lite, two shots of Cuervo, some limes, salt, and a sausage and pepperoni pizza." said Frank.

The girl was quick with the drinks. When they arrived Lori started to play with the limes. "Let's do a body shot," she said, smiling mischievously.

"We'll have to tone it down. Keep your shirt on Lori. I'm well known around here." Frank looked around him. Sitting at the bar to the right was a woman Frank had drunk with two months before. Sitting with her was a young man who worked at Frank's bank as a loan officer. Seated at a table were three men with their wives including Ray Bradley who supplied Frank and many of the farmers in the area with diesel fuel and gasoline. Sitting at the bar way over on his left were three middle-aged women who were vaguely familiar.

Lori reached out for Frank's hand and started to lick the back of it. Then she plastered salt all over it and began to lick the salt off. Frank took Lori's hand, wet it down with his saliva, put salt on it, and licked it off. Lori took one of the slices of lime, put it in Frank's mouth, and started to kiss him. They passed the lime back and forth between their mouths. Then they did the same with the second slice of lime. When they had finished Frank observed the young loan officer out of the corner of his eye. The loan officer was giggling. The middle-aged women to his left were watching with disapproval. Ray Bradley got up from his table, came up to the bar, and took a seat next to Frank.

"Who's your friend Frank?"

"Lori, this is Ray Bradley. He keeps sending me these horrendous bills for all the diesel fuel I buy from him."

Ray leaned over the bar, rested his elbows on it, and propped his chin under his hands. He smiled broadly at Frank and Lori. "That's really something what you were doing with the salt and the limes. Where'd you pick that up from?"

"Oh we do that all the time," said Frank.

"Except that Frank usually takes his shirt off so that I can lick the salt off his nipples," said Lori. "Of course I let him suck it off my nipples too." Lori looked at Frank, pleased with herself that she had embarrassed him.

"I've better get back to my table," said Ray. "I'll see you two later."

Lori went off to the bathroom. Minutes later she returned. Parting Frank's legs with her hands she stood between them, took his head in her hands, and started to kiss him. When she finished, she jumped on his lap. Frank noticed that the three women at the bar were watching them intently. He stared back at them as if to say, "Okay, make something out of this. I know you are watching us and you now know that I'm onto you so just come right over and say something, I dare you." They looked away.

Then he pulled Lori around on his lap so that she could look at him without turning around. "Lori, I used to go to the Injection Pump, the Sports Bar, and other places like them so that I could take advantage of the girls. I can't do that anymore. I really don't like seeing what I'm seeing in those places."

Without a word, Lori jumped off his lap, and bolted out the door. Everyone stopped what they were doing and looked over at Frank as if to ask in one unified voice *what happened*?

It was Tom Bradley, a cousin of Ray's, who broke the silence. Standing up from his table, he came over to Frank. "What did you do to that poor girl, Frank? One minute you two are getting along fine, the next she's pissed as hell at you."

"I don't know Tom. It must be something I said. I'd better go find her though."

He found her sitting in someone's doorway a few doors down from the bar. Frank sat beside her. "What's wrong, Lori?"

"You. You set me up in there. Set me up to embarrass me."

"How do you figure that?"

"Everybody's staring at me. To you I'm just something to toy with. I'm just a dancer who works on the East Side."

"Now hold on one minute. You are very special to me Lori, and I'm proud to have you with me. I wouldn't hurt you for anything. And right now I care about you more than anyone in this world. As for their staring at you, why you're the prettiest thing that's probably ever come into this town. And then you're with me besides. They've never seen you before, and you're a lot younger than me. I'm very well known around here. I can't tell you how well known I am. I always feel like I'm living in a glass house. Now let's go back in and eat our pizza."

Lori put her arms around Frank's neck and hugged him to her. He put his arms around her back and pulled her close. They kissed, and then they heard someone walk by. Neither of them cared.

He took her back into the bar. Tom Bradley got up from his table carrying what was left of a pizza. What was left was one piece. He set it on the bar.

"I'm sorry Frank. Your pizza arrived and we didn't think you two were coming back so we ate it. I'll buy you another."

"That's okay, Tom. We'll make do on this one piece."

"Damn right we will," said Lori. "Here Frank, eat this." Lori picked up the slice of pizza and jammed it into Frank's mouth. Frank started to chew on it, but Lori was relentless, smiling malevolently. She continued to thrust it into his mouth until she had crammed it all in. Then she picked up the beer bottle that he had left unfinished at the bar and poured its contents down his throat.

Ray Bradley got up from the table laughing. "I've never seen a woman do that to you before Frank."

"That's because you've never seen a woman like this one before," said Frank. "Let's go home Lori. I believe we're finished here."

"Bring her back, Frank. Bring her back anytime."

He took her back to his house and made love to her. Afterwards, she fell asleep. Stretched out on his bed her face calm, she seemed a child without a care in the world. He didn't sleep. It was up to him to get her back on time. Before it was time, he pulled her toward him. Then he made love to her again. She woke up with him still inside her. Putting her arms around him, she pulled him close. Later she asked, "What time is it."

"It's time to leave."

And they went back. Once again they were lucky. They went inside the Injection Pump and had one last beer together. They were the last to leave.

STAN GOES TO THE CLEANERS

"You mean to tell me that you've lost it all!" Frank exclaimed.

"It's all gone. The whole farm is down the tubes. Never even put in the crop," Stan replied.

"So where's Carl?"

"No one knows. He's disappeared off the face of the earth."

"What about the land you bought in Brazil?"

"It's been repossessed by the Brazilian government. Actually I never owned it in the first place."

"Why?"

"I didn't put in a crop. I couldn't make the payments. Carl never bought the land to begin with. He purchased an option to buy the ground but I didn't find out about it until just recently. Probably only paid the Brazilian government five thousand or so, so we never took title."

"How could he slide that one by you?"

"He showed me a bunch of fake legal documents. It all looked authentic. They showed that we took title."

"What about the machinery?"

"Same thing. I thought I had it all bought, but I left the paper work to Carl. He never paid for it."

"What happened to the money?"

"It's in Carl Chicanery's pocket."

"The whole six-hundred and fifty thousand dollars?"

"And more."

"How do you figure?" asked Frank.

"While I was in Brazil trying to buy machinery and hire my work force, Carl went to one of our local banks, one where he was serving on the board of directors. It was easy for him to convince the board of directors to cut loose of another two hundred thousand so that we could put in the crop."

"For fertilizer and seed?"

"You've got it?"

"And that's in his pocket too?"

"What do you think?"

"So, what are you going to do?"

"Declare bankruptcy. Then if I'm lucky perhaps one of the landowners around here will let me farm his ground."

"One thing for sure, they'll never allow Carl to practice law again. And if he ever resurfaces in the US, they'll get him for fraud and embezzlement."

"He won't need to practice law again Frank. He's got eight hundred and fifty thousand dollars."

"I'm sorry Stan. I'm really sorry that this happened to you," said Frank.

"If anything happens to me Frank, I don't want to be buried-- especially around here. Make sure they cremate me."

THE WARNING

One morning Frank woke up later than usual to the phone ringing. The voice on the other end was Tamara's. "Frank, what are you doing today? My car broke down and I've gotta go to work. Can you take me?"

"I've got a few things planned but nothing serious. It can all wait till the next day," he replied. "When do you want to go?"

"Can we leave here at ten?"

"Okay then, I'll be there at ten, but you've got to buy me a beer." It didn't take Frank long to agree to a day of idleness at the Sports Bar. Tamara was always good company, and if he could get her to buy him a beer, he could probably convince the other girls that he was a little short on cash which should keep them from asking him for drinks. Furthermore, Tamara lived right on the way to the Sports Bar no more than twenty miles from Frank's farm.

"I'll do better than that. I'll buy you several."

"You're on. I'll see you at ten."

They got to the Sports Bar at eleven. None of the dancers were there. Nadine was cleaning up the bar, and the cook was already in the kitchen trying to get the daily special done before twelve. True to her word, Tamara got a bottle of Bud out from behind the bar for Frank.

"Normally I don't start drinking at eleven in the morning," said Frank. "I usually start at noon."

"I don't believe that," said Tamara. "You are too successful to be drinking during the day."

"You are right, Tamara. I only drink during the day when I'm here or at the Injection Pump. And today is going to be different because today I'm going to get loaded."

"Oh no, you're not. I'm limiting you to three. We've gotta drive home, remember?"

"You've got that wrong," said Frank. "You're driving us home which leaves me free to get despicably drunk."

Which is exactly what he did. And if not despicably drunk, at least he did get drunk. At eight o'clock it was time to leave. Frank was not so chauvinistic as to refuse a girl the chance to drive his car if he had a great deal more to drink than her. Instead his attitude was, *if she's willing to keep me from getting a DUI I'll let her.* So he let Tamara drive.

On the way home he told her about how he and Lori had been

driving down to his farm and returning to the Injection Pump just before closing time. He explained how Lori had fallen asleep in his bed and how she didn't seem too concerned about the time. He told her how they had walked out together at 4:15 a.m. while Travis waited outside.

"Sounds to me that she's taking more and more chances," said Tamara. "It's almost as if she wants to get caught. It's only a matter of time and Travis is going to find out about you two. Then they are going to have a big fight, and he's going to leave her or she's going to leave him. What are you going to do if she ends up on your doorstep with five kids?"

"Five kids?" said Frank drunkenly. "What am I going to do? I don't really know. I know my limitations. I couldn't even handle two kids"

"Well, you know that this is a package deal whichever way you cut it," said Tamara.

"There's got to be another way," replied Frank. "I'm not thinking very clearly right now. I've drunk too much. How much time do you think we have before she gets caught?"

"No more than two or three weeks if you ask me. Things are going to come to a head real fast."

The time passed quickly as it always does when two friends are driving together. Tamara pulled in front of her house and got out. "Are you going to be all right?" she asked.

"I'll be fine. In twenty-five minutes, I'll be home. I've faced greater challenges before."

"Okay then, drive carefully," she said.

Twenty-five minutes later he was home. He went to bed wondering what the next week would bring.

THE PROMISE

The shock of seeing Stan's body hanging from the barn rafter wore off after the first day. Stan had left a note requesting that Frank be given the authority to decide what to do with his body. The note had been witnessed and notarized. When Frank told the family that he intended to have Stan cremated, the family protested, but after two hours, Frank convinced everyone that it would be best that they go along with Stan's last request. Stan's mother was the hardest to convince, but in the end Frank was able to silence even her by promising to spread Stan's ashes on one of the farms he had owned, saying "This way Stan will be made a part of the land he farmed forever."

Two days later Frank hired a small plane and pilot and directed the pilot to fly over one of Stan's fields. When the plane cruised over the center of the field, Frank opened one of the plane's windows and opened the small wooden box he had brought with him. Closing the lid just tightly enough that the ashes wouldn't fall out and so that he could still open it easily, Frank held the box out the window and reopened the lid. When he finished, he loosened his grip on the box and let it fall to the ground.

When he got home, Frank made a pot of coffee, poured himself a cup, and sat at the kitchen table. His thoughts returned to Stan, to a Stan who would never sit down with him again to discuss farming, women, or what ailed the world. *Drinking coffee will never be the same again*, thought Frank--*at least not at this table*. Then he thought about Carl.

You did this to him, Carl. You were the one, you selfish, greedy son-of-a-bitch. God, if you are God--I swear to you that I will get Carl. No matter what it takes and no matter where I have to go, I will track Carl down and kill him. And God, or whatever you are, you can take your Ten Commandments and shove them--shove them up your wispy spiritual ass!"

351

FOUR LETTER WORDS

He was a little embarrassed with the bouquet of flowers he had just bought. He had gone to the nursery for twelve long stemmed roses. Frank paid $46 in advance for the flowers, agreeing to pick them up the next day on his way to the Injection Pump. The nursery had put Baby's Breath flowers into the bouquet with the roses. It was the largest and most ostentatious bouquet of roses that Frank had ever seen.

He was lucky. The man watching the parking lot was the man he hoped would be on duty. They had talked on several occasions in the past and Frank had sized the man up as a helpful sort. Frank parked his car and walked over to the attendant.

"Hi. I would like for you to do me a favor. I'll tip you five dollars if you do it."

"What is it?"

"You remember Brittany who works here--the little blonde I've been going out with."

"Sure, I remember her."

"I have with me a bouquet of long-stemmed roses. They are for her. I need to have you go upstairs. Give me ten minutes or so first though; then give the flowers to the man who's watching the door upstairs. I'll talk to him about it so that he knows what's going on. I want Brittany to think that these flowers were specially delivered to her."

"Okay, I'll do it."

"Thanks. I'm going to have the doorman bring them over to our table. Give me enough time to get Brittany and me a drink."

Frank went upstairs and paid the three-dollar cover to the doorman. A waitress came over to take his order. Instructing her to take a Jack and Coke and a Bud Lite to Brittany, he gave her a ten and turned back to the doorman.

"I would like for you to do me a favor. I have bought a bouquet of flowers for Brittany. The parking lot attendant is bringing them up to you in a few minutes. When he does, can you bring them over to her? Then tell her there has been a special delivery from a flower shop."

"No problem. What if she's on stage?"

"Bring them over afterwards. After we are sitting at a table."

Lori was sitting at the bar watching him. He sat on the bar stool next to her. She raised her glass to him in gratitude. "Thanks for the drink, Frank. I was hoping that you'd come."

"And I was hoping that you'd be here."

She had to take her turn up on stage. Twenty minutes later--
after they'd taken a table, the doorman came over and set the flowers
on the table in front of them. Lori studied Frank thoughtfully. Then
she opened the card. It rea:. *To my favorite girl--Sorry I cannot be
here today--Missing you--Love Cliff.* Frank snatched the card away
from her.

"So, you've got your other boyfriends sending you flowers,"
Frank said angrily. "Where does that put me on your list?"

"Thanks Frank."

"What do you mean by thanking me? Thank Cliff." Frank
had used Cliff's name because Tamara had told him that Cliff had
been one of Lori's customers when she worked at the Sports Bar.
Frank had thought that signing Cliff's name to the card would be the
crowning touch to his little prank.

"That card's from you Frank and you know it," replied Lori. "I
know your handwriting. You know I do."

"Okay then. It was a nice try. Hope you like the flowers."

"I do. I love them. I got flowers only once before--in my
whole life."

"Lori, last week, why'd you leave me in that bar?
Remember, I went out to find you and found you sitting on
someone's doorstep."

"You really pissed me off, Frank. All I could think about was
you and Dotie in that limo together. And then, to make matters
worse, you had to come in here and brag to me about it."

"What did you expect? You stood me up. As if I didn't
matter."

"So you fucked my best friend. You fucked my friend.
Imagine how that makes me feel."

"Well, you really set me off. You didn't show and you didn't
even bother calling. There's nothing worse than treating another
person as a nonperson. What you were telling me was, Frank, I
don't really care about you. Something else came up, so fuck you!"

"You fucked my best friend. As if fucking me meant nothing.
I love you Frank. I think about you always. It scares me because
sometimes I think about you more than I think about my kids."

"Love! Love. Lori--that's a four-letter word. Like piss, and
fuck, and shit, and hate. It's something people say to one another,
only they don't really mean it."

"No, you don't understand it, Frank. I've got five kids. You--you don't have a care in the world. I can't always be there when you want me to. That doesn't mean I don't want to be."

"Look, I'm glad that you say you love me. But that just makes you feel good, saying it. I don't really think the word fits into your vocabulary or mine. I feel close to you. I'll admit that. The flowers express my real feelings about you. The card didn't. That was just a joke. But let's not talk of love. That's something other people use to get something from each other. It's a four-letter word and it has no meaning."

"All right then. I luv you. That's spelled L-U-V. That's a three-letter word. I luv you Frank. You are my best friend. You are my best friend in the world."

"Lori, let's grab a table somewhere else."

"Okay, let's find a table near stage five. It's a little quieter over there."

They sat at a table for two close to the men's room. A waitress took their drink order. Five minutes later she returned with two glasses of beer. Lori sipped from hers, then looked up at Frank, her face contemplative. "Did I tell you that I've moved?"

"Moved. Where?"

"I moved to Union, Missouri. It's a long way out, but Frank, I had to get out of the city."

"Why'd you move out of the city?"

"Because there's so much crime there. They shot up our house three weeks ago. Do you remember Frank?"

He remembered her telling him about it. The trouble was that he didn't believe it. It had gotten to the point that he didn't believe anything she told him. The story had made no impression on him whatever.

"Don't you remember how I told you once that some people started to break into our house? Travis caught them and shot three of them."

"It seems that I remember your telling me that," Frank replied.

"This time some of their friends came by and shot my house up. There's bullet holes all over the place. My little three-year-old was in the kitchen and some of those bullets came damn close. When that happens to my kids, it's time to leave."

"So, that's why you moved to Union, Missouri."

"That and the fact that I'm getting tired of the fast pace. When I saw your farm, I was inspired. You've done so much with it. You don't realize, Frank, how much you've changed me."

"So how do you like it out there."

"I live on the outskirts of town. More or less in the country. I went out and got me some chickens. I got me these little baby chickens. But I don't know how to take care of them. Frank, you've got to show me how to take care of the chickens. Will you show me how?"

"Jesus Lori. I raise corn. I don't know anything about chickens, but I'd guess they are very easy to take care of. Just give them some bird seed or ground up corn and watch them grow. Anyone can raise chickens."

"Frank, I'm so worried about the chickens. I don't know what to do. Please show me how to take care of them."

It is getting a little deep, thought Frank. *Chickens. What next? Baby foxes? A pet orangutan from the zoo? Lori with chickens? Now is an outrageous thought. Girl moves out to the wide-open spaces less than a week ago. Probably not fully moved in yet, and the first thing she does is get chickens?*

"Okay. I'll come out sometime and see your chickens. Hey, I have an idea. You and I have never spent the night together. I want to spend the night with you, Lori. Is Travis picking you up?"

"Yes. Unfortunately."

"When he comes just tell him that you are spending the night at a girlfriend's house."

"That might work, but who?"

"How about Tamara? She only lives twenty miles from me. You could even leave with her. Meet me on the road and switch cars."

"Tamara won't do it. She doesn't like me."

"But she likes me. Besides, she owes me a favor."

"What are you going to do? Have her leave the Sports Bar and come here for me? She won't do that. She's been banned from the premises."

"Why?"

"I don't remember exactly why, but she created a bad scene when she quit here."

"Then that leaves her out. I got it! How about Susan? You and her are good friends. Susan and I have known each other for over a year."

"Then let's get her over here," said Lori.

Susan was already sitting with a customer close to one of the pool tables.   Not one to chase anyone down after she had a few, Lori called out to her. "Susan, come over here." Susan left her customer and came right over.

"Susan, Frank and I have a favor to ask you. He wants me to visit him tonight except that Travis is picking me up. We were wondering if you would go outside and talk to Travis about my spending the night at your house."

"Sure Lori. I can do that."

At 8:15 Susan went out into the parking lot to talk to Travis. Lori and Frank drank a pair of Bud Lites. Ten minutes later, Susan came back upstairs.

"I tried but he's not going for it. Lori, he's really pissed. He told me to tell you to get your butt down there right now."

Lori turned to Frank. "I'll call you tomorrow. What time do you want me to call you?"

"Call me at 8:00. I'll wait for your call."

Then she went back into the dressing room returning with her bag and flowers. She stopped at the table to kiss Frank goodbye. Then she walked out of the room and down the stairs dragging her bag across the floor. This time Lori walked slowly, dejectedly like a little girl who had just been disciplined by her parents. Yet, she carried the flowers out with her.

Frank was surprised that she didn't leave the flowers behind. *How was she going to explain them to Travis?*

INCOGNITO

The next day, Frank went to Springfield, Illinois where he did his grocery shopping. Then he went to a favorite pub of his on the way home where he had chicken wings and a beer. His waitress, a friendly and pretty brunette, asked him if he was going to stay longer. The prospect was tempting, but he had a phone call to catch. By eight o'clock he was home, and she never called.

By Saturday he had an idea--a great idea. He sat at his computer and whipped up a four-page paper which criticized the sports program of the Union, Missouri School District. He didn't exactly whip it up from scratch, for he had long ago written a letter to the editor of his own local paper in which he had lambasted the sports program of his local school district. Then he had taken that letter, which still lurked on the hard drive of his computer, and made the necessary changes to make it appear as if it were written about the Union, Missouri School District. Changing a word or two here and a phrase there did the trick. The whole thing took only five minutes. It took another five minutes to print out four copies of the letter. Then he went into the bathroom and shaved off his mustache. The last thing he did was to change into a white shirt, tie, suit, and dress shoes.

An hour later he was at Tamara's. He was in luck. Both Tamara and her husband, Charles, were home. It was eleven o'clock in the morning when Charles came to the door in his underwear shorts and a T-shirt. Frank had come to expect this sort of thing from Tamara and Charles. She got off of work at eight o'clock in the evening. Since she lived almost as far away from the Sports Bar as Frank, she usually didn't get home before nine. After that she either prepared supper or went grocery shopping, then prepared supper. Her schedule had by necessity become her family's schedule which lent itself to late nights and mornings. Saturdays and sundays were for sleeping in.

"Good morning Charles. Everybody home?"

"Tamara just got up a few minutes ago. Come on in. She's decent."

Frank followed Charles into the living room and sat on the couch. It was one of those old comfortable couches. Frank had drunk beer there on many occasions talking with Charles and Tamara, and had even fallen asleep there. Tamara heard him come in. Coming out of the kitchen, she took him in with a glance and started to laugh.

"God, you look different. What did you do with your moustache? And why are you wearing a suit? You never wear a suit."

"I'm paying Nipples a social call. Do you or Charles or both of you want to come along?"

"You are what? You are going to go see Nipples? What is Travis going to say?"

"That's one of the reasons I'm going to go out to see them. Actually I'm going to make a social call on Travis and Lori."

"You're crazy. You are absolutely crazy. You are fucking Nipples, and Travis is suspicious of you already. He's probably seen you, and you are going to go out and meet him? Watch yourself Frank."

"Do you know that Travis has killed several people?" replied Frank, raising his eyebrows skeptically. "That's why I want to meet him. I want to see what someone who has killed three people looks like."

"He what? Travis has killed three people?" With this, Tamara broke out into spasms of laughter.

"Killed three people my ass!" Charles replied. "That little punk. He's nothing."

"You would think he was a big time hood," said Tamara. "Nipples told all of us that he was in the mafia. He's just a boy. But I understand that he beats her."

"She's finally admitted that to me too," said Frank. "I just want to meet the guy--take his measure. I also want to see the expression on Lori's face when she sees me in her house with Travis. I also want to see where she lives. See if she really lives in Union, Missouri and if she does, what the place looks like."

"You look a lot younger without the moustache, but I don't think it's going to be enough," said Tamara.

"We've got to get some black hair dye-- the kind that rinses out," replied Frank. "Do you know where I can get some?"

"Tell you what. I have to buy a few things at the grocery store. I'll pick up some for you. You and Charles sit here and talk and I'll be back in half an hour."

Frank had found from experience that Tamara did not half step around about anything she did. With three children she couldn't afford to. She did everything fast and efficiently. Not only was she a top money maker in the clubs-- she was a good mother as well. He had found her to be a woman of formidable intelligence and to be very disciplined as well. This applied to shopping as it did in everything else. Tamara returned half an hour later.

Frank went into the bathroom and doused his hair with a half bottle of black hair dye. Using his fingers, he massaged the thin liquid into his scalp. He didn't quit until every hair was soaked in the dye. Using a Kleenex Frank wiped off the excess liquid which had run down his face. He peered into the mirror and carefully regarded the new Frank Harring. Yes, no doubt about it--he had just taken sixteen years off his life. Without the moustache and with his hair a dull black, Frank looked only thirty years old. He walked out into the living room.

"I can't believe it man. You really do look different," said Charles.

"You might, you just might get away with it," said Tamara. "Now when you come back, stop by and tell us how it went."

It took better than two hours to reach Union, Missouri. Frank went to the first service station off the highway to get directions. The young woman at the counter acted surprised when he told her the address. Then she sketched out a map to Lori's house.

"It's in a bad section of town," the woman said.

"What do you mean by bad?" he asked.

"People live there who can't afford to pay rent anywhere else."

"I don't want the people who live there to see my car. I don't want to be seen just driving up. Have any ideas?" asked Frank.

"Just before you turn right there's a community center with a little parking area over on the left. It's got sort of an embankment on its south side. You might hide your car there."

The place was easy to find. It was, as Lori had described, on the outskirts of town. Her street turned off to the right. To his left Frank found the community center, which was a small building with a pay phone just outside. A ball diamond next to the building was the only visible form of outdoor activity. Just in front of the building was a small parking area just off Lori's street. Frank had to drive down a little driveway to get to it. As the girl had explained, the parking area would hide his car from the street as it was four or five feet lower than the street with a shallow embankment to the south. Frank was glad that he had driven the sports car since the embankment was too low to hide his pickup. He parked the car, walked back up the driveway, and turned right into Lori's street.

Grant Street was only two blocks long. Old cars were parked along the street or in driveways. Some appeared to be abandoned, already past the point of repair. Number twenty-four was only seven or eight houses down the street. It was a medium sized white building that already needed repainting. Frank guessed that it was seventy or eighty years old. A large porch adorned the front of the house. A teenage girl and several boys in their late teens were talking in the front yard. Several men whom Frank sized up to be in their early twenties lounged around the porch. One of the men was wearing a baseball cap whom Frank judged to be five foot eight or so. The man or boy--Frank didn't know what to call him--was stocky, and was already growing a bulging pot belly.

Bingo. Gotta be Travis, thought Frank. *But sweet Jesus, the man sure isn't much.* Short and squat the man was neither handsome nor striking. And even though he was not yet out of his early twenties, he already sported the beer belly of the middle-aged couch potato. Frank walked up to the man hoping that he was Travis.

"Hi, my name is Jim Hawkins. I'm running for the Union Missouri School board. Does a Lori Mellon live here? I just contacted our local post office over who was new in town. The postmaster gave me her name with some of the others."

"Yeah, she just moved in. I'm her boyfriend, Travis."

"Travis, I brought several copies of a letter I sent to the Union School District board members in which I criticized the district's sports program. If you don't mind, I'd like you to read it. I'm going to tell you right in front that I am totally against the district's emphasis on sports over education and it's because of this that I'm trying to get elected to the board."

Frank handed one of the four page printouts to Travis. Travis started to read the first page. Then, a few moments later, he handed it back to Frank. *Probably didn't get past the first paragraph*, thought Frank. *Probably incapable of absorbing the contents of the handout and obviously wouldn't care even if he could.*

"Where do I vote on this?" Travis asked.

"You go down to City Hall. The same place you go to vote for your Congressional candidates, President, or whoever. Election's in September," said Frank. *I hope he doesn't ask me where City Hall is*, thought Frank, *because I don't know where anything is in this town.* "When I talked with the post office, I found out that Lori just moved in a week ago. The postmaster didn't tell me you were living here too."

"The house is in her name, but we've been living together now for a few years," said Travis.

"Where's Lori now?"

"She's in the kitchen flipping hamburgers."

"I'm going to go in and let her have a copy of my letter. I need both your votes."

"I don't know. She's pretty busy right now," said Travis.

"I'll just go in and watch her flip hamburgers," said Frank. "You never know, I might learn something. I'll give her my little spiel while she's flipping. Then I'll leave my handout for her to read later when she's not busy. Do you mind taking me to the kitchen and introducing me to her?"

"Follow me then."

Frank followed Travis onto the porch and into the house. They walked past several small children and three or four women in their fifties. Frank paid little attention to his surroundings, his concentration focused on finding Lori and what he would say to her when he did. He saw her as soon as he entered the kitchen sitting by herself at the kitchen table talking to a teenage girl who stood across the room. Lori wore shorts and a T-shirt--not the kind a girl would wear to impress someone--but the kind that a girl wore around the house when she expected no one to stop by. The T-shirt accentuated Lori's slenderness--made her appear as a high school girl on the brink of womanhood.

"Lori, someone wants to speak to you. Something about the school." Travis turned to Frank. "I'm sorry, but I forgot your name."

Frank crossed the room over to Lori ignoring Travis. "Hi, I'm Jim Hawkins. I'm running for School Board on an anti sports program. If you don't mind, I've brought something for you to read." Frank handed Lori one of the four page printouts.

He studied Lori's face closely. For a fraction of a second there was the trace of a smile. The moment was brief, and the hint of the smile could not even be called a slight upturning of the lips. Yet, it was there. Then she looked as if she had just swallowed a dill pickle. Frank became the unwanted salesman who had just intruded into her kitchen. Her eyes showed a total lack of interest. Only one thing betrayed her, and Frank was the only one in the room who caught it. Lori started to read the handout, and although she acted uninterested in its contents, Frank knew that she was scrutinizing the handout carefully.

"So, you just moved here. As I was telling Travis, the postmaster gave me the names and addresses of the new residents. Are there any other adults in your household who will be voting in the next election?" Frank asked.

"No, there's just Travis and me," Lori replied.

"Well, you two look like an interesting couple."

Lori barely suppressed an expression of distaste. She continued to read the document never once looking up at Frank--then stood up and started to walk to the refrigerator.

"Are you going to the refrigerator?" asked Frank. "I've been walking door to door trying to get people to vote for me. It must be close to a hundred degrees out there. Lori, you wouldn't have an extra beer for me, would you?"

"Do you really want one?" Lori did her best to make herself sound unfriendly.

"Yes, I insist."

By this time Travis had left the room. A girl 14 or 15 years old stood in the hallway outside the kitchen staring at Frank. She wore a dress whereas everyone else in the place was dressed casually. Her long dark hair hung loosely around her shoulders. She didn't look at all like Becky, the girl who had met Frank at the door the day he took the limo with Lori. Yet it had to be her. The girl stood staring at Frank as if she were saying *I know who you are. Now just what are you doing this time.*

It's time to leave, thought Frank. He turned to face Lori. "You can read that later. I'm leaving it with you. I'll return in a few days to see what you think of my views. I want you to vote for me and I hope that handout convinces you. I've gotta leave. I'll just take this beer with me. Thanks for your time, Lori."

Frank walked out of the kitchen past the girl in the dress whose eyes never left him. He walked onto the porch and down the steps into the yard where Travis stood talking to a brunette. The woman was in her mid twenties and a little taller than average. As he started to walk past, the woman grabbed his arm gently.

"So you're running for school board. Do you know any of the other Hawkins here in town? I know them all. I went to school with some of them."

"I moved here less than two years ago," Frank replied. "I might be related--distantly related to some of the Hawkins. Really don't know a lot of people here yet. Work keeps me busy, but now that I'm running for school board, I'm meeting some people. I have a cousin, a Dr. Hawkins, who lives in St. Claire, Missouri."

"Well we don't know any Dr. Hawkins or anybody like that," said Travis. "We're from the poor side of town."

"Well, I must get going. More people to see and convince that they should vote for me. It was nice meeting you, Travis. And nice meeting you-----------" Frank turned to the brunette.

"Alice. Mr. Hawkins, you definitely look familiar. Really familiar."

"A lot of people say that about me, Alice. Well, nice meeting you."

Frank walked out into the street and headed uphill where his car awaited him. After he got several houses past Lori's, he turned to see if anyone was following him. Then, satisfied that he was not being observed he walked down the driveway into the community center parking lot. He got into his sports car and started it. Then he got out and looked out into Grant Street for the last time. Finally, convinced that no one was watching him, he got back into the little car and drove out of the parking lot.

Five minutes later he was out on the highway. *Everything had gone perfectly*, thought Frank. Travis had not suspected a thing and he had gotten Travis's measure. Best of all he had gotten one over on Lori. He didn't know anyone who would do what he had just done. It took intelligence, nerve, and a don't give a damn attitude. *And what about her? Her acting job was outstanding. What is a girl like that doing with an idiot like Travis?* He went home believing that Lori would never forget what he had pulled off--not in her lifetime.

FOUND OUT

The voice on the other end was urgent. "Frank. We've gotta talk. Can you come here? Now?"

"I can make it at six."

"Can you come sooner? I need to talk to you."

"Lori, I'm leaving in one hour. I can't be there any earlier."

"Hurry up then."

Frank walked up the stairs into the Injection Pump at 5:45. He took a seat at the far end of the bar and ordered two Bud Lites. Suddenly, she was there sitting next to him.

"We're in deep shit Frank. Travis knows about us. He's known about us for weeks. The last time we went out--he was outside in the parking lot watching us. He knows it was you who came out to Union. Frank. He's been watching our every move."

"How did he find out?"

"I don't know. Maybe someone told him. Frank, he knows everything. What are we going to do?"

"Beats the shit out of me. Keep going out with each other. That's what we're going to do."

"He hasn't done anything to me, yet. I think he's waiting for the right moment, and then he's going to beat the shit out of me. Then he'll probably go after you--with a gun. He carries a sawed off shotgun in his car all the time. He hates you. We've gotta do something."

"We'll figure something out. Jeff Shannon's going to come in at 8:00. We can go somewhere then and between the three of us will come up with something."

"I've got it. Let's all go to Ciceros. Rozanne's supposed to wrestle one of the other girls. She wants me to come watch her."

"You mean she's going to get in a ring and wrestle?"

"It's just like the boxing matches they have here and at Ciceros. Only this time it's wrestling. We can all go watch her. Then I'm going to kick the shit out of her."

"Why do you want to do that?"

"Because she told Travis about you and me fucking in the hot tub. The little snitch."

They knew it was eight o'clock when Jeff Shannon came in. Always on time and utterly dependable, Jeff was one of those rare friends you could always count on. If Jeff promised he'd be somewhere at 4:00 p.m. one month from now, Frank knew he'd remember--every time. Frank contrasted his friend with Lori. *If she promised she'd be somewhere twelve hours from now, there was a 50% probability she'd forget or say to hell with it. Undoubtedly it was the same way with her friends. They'd show up for her if they felt for it.*

Jeff came in, mouth wagging and hand extended. "Hey what do ya say bro. Let's get a drink. You're buying." Jeff pointed at Frank as he caught the bartender's eye.

"Miss. He's buying. No. Not me. Him. He dragged me in this place, and it'll probably cost me my marriage. I'm having him pay my damages ahead of time. That way I won't have to hire me a lawyer."

Jeff noticed that a man was sitting close to Frank and Lori at the bar. He grinned and grabbed the man by the shoulder not even noticing that the man outweighed him by more than a hundred pounds. "You know you're not supposed to be here either. If your wife knew you were here you'd be in trouble too. Am l right or am I right?" Without even waiting for an answer, Jeff continued. "Bartender, get this man a drink." Then he turned to the man once again. "You've been sitting next to Frank all this time. He's single-- or almost. And you--you are probably married like me. We're both having drinks on him just for allowing him to be a bad influence."

For the first time the man spoke. "Oh hell, you guys don't have to buy me a drink. I don't even know you guys."

"Bartender"--Jeff focused once again on the bartender--"Will you please get this man a drink and get me one too. I'll have a vodka gimlet." Jeff turned to the man again. "You've met my friend Frank here?"

"No. He and the girl have been just sitting here in their own little world."

"That's what I'm telling you. He's a bad influence. He's got Lori here. Now she's a true derelict. What does that tell you about him now?"

"Jeff, don't call me a derelict," Lori replied. "It's Frank. He's the derelict. And he ought to buy us each several drinks just for putting up with him. Except we've gotta all leave. I'm supposed to meet Rozanne and watch her wrestle. We've only got a few minutes so we'll just have to have Frank buy us our drinks in the next place."

"Then what are we waiting for?" Frank replied. "Let's get the hell out of here. Jeff, you know how to get to Ciceros. We'll meet you there."

"No, I'm going with Jeff," said Lori. "Travis knows what you're driving, Frank. He's probably laying out there for us right now."

"See you two there then."

"Why don't we have a drink at the Sports Bar first?" suggested Jeff. "You two met there and I wrecked my car leaving there that same day. You got time for one drink, Lori?"

"We can have a couple."

"The Sports Bar then. Lori and I will meet you there, Frank."

Frank was the first inside. Nadine had a bottle of Bud out for him before he could seat himself. *Gotta hand it to the old girl,* thought Frank. *She doesn't sparkle with good fellowship and goodwill to the clientele the way some of the waitresses and bartenders do, but by God she has that beer out for a man right now. And that little action by itself speaks louder than words could possibly convey that the customer is special and welcome.* That promptness more than anything showed Frank that this was his bar. In here he was safe. If he got into a fight the bar would probably back him and kick the other guy out. If he got out of line and did something really stupid such as taking all his clothes off, he would be asked to put them back on whereas someone else would be escorted out the door. He felt good inside this place for this reason. He also felt good because he had met Lori here.

Jeff and Lori came in five minutes later. Lori immediately went over to Janey and threw her arms around the other girl's neck. Janey hugged Lori around the shoulders.

"Where you been, Lori? Haven't seen you in a long time."

"Oh, I've been working down at the Injection Pump. And seeing him." She pointed at Frank.

"We've missed you," said Janey. "Things haven't been the same since you left. It's a lot quieter now."

"I've missed you too. God, I've missed all of you." A tear started down Lori's cheek, followed by another. Then another. Lori started to sob uncontrollably and pressed herself tightly against Janey. "Janey, I want my job back so badly. I'd do anything to have it back. I miss you girls so much."

"I don't think they'll let you have your job back, at least not just yet," replied Janey. "Not since you called all of the girls a bunch of holes. You even called me a hole and you know very well that I don't fuck anybody but my husband."

"I want to come back. I really miss you guys," Lori sobbed.

Frank bought Jeff a beer and had a waitress bring a Jack and Coke to Lori. Then he motioned Jeff toward the back room. They took a table in the back so that Lori could easily find them. Frank leaned toward Jeff. "Did she spill her guts?"

"You bet she did. She's one scared broad, Frank. She's afraid this Travis is going to kill her."

"What do you think we should do, Jeff?"

"I tell you what I'd do. I'd get rid of her. She's going to do nothing but cause you trouble from now on."

"That's easy for you to say. I don't know that I want to."

"Look at it this way, Frank. You've gotten everything you've wanted from her. You've been fucking her. You've gotten drunk with her. You've partied with her. Right now you and Lori are at your peak. Her stock is at its all time high. From now on it's going to rapidly lose its value."

"Go on Jeff. I'm listening."

"Let's look at the best case scenario. She falls in love with you and somehow she manages to get rid of this boyfriend. She's still got five kids. Plus, she probably doesn't know how to take care of herself. Oh, she can do that in a way. She's street smart, but it's the usual everyday stuff--the grocery shopping, managing a check book, keeping herself out of trouble--that's going to drive you up the wall. You remember my ex girl friend Alicia. This broad is just like Alicia only worse. And you remember how Alicia almost set our apartment on fire with her hair dryer?"

"I'll never forget. A good thing I went back to the apartment. The bed was on fire. Alicia was on the floor crying, unable or unwilling to do anything about the fire. Alicia never left the room-- just kept on crying how you were going to kill her. In minutes the fire would have spread from the bed to the carpet and Alicia would have died of smoke inhalation before she even realized what was happening."

"Believe it. This Lori is worse."

"And much better looking," added Frank. "And a lot more fun. One hell of a lot brighter as well."

"Okay, now let's look at a more realistic scenario. Do you think this Travis is going to let Lori get out of his life? He's her pimp for God's sake. You move Lori to Springfield, Illinois. He'll find her. He's going to check all the strip bars first. Then he's going to check the other bars, the restaurants, whatever. And he probably already knows where you live. So, he's going to come looking for you with his shotgun."

"Not if I get him first. I'll kick his butt."

"But that's not the way it's going to happen. First, this guy
doesn't work. He's unskilled and totally useless. Without Lori, he's
just not going to make it, and he knows it. So he's going to track her
down. And if he thinks she's with you he's not going to care what he
does. The man has nothing to offer and he knows it. What's it to
him if he shoots you in the back. He's got nothing to lose, and I
guarantee that whatever confrontation you have with him is not
going to be fair. You'd kill him with your bare hands and he knows
it. This guys a punk, Frank. You're going to get hurt when you least
expect it."

"I think I can hide her from him."

"I doubt it, but suppose you do. What do you know about this
girl? Can you trust her? Has she given you any reason to trust her?
She might live with you for a while, and then sometime when you're
not home, steal you blind. It could even be that she and Travis are
setting you up right now. Do you even know her name?"

"Sure I know her name."

"How do you know?"

"Because everyone calls her by that name and because she
told me that was her name over a year ago."

"So in other words, you don't even know her name. I rest my
case," said Jeff. "Now do you know her age? Do you know that
she has five kids? Do you know where she was born? Who her
parents are?"

"I hate to say it Jeff, but you do have a point."

"See. I told you so. So you don't know a goddamn thing
about this broad. She might have a record a mile long. She might
have done things that would make your hair curl. Stay away from
this broad Frank. She's trouble and she's a loser. You can't help her.
You can't save her. She's made her bed and she's never going to
crawl out of it. Here she comes. We'll talk about this later."

"We've gotta go next door." Lori approached them from the
front room.

They walked over to Ciceros which was less than a block
away leaving Jeff's van and Frank's car parked at the Sports Bar.
Lori walked over to Rozanne who was standing with two other girls
across the bar. One of the stages had a rope stretched around it
forming a make shift ring. Lori talked with Rozanne for a few
minutes, then came back to Frank and Jeff.

"Let's sit over there at that table next to the ring." Then she turned to Frank and smiled. "Buy me a drink, Frank. I'll take a Jack and Coke."

Frank found a waitress who brought him two beers and a Jack and Coke while Jeff led Lori over to the table. The match started soon after Frank got back with the drinks. Rozanne stood in the center of the ring facing a taller woman. The doorman, acting as referee, blew on a whistle signaling the beginning of the match. The taller girl grabbed for Rozanne's arm as Rozanne jerked away. Then she reached for Rozanne's other arm. This time Rozanne let the woman grab her arm. The woman clasped her other hand around Rozanne's arm and started to pull Rozanne toward her. Suddenly the woman lost her balance and started to fall backwards. Seeing her opportunity Rozanne shoved her body forward which took the woman completely off balance. She fell backwards to the stage floor. Rozanne jumped on top of the woman, struggled with her for a few seconds, and pinned her. The referee counted to three and then blew his whistle to announce the ending of the match.

Five minutes later, Rozanne sat down next to Jeff. "How about a drink for the winner? Who's buying?"

Jeff pointed at Frank. "Sugar Daddy over there's buying."

"Okay Rozanne. You get the waitress over here; then I'll buy you a drink," said Frank.

"Lisa, come get me a vodka gimlet. I need a drink." Rozanne's voice carried across the room.

"I'm going to the little girl's room," Lori announced as she got up from the table.

Rozanne's drink arrived while Lori was in the restroom. Frank tipped the waitress and started to study Rozanne. *Definitely young*, thought Frank, *and not too bright either. Thinks constantly about her boyfriend who's probably not worth thinking about in the first place. That and having a good time.*

"Rozanne, how's Lori and Travis getting along?" Frank asked.

"Not bad. Why?"

"I'm always interested in Lori. You know that. What does she see in Travis? I can't figure a girl like her having anything to do with someone like that."

"I guess she loves him. That's why."

"What does she see in him to love anyway?"

"I don't know. She just loves him."

Lori returned from the lady's room and sat down. "You did

good, Rozanne. I'm proud of you."

"Brigitte's just slow and uncoordinated, that's all."

Suddenly a waitress appeared. "Lori, someone's outside waiting for you. He doesn't seem very happy."

"Shit, it must be Travis." Lori reached under the table and picked up her duffel bag. Without saying another word, without so much as a goodbye, she was gone. Within seconds the room seemed empty to Frank. Yet there he was surrounded by people, half naked women running around, one of his best friends sitting close by.

"Well, we'll never see her again," said Frank. "Come on, Jeff. Let's go next door."

Forty-five minutes later Frank and Jeff were standing at the Sports Bar talking to two of the dancers. One of them, a short plump blonde named Sherry, had always been especially friendly to Frank every time he had gone into the Sports Bar. Once, she had sat with Frank and Lori when he had jokingly asked Lori whom he should choose as her substitute when she wasn't there. Lori had pointed at Sherry, announcing in a serious voice that Sherry should be her substitute.

"Can I have another drink, Frank?"

"Go right ahead. You order the drinks. I'll buy."

"I forgot. I'm up next. Will you join me up on stage, Frank? You too, Jeff?"

"We'll come up. And I'll bring your drink over to you."

Sherry punched her three selections into the jukebox, and went over to the stage. The bartender brought the drinks over to Frank--two beers and a rum and coke. Frank led the way to the stage, taking a seat over on the left side, Jeff close behind him. Placing Sherry's drink on the edge of the stage, Frank reached into his pocket for a cigar. Pulling the pack out he took one cigar, an Anthony and Cleopatra, for himself. Then he placed the pack on the stage in front of Jeff.

"Have one Jeff."

Jeff reached for the pack and searched his pocket for a lighter. Suddenly he stopped, one hand remaining in his pocket, the other still holding onto the pack. "Look who's here."

Frank looked away from the stage toward the bar. His eyes immediately found Lori. He didn't have to see her face to see in a second that she had been beaten up. Her dejected posture and the way she walked, told him everything he needed to know. She sat next to him.

"Travis and Steve beat me up, and now I have nowhere to live. Look at me, Frank."

Lori's face was bruised in several places. One eye had started to close. Her arms and legs were lacerated in a number of places. Frank caught Jeff's eye, but only for a second, but that second expressed an understanding that Frank would finally have to deal with her--that he would have to take her in and take care of her. The two men had known each other a long time and had gained the ability to read each other like a book. Jeff knew that Frank would feel obligated to take Lori under his roof since he had led her to this. Time had run out. That one little glance between them meant, *I wish I could have warned you off of her earlier and that you would have heeded my advice, but you're caught. First her; then her kids and I know that's not what you want, but you love her and now you're going to have to do something about it.*

"So what happened?" asked Jeff.

"I got in the car with Travis and his brother, Steve. They took me somewhere and threw me out of the car when it was still moving. They got out, and Steve held me down on the street while Travis beat the fuck out of me."

"Why'd they do that?" asked Sherry.

"For going out with Frank. Travis came into Ciceros and saw me sitting with Frank and Jeff. And he knew all the time that I was going out with Frank."

"So what are you going to do?" Sherry asked.

"I don't know. I don't have a place to live now. Unless Frank lets me stay with him." Lori took Frank by the arm. "Let's get out of here. You're taking me to the 3rd Precinct station."

"Are you going to press charges?" Frank asked.

"I already did. I just want to find out if they've done anything with them. Come on, let's go."

"See you later, Jeff." Frank nodded at Sherry. "Take good care of my buddy, and make sure he buys you a drink." Then he led Lori out of the bar to his sports car.

THE POND

They walked into the police station together. A police officer sat behind a broad counter. Lori grabbed Frank by the hand and led him over to the counter. The officer looked up from his paperwork.

"What can I do for you?"

" I want you to check on the complaint I just made tonight," said Lori. "It's on Travis Johnson. Is anything being done about it?"

"What time was the complaint made?" asked the officer.

"Around ten o'clock tonight. He beat me up."

"Be right back." The officer got up and went into one of the back rooms. Lori pulled out her cigarettes, took one out of the pack, and lit it. She inhaled from it, puckered up her mouth into the form of an exaggerated O, and blew the smoke out in a perfect ring. Suddenly she threw the cigarette on the floor and ground it out with her foot.

"Let's get the hell out of here, Frank."

"Why? The officer's not done yet. You can't leave now."

"The hell I can't. They've got a lot of parking ticket violations on me. When he finds them, I'm going to be in big trouble. Let's go. Now!"

"Okay then."

They got in the car. Frank started the engine, threw the sports car in gear, and eased out of the parking lot. Five minutes later they were on I-55 heading for the St. Louis Skyline. Frank turned onto the entrance ramp for the Poplar Street bridge and headed for Illinois. Lori reached out and touched him lightly on the arm.

"Looks like you're stuck with me. I have nowhere else to go. Think you can handle it?"

I'd love to handle you, Lori, Frank thought. *Don't know if I can, but it sure would be fun trying. Your kids, now that's a different story. No way can I handle five kids living in my house for any length of time. We'd have to work out something offbeat and nontraditional. But right now it's just the two of us. Two faces in the crowd who have found each other--found something there that neither could understand. We need each other--forget about the impracticality of it all or what others might think.* "I'd like to handle it Lori. I'm just glad we've found each other," said Frank.

The next morning he made coffee while she slept. He was used to getting up early because no matter how late he stayed up, no matter how much he drank the night before, there was usually work to be done the next day. He was a farmer and because he worked alone, there was no one else to fall back on. If a job had to be done, it had to be done, and his success or failure as a farmer depended upon his ability to come through every time. Today, he had trucks to load up. They would be arriving for his corn, and even though his grain handling systems were state of the art, he had to be available at all times in case something went wrong.

Lori slept as if she had never slept before. She was a dancer who lived for the night and slept throughout the day. Frank went upstairs with two cups of coffee. Lori snored underneath a sheet. He pulled it off only to find that she was still naked from last night. She had her legs tucked up so that she was in a semi fetal position, her face smooth reflecting an inner peace that she probably experienced only in her sleep. He saw once again that her body was perfect with hardly a trace of body fat, beautifully muscled, and put together in one trim wonderfully coordinated package. At this moment she appeared a child, almost grown up, a child woman stuck in a hostile world, who had been forced to struggle constantly under the most adverse circumstances to survive. *And Good God* thought Frank, *what she had to do, or felt she had to do to survive.* He didn't want to know.

"Lori, wake up. I have some coffee for you," he said gently. There was no response. Frank lay down on the bed next to her and kissed her tenderly on the lips. "Lori, wake up. I'm not going to let you sleep any longer. We have too much to do." Again, no response. Suddenly an idea hit him--right in the balls. He pulled off his pajama bottoms and pulled her up close. Then he reached around her slim body using both arms to pull her even closer, but this time he pulled her against him with his hands which were by now resting firmly underneath her. Still getting no response, Frank took his hands off of her and brought them around in front of him. He started to ease into her. He moved slowly, not wanting to hurt or to alarm her.   Frank took his time putting it in a little deeper, then working it back and forth inside of her before easing it in a little more. At last, he was all the way in, which meant that she was waking up, aware that something was happening. At last she gave a little audible moan and opened her eyes. He reached around her once more, twisted around onto his back, and pulled her on top of him. She was light as a feather while his movements were slow and controlled so that he didn't come out as she straddled him. At last, her body began to come alive and she started to thrust back and forth. Still sleepy himself, Frank's body wasn't fully awake and not as sensitive as it would be later. It took a long time for him to come, but by the time he finally did, Lori's body was fully awake. At last they lay there together in each other's arms while she kissed him softly on the neck.

"How long were you doing that to me?" she asked.

"Not too long. I just wanted to wake you up before your coffee got cold, and you just slept on no matter what I did. Now it's cold. I'll get you some more."

Frank jumped out of bed, his movements those of a twenty-year-old athlete, quick and lithe. He went down the steps and poured another cup of coffee for each of them; then returned to her.

"You are really despicable, Frank, raping me in my sleep that way."

"I had to. I'm not going to sit around and watch you sleep all day. Now get out of bed and come downstairs so that I can feed you. We are going to load trucks and then we're going swimming."

"I can't swim, Frank."

"The way we're going to do it, you don't need to know. Now put some clothes on and come downstairs with me."

"I'm wearing your bathrobe. Do you mind?"

Suddenly Lori was out of bed, pulling on Frank's blue bathrobe which had hung over the foot of the bed. *God, she looked good*, thought Frank. *She looks perfectly at home here wearing my bathrobe as if she's been wearing it forever. It's hard to believe she's a dancer--she seems such an innocent.* He took her downstairs and made her some English Muffins, laying out for her a stick of butter, a jar of strawberry jam, and a container of peanut butter. She ate one piece--then looked up at him.

"So what are we going to do now?"

"Put on some clothes so we can meet that truck. Then we're going swimming."

"I don't have a swim suit."

"Just put on your shorts and one of my T-shirts."

Frank went to his dresser which he kept downstairs in the family room and pulled out a red T-shirt which had always been too tight for him to wear. *It would be way too loose on her*, he thought, *but it is the best I can do.* Then he grabbed a pair of swim trunks and put them on. When he came back into the kitchen, Lori was sitting bare breasted at the table in her red shorts. Frank tossed the

T-shirt to her.

"Let's go. The first truck's due in fifteen minutes."

He led her out to his machine shed where he kept the inner tubes. He found two of them and pumped them full of air with the electric air compressor which lay on the floor. Next to it was a Playmate cooler. He took this, one of the inner tubes, and two twelve-foot sections of rope which lay on top of the cooler and walked out of the shed. She followed him to his truck carrying the other inner tube. He put everything in the back of the truck as she got in the passenger side.

"One more thing," he told her. "The most important thing."

"What's that?" she asked.

"The beer."

He went back into the house, took a six pack of Busch and a container of ice out of the refrigerator and returned to the truck. Reaching into the back end of the pickup he took out the cooler, dropped six cans of cold beer into it and packed the remaining spaces with the ice. Then he got in on the driver's side, started the engine, and drove to the farm next door.

It was the farm with the grain leg, the one Lori had so adroitly climbed several weeks before. They waited a short time and then they heard the truck coming down the driveway. The driver got out of his truck and walked over to a wheel which had once been a steering wheel off a tractor. The wheel was attached to a steel cable which rode on pulleys attached to the ceiling. The driver turned the wheel to the right which pulled on the cable which opened a trapdoor on the bottom of one of the overhead bins. Corn started to fall into the truck. Frank went over to a control panel and pushed three buttons. One started the grain leg. Another started the pit auger. The other started another auger which went to the Southeast bin. This last auger, which resembled a giant corkscrew, pulled corn out of the bin into the pit. The pit auger then channeled the corn underneath a concrete floor into the bottom of the grain leg. The grain leg then transported the corn one-hundred feet into the air and dropped it into a long steel tube which went into the overhead bin. If Frank and the driver had wanted to, they could have used a different bin auger and emptied another bin into either the overhead or one of the other overheads. Or they could have turned another wheel thus turning a valve one-hundred feet in the air which would have rerouted the corn into still another bin.

"Dave, I'm going to have to leave you. You know how to stop

everything. I want you to meet Lori over in my pickup."

The driver followed Frank over to the pickup. Lori lowered her window, a look of surprise on her face. "Lori, this is Dave. He's been driving his truck over here for years."

"Glad to meet you, Dave."

"Dave, we have to go. If you have any trouble, you know where to find us. It's that pond you pass just before you make your left turn down my road, the one with the Sycamore trees around the banks. Or if you want, forget about hauling all that grain. Come join us."

"Gerald would kill me if I did that," said Dave. "He wants to keep his trucks rolling and besides I can't swim."

"Neither can Lori. We're just going down to drink a little beer. See you later, Dave. Probably tomorrow."

Frank drove Lori down to the pond. Years earlier he had built a dock which stretched thirty feet out across the water. He walked out onto the dock, threw his inner tube down into the water, and dived into the water head first. He surfaced and looked around for the inner tube, then seeing where it had drifted to, swam over to it. Frank pushed the inner tube to the ladder which hung over the side of the dock.

"Come on over here, Lori. I'll hold the inner tube while you climb into it. But first, bring over those two sections of rope and the other inner tube."

Lori went back to the pickup truck and returned with the two pieces of rope and the inner tube, which she placed on the dock. Then she started down the ladder. Frank dropped the inner tube into the water and held it next to the dock while she eased into it. Satisfied that she was securely ensconced in the inner tube, Frank swam the short distance to where she had laid the sections of rope and the other inner tube. He grabbed the two pieces of rope and put them between his teeth. Then he pulled the inner tube into the water and started to swim over to Lori pushing the inner tube ahead of him. When he reached her, he took one of the pieces of rope from his mouth and tied one end to the inner tube, the other end to the dock. Then he turned to her and gave her one end of the other piece of rope.

"Here you tie this end to your inner tube just as I have while I tie the other end to the dock."

Lori tied her end to her tube while Frank tied the other to the dock. Finished with securing the two inner tubes, he swam back to the ladder and climbed back onto the dock bringing the beer over from the pickup.

"Now this is the important part, Lori. Any time that you're thirsty use your rope to pull yourself and your inner tube up close to the dock. I'm leaving the cooler right here on the dock. Grab a beer any time you're ready."

Frank placed the cooler on the edge of the dock, and pulled on the rope which was attached to his inner tube. The inner tube came right up to the dock. Frank climbed down the ladder and eased into the inner tube so that his rear was in the water, pressed tightly against the inside of the tube while his legs were draped up and over its opposite end. The movement of getting into the tube had caused it to drift away from the dock. Frank took the rope and pulled himself in close to the dock and took two cans out of the cooler. Placing his feet against the dock, he pushed off causing the inner tube to drift up next to Lori's. He handed her a beer and placed one foot onto her inner tube. It didn't take much, for the downward pressure of his foot against the top of her inner tube kept his inner tube from drifting away from hers. Since the prevailing wind was from the South, both inner tubes would tend to drift North away from the dock stretching both ropes' taut.

Frank opened his can and took a long swallow of beer. "Now Lori, this is the way to really fuck off."

"I can see that you've done this before," said Lori.

"A few times. It takes you out of the world you're living in. Makes you forget. That's why I brought you here."

"You find something wrong with the world I'm living in?"

"Yes. Don't you?"

"Sure I do. I didn't always dance, you know. I didn't always do the things I do, and I didn't always think the way I think now. I've made some mistakes and now I have to live with them. Five of them: Jenny, Charles, Roger, Sarah, and Jamie. Those are my five children."

"You made a sixth one," said Frank. "Travis."

"Oh yes. Travis--my sixth child."

"How'd you get mixed up with him?"

"I was married at the time. In fact, I'm still married. My marriage was good for a while. Had three kids by my husband, but then he started drinking heavily, and he started beating me. And Travis was there living next door. He used to come over a lot. Travis was sixteen at the time and I was twenty. I had nowhere else to turn so I turned to him, and then he gave me two more kids."

"So, do you like dancing?"

"I did, but I'm burning out. Frank, I'm really starting to burn out. I probably told you this before, but I worked at one of those places as a cocktail waitress. One night some of the dancers got me drunk, got me up on stage, and the rest is history. So now I support my five mistakes with my dancing."

"Six mistakes," said Frank. "Who else do you support?"

"Too many of them. Too goddamn many of them. Let's see. There's Travis. Then my five kids. Then there's Travis's brother Steve. He's got another brother who lives with us time to time. And then there's his little sister Becky. She's only fifteen years old. And, did I tell you this? She's already pregnant. Fifteen years old and she's already pregnant."

"Sounds like you."

"Me?"

"Yeah. You had to have gotten pregnant when you were around fifteen."

"No. I was a little older than that. Maybe, I'm a little older than you think."

"You are twenty-five, almost twenty-six. Your oldest is how old?"

"Eight."

"So there you are."

"You don't know a damn thing about me, Frank. I can be anyone. You don't know who I am and you don't know how old I am."

"And you could disappear out of my life in an instant, and I might never see you again, and I might never have known you--who you really are."

"Oh, you will find me Frank. I know you will."

"So who are you?"

"I am just a little girl wanting something. I want to love someone like everybody else. I want to be a housewife. Can you believe that--me wanting to be a housewife? Is that too much to ask? Is that too much to ask of life?"

"No, it's not."

"I'm getting me another beer. Want one?"

Frank pulled the rope toward him dragging the inner tube up to the dock. He reached into the cooler and took out two cans of beer. The inner tube lay in the water just beneath the angle iron beams which supported the dock's deck. One side of the inner tube rose against the angle iron as Frank transferred his weight to get the beer. Nothing would have happened except Frank had put the cooler at the end of the dock. The inner tube rubbed against the corner of the angle iron brace where it had been welded to another brace. Since the weld was down low beneath the cypress platform and out of sight, Frank had not bothered grinding it smooth. Suddenly Frank heard the tube blow. Air rushed out of the gash that the weld tore into the inner tube and the inner tube started to sink. Within seconds Frank was left in the water holding two cans of beer while he tread water with his legs.

"It looks like we're sharing," said Frank. "Bring your tube over."

Lori pulled on her rope which brought her inner tube close to Frank. He handed her one of the Budweisers and rested his hands on the inner tube. "Now move over so that I can swim underneath the inner tube and pull myself into it," he ordered.

Frank ducked under the water and swam underneath the tube. He brought his head to the surface in the center of the tube. Reaching upwards with both arms he grabbed both sides of the tube and pulled himself up. Lori spread her legs wide giving him room to come up between them. Frank brought his body up between them; then quickly opened his own legs and put them around her. Within seconds they had managed to get him into the inner tube so that his groin rested tightly against hers. His legs enveloped her but rested across her end of the tube while her legs rested on either side of him. Not too many people could have done it without capsizing the inner tube. Frank was slender and strong. Lori was well coordinated and built small for a woman who was five foot six. Although she could not swim, she had shown no fear at any time during this maneuver. Moreover both Lori and Frank had managed to hold onto a beer can while performing the gymnastics that had brought Frank into the inner tube.

"You sunk that inner tube on purpose just so you could climb in here with me," said Lori.

"I wouldn't put it past me, but that just happened," said Frank.

They left the water in the middle of the afternoon. Frank had to meet another truck. Not that there was anything that he really had to do, for everything had been going smoothly--it was just that he believed good management meant that he had to be there to keep track of things. Swimming in the pond with Lori when trucks were loading up with his corn was an example of derelict management.

He made love to her twice when they returned. Afterwards as they sat together on the couch in the family room, Lori became very quiet. Then she asked if she could use the phone. First, she called someone--Frank wasn't sure who it was--about her kids. He gathered that they were staying with a friend somewhere in the City and were not in Union, Missouri. Or was it that they were staying with Travis's mother? He had long ago decided against believing anything Lori told him so he didn't pay attention to the telephone conversation. Then she made another call, this time at his urging, to the St. Louis police station. This time he listened to her end of the conversation.

"Do you have the report on file for an assault and battery committed by Travis Johnson?" she asked. "When did it happen? It happened last night. Yes I made the report." Then there was a long pause in the conversation. She spoke with Frank for a few moments before the police officer on the line came back with the report. "You have it. Good. Yes I'll stay in touch. Where can I be reached? I am staying somewhere near Springfield, Illinois. Telephone number? 217-631-2267. Yes, that's where I'll be." Then she hung up.

"What are we doing now?" she asked.

"We are going out for dinner," Frank replied. "Then we are going to go to a little town called Chatham. I'm going to have a friend meet us at a pub. It's time that you start meeting more of my friends since you are going to be staying here awhile."

"What should I wear?"

"Your shorts will be fine. You'll have to put them in the dryer first. Face it, Lori, you don't really have a lot of clothes here you know."

"Sometime soon you can take me back to Union so I can get all my stuff."

Your kids too? What am I going to do with them now? Frank asked himself. "We can do all of that tomorrow," he told her. "Tonight we are going to just enjoy ourselves and not do anything that really needs to be done."

Two hours later they sat at a large cooking table in Springfield's Benihana style Japanese restaurant. Cooking table was the appropriate term for the counter at which they sat since all meals were prepared in front of the Diners. A slender Japanese came over a few minutes after the waitress had taken their order. He stood in the center of the cooking table which surrounded him carrying knives, forks, and other assorted weaponry. He put a cucumber on the table and sliced it into thin slivers with a sharp knife, his hand moving rapidly. The Japanese did the same with the meat and other vegetables so that everything was accomplished with blinding speed. He did this partly for expediency but mostly for show. Then he took a bottle of seasoning and nonchalantly tossed it in the air catching it with his other hand. The man made a great show of showing reckless abandonment with seasoning bottles, knives, and forks. Frank asked the waitress for chopsticks and an order of saki.

It had all started with this in mind, he thought. *I was planning to take her to a Japanese restaurant in St. Louis, and she had stood me up. Afterwards I gave her a lesson in chopsticks. Now she's planning to move in with me at a farm in Central Illinois.* Then he poured Lori a cup of Saki and handed it to her.

"This restaurant's not bad," he said, "but it's not at all like the one I was going to take you to in St. Louis. Here, as in many so-called Japanese restaurants, they put on quite a show. They don't do that at the Tachibana in St. Louis. It's rated tops for the area. There the emphasis is on the food, and it's quiet with no knife throwing. They serve sushi and quite a few other things, but the sushi's the interesting thing, which as you probably already know is cold fish."

"Sounds horrible."

"Not so," Frank replied. "You don't think tuna fish is terrible, do you?"

"Not really."

"How about lobster? Or pickled herring? Or shrimp cocktail?"

"I've never had herring or lobster before?"

"See, you've been hanging around the wrong people. But anyway, you've heard that most people like herring and lobster. It's all sushi or cold fish. When the Japanese serve sushi they serve it in little servings arranged in a very appealing manner, often in various floral arrangements. The only thing about it that's bad is the price."

"I don't know Frank."

"Hang around me and you'll find out that you like it."

"I'm planning to Frank."

They left after they finished the saki. Instead of going directly to Chatham Frank decided to take her to a topless bar in Springfield. He had been there once before, but only for half an hour, after having left a bachelor's party in a late attempt at finding a girl or two to perform at the party. The girls didn't know him there so the attempt failed and he and the two friends who had driven there with him returned to the bachelor's party empty handed. One reason he took Lori there was curiosity--his and hers. The other was because he wanted Lori to have the opportunity to size the place up as a possible source of employment just in case she wanted to permanently disappear from Travis. They had not discussed any long range plans of what she planned to do. Having her five children in his house for an extended period of time was out of the question. Perhaps she would move to Springfield, temporarily get a job as a dancer, then move onto waitressing or something else. He could then supplement her income so that she could make ends meet.

The topless bar did not serve alcohol; the good citizens of Springfield, most of them women, had seen to that. Frank and Lori ordered cokes from the waitress. The waitress returned to their table before the first dancer had finished her set.

"May I ask you something?" Lori asked the waitress.

"Sure, go ahead."

"Do the girls ever do table dances?"

"What do you mean?" the waitress asked.

"Over on the East Side of St. Louis, at some places the girls jump on the men's laps. They go from man to man collecting a tip from each one."

"No, they don't do that here."

"Then how do the girls make their money?" Frank asked.

"They make their money up on stage," the waitress replied. "Any man who goes up on stage with them is expected to tip them. Of course they do privates also."

"Well, we know what privates are," replied Lori. "How much do they get for them here?"

"They usually get $15 for a private. Out of that they have to give the bar $5.00. Sorry to rush off, but I've got other customers waiting."

After the waitress left Lori turned her attention back to the stage. A new girl was up there now, but only one customer sat in front of her stage. She did three songs for her set before the man tipped her. They stayed to watch one other girl perform after which Frank pulled a dollar from his pocket and put it on the table.

"I don't know about you, but I've seen enough," he said.

"I have too. Besides, we have to go back to Union to pick up my stuff."

"Can't it wait until tomorrow?"

"No, it can't. We've got to go up there Frank."

"I was hoping to introduce you to my friend in Chatham. When you were changing back at my house, I called him to tell him that we would probably meet him at a bar there. He's waiting for me to call him right now."

"Well, he will just have to wait for some other time," Lori replied.

"Let's go then," said Frank.

They left Springfield, not bothering to stop at the farm. Lori rode back in silence. *What is she thinking about*? thought Frank. *Her kids*? He took her hand and held it to assure her that he understood. Except as it later turned out, he didn't.

"Do you really think it's such a good idea you and me going up to Union together and barging into your place? I mean, Travis knows about us and if he's there, there's going to be trouble and you know it."

"I don't think he's going to be there," Lori answered. "He's in the City no doubt, but you're right. I have some things with Frances in St. Louis. I have to pick them up first. Then I can have Paul and her take me out to Union to get the rest of my things. That will only take forty-five minutes once I'm in the house, and after that's done I can have them drop me off at the Sports Bar where you will be waiting for me."

"That sounds reasonable," said Frank. "I'll just have a few there while I'm waiting for you."

He drove her into the City not far from where he had found her the day they had done the Limo together. She gave him directions to France's and Paul's house.

"They're home," said Lori. "Drive me around the block. I'll tell you where to let me out."

"Why shouldn't I just let you out here?" asked Frank.

"Because Travis or one of his friends might be watching."

He drove about a block when she asked him to stop. She was about to get out of the car when he stopped her.

"I'm going to be at the Sports Bar now. I know this thing's going to take several hours so you tell me right now whether you are going to be there or not."

"I'll be there, Frank. Just wait for me. Okay?"

Then she got out and walked up the street without looking back. Frank drove to the Sports Bar which was only fifteen minutes away. He sat at the bar alone and ordered a Budweiser where he was joined by a plump brunette.

"Will you buy me a drink, Frank?" My name is Promise.

Without waiting for an answer, the girl took a seat on the bar stool next to him. He bought her a beer and brought her up to date on what he and Lori had done and about their plans to take her things back to his farm. Promise shared with him her relationship with an ex-boyfriend who used to beat her, and how she kept on coming back to him until finally she had enough of it. "I had to really struggle with myself," said Promise, "for it took a long time for me to feel I was worth anything. I won't let any man ever beat on me again."

"Frank, you really like this girl, don't you?"

"I really like her and she really likes me. But how is she ever going to get rid of her boyfriend?"

"She'll just have to make her mind up. I did." Promise sipped from her drink, then looked up at Frank. "I've got an idea, but you can't tell anyone, okay?"

"I won't."

"I have a little flat which I'm not using right now. No one here knows I've got it. It's not all that much, but it's mine. If Lori wants to leave her boyfriend, I'll let her stay there for a while. She can disappear from him until things blow over. Then perhaps you and she can work something else out."

"That's very generous of you, Promise. You don't even know me. Why would you do it?"

"Because I've been where Lori's at. She's being abused like I was. She needs help. And I know I can trust you, Frank."

"But you don't know me."

"I'm a shrewd judge of character. You're all right Frank."

Four hours and seven beers later Lori had still not come in. Promise looked down at her watch to check the time; then put her hand on Frank's leg.

"It's close to closing time Frank. I guess she's not coming, is she?"

"It doesn't look like it, Promise."

"Maybe something's happened to her."

"Very possible," Frank replied.

He stayed until the bar closed. Then he drove home. *Something's happened to her all right*, Frank thought. *She got lonely for Travis and changed her mind. Soon as I got her in the city she made a beeline right for him. Didn't give a shit about me and left me to rot in a bar without giving the matter a second's thought.* Then he went to bed.

DETECTIVE GORDON

The insistent ringing of the phone woke him up at 3:00 in the morning. It had been an uneventful Saturday night, so uneventful that Frank had turned in early. The voice on the other end seemed to be from another planet. It was the police.

"Are you Frank Harring?" the voice asked.

"Yeah. You've got him. Who are you and why are you calling so late?"

"This is Detective Gordon from the St. Louis Police Department. I'm calling for Lori Mellon. Is she there?"

"No, she left a couple days ago."

"Do you know how to reach her?"

"Not really. She doesn't have a phone and she lives way out in Union, Missouri."

"Oh no. Is she out there again? That's Travis's old address. Her boyfriend. You know him?"

"I've met him. He beat her up again the other day. I brought her home here with me afterwards so I know all about it."

"Yeah, well, we've picked up Travis just last night and put him in jail. Look, if you can get hold of Lori, she has to file an appearance by 10:00 a.m. to keep him there a little longer."

"Mr. Gordon, is this the first time she's filed charges against Travis?"

"No, she's done it several times before. Then she either drops the charges or doesn't show up for her court appearance. They always do that. The same thing's going to happen this time, but I've got to follow through on my end since that's my job."

"Sounds like it won't do any good for me to drive out there then and tell her," said Frank. "It's 120 miles for me one way. If it would do any good I'll go out there."

"You'd probably be wasting your time. Stay home and get some sleep."

"Mr. Gordon, I want to ask you one question. What do you think of Travis?"

"He's always getting in trouble. We see him in here every so often like clockwork. The way he's going, he'll be in the penitentiary before long. I have to get going Mr. Harring. If you can get hold of Lori, it would be helpful, but I can tell you right now that she's going to let this whole matter drop."

"Why's that?"

"She always did before. This is not the first time she's filed charges against Travis. They're all like that. These girls get beat up by these assholes, file charges, then go right back to them."

"Thanks for calling," said Frank. "I doubt if I'll get hold of Lori, but I'm going to think about going up there."

By 7:30 a.m. Frank was on I-44 on the outskirts of Union, Missouri. Lori had stood him up by not showing at the Sports Bar after he had let her out of his car several nights before. Nevertheless, he thought the situation over carefully, and not being able to get back to sleep, got in his car and committed himself to the long drive to Union. *Travis is in jail but will be out around 10:00 a.m.. If Lori is in Union, Travis will return somewhere around eleven. Knowing that she had put him there and after spending the night in jail, Travis will be mad as hell and bent on beating her up again.* Although Lori had never been a loyal friend to him, she had nevertheless shared a part of her life with him. The girl needed help. Frank reasoned that she needed three things to start getting her life in order again: 1. Control over her car, 2. Control over her home, and 3. Control over her money. *Travis is a parasite who takes money from her, drives her car whenever he pleases, and lives in her house without contributing to the household expenses.*

Frank knew he could help her get control over her life if she would let him. He asked himself, *If I'm not her friend, who is?* He wanted to roll over back to sleep, but decided instead that he would not be a friend if he did. *So what if the friendship had so far been one-sided, and so what if she might end up going back to Travis no matter what he did. He'd give it a shot--his Code of the West compelled him to--and he didn't care whether going all the way out to Union made sense or not.*

A Missouri State police car passed him. Frank accelerated, bringing his car up close behind the speeding patrol car and switched on his emergency flashers. The patrol car stopped and pulled onto the shoulder of the highway. Frank pulled up behind it, got out of his car, and went over to the officer's window.

"I need your help officer. I have a girlfriend who lives in Union who lives with a guy who just assaulted her several days ago. He's in jail and will be out in a couple of hours. He's likely to come back here and beat the hell out of her unless I can warn her."

"Do you know where she lives?" the officer asked.

"I know where she lives, but if I go over there myself, the people she lives with will tell her boyfriend. I need to have a police officer go over and warn her."

"You'll need to talk to the municipal police in Union. I'm a state cop. Tell you what. You can follow me over to the station."

Frank followed the officer to the station and went inside. A police officer sat just inside the door going over his paperwork. Frank spent five minutes explaining to him why he had driven 120 miles to Union, Missouri, and the man agreed to help. *It didn't take much to convince the police officer to help*, Frank thought. *The man obviously despises men who beat women.* Frank followed the officer over to Lori's house being careful to park his car a block away. The officer went to the door and rang the doorbell. When no one answered, the officer knocked on the door. Still, no one answered. The officer waited on the porch for five minutes, knocking intermittently. Then he walked up the street to talk to Frank who was standing on the sidewalk just out of sight of anyone who might come to the door.

"There's no answer," said the officer. "I knocked a number of times. My guess is they're all inside asleep."

"Can we try again later?" asked Frank. "Say one hour from now. Can you meet me right here at 8:45?"

"Yes. We can give it another try. I'll meet you here at 8:45 sharp."

Frank drove downtown where he found a little cafe, went inside and had breakfast. An hour later he drove back to Lori's house and waited for the officer to appear. Frank waited fifteen minutes, but the officer didn't come. *I'm running out of time,* thought Frank. *What the hell, I'm going over alone--I didn't want to do it this way, but now I've got no choice.* He walked up onto the porch and knocked. He heard movement inside the house; then someone opened the door. A skinny young man stood there, sleepy eyed and listless. Frank recognized the man from the time he had looked Lori up in the City--the day he had done the Limo with her. It had to be Steve, Travis's brother, who had helped Travis beat Lori up.

"Who are you?" asked Steve.

"I'm Jeff Shannon. Is Travis here?" Frank decided to use Jeff Shannon's name. Lori would know Frank had been there. Travis wouldn't--that is unless Steve recognized him from the day they did their first limo.

"No. He's in the city."

"Oh really, where can I find him? I'm a friend of his and

Lori's."

"He's in jail. He'll be back sometime this afternoon."

"Well, how about Lori then? Is she home?"

"No. She's in the city also."

"Okay then. Tell them I was looking for them."

"What is your name again?" asked Steve.

"Jeff Shannon."

Frank idled around town for a half hour, driving aimlessly up first one street, then down another. Then he drove back to the police station where he found the officer inside. The man looked up from his paperwork and smiled.

"Sorry I couldn't meet you. I got a call, but I went over afterwards. Someone was home after all. The guy explained that his brother was in jail and that your girlfriend was somewhere in the city. Did you tell me that two guys beat your girlfriend up?"

"That's correct, officer. The guy you talked to is Lori's boyfriend's little brother. He's the one who held her down."

"Nice people," the officer replied sarcastically.

"Is there anything Lori can do to protect herself from Travis and his brother while she's living in Union?" Frank asked.

"What she can do is she can go to the courthouse right here in Union and meet with the judge. At her request he will give her an order of protection against both of them. This order of protection can specify a radius of say one-half mile. Then, if either one of those guys ever gets within one-half mile of her, he is in contempt of court and we can throw him in jail."

"That sounds like the route to go," Frank replied. "In effect then, the two brothers will be banished from Union, Missouri."

"That's right," the officer replied, "because sooner or later one or both of them are going to come within a half mile of her."

"Officer, thank you very much for your time. I'll keep in touch."

It took him two and a half hours to drive home. On the way Frank considered Lori's situation. *She could get rid of Travis and his brother. The local police would make sure of that. With Promise's help he could get her a place and make her disappear so that Travis would never find her.* After that, he would work something out with her--he didn't know what exactly--but he'd do something to make her life better. A whole lot better. The question was, *would she want that?*

LORI'S STORY

Lori's voice was insistent. "You have to come see me. We've gotta talk." The phone had rung at 12:30 which meant that she had been at work for only a few minutes. This time Frank knew that the news would not be good.

He walked into the Injection Pump two hours later and found her at the bar. Hardly looking up at him, Lori asked a waitress to bring them two bud Lites; then she motioned   toward a table in the back. He followed her to the table and sat next to her. "Guess where I've been?" she said.

"I have no idea," Frank replied. "I know one thing, and that is you didn't show up at the Sports Bar the other night."

"Travis found me and made me go with him," said Lori. "And I've been in jail the last three days."

"Come on now, Lori. What in the hell got you in jail?"

"The cops picked Travis up Saturday night for beating me up. He was driving around in the city in my car and they found a bunch of stolen stuff in it. They came and got me out in Union and put me in fucking jail. Frank, I just got out, and then I had to pay sixty bucks to get my car out of the impound yard. Then I had to put up three hundred dollars bond. I had to go back to Union and sell some things to come up with the money. I had to sell my $2000 stereo for $200."

"Lori, that's quite a story."

"Look, if you don't believe it, here's the impound papers for the car." Lori reached into her pocket and took out a form which had Saturday's date on it and information pertaining to the impoundment of her car. Frank tried to read it, but the writing was difficult to read in the dim light.

Of course there would be an impoundment paper for the car, thought Frank. Even if Lori hadn't been arrested, he knew that Travis had been. If Travis had been driving Lori's car at the time of his arrest the police would have confiscated and impounded her car.

"You don't believe me, do you Frank? Why you lying motherfucker."

The waitress came over with their drinks. "Lori, it's your turn up on stage. Bogart's already upset that you're late."

Lori turned to the waitress. "Tell Bogart that I'm coming right up." Getting up from the table Lori looked down at Frank. "You've gotten me in a lot of trouble. You're always getting me in trouble."

Lori crawled onto his lap and remained there for her set, never once getting up. "And you had to come out to my house again. Steve told Travis it was you. And then you had to send the police over. What are you trying to do, Frank--get me killed? Do me a favor, will you, and never come out to my house again."

"I came out to your house for a reason, Lori. A Detective Gordon called me up at 3:00 a.m. on Sunday to tell me to get hold of you. He told me that Travis had been arrested and that you had better make an appearance at the courthouse to make your complaint stick."

"You lying mother fucker. How in the hell did he get your number, Frank? I know Gordon. He told me that you called him. They would never had put me in jail if you hadn't called Gordon. I had to sell my stereo for $200 and I had to sell my T.V. just to get myself out of jail. You owe me Frank. Plus it cost me $60 to get my car out."

"Gordon's lying to you Lori. I never called him, and I lost a whole night's sleep over that phone call. And then I went out to Union all the way from my farm just to save your ass. I did this as your friend, and I certainly didn't do it to cause you any trouble. I even went so far as to get the police officer to go over to your house just so no one would recognize me. He knocked on your door early in the morning while I hid up the street, but no one answered the door. He and I agreed to meet near your house one hour later, but he got tied up and didn't show. To warn you that Travis was in jail and soon would be out, I went up there myself, not knowing that the officer would appear later. I did this for you because I care about you Lori--more than you will ever know, and believe me, it wasn't easy driving way out to Union. It's 120 miles from my house."

"You're lying, Frank. And I know when you are lying."

When the set was over, Frank pulled a ten from his wallet and handed it to her. She shook her head refusing to accept the money. They went to the bar and ordered two Bud Lites and two shots of Tequila. Without offering to do a body shot, Lori chugged the Tequila, looking straight ahead without smiling.

"You've wrecked my life, Frank. You've got me all screwed up. And then you have to come visit me!"

"I don't quite see it that way," Frank replied. "If your life is messed up you only have yourself to blame. I didn't set you up with Travis, and I never told you to go back to him. You chose Travis, Lori. No one else chose him for you."

"Yeah, and what would you do, Frank? I have five kids, Frank. You have no one to be responsible to."

Let me remind you, Lori, that you had two of your children with Travis. But Frank didn't say it aloud. The conversation was going badly enough as it was. He wanted to tell her that she had to take responsibility for the rest of her life, but he knew that she didn't want to hear it so he kept silent.

"I have to get going," said Lori. "There's a group of guys over there--Lori pointed across the room to four men who were sitting at a table close to stage 2--who are going to tip me heavily. I've gotta make some money, now more than ever, and you were right that time you told me that you scare my customers away. You do scare them away, Frank." Lori got up, turning her back on Frank, and joined the four men who were sitting by themselves. He left in the middle of her next set. She had started on stage two where the four men had joined her, but she was now off the stage half standing on the floor while using a chair for support. One of the men had positioned himself behind her so that his groin was jammed against her rear end. Kneeling over the chair, Lori placed both elbows on its seat as she thrust her backside into the man's groin. For the first time since he had seen her, Lori smiled over at him as he walked over to the stairs. There was no humor in that smile, for it seemed to be directed at him as if she meant to say--*see, I don't need you after all for these guys think I'm terrific, and I am. Look what I'm doing with them. Who will I be with, Frank, tonight, tomorrow, next week--and what will I be doing with them?*

He went straight home, got himself a beer, and sat on the couch in the family room. He reflected on the last few months with Lori. *So she wanted out after all,* he concluded. *Chose Travis after all because it was too difficult to better herself and even went so far as to construct a fantasy--a fantasy that she herself believed--about being in jail, having to sell her stereo, and my putting the police onto her.*

The next day he called the St. Louis police, introducing himself on the phone as the manager of the Injection Pump. He didn't believe that she had been in jail, but he had to know for sure.

Frank told the police officer on the line--"Lori Mellon is one of our dancers. We have a policy at the Injection Pump of fining the girls if they don't show up for work for any reason short of an emergency. Lori informed us that she had spent three nights in your jail beginning on Saturday, and that's why she missed work. Can you confirm this?" The officer excused himself for a few moments after which he returned to the phone.

"Lori Mellon was not in jail on any one of those nights. Not in our jail nor in any of the county jails. We have our information linked on computer with all of the other police agencies in the St. Louis area. This includes the surrounding areas. Lori was arrested on three occasions since 1990--once on July 2 of 1990, a second time on April of 1992 and a third time on October 7, 1992."

"What was she arrested for?" asked Frank.

"In 1990 for disturbing the peace, and both times in 1992 the charge was for assault and battery."

"Thanks officer," said Frank. "It looks like we're going to have to fine her."

After he hung up, Frank concluded that the only way he could continue to see Lori was to accept her fantasy as reality and to take his part in her fantasy world. He was almost willing to do it. Instead he decided to look for her replacement.

THE REPLACEMENT

Nadine already had the can of beer waiting for him before he reached the bar. He paid her four dollars, leaving her a dollar tip and pulled up a bar stool. It would be a good night. A friend who farmed close to him had let him out at the Sports Bar and had driven onto St. Louis for a business meeting. The friend would return in a few hours and drink with him until closing time. Dennis Barry was a good friend, good enough that he would return without fail and not breathe a word to anyone about the night's activities--and he would drive Frank home drunk or sober. Tonight, perhaps the last time for a long time, Frank had the luxury of being completely irresponsible. He could drink as much as he wanted without having to worry about driving. Over the last few months Frank had been coming to the Sports Bar and the Injection Pump alone, driving seventy miles home at four o'clock to seven o'clock in the morning. Once, he had fallen asleep at the wheel waking up just in time to avoid hitting a post. The little car had slalom ed off the road and Frank had barely regained control.

Looking around him, Frank noticed three or four new girls, all of them pretty. He thought about Lori. She had not called him during the last two weeks, and he had concluded that she had decided that he was too much of a threat to her way of life and that she had subconsciously created the fantasy that he had gotten her in trouble with Travis, with the police, and God knows who else. He had brought more money with him than usual and was determined to find a girl who could take her place. One of the new girls was standing close by. Five foot seven or so, perhaps 120 pounds, and blonde, the woman would have been pretty except for the hardened look around her eyes. However, there could be no question about her figure. She would do--at least for tonight. The woman talked with Nadine for a few moments, then looked over at him. Frank caught her eye and smiled. *It should be easy to get her to come over*, he thought. She smiled back at him and came over, standing next to his bar stool.

"Will you buy me a drink?" she asked.

"What can I get you?"

"How about a screwdriver?" the girl replied.

"Are you buying Julie a screwdriver, Frank?" asked Nadine.

"Yes."

Frank turned to the girl studying her carefully. *I know her from somewhere*, he thought, *but where was it and who is she*? "So you're Julie. I'm Frank."

"Yes. I know," the girl replied.

"Come again?"

"You're Frank. You're Lori's friend. I worked with her at the Injection Pump--that is until last week."

"Okay, now I remember," Frank replied, except that he didn't remember. Then it slowly started to come back to him. Vaguely he remembered her walking around the Injection Pump, one of the better-looking girls, but not nearly as pretty as Lori.

"So you really don't remember me, do you? You always had eyes only for Lori."

"But not now. She's not here, but we are," Frank replied.

"Will you buy me another drink?"

No more than five minutes had gone by since Nadine had brought the screwdriver yet Julie had quietly drunk most of it. Frank finished his beer and looked up at her once more in an effort to size her up. *She'll do almost anything,* he concluded. *Probably pretty wild. It will be worth the chance.*

"Nadine, could you get Julie another screwdriver and bring me another beer."

"Thanks. I can use it. It's been really slow here so far," said Julie.

"Julie, I feel like doing something a little different and right away," said Frank. "Ever do any limos?"

"You don't beat around the bush do you?" the girl replied.

"Not if I don't have to. I guess your answer means yes?"

"I might consider it. What do you have in mind?"

"The limo. You and I both know what goes on. I'm asking from you the same that I ask of the other girls."

"And what is that?"

"No limit."

"Okay. What are you going to give me?"

"The establishment gets seventy bucks regardless, and then the rest is between you and me," said Frank. "Normally the girl gets a hundred. That's what I'll give you."

"You've got to give me more," said Julie.

"Not if the other girls don't," replied Frank. "Do you want to do it or don't you?"

"Okay. You're on."

"Our understanding is that there are no limits. You get a hundred, and the bar gets seventy," said Frank.

"Yes. That's right."

"Nadine. We need you to get us a limo and please bring me the forms," said Frank raising his voice just loud enough that Nadine could hear.

"Do you want to pay cash or do you want to put it on your Visa?" asked Nadine.

"Visa."

Nadine went over to the cash register, returning with the Visa form. Frank handed her his card. She returned with a hundred dollars cash and gave it to him after he signed the carbon form. Then she pointed to a man in his early thirties who was sitting at the other end of the bar.

"That's Ted. He's the limo driver. Just tell him when you're ready," said Nadine. "The limo's already outside. It always is during the night shift."

"Come on Julie. Let's meet Ted."

Ted was slightly shorter than average and compactly built. Dark headed and handsome, Ted stood out from most of the customers who were either older or less attractive. A ready smile told Frank that he and the limo driver would get along. Frank and Julie followed Ted out the rear entrance, climbing into the back seat of the limo after Ted opened it for them.

"Do me a favor," said Ted. "Keep your clothes on as much as you can. That way if I get pulled over none of us will get into any trouble."

"Sure, I'll keep my clothes on," said Frank. "But can I keep my jeans pulled around my ankles?"

"You know what I mean," laughed Ted. "Just be careful, okay."

Ted closed the limo's door behind them, then got into the front seat and closed the window between the driver's and passengers' compartments. As soon as he was satisfied that Ted could not observe anything in the back seat, Frank took off his clothes. Without saying a word Julie took hers off as well.

Thirty minutes later, Frank was still inside her and still had not finished. She had been thrashing wildly, screaming at him to finish yet he had not been able to. Together they had tried several different positions. *Odd that I didn't get off*, he thought. *Must be those Peter Downer Pills that the doctor has prescribed for me.*

Those antidepressant pills that I'm taking for sleeping must have some side effects that interfere with a person's sexuality--in my case they allow me to get it up, but they make it difficult to get off. Here Julie's the prostitute. It's her business to get guys off, but she's the one who's getting off, not me.

They walked in together and ordered another drink, sitting down at the other end of the bar far away from the front entrance. "Yeah I know all about you, stud. Lori's told me a lot," said Julie.

"How's that?" Frank replied.

"Oh she's told me that you're the wildest guy she's ever met and that you have this big ranch out in the country."

"I'm surprised she's told you that."

"Well she talks about you a lot. I'm calling you stud man. You've got a great build, not to mention a big dick."

"It's not that large."

"I say it is. Hey, wait here. I'm going to the bathroom."

Frank waited for her to return and ordered another beer. He saw her come out of the ladies room, walk down the length of the bar, and sit with another customer. *Well, who needs her anyway,* Frank thought. *There's other girls here too. Doesn't she realize that?* He noticed one of the new girls--it was hard not to. The woman appeared to be in her mid twenties, was blonde, blue eyed, and slender. So far she had not singled out any of the male customers. She would chat with a couple of the other dancers, sometimes standing up, other times sitting with them at a table. She flit around the room seeking out one of the other girls or several of them at once. Always laughing, but never so loud that one could hear her at a distance, she seemed full of enthusiasm and nervous energy, her shoulders bouncing from side to side as she talked.

The girl started toward him on her way back to the table she had just left. Frank got off the bar stool and started to walk toward her, pretending to go the men's room. They met head on between one of the tables and the bar, and then Frank noticed one other thing about her. *Was it the product of an inebriated mind or was he seeing things as they really were?* The girl was a dead ringer for Lori--except that the new girl had straight very yellow blonde hair whereas Lori had hair that had a slight curl to it, which was darker yet still blonde. This girl was slender just like Lori, was the same height, had pretty legs, and resembled Lori so closely in the face that they could be twin sisters.

Frank looked directly into the girl's eyes and held her gaze when she looked back. She looked back at him as if to say, *what is it?*

"You. You look just like a friend of mine. A very pretty friend of mine," said Frank.

"I do?" the girl replied.

"Enough to be her twin. This is unbelievable."

"And who is that?"

"A girl who used to work here. Her name is Lori, but she went by the name of Nipples."

"Sure. I know her."

"They do look a little alike, but Lucy is better looking. Not that Nipples is bad looking I mean." Sherri had just come up behind Lucy.

"My cousin's sitting over there." Lucy pointed to a tall blonde sitting at one of the tables with two other girls. "I promised her I'd buy her a drink so I'd better get over there. What did you say your name is? Mine's Lucy."

"I'm Frank."

"Well Frank, perhaps you'd better get over to the bar. It looks like Julie is looking for you. You took a limo with her, didn't you?"

"I was trying to be discreet about it. How'd you know?"

"Nothing gets by us here. Word travels."

Frank looked over at the bar. Julie had left her customer and was sitting by herself playing with her drink, stirring it absentmindedly with a straw. He strolled over and took the bar stool next to her.

"It looks like you're alone again. That other guy, the one you were just sitting with--I guess he's not a good paying proposition?"

"He's weird. I just went over to get a free drink."

"You're not very far along with it."

"Hey stud man, I want to give you my phone number. You're a pretty good fuck, did you know that? Give me a call sometime, and if my husband answers, hang up and call me back later." Julie took a paper napkin off the bar and wrote a number down on it. She was about to hand it to Frank, when she hesitated a moment, and wrote a second number below the first. "If you can't reach me at the first number, try the second. You should be able to reach me at one or the other."

Frank bought her a drink. Several minutes after it arrived, she excused herself to go to the dressing room. Ten minutes later Julie had still not returned. Even from the far side of the bar Frank could see two other dancers inside the open door of the dressing room talking animatedly. *Obviously*, he thought, *Julie is with them just out of sight. It's time for me to move on.*

He looked over at the stage. Lucy was sitting with her cousin and a customer close by. Lucy was sitting to her cousin's left; the customer, a heavy set man in his forties, was seated across from the two girls. Frank went over to the table and sat down across from Lucy.

"Hi, I thought I'd just come over to your table. There's one girl too many so I'm here to help him out." Frank nodded at the man.

"I'm Fred Lloyd," said the man.

"I'm Frank Harring. You need help, don't you?"

"Sure I do. I can't keep up with these girls. They're drinking me under the table."

Frank was surprised that Lucy hadn't looked up at him since he had sat down. He was just as surprised that she had not offered to introduce him to her cousin, not that he had found girls in bars to be exceptionally friendly, but because dancers who made their money off their customers usually made every effort to be congenial. He didn't remember this happening to him in any of the clubs. Frank finished his beer, excused himself, and went back to the bar. By this time Julie had come out of the dressing room and had gone over to another customer who was sitting several seats down from Frank.

He had gone to the right side of the bar which was close to the front entrance and far away from most of the tables and the stage, preferring to have the next beer or two by himself. He drank the first one quickly and was halfway through the second when he saw Lucy walking toward the dressing room. Since the dressing room was on the opposite side of the room from the stage and tables, she would have to pass him. Pretending not to notice him, Lucy drew close, for the passage between the bar stools and the wall was narrow. He decided to force the issue and stuck his arm out in front of her.

"Are you trying to avoid me, Lucy? You weren't very talkative over at the table."

"I just don't want to horn in on you and Julie, that's all. I don't like to steal another girl's customers."

"Well, look over there." Frank pointed at Julie who was sitting close to her customer. "Doesn't it just tear you up how loyal she is to me?"

Lucy looked over at Julie and arched her eyebrows with surprise. "You have a point."

"I know I do. Tell you what. Let me order you a drink and when you come out of the dressing room it will be here for you. Why don't we do a shot together?"

"Okay. I'll try and hurry. Just get me a shot of Tequila."

She came out of the dressing room right after the shots arrived and sat next to him. The lighting over at the tables was bad being close to the neon and the stage. Here the light was better giving him a good look at her for the first time. She was bigger than Lori-- perhaps an inch taller--but she was more in proportion to her height. Lori, even though she was five foot six, had the build of a smaller woman. Yet Lori was perfectly proportioned just as Lucy was. He couldn't put his finger on it. Both girls were thin. Lori was like a rapier, almost ferret thin, and like a ferret, was unmistakably strong and quick. Lucy was more long-legged and larger boned, but the larger boned ness was relative to Lori only. Lucy was still a slender woman. Lucy's eyes were blue whereas Lori's were brown. Her face betrayed a lighthearted temperament whereas Lori's was one of many moods. *A tossup*, thought Frank. *Neither woman has anything over the other. Personality, one way or the other, would in the long run be the decisive factor which would make one woman more appealing than the other. Lucy's personality, no even more than that--her essence, is an unknown.*

"Lucy, before you even start on your drink, you have to propose the first toast."

"Must I?"

"You must because I'm proposing the toast on our second Tequila."

"Okay then. To a good night."

"To a good night," said Frank.

They drank the Tequila down the way they always did in the clubs, chugging the contents in one long swallow, only this time Frank was drinking with a girl he had never drunk with before. He decided to try her--to see if she could keep up with Lori and some of the others. He ordered another round, then another. Frank proposed the toast on the second, then let her off the hook on the third.

"To us becoming better acquainted, and soon." Frank held her eyes for a moment, then when she didn't look away decided to risk the rest of his funds. If she'd refuse, at least he would have tried. He doubted that she would go with him, at least on the first meeting, but with all the beer he had drunk and after three shots, he had lost all his inhibitions.

"Lucy, have you done any limos?"

"Once since I've been here. I really don't like many of the men I've met here."

"Will you do one with me?"

"I wouldn't for I don't believe in them, but I've got to make some money, and I'm a greedy bitch. I've got two kids to feed."

"Let's do it then."

"Okay, but on one condition, and that is that we do it real quiet like. I don't want anyone to know I'm doing one, especially my cousin."

"Why don't you go to the dressing room for a few minutes. I'll pay Nadine and make sure the limo is ready. That way we can just slip out of here and no one will miss us."

When she came out of the dressing room, he had already paid Nadine, this time in cash, and had talked to the driver. Ted was waiting for them in the back quietly sipping his beer in the hallway that led first to the back bathroom and then to the rear door. Lucy looked nervously about the room. Satisfied that her cousin was preoccupied with her customer and looking away, she walked briskly to the back hallway. Ted opened the door for them, led the way to the limo, and held open the back door of the car until they got in. Lucy entered the passenger compartment first, turning her back on the two men as she stepped into the limo. Frank handed Ted a twenty while she still had her back turned.

"Can you get us some extra time?" he asked.

"I can give you ten more minutes, maybe a little more," said Ted.

"How about getting a flat tire on the way," Frank suggested. "Make it more than an hour. No one will know the difference."

"The hell they won't. I've got to put all car expenses on my expense report."

"Okay then, I understand. Just do the best that you can," said Frank.

Lucy had brought her cigarettes with her. She lit one up as soon as Ted started to ease the limo out of the parking lot. Frank started to take his clothes off, but when he got to his jockey shorts, Lucy looked at him first with surprise, then offered him a cigarette. "Here, have one of these. You're going to get us in trouble taking your pants off like that."

"No. I always take them off."

"It's against the rules you know."

"Rules are meant to be broken."

"Well, let me finish my cigarette first, okay. We have plenty of time."

"Not as much as you think. Usually I get all my clothes off, even my socks, before the limo gets out of the parking lot."

"Can't you see that I'm nervous?"

"Sure, but I feel pressured for time. I wish I could just take you home with me since we wouldn't have to hurry. Then we could just ease into things, and you wouldn't get so nervous. This is not the way to do this--rushing into things this way--but it's the only way for now."

"Did you bring a rubber?" Lucy asked.

"No. Did you?"

"No. I thought you did."

"Why don't we have the driver turn around and get us one?" suggested Frank.

"No, I don't think that's such a great idea since everyone will know what we are doing, and I don't even want the driver to think we're actually fucking."

"Why not?"

"Because I really don't do limos, and I don't want him to think I'm a slut because I'm not."

"Lucy, that's okay. We don't have to do it all. I just want to know you a little better, okay? We can just fool around and do everything short of it. Besides, I really don't know how good I'd be at it."

"I almost forgot. You just did a limo with Julie."

"I think we'd be better at it, but we'll just have to wait till next time to find out."

"Why do you feel that way, Frank?"

"Just have a feeling. Besides, Julie is not my type. By the way, you just finished your cigarette."

There was something fresh about Lucy--something different that he had not experienced with any of the other girls except for Lori. So inhibited at first, Lucy started to come alive when he began kissing her, first on the lips, then on her breasts, and finally between her legs. She responded, not like Julie, intent on fulfilling herself, but like a woman who was fully attracted to her partner and who had sensed it before she became fully aroused. She returned his kiss, reluctantly at first, then with increasing enthusiasm as she felt his excitement grow. They didn't make love--not this time--but they did everything else. More than enough. The rest could come later.

"Goddamn that was good," said Frank. "Why didn't we get together in the first place?"

"You should have. You were just wasting your time before," said Lucy.

"You were great, Lucy."

"I know."

When they returned from the limo, Dennis Barry was there waiting for him. They had a couple of beers together while Lucy went back to her friends. The beer started to really hit him now. One moment he was drinking with Dennis, the next he was watching Dennis take Julie into the back for a private. He didn't even notice his friend meeting or talking with Julie. The next moment--it seemed like only two minutes had gone by--Dennis and Julie were returning from the room. Suddenly people were leaving.

"It's time to go," said Dennis. "Come on, I'm taking you home."

"First, I've gotta say goodbye to Lucy." Frank looked about the room but his eyes didn't find her. Only then did he notice that most of the girls had gone to the dressing room. *Perhaps she's already left*, he thought. *Why does it have to end like this? I have a great time with her, and then, she's gone. I'm so drunk, I never thought about saying goodbye.*

He fell asleep in the car before they left the parking lot. Then he heard a voice urging him to wake up. He opened his eyes only to find that they were driving into Dennis's driveway. For Frank the one hour drive took only five seconds.

"I'll drive you home if you want to leave your car here," said Dennis.

"No. I can do the last seven miles by myself," said Frank. "I've made it through a whole lot worse." Then he went home.

SHY GIRL

Lucy lay back in the rear seat of the limo averting her eyes. This time--three days after first meeting her--Frank made sure he had a rubber. He tried to get her to look him in the face, but ever since he had plunged deep inside her, she had looked away, focusing her eyes on the rear door knobs of the limo, the roof, one of the rear windows, or anything within range of her vision so long as it wasn't Frank. Once again she had insisted upon having her cigarette which had delayed their having sex by five minutes of the thirty minutes the limo driver had allowed them.

Now that is really stupid, thought Frank. *Here I am paying one-hundred and seventy dollars for this thirty minutes and she pulls out one of her goddamn cigarettes as if we've got all the time in the world. That comes to around twenty-eight bucks for that cigarette. It would be one thing if I'd finished already, but here I am banging away still trying to get off, and there might not be time. I probably would be okay except for those peter downer pills.*

He finished at the last minute, just as the limo pulled off the interstate and had gotten within the last mile of the Sports Bar. Frank pulled himself away from Lucy and started to look for his clothes. He found his jeans first, then his shirt, but it took longer than he expected to find his jockey shorts. For a moment he was tempted into pulling his jeans over his naked body. Later, when he finally found his jockey shorts he could slip them into his jeans pocket. He could slip in the men's room and deal with the problem after he got inside the bar. Finally he found his shorts, which didn't leave much time for his socks. Frantically he looked for them in the dark interior of the limo.

"What are you looking for?" asked Lucy.

"My socks."

"You should never have taken them off. Come on, you've got to hurry. We're almost there."

"Tell me about it."

Finally he found his socks, putting them on just as the limo was pulling into the Sports Bar's parking lot. They walked into the bar together where he bought them both a drink. Sitting together at the bar it was Frank who broke the silence.

"Lucy, what we just did in the limo is not the way I want to do it."

"What do you mean?"

"I don't like to rush into things, but they're really not giving us much time, so I feel that I must be crude and get right down to business. I'd much prefer bringing you to my house, perhaps even go out to a bar first for some drinks, then lay back with you, listen to some music, drink a little more, smoke some cigarettes, and just ease into things. It would be much more natural. Would you come to my house sometime?"

"Perhaps."

"Back in the limo, you didn't even look at me. The last time

405

you were different."

"I was much drunker then. This time I didn't drink nearly enough."

"Do you really want to forget what you are doing?" asked Frank.

"I don't respect myself doing what I was doing," Lucy replied. "I don't do limos. You are the only person I've done a limo with except for once when I went out with another girl and one of the customers. I'm no whore. But I need the money."

Five minutes later she was gone. She had stayed with him from the first moment he had walked in until now. This time it had been Lucy who had suggested the limo hinting that she needed money to support her children. Lucy flit around the room, sat with her cousin for a few minutes, then sat at the bar with one of the male customers. Frank sized the man up as one to buy her a drink or two, but nothing more than that. *Clearly the man either has no money or is a tightwad*, thought Frank. *Obviously Lucy isn't the sharpest businesswoman around leaving me right after the limo for a man who's not going to contribute substantially to her earnings.* He talked with Promise for the next hour, buying her a couple drinks. Promise had seen him leave out the back door with Lucy, and knowing that he was willing to pay for a limo, asked him to do one with her.

"Come on Frank. Let's do a limo together."

"I don't think so Promise. I just did one, and I think that rushing into one right now with you would be doing both of us a disservice." He remembered how he had done two limos several nights before, but he knew he couldn't keep doing it--not at $170 a pop. Moreover, Promise, although a nice girl, didn't have the figure for doing this sort of thing.

"Tell you what, Frank. When you get tired of all the bullshit. When you get sick and tired of Lori and Lucy and all their game playing, come and get me. We will have a good time, I promise you."

He bought Promise one last drink, then left thinking about what the next week would bring. This week had cost him $400. *This couldn't continue*, he thought, but then he thought about the night he had done two limos and resolved that he couldn't ever do that again either.

NEW NIGHTCLUB, SAME GIRL

There was one message waiting for him on his answering machine. It was Lori, and she had called at 1:00 p.m., but now it was 4:00 p.m. He played the machine back only to find that she was working at a place called Risque. She also had mentioned another place called Gals. Risque was a new place owned by the same man who owned the Injection Pump which was in a small town ten miles from the Injection Pump. He called information for the telephone number; then he called Risque only to find that Lori had left after working only one hour. His next call was to the Sports Bar. Janey, now working as bartender, answered the phone.

"Hello Frank," said Janey, "Nipples was in here this afternoon. She's starting tonight at Gals."

"What happened at the Injection Pump?"

"I don't know except she quit."

"Where's Gals?"

"It's just down the road from us. It's off Sevin Street one mile South of us. You can't miss it since there's a sign out."

"Thanks Janey. I know where I'm going tonight."

"You two just can't leave each other alone, can you?"

"Looks that way Janey. We have too much fun together."

Gals was a small place. Suddenly he remembered that it was the same place that Jeff Shannon had taken him two years ago, that night he had gone to the Injection Pump for the first time. This time there were only four dancers working, but one of them was Lori. She was waiting for him at the bar.

"Hi Frank. How'd you like my message?"

"It was hard to understand. I thought you were working at Risque."

"The Injection Pump chose several of us and told us that we had to work there. I told them that I didn't want to drive all that extra distance since I lived way out in Union, Missouri. They sent me there anyway, and after an hour I realized that the place was not getting any business, so I quit."

"What do you have to do to get a beer around here?"

"I have to get it for you. What do you want?"

"Budweiser. And you?"

"I'll have one too. Pay me now, Frank. That's the way it works here."

Frank gave her a ten-dollar bill. A scruffy looking man

wearing a black T-shirt and dark pants stood behind the bar. Lori gave him the ten and waited for her change as he brought out the bottles. Looking around him, Frank noticed that the place was different from what he remembered. A single dance floor that was just large enough to hold several dancers stood in the center of the room. Several tables were lined up on each side of the dance floor. The bar, which was not all that large, took up the whole side of the room at one end. This bar was very ordinary, being neither ornate nor pretty to look at. The floor was linoleum while all the tables and chairs were cheap looking. Frank gave it a D rating, giving the Sports Bar a C while giving the Injection Pump a B and the Pink Giraffe an A.

After Lori got done collecting his change, he followed her to a table. Before they had a chance to finish their beers, it was her turn to dance. Then it was someone else's turn, and they went back to their table, this time for body shots. He left at 1:00 arriving home at 2:00.

The next morning Frank vaguely remembered doing shot after shot with Lori. Then he remembered how she got him up on stage with her, and how she had slipped her hand into his underwear when no one was looking. He remembered what she did to him with her mouth through his jockey shorts, and how no one else seemed to mind. But she didn't go home with him, and she didn't go to a hotel when he asked her to. Travis was picking her up, she had told him. And that's why he left early.

CHICANERY RESURFACES

Since filing for divorce, Frank didn't hear from Karen nor did Frank's attorney hear from Karen-- for over a month. Finally a letter arrived from Karen's attorney. The phone in Frank's office rang-- three times before he could get to it.

"Frank, this is Randy Green. Just got a letter from Karen's attorney, and you'll never guess who he is."

"Who is he, Randy?"

"Carl."

"But that's impossible. After what he did to Stan Osterman, they'll crucify him for fraud and embezzlement."

"Not quite, Frank. He's moved to another city. Practicing law in Springfield now where they don't know him. No one will know or care what he did to your friend."

"But the courts, Randy. They'll get him on the whole business with the bank loan that was to be used for fertilizer and seed. You remember how he convinced the board of directors to lend out that last two-hundred thousand dollars, don't you?"

"Sure I remember. But he's paid it off."

"What? I'm afraid I don't understand."

"When Carl disappeared, it seems he bought another piece of ground from the Brazilian government. Not the acreage that he and Stan had purchased the option for, but land hundreds of miles away. Brace yourself Frank. Carl bought machinery, hired a labor force, paid to have fertilizer put on the land, and now he's going to have that land raising a soybean crop. The only thing is that he did it a few months later than he and Stan planned."

"So he disappeared thinking that he had enough money so that he'd never have to practice law again," said Frank. "Then when he found out about Stan's suicide he decided to use the money to start up the Brazilian operation, only this time he'd run the whole show."

"I don't know how he's done it," Randy replied, "but somehow he's probably managed to acquire Stan's interest in the corporation. With Stan being dead, there's no one who knew enough about the corporation and the various documents that he and Stan signed between them. He's probably forged some of them. As far as cheating Stan, he's clean, since Stan's not around any more to say otherwise. The bank doesn't have a problem with either of them since Carl's paid off the note plus any accumulated interest. This leaves him free to practice law."

"And to help Karen steal a farm from me or at least try to," Frank added.

"That's about the size of it, Frank."

"I'll deal with Carl, one way or the other," Frank replied.

"You'd better let me handle it," said Randy.

"You'll get first shot at it Randy."

"I don't know if I like the way you put that."

"You don't have to like it. I'm paying you to handle my case, no more nor less."

THE HEARING

"Mr. Harring, your petition states that your wife was repeatedly guilty of mental cruelty. Could you please state how this was so?" asked the judge.

"Your honor, early on in our marriage my wife sought to discipline me as if I were a child yet she did not allow me to discipline her children, and . . . ..."

"Your honor, my client has changed her mind, we are not going to contest the grounds' issue in this hearing. I believe that it is in the best interests of all concerned to dispense with the grounds part and move onto the more important issue of Temporary Maintenance." Carl had stood up to object to Frank's continuing to give testimony on what had occurred in the marriage.

Randy Green had informed Frank that he would probably be divorced sometime the next day when the formality of the paperwork could be filled out. Since the state of Illinois required that a grounds for divorce has to be established by one or the other of the parties before a divorce could be finalized, Randy had drilled Frank on stating the reasons he wished to divorce Karen. In his office he had insisted that Frank state what his wife had done, secondly what effect her actions had on his mental state, and thirdly what the effect this diminished mental state had on his work, outlook on life, sleeping patterns, and health. Frank had called Randy the day before the hearing and had asked him if he could pretty much count on being divorced once the grounds had been established and the mandatory paperwork was completed the next day.

"Be it noted," the judge replied, "that counsel for the respondent has moved that his client admits that there is grounds for divorce and that she wishes to move on in these proceedings."

I don't blame Carl for wanting to dispense with the grounds' part, thought Frank. *He probably doesn't want me to prove to the judge that I had absolutely no say over what went on in my house. I doubt if the judge would think much of Karen agreeing to have her son being taken off the football team because of poor grades, then after I wanted to enforce the threat we had made jointly, going to war with me until I allowed him to play. There is of course a lot more to it than that, but this is an event, the validity of which can be established in court. Others can attest to the poor grades and the fact that we parents allowed the boy to continue to play football.* Witnesses from the area could then testify that other parents

411

disciplined their athlete children when their grades sagged, and that Karen and I were exceptions to the norm. It could then be established that my status in the community had declined as a result. *No, I doubt if the judge would think much of that,* thought Frank. *Even he will be reluctant to award Karen, now established as the dominating female, the big boss, any kind of award on the basis that she is a helpless female who was railroaded into signing a Prenuptial.*

"Since he is already in the witness box, I would like to ask Mr. Harring some questions regarding his financial affairs," continued Carl.

"Please continue counsel," said the judge.

"Mr. Harring, I have prepared a summary sheet based on your financial operations that uses the same numbers you have given us. Allow me to hand you this sheet." Carl approached the witness box and handed Frank, not one, but a number of sheets which Carl had prepared.

"Now Mr. Harring I would like you to look at page 1. You will notice that your corporation and you made $63000 last year. Wouldn't you say that is more than the average man makes particularly in view of the fact that you have a house provided for you on which you are not making payments, are not in fact paying rent?"

Frank looked at the numbers Carl had prepared. *Yes, that was right,* he observed. *His corporation had made $10000, and yes, he had reported $33000 net income on his personal tax return. That came up to $43000 net income, and he had to make land payments of $12000 per year out of that, but Carl had omitted that on the summary sheet. Still, he was $20000 off of the $63000 net income he had just told the judge Frank had made.* Then Frank saw that Carl had included $20000 depreciation as part of Frank's net income.

Surely Carl had to know that depreciation was a means that businessmen employed to spread out the costs for large equipment expenditures. If, for example, a factory owner bought a machine that cost $100000, and the owner made $50000 the government would not allow him to deduct the whole $100000 as an expense. For one thing this would mean that the man would have lost $50000 for the year and would therefore not have to pay any taxes. The government had therefore enacted a series of complex Depreciation rules which it was constantly changing. Basically, if the type of machine the man had just purchased had a useful life of 10 years, he would be allowed to divide the amount he had paid for it by 10. Since $100000 divided by 10 equals $10000, the man would be allowed to deduct $10000 off his earnings of $50000 giving him a net income of $40000. However, the man could deduct $10000 each year for 10 years so that the cost of the machine would be totally accounted for.

"Your honor," said Frank, "Carl's figures are not accurate. He is using $20000 which I had as depreciation as a means of overstating my net income."

"Mr. Harring, said the judge, "I must remind you that you must reply to Carl's question. You cannot address the bench directly unless spoken to."

"Okay then." Frank stared at Carl malevolently. "Your $63000 is deceptive as it contains depreciation. It also does not include the $12000 I am paying on land that I have purchased which of course decreases money I have available to live on."

"Mr. Harring," interrupted the judge, "Let me caution you that you must answer counsel's questions. Please do no more unless instructed to do so. It is up to your attorney to bring in anything that you might want to add."

"But Your Honor," replied Frank, "these figures are totally misleading. I think I have the right to explain how they are misleading."

"Please allow your attorney to do so, Mr. Harring."

"Mr. Harring, the $20000 which you used on your tax return as depreciation-- you didn't write a check for that or part with any cash did you?" Carl had raised his voice slightly to show everyone in the room that he was taking control again.

"No, I didn't write a check during that year. However I did write a much larger check during a previous year, and I am making large payments to the bank for the machinery which you did not include in your figures."

"Mr. Harring, let me remind you to please simply answer my questions. If any additional information is required, your attorney can request it," said Carl. "A simple yes or no will do for now."

"I am sorry," said Frank, "But that $20000 represents expenses that I have already paid for and that it is not net income available to me. Every accountant knows that."

"Mr. Harring," said the judge this time raising his voice, "Will you please stop arguing with the respondent's counsel."

"Okay then," Carl continued, "we have here $20000 which is available to you which you did not spend in that current year." He looked at Frank expecting a reply.

"I don't know how to answer your question," Frank replied.

"In other words you had $63000 available to you during that year," Carl continued.

"I already said I didn't," said Frank.

"Okay then," said Carl, "if we add the $20000 to the $43000 that you and your corporation made we have $63000 that you have available to live on. That's a lot of money, wouldn't you say?"

"No, that $20000 is money that the accounting profession and the Federal government recognize as replacement costs for machinery that I have already paid for and that must be replaced at some time. If I can't replace that machinery, and if I don't have the money to pay for it, I won't be able to continue farming."

"Mr. Harring, please limit your answers to what Mr. Chicanery asks you. I must warn you that if you continue to argue with Mr. Chicanery, the court will be forced to discipline you. You can be cited for Contempt of Court if you continue to ignore my warnings."

"Your honor, I am going to state my argument now," said Carl.

"Please go on, counsel."

"Mr. Harring has $63000 available to him out of which he has ample funds to pay for the Temporary relief my client is requesting."

The judge now turned to Frank's attorney. "Mr. Green, would you like to ask the witness any questions?"

"Yes, I would your honor." Then addressing Frank. "The $20000 that you and Mr. Chicanery were discussing which you referred to as depreciation. Does that reduce the income that you have available to meeting household and living costs?"

"Yes it does. Over the last few years I bought a planter for $14000 and two tractors for more than $40000 each. I had to borrow the money at the bank to pay for them and the other machinery I purchased during the same time period. The bank requires me to not only pay the interest on what I borrowed, but timely payments on the principal as well. The Internal Revenue Service does not allow principal payments as a deduction yet I still must write out checks to pay for this machinery. My checking account is noticeably depleted as a result. But the IRS does allow me to take depreciation as an expense. I have probably paid a figure close to $20000 to the bank last year as principal payments on the machinery I have purchased. And I have taken $20000 as depreciation. Although the two are not one and the same, they are comparable."

"And Mr. Harring, you did mention earlier, did you not, that you are making payments on land that you have purchased of approximately $12000 per year."

"Yes I did."

"That represents principal and interest?"

"Yes, it represents both."

"How much would you say is principal and how much is interest?"

"I'd say about $4000 is in interest and $8000 represents the principal."

"So in other words, every year you reduce the amount you owe on the land by $8000?"

"That's right."

"And since you've already reduced your net earnings on your financial statement by the $4000 in interest, the $8000 represents money that you have to pay out every year that is not available to you for groceries or any other form of living expense?"

"That's correct," said Frank.

"Your honor, I am done with this witness," said Mr. Green. "However, I want to have it noted that Mr. Chicanery's figures are grossly in error. Out of the $63000 one must take $20000 as depreciation which gives us $43000 net income between Mr. Harring and his corporation. That is precisely the amount given on his tax returns, figures that Mr. Chicanery has conveniently ignored. Please note further that this figure of $43000 should be further reduced by the $8000 my client must spend each year to reduce his land debt. This leaves him with $35000 a year which is a far cry from the $63000 that Mr. Chicanery says he made."

"I will determine what Mr. Harring made," said the judge.

Now just what does what I made have to do with anything in these proceedings, thought Frank. *I know that they are all trying to establish whether or not I have the ability to pay temporary maintenance to Karen and how much. However, the Prenuptial clearly states that I don't have to pay her any temporary maintenance. Everything we've covered so far is irrelevant except that it's costing me a lot of money by the hour for us all to get into all this crap. They are looking at me as the chief financier for this little farce. If you ask me, they ought to burn this courtroom down.*

"I am now ready to call to the witness box my next witness, Mrs. Karen Harring," said Carl.

Karen approached the box and stood next to it as the judge took her oath.

"Do you solemnly swear to tell the truth so help me God," said the judge.

"I do."

"Please be seated then."

Carl looked over at Karen and smiled. "Mrs. Harring, can you please describe the house you once lived in with Mr. Harring."

"It is a beautiful house in the country with a four-acre yard, a barn, a recreation room with a pool table, and it is surrounded by two hundred trees. It has eleven rooms. We had two microwaves, two television sets, a state of the art stereo system, two Vcrs, two computers, and a whole lot more."

Eleven rooms my ass, thought Frank. *She's counting the two bathrooms as rooms and she's also counting the utility room as a room and that's nothing larger than a closet.*

"And Mrs. Harring, where are you living now?"

"I am paying $550 a month for a 3-bedroom Condo. There is no yard and no trees. I have one microwave which works only part of the time. I don't own a stereo, and I wouldn't be able to afford a television set except for the one that the kid's had."

"So Mrs. Harring, would you say that you have gone downhill as far as where you are living?"

"Oh yes, there is no comparison."

"Mrs. Harring, did you and Mr. Harring take any vacations while you were married?"

"Yes."

"Where did you go?"

"We went to Japan, Lake Tahoe several times, San Francisco, Virginia, Vail Colorado, Miami, Mexico, San Diego and other places as well."

"Do you anticipate any such trips in the near future?" Carl asked.

"I wish, but I can't afford to."

"Why not?"

"For one thing I am currently spending more than I am making."

"How much more?"

"Thirteen hundred dollars per month more?"

"May it please the court," Carl continued, "to look at exhibit one which contains Mrs. Harring's income and expenses for 1993. The court will notice that there is a shortfall of $1300 between what she is making and what she is spending." Then he turned to Karen.

"Mrs. Harring, what kind of expenses do you have now that contributes to this shortfall?"

"Well, for one thing, I have to pay rent--$550 per month to be exact. Another thing is that I have to pay for tuition. Also, I've had to have a lot of work done to my teeth. That was $2800. Plus, I owe $5000 for attorney's fees, and oh yes, now that I'm working in outside sales, I have to buy clothes. That costs me $350 per month. Then there's the medical bills that I have incurred."

Yeah, and if you had settled with me, you would not have to pay $5000 attorneys' fees, thought Frank. *You would have waited for a few years to have the dental work done. You were taking care of the problem with a splint that was already paid for, but you've decided to rip me off for it. And no one, but you, dear old Karen, can manage to spend $350 a month for clothes. Not to mention the tuition--I suppose you feel that I have to pay for your children's tuition because they had to put up with me during the years of our marriage. Well, I had to put up with them, and it sure wasn't easy.* Frank wanted to throw up--hopefully on Carl and Karen.

"Has your husband helped you pay for any of this?"

"No, he has not."

"Then how have you been able to do so?"

"I borrowed $10000."

"From whom?"

"$5000 from my father and $5000 from the bank."

"I notice," said Carl, "that during the first year of your marriage that you were employed. Is that true Mrs. Harring?"

"It is true."

"Why did you quit work?"

"My husband asked me to quit my job."

"Why?"

"He wanted me to help him on the farm."

Aha, thought Frank, *the old loss of earnings ploy. Truth of the matter is your little loved ones--those kids of yours--were being such a pain in the ass that you could not continue working. You had to quit in order to guide them and to take care of them.*

"And do you feel, continued Carl, that today you would be making more money if you had not quit working during your first year of your marriage?"

"Definitely. I'd be making a lot more."

Sure you would, Frank said to himself not believing what he had just heard.. Frank almost wanted to spit the words out for everyone to hear but he kept quiet. *I paid for your college degree. You didn't have a single hour of college credit when you met me, and now that you have earned your four-year college degree, you are more marketable and you know it. Why don't you tell the court about that?*

"Your honor, I am done with this witness." said Carl.

"Mr. Green, you may examine the witness if you wish," said the judge.

Frank's attorney stood up, then approached the witness box. Smiling at Karen, Randy asked her the first question. "This apartment of yours, is it a three bedroom?"

"Yes it is."

"Why is it a three bedroom instead of say, a one bedroom?"

"I need a place for the kids to stay when they visit me from college."

"Mrs. Harring, I notice that you have in your budget clothing at $350 per month. Is that for you only, or does that include your kids as well?"

"That's for me only."

"Wouldn't you say that it is a little excessive to say the least?"

"Not at all. I have just had to get into the work force again, and being in outside sales, I am expected to dress well."

"Mrs. Harring, according to the information that you have supplied all of us, you are currently making $35000 a year. Is this correct?"

"That is correct."

"Next year, do you expect to be making more or less."

"More."

"Why is that?"

"Because I will probably be promoted. Either that or I might get a new position in the Governor's office."

"Yet you are spending $1300 more per month than you are making?"

"That's right."

"Your honor, I am done with the witness."

Karen Harring stepped out of the witness box and sat next to Carl with just a hint, though barely discernable, of a self-satisfied smirk on her face. Randy Green caught it, didn't like what he saw, and quietly promised himself that he would roast her in his final argument. The judge then turned to Carl.

"Counsel, it is your turn for your final argument."

"Very simply, your Honor, I think the issues are the relative needs and the ability to pay. And I believe the Defendant has amply shown, met both burdens of proof here and on her affidavit which has not been seriously challenged. Her net deficit is $1300, and I think that it has become self evident she has, inside the short time that she has been operating, she has been required to borrow an additional $10000. Admittedly $5000 was for her attorney fees, but the rest is for legitimate expenses that she has set forth in her affidavit, and that she has been accustomed to as expenses throughout this marriage. It becomes very evident here when we listen to both of these people talk and their different points of view that they have indeed lived a very high standard of living. I think even Mr. Harring would admit, has admitted to that. The numerous trips they have taken, various lifestyles they enjoyed, the various property acquisitions. They have got all the toys in the home. The 17 room house-- they have the computers, they have got the VCR's, got the TV's, all of the things that all of us would like to have-- they have been very fortunate in which to have. And it seems evident when you look at Exhibit number two, which in this period of time they have accumulated and paid out and bought in excess of two hundred thousand dollars of property. Now, you don't do that on an income that the Plaintiff suggests that he makes, thirty thousand a year. I think that Mr. Harring has done with the expert advice of his accountant and legitimately so for tax purposes, they have a very good tax scheme in which to reduce the overall tax liability that one has to pay. And I think we have to look at both the returns, the corporate return and the personal return to get a true picture of what spendable dollars Mr. Harring has at his disposal. Remember we can talk about a corporation, but it's a one man show. He is the sole shareholder, owner, president, vice president, sole director, sole employee. It's him. So, when you say the money comes to the corporation he is the one who writes the checks. He is the one who has it at his disposal to spend. I suggest to you that Exhibit 1 is an honest attempt, is an accurate attempt, in going through both tax returns and identifying that Mr. Harring, through the use of his corporation and his personal rental income from the farming operation, is accumulating $63000 on an annual basis of which through legitimate tax deductions is only paying income tax of a little over five thousand dollars a year. He is able to minimize social security by taking a management fee, by taking a rental income which is not subject to FICA and social security considerations. All legitimate, but they don't give us the true picture of the dollars and cents that go into his pocket. I think the Court is well aware of what depreciation is all about. It's money, $20000 that goes in Mr. Harring's hands, either with his corporate hat on or with his farm hat on. It's still money that he has got in his pocket to buy sports cars and to buy computers, what have you. And not have to pay taxes on, legitimately so."

"When we look at the ability to pay, I am suggesting that he has close to $58000 after tax income in which to meet his financial needs and expenses. And you would have to make that kind of money to spend and acquire two hundred thousand dollars like he is spending here."

"If you look at his affidavit he has got here nearly $18000 in the bank at his ready disposal, he can pay that out to Karen for a temporary maintenance scenario. As far as his expenses I think, I, hopefully I did my job correctly in going through and identifying for the Court that many of the line items that he has down as to expenditures are indeed taken as tax deductions."

"The point is, your Honor, I am suggesting to you that we have a fellow here who is well to do. He has substantial income. He has substantial earning power and he does indeed have the ability to pay substantial maintenance for my client and we ask that, we ask that we have on a temporary basis the amount that we are deficient and that is $1300 a month. We ask that to be made retroactive to the date we filed our petition which I believe was sometime in April. I believe that was the intent of Judge Smalley as well. We would ask that we need that sum of money so that she can adequately defend herself in these proceedings. There are eight boxes, seven boxes, what have you, an enormous amount of paperwork. Mr. Harring himself has kept records galore on his computer and manually. We need assistance. He has the advantage of his own accountant to go in and help him. She likewise needs those services of an accountant, a CPA, to go through these documents for her lawyers, to analyze it. One talks in terms of the issue of contributions tracing. We know that we have our burden. We need some funds in which to pay an expert to do that. I would suggest that based upon prior experience in my practice with CPA's that I have used that we are talking about, looking at a $2500 tab to get the gentleman to go on an hourly basis and look through these eight boxes of records. We ask for an additional $2500 to help toward her attorneys' fees. She already borrowed the $3600 to pay us so far. She is already in the hole to us another thousand. We are asking for a $2500 contribution for fees.

"Where does Mr. Harring get it? He has got $17000 in the bank, more than sufficient. He can write a check and take care of that," Carl continued.

"We would ask likewise that Judge Smalley's ruling in regard to life insurance premiums continue in effect. We would ask that the life insurance on his life be maintained at his expense, the corporation is paying it, the beneficiary as Judge Smalley had previously ruled would be hers as the sole beneficiary pending the resolution of these proceedings. That the health insurance, she has health insurance and we would ask that he be responsible to pay for all of those health care related expenses that she already has prescriptions for and that she has not had the funds in which to pay. And those medical expenditures which I think are around twenty some hundred, that are not in her monthly budget. It's something that is prescribed. She needs the money in which to do it."

"Again, I suggest Mr. Harring has the funds at his disposal in which to pay them."

"I think with respect to, we would ask, we are all aware of the automatic dissolution stay is in effect and we would ask that be incorporated into our order. But, we would like that the dollar amount be reduced to a reasonable amount of a thousand dollars. No disposition of assets without coming to court and defining what an extraordinary expense would be so that the status quo can be preserved."

"I think, your Honor, we are asking something that is reasonable. I think we have satisfied all of the criteria of the Statute and we are very serious in our request and thank you for your time."

Bunch of crap, thought Frank as he contemplating dragging Carl behind his pickup with a log chain. *The little turd really thinks I should pay for his attorney's fees? And speaking of all those boxes of my records--I can't access my own records to carry out my business because they are in Carl's office. And he expects me to pay for another CPA to drag me into argument and counterargument over how much I made or what my assets were for a given year?*

This judge should throw all of this out for being irrelevant. He should take one look at the Prenuptial which says clearly NO TEMPORARY MAINTENANCE and that I DON'T HAVE TO PAY FOR KAREN'S ATTORNEY'S FEES, and throw the scoundrel and all of his figures and arguments out of court.

Then it was Frank's attorney's turn. The Judge turned to Mr. Green. "Mr. Green, you may proceed."

"I would ask the Court before I begin to go ahead and enter, make a finding that the dissolution of marriage is allowed."

"You prepare the order, I will, the Court will enter into such an order," said the Judge.

"I will, your Honor," said Randy.

"Excuse me, your Honor, it would be my understanding that the grounds would be . . . " interrupted Carl.

"Yes," Randy replied. Then turning to the Judge, he continued. "Your Honor, the context of anything that is said with regard to temporary support in this thing must be taken in terms of the totality of the marriage. When it began. When it ended. Was it by accident we went back and visited the question of Karen Harring in 1985 when they got married? There is a Prenuptial agreement that despite what Judge Smalley has said, that says there won't be any temporary support, won't be any temporary attorney's fees, goes on to say the reason for that."

"Prenuptial?" asked the Judge.

Yes, you idiot. Prenuptial! Frank said to himself through clenched teeth. *You assholes are costing me $200 an hour or so for this little jerk off session and you really don't know what the fuck is going on.*

"Prenuptial, before marriage," suggested Randy.

"Your honor, excuse me, I hate to interrupt. I thought we started at the beginning of this hearing, that the issue here was the amount. That to go in and try to rehash this again, I object to it," said Carl.

Yeah, and I object to your being in the same room with me, Frank muttered to himself. *And in being on the same planet, you unscrupulous, pompous cretin.*

Randy continued, "It's argument, Counsel. But, the relationship of these parties throughout their marriage, the style of life they had, what they did, what happened with regard to Karen's two kids were all done with some thought about that agreement. There would never have been a marriage but for that agreement."

"If you read the agreement which you have almost got to do to come, to make a finding, you will see that permeates where we are at today. We talk about lifestyle. What lifestyle was during the marriage. That has to do with what the marriage was supposed to be and gets distorted when we start adding some other things."

"I will ask the Court," Randy continued, "to look very carefully at the following facts which are clearly shown by the evidence. Frank Harring has an income not of $58000. He has got an income, had an income in 1992 of $34363. That is precisely what is on that tax return. Karen was already working. She came into this marriage with a high school degree. Last year she got her college degree. She went into the work force. She is a professional woman. It goes without saying that she is going to make more next year than what she is making this year. This woman said on the witness stand that she is going to be in an executive position in the Governor's Office, or somewhere very quickly."

"No," said Karen unable to stop herself.

"She has got ability," said Randy. "No question about that. I don't have to carry on about that. But that is part of what we are doing. She has an income by her own financial affidavit of $35633. She makes more money than he does."

"Now, I know Mr. Chicanery wants to make a big deal out of the fact that Frank has some depreciation expenses in here, but he shot his goose when he also talks about the expenses that were made. You get depreciation expenses when you buy machinery. That is where they come. You buy it. It you don't buy machinery, if you don't make improvement to the actual systems, if you don't work on what you are doing in the agricultural field you don't get anything. That is the return, what you plow back into the business constantly. The gravest error and I really didn't know he was going to make that argument here or I guess I would have brought Mr. Harring's CPA along. The gravest error somebody can make is to mix depreciation which is actually money that you don't spend out in terms of putting it on a balance sheet. That goes in different places. But, to call that income, it's not income. Income is the total return you get back on the capital you invest. His total return on capital that he invested is shown here. If you look at the tax return for his corporation for the year ending October 31, 1992, it was none. He actually had some income, taxable income before they carried forward a net operating loss."

"Now, as to this exhibit number one as Frank exhibited in his testimony, it is just plain wrong. It's just plain wrong on its face. It's wrong."

"I do hope the Court understands if you are going to make a finding that is based upon Frank's income it would be nice if you indicate a written thing of what you think his income is. I am concerned where we are going."

"So," Randy continued, his voice getting louder and louder, "Mr. Chicanery says that we have a discrepancy of $1300 between the two. Well, that on its face is wrong. I just did the addition here somewhere, how much it is, some $350 on one page, $200 on another page. $335 for Karen Harring's two children. She has a three-bedroom house which she maintains so those two kids can come home. A good part of these expenses she has testified are for those kids. Those are not Frank Harring's two kids. They belong to her first husband and she has not in anyway stated anywhere that she has made any attempt to exercise the Section 513 of the Code and ask him to pay for some of the bills. She wants to tap Frank."

"I guess I shouldn't, at 4:30 I shouldn't get loud, but that was the whole prenuptial agreement. He knew that she was going to sock him for, for her two kids. Now she is doing it. Right now in this affidavit she has stuck every dime she takes to support her two children by her first husband and wants him to pay for them. That is why I wanted a hearing so somebody could sit down and look at what is going on. You take out everything it costs to support her kids and we don't really know the total amount. These people were going to come out about even. They are both adults, over forty, intelligent, lower middle age. Yuppies they call them in some places. They both like to ski. Karen has got parents that can loan her the money. Frank has a farm so that he has some money. Karen has got skills. She has got appearance. She has got the ability to do. So does Frank. But, she doesn't need to lean on him anymore. She can take care of herself. She is a modern woman with all the ability to be her own boss and run her own life. And Frank is not responsible for her kids. That is what she is trying to do. The whole ball of wax is that there are some things that don't make any sense in here. In addition to that she has health insurance. She has dental insurance. She tells us she needs a whole bunch of money to pay health bills and dental bills. She doesn't tell us what the insurance is for. Sounds like to me that she is trying to bill us for the whole thing and stick the insurance money in her pocket. I don't doubt but what she probably has some health care needs. Everybody does. I don't know how much of this, of the bills, I do know because she did say that the health insurance was only for her. So it doesn't cover her children. And she does have some money elsewhere. The kids are covered by something else, I guess, I assume then. That is correct."

"We have then a rather clear case shown by the evidence and I think the Court can, if the Court wants I will be happy to volunteer my own brief in support of what we have here in terms of how I add the numbers up. A case of expenses, incomes that are about equal. Mr. Harring has his own occupation. He works in the farming world. The farming world generates business income and deductions. You can't hold it against him that he tries to replace worn out equipment that the government allows him to, not to take all of the capital expenses every year, but requires him to distribute them out over a period of time."

"Thank-you." Randy concluded his closing argument, his voice raised as his face dripped sweat.

"I am not going to decide this today," said the Judge. "I know what the limitations are with regard to the hearing, but I think I have to review the file before I would feel comfortable making a ruling on temporary relief."

Frank drove home feeling mixed emotions. This ordeal was costing him a lot more than it should. *The Prenuptial is very simple. A greedy lawyer and the judges are making the whole thing a joke which I am paying for. However, sometime the next day I should be legally divorced now that the grounds have been firmly established.*

He had called Lori the day before asking her to celebrate his divorce. Entering his house, he walked into his office to check his recorder. *No message from Lori. Damn her. She should be the one to help me celebrate my divorce.* He would have to go to the Sports Bar then. Perhaps he would be able to buy Lucy out of the bar.

CELEBRATION

He found Lucy standing close to the bar talking with her cousin. Not one to wait Frank went up to the girls to bum a cigarette from Lucy. He considered himself a nonsmoker until Lori had jammed a lighted cigarette into his mouth when both of them were drunk. Ever since then he occasionally smoked in the East side nightclubs, particularly when he was around Lori.

"Sure go ahead and have one, "Lucy replied after he motioned toward the pack of Marlborough Lights lying on the bar in front of her. "But you have to buy me a drink."

"No problem. What can I get you?"

"How about a"-- she paused for a moment to consider all the different choices she had which he would pay for-- "Oh just get me a rum and coke, but make the rum Myers, and can I ask you something?"

"Go ahead."

"Buy Linda a drink too. She's drinking Black Russians. Frank, have you met my cousin, Linda, before?"

"Not really. I've seen her here a lot, and we all sat at that table together that first night but we've never introduced ourselves."

"Linda, this is Frank," then turning to Frank, "And Frank, this is my cousin Linda. I'd do anything for you, wouldn't I Linda?"

"Yes you would." Then addressing Frank, "I'm Lucy's cousin. We grew up very close to each other, closer than most cousins, so we both feel that we have to look out for each other."

Frank studied Linda. She wore a green Greek Fisherman's hat--the same hat he had seen her wearing every time he'd seen her. For this reason alone he had noticed her the first time he had seen her. A brunette, she was heavier than Lucy and an inch or two taller. *In the face you can tell that both girls are cousins*, thought Frank. *Linda might be slightly prettier in the face*, Frank conceded, *although I like Lucy's figure more.*

Frank reached for the pack of cigarettes, pulled one out, and lit it with a cheap lighter that lay next to the pack. The bartender was not in sight so he couldn't very well order the drinks. He turned to Lucy and offered her a cigarette.

"What about our drinks?" asked Lucy. "I'm getting thirsty."

"I don't see Nadine anywhere. Tell you what . . . you get the waitress's attention and I'll buy us all a drink."

"Nurse." Lucy's voice carried throughout the room. Frank

was amazed that she could yell that loudly.

"Coming Lucy." An older woman, in her fifties, scurried over to take their order. The woman had short black hair and was slightly out of breath from rushing around between tables. She was the only waitress on duty. "Okay now, what can I get you?"

"Linda's having a Black Russian, and I'm having a Rum and Coke, and what are you having Frank?" Linda put her hand on Frank's arm to regain his attention which had drifted to some new customers who were just then coming into the bar.

"Oh me. Just get me a Bud, Nurse."

As Nurse rushed off to get their drinks, Frank looked at Linda, who had been quiet, but who had been studying him carefully, measuring him as to what kind of person he was. "Linda, why do you girls call the waitress Nurse?"

"Because she looks after us. Or at least that's what Lucy thinks," Linda replied. "She's quite a lot older than us, and she's one damn good waitress. And we depend upon her to get our medicine to us--our alcohol."

"Your medicine?"

"Yes, our medicine," said Lucy. "I for one don't like what I'm doing here to make a buck, and the alcohol helps me tolerate it."

"Lucy, I just got divorced today. I've been in court, and all that needs to be done is to have the correct papers filled out tomorrow which my lawyer is handling. I want to get to know you better, and I want to have someone to celebrate with tonight. How about my buying you out of the bar?"

"Sounds good to me. Let me have another drink or two to think about it," Lucy replied.

She went with him--one hour later--after two more drinks, and only after she asked Linda about it. Apparently he had created a favorable impression with Linda since Lucy was leaving with him. It cost him $100 to buy her out of the bar, and he only had five hours to spend with her since he had to get her back by 2:00 a.m.. Bill, the owner, hadn't helped any. Frank had asked Bill if he could buy Lucy out. Bill had hesitated at first and then replied that it all depended upon how things went, and that he didn't really know if he could spare Lucy. Acutely aware of the clock ticking and wanting to get out and celebrate with Lucy, Frank spent the hour waiting for Bill to give his approval. Finally, unable to contain himself any longer, Frank asked Lucy to remind Bill that he had not made up his mind yet.

"Oh Bill--just ignore him Lucy," said Linda. "Go out and have a good time. Frank, just give Nadine a hundred bucks and take my cousin out of here. You don't need Bill's approval because he's already got a rule that $100 gets the girl out of the bar."

They drove to the Injection Pump since Lucy had never been there before. The owner's girlfriend whom he had employed as overall manager was tending bar. In her late twenties, the girl was perhaps five foot five and perfectly proportioned. Green eyed and vibrant she wore her blonde hair long so that it hung about her shoulders.

"Helen, come over and meet Lucy," said Frank. "I've gotten divorced today and she's helping me celebrate it."

Helen sauntered up to Frank and Lucy who had seated themselves at the bar. She swayed her hips as she walked, not even going through the pretense of modesty. Helen knew she was great looking, thought Frank, and she has made it her mission in life to let the world know it. The way she walked, the way she carried herself, and the things she said, would have been sickening except she was so outrageously conceited that Frank had begun to think it was all a show which she was performing tongue and cheek. It was almost as if Helen were saying, "Okay all you men out there, you're all out for a fantasy, cheap thrills and the lure of easy women--so look at me-- the ultimate fantasy, something I've made up just for you that's not really real and we all know it, don't we?"

"And you've decided to buy us all a round of drinks. I'll have a Jack and Coke. Do you mind?" asked Helen flippantly.

"Now Helen, you will have to admit that I've bought drinks for you before. I really did get divorced today so I'm kind of wondering if you'd buy Lucy and I a drink considering you are the manager and keeping in mind that I've been a good customer."

"You really did get divorced?"

"Paperwork will be completed tomorrow."

"Okay, what can I get you two."

"We'll just have a Rum and Coke and a Budweiser," said Frank.

While Helen was preparing the drinks, a cocktail waitress came over. Frank knew her, but he could never remember her name, perhaps because she had not waited on him that often.

"Hi, how's it going, Frank?"

"Great. Today's the day for the Big D. I went to court and she agreed that I had reason to divorce her. The papers will be drawn up tomorrow. Want to buy me a beer?"

"Sure, why not. What kind do you want?"

She's a good sport, thought Frank. *She's willing to buy me a beer, and I'm sure that she's got kids to support. She probably doesn't make much money either. And I can't even remember her name. Saw her a few times over at the Pink Giraffe when I was chasing Lori. She was working as a dancer there.*

"No, you don't have to buy me a drink. Helen is already buying both of us drinks and they'll be here in a moment."

"How's Lori? Have you seen her lately?"

"Saw her briefly the other day. By the way this is Lucy." Frank nodded toward Lucy. "She's with me tonight celebrating my divorce."

"I almost forgot to tell you, I'm getting divorced Friday," said Lucy.

"You're kidding. Y-O-U A-R-E G-E-T-T-I-N-G D-I-V-O-R-C-E-D T-H-I-S F-R-I-D-A-Y," said Frank incredulously as he spoke each word out in disbelief. That is a coincidence."

"I've been separated now for two years, and now finally we're actually getting divorced."

"Then consider this a dual celebration."

"I don't know," Lucy replied, "I might ask you to celebrate with me later."

"I'm leaving you two to your celebration," said the cocktail waitress. "I must go wait on some of the other customers. Drive carefully."

They finished their drinks and left in Frank's pickup. One hour later they were pulling into his driveway. He took her into his house and made both of them a drink while she walked around. He looked at his watch, noted that it was already eleven o'clock, and that with one hour's driving time to get back, they would have less than two hours.

"Frank, you've got a long way to drive when you come up to the Sports Bar. I don't know that I could handle that."

"Well, I've been doing it, but I don't know how well I've been handling it. Sometimes it's rough coming home at nights with all the drinks I've had." Frank returned to Lucy who was now sitting on the couch in the family room. "Look Lucy, I don't know what you are expecting, but I've told you that I want to get to know you. Well, we've done the limo, and we're going to do it again. I hope to have you over here again. Tonight though, that's another matter.

Tonight's for fun, and we are going to drink and celebrate, so I'm not asking you to go to bed with me--not tonight. Let's go to one of the local bars."

"That's fine with me except I'm not really dressed for it."

Frank noticed for the first time that Lucy was wearing shorts, not ordinary shorts, but the short short shorts that go way up the thigh exposing the maximum amount of leg. He considered for a moment that if he had her legs and were a woman he would be wearing them also.

"Don't worry about it," said Frank. "The only people who will condemn you for wearing those shorts will be women who will be jealous of you because of your good figure. Who needs them anyway. Let's go."

The tavern was only five miles away from where he lived. They were sitting at the bar when a heavyset woman in her late twenties came over. Frank had known her for years, ever since she was a teenager. The woman had taken a special liking for Frank seeing him as an older brother type.

"Frank Harring, now just what in the world are you up to bringing younger women into this bar?" she whispered.

"What younger woman?" he replied with feigned innocence.

"The one sitting next to you."

"Oh-----she. Barbara, I want you to meet Lucy. I got divorced today and Lucy's helping me celebrate it. Lucy, this is Barbara. I pulled Barbara out of the ditch after she got drunk. That was a few years ago. Ever since then, she's been trying to mother me."

"Yeah, and you never take my advice, do you?" Then looking at Lucy closely for the first time. "Lucy, now that I'm getting a good look at you, I'd say you are even younger than I first thought. How old are you anyway?"

"I'm twenty-four, but I'm almost twenty-five."

"You know how old Frank is, don't you?"

"He never told me."

"I believe he's somewhere in his late fifties, aren't you Frank?"

"Barbara you are over ten years off." Frank turned to Lucy. "I'm only in my forties. Barbara's just trying to be the big bad wolf."

"So today you just got divorced," said Barbara. "Well congratulations, although I'll have to admit, I did like Karen."

"Barbara, every woman I ever bought a drink for that I've

caught in a bar tonight has had to buy me a drink. Have I ever bought you a drink?"

"Well, sure you have."

"Good. Lucy and I both need something to drink. She's drinking Rum and Cokes. Myers Rum please. I'll have a beer. Make it any kind--maybe even the kind you are having."

"Yeah, I'll buy you a drink all right." Barbara looked at the bartender, a slight woman in her early thirties, and winked. "Jennifer, you still have those Big Mamas?"

"I think we've got some left. Barbara, look in the jar."

On the top of the bar was a large glass jar. Plastered to the outside was a white paper label on which was printed BIG MAMA. Inside were several large franks which floated around in a light greenish juice. Frank knew from experience that Big Mama's were spicy and that they got their spiciness from the juice in the jar.

"Jennifer, pour Frank a glass of some of that juice out of the Big Mama jar."

"You've got to be kidding, Barbara."

"No, I'm not. I'm betting that he will drink it. He's always bragged about what a cast iron stomach he has. Well now, he has a chance to prove it."

"What do you think, Lucy? Should I take Barbara up on this cocktail she's getting me? I always liked hot food."

"Definitely. It's your divorce night."

"Okay then." Then he shouted at Barbara. "I'm ready Barbara. Bring it on over except you're having some too."

"What do you mean, I'm having some too?" asked Barbara.

"Have her pour some out of the jar into a glass for you," said Frank.

"I will not. Here drink this." Barbara put the beer glass that Jennifer had just filled with Big Mama juice in front of Frank.

"Have her put some in a shot glass for you," ordered Frank.

"Oh no. You're the one who says he's got the cast iron stomach, not me."

"Come on Barbara. You really are a wuss."

"All right then, but I never want you calling me a wuss, ever."

Jennifer filled a shot glass from the Big Mama jar and handed it to Barbara who promptly chugged its contents. Frank looked at his glass, much bigger than Barbara's shot glass, then put it up to his lips. He started to drink it and managed to chug half its contents before he took it from his lips.

"Oh no, you don't," said Barbara. "You are chugging the whole thing," after which she grabbed the glass and placed it up against his lips at an angle so that the juice ran down his throat. After it was all gone, Barbara placed the glass on the bar and beamed at Lucy.

"Well done, Barbara. He deserved it," said Lucy.

Frank looked at his watch. It was already 12:30 and it would take him more than an hour to return to the Sports Bar. He had never asked Lucy if she had driven to work. *Probably*, he decided, *she has a boyfriend and has him drive her to work. If that is the case, the same guy will be picking her up. That would explain why she insisted on my bringing her back by 2:00.*

"Lucy, is your grandmother babysitting for your kids?"

"She's the one."

"Then let me ask you this. Why don't you call her and tell her you'll be an hour late or so? This way we can stay here longer."

"I can't do that, Frank. She's an old lady and little things bother her. She doesn't expect me to be out with someone tonight, and if she found out I was out with one of my customers, she'd be pretty upset."

Bingo, thought Frank. *The girl's got a boyfriend. Substitute boyfriend for grandma and we find the babysitter. Guy's probably unemployed just like most of them. He's making his money off his girlfriend's body like a pimp.*

"We'd better go then," said Frank. "We're about out of time."

"Okay then," said Lucy. Then she looked over at Barbara her eyes sparkling with good humor. "I've enjoyed meeting you Barbara. Hope I see you again. Soon. Frank needs someone like you to put him in his place."

"You're welcome around here anytime Lucy," said Barbara.

Frank got her back to the Sports Bar by 1:45. They went in to have one last beer together. Inside Lucy took him by the hand and looked directly into his eyes. "Thanks for a great time, Frank. This has been one of the best times in my life. And thanks for not fucking me."

"What do you mean?"

"You promised that you would not fuck me and you kept your promise. I think you've also shown that you are interested in me as a person and not just as a pretty body."

"I want to get to know you, Lucy. The Limo is fine, but I'm afraid I want more than that. Besides, it's terribly expensive. One more thing Lucy." Frank handed her a scrap of paper on which he had written a phone number. "That's my 800 number. They charge me a small amount each month for it, much less than you would think. You can call me anytime and from anywhere. It will be charged to my phone always. No coins to mess with or any other problems. It's a lot cheaper than collect, and you can use it to leave a message on my answering machine which you can't do when you call collect. Use it Lucy," he urged.

"What's this access code thing?"

"After you dial the number a voice will cut in asking you to dial the four digit access code. Try it. It's real easy."

As he drove home Frank considered his situation. Lori was still calling him while Lucy seemed genuinely interested in him, boyfriend or no boyfriend. *And after all*, he reminded himself, *boyfriends don't really matter anyway. They are as irrelevant to my success or failure with the girls as they are to the economic well-being of their girlfriends. About as useful as an appendix and just as easily cut out.*

TROUBLE

Both girls had been calling him, and each had called him once today. On the phone Frank had been noncommittal telling both Lucy and Lori that he would probably drop in on each of them. He put a small cooler in the trunk of his sports car which he had filled with ice and two six packs of German beer. A bottle of coke and a fifth of Jack Daniels went in next to the cooler. Frank didn't know if he would end up with Lori or with Lucy, but he fully intended to be equipped for the hotel room.

He went to Gals first thinking he would stay with Lori for an hour or two, and that he would leave from there for the Sports Bar. Once there he would buy Lucy out of the bar after which he would take her to a motel for several hours. Without the time pressure imposed by the Limo, Frank was looking forward to making love to her. Lori greeted him at the door, seeing him as soon as he came in. This time she bought him a beer and led him to a table.

"I'm glad you made it Frank. Is it my imagination or do you like me less than you did several months ago?"

"I like you just as well. More in fact, except that you disappoint me too often. I got divorced last Wednesday. You were going to work that night, and you were going to call me except you didn't call, and you didn't show up at work. My divorce--Lori-- probably the only divorce in my life. A thing that is monumental, and I couldn't get hold of you, and you didn't try to get hold of me. So I had to find someone else. I took Lucy out of the Sports Bar and took her home with me. That doesn't mean I like you less. It's just that when you disappoint me or when you break a promise, I'm going to find someone else."

"I wish you didn't do all those limo rides."

"Why not?"

"Because you are lowering yourself when you go around just fucking anyone."

"How do you know I'm doing limo rides?"

"Frank, c'mon. Think I'm stupid. I was down there that night you did that limo with Lucy or were you doing it with someone else? I was looking for you. Imagine how I felt when they told me you were doing a limo with some broad."

"I didn't see you there."

"No. You were in the limo. And then I left."

"Lori, I'm proposing a toast."

"Go ahead."

"To your looking me up and checking up on me--it all shows you care about me. Now drink up."

"You can be such an asshole," said Lori.

"All right then. To a good night together and to you and me."

"That's better. I'll drink to that."

Two hours later he was still drinking with her. Somewhere in the back of his mind Frank knew that he should be leaving for the Sports Bar to get Lucy. He would have her in a hotel room in half an hour, but he had entered the little Lori-Frank world from which there was no return. He thought about how the hours always passed so quickly when they were together. There was never a dull moment when they were together as there was when he was around any of the other girls. Frank decided he wanted her more than anyone else.

"Lori, I want to take you out of this bar."

"Sounds good but I doubt if they will let us."

"Why not?"

"They are short of dancers so they are not going to want to spare me."

"We can arrange for a family emergency." Frank's eyes sparkled as the idea of pulling one over on the bar took shape in his mind.

"What do you mean?"

"You just had trouble with the kids, and your brother just called the place. You have to leave."

"But my brother wouldn't call me. Besides, he doesn't even live with me."

"I'll be your brother. I'll quietly slip out of this place and call from a phone nearby. When the bar finds out you have a true emergency it is going to have to let you go."

"It's worth a try."

"Then let's do it."

He found an outdoor pay phone only one mile from Gals. Frank shivered as he put the quarter in the phone and waited for the bar to answer. After a few seconds a gruff voice answered.

"Gals."

"This is Brittany's brother," said Frank. "There's been an emergency with one of her kids so she needs to get off work early."

There was a long pause on the other end. Then the voice came on again and asked. "What did you say your name is?"

Frank groped for a name, hesitated a moment, and said, "This is Jim." There was a brief pause on the other end after which the voice said "No. Brittany doesn't have a brother named Jim."

Frank slammed the receiver down and got back into his car. He was only one block from the Sports Bar. *Should I go there? Somehow Lori fucked it all up, and she probably did it on purpose. I should not have failed and would not have failed unless someone sabotaged me on the other end.* Against his better judgement he headed back to Gals.

He walked in thinking, *the gig is up. Wonder if the owner and bartender are looking at me.* He came up to Lori as if nothing had happened. Then he sat next to her and unloaded.

"What in the hell are you trying to pull? Telling them I'm not your brother!"

"Frank, they got suspicious and asked me what my brother's name was. You told them Jim. You should know that I don't have a brother named Jim."

Perhaps she's telling the truth for once, thought Frank. *They might have asked her, but I still think she's set me up.*

"How are you getting home, Lori?"

"I don't know. No one told me anything."

"Is anyone coming to get you?"

"Not unless I call someone."

"Then Travis isn't coming?"

"No."

"After you get off, let's go to a motel. The only thing is that I've just started harvest and I haven't had much sleep. I'm really under par."

"Let's do a shot. That will keep your mind off how tired you are," suggested Lori.

They did a shot; then they had several beers, followed by more shots. It all started to go to his head, yet he had another beer. He wished it were not on the weekend since the place would have closed at 2:00. Being that it was Saturday, Gals was open until 4:00 a.m. With the farming that he had been doing, it was just too much. Finally four o'clock arrived. A loud voice bellowed: "Everybody out. We're now closed."

"I have to get dressed," said Lori. "Be right out."

While she was in the dressing room, a large man weighing nearly 300 pounds came up to Frank. "You're going to have to leave," the man said.

Then Frank remembered the Pink Giraffe, and how they had kicked him out of there so that he couldn't wait inside for Lori. He remembered that night she had walked by his car, trying to ignore him, because Travis was there to pick her up. They were rude there when they asked their customers to leave, and they were just as rude here. He went out to his car, got in, and started the engine. Five minutes later Lori had still not come out. Then Frank saw the large man walking toward him.

"You are going to have to leave," the man said.

"I'm Brittany's ride," said Frank.

"No, you're not. Her boyfriend's here to pick her up."

"What do you mean? I am her boyfriend."

"No. He's over there in that Grand Prix. Now get out of here."

Frank looked around him, but didn't see the Grand Prix immediately yet he knew it was there. Blood rushed to his head and anger took over. *She betrayed me. She betrayed me the whole night, and that little punk Travis is over there somewhere hiding in his car like a scared puppy. Well fuck him and fuck Lori, and fuck this goddamn rude bastard for trying to kick me out.*

"Okay then, I'm going." Frank drove off the lot and out into the street where he parked next to the curb. The large man walked over to his car, hands hanging down at his side, bristling for a fight.

"I told you to get the hell out of here. Now leave!" the man bellowed.

"Fuck you. I'm off your lot and I'm into the street. That's public property. I'm still waiting for Brittany to come out."

"I'm calling the cops. When I get back, you'd better be gone," the man threatened.

The large man went back into the building but came out just seconds later. He went up to Frank's car stopping thirty feet away from it. "We've called the cops. Now get the hell out of here."

"You really are an asshole," said Frank.

When the man started to run toward his sports car, Frank began to reconsider his position. Deciding that the man could easily damage the light bodywork of his sports car, Frank drove away spinning his tires and throwing gravel onto the approaching man.

One mile up the road he saw the flashing lights come up behind him. Knowing they were for him, he pulled over. The police officer pulled up behind him, got out of his patrol car, and came up to Frank's window. A second car pulled up behind the police car, and the large man got out.

"That's him, officer. That's the man who refused to leave our lot."

"Look officer," said Frank, "there really is no problem. Obviously I didn't refuse to leave the lot since I'm no longer there. I'm driving this car instead. There's really nothing to argue about."

"I can see you've got a point," said the officer. "Drive carefully now." Then the officer got back into his car. Frank let out the clutch and headed home. It didn't take long for him to reach the interstate. He got onto the northbound lane for Chicago. It was the next entrance ramp that got him in trouble.

Somehow he turned onto the wrong ramp and ended up on the wrong interstate going in the wrong direction. His contacts had started to get blurry for he had worn them for over twenty hours. He couldn't see the signs very well and simply ended up going the wrong way. The trouble was that he couldn't just turn around. He waited until he got to the first exit, took it, and ended up on an unfamiliar road. However, it seemed to head in the right direction.

Later, he wouldn't remember how he did it, but he managed to turn an hour long drive into a two-hour long trip. Finally he ended up on route four, took it for a few miles, and found himself in a small town where he had spent a lot of time years before. It was close to six in the morning, but he knew exactly where he was, and he felt he could find his way home blindfolded. Then he remembered the German beer.

He pulled onto the shoulder of the road, got out, and went back to the trunk. Pulling a bottle out of the cooler, Frank grabbed the bottle opener, and got back in the car. He opened the bottle, took a small sip just to taste the beer, and slipped the car into gear. One mile later he saw the flashing red lights following him.

The officer came right up to his window. *What should I do about the bottle of beer*, Frank asked himself. Suddenly it hit him that his car had only two seats and that the interior was extremely small. Since he couldn't think of anything else, he shoved the bottle between his legs. "Where are you going?" asked the officer.

"I'm going home officer."

"Where have you been?"

"Off visiting a woman."

"Did you know that you were weaving back there?" asked the officer.

"No, I didn't. Must have been dodging potholes."

"Well, I think you are drinking. What's that between your legs?"

"A bottle of German beer officer. Want some? I might as well offer you some because you've got me cold."

It was his first DUI. He spent the next two hours taking breath tests and waiting for Dennis to pick him up. They had him in a little room at the station. By the time Dennis came in, Frank was already asleep.

LORI'S TURN

She was going to come to his farm Sunday night. When Lori didn't call on the day she said she would, or the day after, or the day after that, Frank wrote her off. He was planning to do his grocery shopping that night. Then the calls started coming in.

He came home from one of his farms at 6:00 and found Lori's voice on his answering machine. The machine used a synthesized voice to tell Frank the time of each message. Lori had called at 5:21 p.m.. Frank replayed the following message: "Frank, this is Lori. I want to see you tonight. Hope to get hold of you in the next hour." He waited until 6:30 for her to call back--then, when she didn't call, he left an announcement on the machine that he had to go grocery shopping and that he'd be back by ten.

When he came back, the trunk and the passenger seat of his sports car full of grocery bags, there were three new messages on the machine-- all from Lori. The first was at 7:19 p.m. in which she said "Hoping to get hold of you. I might leave work early." The second message--this time there was music in the background from the nightclub Lori was calling from--was at 8:22. The third message was at 9:07. This time Lori said she would call back at ten.

At ten o'clock she called. Once again Lori explained that she wanted to see him, and that she wanted to drive out to his farm, but that she was not sure how to get there. Frank thought that she should have known considering how many times she had been to his house. They agreed to meet at a nearby motel, and that Lori would follow him home from there.

He walked in the motel at 11:15 and found that the bar had closed at eleven. He would have to wait in the lobby for her and it could be a long boring wait. Frank walked out into the lobby, and then suddenly she was there coming in the door. She had come by herself to his territory on her initiative and here she was. The moment he saw her, he knew that everything was right with the world. For the first time he decided that it didn't matter what she did for a living. What mattered was that she was with him now--she and not someone else. *That was the difference then--something about her that makes me want to be with her and no one else.*

"Lori, the bar is closed, but I brought some beer. We can have one on the road on the way to my house."

"That'll work," said Lori.

He took her outside into the parking lot and opened the trunk of his sports car. Grabbing two bottles of the German beer, he looked for the bottle opener, and didn't find it. Frank looked at Lori and grinned.

"I am a farmer. I'll find something that'll open these bottles. It might be a board or a sign or whatever, but we are going to get these bottles open. I'd use my car door hinge--they always seem to work well on bottles--but mine is too small, and I might damage it."

"Give me your bottle, Frank. I'll do it."

He gave her his bottle wondering how she was going to open the two bottles. Grinning wildly Lori ran over to the old Grand Prix she had driven over. Within five seconds she had the caps off of both bottles using the outside door handle of her car. Running up to Frank she offered him one of the opened bottles smiling at him as if to say--*see, I'm pretty smart aren't I and I've done this for us.*

The whole thing only took two or three minutes. Lori moved fast--it was as if her brain came up with an idea and the idea was attached directly to her body which reacted instantly. Frank was proud of her--proud to have her with him and glad to be associated with her. He didn't give a damn what others might think. He felt good around her, he liked the way she looked, he liked the way she moved, he liked the way she talked. *She was for him. No substitutions please.*

He drove the ten miles to his farm with her right behind him, the front end of the Grand Prix less than a hundred feet from his rear bumper. The glare of her headlights in his rear view mirror almost blinded him. He had never known anyone to have followed so closely behind him. *Was this symbolic of the way she felt about him?* he thought. *Was she totally dependent upon those she was close to? Was she afraid of losing him?*

A few minutes later they were in his family room, Lori on his couch, while he prepared a Jack and Coke in the kitchen. He grabbed a beer from the refrigerator and brought Lori her drink as she sat at the other end of the couch. Several drinks and an hour later they were still sitting apart from one another deep in conversation.

"I have to leave at 1:30 said Lori."

"Why?"

"If I don't come home then, Travis will be out looking for me."

They were still talking at two. It was that Frank-Lori world again that betrayed her--a world in which time flew by and other people around them faded into the background. Suddenly Lori looked at her watch, shuddered involuntarily, and jumped off the couch.

"I've gotta go, Frank. Now."

He helped her with her coat and kissed her gently on the lips. "Come on, I'll walk you to your car."

"Won't you drive ahead of me so that I can follow you to the interstate?"

"Sure, I'll do that."

Frank walked Lori to her car, kissed her goodbye, and then got in his four wheel drive. Now that he thought about it, he could see why she wanted to follow him even though she had been to his place a few times before. The prairie, especially at night, was a flat forbidding place with few landmarks. He drove seven miles down the frontage road to the overpass which Lori could use to get back on the highway. He pulled over to the shoulder and waved as she drove by.

Fifteen minutes later he was back in his family room, the stereo turned up all the way, drinking a glass of wine. He had made a date with Lucy for the next evening and was planning what they would do that night. Frank barely heard the phone ring, its sound drowned out by the stereo. It was Lori.

"Frank. Where have you been? I must have called you six or seven times. I've been picked up here in Springfield for speeding. They got me doing 95 miles an hour in a 55-mph zone. They gave me three tickets, Frank." Lori spoke in short bursts as if she were out of breath. "Why didn't you answer the phone?"

"Because I had the stereo turned up too loud," he replied. "What are the other tickets for?"

"They are for driving without a licence and for moving my car when they told me not to."

"Why'd you move your car?"

"I was across the street. I had to call you, and someone was on the pay phone, so I drove across the street to another pay phone."

"Where are you at?" he asked.

"I'm right next to the Econo Lodge. Do you know where that is?"

"Damn right I do. Look, I'll be there within 45 minutes."

"Oh c'mon Frank. Can't you get here sooner?"

"All right. I'll try."

"Hurry Frank. The cops are all over here. I don't know what I am going to do."

"I'm coming right over Lori. Bye."

Frank went into his office and saw that there were seven messages on his answering machine, all from Lori. As he replayed them, a synthesized voice announced the time at which each call had been made. The first, which was at 2:35 a.m. went: "FRANK-- PICKUP THE PHONE NOW." (Then there was a slight pause) "FRANK PICKUP THE PHONE." Lori's voice was loud and demanding. The second message which was at 2:38 went "FRANK, PICKUP THE PHONE PLEASE. IT'S LORI. PLEASE PICKUP THE PHONE." The next call which was at 2:40 went "FRANK PICK UP THE PHONE." (Then a slight pause) "FUCK YOU." Then the fourth at 2:45--"YOU DID THIS ON PURPOSE DIDN'T YOU PRICK." By the fifth message which was at 2:48 Lori's voice was no longer belligerent, having a pleading quality instead. "FRANK IT'S LORI . . . PLEASE PICK UP THE PHONE." (pause) then "FRANK, PLEASE." Then at 2:50--"FRANK, I'M GETTING" (unintelligible words which Frank couldn't quite make out but obviously spoken by a frightened woman) "WILL YOU PLEASE ANSWER. PICK UP THE PHONE." The last message showed that Lori was bewildered and frightened since she probably thought she'd never get hold of him. It went--"FRANK, IT'S LORI. PLEASE PICK UP THE PHONE." (Long pause) "PLEASE."

He started off in his pickup; got two miles down the road when he heard the tire go flat. He got out to make sure and saw that the tire had collapsed around the rim. Frank considered the situation. Since the spare tire was held in a bracket underneath the truck, it would take him longer to get the spare out than to change the tire itself. Lori was in trouble. He might even find her in jail. How she ended up going north instead of south on an interstate that was clearly marked he'd never know. The recording on his answering machine clearly showed that she was frightened, bewildered, and lost. Frank didn't even consider stopping to change the tire--he had to help Lori no matter what the cost. Deciding to sacrifice both the tire and the rim, Frank turned back.

Frank was having a hard time getting 40 Mph out of his pickup because of the extra power it took to drive on the rim as it cut into the oiled road. He shifted the machine into four wheel drive and was able to get up to 55 Mph. He pulled into his driveway, got out, and ran to the garage where the little sports car was parked. He drove it 100 MPH to the interstate where he slowed to 90 MPH using the radar detector as he drove. Frank considered his situation. He was driving on a DUI. Frank had not really thought about whether he was legal or not. *Had the DUI gone into effect? No matter. Lori is out there, and she is in trouble.* He drove as if he had eyes in the back of his head, his senses alert, looking relentlessly ahead for any signs of a patrol car. He tried to see into the night trying to judge the width between an approaching car's headlights in an attempt to judge whether it was a semi, compact car, or a larger automobile which could be a patrol car.

Would he find Lori near the Econo Lodge or would he have to go to the police station to bail her out? Frank decided that it was unlikely that he'd find her anywhere near the Econo Lodge. *She had been, after all, driving 95 mph within the city limits of Springfield, Illinois and without a licence to boot.* Thirty-five minutes from the time he started Frank pulled into the Econo Lodge parking lot. He saw the Grand Prix sitting by itself--no police cars anywhere near-- and pulled behind it. He had decided it was empty when suddenly Lori's head rose from the seat.

"Thank God you are here," she said. "Let's go home."

They walked into Frank's family room relieved to be off the road and happy to be together. He went to the kitchen and brought back two beers before settling into the couch with her.

"You saw my tire and rim when we came in, didn't you?" asked Frank.

"Yes. You destroyed the tire."

"And the rim. Probably will cost $150 to get a new tire and rim. I drove like that for 2 miles so I could get to you as early as possible. Lori, I always want you to remember that. Remember that you are my friend-- that you will always be my friend no matter what. It doesn't matter what you do, I will always be there for you."

"For how long?"

"Forever."

Then he took her to bed--only this time he made sure that they made love first. He woke up at 9:00 the next morning and quietly slipped downstairs to make coffee. While it was perking, he went to the bathroom, brushed his teeth, shaved, and put in his contacts. Pouring two cups full, he went back to the upstairs bedroom. She was still sleeping soundly her features childlike, her body slender and beautiful to look at.

"Lori, I've brought some coffee for you," he said softly. When she didn't answer he got on the bed with her and bent down so that he could speak in her ear. "Lori, wake up. I've got us some coffee." When she still didn't stir, he decided upon a more effective means of waking her.

Frank lay down next to her and gently pulled her close to him. Positioning his body so that he hovered over her, he eased into her being careful not to put all of his weight on her at once. She started to wake up, slowly becoming conscious of her surroundings, then when she realized that he was inside of her, she started to smile.

"You are a derelict Frank. Raping me in my sleep like that."

"It was the only way I could wake you up."

He reached around her so that he could get his arms beneath her and pulled her around so that she lay on her side next to him at the same time settling back on his right side. Then he lifted her upwards so that she was on top staying inside of her the whole time.

"Go ahead, Lori. Grab your cup of coffee and hand me mine. We can drink and fuck at the same time."

"But not for long." Lori handed him his cup, then took hers off the dresser.

They sipped their coffee together like that for a time. By the time she was thrusting rapidly up and down on top of him she had long ago set her cup aside. After he came, she said, "Let's go downstairs. There's something I want you to do for me."

"What?" he asked.

"Something on your computer."

He took her into his office bringing his coffee cup with him. "Okay, what do you have in mind?" he asked.

"Frank. I spent the night with you last night. The whole night. That means that someone is wondering where I've been. He's going to beat me up when I get back."

"And you have an idea. Am I right?"

"If only you could make something up on your computer. Something official showing that I spent the night somewhere else."

"Simple," said Frank. "You spent the night in jail. Somewhere far from here. How's Granite City sound? Your crime was driving 95 mph without a licence. By the way, why were you driving without a licence?"

"Because I never had one. Never."

"You never had a licence. Why not?"

"I was born in Trinidad. In fact, I'm not even a U.S. citizen. I don't have a birth certificate and no one's helped me get one. I tried once, but there was so much red tape."

Oh no, thought Frank, *it's whopper time again. When is she going to ever quit* lying? "So what are we going to do here to fool dear old Travis?"

"Perhaps we could make up some kind of special recognizance bond," Lori suggested.

Frank sat down at his computer and brought his Wordprocessor up on the screen. "Okay Lori, we're going to start by calling this Recognizance Bond Form 2312-2Z4. Pure bullshit but it sounds official to me." Then he typed it on the screen so that it appeared in the center of what would become the printed page.

"Here Frank. You can have my three tickets. Read off them if it will help. Then keep them. Just let me know when my court date comes up."

Using the information on the three tickets and by asking Lori a number of questions Frank constructed the fake form which hopefully would convince Travis that Lori had spent the night, not at his farm near Springfield, Illinois, but in a Granite City jail which would have been just a few miles from where Lori worked. Then he ran a copy off for Lori. The form appeared as follows:

RECOGNIZANCE BOND FORM 2312-2Z4

STATE OF ILLINOIS   DATE OF DETENTION
10/11/93
COUNTY Madison
CITY   Granite City

Jurisdiction Municipal Police Dept. Granite
City

Defendants NAME   Lori R. Mellon
Defendants ADDRESS #37 Grant St.
                    Union, Mo. 63077

DRIVER'S LICENCE # Not given
HEIGHT   5'6"
WEIGHT   115
COLOR OF HAIR   Blonde
COLOR OF EYES   Brown

REASON FOR DETENTION Improper lane usage

LOCATION OF   Madison County, Il

DETAIL   Defendant was driving ahead
of arresting officer to the left of the center
line. Officer stopped defendant and was
unable to acquire defendant's driver's licence
or other form of id.

ARRESTING OFFICER Gerald Holloway

SIGNATURE   *Gerald Holloway*

Defendant's SIGNATURE   **Lori R. Mellon**

COURT DATE   11/15/93
     "I don't like the light yellow paper that you used," said Lori.
"Can you try white?"

"That will be easy," said Frank as he ran off another copy. This time he used the continuous forms that he used for most of his printouts.

Lori tore the sheet off the continuous form as soon as the printer had completed its work. Reading it carefully she started to nod her head in approval. "Yes, this might work. It just might save me from getting beat up again."

Satisfied with his work, Frank put two English Muffins in the toaster. He was surprised that Lori only ate half of one of the muffins. Then he drove her to Springfield. After he pulled into the Econo Lodge parking lot he saw Lori to her car and watched her drive off, not thinking about his date with Lucy--but wishing instead that Lori could stay longer.

The next time he saw her, she told him that the counterfeit form worked.

BIFURCATED COURT SETTLEMENTS

"What do you mean I'm not divorced yet?" Frank asked Randy Green.

"Carl is raising an issue with the Judge over this whole divorce thing," replied Randy. "I just forwarded to you a copy of the six page letter he sent to the judge."

"When will it arrive?"

"You will probably get it in today's mail."

"What's the gist of it?"

"The trend of the court cases in the State of Illinois has changed through the years," replied Randy. "It used to be that the two issues--that is the causal issue and the monetary issue-- had to be decided by separate judges. The reason for this is that if a husband established the grounds for divorce by showing the court that his wife cheated on him repeatedly, was a prostitute, did drugs, etc., that judge might be prejudiced in his favor. In all likelihood that judge would not be too willing to give the wife a good financial settlement. So, the trend of the court decisions changed. Two separate judges would decide the two issues, one deciding the grounds issue, the other the financial issue. The problem was that the court system became overloaded with too many cases. The trend then shifted to what it had been before. That is, the same judge was required to decide both issues."

"So, what does this have to do with me?" Frank asked.

"The judge who presided over your hearing went to Law School with the attorney who advised your wife on the Prenuptial before you got married. Since both Carl and I are going to take this attorney's deposition, the judge has removed himself from the case on the basis that he is prejudiced either for or against that attorney."

"My understanding of a deposition is that you and Carl will question that attorney in a formal setting in which all parties obey the rules of Civil Procedure," said Frank. "The judge is not likely to be present."

"You are correct, but there is a possibility that during a later hearing the attorney who advised your wife on the Prenuptial might be required to be at the hearing as a witness."

"But the judge promised to enter a court order that would dissolve our marriage," said Frank.

"That's what I thought he said also," replied Randy, "but apparently that is not the case."

"Okay then. That's what we heard," said Frank. "Perhaps I should have gone on to explain what a bitch Karen was during the marriage when I was giving testimony. The only reason we dispensed with this is that Carl said he would not contest the issue of cause."

"That is correct," said Randy. "He admitted there was cause for a divorce and that cause was your wife's mental cruelty toward you, but apparently he did not agree that the dissolution should take effect immediately."

"Meaning."

"Meaning that the dissolution will in all likelihood be entered after all financial considerations are taken care of."

"All of which is to be decided by a new judge," said Frank.

"That's correct."

"Which means I get to pay court costs twice. Or perhaps this legal establishment might somehow come up with a reason to get me to pay three or four times what I should have to pay."

"Well I don't know about that."

"Come on Randy, you and I both know this is a bunch of bullshit. The only reason that these assholes are pulling this off is that they perceive that I have the money. If I didn't have the money, this little farce would have ended a long time ago."

"I don't blame you for feeling the way you do," replied Randy. "Unfortunately the way the system works is that it allows the other attorney to extort money from you to the extent that you will settle for a lesser amount when you shouldn't have to pay in the first place."

"Anything else I should know about, Randy?"

"Yes. The judge has ordered you to pay $5000 to Carl to cover his attorney's fees."

"In spite of the fact that the Prenuptial specifically provides that I don't have to pay for my wife's attorney's fees!" said Frank.

"That's the size of it. In any case, we can make it the grounds for an appeal."

"Right. So that they can rip me off some more. This judge belongs on a park bench drinking Mogen David wine from a milk carton. He certainly doesn't belong in a courtroom."

"I won't comment on that," said Randy.

"Well I have this to say," said Frank. "I have to pay you to defend me or shall I say to plead my case. Then I pay the other attorney to rip me apart. He digs up more issues--more crap that the two of you can argue about at $100 an hour apiece. That all comes out of my pocket. As long as I have any money left, this thing--this whole series of court actions over my divorce will feed itself. I have never seen anything more dishonest, more self-serving, and more disgusting in my whole life."

........Then calming down--"Look, Randy, I believe you've done a good job for me. Sorry I've got to come down on you, but I just--I just want to puke."

Frank made a beeline for the physical fitness center as soon as he read the six page letter that was in the day's mail. Clad in black shorts and a black tee shirt he walked past everyone working out on the machines straight to the rowing machine. He walked as a man possessed looking to neither the right nor the left. The machine was computerized and could be set for varying degrees of difficulty. Frank set it on Olympic which was the hardest and set the timer for 12 minutes. Then he hit the start button. The images of two boats appeared on the screen ready to race one another. One was the pacer, the other was the boat which was to be piloted by Frank. The words-- get ready, get set, go--appeared on the screen and Frank started to row. With four minutes left to go, Frank was beating the pacer boat by seven lengths. He took his left hand off the pulley bar which exercised the arms and continued to row with his right arm alone. Two minutes later he started to row with his left arm. He did this for one minute, then finished the final minute with both arms. He heard a noise as the cable he was pulling strained. *It's going to break*, he thought. *People don't pull this hard on the machine, People normally aren't as mad as I am right now.*

Done with the rowing exercises and having already run five miles on the indoor track, Frank went over to the bench pressing machine. He adjusted it for 200 pounds and did three sets of three repetitions each, which was more than he normally did. As he did the three sets, he kept repeating to himself *before this is all over with I believe I am going to fuck a lawyer and a judge up.*

Two hours after he left, he found himself sitting at a table with three women in the Sports Bar. First, he had sat with Lucy who was immediately joined by Linda. Later, Julie joined them. Frank had deliberately placed the six page letter on the table to show Lucy that he had not after all gotten divorced but that it really wasn't his fault. Frank was concerned about losing his credibility with her. Her divorce had gone through on Friday, and he was afraid that she might think that he had been lying to her about his own.

Julie picked up the letter and started to look at it. Then she looked up at Frank and grinned. "So these are your divorce papers?"

"I wish. Julie, those six pages are the reason that our ignoble legal system has decided that I should not be divorced."

"Mind if I read it?" she asked.

"I don't mind, but let me tell you first that it's six pages long and that I've only read the first page. That was enough for me. The whole thing is a perversion of words. It's a total crock of shit that justifies the judges and lawyers charging me more than I should be charged. One page--that's all I'll ever read. I don't deal with diarrhea very well, particularly diarrhea of words."

Julie started to read the letter--read the first page--then turned to the second. She looked up at Frank and frowned.

"That's right. All it is, is a citation of court cases which justifies the legalized stealing from honest hardworking people. Don't read any more. It's really not worth your time," said Frank.

Julie pulled out a cigarette, lit it, then held the letter up high over the table. "Can I burn it then?"

"Do it," ordered Frank.

"Sure?"

"Just do it."

Julie flicked the lighter with her thumb. A small flame jetted out. Smiling maliciously, Julie placed the flame underneath the letter which caught fire immediately. The flame grew until the letter became too hot for Julie to hold. She threw it on the ashtray in front of her and started to pour beer on it.

"A fitting end to bad rubbish," laughed Frank. "First you torched it, then you drowned it."

"I think we should do a limo," suggested Lucy.

"What? You are going to admit to your cousin and Julie that you are doing limos," said Frank.

"Sure, Why not?"

"I thought you were secretive about doing limos."

"Well they know I don't do them. Except with you."

"I don't know Lucy. A lot has happened today. I wonder if it's a good idea."

"Come on Frank. Lighten up. Christmas is coming right up and I have to get presents for my kids. You'll help me do that won't you?"

"You make it hard to refuse."

"Come on Frank, do a limo with Lucy," said Julie. "That way we can all hear about it later."

"Not a chance," said Lucy. "What Frank and I do stays with us."

A few minutes later Frank was in the limo watching Lucy smoke her cigarette. When she finished, she took off her clothes, this time quickly and without any false modesty. She didn't avert her eyes as he made love to her. He had never seen her this aggressive before nor did she seem to have enjoyed it as much.

"You were different from the last time Lucy. You didn't or couldn't look at me then as I made love to you."

"That's because I've been to your place, and you didn't try to fuck me. I trust you now."

When they returned to the bar, one of the girls came up to Lucy to tell her that it was her turn to dance. Lucy went over to the jukebox and punched in her four selections. Then she came back to Frank.

"Frank, will you come up to the stage with me?"

"You really want me to. I feel like a real idiot sitting up there the way the other guys do, mouths hanging open, sneaking a cheap feel whenever they can."

"Please come up with me Frank. I'm nervous. I'm not drunk enough yet and I feel like such a fool up on stage."

He followed her to the stage, bringing both drinks with him and sat down in front of her. She danced, paying attention only to him, her slender form reminding him of Lori's. It was uncanny how up there in the neon she not only looked like Lori but danced like her as well. And Lori was very good. *So why is Lucy nervous?* He thought. *She is the best dancer and the best looker in the place.* On the fourth song Lucy put her crotch up to Frank's face, placing her hands around his neck, as she jammed his face against her groin.

When they returned to the bar, she turned to him and said, "I'm not going to work here much longer. I can't stand doing all this. I don't respect myself and I don't like many of the men who come in here. I don't really give a shit. I'd rather be flipping hamburgers or doing anything other than being here."

"How much longer will you be here then?" Frank asked.

"Two weeks or so. That's all."

"And then what?"

"I don't know. I won't be here though. This just isn't me."

He went home that night respecting Lucy more than he ever

had before. He too had gotten tired of the cheap feels and of sitting in front of stages like a dork. Then he reminded himself why he went there and to other places like it. He liked the girls. Frank enjoyed talking and drinking with them. He liked the music, and he liked the fast pace. Above all, he liked taking the girls out.

THE KIDNAPING

"I think I'm going crazy. I'm going out of my mind. Frank, I need you to be here." Frank had been outdoors harvesting corn, and had just gotten in. This time, on her third call, she had gotten hold of him after having left two messages.

"Where are you at?" he asked.

"At work. Frank can you see me?"

"I could, but I've just come in from the field. I'm tired, and I'm hungry, and I don't have any money on me."

"That's all right. Just come over and see me."

Frank walked into Gals with seventy-five cents in his pocket. It was obvious from the way she walked that Lori was drunk. Nevertheless, she bought both of them a drink. "How much money do you have?" he asked.

"I just made $30. That's all, but I've got to pay 10% of what I made as a tip out which means that I've made only $27. How much do you have?"

"Seventy-five cents. I take it that your shift is off now and that you can leave with me."

"Yes. Let's get the fuck out of here."

He helped her out the door and across the parking lot to her car holding onto her arm as they walked. "Where do you want to go?" he asked.

"Anywhere's fine with me."

"How about the Injection Pump? It closes at four and it has a plastic machine. I might only have seventy-five cents, but I have my Visa. Follow me there."

He waited until she started the Grand Prix before he left the parking lot. Frank looked into his rearview mirror to make sure she was right behind him and discovered that she was driving without her lights. Frank pulled over to the curb, got out of his car, and ran out into the middle of the street frantically waving his arms.

Lori stopped her car and lowered her window. "What's wrong?" she asked.

"You're driving without headlights. Turn them on, please?"

They walked up the stairs into the Injection Pump. Jimmy, a large black man, waited at the top of the stairs. "Five dollars please," he said. "She gets in free."

"But she's treating me," said Frank. Frank raised his eyebrows mockingly and turned to Lori. "Pay the man Lori. Then you can buy me a drink. You know what I want."

Jimmy looked at them with surprise as Lori grimaced. Frank walked into the room while she stayed back and paid. A waitress came up to him to get his drink order. Lori waited until Jimmy gave her back her change; then ran up behind Frank, snuggled up against him, and kneed him in the rear end.

"Take that. Serves you right for being such a pain in the ass. Now you've got one too."

"Waitress," said Frank, "I'll have a Budweiser, and she'll have . . . well she'll have whatever she's having. And please have my secretary here pay the bill." He nodded toward Lori. "Actually Lori's my maid."

"You can be such an ass," said Lori.

"And you love it, don't you?"

The waitress brought the drinks back which came to $9.00. Frank moved over to the bar. Lori sat on his lap as he tried to get Helen's attention. Helen sashayed back and forth behind the bar, finished making the drink she had been working on; then came up to Frank.

"What can I do for you? Or should I say, what can you do for me? Want to buy me a drink?"

"Helen, we are short of money right now. Can you run my Visa through?"

"Oh no, not another one. I'm afraid you're out of luck. The visa machine is broken down."

"You've gotta be kidding," said Lori.

"I'm not. You can try Risque. I'm sure their machine is still working."

"Anyplace closer?" asked Frank.

"Not that I know of."

Frank turned to Lori. "I think I know how to get there. It's a few miles from here. You worked there for part of a day. Can you find it?"

"No, Frank. I can't."

"Let's get in my car and try. We can always come back here later."

They drove down route 64 looking for the exit that Frank thought would take them to Risque. He had been on a number of limos. Once or twice he thought the limo had gone to a topless nightclub next to Risque to turn around. He couldn't be sure since he wasn't paying attention to where the limo was taking him, but he recollected seeing the large sign in the parking lot with the nightclub's name on it. Frank came to a familiar exit and took it, merging onto a Southbound two lane highway. He drove two miles anxiously looking to his right and to his left for the nightclub. Then he turned around.

"Must have missed it," he said. "On the way back you look to the right while I look to the left."

"I thought you said you knew where it was," said Lori.

"I thought I did, but it looks like I didn't know what I was talking about."

"You never know what you're talking about."

"Come on Lori. We are in this together. Don't get mad at me."

"Why shouldn't I?"

"Keep looking, Lori. It's gotta be around here somewhere. All I know is that the limo stopped by the place once or twice."

"You and your goddamn limos."

Frank drove back toward route 64 even pulling into a small shopping center in an attempt to find Risque. Then he doubled back once more taking the Southbound Highway a mile further this time. Still no luck.

"Take me back to my car," Lori ordered.

"What are you so mad about?" asked Frank.

"You're doing this on purpose. You know where it is but you'd rather give me a hard time."

"Look, I haven't had much to drink. I've been farming all day and into the night. I'm ready to relax with a beer. Then another and another. Lori, I am not doing this on purpose. I've never been to Risque. I just thought I knew where it was."

Frank turned into the Injection Pump's parking lot and pulled in thirty feet from the Grand Prix. Lori looked straight ahead not once looking at him.

"You've been drinking up all my money. Now I don't have anything left to bring to Travis. All I've got is seven dollars. I can't even get gas."

"I told you that I didn't have any money and you told me to come visit you anyway. And you've got to admit that I can't help it if the Visa machine broke down."

"You can help it," Lori said bitterly, "You can help a lot of things."

"You called me tonight and asked me to be with you. Now

let's enjoy each other."

"I hate men. All they do is sponge off of you and then they want to fuck you all the time."

"Lori, I have never sponged off of you, and I never will, and yes, I admit, I do want to fuck you all the time."

"And you're damn good at it. I haven't had anyone fuck me as good as you have in the last ten years. But you, you're lucky. You get to go home tonight and not worry about anything. I go home, I have to worry about getting killed or beat up."

You chose Travis, thought Frank. *I did something about Karen. Can't you grab hold of yourself and change your life, Lori? You don't have to put up with his shit.*

"I'm leaving." Lori got out of the sports car and started the Grand Prix. Quick as she was, Frank was even quicker, catching up with her immediately. Running up behind her, he grabbed Lori by her arm.

"We're not done talking," he said. "You called me to tell me that you needed me. Now here I am. I'm seventy miles from home here with you."

Frank didn't see it coming. Suddenly her fist caught him in the face. He felt no pain at all, just surprise that she should hit him. Jumping into the Grand Prix, Lori started it, slammed it in reverse, and drove it into his sports car. The big car caught the sports car on its rear bumper. Nevertheless, it still managed to put a scratch on the MG's paint. Jamming the Grand Prix into reverse again Lori spun into the middle of the parking lot. Shoving the automatic transmission into drive, she saw Frank looming in front of her. She stomped on the accelerator as the car leapt toward him. Frank saw it coming, sidestepping swiftly to his left. The car missed him, either because he was just quick enough or because Lori had only half heartedly tried to run him down, perhaps only to scare him. The night watchman, who had been employed by the Injection Pump to watch the parking lot ran over to the Grand Prix. After running into the back of Frank's car and after almost running him down, Lori hesitated a moment, stopping her car. The watchman ran up to her shouting "Hey. Stop the car."

Lori brought the Grand Prix to a dead stop, turned off the ignition, and lay her head across the steering wheel. The watchman walked up to her door.

"Hey, you can't park there. Either leave or park over there and behave yourself." He pointed to the back of the building that was the Injection Pump. Several cars were parked there including Frank's. She started her car and eased up against the building next to Frank's car.

Frank ran up to her window motioning for her to open it. She looked up at him, looked down at the steering wheel, hesitated a moment, then lowered her window. "What do you want?" she asked.

"You're not going to be able to go home without gas," he suggested.

"No."

"What are you going to do and where are you going to sleep?"

"Stay out all night, I guess. It's better than getting beat up."

"Come on. I'll buy you some gas. All the gas you want."

"How?"

"Visa. Unless the Shell Station's plastic machine is broken down."

"Okay. Get in."

Frank slipped into the seat beside her. The Shell station was less than a quarter of a mile away. After the station accepted his Visa card, he filled her tank. Then she drove him back to his car and pulled next to it. When she looked at him, he noticed that her eyes had become yellow slits from all the drinking and the lack of sleep.

"You--you've fucked up my life Frank. I don't know which end is up. All because of you. I quit my job at the Sports Bar because of you. Then I lost my job at the Pink Giraffe because of you. I started to work at the Injection Pump because you always wanted me there. And you--you're out there doing all those limos with whomever."

"Only because you've stood me up or not called me in a week or two," said Frank.

"Well how can I trust you when you're fucking all these other girls?"

"How do I trust you when you keep breaking your promises, Lori?"

Without warning Lori twisted out from behind the steering wheel so that her back faced him. Lowering the upper part of her body so that her head fell in his lap Lori lashed out against the window of the car with her right foot. Her shoe caught the glass squarely almost breaking it. Then she lashed out with the other leg, this time catching the upper part of the door just beneath the window. Suddenly, she was out of control, kicking wildly at the window with both feet. Frank was surprised that the glass didn't break.

Then she stopped, as abruptly as she had started, and began to wheeze. Frank had never seen her out of breath before yet here she was breathing in fast short bursts. "Frank. On the floor there," she gasped, "hand me that inhaler." He fumbled around in the dark looking for an inhaler. "It's there," she said, "right next to your hand." He found it, a small plastic appliance that could have been anything, and handed it to her.

Lori put the appliance up to her mouth and breathed deeply into it. Gradually her breathing slowed, finally becoming deeper and more settled. When he was certain that she had caught her breath, Frank put his arms around her and said softly: "Lori, if you can remember one thing and one thing only, I care about you. I care about you a lot."

Without warning Lori sat up and grinned impishly. He should have remembered that with Lori action followed thought immediately as if the one was attached to the other. Before he had a chance to guess what she was doing she had the engine started, thrust the transmission lever into reverse, and squealed out of the parking lot. Her right hand moved quickly, flicking the lever into drive as her foot mashed down upon the throttle. The Grand Prix leaped forward, gravel flying off its tires, as she drove it out of the lot.

"This time you're coming with me and I'm not letting you out until I'm ready to let you out."

She drove the Grand Prix onto route 64, westbound toward St. Louis and buried the accelerator into the floor. The big car lurched forward. Frank looked down at the dashboard for the speedometer. It didn't work and there was no dash light to illuminate it. The first curve came up as the car picked up speed. *Surely she is going to slow down*, he thought. Then he saw the concrete guard rails on both sides of the road. Lori took the curve with her foot still pressed tightly into the floor. The heavy car started to drift toward the left guard rail missing it with only two feet to spare.

"I don't give a fuck about anything!" exclaimed Lori as the car approached the next curve. Frank estimated their speed at 100 MPH. He remembered how she had been so drunk several hours before that she could hardly walk out of Gals. *Well, she's drunk, and I believe her when she says she doesn't give a fuck*, he thought. *When this car hits the next guard rail or the one after that they won't*

be able to tell who is who, our bodies will be so mashed up together.
The next guard rail came up rapidly as Lori took the right-handed
corner. The Grand Prix veered to the right as she over steered and
almost caught the guardrail. At the last moment she jerked the
steering wheel to the left which brought the car over across two
lanes of traffic.

"Lori, for God's sake slow down!" he yelled.

"No, I won't. Not until I decide to."

"Lori, this is a cheap ass way of dying. If we're going to do it
together let's think of something a little more original."

"How does it feel Frank? How does it feel to be afraid?
You've never been afraid of anything in your whole life. I live in
constant fear--of the future, of being beat up, of being killed. What
does it feel like Frank? Do you like it?"

"Okay, I'll admit it. I'm afraid. Now slow the fuck down!"

The next corner came up way too fast, but the heavy car
skidded around it, once again barely missing a guard rail. After that
she eased up on the throttle. She was doing around seventy when
they crossed the river over to the Missouri side. Lori drove him to
her old neighborhood, not far from the police station they had visited
after Travis had beaten her up. Then she headed back to the river
where she crossed the bridge into Illinois.

"I'm not letting you out until I see the sun come up," said Lori.

"You've got to get me back in time for harvest," said Frank.
Ron is driving the combine tomorrow. I have to haul in the grain
with the harvest wagons, and I have to be there by 8:30 a.m. at the
latest. I didn't mention it, but I've hired Tamara's husband, Charles,
to help me haul in tomorrow. I'll probably have to pick him up
before 8:30.

"Not letting you out till the sun comes up," Lori repeated.

She took him to Belleville; from Belleville she drove to
Granite City; from Granite City she drove back to St. Louis. Then
back to Belleville, both of them smoking cigarettes, Frank bumming
from her now, the cd player turned up full blast. She drove to
Collinsville, then back to St. Louis, then back to Belleville. This
time she headed to a place she had wanted to take him for some time
now.

"Where are you going?" he asked.

"I'm taking you to the cemetery."

"Who are we digging up?"

"We are looking up my half brother, the one who was

supposed to have shot himself, but who was actually murdered."

"That's the grave you wanted to show me--the one you always talked about," said Frank.

She found the cemetery and drove through the gate. "This place is a lot bigger than I remember," said Lori. "I hope I can find it."

"I remember that you told me how you used to come here quite often," said Frank. "You shouldn't have any problem."

"It's different at night, and I really haven't been back here in awhile," said Lori. The grave is beneath some trees. I remember that.

The cemetery was huge. Lori drove around it several times, looking for the grove of trees that marked the grave. On the fourth time around she observed a little side road off to the right that she hadn't noticed before. Turning down the side road she discovered that it formed a long loop coming back on the road she had just been on.

"I think we've got it. Now look for a grove of trees," said Lori.

She brought the car down to an idle. Then she saw the grove of trees, stopped the car. and motioned for Frank to get out. He left the heated interior of the car in his shirt sleeves. The night sky, which had been black as ink, had started to get lighter, which meant that the sun was about to come up. He followed her to the grove of trees and watched her start to look among the graves.

"We are looking for Tommy Exposito," said Lori. "He's gotta be here somewhere."

It must be a section used by poor people, thought Frank. He noticed that the tombstones here were small slabs dug into and almost flush to the ground, their inscriptions chiseled into the tops of the stones. Elsewhere he knew the stones would be much larger and dug in vertically rather than horizontally. Frank started to shiver, wondering what he was doing here looking for the grave of a petty hoodlum. Suddenly Lori stopped walking through the little headstones.

"Here it is. It says Tommy Exposito. And see here on the tombstone--he was only twenty-four years old when he was killed." Lori pointed at the tombstone for emphasis. "We were close. Very close," she said sadly. Then she looked up at Frank. "We can leave now. I've always wanted to show you this."

They drove out of the cemetery together, closer than ever.

Frank felt sad that the grave was so shabby. It showed poignantly the different roads their lives had taken. Once Lori had been a small child, bright, eager, and innocent just as he had been. She had become a stripper and probably a whore, abused and an abuser of men, an alcoholic, a woman who hurt deep down inside and who turned around and hurt others, a child-woman who hung around with men like Tommy Exposito, who would end up in a tawdry grave. He thought of her lying beneath a small stone with her name on it only inches above the ground. He thought of her trying to kick her own car's windows out, frustrated and tormented by the life she found herself in, seemingly unable to change it.

Frank closed his eyes and silently cried for her. He couldn't stand the thought of her dead. Worse, he could not, would not contemplate her lying in a pauper's grave, forgotten. She had stood him up many times. She had betrayed him before and she would betray him again. For the first time Frank understood the meaning of unconditional love. The thought of Lori dead or in trouble was intolerable. He asked himself a simple question: *If she didn't have me who does she have*?

She drove him back to the Injection Pump. *She's taking me back*, he thought. *The sun's coming up*. She turned on her left turn blinker, started to turn in at the light, then, just as he thought she was going to take him to his car, continued to go straight at the last second.

"It's getting brighter, but so far I haven't seen the sun. I'm not letting you out until I see a little yellow ball above the earth."

"Lori, let me out. I've had a good time, but I've got to harvest corn today and I've got to be at Ron's by 8:30."

"You'll just have to drive faster then. Where would you like to go?" she asked.

"Home. I'm going to wuss out on you Lori. I've got to get home."

"We're going somewhere else instead. I just want you to know how it feels to be out of control. You are not going to stop me from taking you where I want to take you. Now you know how I feel. I am not in control of my life."

She drove down a back road which led to another back road. He didn't know where he was. Perhaps she thought that he was about to jump out of the car to hitch a ride to his sports car. Perhaps that is why she was taking him on the back roads--so that he could be her captive a little longer. Twenty minutes later she drove onto a road that he knew well--the road to the Pink Giraffe. As if she sensed what he was thinking, she pulled onto the little street that went by it. It was the place where they had first made love, the first time in front of 125 people, the second time for two hours straight in the hot tub. It was the place where they had truly become friends after which she had let him into her life.

Then she headed back the Injection Pump. Once again, she did not turn into the night club, driving past it, perhaps on her way to Belleville or to St. Louis again. Now he would be late for harvest. How could he explain it all to Ron? This time his anger showed.

"Lori, goddamn it! Let me out of the fucking car! I don't care if you go sixty miles per hour--I'm jumping out if you don't let me out first!"

She did a U-turn and headed back to the Injection Pump. She pulled up next to his car and sat there, stone faced, waiting for him to get out. He bent over to kiss her, but she turned away. Getting out of her car, he got into his, and pulled away. He didn't get home till after nine o'clock, the first time he had ever held anyone up at harvest time.

As he drove home, he thought of her. *She had a good time all night long. Then I had to bring it all to a close. We must have driven more than two hundred miles together, talking and smoking in our little fantasy world. Then, suddenly it all ended when I finally said it had to end, and she had to face the reality of her life--going back to Travis and getting back to her five kids. No wonder she didn't kiss me.*

THE BOXING MATCH

Charles had been working out in the field for one hour. Time to check Frank's messages again. Working close to Frank's house, Charles brought the big tractor to a stop on the end rows. Leaving its engine idle, he walked to Frank's house one hundred yards away, went into the house, and studied the answering machine in the office. The digital counter still read zero which meant that no new messages had been received. Charles went into the kitchen, grabbed a glass from the cabinet and poured himself a glass of water. Deciding to take a five minute break he sat down at the kitchen table and stretched out his legs.

Fifty minutes later he was back at work shredding corn stalks. He was pulling a fifteen-foot Brady shredder behind the tractor with a disk mounted behind the shredder. A number of flail type knives spun around a heavy rotor which was powered off the tractor engine. As Charles drove the tractor through the field he was able to cut and grind the standing corn stalks left by the combine into small pieces. Ten minutes later he would have to check Frank's phone calls again. Since the tractor was gradually working away from the house, he would have to walk a quarter of a mile this time.

Suddenly Frank drove up in his pickup. Stopping the pickup at the edge of the field, Frank turned off its ignition and waited for Charles to turn the tractor around at the opposite end of the field and drive up to him on his end. He waited five minutes as Charles ground up stalks all the way back at a steady six miles per hour.

"Charles, any phone calls?"

"None," said Charles, as he walked to Frank's pickup.

"It doesn't look like Lucy's going to call," said Frank. "Damn her, doesn't she realize that one o'clock means one o'clock." *Does she really think I'm lying in bed all day catnapping while I wait for her to call*? he thought. *My time is valuable, especially now that the field work must be done. And what about Charles? Here I am paying him $6 an hour to shred stalks, but out of each hour he's probably spending an average of fifteen minutes checking my messages.*

"I don't know if I mentioned it to you earlier, but I've got to quit at seven tonight," said Charles.

"I'll come get you then," said Frank. "Then I'll take you home. Charles, I'll catch my messages this time, but I want you to check them at the end of the next hour. If Lucy hasn't called by five, I'm figuring she's not going to call and our date is off. You don't have to check them after five."

"Sounds good to me," said Charles.

"How's everything going otherwise?" asked Frank. "Any problems with the equipment?"

"None that I can see."

"Then I'll check up on you later. By the way, if she's left a message this time, I'm coming back for you. You'll still have time to pick her up, bring her over, and still get home by seven." Frank checked his watch, which showed three o'clock which was two hours after the time Lucy promised to call.

His answering machine showed that one person had left a message. He hit the play button and was rewarded by a woman's recorded voice. Except that it was Lori's. "Frank, this is Lori. I'm no longer working at Gals. I am at the Club Shangrila. I suppose you're out in the field so I'll just have to call back later."

So, it didn't look like he'd end up with Lucy after all. He had almost forgotten how she had stood him up the day after Lori had gotten her three tickets. He had driven all the way to Ciceros which was one hour away from home, and she had not shown. The next week she had told him in the Limo that she had lost his phone number, had one of her children get sick on her, and had not been able to call him. He had asked himself, *if she couldn't have reached me at home, why didn't she at least call Ciceros so that I wouldn't wait there for her?*

Frank thought of Lucy--first standing him up on that Monday, then not calling today as they had agreed upon. *Oh well*, he thought, *Birds in the Attic Nobody at Home.* But Lori had called, so he would see her instead. He pushed the record button and spoke into the little machine's mike, "You have reached the Frank Harring residence. If you are Lori Mellon stay on the line. If you are anyone else, please leave a message at the sound of the tone. Now, as for you Lori, I got your message. I can leave the field sometime after seven. If you want to go with me somewhere after work give me a time and I'll be there to pick you up."

What if Lucy calls and hears this message which is directed to Lori? thought Frank. *So what if she does. She didn't do what we agreed upon. Didn't even come close. Well, fuck her then. I've hired Charles to work today when I didn't really have to. And I'm paying him to check my messages. Not to mention the fact that I had to pick him up and that I have to take him home which is one half hour each way. I would have done just as well staying off the other tractor and done what he is doing.*

At six-fifteen Frank got off the John Deere and walked over to his pickup. He had been chisel plowing a field which was seven miles from the one Charles was shredding. He pulled into his driveway and went into his house. Lucy had not called. Lori had however. He was to pick her up at eight p.m. which was the time she got off of work. He went into the bathroom to wash up, quickly changed to a clean pair of jeans, and went out to pick Charles up.

Frank walked into the Shangrila Club a few minutes after eight, found Lori, and bought her a drink. They sat at the bar together both drinking beer. Frank had looked in the parking lot for the Grand Prix when he first walked in half expecting Travis to be out there to pick Lori up.

"Travis is picking you up then?" asked Frank.

"Yes, but I am going to tell him that I am working late."

"We tried that before, and we got caught--remember?"

"We did, didn't we. Travis likes to see me make money since he has none of his own, and he's not too bright to begin with so he probably will hardly remember what we used to pull on him."

"It's twenty after eight. Don't you think you should go out to check on him?" Frank suggested.

"No. Let him wait."

At 8:30 Lori went outside to look for Travis, leaving her bag at Frank's feet next to the bar. Three minutes later she came back grinning in triumph. When they finished their beer, they left together in his car and went to the Sports Bar.

He didn't care if he saw Lucy there or not. She had cost him a lot of money not to mention time and worry. He ran his farm operation methodically and did not normally leave the field unless he had to--and women had in the past not been an appropriate excuse for quitting early. However, this time he had made an exception for Lucy and for Lori. Nevertheless, he had still put in a twelve-hour day.

They sat at a table together and called Nurse over to take their drink order. Looking around the room, Frank did not see Lucy, but he did see her cousin, Linda, who gave him a dirty look when their eyes met.

"You want to sit down in the backroom?" asked Lori. "That way we won't be disturbed."

"That's a great idea, Lori."

Just then Nurse came back with their drinks, put them on the table in front of them, and waited for Frank to tip her. Frank pulled out a dollar bill as Nurse stuck out her chest. He stuck the dollar into her bra being careful not to feel her breasts as she bent over to kiss him chastely. Frank liked Nurse, who was an older woman and a fine waitress to boot.

"Nurse, we're going to take a table in the next room. Can you wait on us there?"

"Gwen's working the back room tonight for the most part. I'll get back to you every now and then, but you'll probably see more of her," said Nurse.

"Nurse, can you bring us some salt and limes and two shots of Cuervo?" Lori asked. "Frank and I are going to do a body shot together." Then she turned to look at Frank and smiled. "Unless you don't want to do one with me."

"What? And spoil our tradition? Not a chance," said Frank.

They sat in the back drinking beer until the waitress arrived with the Cuervo, limes, and salt. Gwen, a brunette, who was around five foot eight, came up to them. Frank remembered the first time he had met her--how Gwen had walked up to him and asked him to tip her after she had danced. Since she was far better looking than most of the other girls, it had been difficult for him to say no, yet he had replied "I don't tip anyone except the girl I'm sitting with." She had answered, "You've got a high opinion of yourself, don't you?" Since then they had learned to appreciate each other. He liked her because she had the guts to tell him what she thought and had put him down cooly--because he thought she was more intelligent than most of the other girls, and because she always handled herself in a ladylike manner which was a difficult stunt to pull off in a place like the Sports Bar. He had never known her to do a limo, and he had never seen her do a private. She was a good waitress when she was not dancing, and when she was dancing she was the best dancer there, Lucy included.

"Here's your Cuervo," said Gwen. "Enjoy your body shot."

"Lori, do you know Gwen?" asked Frank.

"Can't say that I do." Lori replied.

"Lori, this is Gwen. She used to hate me."

"That's because you used to be so pompous," Gwen replied. Then looking at Lori, she continued: "He told me the first time he met me that he wasn't going to tip me or anyone else. I told him that he had a high opinion of himself, but actually he's turned into a real sweetie."

Frank gave Gwen a dollar, stuffing it into her bra as he had done before with Nurse. Gwen bent over and kissed him on the lips, set the drinks, limes, and salt on the table, and hurried off. Lori turned to Frank and glared at him. "So she's one of your little girlfriends. How many limos have you done with her?"

"I don't think she does any limos, Lori. As a matter of fact, I don't even know if she does any privates. I've never actually sat down to talk to her for very long, but she's certainly one of the more likeable girls here."

"Yeah, I'll bet. You are a liar Frank. You are a lying motherfucker."

"Look, you've got to admit that I've told you who I've done the limos with. Now, why should I lie about Gwen?"

"No reason, I guess. Let's get up and dance," Lori said.

They got up from the table, walked away from it, and started to slow dance next to the corner where the girls did their privates. Lori snuggled up to him inside his arms as he bent down to kiss her. She fit into him perfectly, her slenderness making her appear vulnerable and attractive at the same time. He reminded himself once again that large breasts, and the large female bodies they were often attached to, simply got in the way. Several songs later they went back to their drinks.

She took his shirt off and started to lick his nipple until it became hard and wet. Dumping salt into her hand from the shaker, Lori rubbed the wet nipple until it was coated with salt which she started to lick with her mouth. Then she took the lime and passed it from her mouth to his, but she couldn't wait for the last step. Grinning maliciously, she raised the shot glass above his lips and poured Cuervo into his open mouth, being careful to spill some of it on his chin and shirt.

Then it was Frank's turn. When he got to the chugging part of the ritual, he poured half the Tequila down Lori's throat--then poured the other half on her head. Grabbing him behind his neck with both hands, Lori pulled his face up to hers and stuck her tongue in his mouth as she sucked his tongue into hers. Biting his tongue, she pressed her face firmly against his. Keeping her hands against the back of his head she crushed her lips against his as she continued to bite his tongue.

They stayed there until the bar closed at 2:00. Then he took her to the little motel which was one half of a block from the

Injection Pump. She followed him inside the door and watched him ring the buzzer. A young woman came up to the window to take his money. He asked the woman several questions most of which she could not answer. This surprised him as she looked Indian, and everyone he had ever met from India spoke good English. After he filled out the registration form, the woman pushed a button which unlocked the door. Lori followed Frank down the hallway to the room.

"Can't these people speak English? What's wrong with them?"

"Most of them do," replied Frank, "For most of them English is a primary language. I don't know how we ran into one who doesn't speak English."

He made love to her once. Then they lay in bed next to one another smoking and talking. Later, he scooped her up in his arms as he kissed her on the lips. Holding onto her tightly he got out of bed carrying her with him as he rose to his feet. She wrapped her legs around his waist as he carried her around the room. Finally he walked back to the bed, lowered her into it, and covered her body with his as he plunged inside her. This time he made it last a long time. He was still going strong long after she started to come. Afterwards they lay there for several minutes. Suddenly, without warning Lori got up, took a pillow off the bed, and started swinging it at Frank. He took the other pillow and went after her.

Tired of the pillow fight at last, Lori threw her pillow on the floor and raised her fists in the classic pose of the prize fighter. "Come on, Frank, let's see who's faster."

"That's easy," he replied, "that'll be me."

Then she went after him striking him in the face with an open left hand. He couldn't believe how fast she could move. *Not only is she fast--she also has all the moves. It's time she gets just a little hint of what I can do,* thought Frank. This time he was the aggressor, coming in with a little left jab at her face that he pulled at the last second. He feinted with his right as she raised an arm to block the blow. Then he came in quickly with the left, still open handed, but harder than he intended.

She had been good--good enough to put him at his best, but in the end instinct took over. He forgot for a moment that she was a woman. The left took her in the face before he could pull the punch. Although it was only a slap, it stung. Now it was Lori's instinct that took over. Turning inside of him as she brought her body into his, she brought her knee up into his groin. The blow took him by surprise almost putting him down. If he had wanted to he still felt strong enough to go after her.--barely. She had gotten him square in the testicles and it hurt. By the time she started to run out of the room he was feeling two things: pain and anguish over having struck her. Anguish prevailed over the pain for it was the longer lasting of the two.

"I'm getting the fuck away from you," she yelled. "I can't believe you would hit me like that."

He ran after her and threw himself in front of her. "God Lori, I'm so sorry. That's the last thing I want to do is to hurt you. I didn't mean it. I just got caught up in it and my instincts took over."

"That's the last time you're going to hit me."

"Look at it this way. We got in a pillow fight. Then we started to box open handed. One thing led to another. I didn't suddenly decide to beat up on you. The open hand just slipped out almost of its own accord. I've done a lot of boxing. I don't know if I've told you before, but I'll tell you this, and that's when you've done it awhile you don't even think when you see a punch coming. You just react. That was the whole trouble here--my instinct came out, and Lori, I'm so sorry. Look at it this way--you got me a hell of a lot better than I got you. I'll forgive you if you'll forgive me, okay?"

She tried hard not to, but in the end she couldn't help herself. She smiled a little smile at first, then she started to laugh. "Okay, I'll forgive you if you will allow me to kick you just one more time."

He took her back to the Shangrila half an hour before closing. They had two last drinks together, then he left her. As he pulled away in his car, he said to himself, *that's the worst part of it--leaving her. I just wish I never had to leave her.*

"Hi, what are you doing?" Lori asked.

Frank was on his way out the door when the phone rang at 8:30. Lucy had called at 3:30 and had asked him to visit her at the Sports Bar. He had been out in the field all day harvesting corn, but he had been able to check his messages from inside Ron's combine cab. Several years before, Ron had a radio tower installed on his farm. In his combine he had a special phone which broadcast its own radio signal to the tower which could be picked up by one of several portable phones which he kept in his pickup, tractor cab, or which he could carry around with him on his belt. The tower was connected to Ron's home phone so that what had started as a FM radio broadcast could be transmitted through the phone lines to any phone in the world. Ron could stand in the middle of a field and talk on one of his hand helds until his battery went dead without incurring any telephone usage charges if the call was local. The system had initially cost him six or seven thousand dollars, but once it was installed he had a free ride. Every hour or so Frank crawled in the combine with Ron to check his messages. *This is a good setup,* he thought. *I can use this phone to call my home phone number. When my announcement on my answering machine starts I punch in my access code and the machine replays my messages. The girls have my 800 number so they don't have to pay for their calls. The only thing that I still need is my own cellular phone. I can carry it with me in my tractors or pickup and always be in touch with them.* At 8:15 he had called the Sports Bar to tell Lucy he was coming.

"Lori, I was just going out the door. You barely got me."

"Can you come see me?"

"I can't. Somebody else called me earlier and I promised to see her. I wish you had called earlier."

"Oh, that's okay. I guess I'll see you some other time then." She tried hard not to sound disappointed, doing her utmost to sound upbeat, but she was not quite able to pull it off.

"I'll see you soon, but I just can't do it right now."

"Bye."

After he hung up, Frank reconsidered and called the Shangrila. A woman's voice answered the phone.

"Brittany just called me here at home," said Frank. "Please give her a message."

"What shall I tell her?" the woman asked.

"Tell her I am going to come see her tonight but that it will be late. Please do that. It's important."

"Okay. I'll tell her."

He was on his third beer when Lucy kicked him under the table. "Lighten up Frank. Come on." This time both cousins were sitting with him, Lucy becoming more talkative with each drink, Linda quietly sitting across from him sipping her drink as she studied him carefully.

"Sorry girls. I've been farming and putting in a lot of hours. I've worked the last seven days straight so you'll just have to excuse me."

"The real trouble with you Frank is Lori. You're infatuated with her, admit it. Oh, and by the way, don't think I didn't hear about your bringing her in here last week. Linda and the other girls told me all about it."

"That's because you never called me as you promised," said Frank. "If you and I had gotten together at my farm as we had planned, I would never have brought Lori into this bar."

"She's already got a husband Frank or a boyfriend who might as well be her husband," said Lucy.

" I don't know if they are getting along all that well," said Frank.

"She's with him, isn't she?"

"Yes, but . . . "

"Frank, she's either with him or she isn't. If she doesn't like him, she should get out. Has she gotten out?"

"No."

"Okay then. I don't like the fucking bitch."

"Why not? You don't even know her."

"There's something about her that I just don't like."

"Yeah. She's going out with me."

"No. It's more than that."

"Let me warn you, Lucy. Don't fuck with her. She'll fight you at the drop of a hat. She'll fight anybody."

"I'm not afraid of the little bitch. Am I Linda? She messes with me and I'll fuck her up."

"Frank, Lucy can take care of Lori. She's my cousin. I've seen her in action," said Linda.

"Take us both on a limo Frank. Linda and I will make you forget about Lori for a month."

"Oh, you think so," said Frank not quite believing what he had just heard.

"We'll make you smile for a week, won't we Linda?"

"If Lucy says so, then we will," said Linda. "You won't know what hit you."

"Take us on a limo, Frank. We need the money and you need to forget about Lori."

Frank thought about Lucy's offer. He would have to pay for both girls, and he really couldn't quite afford it. On the other hand, he could put it on his plastic. He had never had two girls at once, and he didn't know when the opportunity would come up again. *And how many times does a man have the chance to have sex with two cousins at the same time? And Lucy, who was shy little Miss Lucy during my first several encounters with her, is she really going to come out of the wood work and do it in front of her own cousin? This could get very interesting.*

All three of them took their clothes off at once. This time even Lucy dispensed with the "cigarette first" ritual. At first both girls played with him, stretching him out on the back seat of the limo as they took turns sucking him. After he got hard, Linda straddled his chest facing away from him as one of them, Frank thought it was Lucy, put on the rubber.

"Scoot on down him, Linda. Sit on his face while I fuck him."

Lucy got up on her knees next to Frank's knees, stroked him several times with her hand, and mounted him as Linda backed into his face. Spreading her upper legs Linda hovered over him, then gradually lowered her body until it rested upon his mouth. Because of Linda, Frank could not see Lucy thrusting up and down, slowly at first, then faster and faster as she became aroused. His attention became more focused on the closer woman straddling his face.

By the time the limo got back, he still had not finished. After the three of them went back into the bar, the two cousins disappeared. Frank bought himself a beer and waited for them. When they finally got back, it was as if they were done with him and it was time to get to the next dollar. He laughed to himself, *They said they'd do me so thoroughly that I'd forget about Lori. Well, I'm going to see her right now.*

His watch read 2:00 a.m. when he went up to her in the Shangrila Club. She was sitting at the bar with a middle-aged man who was slightly overweight. At first she ignored Frank, looking away from him as if she hadn't really seen him. Putting her arms around the customer's neck, Lori started to kiss him. Frank walked up to the bar, sat at one of the stools a few feet away from them, and got a beer from the bartender. He waited until Lori went up on stage. Then he took a seat in front of it. Lori smiled a little half smile before coming over to him as she sat on the edge of the platform touching her knees against his.

"Where have you been?" she asked.

"Over at the Sports Bar. Did you get my message?"

"What message?"

"I said I would come in, but that I wouldn't get here until late."

"No. No one told me that you called."

"I'm here."

"Finally."

He left her after two songs, went back to the bar, and sat next to her customer. "Hi, I'm Frank Harring."

The customer shook hands with him. "And I'm Doug Magill."

"It looks like you've gotten pretty well acquainted with Lori. I've known her now for one 1/2 years."

"And I just met her tonight."

"Doug, tell you what, I'll buy you a beer. What are you having?"

"Just get me a Bud."

Lori came back to the bar just as the bartender was bringing Doug his beer. She sat on the bar stool she had been sitting on earlier with Doug sitting between her and Frank. This time she edged up close to Doug, closer than she'd been sitting before. Ignoring her, Frank turned to Doug.

"Doug, have you spent much time at any other clubs?"

"Not really. I don't get out to them very often."

"Ever been to a place called the Sports Bar?"

"Can't say that I have. What's it like?"

"I like it a lot. They've got this limo there, and in the limo you can do anything you want with the girl."

"We're going to get a limo here also," Lori interrupted.

"Yeah, but the difference is that at the Sports Bar you can go on the limo today or tomorrow. You don't have a limo here, and that's what counts."

"What's the deal with the limo?" asked Doug.

"You pay the bar seventy bucks and make your own arrangements with the girl or girls. Normally the girl gets a hundred. The girl should screw you for that. Make sure you agree on that before you go on it with her. I just got back from doing a limo--with two girls at once." He couldn't help himself. Lori had not called him for a week. Then she called him at the last minute. Now she was trying to make him jealous. *Well, two can play that game*, he said to himself.

This time Frank looked over at Lori to see her reaction. It was obvious that she was seething although she was doing her best to cover it up. "There's a table over there," she said. "Let's take it." She looked at Doug, including him by the gesture but not Frank. Just then two girls walked in. Frank recognized them from the Sports Bar which must have just closed. Taking his beer with him he joined them at the other end of the bar. One of them was Promise, who had been trying to get him into the limo for weeks.

"Can I buy you two a drink?" he asked.

"Frank, what are you doing here?" asked Promise.

"Nipples." Frank motioned over to the table Lori and Doug had taken.

"You're still chasing her, aren't you?" asked Promise.

"Sort of."

"That's right. You did a limo tonight with Lucy and Linda."

"And I made sure Lori knows about it," said Frank.

"And she's making sure that she's going to get you jealous," said the other girl.

Frank looked back at Lori and Doug who were making out at the table. "Yes, but I don't think she's in love with him. Do you?"

"Not hardly," said the other girl.

"I'm telling you, urged Promise, "you should take me on a limo and forget her. She doesn't treat you right, Frank."

"And it could be said that right now I'm not treating her well either," Frank replied.

Half an hour later, both girls left, leaving Frank alone at the bar. He looked over at Lori and Doug who were by this time quietly sitting by themselves at the table. Then he noticed Doug fiddling with his coat, a sure sign that he was about to leave. He walked over to them.

"Doug, it's not closing time yet. You're not leaving are you?"

Lori gave him a dirty look--then thinking better of it--forced a smile. "Did you come over to buy me a drink, Frank? You haven't bought me one all night."

"What do you want?"

"Jack and Coke. I'm not up to a shot."

"Nice meeting you, Frank, I've really got to go," said Doug as he put on his coat.

"Nice meeting you, Doug. Try the Sports Bar sometime. I think you might like it," said Frank as Lori stiffened.

Frank went up to the bar and returned to Lori with her drink and a beer for himself. She bristled--took a little sip from her glass-- then chugged the rest. "Now get me another. You owe me one. You've been such an ass."

"You drive me to it Lori."

"Sure I do. Just like you can't help doing all of these limos."

"You should have called me earlier."

"What is this--a contest? What am I supposed to do, Frank?"

He motioned for the waitress who came over to take their drink order. After they ordered Lori stood up and took him by his arm. "Come on, let's dance."

"Right here!" said Frank.

"No, in the parking lot," she said, her voice seething with sarcasm. Then she pulled him from his chair and led him halfway to the bar. Luckily the song was a slow song as he didn't care to dance fast. Lori put her arms around his neck and pressed her body tightly against his. Then her body started to quiver. She tried to get it to stop. When she was unable to, she pressed herself into him tighter than ever.

Am I that drunk, Frank thought, *or is she really shaking? Lucy and Linda are in this whole thing for the money whereas this girl is real. She is flesh and blood, and she's very emotional right now. I can feel her flesh tingle against mine. I can feel her pain, and I can feel her like I haven't felt anyone for a long time. God, please do not let me forget this moment. Whatever happens tomorrow or some other day, this girl loves me-- at least she loves me today just as she has on other days.*

"Travis picking you up?" asked Frank.

"Yes. Unfortunately."

"That's too bad."

"Why?"

"I want to make love to you."

"But you just did, with two other women. Remember?"

"I didn't make love to them. I fucked them and they didn't even make me come. Lori, they are in it just for the money. There's a big difference between you and me and me and them. That became obvious tonight."

"I hope you learn someday."

"I think I just did. I came back to you."

"Travis has been coming here late. Maybe we can sneak out to your car and fuck each other before he gets here."

"Wait right here. I'm going out to move it to the other side of the building so he can't see it very easily," said Frank. "Then right at 4:00, earlier if you can make it, we'll go right out there."

He went out to move his car. Driving it to the side of the building he noticed there were some little flags set out. He drove over them so that he could get the little sports car as close to the building as possible which would make it difficult for Travis to see it. He started to feel a loss of traction after he had gone twenty feet. Looking behind him he saw the deep ruts his tires were cutting. *Mud! Goddamn it! I didn't even see it! Now I've gotta be stuck.* He slipped the car into reverse. The car didn't have much traction. It weighed only 2200 pounds, had rear wheel drive, and had tires that were meant for excellent handling instead of for navigating through snow or mud. The little car started to spin its tires; then as if by some miracle, started to grab hold. Slowly it started to gain momentum sliding from side to side as he backed it onto solid ground.

He went in and found her at the table. She leaned over and kissed him. "God, I hope he doesn't get here for a while."

"Why don't you just get rid of him?" suggested Frank. "He's nothing but a millstone around your neck."

"That's easier said than done."

Four o'clock arrived. Lori turned to him and said, "Frank, please go out and see if he's there." He got up to go out. There just outside the door he saw the yellow Grand Prix. A doorman stood just outside the door. Frank stayed and talked with him so that it would appear he had gone out to ask the man a few questions. Then he went back in.

"He's out there."

"Then I'd better go."

He waited inside, giving her enough time to get Travis out of the parking lot. The doorman asked him politely to leave, but when Frank explained to him why he wanted to stay an extra five minutes, the man nodded his head. Frank waited a few minutes as the place closed down. Then he went home.

UNCLE FRED

Once Lori had given him the phone number of a 55-year-old man she called her uncle Fred. She was staying there she had told him. The other girls had told him that he was not her uncle but a former customer who had ended up taking her out West for a week. A Christmas Party was coming up to which he wanted to take her and no one else. She had not called him for a week and he had to get hold of her. He dialed the number. A man's voice answered.

"Hello."

"Is this Fred?"

"Yes."

"Fred, this is Frank Haring. I believe we met briefly at one of the East side nightclubs. We're both good friends of Lori."

"Sure. I remember you, Frank."

"Fred, I understand that Lori's staying with you."

"On and off. She usually comes over when she and Travis are having trouble."

"I'm glad she's got someone like you," said Frank. "She needs someone to go to and I'm too far away."

"I wish she'd get away from this Travis. He's no good."

"Look, Fred. I'm going to go to a place in Collinsville called The White Kangaroo. If you hear from Lori, could you have her call me. Perhaps we can all meet there for a beer."

"I should hear from her this afternoon. I'll have her call you, Frank."

That night he was on his way to meet her at the White Kangaroo when his contacts started to give him trouble just as they had on the night of his DUI. He had never been to the White Kangaroo before. Suddenly it appeared on his left. By the time he could read the sign he had already driven by. He drove a mile up the road, saw a roadhouse, and started to turn around in its parking lot. He stared at the sign in disbelief which read Ducky's Paper Dolls and More. *Unbelievable.* Here he had just missed turning in because of blurred vision and the place he pulls into, just to turn around, ends up being a strip joint. Frank drove back to the White Kangaroo and went in.

He was almost an hour early. The bartender was a woman who had once worked with Lori at the Sports Bar, and he had gotten there early just to talk with her. The place was packed. The crowd was young, and he didn't know anyone with the exception of Patty, the bartender. He had a quick beer and found that the place was so busy that Patty was on the go constantly. Alone and bored in a strange place Frank decided that he was not going to sit alone at the bar like a lost barfly. *No, not him.* After telling Patty to tell Lori and Fred that he might be a little late, Frank drove to Ducky's Paper Dolls and More.

Just like me, he thought, as he walked in the door, *I wander into a strip joint without even trying. That should tell me something. Now I've got to stay away from these girls. Keep them out of my pocket. All I want is a quick beer and then I'm off to join Lori.* He went up to the bar. A tall skinny woman who seemed to be missing half her teeth went up to him.

"What can I get you?" she asked.

"Are you the bartender?"

"No. Oh, I can see that you've never been here before. Whichever girl you are with is responsible for getting you your drinks, and," she added after a slight pause, "any drinks you might get her."

"I'll have a Budweiser."

"And will you buy me a drink?" the woman asked.

"Sure. Go ahead," said Frank, not trying to let on that he was unhappy with the way things were progressing.

"Go ahead and sit down," said the woman.

Frank sat at a cheap table that was in front of the stage. Then he looked around and studied the place. All the tables were in front of the stage. They had to be since the place was that small. Only three girls were working, none of them very attractive. The bar was seedy, a typical roadhouse, which made it his kind of place except that it was a strip bar and the women would end up hounding him for money. His girl--he supposed that she was his girl now--came back with the drinks, a Budweiser for him and a scotch and soda for herself.

The woman pulled up a chair across from him. Like most of the women he had met in the East Side bars, she was pleasant to talk with, telling him about her three divorces and how she had gotten started dancing. She rolled up her eyes as he told her about the soap opera that was his divorce and empathized with him throughout his story. Then she got up to dance.

She looked down at him from the stage, smiling, her mouth half empty from the missing teeth. He smiled back at her wishing he had already left. *Now how did I get into this?* Here he was spending money to watch this woman dance or to spend time with him and in just a few minutes he was meeting Lori, in his book the top stripper of all his experiences?

She asked him for another scotch and water when she came off the stage. Buying her the drink, he told her that he had to meet Lori in a few minutes, politely excused himself, and left. When he got back to The White Kangaroo, he found Lori and Fred already standing at the bar. Lori saw him come in and ran up to him.

"Let's get a table. Guess what, Frank, I just set up Uncle Fred."

"You what?" asked Frank. Then he noticed that there was another person who had been standing next to Lori and Fred. The tall brunette was young, in her early twenties, slightly overweight (by Frank's standards but hardly so by anyone else's), and ample in the bosom. Lori took Frank's hand and led him to a table that was next to a large window. The brunette walked over to them followed by Uncle Fred.

"You must be Lori's Uncle Fred," said Frank.

"Right. I'm her Uncle Fred," the man said with a touch of sarcasm. "That's what she calls me." Then he put his arm around the brunette and nodded toward her. "This is Peach. Lori just introduced me to her. They work together."

Peach took Frank's hand and shook it. "Glad to meet you Frank. I've heard a lot about you."

"Good or bad?" Frank asked.

"Oh all good," said Peach. "Lori would never say anything bad about you, would you Lori?"

"Yeah, except when he dressed up like a school board member and came to my house with his hair dyed black or when he tried to kill me in his tractor," said Lori, her eyes lighting up as she recounted the past.

They almost ordered food, but when the waitress told them it would be awhile, decided to wait until later. Several drinks later, it was Lori who decided on the game of pool. They played as teams, Lori and Frank taking on Uncle Fred and Peach. Every time Uncle Fred lined up for a shot, Lori would watch, mentioning something to Frank about Uncle Fred each time.

"Fred didn't use to play pool until he met me," said Lori. "Now watch him shoot. See, he's got a nice touch. He made it. Good. I taught him how to play pool. The trouble is I think he's better than me."

"No Lori. No one's better than you," said Frank. Then after a slight pause. "Except for me."

"Bullshit. You're not better than me, and you know it."

"Just watch me then. I'll show you who's king of the hill."

It was Frank's turn to shoot. He was shooting at the six which was a straight shot into the right corner pocket. The queue ball was almost up against the back rail which made for a long shot. Frank wished it was not a straight shot. That way he would have an excuse if he missed. He considered himself a mediocre shooter when it came to shots like this. Just then, as he stooped over lining himself up for the shot, Lori came up behind him, pressed her groin up to his rear end, and started to hump him. He missed the shot.

Fred hunched over the table looking older than he actually was. He made the next three shots, shooting deliberately as he moved slowly to whatever side of the table the queue ball ended up at. Then he missed and it was Lori's turn. Lori made her next two shots, then missed a bank shot to the side pocket. Peach missed an easy shot and it was Frank's turn. He borrowed a cigarette from Lori, lit it, and stuffed it into his mouth. The first ball was up tight against the rail. Frank hit it just right, gently tapping it on the far left side so that the queue ball hit it and the rail simultaneously. It went into the right corner. Lori nodded with approval. His next shot was a long one--the ten ball into the left corner. This time he did not miss. This left the twelve which was lined up close to the right side pocket. He knew that side shots were difficult leaving little room for error unless the ball was lined up so that it could be shot straight in. This one wasn't. The side pocket presented a narrow angle requiring a perfect shot. He lined up, cigarette dangling from his mouth, and shot with a soft touch. The ball went in, which left the eight. Frank called the shot, an easy one to the left corner, and made it.

He looked over at Lori who was beaming. This time he could read her mind. He was her boyfriend after all, and he had just shown both Fred and Peach that he could shoot pool. Others too had seen the game. A number of young men and a few girls in their early twenties stood around close to the pool tables watching. *Her Frank had just put on a good show for everyone.* The music was blaring loudly out of the jukebox. The selection changed to one that she liked. Without saying a word she took him out to the middle of the room and started dancing. Suddenly she pulled close to him and pressed herself up tightly against him as she humped him to the beat of the music. She reached down to fondle him as more people started to watch them.

"Come on. Let's go over there." She pointed toward a little alcove which was occupied by several small tables and a dart board. Four or five young men and women were playing darts there. Otherwise, the alcove was unoccupied. "Let's leave Fred and Peach to get better acquainted. It's their first date." She went over to one of the tables and sat down where he joined her. A waitress took their drink order and returned with two beers.

"I thought that you and your Uncle Fred were going out," said Frank.

"Fred and I. You've got to be kidding me!" Lori replied incredulously.

"I just heard it from the other girls," said Frank.

"What would I be doing with an older man like him?" she replied. "No. I like him and all that, but I'm not fucking him."

"So. He's not your uncle after all."

"How would you know?"

"Because you said you wouldn't fuck an older man like him. You didn't say that you wouldn't because he's your uncle. So he is an ex customer of yours after all."

"Okay, so he is, but I'm not fucking him."

"I've got an idea," suggested Frank. "Let's go to the Sports Bar. I bet that I can talk to Bill and talk him into getting your old job back."

"Think you can?"

"I've got a good chance. What do you say that we try?"

Lori was able to talk Fred and Peach into meeting them at the Sports Bar. She and Frank pulled into the Sports Bar's parking lot but there was no Uncle Fred. They had to wait five minutes for him. The red mustang finally pulled in and the four went in together.

"I thought Fred and Peach would get here first," said Lori.

"I didn't," said Frank.

"Why not."

"Because my car's faster than his," said Frank.

"You weren't driving it that fast," said Lori.

"I was driving eighty on the interstate," said Frank.

"I didn't notice. What! You were driving eighty on your suspension?"

"I know. I'm not supposed to be driving for 30 days because of the mandatory suspension. But what the hell," said Frank. "The law also told me that I had to pay Karen's attorney's fees. FUCK

THE LAW."

Lori left him for five minutes to go into the lady's room. Linda found him buying a pack of cigarettes out of the cigarette machine. "How can you bring her in here?" she asked.

"What do you mean?" asked Frank.

"Nipples. That's who I mean. My cousin's not here. You're lucky on that, but you know and I know that the other girls will tell her that you were out with Nipples and that you brought her in here."

"Look, Linda, I wouldn't do this sort of thing, but you've got to figure that Lucy has stood me up several times. In fact, she hasn't made a single date with me yet, so the way I figure it, I don't owe her a thing."

"And Nipples has never let you down? Come on Frank, we both know better than that. You know my cousin likes you."

"She doesn't show it when she stands me up. Besides, Nipples isn't standing me up like she used to. She doesn't charge me for sleeping with her like some of the other girls including your cousin. We've known each other for a year and a half now, and we've had a lot of fun together. Now if your cousin really wants to get to know me, she's going to just have to try as hard as Nipples has."

"I guess you have a point there," Linda conceded.

Lori came out of the Ladies room, saw at a glance that Frank was talking to one of the dancers, and came right over. Linda left for the dressing room.

"Wait right here," said Frank. "I almost forgot our main reason for being here, and that is I promised to talk with Bill."

He found Bill standing at the other end of the bar talking to one of the waitresses. "Bill, you know what you need to do?"

"What do I need to do, Frank?"

"You need to hire Nipples back."

"Why should I do that Frank?"

"Because she's a top draw, that's why. She'll pull a lot of men in here."

"I like to sleep at night. The minute I hire Nipples back, I've got problems. When I go home, I like to sit in my lazy boy and relax. When I've got her working for me, somebody's always calling me to say there's a problem. She's either started a fight or she's instigated something that gets someone in trouble."

"Okay, I'll give you that Bill. So she's trouble. What would the television series Dallas have been without JR? Without Larry Hagman it would have folded right away. And what would history be without Attila the Hun or Genghis Khan? Now Bill, you have the opportunity to hire the Attila the Hun of strippers. You might lose a little sleep but we'll all have fun and you'll make even more money than ever."

"Well, I'll think about it.

Lori was talking to one of the other dancers about doing a Christmas Party when Frank returned. "Did you talk to him?" she asked.

"Yes. He said he'd think about it."

"I'm going to go talk to him about it right now," said Lori.

Suddenly she was gone and he was left talking to the dancer. Her name was April. She was brown headed, reasonably attractive, and very sharp. He had talked to her on several occasions and had found out that not only was she sharp, but that she was a woman of her word, which was rare among dancers.

"So, you're going to do a party with Lori?" he asked.

"Yes. We've done one before together, and we just had a blast. Nipples kept me in stitches the whole time."

"Why do you like doing them with her?"

"Because she really doesn't care what others think."

"So she gets pretty wild when she entertains at a party."

"Definitely, but then we both do. I can get just as bad, especially when we are together. I'd stay here and talk with you Frank, but I've got a customer waiting on me. Besides, you're with Lori. Speaking of the devil, here she comes."

"I'm never going to get my job back!" Lori exclaimed.

"Why not?" asked Frank.

"Bill just mentioned that he could not rehire me because of my calling all of the other girls a bunch of holes. Then he mentioned that he might reconsider if I'd fuck him. I might as well fuck him and get it over with. I want my old job back."

"He'll rehire you anyway if you're persistent enough."

"No, he won't."

"Well, don't fuck him. He won't respect you if you do that and you won't respect yourself."

"I might have to."

"It's up to you." The thought of Lori putting out for Bill was disgusting. The idea that any man could exert such power over a woman, especially if that woman were his Lori, was sad. Then he thought how he once thought he could come into these places and buy the women. It all seemed so far away now that he had become friends with them. He didn't want to buy these girls--not anymore. He wanted to drink with them, talk with them, and to party with them--not bludgeon them into going to bed with him for money.

They closed the place after which he took her to the little motel that was next to the Injection Pump. He would have preferred spending the night with her at his farm. Instead he ended up taking her to Fred's and returned home alone.

The date with Lucy had been planned for tonight. Then she had called him to tell him that she could not spend the night with him on Friday but that she could on Saturday. This meant that he didn't have anything planned on Friday, so he told her he'd see her at work.

Frank pulled into the parking lot and walked toward the door of the Sports Bar. Before he even reached the door, a voice called out to him from inside: "Hey Frank, guess who's here?" Then Cindy came to the door. "Nipples is inside."

Lori was just inside the door, standing at the bar smiling at him. "Come on outside Frank, there's something I've got to show you," she said unable to hide her excitement.

"What are you doing here, Lori?"

"I came to see you. I figured the chances would be good that you'd be here. I just bought a new car. Come on. I've got to show it to you."

He followed her into the parking lot to a dark blue Pontiac Grand Prix. Lori got in behind the wheel and leaned over to open the passenger door for him. The car was nearly ten years old, but it had a CD player in it. Lori brought out her cds, put one in the player, turned the ignition on, and started the player. Loud music started to come from the car's four speakers.

"See, I've got my own wheels now," Lori said proudly.

Frank listened to the selection. Before it had finished, Lori pushed a button which started another. "Come on," he shouted, "I've got something to show you in my car." Then he took her to the little sports car to show her his cellular phone.

"Just got it today--on the way over here in fact," said Frank. "Let's see if we can check my messages." He dialed his home number. After four rings his answering machine answered. He dialed the access code after which a synthesized voice cut in stating "There are no new messages." He hung up and dialed his number again after which he handed the receiver to Lori. She hung up thirty seconds later.

"That's pretty cool."

"I don't know if I've mentioned it, but that same voice that said there were no new messages, announces each message, if there are any, and gives the time of the call. Let' say you called at 6:19 p.m. and you left a message that you were at a certain phone number and I retrieved my messages at 7:00 p.m., I would have a pretty good idea that you might still be there. I can plug this phone into my car, my truck, or into any of my tractor's and stay in touch with you Lori."

"You'll have to give me the number of that phone," said Lori.

"There's something else I have to talk to you about," said Frank. Suddenly he got very serious. "Lucy called me up on the phone tonight and I promised her that I'd come in to see her. You know me, Lori--I've got to keep that promise. So I have to stay with her for a while. Perhaps you and I can meet somewhere else later."

"Sure. We can do that. Where?"

"How about next door at the Swinger's Club?"

"That'll work. I'll go over there and wait for you."

"Stay over there, Lori. I'll come. I promise. But it might be awhile-- possibly as long as a couple of hours."

"I'll be there, Frank. Just come in when you're ready."

They went back inside where Frank found Lucy and Linda sitting at a table with a man who was around ten years younger than Frank. Lori went up to the bar, bought herself a drink, and talked with two of the dancers. Frank looked across the table at the man who had been talking to Linda and grinned, stretching out his hand.

"Hi, I'm Frank Harring."

"My name's Alan. Alan Rickoff."

"Known these two for long Alan?"

"I've known them for a few years now."

"He thinks that gives him the privilege of giving us advice all the time," said Lucy. "He's the one who needs the advice however."

Just then one of the girls who had been talking with Lori came over to their table and motioned for Lucy to follow her to the dressing room. Lucy excused herself and followed the girl. A few minutes later she came back, her face red with anger. "Why that goddamn bitch!" she shouted.

"Who's a bitch?" Alan asked. Then he turned to Frank. "I don't see a bitch. Do you?"

"Knock it off Alan," said Lucy. Then looking directly at Frank: "That goddamn bitch friend of yours--You know what she's telling the girls in here?"

"I wouldn't have the slightest," Frank replied.

"She's told them that you're her husband, and then she said, "What's that whore over there doing with him?""

"She said that," said Frank. "You have got to be shitting me?"

"No, I am not!" Lucy exclaimed. "Where is that bitch? I'm

going to kill her fucking ass!"

"I don't see her," said Alan. "She's probably left. Pretty wise of her to flee the scene of the crime. Now Lucy, I think you had better calm down."

"Yes Dad," Lucy said derisively.

Linda went off to another table to sit with one of her customers. A few minutes later Lucy disappeared. Frank bought Alan a beer and ordered another Budweiser for himself. By the time he had finished it, Lucy still had not come back. He went into the backroom and saw her sitting at a table full of people. *Lucy*, he said to himself, *it's a competitive world out there. You just don't know how competitive*. Then he went next door.

Lori was sitting at the front bar drinking with the bartender, who was an attractive plump blonde around thirty. Frank walked up to Lori and stood next to her. Lori turned around, put her arm around his neck, and addressed the blonde. "Frank's buying me the next drink. Make it a shot of Cuervo and get him a Budweiser."

Five minutes passed after which he looked at her and asked: "Lori, shall we go in the back? I've never been back there before."

"Sure, follow me. I'll show you."

The front bar was a typical neighborhood pub. Frank had been inside a number of times before. Many of the dancers from the Sports Bar went there to drink after hours, and Frank had gone with them on several occasions. A small room adjoined the main room just to its rear. This room was open to the main bar and had a pool table and two small tables inside. The next room was behind this room. There was a small door leading to it which was shut against anyone who might casually walk in. Behind this door was the Swinger's Club. Frank followed Lori inside. In front of them was another bar. They sat down across next to each other on the bar stools still drinking. Frank noticed that they were the only people in the room. A pornographic movie was playing on a wide screen television just behind them. A man in his middle thirties came into the room from the main bar. It was Greg, who managed the bar for Bill.

"Do you need anything?" Greg asked.

"No. We brought our drinks with us," Lori replied.

"I'm going back into the main bar," said Greg. "If you need anything, holler."

"Anyone in the hot tub?" asked Lori.

"I think so," said Greg. "Why don't you check and find out?"

They finished their drinks together after which Lori went off to find Greg. She returned to the bar. A few minutes later Greg brought them a Jack and Coke and another beer for Frank. Then he went back inside the main bar. Lori disappeared behind a door that Frank assumed went to the hot tub room and came back a few seconds later.

"He's right. There are people in it, but I think they are about to get out."

A few minutes later, they both went in. A fat black woman stood naked in front of them, drying herself off with a towel. "Welcome to the dressing room," she said. "The hot tubs in there. They're coming right out." The woman pointed to a small room accommodating a small hot tub. A man and a woman, both fat, were just getting out of the hot tub. Frank and Lori slipped by them, took off their clothes, and got into the hot water.

Lori sat in the water at the opposite end from Frank. The tub was large enough to hold perhaps six people and no more. Frank was surprised that she didn't come over to him. He had never been to a Swinger's Club before, but he had always figured that the truth was different from the myth, the myth being that a lot of high powered attractive people went to swingers clubs to switch to different partners. Frank had always assumed the opposite--that a truly attractive man, who had an attractive partner, would not want to take her to a swinger's club to share her with others. He, for one. would never have considered taking Lori to one with the intention of trading her off for someone else.   "I think I'm going to get sick," said Lori.

"Why?"

"Take a look, that's why." She nodded toward the dressing room which was behind Frank's back.

The door to the dressing room was open. Because the room was behind him, he could not observe what was going on there. Lori, sitting opposite him in the hot tub and facing him, could see everything that was happening there. Just outside the door was an old couch. The fat man was lying naked on the couch while the black woman nestled next to it on her knees. The man's penis stood stiffly away from his fat gut in full view of Lori. The fat black woman bent over, put his penis in her mouth and sucked it enthusiastically. Then the fat white woman climbed on top of the man and pressed her head into his groin. Waving the black woman off she started to give the man a blow job.

"Let's get out of here," said Lori. "I've seen enough."

They returned to the bar where they had another drink. Lori looked at her watch, then looked up at Frank. "You've been over here a long time. If I was Lucy, I'd be getting pretty upset. Perhaps you should go over to her for a while. I'll wait for you in the front bar. When you come back, I want to fuck you in my car."

"Where?"

"In the car. It doesn't matter where. In the parking lot for all I care. I just want to fuck you."

Lucy, Linda, and Alan were sitting together at a table close to the stage. One and a half hours had passed since he had last seen them. Frank pulled up a chair and sat down, then looked up at all of them in order to observe their reactions to his late arrival. Alan was studying him carefully, a half-smile on his face.

"Where have you been, Frank?" Alan asked. "I notice that your hair is wet. How'd that happen?"

"My hair? Wet?" asked Frank, feigning surprise. "Is it wet?"

"Yes, it is wet," said Lucy. "You've been next door, haven't you--with that little bitch?"

"Yeah, I went next door, and she just happened to be there."

"See. I knew it," said Lucy.

"Lucy, you've got to figure that I get bored very easily," said Frank. "When I was in here, you took off to a different table leaving me to entertain myself. So, I just went next door to entertain myself."

Frank bought Lucy a drink and a Budweiser for himself. When they finished their drinks he pulled her over to him and whispered in her ear: "Lucy, I've got to be shoving off. I don't want to stay out late since I've got to get up early tomorrow morning not to mention our date tomorrow night."

"You've got to get going because you're going back next door to that bar to meet her. If you do that Frank, you can forget our date tomorrow night. As a matter of fact, you can forget the whole thing. I mean it!"

"Okay, okay. I'll go next door and tell her. Then I'm coming back here."

He went next door, the bar being less than a hundred yards away from the Sports Bar. He found Lori seated at the bar, drinking and laughing with the blonde bartender. Then he noticed the big man sitting to Lori's left. It was the same man who, on the night of his Dui, had chased Frank around the parking lot at Gals--all 275

491

pounds of him.

"Lori, look I'm sorry, but I can't go with you tonight. I promised Lucy I'd visit her tonight, and when I just told her that I had to leave she knew I was coming over here to you. She's really upset and I just can't do that to her. I knew that you'd understand . . . "

"Get away from me Frank." Lori scooted her stool away from Frank's. "Just stay the fuck away from me."

"Hey, is he giving you trouble?" the large man asked Lori.

"He's being a pain in the ass as always."

The blonde who was tending bar came out from behind the bar and stood next to Lori. Lori got off her stool, put her arms around the blonde, and started to cry. The blonde looked over at Frank and said: "I'm sorry Frank, but you've got to leave. She was having a good time drinking and laughing and dancing on the bar even, and then you had to come in and make her cry."

"But I didn't do anything," said Frank.

"Yes you did. You made her cry, and she's my friend, so you will just have to leave."

"You heard the lady," said the large man. "Now leave."

"Okay," said Frank. "I'm leaving. In fact, I'm gone." He gave Lori a dirty look and walked out the door.

He had been sitting with Lucy, Linda, and Alan for no more than thirty minutes when Lori walked in with the large man. Walking past the bar and refusing to acknowledge Frank or his companions, they went into the back room. Frank had two more beers, buying Lucy several more drinks at the same time. He had not seen anything more of either Lori or the large man so he assumed that they were still in the back room. Finally, close to closing time, Lucy excused herself and went into the dressing room to change. It was a quarter to four.

The timing is right, he told himself. *I've done enough damage for one night. Think I'll slip out of here unobserved. That way neither girl will be able to accuse me of staying with the other.* He went to the bar alone where he spent a few moments finishing his beer. Then he went outside.

Oh shit, there she is, he thought. *How'd she know I was leaving?* There, across the parking lot Lori stood next to his sports car, her right hand resting on the soft top. She stood there facing him, a big grin on her face. "Let's go, Frank. I'm ready to go somewhere else," she called out. Then he saw the two dancers who stood talking next to another car close to where Lori was standing. It was Julie and another dancer, and Julie was the worse girl to see him leave with Lori. Julie would be sure to tell Lucy. She'd tell her out of spite, just to stir things up.

Frank hurried over to his car, looked at Lori, and said "Get in. Right now."

Lori got in the car as he pulled behind the wheel. "We're getting out of here, immediately. I don't want Lucy to see us leaving together. By the way, how'd you know I was leaving the bar?"

"Simple, I was watching you. I saw you go to the bar for that last little swig or two. I know you too well, Frank."

"We're going to drive around for a while. It doesn't matter where just so long as we give her enough time to get out of the bar."

Fifteen minutes later he drove her back to her car which was still parked at the Sports Bar. He followed her into her car and she drove them to the Swinger's Club parking lot. After she stopped, he put his arm around her and started to kiss her. He undid his jeans as she took off hers. Then he reached up underneath her and gently lifted her up onto his lap. He slid in easily. Afterwards he took her to the hotel and they did it again.

PIECE OF SHIT CAR

Janey sat at the bar sipping the Bloody Mary he had just bought her. Janey's eyes almost had that far away look some girls have who are not quite there but somewhere else. But Janey was there perceptive to her surroundings and to what was being said. The eyes, Frank decided, were those of a woman who had been around, who had seen much, and who had been tender enough to be affected by each tragedy, great and small throughout all the years.

"I've got to leave right after this drink," said Janey. "Bill won't let the day shift hang around for more than half an hour after eight. The night shift figures we're interfering with their customers, and they're right."

"Then let's go next door," said Frank. "I've always wanted to have a few with you Janey, but it just seems we've never been able to do it for some reason or another."

"I can do that," Janey replied. "I don't have to be home tonight until late."

They sat at the front bar next door drinking together. The Swinger's Club in the back was open, but Janey and he were friends, not lovers. Besides, Frank had heard from the other girls that Janey didn't do limos, that she didn't do nasty things with the customers, and he respected her for that.

"Janey, I have offered to take Nipples on a ski trip. We went to Springfield last September to the Springfield Ski Club Wine and Cheese party and I signed her up as a member. She's getting their newsletter every month in the mail. We didn't sign up for any of the trips, but I promised to take her to Sun Valley, Idaho, and I meant it."

"She went out to Las Vegas to gamble with Fred. They were out there for a week together," said Janey.

"I predict that she won't go with me. I really want her to go, and I keep reminding her of the trip, but I believe that Lori would rather grab a piece of shit with both hands than grab a diamond with one. She's going to blow this thing somehow because . . . somehow . . . she doesn't think she deserves it."

"Well, if it were me, I'd be out reaching for the diamond with both hands," Janey replied.

"I really want to take her. And if we'd have a good time, I'd probably take her somewhere else the next year. You never know what this could lead to. She is such an athlete. She really doesn't know what talent she has, and she probably never will know because as long as she limits herself to Travis and his little world and the kind of friends he keeps, she'll never know what could be available to her."

"Frank, why don't we go to the White Kangaroo in Collinsville," Janey suggested.

"Sure, why not?" Then he thought about his DUI. *Yeah,* he wondered, *who's driving?*

"Tell you what. Let's leave right now. You follow me in your pickup to my house, and I'll leave my car there. Then we'll go together in your pickup to Collinsville."

Sounds like DUI number two thought Frank. *No, they won't even bother about the second DUI. They'll just lock me up for driving during the 30-day mandatory suspension and I'll be SCREWED, SCREWED, SCREWED.* Then he laughed to himself. *But I'm Frank Harring, and I can do anything I want so fuck them.*

They walked next door to the Sports Bar to their vehicles. Janey was about to get into her car, stopped just before getting in as if she had forgotten something, then came over to Frank. "Tell you what, Frank, why don't we switch vehicles. I drive your truck, and you follow me in my piece of shit car."

They exchanged keys and he followed her out of the parking lot, thinking *this is not a good idea.* He followed her out to route 64 and into the West bound lanes. Then she took off. He hadn't paid attention to what he was driving--it was an older car and that had been that. He was now driving 75 miles an hour and she was still pulling ahead of him. *75 miles per hour in a 55. I'm going to get caught and then it's hello jail.*

All he could do was to keep her in sight. The car's handling was sloppy, and Frank could barely keep it on the road let alone weave in and out of traffic with it. And here he was approaching the Poplar Street Bridge over to the Missouri side--and she still wasn't slowing down. *This must be Lori's cousin*, he thought. *Wild and reckless--shades of Nipples.* They crossed the bridge--how he kept the car from hitting one of the concrete embankments on the way over--he'd never know--and they got on I-55 going South. By now the pickup was three quarters of a mile ahead of him. He tromped on the gas in order to close some of the distance. After all, he had no idea where she lived and he couldn't afford to lose her.

Suddenly, the car died. The engine just quit and he started to coast. As the car slowly came to a dead stop he tried to restart the engine several times but the thing would not fire. Frank flipped on the emergency blinkers and waited for Janey to turn around and come back to him. Surely she would realize that he was not behind her, take the first exit, and drive back to look for him, he thought. Five minutes passed, and still no Janey. Suddenly the thought crossed his mind of a helpful cop pulling over to help him. The police officer would probably smell the alcohol on him and then ask him for his driver's licence. And then the big trouble would start. He waited two more minutes, then decided to bail out.

He started to run along the shoulder of the interstate. Frank ran perhaps a mile to the first exit, as the cars whizzed by him, only to discover that he had probably found the only exit off 55 in St. Louis that didn't have a gas station nearby. He found himself running off the highway into nowhere land. No gas station, no restaurant, no phones, no nothing. He ran another half mile down the city streets, past vacant lots, and through a neighborhood of small brick homes. Then he saw the diner, which thankfully still had its lights on. He ran inside all out of breath.

"Can someone help me?" Frank gasped. "I've got a car down the road that needs to be towed. Anyone know of a tow truck nearby?"

"There's a gas station just one block up the street," a woman behind the counter said. "The owner's got a tow truck and he's still there."

A man stood behind the counter with the woman. Frank sized them up as the diner's owner and the owner's wife. "What kind of car is it?" asked the owner.

"I don't know," Frank said. "Some kind of piece of shit car."

"You mean you don't know what you're driving?" asked the woman.

"That's right," said Frank. "However, I know where it's at. It's out on 55 on the southbound lanes just one mile before you come up to this exit."

"How come you don't know what kind of car it is?" asked the owner.

"Because it belongs to this topless dancer. She's driving my pickup truck and I'm following her in her car when suddenly her engine quits on me."

"Did you just say you were following a topless dancer?" asked the owner.

"Yes. She's in my pickup," said Frank.

"Well, you can kiss that pickup goodbye," said the owner's

wife.

"I don't think so," Frank replied. "I've known this woman for a year and a half. I know where she works. The only thing I don't know is where she lives."

"Aha," the woman replied knowingly, "She's got your pickup. She'll quit her job tomorrow and you'll never find her or your pickup again."

"These topless dancers, they're all alike," said the owner.

"I think you're wrong," answered Frank. "Look, I've had a lot to drink. So has she. Will one of you call the gas station and put me on the phone?"

The man took a phone book out from behind the counter, looked up the number, and dialed. Then he handed the phone to Frank. A man's voice answered.

"Shelby Mobil."

"I'm stranded at the diner down the street from you," said Frank. "The car I was driving just quit on 55 and I ran down here. Can you pick me up and I'll take you to it?"

"What kind of car is it?" the man asked.

"I don't know," Frank answered. "A piece of shit car if you ask me."

"Where do you want it towed to?"

"I don't know," said Frank. "Look, I know this conversation might seem odd to you, but why don't you just bring your tow truck down here. I've got a Chicago Motorists Card and plenty of cash so I'll just explain everything when you get here."

"Okay. I'll be right over."

Frank sat next to the driver in the tow truck and directed him to Janey's car. Then he told the man his story. They got onto the North bound lanes of the highway and soon saw that there were two vehicles where he had left Janey's car. The emergency blinkers of both vehicles were flashing. The gas station owner took the next exit off the highway, merged onto the Southbound lanes and came up behind Frank's truck which was parked behind Janey's car.

Janey got out of the pickup and ran up to the wrecker. "I didn't leave you Frank. I was wondering what happened. Suddenly you weren't behind me, and I came back looking for you."

"I knew you wouldn't leave me in the lurch Janey. The people over at the diner said you would since I told them you were a topless dancer, but I said that you were a good friend of mine and that you wouldn't."

"No baby, I wouldn't ever do that to you."

"Where do you want it towed to?" asked the man.

"To my house," said Janey. "Just follow us."

Janey lived four miles away. She had Frank park on the street next to her house and directed the tow truck owner to her driveway. He took the car off the hoist there and went up to Frank.

"I'm paying this," said Frank. "How much do we owe you?"

"Seven dollars," said the man.

"Here's seven," Frank said surprised that towing a car 4 miles would be so inexpensive, "and here's another eight for your trouble." He reached into his pocket and paid the man. The owner then got into the wrecker and drove off leaving Janey and Frank just outside Janey's house.

"Nothing's changed, Janey. We are still going to Collinsville," said Frank.

"Do you want to come in for a few minutes, Frank?"

"Sure. Is your husband home?"

"No, of course not. Come on. Follow me."

The place was well kept. There was a small living room, a single bathroom, a kitchen, a bedroom, and a utility room--enough for two people. Janey directed him to a picture that was hanging on the wall of the living room. "That's my son. He's only twenty years old. And now he's in the pen," she said sadly.

"What happened?" asked Frank.

"He was with the wrong people when they committed a robbery. He says he had no part in it but was with them when they suddenly pulled into a store to rob it. My son didn't know what had happened until it was all over. He sent me a six page letter for my birthday. I still have it. I shouldn't dwell on all that. Come on Frank. Now that you've seen where I live, we've got some serious drinking to catch up on. Let's get going."

The White Kangaroo was crowded. Janey walked in just ahead of him, saw Patty tending bar, and rushed up to her going behind the bar where she threw her arms around her. "Patty, I was hoping you would be tending bar."

They had several more drinks there; then they decided to go back to the Sports Bar. Mary, the bartender on duty tonight, ran up to them as soon as they walked in. "Frank, Nipples has been calling here ever since you've left. She must have called three times already. Said it's a matter of life and death."

"You're shitting me Mary. Nipples hasn't been calling here for me. How would she know that I'd be here?"

"Because you're here a lot, Frank, that's why. She knows that."

"I think you are full of it Mary."

"No, I'm not. Just ask Bill."

Frank noticed that Bill was standing several stools over from him at the bar. *Surely, Bill wouldn't lie to me*, he thought. *Mary might. After all, she is one of my favorite bartenders and she probably knows it.* She always recognized Frank's voice whenever he called and ended up kidding him as much as he kidded her.

Going up to Bill, he asked: "Bill, has Nipples been calling me?"

"Called three times," Bill replied. "I don't know what she sees in you but she must see something. I've tried to get her to fuck me before, but I've never been successful."

"Well, I think you're both bullshitting me," Frank replied. *Maybe she has been trying to call me*, he thought. *Chasing me down--God, I hate that in a woman. But I feel good about her doing it--her feeling dependent upon me. Something about her that's special that enables her to break all the rules--something very special about that girl, and I don't know what it is.*

Half an hour later the place closed. Frank took Janey home, walked her to her door, then went back to his pickup. He got home a little after five Saturday morning, went into the kitchen to make English muffins, and went into his office to check his messages. There were three of them, one from Lori, one from Lucy, and one from Tamara. He heard the toaster pop and went back to pull the muffins out, and then he heard the phone ring.

A woman's voice answered: "Frank, what are you doing?"

"Who is this?" he asked.

"Take a good guess," said the voice.

"Lucy?"

"You asshole."

"Lori then. Sorry to call you Lucy, but she called and left a message."

"I need you Frank. Will you come and see me?"

"I just got in from the Sports Bar and I'm still drunk and tired. How about some other time?"

"It's real important. As in life and death."

"Lori, it will be my death getting back on the road in my

condition."

"Frank, you told me once that you would do anything for me if I really needed you. Well, I really need you. Will you please come get me?"

"All right, Lori. I'll get in the car right away. Where shall I meet you?"

"At the gas station just off of 55. You know the one."

"I'll be there in one hour and fifteen minutes."

It was the same gas station they had planned to use as a meeting place months earlier at the Pink Giraffe only this time she showed up. Frank had just finished paying for a large coffee when he saw Lori walking up the street. *One can say this for her,* he thought as he watched her striding toward him, *she's totally unpampered. She will walk, run, hitch a ride, and do whatever it takes to get to where she wants to go.*

"Where'd you just walk from?" he asked as she came in the station.

"Uncle Fred's. That's where I called you from. Let's go back there for a little while."

"Okay, but just for a little while."

"He's got a new girl friend since I set him up with Peach. She's only twenty years old. You're about to meet her."

They went into the apartment into a small living room. A young woman sat in her bathrobe on the couch drinking a cup of coffee. The girl had brown hair, blue eyes, was ten pounds overweight, and looked--only twenty. Seeing Lori again the girl grinned. Frank liked her from the start.

"Back already?" the young woman asked.

"Rose, this is my friend Frank."

Rose climbed off the couch, came up to Frank, and shook his hand. *Very rare,* thought Frank, *for a woman to shake my hand, and rarer still for a woman to get off a comfortable couch to greet a man. This girl is one I feel at home with instantly.*

"Where's Fred?" asked Lori. "Still asleep?"

"You've got it. I tried to get him up, but he had to work late, so I passed."

"Let's get him up," said Lori. "It's time to party. Come on Rose, let's get him out of bed."

The bedroom was directly behind the living room. The girls opened the door that led to the bed room. With the door open, Frank could see the bed in the middle of the room. Both girls lay on the bed next to a large lump in the covers which Frank assumed was "Uncle Fred." The girls started to tickle him. Suddenly Fred jumped out of bed, exclaiming, "Okay, okay, I'm getting out of bed goddamn it. Lori, you put Rose up to this, damn you." Fred went into the bathroom, coming out into the living room five minutes later wearing a pair of work pants and a v-necked T-shirt.

"Sorry Frank that I'm not presentable but I had to work late. I was sleeping like a baby until these two witches woke me up." He frowned at Lori who had just followed him in. "This one especially is bad news."

"Fred. Can I get out that bottle of Jack that you've got somewhere around here?" Lori asked.

"What--at seven o'clock in the morning!" said Fred.

"That's a good time to start. Where can I find it?" Lori asked sweetly.

"Back in the kitchen where it always is. You should know that. Rose, can you bring me a cup of coffee?"

"I'll bring it to you Fred," said Lori. "I'm going there anyway."

"No. Let her do it. That's what she's here for."

Lori returned a few moments later carrying a bottle of Jack Daniels and three glasses, followed by Rose carrying two cups of coffee. Rose handed Frank one of the cups, then took a seat on the couch to Fred's left while Lori sat to his right. Lori filled one glass from the bottle, then looked up at Frank who was sitting by himself on the floor.

"Want some Frank?"

"Not really. This coffee's fine."

"How about you Rose?"

"Not yet. Later."

"Lori, you've got to cut that out," said Fred. "It's too early to be starting on that crap."

"Fred, it's not crap. It's Jack Daniels, and it's seven o'clock in the morning," Lori replied.

"Girl you drink too much," said Fred. "Some day you're going to be sorry."

"Is Fred worried about his little Lori?" Lori teased as she leaned over and kissed Fred on the cheek.

Frank had seen enough. *So this was the matter of life and death*, he thought. *She expects us all to hang around this little apartment and get drunk with her while she makes over this Uncle*

Fred of hers who's really not her uncle in the first place. Well, it's a nice day outside, and I'm taking the top down.

Frank got up and announced, "I didn't sleep last night. Thanks for the coffee Rose. I've got a lot of things to do. I'm going home. Fred, catch up on your rest." Lori sat on the couch sipping from the glass, her face impassive. Frank looked over at Lori. Not saying a word about his leaving, and not making a move to jump out of the couch to stop him, Lori seemed indifferent to whether he stayed or left. Then he walked out the door.

He got five miles away looking straight ahead as he drove with the top down looking neither to the right nor the left. He drove without thinking. Then it hit him that before he'd know it, he'd be pulling into his own driveway seventy miles away. *What am I doing,* he thought. *I am in St. Louis. Lori's in St. Louis. It's early in the morning. I've come all this way to see her, and here I am driving away from her. Sure, she's making a horse's ass out of herself, but she'll snap out of it.* He turned around to go back.

When he came back in, he noticed that Lori had been crying. Frank lay down on the floor as she drank Jack Daniels from her glass. "Okay, I'm back," he said.

"Frank, how many pushups can you do?" asked Lori.

"After a night of drinking and no sleep, I don't really know," he replied.

"Can you do twenty-five?" asked Rose.

"In my sleep I can do more than that."

"Let's see you do them then," Lori added quickly.

"All right, but you girls have to count. I never could do two things at once."

Frank turned over on the floor and assumed the pushup position. Lori got off the couch and lay next to him on her stomach. "Now don't cheat," she ordered. He started slowly, trying to clear his head and to get used to the idea of strenuous physical activity. He picked up speed after he had done ten pushups and started to slow down after he hit thirty-five. Frank quit at fifty-five and lay on his back catching his breath although he might have been able to do two or three more.

"That's twenty-five," said Lori.

"Bullshit. You counted me doing fifty-five."

"Yeah, but you cheated. You only did the first twenty-five right."

"It's too early in the morning for this," Frank muttered.

Suddenly Lori jumped on top of him and started to tickle him under the arms. Then Rose came over and held his arms against the floor as Lori straddled his chest.

"That's enough!" Fred bellowed. "I'm going back to bed. Why don't you kids go somewhere else to play?"

"I think Fred's pissed," said Lori.

"That means we've got to go somewhere else," said Rose.

"We'll have to find a bar somewhere that's open," said Lori.

"On a Sunday morning? Good luck," said Rose.

"Don't worry, we'll find one, won't we Frank?"

"I'm sure we'll manage," said Frank.

"Hey Fred, do you have a paper cup for my drink?" asked Lori as she got off the floor.

"If it means getting rid of you, yes," Fred replied.

Fred went into the kitchen returning a few moments later with a large paper cup. "Here's one that's large enough for all of you," he said. "Now get out of here! All of you, and let an old man get his rest."

Lori poured straight from the bottle filling the paper cup all the way with Whiskey. Then they went out to Frank's car. Rose looked at it for a few moments studying its interior. "How are we all going to get into that little car?" she asked.

"Simple," replied Lori, "You are going to sit on my lap."

"But I'm bigger than you, Lori."

"Yeah, but I'm stronger and tougher than you."

Frank got in behind the wheel as Lori sat in the passenger seat. Rose was the last to get in, wedging herself tightly in between the dash and Lori. "Here, let me spread my legs just a little," said Lori. "Take your weight off me for a moment, Rose. This is uncomfortable."

Rose stood up, raising herself several inches off the seat, as Lori repositioned her legs. Then she lowered herself once more onto Lori's lap. Satisfied that both girls were somewhat comfortable, Frank started the engine and pulled away from the curb. "Where to?" he asked.

"I'll bet Jack's is open. What do you think, Rose?" asked Lori.

"They've gotta be open," said Rose.

"Go up two blocks and turn left, Frank," Lori directed.

He drove briskly, shifting through the gears quickly, as he revved the engine to 5000 rpms in first and second. He turned left at the end of the two blocks. "Now where?" Frank asked.

"Continue straight," said Lori. It's three or four blocks away.

He pulled next to a little tavern and parked along the curb. Once inside, they sat at the bar, Lori sitting to his right with Rose on his left. It was just a neighborhood pub, nothing special, several men sitting on bar stools talking while a woman in her fifties tended bar.

"Alice, get me a Jack and Coke," said Lori.

"Just get me a Bud Lite," said Rose.

"I'll have one of those also," said Frank. "But more important than that, what do you have to eat?"

"Mostly sandwiches," the woman replied.

"How about a Ham and Cheese," said Frank as he read from the menu that was on the wall.

"That can be done," replied the woman. Then she turned to the girls. "How about you two? Anything to eat?"

"No thanks," said Rose. "I already had breakfast."

Frank looked at Lori. "Have something to eat Lori. I'm buying."

"I'm not hungry," she replied.

They left an hour later.

The Jack and Coke Lori had left in the car was still cool. After they got underway, Lori took the cup off the floor and held it to Frank's lips. "Come on Frank, you've got some catching up to do." Frank sped through the gears and headed out toward I-55.

"I've got an idea," he suggested. "Let's the three of us go to the Injection Pump. It opens at noon."

"Great idea," said Lori. "We can have a few there, agitate Bogart, and then we can go to the Sports Bar."

"It's not open until three p.m. on Saturdays," said Frank.

"Hey Rose, lean forward will you, you're scraping my titty nipples," yelled Lori.

"What titty nipples," Rose replied. "I didn't know you had any."

"Lean forward, will you. It's starting to hurt."

As Rose leaned forward, Lori bit down on Frank's earlobe. "Just getting your attention, Frank. This does it--I'm getting silicone injections. When the girls say that I don't have any tits, then it's time."

"Don't change them, Lori," said Frank. "You've got a great body and small breasts are just part of you. You wouldn't look right with large breasts. Besides, when you climbed that grain leg, you would have never made it with large tits. A gear, pulley, or even a steel cable would have grabbed onto your large breasts and would have dragged you off the ladder to your death. Don't do it. Hear me. Don't do it."

They took a small table close to the stairs at the Injection Pump. A new waitress, a small blonde no taller than five -one, came to get their drink order. Bogart sat in the bouncer's seat next to the stairs. Frank and Rose stuck with beer, while Lori ordered a Jack and Coke.

"What's your name?" Frank asked the waitress.

"Polly," the girl replied. "What's yours?"

"Frank. And this is Lori and Rose. Rose is the girl on the right. Lori's . . . "

Suddenly Lori got off her stool and came up to Frank. Shoving the table back she inched between Frank and the table so that she was standing against his crotch between his legs. "I'm the one who's with him," said Lori.

"Oh in that case, I'm staying away from him," said Polly.

"You'd better," Lori laughed.

As Polly returned to the bar to get the drinks, Lori jammed herself up against Frank's crotch, put her arms around his neck, and started to kiss him. Pulling her tongue out of his mouth she opened her mouth wide around his lips and bit down. Suddenly she let go and started to drag her mouth down his neck. Without warning she bit him on his neck. When Frank pulled back in pain, she let go and jumped up into his lap.

"Don't ever fuck with me Frank," Lori warned.

"What did you do that for?" he asked.

"Just for the hell of it," she replied. "I love you Frank."

"Why?"

"I don't know why. Because you put up with me, I guess."

When he finished his drink, he went to the bar and ordered another round. He stood there waiting for the bartender to bring him his change when he felt a nudge in the middle of his back. Turning around he saw that it was Lori. She had followed him over to the bar, sneaked up behind him, and was now smiling at him. Grabbing him by his arms she pulled him away from the bar and started rubbing herself against him to the beat of the music. Arms around his neck now and thrusting her pelvis into his to the beat she worked her way back toward the table, pulling him with her. Polly had just finished setting their drinks down when they danced up to the table arms around each other's necks, their bodies entwined. Now seeing his chair in front of him, Frank reached under Lori's thighs and lifted her up in his arms as he fell into it. Her lips still pressed tightly against his Lori dropped into his lap, flinging their glasses off the table and onto the floor with her elbow. There was the sound of breaking glass as heads turned to see who was causing the disturbance. Bogart looked their way, frowned, and slowly shook his head like a disapproving school master. Polly scurried over to them, kneeled in the middle of the broken glass, and started to pick up the broken shards.

"Sorry Polly. We just got carried away," said Frank. "Too bad that you have to put up with us when we get like this."

"When you're done, get us another round Polly," said Lori. "Frank can't hold his alcohol. It's all his fault." Then she continued kissing him until Bogart came over.

They were sitting at the large table just inside the door, the one Bogart normally sat at. Here he could keep an eye on the door while watching for troublemakers like Lori and Frank. Bar stools surrounded the table since it was too high for chairs and was large enough to seat ten people. Usually there were several dancers sitting with Bogart as he drank his forty-eight ounce mugs of beer. There the girls talked and flirted with him or begged him to lend them money. Bogart sat at the head of the table.

"I'm keeping an eye on you two," said Bogart. "You'd better watch it."

"Oh don't worry, Bogart," said Lori, "we'll be good." Then she lifted Frank's shirt out of his pants past his armpits and bent her head to suck one of his nipples."

"Hey Frank. They make hotels for this sort of thing," suggested Bogart as he rolled his eyes in disbelief. "There's one right up the street."

"Now that's a great idea," said Rose. "Let's all go to the hotel. Bogart, are you coming with us?"

"No, I can't, but I think it's a great idea for all of you."

Still sucking Frank's nipple Lori bit sharply into it and raised her mouth to his ear. "Let's just you and I go to the hotel, she whispered. I want to fuck your brains out."

"And what are we going to do with Rose?" he asked softly.

"I don't give a fuck what we do with her. Let's just ditch her somewhere," said Lori.

"We can't just ditch her just like that," said Frank. "After all, we brought her here and it's miles to St. Louis. You might think it's all right to do that to her, but I don't."

"Well then, let's just take her to the Sports Bar. You can order us a round of drinks and we'll leave her with a little beer money. She'll find someone who can take her home."

"Lori, you're drunker than I thought you were. You know the Sports Bar is not open until 3:00 on Saturdays. After all, you used to work there."

"What! It's not open?"

"What's not open?" Rose asked.

"The Sports Bar's not open. We thought we might all go out there to drink since Bogart thinks Frank and I are derelicts."

"No thinking about it," said Bogart. "I know you two are derelicts."

"Let's go to the hotel then," said Frank. "We can all get in the shower together, all three of us."

"I'm not going to the hotel with her," Lori whispered. "First thing she's going to do is to tell Uncle Fred and then he'll tell Travis."

"He wouldn't do that, would he?" asked Frank.

"The hell he won't."

"Let's take Rose home then, and then you and I can go to the hotel," suggested Frank.

They dropped Rose off at Fred's. Lori followed Rose inside and came out a few moments later. Frank drove one block, accelerating rapidly through the gears, hitting sixty before slowing down.

"Go left," Lori ordered.

"But I was heading for the interstate. We're going to the hotel aren't we? Remember, you wanted to fuck my brains out."

"First, I've gotta piss. Take me to the Shell Station."

They walked in together. Then Frank went into the men's room as Lori disappeared into the ladies room. Coming out, he expected to see her since she usually didn't take as long as he did. He went over to the little counter fifteen feet off from the register and poured her a large Styrofoam cup of coffee from the coffee maker being sure to add the right amount of sugar and cream. *Surely Lori has to be still in there*, Frank thought. He smoked a cigarette, finished it, and checked his watch. *She's been in there fifteen minutes already. Must be some piss.* Then he went to the register where he paid for the coffee and bought a pack of cigarettes. A large woman took his money.

"My girlfriend's been in the ladies room for fifteen minutes now. Can you go in there and see if she's all right?" Frank asked.

"Sure, I'll check on her."

The woman came out alone. For a moment Frank thought that Lori had somehow slipped out until the woman said to him: "She's in there all right. Asleep on the toilet."

"I'm going in then to get her," said Frank.

"You think that's a good idea?" asked the woman. "I mean, she's on the toilet."

"I've seen her before," said Frank. "Do you mind?"

"No. Go ahead then."

Frank went to the ladies room and went in. Lori sat on the toilet slumped over the throne, her jeans and panties pulled down around her ankles. Her head rested on her lap, her hands clasped tightly around her thighs. Frank wanted to laugh--No, he wanted a camera. He would have given a hundred dollars for one. He kneeled next to her, speaking gently: "Lori, it's me, Frank. You are asleep on the toilet at the Shell station. We've gotta leave." When there was no response from her he started to shake her.

"What? Where am I?" Lori asked.

"On the toilet in the Shell station."

"I must have fallen asleep."

"Here, let me help you." He put his right arm around her back while he reached underneath her legs with his left. She was light as a feather in his arms as he carried her out to the car. He set her down in the passenger seat, then went back into the station for the coffee. He came out, got in behind the wheel, and handed Lori the Styrofoam cup.

"Here, have some coffee. You need it."

She drank greedily from the cup. "I really fell asleep on the toilet?"

"Sure did. Good thing I brought my camera along. I've got some great pictures."

"You bastard. You didn't, did you?"

"No. Unfortunately I didn't have my camera along. I'd have some classic shots if I did. I'd show them to all the girls you used to work with. Tamara especially would get a kick out of them."

"How did I look?" asked Lori.

"Beautiful. Absolutely stunning with your arms clasped around your legs, panties and jeans hanging over your ankles."

"Let's go to the hotel then," said Lori.

They went to the place next to the Injection Pump. The Indian woman came to the night window to take his money giving him a faint smile of recognition. When they got into the room, he left Lori on the bed while he took a shower. When he came out, he saw that she was asleep in her jeans on her back exactly as he had left her. Frank lay next to her and kissed her gently on her lips. "Lori, I'm back. Wake up." When she didn't answer or respond he started to shake her gently. "Lori, it's me. It's only five o'clock. Wake up."

Lori started to snore, her snoring low and guttural. He looked into her face while she snored. He had never heard sounds like that coming out of a sleeping person before. She reminded him of the movie "The Exorcist"--of Megin possessed by the Devil speaking in another voice. Shaking her harder this time he was still unable to get a response. He considered pulling off her jeans and fucking her awake. He undid her belt, took off her socks, and tried to pull her jeans off, but they were tight and she was asleep, unable to help him. Through it all she slept, not moving or responding in any way. He thought about making love to her--thought real hard about it--then decided that it would be too much like rape. There would be other times for this, and even though he had woken her up before by making love to her, this time he decided against it. It was those damn jeans--with her wearing them, it would be too much like violating her whereas before she had been naked and he had already made love to her just hours before.

Although he hadn't slept the night before, he didn't want to sleep now. He watched her snore on. *She'd probably be out for hours.* He decided that he had more exciting things to do than to stay in the room with her so he looked around the room for his dop kit. Taking an aerosol can of Edge shaving cream out of the kit, he sprayed a message on the mirror which faced the bed in the main room. It read: LORI. PLEASE SEE NOTE ON DESK. Then he went into the bathroom and sprayed the same message on the mirror above the wash basin. Going back into the main room he took pen and paper and wrote a note which he put on the desk which said: LORI, WENT TO THE SPORTS BAR AT 5:00. BE BACK AT 7:00. IF YOU WAKE UP BEFORE THEN CALL ME THERE AT 522-6753. THERE IS A PAY PHONE OUT IN THE HALLWAY. LOVE FRANK. He picked up the pack of cigarettes, pulled two out, and set them on the note. Then he took two quarters from his pocket and laid them next to the cigarettes. *She should be in good shape,* he said to himself as he drove to the Sports Bar.

"You what"--exclaimed Tamara--"You left her in a hotel room! Asleep! Well, you had better be back at seven. If you don't, she's going to wake up and she's going to kick your ass."

Frank was sitting in the rear section with Tamara and her number one customer, an older man named Jeff, who had been with Lori in the past. Jeff smiled broadly, shoved his drink forward scooting the glass several inches along the table top, and leaned back in his chair.

"That's great, Frank. So you left Nipples asleep in the hotel room so you could come here."

"What are you going to do, Frank? Hustle other women while she's asleep? She finds out about that, she's not going to like it and then there's going to be hell to pay," said Tamara.

"What else is there to do here, Tamara, besides hustle the girls or allow them to hustle me."

"Well, you could just sit here and drink."

Frank went back to the room at seven only to find Lori sprawled out on the bed in the same position he had left her. He stayed ten minutes and tried to awaken her with the same lack of success he had before. Finally giving up he grabbed another sheet of paper from out of the desk drawer and wrote on it LORI. CAME BACK AT 7:00 BUT COULDN'T WAKE YOU UP. WENT BACK TO THE SPORTS BAR. BE BACK AT 9:00. He went back into the Sports Bar, found Tamara and Jeff, and sat with them until Tamara left at 8:00. Fifteen minutes later, Lucy came in, finding Frank sitting alone at the bar. "Came in to see me?" she asked him.

"For a little while," he answered.

"Why just a little while? You got a hot date or something?"

"I've got a situation. I might come back in and I might not. I just don't know."

"Want to do a limo before you leave?"

"I would, but I really can't stay that long. Can I buy you a drink?"

"Get me a Tom Collins."

He ordered from the bar as she pulled up a stool next to him. Janie brought the drinks over to them, which he paid for, leaving her a dollar tip. He stayed until a quarter to nine, looked at his watch, then turned to Lucy. "I've gotta go. Like I've said, I've got a situation on my hands and I've just got to deal with it. I might see you later. I don't know." Then he went back to the hotel room.

She was still asleep. Once again he failed to awaken her. This time he was tired so he lay next to her. They woke up together at eleven when she started to move around on the bed. "How long have I been asleep?" she asked.

"About six hours," Frank replied. "I've already been to the Sports Bar twice. Left you notes all over the place. Look at the mirror."

She saw the shaving cream on the mirror and started to laugh. Then she climbed out of bed and went into the bathroom. He heard her laughing there as she took her shower, then got out of bed himself and lit a cigarette. When she came out she went to the desk and started to read the notes that he had written her.

"What! You left me only two cigarettes! You fucker. And two quarters for phone calls?"

"That's right. I wanted you to get hold of me as soon as possible."

"Who'd you see there?"

"Tamara. Some of the other girls. Lucy."

"I suppose you did a limo with one of them."

"Come on Lori."

"Come on Frank. As if you wouldn't stoop so low as to fuck one of those girls in the limo. You'd do it. I know you would."

"Well I didn't. Let's put our clothes on and go over to the Sports Bar."

They walked in together, Lori going over to talk to one of the other dancers, Frank going to the bar for drinks. Linda saw them come in together, gave him a dirty look, and came over to the bar.

"I don't believe you. I just don't believe you. You sit at the bar with my cousin telling her 'you've got a situation' and all the time you had Nipples in a hotel room. You've got to stop pulling this shit on my cousin."

"What am I supposed to do?" replied Frank. "Lori fell asleep and I couldn't get her up so I got bored and came over. How am I supposed to know that your cousin would be here? She probably only works two days a week and one never knows when those days are. She hasn't been the epitome of reliability either at work or with me."

"You shouldn't do what you're doing. She likes you, you know, and I don't want to see my cousin get hurt."

Lori looked over, saw Frank talking with Linda, hugged the dancer she was talking with, and walked over.

"What are you two talking about?" she asked.

"You. Who else?" Frank asked.

"Bullshit."

They closed the Sports Bar at 4:00 and went back to the hotel. Just before driving in Frank decided that he didn't want to sleep there after all. "Lori, the room is paid for, but I'd like to go to the farm. Wouldn't you?"

"You know I don't like that room. Are you sure you're up to driving?"

"Just keep me awake in the car. I can do it if you promise not to go to sleep on me."

He drove home in the dark, his favorite girl next to him, tired yet ecstatic that she wanted to go there with him. This time he was careful to point out the major landmarks along the way so that she could find her way to his house in the future. When they got to his house, they went straight to the bedroom where Lori promptly fell asleep. She didn't wake up until three in the afternoon.

"I've gotta check on my kids," Lori told him after she got up. "Can I use your phone?"

"Help yourself."

She went into the family room where she snuggled into the couch with the cordless phone in her hands. He went into the kitchen and made a pot of coffee. Taking a cup to her, he caught the tail end of the conversation just before she hung up.

"I'll be over in a little more than an hour. Did you say that Travis is playing soccer?"

Then she hung up and looked up at Frank as he handed her a cup of coffee. "I've got to go check on the kids. It will take just a little while. Then we can come back here."

He drove her back to the Shell station where he had picked her up the day before. They sat there in his car sharing a coke as she jotted down a phone number. "Call me here if I'm not back in fifteen minutes. Travis is still playing soccer so I should be able to get out of the house before he gets back."

"Who lives there?" Frank asked.

"Travis's parents. His mother's an alcoholic, so I don't want to stay there very long."

"I have a feeling that you are going to leave me waiting in my car while you wait for Travis to get back," said Frank.

"Not. Just wait here."

Fifteen minutes passed. He called and asked for Lori, who came to the phone and asked him to wait another fifteen minutes. Then he called again. The voice on the other end, the same woman's voice that had answered the phone the first time, told him that they had already left--Lori and Travis.

She dumped me just like she was planning to do to Rose yesterday. What's wrong with Lori? he asked himself. *What makes her keep coming back to Travis, and why does she keep telling everyone that she's no longer with him?*

Later she would tell him that Travis came in before she could return to Frank's car, and that he beat her up. Frank would ask himself again as he had many other times: *Is she telling the truth?* He answered himself with "a probably not".

HARRING BLOWS IT

He walked into Risque and was immediately mobbed by the two dancers as he was paying his cover. Lori and Susan saw him come in the nightclub, jumped out of their bar stools, and hurried over to the door as he was reaching in his pocket to pay the doorman. It was Lori who kissed him first, kissing him on the lips as she hugged him tightly. Susan pushed Lori aside and started to kiss him while Lori watched.

"Very boring here, isn't it, girls."

"Damn right it is. This is all Susan's idea. I just got back on at the Injection Pump last week. Susan decided that we should volunteer to work here today and I agreed in a weak moment. There's nobody here."

The place was dead. Only four dancers were working and there were even fewer customers. Frank had a date with Lucy at eight o'clock, and he was supposed to pick her up at the Sports Bar. They had arranged to go to his farm where she agreed to spend the night. Since Lucy usually arrived for work late--getting there between 8:15 and 8:30--he had thought that 8:00 was the perfect time for them to meet, before she checked in. Then Lori had called from Risque, and he had decided to have a couple drinks with her before taking off for the Sports Bar. He had walked in at 6:00 when the girls spotted him. He had it all figured out. Lucy would stand him up as usual. In the meantime he could set something up with Lori--say for 8:30 or 9:00.

"Let's go to the bar and have a drink," Lori suggested.

They sat at the bar where he bought each girl a drink. Then they took Frank to the stage where they stripped him to his underwear. They made him lie on his back on the cold floor. Lori lay across his chest, her top off, bare nipples rubbing up and down his body. Suddenly she got off and Susan mounted him so that she faced away from him with her backside in his face. Hovering over him she stuck her groin next to his mouth so that he could part her G-string with his tongue. Lori kneeled at his feet and stuck her hand between his legs. Rubbing him through his underwear she watched as Susan pressed her G-string up against his mouth.

Afterwards they went back to the bar, Lori sitting close to him on his right. Frank decided he couldn't just get up and leave at 7:30. He had to tell her about his situation so that they could make their own plans, so sure was he that Lucy would blow it once again.

514

"Lori, there's something I've got to tell you."

"What Frank?"

"I've got a date with Lucy for eight. I'm picking her up at the Sports Bar. That's the bad news. The good news is that I'm not too excited about it, and I don't think she's going to be there anyway. Just have me call there at eight. They'll say she's not there, and then you and I can do something."

"That's cool."

Frank didn't call the Sports Bar until 8:15 both of them losing track of the time. Once again the Lori-Frank magic had taken over, leaving both of them out of touch with their surroundings. When he finally called, it was Mary who answered the phone, recognizing his voice immediately.

"Hello Frank. Are you coming in?"

"Probably. Is Lucy there?"

"She's here."

"Did she sign in yet?"

"She signed in as soon as she got here."

"In other words, if I wanted to take her out tonight, I'd have to pay the bar one hundred bucks."

"That's right Frank."

"Probably see you in a little while then." He looked at Lori after he hung up, noticing that she was watching him the whole time.

"Well?"

"She's signed in. It would cost me a hundred dollars to take her out of the bar. If she wanted to go out with me, she should never have signed in. She has very little regard for my money. Tell you what Lori, let's just go over there."

"Why don't we take Susan and Brian with us? They'll probably want to go."

Frank looked across the room where Susan was up on stage. A man in his early thirties was sitting in front of the stage. Frank recognized the man from the Injection Pump, remembering that he was an interesting conversationalist. Several minutes later, Susan came off the stage, coming back to the bar with Brian.

"Our shift is over," she said. "Lori, what are you doing now?"

"Frank's taking me to the Sports Bar. Want to come? Both of you?"

"I've always wanted to go there, but never did. Yeah we'll meet you two there."

When Lori and Frank pulled into the Sports Bar's parking lot,

Susan and Brian were already parked, waiting for them. They went in together taking a table not far from the stage. Frank noticed Lucy standing at the bar looking glum and dispirited. *Time to cover my bases*, he thought. The waitress came and took their drink order. He excused himself from the table after she returned with the drinks and went up to the bar.

"Lucy, I didn't think you were going to make it?"

"Well I did. Didn't I?"

"Why'd you check in. We were going to go to my house tonight."

"I don't want to talk to you. Not ever."

"You know that once you checked in I would have to pay a hundred dollars to get you out. Why'd you do it?"

"Look Frank, I got here early. I waited fifteen minutes in the parking lot so you wouldn't have to buy me out. When you never showed I came inside and checked in."

"I thought you were standing me up again."

"I was planning to spend the whole night with you. Then you had to bring her in here again." Lucy pointed angrily at Lori. "I don't want you ever to talk to me again. Not ever again. And by the way, this is my last week here. I'm quitting. Anything's better than working here. I don't care what I have to do for a living so long as it's nothing like this."

"Look Lucy, I'm so sorry. I really didn't think you'd be here."

"I was sitting at the bar when you called. I listened to Mary's side of the conversation. You knew I was here, and you still brought that woman in here. And I was really beginning to like you."

"I don't know quite what to say other than what I've already said."

"Well don't come crying on my shoulder the next time she decides to fuck you over."

Lori and Frank stayed late well after the time Brian and Susan left them. Cavorting together at their table and forgetting where they were he started to do something with her that brought the bouncer over. Short, stocky, and in his early fifties, Jack was not the biggest bouncer in the world; nevertheless he had been working for Bill for the past twenty years and had managed to keep the peace at the Sports Bar and the other bars that Bill had owned.

"Now cut that out or I'm going to have to evict you two."

A week later, Frank would have to ask Lori what they had done to provoke Jack since he couldn't remember what they had done. Lori remembered, telling him that he had kneeled between her legs and tried to lick her there right at the table. Frank couldn't remember having done anything that bold in a bar before, but after thinking about it for a while, he had decided that he probably had with Lori, given their ability to forget their surroundings whenever they were together.

He took her home--the long way. It took them three hours to get there. This time he did the driving, taking a detour to Belleville, to Collinsville, to East St. Louis, to St. Louis, back to Belleville, and finally to Granite City. He remembered Lori sitting up close to him, shifting the gear shift as he clutched, both of them trying and usually succeeding in synchronizing their movements. When daylight broke, she had him take her to a spot that was a block from the place she and Travis were staying.

One of the last things she said to him before he let her out was: "Frank, when you give up these limos, you can have me." When he asked her what she meant, she added, "I'm yours, but only after you give up those limos."

THERE'S AN OLD MAN IN THE BATHROOM

They had been playing pool in the nightclub, neither one of them winning. One of the other dancers, who worked with Lori at the Injection Pump, was cleaning up, hardly missing a shot. A doorman, who worked at the Injection Pump shot almost as well as the dancer. Unfortunately Lori and Frank were on the same team, and this time both of them were badly overmatched.

It was a large nightclub having four or five large rooms including its own pool hall. The place was owned by the same man who owned the Injection Pump, Ciceros, and Risque, but this nightclub, unlike the others, was not a strip bar. There was a large dance floor to which Lori now led him. Frank and Lori started to dance when suddenly she wrapped her legs around his waist as she held tightly onto his arms. Leaning back as she mounted him, Lori ground her pelvis into his in time with the music. Arching her back she leaned backwards until her head touched the floor. When the selection ended, Lori regained her feet and the two of them danced conventionally. Suddenly, Frank felt that they were being watched. He looked away from Lori, his eyes searching for whoever might be observing them. It was then that he noticed the two girls who had been dancing together close by. They had stopped dancing and were watching Lori and Frank.

"Excuse me, one of them asked, can you do that again?"

"Do what again?" asked Frank.

"Whatever you two were doing before. You know, her straddling you and all."

"Sure, we can do that for you," Lori replied.

Once again she mounted him, wrapping her legs around his waist while he held onto her arms. Then she arched her back as she ground herself into his groin. "How's that?" Lori asked.

"Can you touch the floor again?" the other girl asked.

Lori leaned way back arching her back as she brought her head downward. This time she raised her head slightly off the floor as Frank started to spin her around. When the selection ended, Lori walked Frank off the floor and headed for the restroom. "Come on. You're going to the ladies room with me," she said.

When they came up to the lady's room Frank turned off toward the men's room. Without warning Lori grabbed him by his arm and yanked him through the door of the restroom. He followed her inside as she led him into the stall, closing the door after them.

He heard the door open behind them, decided that a woman or women were entering the lady's room, and stood up on the stool. Lori was already sitting on the stool as Frank placed one foot on either side of her hips. *At least they won't be able to see my big feet underneath the stall*, he thought.

"Did you see that," one of the women asked the other, "an old man just came into the lady's room. He's in here somewhere."

Thanks a lot, Frank thought, *for calling me an old man. So my hair's grey or white. That doesn't make me old. I still have the body of a much younger man, and my maturity level--well this speaks for that--my being in the ladies room with Lori.* Lori started to urinate into the bowl as he straddled her. Then an inspiration struck him. Undoing his belt, Frank let his jeans down so that they reached his ankles. Then he pulled down his jockey shorts and whipped his penis out. Bending over he offered it to Lori who was still urinating. She took it into her mouth as they heard the door open and shut.

Good, they are leaving, thought Frank. And then he heard it open again. More women entered the restroom. They couldn't leave--not yet, as Lori continued to suck his penis.

"There's a man in here," one of the women said to the other. "Can you see him?"

"No, I can't," the other woman replied. "You say he's in here."

"He sure is. Somewhere."

One of the women went into one of the stalls as the other stayed to powder her nose at the mirror. Frank and Lori walked out of the stall trying to sneak by her. Frank could see the woman's reflection in the mirror, her eyes wide with surprise at seeing him exit from the stall. He turned to address her as he and Lori walked out.

"Don't worry, I'm leaving." He pointed at Lori. "She dragged me in here to help her do something."

They went back into the poolroom. The dancer who had been shooting so well had already asked them for a ride home. Frank had assumed that she was a good friend of Lori's and had agreed to take the woman home. He knew it was a long way from where Lori was staying and in the opposite direction from where he lived.

"We're leaving," he said. "If you want that ride home you'd better come with us."

The three of them crossed the river to the Missouri side.

Mercifully he had brought his pickup. Frank noticed that Lori had been very quiet on the way to the river.

"Take me home first!" she demanded.

Frank looked at her in disbelief. *It's your goddamn friend, not mine*, he thought. *And why would you let me take another woman home first? Especially the way you get so upset about my doing limos.* "Okay Lori, but if I take you home first, she and I are going somewhere to make love. You don't mind, do you?"

"I don't give a fuck what you do. Just take me home first."

"Sorry Lori. I'm taking her home first. You and I are in this together and we are staying together until after I've taken her home."

After they dropped the girl off, Frank turned back toward the city. Lori didn't say a word until he had almost gotten her back. "All right then, turn right," said Lori. Frank followed Lori's directions until they were two blocks from where Fred lived.

"You can let me out here," Lori said. "Why didn't you take me home first?"

"I already told you why," he replied.

"Stop the car," she demanded. "Next time, take me home first." Lori got out of the car, and in a matter of seconds disappeared out of sight.

CENTER OF ATTENTION

Lori stood up against the desk in the cold motel room still wearing her winter coat as Frank adjusted the small heater's controls. The heater's fan produced a weak current of warm air, which would eventually warm up the room given enough time. Frank was willing to accept the cold knowing that eventually the heater would do its job. Satisfied that he had done what he could, he took his coat off and sprawled out on the bed.

"That heater won't work," Lori complained. "It's not producing any heat."

"It's giving off a little heat," Frank replied. "We can wait it out."

"It isn't working Frank. You can feel it isn't giving off any heat."

"Give it a chance Lori."

This time Lori had picked the motel, choosing an inexpensive place two miles from the Injection Pump. She had followed Frank into the office, when he checked in, only to discover that the woman at the desk, like the woman at the motel they had used several times before, was Indian. After he had gotten the room key, she had followed Frank to his car muttering, "Can't any of these people speak English?" Worse, Lori found the room to be even smaller and more claustrophobic than the rooms at the other motel.

Still leaning against the desk and uncomfortable from the cold Lori studied Frank, carefully waiting for his reply to her question: "Frank, why do you hang out at all these topless bars?"

"I have always wondered why certain women behave as they do," he replied. "Why does a good-looking woman who seems to have a lot going for herself go out with men who are unattractive, boorish, and stupid and not go after men who for the most part have all their shit in one sock? All my life I've asked myself that question."

"Bullshit!" Lori replied. "Frank, you are full of shit, and no one knows that better than me."

"Okay then, that's part of the reason. I also like the music and I like the fast pace. It also allows me to escape from what I am going through with my divorce."

"Wrong. Wrong. Face it Frank, you don't know why. Admit that you don't know the real reason why."

"I just told you the reasons. If you don't like them, then I'll agree with you. I really don't know. Now, are you satisfied?"

"Yes. This place is cold. Let's get another room."

Leaving her alone in the room, he walked back to the office to complain. The Indian woman scowled at him when he asked for another room; then grudgingly gave him the key to another room. They found the next room to be worse than the first since Frank couldn't get the heater to work at all. Then, only minutes after they had gone to the second room, they heard the car driving back and forth through the parking area outside. The car rumbled past Frank's pickup to the opposite end of the motel, turned around and rolled to the other end, its engine obviously needing a tuneup. They could hear it go back and forth, back and forth from one end of the motel to the other and then back again.

"It's Travis," Lori whispered. "Keep still. He knows we're here."

"Now how would he know that, Lori?"

"How in the fuck should I know? It's him. I should know what my car sounds like."

"Should I prepare for a shotgun blast through the door?" Frank asked. "After all, Travis drives around with a shotgun or at least that's what the other girls tell me."

"No. He's not going to do that."

"Why not? You tell me he's shot people."

"Because I don't think he's going to try that here."

"Just thought I'd ask."

Five minutes later the car left after which Lori walked to the door. "Come on Frank, let's get the fuck out of here. I want to go out and have a drink. Take me to Gals."

"Let's get another room," he suggested.

"Let's get out of here," she demanded. "I don't like this place."

He didn't want to take her to Gals but felt he had little choice. They walked in as the place was about to close. However, it was obvious that neither the owner nor his employees were in the mood to shut down. Lori took him to a table and introduced him to the couple sitting there. Buying Lori and himself a beer Frank sat across from the couple as she sat next to him. The door opened, and Mary and Greg walked in, came over, and sat with them. The Sports Bar had just closed. Frank didn't have to look at his watch to determine that--since Mary was the bartender on duty there, and Greg, her husband, was managing the Swinger's Bar next door.

Suddenly Lori jumped up from the table and went up to the stage to talk to the dancer who was descending the steps, her last set for the night finished. Frank watched Lori take off her clothes and lie down on her back, naked. The other woman kneeled between her legs, extended her body across Lori's, and started kissing Lori's breasts. Frank turned away to talk to the woman sitting across from him. Ten minutes later, Lori was still lying on the stage as the dancer either licked or pretended to lick her crotch.

Frank went to the bar, bought himself a second beer, and returned to the table. Once again he turned to the woman sitting across from him. "Have you ever been a dancer?" he asked.

"No," the woman replied. "But I've always wondered what it would be like. I used to want to try it but I guess I never had the guts to do it."

"Most of the women in these places have to do lap dances for a lot of men. You know what those are, don't you?"

"Sure. I've gone to these places before. Tonight's not the first time."

"Look. What Lori's doing up on stage is really starting to get to me. This place is officially closed and she's not making a dime on what she's doing up there. What do you think of practicing a lap dance on my lap. Just pretend that you're a dancer."

Frank then turned to the woman's escort, not knowing if the man was her husband, boyfriend, or simply a friend. "You don't mind, do you? I don't know if your date is your wife or your girlfriend or what your relationship with her is. I just want to see what Lori's reaction will be if we do a lap dance together. Lori is my date, and we've been out a lot in the last few months."

"Go ahead," the man replied. "I don't mind at all if my girlfriend thinks it's okay."

"It seems safe enough to me," the woman replied.

The woman got up and came over to Frank's side of the table. Smiling down at him she straddled his lap and started to rock back and forth against him. It was then that Frank noticed that she was older than he thought, being in her upper thirties, perhaps even in her early forties. She was also heavier than he had judged her to be. The woman put her arms around Frank's neck holding him close against her chest.

Lori came back to the table just as the woman was completing her lap dance with Frank. She sat next to him as the woman climbed off Frank's lap and went back to her boyfriend.

Then Frank turned to Mary, who was sitting on his right. "When do you think they're going to close Mary?"

"I have no idea. Sometimes they go to five or six in the morning. It all depends."

Frank pretended not to notice Lori taking off his belt as he continued to talk to Mary. He felt Lori loosen his belt; then he felt it being removed from his belt loops. Frank continued to ignore her.

She preferred to bring me here after I paid for a hotel room. She could be in the room with me, just the two of us. Then she does a lesbian show when she's not even being paid and after the place has closed. She's cheapened herself and made a mockery out of our relationship. Why?

Then he felt the belt being placed around his neck, felt her draw it tight against his throat, and right then he decided that he wouldn't give her the satisfaction that he noticed. But he didn't quite pull it off. For several seconds Frank observed her face from the corner of his eye as she tightened the belt. Lori's face had changed. Was it the dim lighting in the bar or was that face really hers? Lori's face had taken a yellowish cast as her eyes became slits. Her mouth became set, unsmiling, yet her eyes were focused, not on his face, but on his throat. Her face was resolute, her mind somewhere else, as she drew the belt tight.

Suddenly Mary jumped out of her chair. "He's turning blue," she shouted. "Lori, stop! Stop that! Now!"

As if awakened from a dream, Lori looked at Mary and smiled as she loosened the belt around Frank's neck. Mary reached over and grabbed the belt as she took it off Frank's neck. "What's wrong with you Lori? You were choking him. Couldn't you see him turning blue?"

A few minutes later, the woman who had been sitting across from Frank left with her date. Lori got up from the table and walked over to the bar as Mary joined her husband who was busy talking with the owner. Two employees of the bar, both large dark haired men, sat on the left side of the bar talking with Lori as Frank sat at the bar at the other end.

Frank had been farming that day having put in fourteen hours on the tractor. He had only two hours sleep the night before, having worked late into the night. The lack of sleep had finally caught up with him. Now merely sipping his beer and thinking about sleep, Frank saw Lori taking off her clothes while the two large men watched. The owner, who had been talking with Greg, saw it too--

left Greg standing in the middle of the room, and joined Lori and his two employees. Frank saw the two employees lift Lori, now naked, up onto the bar. He turned away, climbed off the bar stool and went over to Greg who had just been joined by Mary.

"Mary, have you ever seen her act like this before?"

"Oh Nipples," Mary replied. "Who knows about her."

This is too much, Frank thought. *I don't know if I ever want to see her again. She's not fucking the men over there, but she's letting them play around with her. What is she doing this for? Doesn't she know that she's better than that? Or does she? There's nothing left but to sleep. I'm going home.*

Frank went up to the men and addressed the owner. "Lori came in here with me. If she wants to leave with me, she has to go now because I'm going."

The owner looked at Frank and replied: "I don't know you and I don't know what your relationship is with Lori, but she might end up working here tomorrow night. I don't want to interfere with the two of you tonight. You'll just have to talk with her about it."

Frank turned to Lori. "I'm leaving. Do you want to leave with me?"

"I need just five more minutes Frank. Then we can go."

Frank went back to Greg and Mary, carefully checking the time on his watch. Five minutes later he returned to Lori and the three men. "Lori, your five minutes are up. Let's go." Lori was facing the bar, facing away from him as he strode up to her. Not even turning around, she continued to talk with the three men.

"Okay then, have it your way. I'm leaving now. If you want a ride with me, you'd better follow me out of this place."

He stalked out of the bar, unlocked his pickup, and slid onto the seat. She came out as he started the engine, walked over to the passenger door and got in with him.

"Let's go for a ride," said Lori.

"No, I'm taking you home," said Frank. "Let me just say this, Lori. This has been a very enjoyable evening for me. In fact, it's been one of the most fabulous evenings of my whole life," he added sarcastically.

He took her back to Fred's not saying a word to her until he dropped her off. He waited for her as she got out and went to the door of the little apartment. Then he drove off as soon as he saw her go inside.

JUDAS

There were some good times too. They met several times in the bars after that night--drove around together in his sports car into the wee hours of the morning, but each time she had him take her to Fred's or to a house nearby in the City where Travis was staying. Each time she avoided any opportunity or situation he proposed which would bring them together sexually. Then she called that Saturday afternoon in December.

He met her at 6:30 in the Injection Pump. She had been scheduled to work until 8:00, but this time she quit early. He found her at the bar talking to two men, either customers of hers or potential customers. He noticed that she had a black eye, and he knew without asking her that she had gotten it from Travis.

"I want you to meet my boyfriend, Frank," said Lori. "Frank, this is Al and Sam." Then she turned to Frank and smiled. "Guess what? I get to quit early. I'm going to the dressing room. Be right back."

Leaving the two men at the bar, Frank strolled through the nightclub and then he saw the seven men--seven men, neighbors of his, sitting at a table far from the door on the way to stage five. It was the last thing he wanted to see--men from the farm area in which he lived. No matter what happened and no matter that all the men were married--it would get out in his community that he was seen frequenting topless bars. The rumor was already out for it was already common knowledge that his best friend Stan had frequented such places and that he had introduced Stan to them. The men would pass it onto their wives that they had gotten drunk and had gone to the Injection Pump just this once, and that they had seen Frank with one of the girls in the topless bars, obviously not for the first time.

He saw Lori come out of the dressing room in her red shorts. So far the men had not seen him. He met her close to the bar where she suggested a table close to stage one, far away from the men. Then he told her that his friends were there.

"Bring them over," she suggested. "I'd like to meet them."

"Oh, by the way, you've got a black eye. Want to tell me about it."

"I was in the car with Travis's mom, who's an alcoholic you know. We got into a car wreck and my face hit the dashboard."

"I see," replied Frank not believing a word of her story.

527

"About those men again--They're going to know that we've been together, that you are a dancer, and that I come to these places often. Later, when I bring you to one of the local bars one of them is going to see you there and it's going to be all over the country that you are my girlfriend and then everybody's going to know what you do for a living."

"It's up to you," said Lori. "I don't care much one way or the other, but if you want to slip out of here without them seeing you, we can go somewhere else."

Frank thought about it. He thought about the men. One of them was Dave McGuire, the super mechanic who had installed the supercharger in his car and the man who had been working on his tractors ever since he had started farming. He remembered many years before either he or Dave had gotten married, how they had drunk in a bar listening to the band and how he had dared Dave to walk up the hand rail along the stairs that led to the second floor. Dave had gotten half way up before slipping off onto the stairs. He considered Dave's personality and outlook on life. Dave was charismatic and wild.

To hell with it, Frank decided. *Dave would never condemn him for frequenting topless bars.* Life was short, and what did he plan to do with his life anyway? Was it his mission in life to pretend that he was a paragon of virtue? In the long run he would be dead along with everybody else. Life was full of toil, sickness, heartaches--of seeing those close to you die off one by one--then of waiting for your own death. The rest of it was for having fun. Tonight he was going to have fun and to hell with what anybody else thought.

"Fuck it," said Frank. "I'm going to ask them to join us."

The seven men looked up when he came up to their table. Besides Dave, there was Dave's younger brother Phil who farmed in the area; Dan Johnson, an engineer; Bill Johnson who farmed near Frank; Fred Hendricks, another farmer; and two others whom Frank didn't recognize.

"Hi, what are you all up to?" Frank asked.

"We've been goose hunting all day," said Bill Johnson. "Then Dave decided to bring us here. What are you doing here?"

"Just visiting a friend. We're sitting at a table over there." Frank pointed at Lori sitting across the room. "Come over and join us. I want you to meet her."

The men followed Frank over to his table. Seeing them, Lori

grinned and stood up. "Hi, I'm Lori. Frank didn't tell me that there were seven of you. We need to pull up some more tables."

Lori scampered over to the first unoccupied table and began pulling it across the floor. *Her eyes are clear*, Frank observed, *and she's alert as hell. She's not drunk and she's more perceptive than practically anyone in the room. And she moves so quickly.* Frank went over to help her, the two of them shoving the table over to the one they were sitting at. Then they brought another table over, positioning the three tables so that they adjoined one another end to end so that the three tables formed one long table that could seat six people on each side.

After they all sat down Lori waved to the waitress, who came over to take their drink order. Then Lori looked up at the men. "You're going to have to introduce yourselves to me."

One by one each man introduced himself to Lori who sat next to Frank, attentive to her surroundings as she tried to learn who was who and how each man knew Frank. *Jesus*, thought Frank, *this girl has it all over most women. She really knows how to handle herself when she wants to. No wonder that I picked her. Damn proud of her, I am. Damn glad to be with her and not with someone else.*

"Where do you know Frank from, Lori?" asked Bill Johnson.

"We met a year and a half ago," Lori replied. "We've been going out the last few months."

"Ever been to his place?" asked Bill.

"Oh, a few times," Lori replied as she looked over at Frank smiling quizzically. "A few times."

"Have you ever been on one of his tractors?" asked Bill.

"He let me drive one. That is after he practically killed me on it. He was mowing a ditch with me with him and he almost turned it over. He did it on purpose. Almost turned it over on me. Can you believe that?"

"Knowing Frank, I can believe it," said Dave.

"Then there was the time that he took me up his grain leg. Frank took me up one-hundred feet," said Lori. "I think he's trying to get rid of me, don't you?"

"Well, did he carry you up?" asked Dave.

"No, I followed him."

"You what?" Phil asked incredulously, "You went up his grain leg?"

"Sure. Why not?"

"Not the average woman, is she?" said Dan addressing the

whole table.

"I'd say not," Dave replied.

"We're going to the Sports Bar," said Frank as he looked around at each man. "Want to meet us there?"

"What's it like?" asked Phil.

"For one thing, there's no cover," said Frank. "And it's seedier than here."

"The girls are friendlier," added Lori. "They can sit with you longer. You can have a lot of fun there."

"Well, where is it?" asked Phil. "It sounds like our kind of place." Then looking around him he asked, "Where'd my brother go. He was just here a second ago."

"Up there," said Fred. He motioned toward stage two. Dave was sitting in front of it, a pretty blonde on his lap.

"Yep, that's my brother," said Phil. "Give us directions to this place, Frank."

"Tell you what," said Lori. "It's just down the street. Follow us. We'll wait in the parking lot for you."

On the way down the stairs, Lori tugged at his arm. "Do you think I'm getting heavier Frank? All I've been doing is eating and drinking. I really haven't been to work all that much so I haven't been getting a lot of exercise."

"No. Why?"

"Because I'm up to one hundred and twenty-three pounds."

"Bullshit, Lori. You don't weigh any hundred and twenty-three pounds. More like one hundred and ten. Same as usual."

"I'll bet you I weight 123 pounds," said Lori as they walked to his pickup.

"Bet not."

"They have a scale at the Sports Bar. I'll bet you I weight closer to 123 pounds than to 110."

"What do you want to bet?"

"Tell you what, if I weigh closer to 110 I'm spending the night with you at your place. But if I weigh closer to 123, you have to do a limo with me."

"We've done it before," Frank replied. "You were working here--not at the Sports Bar, and Bill let you do a limo with me anyway. He still got his seventy bucks. As I recall, I didn't pay you anything. Did I?"

"You didn't, you cheapskate."

"Watch it Lorry. You know better than to say that."

"Then we've got a deal?"

"Yes. We put you on the scale when we get there, and after I win, you're coming home with me."

"No. You're doing the limo with me when I win."

The men followed them to the Sports Bar. Gwen had to pull two tables together for them all to be seated together. Two dancers, old friends of Lori's, came over and sat with them at their table. Frank ordered two Budweisers for Lori and himself after the others ordered. "Lori, let's get you up on the scale. Where is it?"

"Over by the cigarette machine."

She followed him to the scale and got on it as he inserted a nickel. Lori looked down at the readout and frowned. "There's something wrong with this scale," said Lori.

"It says one hundred and eleven pounds," Frank replied. "Looks like you're coming home with me."

"This scale's all fucked up," said Lori. "I don't weigh any one hundred and eleven pounds."

"The hell you don't."

"Then you try it, Frank. You get on the scale, but first, what do you weigh?"

"Between one hundred and sixty-two and one sixty-eight."

Frank got on the scale, inserted another nickel and read the readout. "See Lori, it reads a hundred and sixty-five. Right in there. Sorry, you lose."

"No, you lose. This scale's off. You know it's off Frank."

"Sorry, a deal's a deal. You've got to pay up."

"Not."

They returned to the table where their beers awaited them. Frank looked up at the men, addressing all of them at once. "I've got an idea. A really derelict idea, but if all of you agree to it, not a word about it can get out of this place."

"What's that?" asked Phil.

"In this bar the girls do limos. Now Lori will verify what I'm saying. It costs one hundred and seventy bucks with seventy going to the bar and one hundred going to the girl. The girls will fuck you in the limo. Here's the deal. Every man puts in twenty bucks. Hell, I'll even put in twenty bucks, and I won't even get into the running. Anyway, it's a little more than twenty bucks--make it twenty-two a man. Then every man's name goes into a hat and we have a drawing. The winner gets the one-seventy and he gets to take the girl of his choice on the limo. But we've got to swear ourselves to secrecy."

"Hell Frank, we're all married," said Phil. "What if our wives find out about it?"

"I'm not talking," Frank replied, "and the rest of you have to make a pack not to tell on one another."

"I don't think it's a good idea," said Dave. "Someone's bound to talk. Let's be realistic. You know that I'd be the first to go for it, but my wife will divorce me if she finds out about it and I can't afford that."

"Okay then. That settles it," said Frank. "Hey, have you ever seen anybody do a body shot?"

"What's that?" asked Dave.

"Lori and I will demonstrate. It's like an old family tradition with us."

Lori had Gwen run up to the bar for the Tequila, limes, and salt as Frank contemplated the wisdom of what they were about to do.

They are all going to know that Lori and I are derelicts. Probably get all over town. I'm drunk and she's drunk so neither of us can be thinking clearly. But what the hell. You only live once, and it's high time that these men find out what I'm really like.

After Gwen brought back the ingredients to the body shot, Frank stood up and addressed the table. "Gentlemen, the body shot. Watch." Lori stripped off her top and stood up next to Frank allowing him to suck her nipples, first with the salt off, then with the salt on. The men watched as Frank and Lori kissed, passing the lime back and forth between their mouths. When it was her turn, she licked his nipple and plastered salt on it, then still stooping over, sucked it off.

"Frank, let's sit up at the bar where we can be alone," she suggested.

They sat close together at the end of the bar drinking tequila and beer. She leaned over to kiss him, closing her lips around his after which she started to blow air into his mouth. Rising to the challenge, Frank began to blow into Lori's mouth even though he hadn't taken a deep breath beforehand. It was so unexpected that this time he gave up before she did, pulling away from her, gasping for air.

"I win. I might smoke more than you, but I can hold my breath longer than you," said Lori.

"Lori, we're both pretty drunk, and you know I've got a DUI.

I'm under a mandatory suspension so if I'm caught driving they are going to take away my licence for a long time. You obviously didn't want to come home with me tonight so I'm asking you to spend the night with me in a motel. Is that all right with you?"

"I can spend the night in a motel with you Frank."

"Good. Now let's really get drunk."

Lori pulled her stool closer to his, took his head in her hands, and kissed him on the lips, this time putting her tongue in his mouth. He started to lean back in his stool as she snuggled up next to him. Suddenly, without warning, the two bar stools started to tilt and fell backwards, tossing Frank and Lori onto the floor. There was a loud clash as the two stools clattered against the floor and everyone in the room looked over at the bar. He fell underneath her, Lori's body ending up on top of his. The beer that she had been holding spilled all over her as she dropped the bottle. There was the sound of breaking glass that was heard throughout the room as Gwen hurried over.

They stood up as Gwen stooped to pick up the broken glass. Kneeling in front of them, Gwen looked up at Frank, her eyes asking "What Next?"

"I'm sorry Gwen. I don't know what happened. We were just leaning back and all of a sudden we were on the floor together."

"It's all right Frank." Then she laughed. "Just don't do it again."

A young man sat at the bar several stools from where they had been sitting. Lori recognized the man and went over to him, turning her back on Frank as she sat on the stool next to him. Looking down at the far end of the bar Frank saw Queeny sitting next to a customer. One could hardly notice her as she slumped down in her bar stool. To her left was a machine on which one could gamble at cards. Suddenly Frank got an idea.

He walked to the other end of the bar, sitting on the barstool next to Queeny as he slumped in his seat.

"Hi Queeny," said Frank as he nodded at the customer. "I'm going to sit here with you if you don't mind. I don't think that Nipples can see me back here with you with this machine on the bar in front of me. Let's see how long it takes her to miss me. Probably take only five minutes and she is going to wonder where her ride went."

Ten minutes passed as Lori continued to talk to the young man. Frank became bored and decided to push the issue. Stepping off the bar stool, Frank ambled over to Lori and the young man. Frank guessed the man to be twenty-one or twenty-two--and definitely green between the ears. *It was time for the boy to leave.*

"You know that you are sitting with my date don't you?" asked Frank.

The boy looked up at Frank, not liking what he saw. Frank could see apprehension settling into the young man's eyes. "I didn't know the two of you were together," the boy replied.

"We are."

"Well, I was just leaving," said the boy.

"Then I'll just sit down here with Lori," said Frank.

The young man left them sitting together. After he left, Lori looked at Frank. Her eyes had narrowed and her lips did not smile. "Where have you been, Frank? Why'd you leave me?"

"I've been over there talking with Queeny." Frank pointed at Queeny who was still sitting with her customer.

"What did you do with her?" Lori demanded. "I'll bet you did a limo with her."

"No way. I've been only gone ten minutes. Limos take at least a half-hour. Besides, I wouldn't do one with her anyway."

"You probably did one with someone else then."

"Lori--look, you came over here and sat down with this kid. You left me. Remember?"

"You left me, Frank. Why do you keep leaving me. You embarrassed me. We're supposed to be together and you leave me to go over to someone else."

"I think you've got things turned around."

"Don't do that to me. Don't ever do that again," she warned.

Noticing that his friends had already gone, they left, walking out into the parking lot together. Without warning Lori reached out to him and grabbed his shirt. Taking it firmly in both hands she started to rip it off his back. Frank pulled away from her just in time to keep her from ripping the material to shreds. As it was she managed to tear off five buttons.

"Why'd you do that?" he asked.

"Just wanted to," she replied. "For leaving me like that."

"Want to go have one at the Injection Pump?"

"Sure. Let's go close the place."

They sat at the bar together drinking beer. She leaned over to kiss him, then pulled away, and stuck her finger up his nose. He started to bleed on the bar and left her sitting there to get some toilet paper from the men's room. He returned to her and sat back on his bar stool as he sopped up the blood that was still coming from his nose.

"Why are you bleeding?" Lori asked.

"Because you gave me a bloody nose."

"You're lying."

"I don't lie. You stuck your finger up my nose."

"Did not. So what happened?"

"I just told you."

For the next half hour, they sat drinking together. Then suddenly and without warning she struck him in the face. Shocked, Frank looked at Lori and saw that her face had just taken the yellowish pallor he had noticed at Gals when she had choked him with his belt. Her eyes had narrowed, and she had become someone else.

"Look, I've got big shoulders. If that really makes you feel good hit me again."

Big mistake. Lori's little fist flashed out again striking him in the face exactly where she had hit him before. Frank got up off his barstool and walked out into the room, paced around aimlessly for a few seconds, then returned to the bar. Lori looked behind her and saw a man she knew sitting alone at a small high table just ten feet off from the bar. Ignoring Frank she went over and sat with the man. Five minutes later she was still sitting with the man.

Frank looked around the room for a moment and saw a short pretty blonde standing at the jukebox making her selections. It was the same girl Dave had done the lap dance with earlier in the evening. The jukebox was only twenty feet from Lori and the man. The area in which privates were done was just to the left of the jukebox. *War is hell*, thought Frank, as he walked up to the girl.

"Hi, how would you like to do a private?" he asked.

"I'll do one with you," said the girl. "Let me just finish making my selections."

After the girl finished punching in her selections, Frank led her to the chair where private dances were held. The girl appeared to be in her early twenties, was perhaps five foot two, had long curly blonde hair, and was the best looking dancer there that night. Frank took off his shirt and sat in the chair making sure to pay the girl first. The girl climbed onto his lap as she thrust her bare breasts into his chest.

Lori sat talking to the man just a few feet away as Frank and the girl did their private. If she saw him doing the private she didn't show it. But then again, that was Lori. Time and time again she had demonstrated to him that she had eyes in the back of her head. She also had shown that she could hide her feelings with the best of them if she wanted to.

After the girl and he had finished doing their private, he decided to introduce himself. "My name is Frank. Can I buy you a drink?"

"And my name is Euphoria," said the girl. "And yes, I'll have a drink with you." Then she pointed at Lori. "Is that your friend over there?"

"She came in with me. Left with me earlier. However, I'm beginning to wonder if she's my friend. She's already given me a bloody nose, slugged me twice at the bar, and now she's run off to sit with that older guy. I don't know what's gotten into her."

"So, you're using me to get her jealous."

"Yes. But you don't care, do you--so long as I continue to buy you drinks?"

"No. I don't care."

They sat at the other side of the bar. Frank had not bothered to put his shirt back on and sat there bare chested ordering their drinks. Euphoria had a screwdriver while he stuck with beer. Lori could see him sitting on the bar stool if she was watching him, but it was difficult to tell. After he paid for the drinks he took Euphoria to a low table on the opposite side of the bar where Lori could not see them.

They hadn't been sitting there together for more than five minutes when Euphoria got the call to collect for the jukebox. This meant that she would have to walk throughout the room as she approached each customer for a dollar for the jukebox. And that would take her to her next set on stage which meant that Frank would be sitting alone at the table for a long time.

He found two young men talking to a friend who had just been doing a lap dance with a dancer up on stage three. The third man was just leaving the stage while the other two were heading for the men's room.

"How are you doing?" one of the men asked Frank.

"If you really want to know I'm pretty pissed off right now," said Frank. "See that blonde over there sitting with that guy." Frank pointed toward Lori. "She just happens to be my date. I'm probably not going to take her home. I'm going to let her go home with that guy or someone else."

"There you go," said the man. "Don't let these women abuse you."

"Well, we're about done with this place anyway," said one of his companions. "It won't be long and this place will be closing and we can hit that six pack we have in the car. It's a hell of a lot cheaper than the beer in here."

Finally, Euphoria finished collecting for the jukebox and returned to Frank's table. "Now I've gotta get up on stage again," said Euphoria. "Bummer. But the money's good. You can come up if you want."

"I'll pass this time. When you come off the stage--no-- I'll do better than that--I'll bring you another drink. How's that?"

"Hey, I'd like that. You're going to bring it right up for me?"

"That's right."

He ordered her a Vodka and Grapefruit, walked up to the stage with it, put it in front of her, and went back to his table. After her set was over, Euphoria pulled up next to him at the table. They were on their second drink when he heard Lori calling out to him.

"Frank, Frank," Lori shouted. "Frank, get your bony ass over here."

He turned to Euphoria, "Just ignore her. She's probably just awakened to the fact that her ride might be gone." Then the implication of what he had just said registered. *What if I leave her there? Better yet, what if I make a big display of taking one of the other dancers home? Would Euphoria accept say twenty bucks to let me drive her home or for that matter just out of the parking lot? Perhaps Lori might learn her lesson then.*

He looked in his wallet, saw that he only had about thirty dollars left, and gave up on the idea, thinking *Euphoria's probably already got a ride, and even if she doesn't, she won't trust me since she doesn't know me from Adam.* Then he came up with another thought that might force the issue.

Excusing himself from Euphoria, he went back to the table where Lori and the man were sitting. It had been an hour since he had talked with her. Lori did not look up at him as he approached the table. "I just came over here to tell you two that I'm leaving," said Frank. "I've got a DUI and there is a mandatory suspension against me. I am very drunk, but I brought Lori over here. I've decided to get a motel room close by. You two seem to be getting along very well." Then Frank spoke to the man. "You don't mind taking her home to St. Louis, do you?"

It was almost as if he had dropped a match into a keg of gunpowder. Lori immediately jumped out of her chair, turned her back on the man, grabbed Frank by the arm, and led him away from the table. Never, not once did she acknowledge the man she had just spent an hour with. "Let's get out of here," said Lori.

Euphoria watched Lori try to lead Frank to the door, then saw him break away from her grip and walk ahead of her. She waved at him just before he got to the stairs as he waved back. Then Frank went down the steps and walked out into the parking lot with Lori following him. She went over to the passenger side of the pickup as he went ahead of her to unlock the door.   They heard a car pull up next to them just as she was about to get in the pickup. The driver of the car pulled down his window and said to Frank, "I thought you said you weren't going to take her home." It was the same three men Frank had been talking to earlier. For he second he considered trying to cut himself in on their six pack.

"Circumstances change," Frank replied.

"Well, I wouldn't be taking the bitch home if I were you," said the driver.

Without warning Lori rushed over to the car and swung through the window at the driver's face. The man pulled his head back just in time as he abruptly closed his car window. Lori swung a second time, then a third at the window, almost breaking the glass. Consternation filled the car. Frank could almost hear the men saying to the driver: "Let's get the hell out of here. This woman's crazy." The driver revved up his engine, put the car in gear, and roared out of the parking lot.

Lori got into the pickup as Frank started the engine. He drove the four-wheel drive one block from the nightclub and got into the left lane.

"Where are you going?" Lori asked.

"I'm finding the closest motel I can find. I'm drunk and so are you. I have no business driving on this DUI."

"You're taking me to Fred's," she demanded.

"Look, I'm not taking you to St. Louis. If I get caught driving, it's goodbye licence. Besides, you and I already agreed to get a motel room."

"Frank, take me to Fred's!" Lori said through clenched teeth. "Now!"

"Get out and walk then," said Frank. "Now!"

Suddenly she had the door open, had snatched up her clothing bag, and was jumping out of the pickup. By the time she started walking toward the Interstate he decided that he could not let her walk alone in that neighborhood. He decided to pick her up and to deliver her to Fred no matter how distasteful this might be. And if he were stopped by the police and were to lose his driving privileges as a result, so be it. After all, he had been responsible for making her dependent upon him for her transportation that evening, and he had been responsible for drinking what he had drunk, which was considerable. Later, some other time, he would explain to her that he could never get into this position again, and that it would be up to her to cooperate with him if they were to continue to go out with each other.

Frank pulled off on the shoulder of the road one-hundred yards from the interstate's entrance ramp and got out of the pickup. At first she tried to run away from him, but running was the one thing that he did better than practically everyone else. Within seconds he caught up with her, grabbed her around the shoulders, and spun her around.

"Look, I'll take you to Fred's. Now please get back in the truck."

"I'm not going anywhere with you," Lori replied angrily.

"You don't understand. I can't just let you walk off like this."

"Just leave me. I'll get a ride."

"Lori, I can't let you get a ride with just anyone."

"Why not? I've done this sort of thing before. Many times. Now leave me."

But he couldn't do it. It had been ingrained in him long ago that he always took the girl home who came with him. Not only that--he had always considered it his duty to see the girl into her house before driving off. Not often, but several times the woman riding with him had been unable to get inside the house because she forgot her key, a defective lock, or whatever. Perhaps it had all started with the King Arthur legend in which a knight would never allow a woman to remain in a situation of distress even if coming to the woman's aid resulted in his death. This code wasn't his alone, for it was shared by all men who considered themselves gentlemen and it had remained in effect for centuries.

"I can't leave you here, Lori. I can't and I won't. I don't want to take you to St. Louis, but I will. Now, get in my truck before the police come."

"Fuck you, Frank."

He didn't expect it when her arm moved forward, hitting him in the face. Lori started to run, got a few feet, when she stumbled and fell. He caught up with her, grabbed her roughly by the arm, and tried to drag her to her feet. Instead he dragged her along the ground as she tried to get up. When she finally managed to stand up, she struck him in the face again.

"Damn, you hit hard, Lori."

"Give me your best punch, Frank. Go ahead. Hit me. You can't hurt me. Go ahead. Hit me."

"Lori, I can't hit you. Your boyfriend, Travis, can hit you, but I can't. I can handle most men so I don't have to beat up on women." Frank reached out, reached around her back, and held her against him, hugging her tightly against his chest, saying, "How can I hit something that I love."

For a moment Lori relaxed. Putting her arms around him she held onto him tightly and started to sob. Then she started to have little spasms as she began to cry. He felt her up against him and felt each shudder against his chest as she started to let go. Suddenly she broke away from him.

"Lori, if we're going to argue, let's do it somewhere else. We can go to a motel parking lot or anywhere but let's not do it here. The cops will see us and then we'll be in for it. Please get in the truck."

Perhaps he said the wrong thing when he mentioned motel parking lot. Lori stood there, backing away from him, unwilling to move toward his pickup truck. Suddenly he heard the siren and saw the flashing lights approach. At first it was only one squad car; then a second appeared as the first parked behind them. A police officer got out as the second car pulled up behind the first.

"What's going on here?" asked the officer as two other police officers rushed up.

"We're just having a little domestic dispute," said Frank. "We had just settled down, officer, when you arrived."

"It looks like the two of you have been having a fight," the officer replied. "Do you know that you've got a bloody nose and that she's got a black eye?"

"Yes officer. We were arguing at the Injection Pump when I got the bloody nose. But we've stopped arguing." Frank looked down at himself and saw that his shirt was wide open. He had been missing five buttons ever since she had torn them off, and he had been forced into wearing his shirt wide open at the Injection Pump although he had tucked it in as well as he could. It was no longer tucked in, his shirt tail having come out of his pants during the argument and his chest was totally exposed.

"Let me see your drivers licence," the officer demanded.

Oh oh, now I'm up shit creek, thought Frank. *The county circuit court has my licence and I shouldn't be driving in the first place. They've got me by the balls.*

"I don't have it with me," said Frank.

"Then let's see some other form of identification."

Frank reached into his pocket, took out his wallet, and handed the officer his Visa card. The officer went back to his squad car, got in behind the wheel, and got on the radio while the other officers looked on. A few moments later Frank heard the officer's radio blaring "Frank Harring. Driver's licence number HJ-5043-22-4566. Driver has a summary suspension still in effect."

Now I've had it, thought Frank. His mind started to race seeking a way out of this mess. An idea started to form in his mind. *I'm off the hook* he thought. *They can't possibly pin this one on me.*

The officer got out of his car and walked up to Frank as another officer came up to help. "Turn around!" the officer demanded. "I'm going to have to handcuff you."

Frank stared at the police officer in disbelief thinking *Handcuffs on me. You've got to be kidding. Handcuffs on Frank Harring.* Then he turned around as the officer put the cuffs on. He felt the cuffs pinch his wrists as the other officer patted him down for weapons.

"Now get in the car. The back seat please." Then the officer turned to Lori. "And you. I want you in the front seat next to me."

Frank walked to the officer's squad car following the first officer, who opened the door for him. A third officer walked behind him shoving him in the direction of the squad car. Frank could hardly walk for the officer had put the cuffs on too tight accidentally leaving a kink in them. There was no play in the handcuffs whatever, for Frank couldn't move his wrists as much as a quarter of an inch apart. He stooped over and got into the back seat of the patrol car as the cuffs tightened against his wrists. Excruciating pain shot up from both wrists as he climbed onto the seat. Painfully, Frank forced himself into a sitting position.

Meanwhile, Lori got into the front seat next to the officer who had just sat behind the wheel. There was a glass partition between the front and rear seats in the car. The officer turned his head and started to speak into it. "Now Frank, I want you to tell me who was driving the truck."

"It was Dave McGuire," Frank replied. "He lives near me. Several men from back home were at the Injection Pump."

"Now don't lie to me, Frank. Tell me the truth," the officer warned.

"I'm not lying officer. I know I've got a mandatory suspension and I know what will happen if I'm caught driving. I'm not stupid enough to drive on a mandatory suspension. That's why I had Dave drive. Then when Lori and I started to argue and things began to get ugly, Dave bailed out and went off with our other friends. I think he was planning on picking us up later."

Now that's pretty good, thought Frank. *Here I am dead drunk and I come up with this. When push comes to shove, my friends will back me 100%. Lori and I were arguing off the shoulder of the road. No one saw either of us driving the pickup. They don't have a thing on either of us so they cannot make this driving on a suspended licence stick. Leave it to Harring to come through again.*

The officer turned to Lori and asked, "Who was driving Lori?"

"Frank was," Lori replied.

What's going on here? thought Frank. *I can't believe she said that. Is she really that drunk? She's surely not that stupid. Or does she plan on getting me in trouble?*

The officer got out of the car and walked up to the other two officers. The three police officers talked briefly with one another after which the first officer started to walk back to his squad car. One of the other officers went to Frank's pickup, opened the door on the driver's side, and let himself in. Frank shoved himself forward in the backseat in an effort to bring himself up to the partition. The cuffs tightened on his wrists from the effort and once again he was wracked with pain. Putting his face up against the glass partition, he started to speak to Lori.

"Lori, listen carefully. Change your story. I was not driving. Dave was. That way neither one of us will get into trouble. Otherwise, they are going to take my licence away for a long time."

Lori started to shake her head. "They've got a bench warrant out for me for my three tickets. I never made it to court like I was supposed to. So help me Frank, if I get thrown in jail I'm going to be in big trouble."

The officer slid into the seat. He took a clipboard off the floor, inserted a form into it, and started writing. Meanwhile the officer who had just gotten into Frank's pickup slid across the seat over to the passenger side and opened the glove compartment. The other officer went up to the pickup and got in the driver's side. Frank watched in horror as the two officers started to search his pickup.

Frank had forgotten about the little leather overnight bag which lay on the floor of the passenger side of the pickup. He had put a pair of pajamas, an extra shirt, some toiletries, and a Seecamp 32 automatic into the bag. The gun had six 60 grain hollow points in its clip. Surely the officers would find the gun, and then they could charge him with carrying a concealed weapon. Then, with Lori testifying that he had been driving the truck and armed with the concealed weapons charge they would probably be able to make the driving under a mandatory suspension charge stick. Frank started to close his eyes as he watched the two officers make a thorough search of his pickup.

The officer finished writing out the ticket, started his engine, and drove out onto the street. "I'm taking you both to the station," he said.

They took him into a little room where they asked him a few questions. Then they told him that he could make one phone call and that he or someone else could post bond for a hundred dollars. Otherwise, he would have to spend the night in jail. He didn't have the hundred dollars. That became obvious when they emptied his pockets and put the contents in a little bag. Finally, they took off his watch and put it in the bag.

"It's too late for me to call anyone," Frank told them. "Besides, I don't know anyone who lives around here. I'll reserve my phone call till later. I guess I'm going to find out what jail is like."

He was taken into a large room which had a doorway that led to the jail. The arresting officer stood behind him for a few moments as Frank faced this doorway. Turning to his left, he saw Lori sitting in a chair next to a seated officer. She looked over at him. For a second their eyes met as the arresting officer opened the door before pushing Frank it.

"Go to the third cell," said the officer.

Frank walked a few feet, stopping at the third cell as the officer followed him. The officer opened the heavy barred door with a key and Frank stepped inside.

"Turn away from me. I'm taking your cuffs off," said the officer.

Frank faced the wall opposite the door as the officer removed the cuffs. Then he slowly turned around to face the officer. "Officer, what am I being charged with?"

"Frank, you are being charged with Assault and Battery against June Whitney."

"That's it?" asked Frank.

"That's what you're being charged with Frank."

"No other charges?"

"No other charges," the officer replied.

Suddenly it hit Frank. Lori had betrayed him. She had pressed charges against him. So they didn't find the gun after all. *No, perhaps not*, thought Frank. *The little Seecamp is very small, and I wrapped it in my pajamas. But this is almost worse. Lori has betrayed me. My friend Lori. And she's used a false name and a fake I.D. with the police. She's sacrificed me to save her own butt. My girlfriend.*

"Goodnight Frank," said the officer as he locked the cell behind him.

Frank was alone in his cell. He could hear an officer asking Lori questions. Although he couldn't make out the words, he caught the drift of what she was saying from the tone of her voice and the rapidity of her speech. She was fabricating a story over how he had assaulted her. Perhaps half an hour later the room became quiet. Either Lori was in a cell near him or she had gotten a ride home.

He waited a few minutes longer. Then he called out, "Lori, it's Frank. Can you hear me?" No answer. *So, she's gotten a ride home*, he thought. *Either with Fred or with Travis.*

The hours passed slowly. Somehow he expected her to appear. Surely she would realize that he was in jail for the night and all because of her. She'd sober up, come to her senses, and get someone to bring her over with bail money. There was a bunk bolted to the wall. On it was a thin mattress and a single blanket. He lay down on the cot and waited until morning thinking about how he had been stabbed in the back.

The next day he called a lawyer he had done business with whose office was not too far away. The lawyer arrived at eleven o'clock in the morning with Frank's bail money.

They walked outside to the lawyer's car. "Where can I take you?" the lawyer asked.

"Just take me to the Sports Bar. I'll direct you to the place. They'll take care of me there."

"You're going to have to get your pickup out of the impound yard. They'll be watching you," said the lawyer, "so you can't just drive it off their lot. Can I help you with that?"

"You're very helpful. It's going to take three of us to get the truck out. One to drive the car, one to drive the pickup, and then there's me and I can't do anything" said Frank. "This is going to get a little complicated. Why don't you just take me to the Sports Bar.?"

The lawyer drove Frank to the Sports Bar. They talked in the lawyer's car for a few minutes during which Frank discovered that the lawyer had used all his money for Frank's bail. Frank gave the lawyer twenty dollars to cover the lawyer's lunch and other incidentals which left him with only ten dollars. As Frank got out of his car and started to go in the lawyer called out, "Are you sure you are going to be all right, Frank."

"Tamara's here," Frank replied. "And I am friends with some of the other girls as well. They've got a plastic machine in there, so I'll have money. They have good food, and they have plenty of beer. I'll be in good hands. Don't worry about me."

Frank walked into the Sports Bar thinking *Not all lawyers are bad.* Tamara saw him come in and rushed up to him.

"Jesus Frank, you look awful. What's happened to you?"

"I should look awful. I just spent the night in jail."

"You what? How come?"

"Nipples accused me of assault and battery."

Frank gave Nadine his Visa card for a cash advance only to find out that the Visa machine did not work. No matter how hard Nadine tried, she could not get the little machine to accept Frank's card.

Frank started to tell Tamara his story when Goldie came up to them and took a bar stool on the other side of him. By the time he had finished Goldie was rolling her eyes and shaking her head.

"Can I get you a beer, Frank? You look like you need one," said Tamara.

"Please."

"Look, if you need money to get your truck out, I can call my husband, Jim," said Goldie.

"I need help. I'd appreciate it if you'd call him," said Frank.

An hour later, Jim came into the bar bringing a friend. Frank took the two men to the impound yard. It cost sixty-eight dollars to get his truck released, but the three of them were soon back at the Sports Bar drinking beer together. Jim and his friend left an hour later, but only after Jim lent Frank another thirty dollars spending money.

At eight o'clock both Goldie and Tamara had to leave. The girls agreed that Frank couldn't drive his truck in the area--not with his mandatory suspension and with the possibility of the police laying for him. Since Janey and Goldie lived near each other and since they had driven to work together Janey drove Frank in his pickup to a McDonalds parking lot ten miles away. Janey then got in Goldie's car for the ride back to St. Louis.

"Hey Frank," Goldie yelled out to him as he was sliding across his seat to the driver's side, "Jim and I are having a New Year's Eve party. We want you to come if you're not doing anything."

"I'll be there, Frank replied

EVICTED

He saw her up on stage five about to get off and rushed up to her just as she was walking off the platform. She had not called him in a week since he had gotten out of jail. Worse, he had called Fred and asked Fred if he had picked Lori up at the jail that morning. Finding out that this was the first that Fred had heard of the incident Frank concluded that Travis had come and gotten her. He could picture them in the car together, laughing at him--Travis who had beaten Lori up and Lori who had battered him, both of them guilty of assault and battery while he, Frank, totally innocent, was spending the night in jail. As he came up to her, he pulled out his ticket.

"Thanks for putting me in jail, Lori. Look at this." He read off the ticket: "Frank Harring repeatedly struck June Whitney with his fists." Then he looked up at her. "You know that's not true, Lori. Why'd you do it?"

"I didn't file a complaint. They just asked me a bunch of questions and I told them a bunch of shit."

"Well, I think we'd better talk about it at the bar."

"Why should I?"

"Follow me."

Frank started off toward the bar. He didn't get thirty feet before he was intercepted by the doorman. He didn't look back to see if she was following him. It was the same doorman who had played pool with them several weeks before. The man was a little over six feet tall, thin, and taciturn.

"I'm sorry but you're going to have to leave."

"Why?" Frank asked.

"The manager thinks it's best," the man replied. "The manager has barred you when Lori's here, but you can come any other time."

"Can you give me a reason why?"

"I don't know why. But you've got to leave."

Frank walked out to his pickup, his sense of having been betrayed complete. *So Lori really doesn't give a shit about me*, he thought as he drove off. *Even signals the doorman to have me evicted while I'm walking away from her with my back turned.*

WHO IS FRED?

Frank had a new girl visit him at his farm. He had met her at the Sports Bar and had followed her home that night in the rain. They had sat close together in her bed talking all night drinking and smoking. He didn't have a prophylactic and hers were in her car. It would be difficult for her to find them, she had told him, so they had decided that it would be better for them to wait for another night--especially since they were both drunk.

One week later she was sitting at his table drinking with him and a friend. Then Fred had called, looking for Lori. Fred and he had come to an understanding a few weeks before. The understanding was that both of them recognized that the other was genuinely interested in Lori's welfare. Each had called the other several times--the subject of the conversation being Lori.

Frank, his friend, and the girl had been drinking heavily and enjoying themselves immensely when Fred called. Frank had put the girl on the phone who had flirted with Fred. Tonight, perhaps his putting the girl on the phone had come back to haunt him.

Lori was sitting at the bar with a customer, an average looking man in his late twenties when Jeff Shannon and Frank walked into Ciceros. Frank had tried to set Jeff up with the woman who had been at his farm. It had been Jeff who proposed that they call Lori and who had called her down at Ciceros. "Sure they could come by and see her," she had told Jeff when she called him back at Frank's house. And "Things can't continue to go as they have between Frank and me and I would like to discuss the situation with him."

The plan was for them to pick the other woman up on the way and to escort her into Ciceros. With Lori working there an hour away from quitting time and with the other woman with them it would be easy to convince Lori to go out with the three of them after work. But the other woman hadn't been home so they had to come in without her.

Seeing Jeff, Lori ran up to him and threw her arms around his neck, a huge grin on her face. "Jeff, how are you?" Lori asked, ignoring Frank. "It's great to see you."

Perhaps she was there next to Fred when he called, thought Frank. *Probably put him up to it just to check up on me. If that's the case, then she probably didn't care about my having the girl at my house. Probably doesn't like the fact that I've told the girls at the Injection Pump my side of the story about being arrested either.*

Lori went back to her customer, still ignoring Frank. Frank and Jeff seated themselves at the bar several bar stools away from Lori. Frank watched Lori lean over and start to kiss her customer and decided that she was trying to get him jealous.

"Don't worry, she'll come around," said Jeff. "She'll be cold and aloof for a while, then watch."

When it was eight o'clock and time for the day shift to quit Lori took her customer to one of the two pool tables. Jeff and Frank watched them play pool for a few minutes; then went to the other table to play. Lori was playing well that night. So was Frank. Jeff, whom Frank had never played before, turned out to be a mediocre shot, whereas Lori's customer proved to be hopeless. Frank turned around to watch Lori shoot only to see that she had been watching him. Looking away he studied the balls on the table and lined up for his shot before sinking the eight ball in the corner pocket.

"Hey, why don't we all play together," Lori said loudly. "Jeff, you and Frank can play against us. I'll bet we can beat you."

"You two don't have a snowball's chance in hell," said Frank.

They played three games, Jeff playing just well enough to not embarrass himself, Lori playing at the top of her game, while her customer missed practically every one of his shots. But it was Frank who was the star. He had never played better-- that is until the next three games.

"I want Frank," said Lori. "I want Frank to myself to see who's better."

"Well, that's an easy one to answer," Frank replied. "I've always been better than you. Always will be."

"Let's go then big shot. Let's see what you can do," said Lori.

He won the first game and was winning the second when she ran up behind him while he was taking his shot. He felt her queue stick being inserted between his legs, felt it being raised next to his groin, and felt it rub his testicles as she worked it back and forth. Frank threw his own queue stick on the table and whipped around to face Lori who stood in front of him laughing. Knowing what was coming Lori started to run away, but he was too quick for her. He caught her and picked her up in his arms. With one arm around the small of her back he reached under her rear with the other and lifted her up. Then he carried her around the room until she started kissing him.

She was winning the third game. One more ball, then the eight, and she would win. He still had five balls on the table-- then sank them all. He looked over at her standing at the other end of the table watching him, holding her queue stick in both hands, its butt resting on her foot. There was a trace of a smile on her face that came from an inner sense of satisfaction that seemed to say "This is my boyfriend. He's a damn good pool player, and I've taught him well."

They all went back to the bar together. Lori now directed her attention at Frank and Jeff. Her eyes were on them, hardly ever on her customer. By the time she started to tell Frank and Lori stories the man looked lost. When she started to discuss her experiences with Frank's penis, the man decided to leave.

The three of them went over to a table and ordered another round of drinks. It was then that Jeff started to play the role of Uncle Jeff, Frank's good friend of more than twenty years, and now a good friend of Lori's as well. More and more, as the years had passed, Jeff had become more serious and less inclined to be the prankster, comedian, and thief of the past. Ultra competent in his work, he had become an outstanding father and had become more disciplined in everything he did. And his mind, as it always had been, was like a steel trap.

"I've decided to act as a mediator," Jeff said seriously. "You have both gotten each other in a lot of trouble. Am I right?"

"I'll say," Lori replied.

"And now the two of you are on rocky ground. I think the problem arises out of jealousy. I think, and I'm speaking as your friend, Frank, that you get a little carried away when Lori spends time with her customers after quitting time. You know that she has to do this to make a living, but I think that you've got to get less uptight about it. When she's in these bars with you after quitting time, she still has to talk with them and to flirt with them a little. It's the nature of the business that she has to keep on developing new contacts while keeping the old ones." Then he turned to Lori.

"But I think you." Jeff continued, "overdo it. You have stayed too long with them. I don't blame Frank for getting mad and retaliating against you when you're sitting with a guy for fifteen minutes or longer. What I propose is that the two of you make a pact. A pact that Lori can spend perhaps five minutes with a guy but no more, and that Frank doesn't go off with other women when he's with you."

"I agree," said Lori.

Suddenly the waitress rushed up to the table. "Lori, there's someone just outside the door waiting for you."

A moment later Lori was gone. Five minutes later she returned, a huge grin on her face.

"Who was it?" Frank asked.

"Fred. He came to pick me up. I told him that I'd have you take me home so he went back to St. Louis."

The little world of Frank and Lori became a slightly larger world of Frank, Lori, and Jeff, the three of them becoming oblivious to everyone else around them. Jeff, finished as mediator, now became the comedian. Frank and Lori did a body shot together. Then the waitress came back.

"There's someone on the phone who wants to talk with you, Lori."

Lori left the table and went over to the pay phone. Five minutes later, she came back, her face sullen. "I have to leave in fifteen minutes. Fred got half way to St. Louis, got pissed off, and decided to come back for me. That was him on the phone."

During the next fifteen minutes, Lori became increasingly moody. At first quiet, she became withdrawn from the conversation around her. Suddenly she got up and walked out of the room without bothering to say goodbye. Frank and Jeff stayed another five minutes, finishing their beer. Then they walked out the door and into the hallway that led to the main door.

It was cold in the hallway. Lori stood there in the cold waiting for her ride. She looked back at them and glared.

"You're waiting for Travis, aren't you, Lori?" Frank asked her accusingly.

"No, I'm not. Fred's going to be here any moment," she shot back.

"I don't believe you," Frank said angrily. "I think it's Travis."

"Wait and see," she replied heatedly. "It will be a Mustang. Travis doesn't drive a mustang."

"Well, we're not waiting," said Frank. "Bye."

As he and Jeff were getting into his pickup, a red mustang pulled up. Then they drove off. "What do you think?" Frank asked Jeff.

"I think she's a lost cause. That' my advice to you. She had the chance to get back together tonight, and for a while things were looking good; then she decided to blow it."

"Meaning that our relationship isn't all that important to her," Frank replied.

"I think she's siding with where her money's coming from," said Jeff.

"Here's what I think," said Frank. "Correct me if I'm wrong. Travis, her boyfriend doesn't have as much influence on her as I thought. And why should he? The guy is a mooch, living off her and not contributing. He's totally worthless. But Fred, now that's a different story. He helps her out whenever she gets into trouble. She hasn't been in bed with me for quite a while so I think someone's laid down the law to her, telling her that if he ever finds out, he's going to let her have it. Well, now

I don't think it's Travis saying it. He hasn't earned the right and she knows it.

"My thoughts exactly," Jeff replied.

"So the most influential man in her life right now is Fred, not Travis," said Frank.

"He lives close to her and he drives her all over. Probably lets her use his car. Let's her sleep over when ever she's having a fight with Travis, and he might even be lending her money."

"And she wanted to be with us. She doesn't want to do what she's doing. Notice how she couldn't wait to leave us and waited out in the cold for Fred, not wanting to piss him off."

"I think you ought to leave her alone, Frank. Find someone else."

"You're probably right. No. You are right."
After he let Jeff off, Frank drove home alone.

CHANGE OF HEART

He was in the exercise room at his farm hitting the punching bag when the cordless phone on the floor rang. Frank barely heard it above the stereo, turned the music down, and answered the phone.

"Hi, what are you doing?" asked Lori.

"Just hitting the punching bag. Then I'm settling down to a good book."

"How about coming to visit me at work?" she asked.

"I can't. I'm barred. Remember?"

"I don't know that you are Frank. I'm sure they'll let you come see me."

I'm sure they will, he thought. *So you want to see me now. Now that it pleases you, you have decided to tell them to let me in. What do you think I am--some kind of* toy?

"Lori, I'd love to come visit you," Frank replied, "but I'm really tired so I'm just going to stay put. I'll come see you later in the week. Just give me a call."

"Okay, I understand," said a tiny voice.

EUPHORIA

He sat on the edge of the stage talking to Euphoria who was going through the motions of doing a lap dance. He had been there once or twice since being evicted, each time looking Euphoria up after first calling to make sure Lori wasn't there. Once he had gone there several days before Lori had him evicted and had talked with two of the waitresses and Euphoria. They had all asked him what happened to him the night he had been arrested. Euphoria, in fact, had driven by as she left work and had seen him stopped alongside the road with the squad cars all around him. He had told the girls what happened, how Lori betrayed him, and they believed him.

The fact that they believed him would not have endeared Lori with her co-workers, and he had decided that was why she had him evicted. His night in jail was now working to his advantage however. Euphoria had been there that night and along with the waitresses had felt sorry for him, warming up to him a little more each time he visited her.

"Lori got fired last night," said Euphoria.

"Why?" asked Frank.

"She wasn't coming to work that often so they started fining her $75 per day every day that she didn't show up. She ended up owing the Injection Pump $750. Then, last night they tried to collect $75 from her from what she made, and they told her that they were going to get $75 a night from her each time she worked. She told them to go to hell. It got to be a bad scene. Lori ended up storming out of here. Jimmie was covering the door, and she swatted him a couple of times in the head with her bag. She must have thought he should have helped her."

"Jimmie had nothing to say about it," said Frank.

"Anyway, she hit him."

"I've seen that in her before," Frank replied. "God, I've seen that violence in her many times."

"I don't want to work tonight," said Euphoria. "I'll bet I can get off early."

"They won't let you do that, will they?" Frank asked.

"Want to do something with me if I can. You see, they've hired me to be a bartender. I'm supposed to start tomorrow during the day. I'm not a dancer any more so I think they'll let me off."

"Well hell yes, I want to do something with you. That is, if you can get off."

Thirty minutes later he was taking Euphoria into the Sports

Bar, both of them having agreed earlier to go to his motel room afterward. Jack carded her at the door. Only then did Frank discover that she was not of age.

"How old are you, Euphoria?" he asked as they went to the next bar.

"Twenty, but I'll be twenty-one in two months."

But the next bar carded her also and they had to go to Ciceros where she got in since she was an employee at the Injection Pump. The bartender there, also twenty, was a friend of Euphoria's which assured them of a steady round of drinks. Then they went to his motel room.

Frank studied the young woman in bed with him. She was only twenty yet it was perhaps more her idea to be there than his. They had toasted each other at Ciceros--had toasted to a developing friendship and to a continuing sexual relationship. She had cut through the chaff faster than any of the older girls. Sure, others had aggressively invited him to go on limos, but Euphoria had gone one step further, proposing a continuing relationship outside the topless bars.

Now she was lying naked next to him, totally uninhibited about her nakedness and what they were doing. Other dancers had told him that most dancers had been abused--usually raped or sexually molested by someone close to them early in life, and that many of them bore the scars of this later in life which usually surfaced in their sexual relationships. Not this girl. She enjoyed what she was doing. Easy going and good natured about it, it was almost as if she was from another culture which didn't have the sexual hangups of the Western World.

He took her home knowing that they would see each other again.

PREMONITION

The large white wolf was running aimlessly through the forest, terrified of the men who were pursuing her. A snow mobile was following her but was hampered by the thick forest, its thick trees and underbrush thwarting the snow mobile's ability to turn with her. Time was, however, on the side of the men in the snowmobile as sooner or later she would tire and the machine would catch her in the end. Out of the brush another wolf appeared, ran up to her in view of the men, and started to run in another direction. The snowmobile veered off to follow the second wolf as the men momentarily lost sight of the female, believing this second wolf to be her. The female ran on when a second snowmobile appeared in front of her. She knew the men in the first snowmobile would catch her mate after they had first tired him out in the chase. She felt a sharp pain in her side as the bullet entered behind her shoulder. Then she heard the crack of the rifle a second afterwards. As she lay dying, she heard several more shots in the distance and knew in her last moments that the bullets had found her mate.

Frank woke up in a cold sweat. Then he saw her at the end of his bed. It was Lori's face, her expression puzzled, questioning. It could be no other--the face was Lori's trying to tell him something. He tried to make out what she was trying to explain only to realize that he was looking at his bathrobe which he had placed on the stand at the end of his bed.

Was she dead? he asked himself. *Was she trying to apologize to him? Or was she trying to warn him about something?* For a moment he considered the prospect of her death, and determined that no matter what she had done and no matter what she was, he would never recover from it.

THE FIGHTER

Frank had been busy all morning and into the early afternoon slogging through the pile of paperwork that had accumulated in his office and it would be well into the evening before he would be finished. Then at 1:30 p.m. the phone rang. He could hear music in the background when he heard her voice, cheerful and confident.

"Frank, I'm back at the Sports Bar. I can't believe it."

It was the best news he had heard in a long time. Frank knew how much Lori wanted her old job back and had done all he could to talk Bill into rehiring her. He had gotten to appreciate the bar more through the past few months. Now he could visit her in the bar of his choice.

"You what? You got back in there! That's great!" he exclaimed.

"I'm calling you from there right now. Can't you tell?"

"I can hear the music. I knew you were working somewhere," he replied.

"Why don't you come in and help me celebrate?"

"I want to. I really do, but I'm submerged in paperwork and the bills are overdue. Do you have your car there?"

"No."

"Can you do anything afterwards?"

"I can't Frank. Someone's picking me up."

"How about tomorrow night then?"

"I'll be here."

"Can you come with me to my farm afterwards? You haven't been there for a long time."

"I think it can be arranged," she replied.

"Then I'll see you tomorrow."

Two hours later the phone rang again. This time it was Euphoria. She asked "Do you want to party tonight?" For Euphoria partying didn't mean drinking--it meant fucking. Before answering Frank thought about meeting Lori the next afternoon. Sure, she had promised that she would go back to his farm with him. She had made the same promise the night he spent in jail when she had bet him that she would go with him if her weight was close to 110. Knowing that he couldn't trust Lori to keep her promise he said yes to Euphoria.

This time he stayed with her in her boyfriend's apartment for several hours. And he wondered why her boyfriend wasn't home or why she wasn't worried that he would come home early when she told him that her boyfriend was over on the North side. *Could it be that her boyfriend knew what she was doing, condoned it, and had left for several hours just to get out of the way?*

He spent the rest of the night in a motel room since he planned on going to an auto show the next day and seeing Lori afterwards. At the auto show he didn't see a car that compared to his sports car the way he had it set up, became bored, and left early. The Sports Bar was only fifteen minutes away.

He found her with a customer and had the feeling that the man was a good tipper. There was a new girl there with Lori. The new girl came over to him right away.

"Hi, my name is Carla Jailbait. I've been living with Lori and she got me a job here."

"Hi Carla. I'm Frank Harring. I guess Lori's told you everything about me."

"She's talked about you, but she hasn't told me everything."

"How old are you, Carla? I know a man's not supposed to ask a woman her age, but I'm thinking that you're pretty young for this place."

"I'm seventeen, but don't tell anyone I said that. They'd fire me in a minute if they knew."

"My lips are sealed." Frank caught Lori looking over at him from the other side of the bar every so often. *Probably checking up on me*, he thought. *She knows that I am acquainted with practically every girl in the bar. That's why she sent Carla over to me--to keep me out of the clutches of the competition.* He saw Lori heading for the women's room, saw his chance, and caught up with her just before she went in.

"Lori, can you stay with me tonight?"

"I've gotta get back to my kids, Frank."

Anger welled up inside him. She had promised him that she would go to his place with him tonight, and he had arranged his plans for the day and for the evening around that promise. *Suppose he had not seen Euphoria the night before?* He would have driven one-hundred and forty miles out of his way on the strength of Lori's promise. He told himself that he had made the right decision to spend the previous evening with Euphoria and not with Lori.

Frank stalked back to the bar to sit with Carla. *What a pimp. Lori will probably spend the next two hours with her customer while*

I'm expected to sit here with a seventeen-year-old girl only to see Lori leave with Travis or Fred. Well, that about puts her out of my life, he concluded.

Janey was tending bar. He left Carla and went up to her. If Tamara was his foremost confident in the bar, Janey had gotten to be his second favorite confidant. Ever since that night that he had her car towed to her house and they went drinking together, he had considered her to be a friend. He had shared with her his feelings for Lori and she had let him in on some of her own secrets. Tamara wasn't in today which was his second biggest disappointment that afternoon.

"Well Janey, Nipples has done it again. Promises me that she'll come home with me if I come and see her, and look--she's with a customer while she sends her young friend over to watchdog me. Then she tells me that she's going home to her kids, and that she can't spend the night with me."

"Looks like you need someone new," Janey replied.

"I do. And it's the same girl who was doing the private with me the night Lori put me in jail. That's ironical that she should sit with that guy that night, which pissed me off enough that I went right up to the girl and asked her for a private. Lori's got some serious competition."

"That's not very smart of her," Janey replied.

"Not if she's interested in me."

The place was busy, and Janey had to rush off to take care of the bar. Frank spied Kim sitting at the other end of the bar. Since Kim never seemed to have liked Lori, Frank decided that she was the ideal person to confide in since she would be sure to tell Lori everything just to upset her.

"Hi Kim. May I buy you a drink?"

"I thought you'd be buying Lori a drink by now," Kim replied mischievously as she glanced at Lori sitting with her customer.

"It doesn't look that way, does it Kim?"

"Yeah, but you will before very long. I know you two."

" I don't think I'm going to be with her for a long time," said Frank.

"I'll bet you that you will."

"I bet I won't."

"Tell you what Frank, I'll bet you a hundred dollars that you two will be back together within the month."

"You're on Kim. Here's some money. Order us a couple beers.

560

I'm going to the men's room."

When he came out of the men's room, he saw that Kim was busily writing something down on a piece of paper. He came up behind her and started to read over her shoulder. She had written 'Today on the 28th day of January, Kim Schoenberg has bet Frank Harring one hundred dollars that he will be back with Lori Mellon by February 28. If Lori and Frank are back together by then, he has to pay me one hundred dollars.'

"Jesus Kim, you are taking this seriously."

"I need the one-hundred dollars."

A few minutes later, Kim had to go up on stage and Frank sat with one of the other girls. Twenty minutes later he found Kim at the bar. A large blonde sat next to her, a woman whom Frank had known for as long as he knew Kim and Lori.

"Hi Paula. You two are inseparable aren't you?"

"That's because we've worked here a long time together."

"Frank, look at the contract. There are a few side bets. Want to sign?" Kim asked.

Frank looked at the piece of paper. On it had been added, 'We the undersigned have joined in on the bet that if Frank and Lori are together within the next 30 days Frank Harring will pay each of us $100. Three more names had been signed at the bottom of the contract.

"That means that I will have to pay four hundred dollars if I lose. You girls really think I'm going to get back with Lori, don't you Kim?"

"We're betting on it," Kim replied. "I'm coming right back as soon as I go to the Ladies room. Have him sign it, Paula."

While Kim was in the restroom, Paula picked up the contract and started to read it. After she had finished reading it, she looked at Frank with raised eyebrows. "I think you had better read this carefully, Frank, but don't tell Kim that I've told you."

"Why, what's wrong?" Frank asked.

"Read it."

Frank read the contract, his eyes stopping on the sentence that read: 'If Frank and Lori are together within the next thirty days, Frank Harring will pay us one-hundred dollars each.'

"Why that damn Kim. She's cleverer than I would have ever suspected."

"See, it says that you have to pay them if you lose, but it doesn't say anything about their paying you if you should win," said Paula.

"You're paid up in full, Paula." Frank was referring to the time that he had a few next door at the Swinger's Bar with Paula and Kim. Kim had been Paula's ride home but had left early with two men, leaving Paula there with Frank. In the midst of her conversation while sitting at the bar with Frank, Paula had slumped over and then passed out with her head on the bar. Frank had found himself in no condition to take Paula home and drive all the way home himself, so he had called a cab. Then he had helped the cabbie put Paula into the cab and had given the driver thirty dollars.

"Yeah, that thirty dollars was pretty cheap in the long run, wasn't it?"

"You're a damn good woman, Paula. I've always liked you."

Just then Kim came back to the bar. Frank eyed her suspiciously, then handed her the contract. "This doesn't say anything about me having to pay you girls anything, does it Kim?"

Kim laughed and said, "I was wondering if you were ever going to catch on."

"You devil. You conniving, sneaky woman, Kim. You're pretty damn smart aren't you?"

He heard a loud voice call out to him from the other side of the bar. "Frank, you're pretty pissed off at me aren't you?" It was Lori, still sitting next to her customer.

He ignored her and went to sit at a table with Kim and Paula. The next time he saw Lori it was close to eight o'clock. She came up to him and asked, "You're pretty pissed off at me, aren't you, Frank? Will you talk to me about it?"

"Where?"

"How about the back room?"

They sat close together at a small table in the back room. Afterwards he would forget what they said to each other, but whatever it was it must have been the right things. A few minutes later they found themselves next door a half hour later drinking with Carla in the Swinger's Bar after Jack had gone back there to kick them out.

Jack had kicked them out because Lori and Carla were on the day shift. The rule was that the day shift had to leave within a half hour after quitting to make way for the night shift since the night shift didn't want the day shift girls to stay with the customers. Frank was buying both girls drinks at a table between the main bar and the Swinger's Bar in the back. While Lori was in the restroom, Carla started to admonish Frank for keeping Lori out.

"Frank, when are you going to let Lori leave so that she can go home to her kids?"

Who does this seventeen-year-old think she is? Frank thought. *She wouldn't know that Lori and I haven't been together for over a month. She has no idea what we've been through together. She doesn't know how thick we were. And now, she's going to be the one to keep us apart.*

"I'm not keeping her from her kids," said Frank. "Besides, that's her business."

"She should be home with her kids and her boyfriend," Carla replied.

"Am I interrupting anything?" asked Lori as she rejoined them.

"No. Sit close to me," said Frank.

They had another drink, Frank buying for himself and for both girls. Both he and Lori were eyeing the pool table next to them. Then they both got up and played a game, this time neither of them caring who won and who lost. Then they sat with Carla again.

"Lori, can you take me home?"

"I will but only when I'm good and ready to," said Lori. "Frank and I haven't talked with each other for a long time."

"If you want, you can give me the keys and I'll drive myself home," said Carla.

Then it was Carla's turn to go to the ladies room. Lori's eyes brightened. Looking at them Frank realized that he had the old Lori back.

"This bitch is getting on my nerves, Frank. Let's leave her here and do the hot tub together. Perhaps we'll get lucky and she won't find us there."

"Go Lori--quickly before she comes out."

Two minutes later they were in the hot tub room undressing. Then, both of them entirely naked, they climbed down into the water. Lori sat across from him watching him moodily as he gazed upon her, wanting her yet wondering how long it would take Carla to appear to spoil everything.

"Oh, here you are. Lori, don't you think we should be going home pretty soon." Carla had come in sooner than expected.

"Carla, come in and join us," said Frank. "This water will make you forget about home."

"I don't know if I should," said Carla.

"Oh come on, Carla. You're among friends. Just take off your clothes and jump in," said Frank.

For a second Carla hesitated. Then she started to take off her clothes. A minute later she was sitting in the hot tub next to Frank. "Hey, you've got some pretty good muscles on you, Frank," said Carla.

"He does, doesn't he?" Lori replied.

But somehow it wasn't quite the same. Frank's attention was riveted on Lori's body. Thin in the waist and still with no belly, Lori sat in the water opposite him, a human ferret. Although she seemed totally relaxed, her body seemed capable of instant movement at any moment. She was, more than any other, perfect.

They went back to the main bar for one more drink after putting their clothes back on. Frank had already seen enough. "Lori," he whispered low enough so that Carla couldn't hear him, "let's go back and do a limo."

"That's one way to get away from her," Lori whispered back. "Let's do it."

"Okay, but let's have an understanding. I'm going to pay you nothing but I'm still going to have to pay Bill his seventy bucks."

"That's all right by me," Lori replied.

Lori and Frank walked out of the bar together with Carla bringing up the rear. "Where are you two going?" she asked.

"Back to the Sports Bar," Lori replied. "You're just going to have to come with us Carla."

When they went into the Sports Bar, Frank let the girls walk ahead of him. Jack met them at the door just as Frank was walking in. "Hey, you two girls can't come in here. Lori, you know that the day shift can't be in here. I've already told you that." Then he turned to Frank and glowered. "And as for you, I've never liked you in the first place."

"And I've never liked you either, Jack," said Frank.

Frank felt the punch before he saw it because he didn't expect it. Jack reared back and hit him as hard as he could while Frank's attention was focused on the girls. Although he was a good boxer, it was instinct that took over. Suddenly all the hatred that he had been holding in him for the lawyers surfaced. The quickness that had been developed by the punching bag flashed out in a single punch, so quick that Frank himself didn't see it. The right hand darted out taking Jack in the face. Whether the left followed the right--whether he threw two more punches or none--Frank was unaware of what was happening. His mind focused upon the destruction of his opponent-- all the strength in his body flowing into his two hands as he moved in on Jack. Within a second, Jack's body recoiled backwards from Frank's punch. Jack almost went down, his eyes widening in surprise. He stood ten feet back from where he had been standing trying to recover. Pulling himself together Jack went into a crouch and shuffled forward. Suddenly, Frank saw Jack go down. His mind focused on putting Jack down, Frank didn't even feel his fists crashing into Jack's face. Didn't feel a thing. Unaware that he had even thrown a punch, Frank saw his man on the floor--as if by magic. Frank hovered over his opponent who was trying to roll over on his back. He heard someone behind him yell "stop" and couldn't.

He felt someone pull him back just as he was about to throw himself on top of the bouncer. Frank felt someone grabbing him by his shoulder. Then he felt a second man grab him by the waist. Both men pulled backwards. Frank pulled away, slipping from their grasp and spun around to face the two men. Only when Frank realized that the second man was Alan, Bill's son-in-law who managed the place in Bill's absence, did Frank regain control.

"Get out," said Alan as he placed his body close to Frank in an effort to keep Frank away from Jack. "Leave. We're calling the police."

Then he heard Jack muttering, "You are barred. You are barred from here forever."

Frank had never had any problems with Alan but he remembered his problems with the police. The prospect of an assault and battery charge against him, and this one would stick, made him back toward the door. Then he felt several hands on him at once as he felt himself being shoved out the door. Suddenly he was outside the place slipping on the ice. He went down on his back as Jack rushed over to get around the other two men. For a second or two Frank lay on his back, helpless, as Jack stood over him and punched him twice in the face while he was down.

The urge to destroy came back to him while he lay there. Twisting his body around on the ground he threw his weight on his left elbow as he jerked upwards and threw the right. Afterwards the nerve in his elbow would hurt for several weeks from his shoving it in the ground as he transferred his weight from the elbow to the right hand. The right hand caught Jack in the face, knocking him backwards. Frank leaped up off the ground as Jack retreated into the building. Alan stood in the doorway barring his entry as Frank ran after Jack. Frank yelled out: "Jack you are a coward for hitting a man when he's down. You are nothing but a coward, Jack."

"The police are on their way," Alan warned. "You'd better leave before they get here."

But Frank waited a few more seconds until the girls were outside with him. Lori ran up to him, her face radiant with excitement. "Frank, you just beat the fuck out of three guys. You should see them. You've really messed them up."

Who's the other two guys, thought Frank. *The only one I remember hitting is Jack. He's the only man I could have messed up.* Then he spoke loudly to the girls. "Come have another beer with me. Meet me in the parking lot over at the Injection Pump." He walked to his pickup, got in, and drove to the Injection Pump.

The girls arrived soon after he got there. Together the three of them climbed the stairs, Frank following the girls upstairs. Jimmie sat at the top of the stairs waiting for them.

"You girls can't come here," said Jimmie.

Frank pushed past Lori and Carla so that he could stand next to Jimmie. "C'mon Jimmie. Just this once give them a break. I just got in a fight with the bouncer over at the Sports Bar. These girls were with me the whole time. I just have to have a drink with them."

Without answering him Jimmie grabbed Frank by the shoulders and shoved him toward the exit as another bouncer rushed up. "You've got to leave," said Jimmie as he pushed Frank toward the stairs.

"Okay, Jimmie, I'm leaving. I'm going peacefully. You don't have to shove me out. I'm leaving."

Only then did Jimmie take his hands off of Frank. Frank walked down the stairs, the two bouncers right behind. He found the two girls outside waiting for him. The doormen followed him outside as Jimmie yelled out to the parking lot attendant.

"Don't let them stay here. Not for one more minute," said Jimmie. "They've all been evicted."

Frank's mind raced as he thought of a place to meet the girls. He looked at Lori and the idea came. "Lori, meet me at the Wagon Wheel. You know it. It's right up the street just past the Interstate. We've been there before."

The girls followed him into the Wagon Wheel. Frank went right up to the doorman. "I need a beer. And with these two girls who have been with me. See, I'm bleeding from the nose. Just got barred from the Sports Bar for beating up the bouncer. He hit me without cause. Just didn't expect me to hit him back."

"That's no big deal," said the man. "That place has a

reputation and it's not good. And the bouncer--I know him. He's a complete asshole. Don't worry--you're welcome here. We won't treat you like that."

Then the doorman asked Carla for her I.D.

"I'm going to tell you right now that she's underage," said Frank. "She's with Lori here who isn't. Just give her an orange juice or something and let me drink with Lori."

The man conferred with the bartender for a few moments, then nodded at Frank. "We have an idea. If the two girls will dance on stage for at least one set, they can both stay here and drink." Then he looked over at Lori and asked: "Is that fair?"

"That's fair," Lori replied. Then she and Carla went out to her car and returned with their clothing bags in which they kept their T-bars. The man then handed each of them a job application. Frank got himself and each of them a beer while the girls sat at the bar filling out the applications. When they had finished, they went into the dressing room, changed, and came out. Frank followed them over to the stage where they danced one set before returning to the bar.

Frank sat on a bar stool with Carla sitting next to him as Lori stood between them. A young man, long haired, and wearing a baseball cap came over to Lori who recognized him.

"I know you. You used to work with me. I forgot your name," said Lori.

"It's Billy."

Once again Frank was left talking with Carla while Lori preoccupied herself with another man. Within minutes Lori pulled Billy away from the bar and started to rub herself up against him to the music. Jerking herself upwards Lori wrapped her legs around Billy and started to grind her groin into his to the beat of the music.

This kid's in my territory, thought Frank. *She's the one who's at fault, but these punks had better stay out of my face. Doesn't he know that I can tear him in half?*

Frank went over to Billy and Lori and took the baseball hat off Billy's head putting it on his own. Then he returned to his bar stool thinking, *Let's see what little Billy makes of that.* Frank started to feel lightheaded from the beer. He remembered seeing the doorman arguing with Billy as Lori tried to intercede. The doorman pointed to the door asking Billy to leave. The girls followed Billy outside. Frank started to say goodbye to the doorman who escorted him into the parking lot. They walked together over to Frank's pickup as the girls got into Lori's car.

"Sorry about all that," the doorman apologized. "Come back here anytime. We'd really like to have your business." Frank didn't bother saying goodbye to the girls as he drove off thinking: *Lori, you can have all the Billies in the world you want.*

Two days later he would find out that he had been barred from the Sports Bar for life. Jack would miss the next two days work. The same day Frank would discover that he was no longer welcome at the Injection Pump. He wouldn't see Lori again until the last time, and that would be the day of their last pact, which she would keep forever.

THE PRENUPTIAL

"Your Honor, I believe it is very clear from the evidence that Mr. Harring is a very wealthy man. He is worth over $600000 whereas Mrs. Harring is making only $37000 per year. I have cited the Warren case where the husband was much wealthier than the wife. In that case the appellate court decided that Mr. Warren should pay Mrs. Warren's attorneys fees," said Carl.

"Since obviously," Carl continued, "Mr. Harring is in a far superior position financially than Mrs. Harring we are asking that he pay her attorney's fees. At this point they are $20000--far more than she can afford to pay. Furthermore, I have said all along that the courts in the State of Illinois have tended to rule that Prenuptial Agreements are void against Public Policy. At the time of their marriage Mrs. Harring did not have a college degree whereas Mr. Harring did. He had been in business for himself for over fifteen years. In terms of education and life experience Mr. Harring was far more worldly than Mrs. Harring and took advantage of her to sign a Prenuptial Agreement. I pray that the court will find that Mr. Harring coerced Mrs. Harring to sign the Prenuptial Agreement, and that he put undue pressure on her to sign it as a condition for marrying her."

"In the proceedings today, I have also pointed out that Mr. Harring did not fully disclose his financial status prior to their marriage. Yes, he did provide Mrs. Harring with a balance sheet which he had stapled to the Prenuptial Agreement. But that only showed what he was worth. It did not show what he was making. What he should have done was to include his tax return and an income statement both of which would have shown exactly what he was making. When Mrs. Harring was coerced into signing the Prenuptial Agreement, she had no idea what Mr. Harring's income was. Therefore, she had no idea what she was giving up in terms of her rights should a divorce occur, when she signed the agreement."

"During their marriage," Carl continued, "Mr. Harring bought 200 acres of farm ground which was worth approximately $1500 per acre. Now it is worth $2500 per acre if he should sell it today. His land appreciated $1000 per acre during the course of the marriage while Mrs. Harring was working on the farm. She cooked his meals, brought them out to the field, helped him by driving his tractors, kept his house clean, and mowed the yard. Meanwhile, his machinery increased in value by $50000. Today Mr. Harring is worth $250000 more than he was before the marriage, largely due to the efforts of Mrs. Harring. Under the laws of the State of Illinois the wife upon divorce is entitled to half of the increased value of the marital assets. In Mr. and Mrs. Harring's case this amounts to $125000 which is half the appreciated value of his assets. In conclusion, we are taking the position that the Prenuptial Agreement be declared void against Public Policy, as being void as Mrs. Harring was forced into signing it, as being void since Mr. Harring did not adequately disclose his financial condition, and as being void due to the inescapable fact that Mrs. Harring, who is making only $37000, will have to severely compromise her living standards because Mr. Harring is divorcing her."

Judge Passabuck, a portly man in his fifties, readjusted his glasses which had been resting too low on his nose, and smiled at Carl who was standing before the bench. "Are you finished counsel?"

"Yes, your honor. We are finished making our final argument."

Judge Passabuck now looked over at Randy Green and nodded. "You may approach the bench, Mr. Green, to proceed with your final argument."

Randy Green stood up from the narrow table he and Frank had been sitting at, but he did not approach the bench. It was sufficient that he merely stand up as the term "You may approach the bench" merely meant that it was your turn. The attorney making his argument in front of the judge was not obliged to stand five feet away or any particular distance from the bench so long as he was easily heard.

"Your honor, there is no clear basis under Illinois State law as to what is against Public Policy as far as Prenuptial Agreements. These things are decided on a case by case basis. In this case both Mr. and Mrs. Harring were in their thirties when they married. Mrs. Harring had been married once before, and had two children by that marriage. Both Mr. and Mrs. Harring were mature responsible adults, of above average intelligence. They both knew what they were doing when they signed the Prenuptial Agreement. Furthermore, Mrs. Harring had her own attorney, whom she had hired, who advised her on the Prenuptial Agreement. There could not have been any coercion from Mr. Harring on this Prenuptial. If there was, her attorney would have said so and advised her not to sign it."

"Mrs. Harring," Randy added, "is making $37000 per year.

That is more than most people make. One of the reasons she is making it is because Mr. Harring put her through college--four years of it--during their marriage. Now Mr. Chicanery has mentioned that Mrs. Harring is largely responsible for Mr. Harring's increased net worth due to her efforts on the farm. Now how can this be possible when she was busy raising two kids--her kids--while she was busy getting a college degree?"

"And speaking of that increase in the value of Mr. Harring's machinery and land, it is important for us to realize here," Randy Green continued, "that Mr. Harring is not in the business of selling machinery and land. He is in the farming business. It is the machinery and the land which he owns which makes it possible for him to make a living. He is not about to sell his land or machinery and quit farming. He needs it, and he needs every piece of farm equipment and every acre of land to make money on the farm. Now if we make him pay Mrs. Harring $125000 which is what Mr. Chicanery wants us to do here, and if we make him pay $20000 in attorneys fees he might very well have to sell some of that land and his machinery."

"But suppose he doesn't sell some of his land. The $125000 plus attorney's fees amounts to $145000. At 9% interest, and he'll have to pay at least that on the money he will have to borrow in order to pay Mrs. Harring off, he'll be paying $22594 a year in principal and interest which he is not paying now.   His tax returns show that Mr. Harring is making approximately $40000 per year. If the court awards Mrs. Harring a $145000 settlement, this means that he will have less than $18000 per year to live on. After Mrs. Harring uses the $20000 to pay her attorney, she will have $125000 in her pocket. If she invests this at 6% over a ten year period, she will be making $53984 over the next 10 years. Her kids are in college. In effect she will be using that money to pay for their college educations. His income will be barely more than one third of hers. That is unfair, and that is against Public Policy."

"Now as to what amounts to an adequate disclosure of Mr. Harring's financial condition at the time of their marriage, we contend that the balance sheet showing his net worth was sufficient. Mr. Chicanery stands before us today and asks that Mrs. Harring be awarded one half the increase in Mr. Harring's net worth. He is using Mr. Harring's balance sheets to determine what he thinks Mrs. Harring should get. I think it is obvious that Mr. Harring adequately showed Mrs. Harring his financial condition at the time of their marriage. An income statement or tax return would not have changed anything as to whether or not Mrs. Harring would have signed the Prenuptial Agreement."

"In closing I would like to point out that 1. Mr. Harring gave adequate evidence of his finances at the time the Harrings signed the Prenuptial Agreement, 2. Mrs. Harring was an experienced woman capable of making intelligent decisions at the time of their marriage and furthermore that she had the advice of a competent lawyer of her choosing, 3. Mrs. Harring bettered herself because of the marriage by getting a college degree and having Mr. Harring provide for her children, 4. Mrs. Harring is making an above average income and is therefore very well capable of taking care of herself, and 5. That any settlement in Mrs. Harring's favor will seriously affect Mr. Harring's ability to make a living for himself."

"Mr. Harring took it upon himself to support two children who were not his. He helped his wife get to the point where she could live comfortably by herself with no further help from him. He had the foresight of entering into a Prenuptial Agreement in order to protect his business and his ability to make a living and to keep Mrs. Harring from asking him to support her children, not his, indefinitely. And he was right because this woman is trying to soak him for those children--to send them to college at his expense. Right now, as we sit in this courtroom, she's doing to him exactly what he was afraid she would do. Now, are we going to punish him for being intelligent enough to protect himself with a Prenuptial Agreement? That is for this court to decide." Randy paused for a moment as he wiped the sweat from his brow. "I'm finished with my final argument, your honor."

"We have now heard the final arguments of both attorneys," said Judge Passabuck. "The issues in this case are complex. In order to be fair to both parties, I am going to give the matter my utmost consideration and will express my decision to both attorneys within a week."

JUDGE PASSABUCK'S DECISION

Frank didn't learn about Judge Passabuck's decision until two weeks later. He was about to walk out of the house when the phone rang.

"Frank," said the voice on the other end, "It's Randy."

"Got any news Randy?"

"Yes, but it's not good. It's the worse thing that could have happened. Of course we can appeal, and we will."

"Tell me, Randy, what did the judge decide?"

"For one thing, you have to pay Carl Chicanery $20000 for Karen's attorney's fees."

"And the settlement?"

"$125000. Half the increase in your net worth. But the good news is that your divorce can now be finalized."

"Skip all that crap Randy. You did a good job. One helluva good job, and you can't help it if the judge was born without a brain. What did he say? What reasons did he give for voiding the Prenuptial Agreement?"

"You should get a letter from me in the mail tomorrow explaining the whole thing," said Randy. The gist of it is that he declared the Prenuptial void against Public Policy. He said or wrote that the institution of marriage is a sacred institution, and one that is not to be taken lightly. He then went on to say that Mrs. Harring went into the marriage in good faith and that her standard of living would be jeopardized if she were not afforded an equitable settlement. Your ability to earn a good living would not be jeopardized by giving up $125000 because of your high net worth."

"Bullshit it won't. The judge is an idiot who doesn't understand a thing about economics--or about anything else." Then taking control of himself, Frank lowered his voice. "Sorry to interrupt, Randy. What else did he have to say?"

"He said that you should have provided a tax return or income statement and attached it to your prenuptial, and that by not doing so you did not give Mrs. Harring enough information as to your financial condition. And that's the crux of it. That is his main reason for declaring the Prenuptial Agreement invalid."

"Bottom line is that the judge felt sorry for Karen having to send her two children through college and decided to tap me for it even though they are not my kids. That is what he decided. Then he looked around for a reason that he could give which would be the official reason from a legal standpoint for why I should have to support those two kids."

"I hate to agree with you, Frank, but off the record, I think you are right."

"I think you did a great job, Randy. You were very eloquent in that courtroom. It's just too bad that you have to work around assholes like Carl and men of subhuman intelligence like Judge Passabuck. Ever wished you were in another profession--one with some honor in it?"

"Often, Frank. I often think about it. I'm sorry we have lost. Perhaps an appeal."

"Let me think about it Randy. Right now I'm going to go out and get drunk. Very drunk."

THE BAD NEWS

Frank had been sitting in the waiting room for only a few minutes when he was ushered into Dr. Quaid's office. This time he didn't have to submit to the nurse's questions, a blood pressure test, or having to stand on the scale while his weight was carefully noted. Dr. Quaid stood behind his desk somber and unsmiling.

"Have a seat Frank. I'm afraid I've got bad news to tell you."

"Then perhaps I'd better take it standing. You're going to tell me what I think I already know--that these headaches I've been having are more than a migraine."

"You have cancer, Frank. Actually a brain tumor, and as you probably already know an operation offers little chance for success."

"So how long do I have?"

"It's hard to say. A year at the best. These things go quickly. Probably no more than six months."

"And what should I expect?" asked Frank. "How's it going to go?"

"You will start forgetting things. You will wind up not even being able to remember your name. But even before that happens, your behavior will become very erratic. First you will experience mood swings. Later you will behave in such a way that people will wonder about you. It varies from individual to individual. Some people become very childish while others become very violent. During the last stages your coordination will go completely, and then you will go into a coma. It will be very unpleasant and very painful."

"So what do you recommend?"

"We can operate. The operation holds little chance for success, but it might prolong your life a few months. As a doctor, I have to recommend this course, but I'm telling you man to man that you will have to make the final decision."

"Skip the operation. I have much to do, and I really don't care to spend my last months in a hospital."

"What do you mean, Frank?"

"I think you know what I mean Dr. Quaid."

"It is your decision, Frank."

"Goodbye Dr. Quaid. You've done your best."

"Best of luck to you Frank."

"The sun's shining. It's going to be a good day," said Frank as he walked out of the office.

He drove home without stopping, his mind racing as he weighed his options.

NO OPTIONS

So, I'm going to die slowly and horribly like an animal--not the best way to go, thought Frank, as he drank beer from the can. He sat alone in his lazy boy already on his fifth beer as he contemplated the next few months--the last few months of his life.

I might have a month--perhaps two in which I can function normally. Then what? Or I can end it on my own terms. But suicides don't go to heaven, do they? he asked himself. *However, that's the only honorable way. Far better that way than to linger in a hospital room going out of my mind, a constant burden on what's left of my family and the whole thing costing thousands of dollars. And for what?*

So, if there is a god, would he want it that way? According to the Book of Genesis, God made man in his own image. My going out of my mind from a brain tumor, not to mention others before me, is hardly anyone's image of God. The idea of God doesn't make sense. And if there isn't a god would it really matter if I take my own life or not? So I'm free to take my own life, and if I can take my own life aren't I able to take others as well? Frank's thoughts turned to Carl and Judge Passabuck.

Carl is an unscrupulous shit, out to enrich himself, not caring whom he hurts. How many men has he destroyed, destroyed them financially until they didn't care if they'd go on or not. He is a member of the lawyer pestilence which is afflicting the whole country. And he caused my friend Stan to hang himself--drove him to it because of selfish greed. Then there's Judge Passabuck, pompous man who believes himself to be a god. Judge Passabuck who ruled against my prenuptial, never mind that Karen and I knew very well what we were signing, who declared it invalid because he found some little technical flaws in it--who in the final analysis ruled against it because he felt like it.

God has erred. Frank remembered his conversation with Stan over coffee after they had cleaned out the overhead bin--remembered how he had told Stan that God had erred by imprisoning men in a state of marriage so that they could perpetuate the human species. God had erred, he had told Stan, by causing men so much unhappiness just to accomplish his goal of creating generation after generation of children.

Frank considered the prospect of God. *God is not God after all. He is not good. He hasn't created good. That is if he exists at all, and if he does exist, he is irrelevant. This leaves me with all the options even though it might seem that I have only one, and that is to die of a brain tumor. I can do what I want, after all, with no fear of the consequences. I can't be arrested for I will be dead before it comes to that, and I don't have to worry about God or heaven or hell since God either doesn't exist or is something entirely different from what people claim--instead he is a dark force for evil who creates only pain and suffering.*

So if there is good in the world at all--then it lurks in the hearts of men, or at least in the hearts of some men. And these men are constantly being destroyed by the Carls and Judge Passabucks in the world. Just because all males zip their pants up the same way and share the same urinals does not mean that they are all men. That is the deceptive part about being male, thought Frank. A male proves by his acts whether he is a man or not. Most lawyers use the legal system to pursue a lifetime of self interest and robbery--then have the audacity to call such pure thievery practicing law. Someone has to expose the Carls and Passabucks for what they are--greedy, conniving little weasels and show that they deserve to be shot like rabid dogs. Frank fell asleep in the lazy boy, but before he fell asleep, he had decided to do something about Carl and Judge Passabuck.

STALKS AND HUMAN FERTILIZER

The big John Deere tractor moved down the field at 6 miles per hr cutting and pulverizing the rows of corn stalks in its path. Frank Harring guided the heavy machine between the rows, the stereo in the cab turned up loud. The tractor was pulling a stalk shredder and disk combo, the disk mounted directly behind the stalk shredder. Fifteen feet wide, the stalk shredder had been designed to cut two foot tall corn stalks left by the combine into two inch long slivers. The machine consisted of a large outer casing which housed a heavy 15 foot long rotor. One-hundred-twenty-eight double-edged L shaped knives were bolted up and down its length. A power take off shaft from the tractor's transmission to the stalk shredder's gear box funneled 190 horsepower to this rotor. Spinning at tremendous speed this steel rotor spun the 128 blades with devastating effect at anything they encountered.

Of course, what the machine was designed to encounter were corn stalks. *But what if the machine could be used to destroy something else*, Frank reasoned. Then there was that heavy disk behind the stalk shredder. Weighing in at 6000 pounds it employed round blades 22 inches in diameter each of which were seven 1/2 inches away from the next one. This machine ground up the soil to a depth of 4 inches while cutting up what remained of the corn stalks. Frank had accidentally run over rabbits and kittens with both the disk and the stalk shredder. Sometimes the badly lacerated animal took a few minutes to die after it had been run over with the disk. Not so with the stalk shredder. The animal was always obliterated into a puree of blood and tiny bits of gore in a fraction of a second.

The image of his wife's attorney buried up to his neck in the middle of the field ahead of his machinery made Frank's mouth water. He had adjusted the stalk shredder's blades to run two inches above the ground. The vermin's head would be taken off two inches above the ground low in the neck. Brains, skull, blood, and hair would be instantly turned into a red mist. Frank dismissed the idea as too easy on the lawyer. *However, what if a whole 80-acre field could be usefully employed to execute as many lawyers as possible*? Now that was an idea that would be worthy of his $6000 investment in the stalk shredder. Frank turned the numbers over in his head--*an 80-acre field was one-half mile long by one quarter of a mile wide--or 2640 feet by 1320. If he and his friends could bury a lawyer every*

579

five feet there would be 264 lawyers along the quarter and 528 along the half mile width. Thinking in terms of rows and columns Frank figured the field would be 528 lawyers wide and 264 lawyers deep. Multiplying the two, he came up with 139392 lawyers.

Now that was a noble idea--the offering up of his farm for the social good of the country. Not only that, but he would save $64 an acre on fertilizer since every inch of his land would be treated with human gore disked and mixed into the soil. Frank visualized 139392 human--no let's not give these attorneys that much--subhuman heads protruding above ground level in the path of his stalk shredder. One hundred-thirty-nine thousand-three hundred and ninety-two mouths would be screaming, but he wouldn't hear them above the stereo in his tractor cab. It would take him roughly 10 hours to finish the job since he could shred and disk 8 acres an hour.

Frank asked himself *if the stalk shredder would eventually plug up on human skulls. After all 139392 skulls were a lot of mass. No,* he reasoned, *properly adjusted the machine would wade right through them. It was built to take a lot of punishment, and after all, a lawyer's skull was not very thick to begin with while the brain was softer than that of the average man's. The job would be an easy task for the tractor's 190 horsepower diesel engine. It would be a pity though that the green paint of the John Deere would be so badly splattered.* What Frank could not visualize was what the freshly shredded and disked field would look like after the job was done.

Ten hours later, Frank had finished the field. It was now 11 o'clock in the evening. He went home, showered, ate a late supper, and went to bed. Some people count sheep at night to get to sleep. Frank counted lawyers by the row and by the column. Just before he went to sleep, he asked himself what the country would think of his idea. All he could come up with for an answer was *a damn good start.*

FRANK CALLS ON JEFF SHANNON

They were drinking beer together in the bar at Calicos close to the St. Louis University campus. Frank's last remark left Jeff Shannon stunned. About to drink from his glass, his beer glass barely grazing his lips, Jeff set it back down on the table untouched, shocked at what he had just heard.

"Say it's not true Frank. In the name of friendship tell me you are joking."

"I'm dying Jeff, and in the name of friendship--our friendship--I'm calling on you--I'm calling on you as a friend to do me one last favor."

"What do you want me to do? Just tell me--I'll do anything you ask."

"I'm leaving a scorched earth behind me, Jeff. It's what Russia did to Napoleon back in 1812. The Russian armies retreated while the French advanced almost to Moscow, but they left nothing behind. The Russians burned their fields, they burned their buildings, and they destroyed their cities. They harassed the French supply columns making it nearly impossible for Napoleon to resupply his troops. Winter set in, one of those long, cold Russian winters, and Napoleon's great army, the same one that had conquered most of Europe, started to die. It was a defeat Napoleon never recovered from."

"Just what the hell are you talking about Frank?"

"When I go, Jeff, I'm taking Carl and the Judge with me. No one's going to stop me, but then that leaves Karen, and when I'm gone the courts are going to give her half of what I've got."

"Then kill her too, Frank. The bitch doesn't deserve it. Don't let her get what you've got."

"There's another way, and that's where you come in."

"There for a minute I thought you were going to ask me to kill her," Jeff said numbly.

"Still like to gamble?"

"Sure, it's my number one vice."

"I want you to have some fun on my account."

"What do you mean--on your account?"

"Just that. I want you to gamble on my account. And I want a scorched earth. Leave nothing for anyone to get."

"Go on Frank. I'm interested and horrified at the same time."

"I want to congratulate you, Jeff. You are now Vice President of Harring Farms, Inc. I have brought all the paper work in my car for us to sign and to have notarized. I have also brought ten thousand dollars cash which I'm handing over to you. There is nothing left in my checking accounts. I am giving you this to place some bets for the corporation in Las Vegas except that this will be all off the record."

"What do you mean off the record?"

"I've cashed in the checking accounts so everyone's going to think I did something with the money. You're going to play with it in Las Vegas and no one's going to be any of the wiser."

"Take the ten thousand dollars and do with it as you want," Frank added. "Play cards. Bet on the fights, horseraces, baseball--whatever. I don't give a shit what you do so long as you do one thing."

"What's that?"

"Lose."

"I think I can manage that."

"And one more thing."

"Name it."

"Ten thousand dollars is nickel and dime bullshit compared to a farm. You have to destroy the farm for me Jeff."

"Just how am I going to manage that?"

"The Board of Trade Jeff. You are going to learn all about the Board of Trade. No. Strike that comment. You don't have to learn much about it. Just learn how to lose."

"What's the Board of Trade, Frank?"

"It's like a stock brokerage. It's in Chicago, but there they trade grain contracts instead of stocks. Say you are a farmer or just someone who thinks the price of corn is going to go up. You buy a contract for five thousand bushels of corn on the board. That contract costs $500 which is the entry fee for playing the Chicago Board of Trade game. Each bushel costs ten cents which is the $500 you put up divided by five thousand bushels. Now if the price of corn goes up ten cents you make ten cents a bushel which is $500 for the five thousand bushel contract. If corn goes up fifty cents a bushel, you are going to make $2500."

"And if the price of corn goes down fifty cents, I lose $2500 on the contract?" asked Jeff.

"You've got it. The beauty of this whole thing is that farmers do this sort of thing all the time. I won't get into all the reasons why, but let's just say that they use it as a marketing tool, and it all gets really complicated. Since farmers routinely buy and sell on the Board of Trade no one will fault you for gambling on it as my corporate vice president."

"I'm going to get into trouble over this one Frank."

"No. You're not. I've got a written power of attorney which we will both sign that gives you the right to place the bets as corporate vice president."

"I don't know that it will fly Frank."

"Yes it will. I've already checked it out. And who's going to complain? The stockholders? I'm the only stockholder, and your authorization comes from the Chairman of the Board, which is me--from the President, which is me--and from the sole stockholder--which is me."

"If you say so Frank."

"Let's say that you buy into ten contracts of corn. That will cost us $5000 up front. If corn goes down fifty cents, the corporation will be out $25000."

"What happens if corn goes up? You want to lose money, right?"

"Turn around and go short. Sell fifty thousand bushels on the board. It's all done on paper anyway, and I'm having a broker friend of mine explain the whole thing to you anyway. What happens is you sell fifty thousand bushels or ten contracts and if the price goes up fifty cents, you can lose $25000 that way too."

"How much do you want me to lose, Frank?"

"The farm. The whole goddamn farm."

"And how much is that?"

"That's hard to say Jeff. It's whatever someone's willing to pay for it. To help you out, I have brought along a bunch of financial reports--balance sheets and things like that. The balance sheets show what I think I'm worth. They show machinery values and land values according to my best estimates. I'm probably not too far off the mark. Just make sure you lose it all and then some."

"But someone's going to get screwed Frank."

"Fuck them. The Chicago Board of Trade is always fucking the farmers. Ask any farmer and he'll tell you that. Just make sure there's nothing in the farm that Karen can get. Make sure the debts on the grain contracts are greater than my net worth. Then when you are absolutely sure that you've lost enough, cancel out of the contracts to guarantee our losses."

"Come again?"

"The market can turn around. If you haven't canceled out of the contracts, before you know it, we might be making money."

"One more thing Jeff. I'm putting Karen into my will and I'm giving her all my personal and corporate assets. Technically she's still my wife so technically she's responsible for all my debts. Oh, she'll slide out of them eventually since the courts will probably decide that this whole thing was set up to screw her over. Nevertheless, she'll have to pay her lawyer thousands of dollars to get her off the hook."

"Yeah, and I can just see them prosecuting me for conspiracy to defraud her," Jeff added doubtfully.

"I don't think so. As I have already said, you as corporate vice president have the perfect right to buy and sell on the board of trade. It is a legitimate tool used by farmers all the time to market their grain. I believe that the only way you can get into trouble is if they proved that you and I agreed to destroy the farm since I was dying anyway. Now I know that I am dying and the doctor knows it, but they don't know that you know it. They would have to prove that you knew I was dying. You could always make the case that I used you to get revenge on my wife and that you had no knowledge that I was doing this."

"So, how am I going to pay my legal bills?"

"From the grain I am shipping right now as we speak. I have one hundred and fifty thousand dollars of grain in my bins. Semi trucks are loading some of the grain right now. I have hired a man temporarily to make sure that the job is done. The grain checks will be sent to me over the next several weeks and I'm going to cash them in. I'm going to make it obvious that I cashed the checks in and not you." Then I'm going to give the cash over to you."

"That leaves one hundred and fifty thousand unaccounted for," said Jeff.

"After I get all the money, or more accurately, after you get all the money, I'm going to take a little trip."

"Where to?"

"Russia."

"Why Russia?"

"Two reasons Jeff. One--since the whole country is more or less falling apart, there is a flourishing black market over there. A lot of money can be won or lost in Russia right now. Everybody's going to know that I've been to Russia. Customs will have a record of my going there for one thing. When this whole thing's done, Jeff, it's going to look like I took off with $150000 and did something fishy with it. It's all going to look like this whole thing was all set up by me with no involvement from you."

"What's the second reason?"

"Remember that I'm dying. I want to have a little fun before I check myself out. I know I'm going to enjoy myself in Russia, and I'd like to see for myself just what the hell is going on there."

"Why even mess with me Frank? Why don't you just lose the farm on the Board of Trade yourself and leave me out of it?"

"I don't like to gamble Jeff. You do. Remember again that I am dying and that I want to enjoy myself before I go. So you are going to do the gambling thing which is your thing. You are going to go off to Las Vegas and enjoy yourself while I'm enjoying myself in Russia. You are going to end up with some legal fees but you are still going to have a lot of money left over so you end up winning. No one will know that you are using my Ten thousand in Las Vegas. Everyone will think I took it with me to Russia. We both get what we want."

"Except I'll lose you as a friend."

"And I'll remember you from the grave," said Frank.

"Jeff, this last act--this destruction of my farm corporation is going to set our friendship in concrete--make it last beyond death into whatever comes afterwards.

"You can count on me, Frank."

"Jeff, it's our Code of the West. We'd do anything for a friend-- each of us would as surely as the sun comes up. Karen is as good as ruined, and I know that because you have promised. Let's go get these documents notarized.

LAS VEGAS

Jeff Shannon was not missing his wife one bit. He had a bad night gambling which turned out to be a good night after all since he had come here to lose. Lying next to him was a woman who had picked him up in the casino, a tall willowy blonde, who had charged him three hundred dollars to spend the night with her.

He had chosen a room in the Flamingo deliberately--to honor Bugsy Siegel who had founded Las Vegas--and who had therefore made it possible for him to gamble there in the first place. He felt close to Bugsy Siegel for another reason as well or at least to the memory of Bugsy Siegel. Jeff had just lost close to a half million dollars on the Chicago Board of Trade.

He studied the blonde who was already asleep and decided to wake her up in a few minutes for another go; then he refilled his glass from the champaign bottle on the bed stand. As he drank from the glass, he reflected on his work during the last month as Vice President of Harring Farms, Inc.

He had looked at the balance sheet for Harring Farms, Inc. and had decided that $478,000 should be the right amount to lose. It took him two-hundred and eight contracts on the Board of Trade to get the job done. Trouble was that sometimes he actually made money on some of the grain contracts. When this happened he had to reverse his position on the board so that if he was winning when grain prices were climbing, he had to get out of the contract, then sell the grain on paper so that he would lose while the prices were still on an upswing. Sometimes, even after he reversed his position, the prices would start to fall so that he would once again start making money on the contract. It had been hard work but eventually he had met his goal, losing just enough to bankrupt Harring Farms, Inc. plus a little extra for Karen Harring to worry about.

By now Frank should be back from Russia, Jeff thought. *I hope he's had a better time than Napoleon did. Wonder what he's up to now?*

THE CODE OF THE WEST

Frank woke up still thinking about lawyers. Sure, there were some decent men in the profession--not many, but some. He went out and started his run. It was a thirty-degree morning. A light snow had fallen during the night. At first the cold gripped him, piercing his body, while making him totally conscious of his surroundings. By the time he had begun his third mile, the Gortex suit had started to do its work keeping his body heat inside the jacket and pants. A cock pheasant flew out of the drainage ditch as he ran by. He heard the crunching of his feet on the frozen ground. He wished his friend Mike was running with him today--Mike the attorney. So much for his fantasy in the corn stalks. Frank told himself that not all lawyers deserved such treatment. Certainly Mike didn't. But Carl did and today was the day for payback. His life had come to this. He could already imagine the headlines of the paper--PROMINENT LOCAL ATTORNEY SLAIN IN HIS OFFICE BY BERSERK LANDOWNER. So what, what others thought. It was his code and his only. He would do it because it needed to be done.

After the fourth mile he went back into his house and poured himself a cup of coffee. That was the best part--that first cup of coffee. He felt vital. He was ready. Frank went over his game plan mentally preparing himself for the coming evening events.

The day passed slowly. He read The *Wallstreet Journal*. He read *Time*. Then he poured over several volumes of the Time Life World War II series. He thought about Lori. Poor little Lori, who never gave in, who never compromised. Lori never took any crap off of anyone and never gave in to the system. Five o'clock arrived. He went out and got into his sports car. He was at the lawyer's office at 5:30. As he pulled into the little parking lot behind the office, he noted with satisfaction that the only car there was Carl's white Mercedes. Carl's legal secretary had left at 5:00 as usual.

Frank pulled the chopped 45 automatic out from under the seat and stuck it in his belt. It was the same pistol he carried in the tractor--his favorite gun. Frank got out of the car and went to the door of the law office. He didn't have to knock. It was already open. He went in. Frank stood at the desk just inside the door--the one used by Carl's secretary receptionist--and waited.

Carl heard someone enter and came out of his office smiling, his black hair slicked back as usual.

"Can I help you?"

Then, seeing it was Frank, the smile faded into a frown. Lowering his eyes, he saw the 45 tucked into Frank's belt. Surprise took over. Then fright.

"What are you doing in here with that gun? I'm going to have you arrested."

"Oh this. I forgot. I had it with me to take care of a groundhog. I mean hog," Frank said absently. Then he looked down at the 45 as if seeing it for the first time. Frank reached down and casually pulled it out of his belt, his eyes off of Carl now, as if he were going to clean the pistol. Then he raised his eyes off of the automatic staring into Carl's. His left hand moved--so fast--that Carl could hardly see it, pulling back the slide, chambering the first round. Then he leveled the gun at Carl's face.

"This gun's for you, you hog. Now I'm going to butcher you. Get into your office," said Frank. "Now."

"Okay, okay, I'm going," Carl whimpered. He went into his office. Frank walked after him shutting the door behind him. Standing between Carl and the door Frank carefully laid the gun on the floor.

"What are you doing?" asked Carl.

"Giving you a chance."

"What do you mean?"

"I see you don't have a lock on your door. I thought I'd lock us in here together and you and I could fight it out so that only one of us would get out of here alive."

"What are you talking about?" Carl asked.

"Lock or no lock you're not making it. But I'm giving you a chance, which is a lot more than you gave Stan. Now Carl, you dear little man, you piece of shit, these are your options. One, you can try to get through me and run for help. Two, you can try to fight your way out of this. Remember Stan, the guy you took $850000 from through your precious legal system? You remember Stan, the guy you cheated over that Brazilian business. He hanged himself."

"He hanged himself. I didn't hang him."

"But you took away his future. You took everything he had to live for. You greedy little bastard."

"I set up the whole Brazilian venture just as we agreed that I would."

"Six months later than the two of you agreed on. After you made it seem he had lost everything he had worked for. You would never have started the Brazilian operation except for the fact that you heard that he had killed himself. Then you knew that it was safe for you to come out of the shadows to pick up the pieces. And you picked up the pieces for yourself."

"You've got all that wrong."

"And I'm calling you a liar, Carl."

"That's where you are wrong."

"The two people who know the truth are in this room and anyone who's not in the room doesn't matter."

"Oh one more thing Carl. You forgot about me. Remember. My divorce. Your tactics were dishonorable, underhanded, deceitful, and disgusting."

"Again, that's a matter of opinion. That's just the way the game is played."

"Carl, let me remind you that most of your business is divorce work. You have developed a nasty habit of using the judicial system to extort money from those who work hard for a living just to enrich yourself. You have exploited the differences the divorcing couple have by widening those differences into outright hatred for one another. You know why Carl?"

"Why?"

"To maximize your fee, you filthy little parasite. Think of all the people you meddled with who might have settled their differences in an amiable way, but no, you had to make bitter enemies out of them with long lasting repercussions not only on them, but on the children involved. Think of all the harm you have done in this world Carl. That's why you must be exterminated."

"Exterminated?"

"Yes. Exterminated. I chose the word deliberately. It's what we do with cockroaches, rats, and other disagreeable creatures. I also chose the word exterminated deliberately because you have as much chance of coming out of your office alive as a mosquito has of flying out of a cloud of Raid."

"What do you mean?"

"Look at you, you fat assed punk. You're a desk monger. Look at that disgusting pot belly on you. Too much spaghetti with too much olive oil. You think you have as much chance at the gun as I do, and in a way you do, but you're not going to make it Carl. Look at me, Carl. Take a good look. I am your executioner. You are going to die Carl, and it is going to be very unpleasant."

"Don't you know what they are going to do to you if you kill me?"

"Sure. They're going to lock me up. My life will be over. So what. Ever hear of the Code of the West?"

"The what?"

"You heard me. The Code of the West. It's when two men stand out in the street and go for their guns. One man wins. The other dies. Only that happened only in Hollywood. Gun fights like that never really happened. In the real West, one man usually snuck up behind the other and blew his brains out with a shotgun. But in my Code of the West, I'm giving you a chance, because we are going to fight it out right here till one of us dies, and that is going to be you. There is another aspect to my Code of the West that you should know about. That is when something needs to be done and you know it is the right thing to do, it really doesn't matter what others think. You just do it and you never weigh the costs. The cost for me is my life and I accept it. I will go down as a madman--that's what others will think, but you and I both know better, don't we? You are a disgusting little turd and you need killing. In your hard little heart you know that's true. And you killed my friend. In my Code, a man does anything for a friend if he's a real friend, and Stan was a real friend, my best friend."

"You are crazy. Absolutely crazy."

"No. Just different. Different from anyone you ever met. You are the one who's crazy, Carl. Now I'm getting tired of talking. Go for the gun, Carl."

"I'm not going to."

"Go for the gun Carl. Go for the fucking gun you whimpering piece of slime."

"I'm not going to."

"Okay then. Have it your way." Frank stepped forward and hit Carl with a hard left jab. The right hand followed quick as thought. Both fists caught Carl in the face. Blood started to stream down the little man's nose. Another left to the face sent Carl to the floor, his body sprawling helplessly. Carl tried to get up, started to raise his head, but his body would not, could not get up. Frank kicked him in the head. Carl lay there, unconscious.

Frank reached down and grabbed Carl's left arm lifting upwards. Then he grabbed him by the right arm again lifting upwards. He got him in a sitting position. Then Frank reached under Carl's armpits and wrestled him into a standing position hugging him to his chest. He dragged Carl to his desk chair and set him into it. Reaching into his pocket Frank pulled out several fifteen foot lengths of bailing wire. Using one piece, Frank tied Carl's arms to the back of the chair. He used the other two sections to strap the lawyer's feet to the legs of the chair. Frank pulled the chair Carl kept for clients around behind the desk next to Carl's chair, took a cigar out of his shirt pocket and lit up. Then he sat in the chair and waited, enjoying the Anthony and Cleopatra more than he ever remembered enjoying a cigar before.

Ten minutes passed. A moan came from Carl that was barely audible. Frank noticed that a coffee maker still had coffee in it. He went over to the pot and poured two cups, one for himself, one for Carl.

"Not bad Carl. Nice touch for your guests." Frank sipped from his cup and walked over to Carl's chair. "Have some coffee Carl." Then he flung hot coffee into Carl's face.

The lawyer's body jerked. His mouth began to sputter. "You were much better in the courtroom. Much more articulate. Not very intelligent, however. You could never have handled me if the judge had allowed me to speak openly. I really don't care much for the way he kept disciplining me, asking me to respond to your stupid insinuations with yes and no responses. I really didn't care much for the way the system works. It really operates the way we are right now, me smoking a cigar while enjoying your coffee. You all tied up, trussed up like a helpless sheep. Of course you are totally responsible for your present situation. You really can't fight worth a shit Carl. You really should have learned how to fight. Really love that courtroom, the way the two lawyers work with the judge. They can bully the witness all they want. They can ask misleading questions. Say what they want. But the witness is allowed to say yes or no. That's it. The witness is tied up in a way just like you are now. Unfair isn't it. I'll bet I could make you look really bad in a verbal debate. What do you think? How do you like my Code of the West by the way?

"Uhhhhh. The Whhhhaattt. Code."

"Code of the West. Tell you what, I'll make it easy on you. Just answer with a yes or a no, okay."

"Whhhhhhhat. Okkay."

"Now Carl, yes or no. How would you like to have your balls cut off?"

"Noooo. You wouldn't do that."

"But I am Carl. I'm going to cut off your balls. Then I'm going to feed them to you."

"Please, don't do that."

"Okay, I won't. I'm going to cut your dick off instead." Frank pulled a straight razor out of his pocket and flicked open the blade. "This is a straight razor. Belonged to my grandfather. I'm going to tell you square that I've never done anything like this before. I never could stand seeing hogs castrated. It's just not me, Carl. So, this operation might take a little longer than it should. Hope you don't mind. You should know, Carl, that after I cut your penis off, I'm sticking it in your mouth. Then I'm cutting your throat like they do to hogs. You really are a hog you know."

"Please, let me go," begged Carl.

"I was going to Carl. But you didn't follow my instructions. I asked you to answer with either a yes or no, and you didn't. Here, let me help you out of your pants."

Frank reached down with the razor and cut open the fabric of Carl's pants. Thirty seconds later, Carl's pants lay in pieces at his feet. Then Frank sliced Carl's penis off. Blood spurted all over the chair and the floor. Carl's dismembered penis flopped underneath the desk. Frank quickly grabbed it. He used the handle of the razor to pry open Carl's mouth and stuck the bloody penis between the lawyer's teeth.

"You know Carl. I always thought you were a cocksucker. Now you've proven it." Then he used the straight razor for the last time, cutting the attorney's throat. Blood gushed all over, spilling onto Carl, Frank, the desk, and the chair. Carl died quickly, his open eyes cross eyed from looking at the severed penis that still dangled from his mouth.

Frank walked out of the office into the parking lot. Then he threw up. When he finished vomiting, he drove away, but only after he took the top down.

THE JUDGE

It took Frank Harring only thirty minutes to reach Judge Passabuck's house. The porch light was on, the bulb not quite bright enough to adequately lighten the area. Instead, it served only to create an atmosphere of gloom and foreboding. Frank left his car a block away from the house and went the rest of the way on foot. He rang the doorbell and waited.

Judge Passabuck came to the door in his bathrobe. Mrs. Passabuck stood behind him curious as to who might be calling at this hour. Not that it was that late--after all it was only eight o'clock in the evening--it was just that the Passabucks rarely received evening callers.

"Excuse me. I'm having car trouble down the road. Is there anyone I can call who can help me?" Frank lowered his voice, purposely muffling it to avoid recognition.

The Judge opened the door anxiously peering out to see who was there. A small chain remained on the door for the purpose of keeping intruders out. Not sure who was there the judge kept the chain on. The door was open several inches. It was enough. Frank hurled his weight against the door, thrusting his shoulder into it. He felt a sharp pain in his shoulder, and then he heard wood splintering as the undersized screws holding the lock to the door were ripped out. His momentum took him into the room past the surprised Passabucks.
"You really should have invested in a better lock, Your Honor. But then you never were a very bright man, were you?"

"Get out of my house before I call the cops." Judge Passabuck tried his best to sound menacing, but his voice quivered, which only made him appear even more frightened than he actually was.

"Let me remind you that you are not presently sitting on the bench," said Frank. "I am." Frank pulled the 45 automatic from his belt. Purposely not pointing it at the judge he studied it for a moment, then looked up at the judge.

"I'm afraid that I'm going to have to ask your wife to leave. Do you have any rooms with an outside lock? So that we can lock her in."

"No, we don't," said the Judge.

"Then listen carefully and do exactly as I say," warned Frank. This time he pointed the 45 at Mrs. Passabuck. "If you don't follow my exact instructions to the letter and immediately I am going to blow your wife's brains out. If you haven't already noticed, this is a 45 automatic. I have it loaded with Glaser Safety slugs. Each bullet consists of a thin outer shell which encloses 250 tiny pellets. The bullet is very light and goes a lot faster than normal. When it hits anything it immediately disintegrates. It is called a safety slug because it acts like a shotgun once the bullet hits something. The tiny pellets disperse and spread out. Therefore, there is not a lot of penetration. But the tiny shot--they go ripping out at tremendous speed and in all directions. And when the bullet hits human tissue these shot bounce around tearing a large hole as they rip through and destroy blood vessels and vital organs. Now just imagine what this will do to your wife's head."

"Okay, okay, what do you want?"

"Take her to the nearest bedroom. Now!" Frank ordered.

"Okay honey. Do what he says. Go up the stairs."

Without saying another word to each other the Passabucks climbed the staircase and went into one of the bedrooms. Frank followed.

"Now listen up Judge. I really don't care what you use. Rip your sheets up. Use up your ties. Belts. Whatever. Tie her up so that she can't get loose. And don't fuck with me. Do it now."

Judge Passabuck went to his closet, grabbed several ties, and several belts. He motioned for his wife to sit in the chair next to the dresser. After she sat down he proceeded to tie her to the chair, starting with her arms and ending with her legs. When he finished, Frank came over to test the knots. Satisfied, he motioned for the judge to leave the room.

"Now let's go downstairs and have a friendly drink," said Frank.

Frank followed Judge Passabuck downstairs to the living room. Frank left the Judge standing as he slouched onto the couch irreverently putting his feet on the marble coffee table. Frank pulled an Anthony and Cleopatra from his shirt pocket, lit it with a cheap lighter, and started to smoke it as he studied the judge. He pointed the 45 at the judge's head.

"What are you waiting for, Your Honor--I'm thirsty. Get me a drink."

"What do you want?"

"Do you have any Tequila?"

"I'll get you some."

"Just one shot please. In a small glass. And be quick about it."

Judge Passabuck went over to a liquor cabinet that stood against the far living room wall. He came back with a small glass of Tequila for Frank and a glass half full of bourbon for himself.

"Who said you can drink in my presence," said Frank. "Put the drink down on the coffee table and hand me the Tequila." The judge handed the glass of Tequila to Frank setting his own drink down on the coffee table.

"Now, sit down Judge," Frank ordered.

Judge Passabuck sat down in an armchair close to the coffee table. Frank eyed the glass of bourbon on the coffee table and kicked it over spilling its contents all over the Passabuck's plush white living room carpet. A brown stain spread over the carpet.

"You've ruined the carpet!" screamed the Judge.

Frank got up and came over to the judge. Grabbing him by the throat Frank jabbed the front of the 45 automatic into the judge's face so that the slide and the barrel struck him in the forehead. Blood started to ooze into the judge's lap and onto the carpet. Frank went back to his couch and sat down, once more putting his feet up on the coffee table. "Don't yell at me Your Honor. It is a sign of disrespect. If I did that to you in your courtroom, you'd have me for contempt, which is exactly what I have for you. Contempt." Frank spat out the words his voice heavy with menace. Judge Passabuck sat in his chair quivering. Frank eased back into the couch stretching his legs and puffed on his cigar. Then he thoughtfully sipped from the glass of Tequila.

"Normally I chug the Tequila. Then I have several more. I am sipping this time because I don't know how many more I'll have--in my life which I suspect is slipping to a close. I had you get me the Tequila because it reminds me of many good times with some pretty good women. For me those times are over just as your life is about to be over."

"My life? Over?" The judge's voice quaked.

"You heard me you slimy jellyfish. OVER. FINISHED. AS IN COMPLETED OR TERMINATED you son-of-a-bitch. You're going to die here, and soon."

"You're going to kill me."

"But not like I killed Carl. I cut his dick off and then fed it to him. You should have seen him, tied to a chair in his own office, his own bleeding penis in his mouth. He was still alive and looking at it--in pain and tasting it as it bled in his mouth--knowing that he had just been castrated--as I cut his throat."

Judge Passabuck, his forehead still bleeding, sat uncomfortably in his chair, his legs close together, his knees touching each another.

His body started to shake.

"Don't worry. I'm not going to do that to you," Frank laughed. "Because you're not really a man Judge. That's why I kicked your drink all over your precious carpet, you spineless turd. I wouldn't have a drink with you for the world."

"You really are going to kill me, aren't you?"

"What did I just say? Now, shut the fuck up." Frank's voice ripped with menace, the impact of his words almost visibly thrusting Judge Passabuck back into his chair. "You are going to die for being a dishonest man who doesn't care about justice."

"Who said the law has anything to do about justice. Every lawyer knows that. It's about statutes and issues and precedents. It's about one lawyer making a better case than the other."

"Enough said. First, you and your brethren--that is your fellow judges-- should take a close look at meting out justice. Second--take my case. Remember the Prenuptial. My lawyer was clearly superior to my wife's. He had the stronger case. But you--you shriveled up little moron--had to rule that I had to pay her attorney's fees. Didn't you?"

"Yes, I did. I had to give her an equal chance. I h---------"

"You gave her more than an equal chance you slime ball. You fixed it so that all the attorneys and judges would win and that she had nothing to lose. You ordered me to pay all of her attorneys fees so that the lawyers could have a huge circle jerk financed by me. You put me in the position that I suffer either financial ruin through exorbitant legal fees or that I pay her off. In other words, you ordered me to pay for her kids' college education--because that's exactly where that money would go."

"I didn't issue an order that the settlement money would be used to finance her kids' college education. She could use that money for anything."

"But you knew how she would use it. And at the same time the father of the children, the real father--was paying absolutely nothing for their support. But you regarded me as a money cow and you and your lawyer bastard friends milked me. You stole from me judge. I worked hard for that money and you slime balls took it from me through your precious little judicial system."

"But the state of Illinois takes a dim view of Prenuptials."

"No. You are the one who ruled on this prenuptial. You took the dim view. You probably sat at home every night with your wife while she browbeat you about how you should give that helpless little wife of mine a break. You caved into your wife's wishes--her point of view. That's why I'm not going to castrate you. Your wife already did that to you a long time ago. You see, your honor, you want to be well respected, a pillar of the community. So you took the middle road, making me pay my wife's legal fees while giving her a nice settlement as well."

"I did what I thought was the equitable thing at the time," said the judge.

"Bullshit you did," thundered Frank. "That prenuptial was very clear. It said that I didn't have to pay her legal fees. I signed it. She signed it. We were both adults in our thirties. We were both advised by legal counsel. It also said that I only had to pay her $7000 yet you awarded her $125000. There was nothing equitable about it, you quivering pussy. On your own you decided that the words of the prenuptial were invalid--that they could be overlooked because you, the big man, said so."

"I felt it was in the best interests of all the parties concerned."

"Then fuck you. You still don't get it do you? Men all over the country are committing suicide because they are being ruined financially because of decisions such as yours. You are truly a power hungry evil man. You decided in my divorce that your opinion was more important than the contract my wife and I made. You sat there smugly in your courtroom knowing that you were the law and that you could ignore everything but what you wanted to do. But you know what, Judge? There is a higher law than you and you are about to find out."

"I suppose you are the higher law as you shoot me. You are insane."

"You've got that wrong. You are insane. I am merely going to carry out what probably 90% of the population would like to see done. They would judge you and your lawyer friends as thieves and as parasites who feed off of honest hardworking people. You broke the law. You definitely broke my law."

"How's that?"

"The Code of the West. My Code of the West. They used to hang horse thieves. Well, you and your lawyer friends stole from me. Impaired my ability to make a living. You did this out of greed and the desire to show that you were a solid and powerful member of the community. But you took what was rightfully mine, and since I have the right to protect myself or to get revenge, I'm going to kill you. Besides--I wish to point out to others who might follow my example-- that they not only can--but that they have the moral imperative to kill any judge or lawyer who makes a mockery out of justice. End of sermon. Now excuse me, your honor, as I scatter your brains."

Frank raised the 45 automatic and pointed it at the judge's head. Then he pulled the trigger. There was a loud explosion as Judge Passabuck's head disintegrated. The Glaser safety slug entered his face just below the eye. The bullet's jacket came apart instantly releasing 250 shot all traveling at more than 1500 feet per second. The 250 tiny shot bounced around inside the judge's skull gelatinizing his brain. Brain matter started to ooze from the large gaping hole where the judge's eyes and nose had been.

Mrs. Passabuck started to scream upstairs. Frank got up off the couch, chugged what remained of his Tequila, and walked out of the house to his car. Settling into the driver's seat, he turned up the stereo and pulled out of the driveway.

He said to himself, *God I hate to make women cry.*

THE LAST TRIP

He drove one hundred miles and stopped at a service station. The car no longer could use regular for it had long ago been transformed into something far different from a stock MGB. He heard a click as the automatic shutoff turned the pump off as he was cleaning off the windshield. Then finished, he went in to pay for the gas. Walking slowly back to the car, Frank admired his creation sitting next to the pump low slung and perfect for its last ride.

He didn't get in right away. Mentally he ticked off the improvements he had made to the machine. The suspension modifications were there underneath where no one could see them. Out of sight, beneath the hood was the small displacement V-6 engine and the supercharger, which Dave McGuire had installed to replace the 94 horsepower four cylinder engine that had come with the car. The car still weighed only 2200 pounds yet it generated 215 horsepower.

The machine had been an expensive project, but he had viewed it as an extension of himself. Sensitive as a thoroughbred she responded like an angel to the slightest nudge of the wheel. Yet, she could overtake all but the swiftest cars on the straights. And nothing could stay with her in the corners. *Too bad he would have to destroy her.*

He drove out onto the interstate and took the little sports car up to 90 and held her there until he saw the flashing lights of the patrol car in his rear view mirror. Without hesitation he downshifted into fourth and jabbed the accelerator into the floor. Even at 90 the car jumped forward. He started to hear the whine of the supercharger as the car approached its redline. Then he shifted into fifth. The car quickly reached its top speed of 145 mph as the patrol car lost ground. Frank took the first exit ramp at 90 mph and held the car there until he was within two hundred yards of the stop sign before he started to slow down. Running the stop sign he turned onto a two-lane country road as he dropped down to second. The car jumped forward at each shift as Frank left the patrol car a half mile behind. Ten minutes later he lost the patrol car's lights in a corner. Out of the corner he saw another two lane, turned into it, and accelerated to 110 miles per hour. Then he saw the old barn sitting by itself on a little side road. An old building, dilapidated, unpainted, and on its last legs, it sat by itself unaccompanied by human habitation. He pulled behind it and cut his lights.

Ten minutes passed with no signs of the patrol car. Frank waited another thirty minutes before he pulled away. Fifteen minutes later he found the interstate, merged onto it, and held the car at seventy. Before, he didn't know where he was going and didn't care. Now he knew where he had been heading, instinctively, his subconscious leading him there. He was close to Lori's house.

She had put him in jail--but she had done it when she was very drunk. Perhaps she didn't know what she was doing, thought Frank. She was the only girl he had ever met in any of the topless bars who didn't try to get him to spend a lot of money on her. At one time, before that night, she would often call him--when she was depressed or simply because she wanted to see him.

The car hit a bump in the road. Frank felt the pain start again in his head, a gnawing, sickening pain that he knew would get worse and worse. The cancer was there, an insidious alien killer, that would first destroy his mind--then slowly kill him. Far better to do it this way, Frank thought, on his own terms.

His thoughts returned to Lori. They had been fated to meet, and both of them had recognized that something had happened that had never happened before. Now he knew why he had pointed his car in her direction. He had come to say goodbye. She would, he hoped, be the last living creature he would see before he plunged into darkness.

He pulled into her driveway and shut the ignition off. She came to the door and walked out onto the porch. *She must have heard my engine*, thought Frank. *Thought I'd have to knock. Thought that she wouldn't be home.*

"Did you hear me pull up?" he asked.

"I thought I did. Got a funny feeling that you were out here," she replied.

"I came to say goodbye."

"Why's that?"

"Because I'm going on a one-way trip."

"What do you mean?" she asked.

"I'm leaving for good. I'm not returning. To you or to anyone."

"I don't understand."

"I just killed two men."

"The judge?"

"And the lawyer. Her lawyer."

Lori started to walk toward his car. Half way there she stopped, riveted in place, as she realized that he had done exactly as he said he had done. She had never seen him like this before. She looked down at her feet, not looking up at him as she took in what he had said. Suddenly she looked up at him and grinned.

"Take me with you Frank."

"No Lori. I came to say goodbye--not take you with me."

"Take me with you Frank," she ordered. "I want to go with you."

Suddenly she was standing next to the passenger door of the little convertible. He wasn't prepared for this, and since he had never considered its possibility, didn't move fast enough. Before he could restart his engine, Lori was sitting next to him slamming her door shut.

"Well, what are you waiting for?" asked Lori. "Move."

"I don't know if I want to let you do this."

"I'm not giving you a choice. You're taking me with you and that's all that's to it."

"Why Lori?"

"Because I love you. That's why."

"That's a four-letter word like piss, and shit, and fuck, and hate."

"Not."

"Yeah, then you've had a funny way of showing it. Like having me put in jail."

"That's because you made me hate you that night."

"Then why didn't you call me afterwards?"

"I was too ashamed to. That was a shitty thing I did. Real shitty. After that, I didn't think I was good enough for you. Ever since that night, Frank, I really got down on myself. Do you know how I got my old job back?"

"Probably."

"I know what you're thinking. You're thinking I fucked Bill. Well, I did. And a lot more than once. I had to keep fucking him to keep my job."

"I knew that would happen."

"And that's not all. I did a lot of limos. With everyone. Any man who would ask, I did a limo with him. Do you know why, Frank?"

"I think so."

"It was because of you. I did it because of you. You see, after I had you put in jail, I knew I wasn't good enough for you. I started to think I was pure trash, and I decided to just go out and prove it."

"You never were trash, Lori. That's the tragic thing. You only thought you were. You could have been anything you wanted to be. You always had the looks, you had the personality, and you had the intelligence. But you had to think you were trash."

"I hated you for doing all those limos with all those other girls."

"Well, I did them after you stood me up or played some other trick on me."

"I know. I'm really sorry I did all those things to you. I did them because I wanted you so much and I knew that I couldn't have you. Then, when you did all those limos, it was like you were telling me, "Look Lori, they're all a bunch of whores, same as you, and now I'm putting you all in the same boat."

"I guess I did, didn't I?"

"When you and I were together I always thought I was somebody special. When you fucked all those other girls you were saying to me, Lori, you really are just a little slut like all the rest."

"Don't try to con me again, Lori. I know that you always did limos, and I heard about some of the things you did at bachelors' parties. You made your money that way, face it."

"Yes, I did, Frank. I'll admit that now. It's just that I didn't want you to think that I was doing all that. You see, in my heart I wasn't really doing it. When you and I made love it was making love. That's why I told you that you were the fourth guy I ever screwed. What I meant was that you were the fourth guy it ever meant anything to me. Making love that is."

"So why did you stand me up so much? I told you not to."

"Because I loved you so much. I wanted you more than anything and I knew that I couldn't have you, and that you'd just go off with somebody else someday and forget all about me--as if I never existed. Somebody without kids. So, I'd be mad at you at the same time as I craved you for jilting me which I knew was going to happen sooner or later."

"So why do you lie so much, Lori?"

"Do you mind driving out of here. Travis might come home."

Frank slipped the little car into gear and pulled out of the driveway. The night air was warm--the evening was--perfect as they drove together in silence. They approached the interstate.

"What do you think, Lori? The interstate or a country road?"

"I always worked around people. Always liked people. I think the interstate."

"So why did you lie to me all the time Lori, not to mention

practically everyone else?"

"Because I hated my life--hated what I was doing, so I made a game of it. It was the only way I could cope, and I never let anyone else in on my game. It was my game and nobody else's."

"Were you always aware that you were lying?"

"I tried to make myself believe that what I was saying was true. The alcohol helped there. The stories and the alcohol were a way of escaping from myself--from what I had become."

"Do you want to stop somewhere for a drink?"

"No. this time I want to be sober. I want to feel the night. I don't want to lose track of anything--least of all the end."

"And how do you want it to end?"

"In a burst of light. With me and you both knowing that we are really together and that we are ending it together. I want to feel everything. For once in my life I want to really feel."

"It'll be easier the other way."

"No. I don't want to get drunk. Frank, why'd you kill the lawyer and the judge?"

"Because I knew I was going to die anyway and because I didn't want my death to be without meaning."

"You sound like a mass murderer, Frank. Sounds like you're saying you can only be somebody if you go out and kill people. Only then will your life have meaning."

"No. I'm not a mass murderer," Frank laughed. "Didn't kill enough lawyers."

"So, why'd you do it?"

"Because it was the right thing to do. Because they caused Stan to kill himself. According to my code--the Code of the West--a man always avenges his friend, and they killed him as surely as if they pulled the trigger on him. And because they stole from me what wasn't theirs in the first place. I believe a man has a right to protect his property if it's being stolen from him, and what was I supposed to do-- call in the law? And because those people would go on stealing from other people after they were done with me. Stealing from lots of people using the mantel of the law--our legal system--to steal from decent hardworking men. I was not the first and I wouldn't be the last they'd ever steal from. And because all their little prick lawyer friends were doing the same thing. I wanted to serve notice that stealing, not to mention ruining other people's lives, should not be tolerated. I wanted to jolt all those little parasites into thinking that they could not commit robbery without paying the consequences. I wanted for them all to have fear in their shrunken little testicles every time they so much as thought about stealing from another human being. So I made their deaths as horrible as possible to drive home my point."

"So how did you kill them?"

"Lori, don't even ask. Horribly and with the maximum amount of bloodshed. Let's leave it at that."

"I believe you, Frank. I believe you did it right."

"Do you want to shift while I drive? The way we used to."

"Sure. Why not."

Frank placed his hand gently on top of hers, held it tightly, not wanting to ever let go. Then he placed her hand on the shift knob. He pushed in the clutch. Lori looked up at him and smiled--then shifted into fourth. He shoved the accelerator into the floor. They both watched the tachometer as the needle approached the red line. Then Frank pushed in the clutch as Lori shifted into fifth gear.

"Fast isn't it Lori?"

"Faster than I thought. You are nuts, Frank. Absolutely nuts to do this to your car."

"I had to make it perfect Lori. I had to make it perfect for us. Somehow I must have realized without really knowing that it would all come down to this."

"So when do you want to do it?"

"I don't really want to do it, but it won't be long and they are going to have a highway alert out for me and they are going to be looking for this car. I don't know about you, but I don't like cops, and I really don't care to have them present when we do it."

"I agree. Tell you what, let me surprise you," said Lori.

"Then let's see what this car will do."

Frank tromped on the accelerator. The supercharger cut in, emitting a noise, noticeable but not obtrusive, that was like a jet airliner taking off. They felt the revs build, watching the speedometer go from 70 to 110. Steadily the needle climbed--120 then 130 until it rested on the dial at 145 as the tach redlined at 7200 rpms. Frank held her at 145 feeling the wind in his face as it whipped into the little cockpit. Lori started to play with her hair trying to keep it from blowing into her eyes. They approached an overpass with concrete retaining walls on both sides of the highway.

"Why am I doing this?" asked Lori. "What do I care if my hair blows all over the place or not." Then she grinned. Frank knew what the grin meant. "Frank, I love you. You must believe that. I've always loved you. More than anything in this world." Suddenly she threw her arms around his neck as she thrust her face in front of his. He felt her tongue enter his mouth as she clung onto him tightly. He felt her hair flutter around his face. Then he let go of the wheel as he returned her kiss.

For a few seconds the little car held a straight course. Then it started to veer off to the left. Neither of them felt the car drifting slowly to the left. The wheels started to turn--slowly at first then more abruptly since there was no one holding onto the steering wheel. The last thing he felt was her hair in his face and her mouth against his. The car hit the retaining wall at 145 mph. For a split second Frank saw a blinding white light as something exploded in his head. Out of the light two wolves trotted together, both white, one larger and heavier than the other.

www.ingramcontent.com/pod-product-compliance
Lightning Source LLC
Chambersburg PA
CBHW020454020726
47493CB00001B/24